The Quarry

Carol Morrissey Hopkins

The Quarry
Copyright © 2021 by Carol Morrissey Hopkins

The Quarry is a work of fiction. Names, characters, places, and
incidents are either the product of the author's imagination
or are used fictitiously. Any resemblance to actual persons,
living or dead; to events or localities is entirely coincidental.

tellwell

Tellwell Talent
www.tellwell.ca

ISBN
978-0-2288-6467-7 (Paperback)

Acknowledgments

The Quarry has been a work in process for many years. It would not have come to fruition without the loving support of my husband, Randy, and my adult children, Anastacia, Ryan, and Kelly, and daughter-in-law, Paula Wells Hopkins. Anastacia's photos are featured on both the front and back covers of the print edition with my sincere thanks for her help in choosing them from her large collection of stellar photographs.

I am grateful for the care and encouragement poured out in immeasurable amounts by my siblings, to whom I owe a debt of gratitude. I thank them all for their unwavering patience, kindness and belief in me.

Gillian Balharry has been a huge part of my journey, assisting with reading and editing my virgin manuscript and helping to make it so much better. Thank you, Gillian. Special thanks as well to Margaret Payne for her constant support and belief in me.

I thank my parents, Anita and Bernard Morrissey, although they are no longer with us, they are the foundation that have allowed my imagination to soar and the bedrock that continues to serve me well in all my endeavors. I am grateful for their examples of faith in a turbulent world and for their love and sacrifices.

I also give a nod to all the wonderful researchers and historians at the Newfoundland and Labrador Heritage Website based at Memorial University of Newfoundland where I found many of the historical items that fired my imagination and are featured in *The Quarry*. Although this is a work of fiction this website was a wonderful source of inspiration in the writing of this story.

Last but certainly not least I thank TellWell Publishing and you, the reader for your interest. I hope you will enjoy *The Quarry*.

Chapter

1

The sun was barely cresting the horizon, its glow reflecting off of the bay, casting light on the hills and cliffs that surrounded the little cove. In the cabins and cottages that clung to its shores people were beginning to stir, filling woodstoves, lighting lamps, or busy with a variety of daily morning chores. Elsie was in her yard tossing chickenfeed from her apron to the hens when she heard it.

The terrifying scream bounced off the rock cliff and reverberated across the water, a fearsome echo that could not be ignored. Elsie clutched her heart as her knees went weak. Seed fell haphazardly upon the ground as the apron she wore fell from her hands. So many of her kinsmen worked at the quarry, including her husband, Joe. Elsie picked up her skirts and raced across the field to her sister-in-law, Fanny, with a sick sense of forbearing dogging her every step. Terror froze her throat and worry filled her mind, churning horrific thoughts as she ran.

Near the dock, where men were loading limestone onto a ship, work slowed as all hands looked the question to one another: 'what was that?' "All ye, just never mind! Get back to work," barked the boss.

The harrowing scream had erupted from one of the laborers, heard even above the din of pickaxes, shovels, and machinery. He was crushed between two full carts of limestone. Joe had been standing in the middle of the narrow track, having released the brake on his cart and was pushing on it, trying to send it on its way. Behind him and further up the track a co-worker had failed to fully engage his own brake, causing his cart to careen down the track, gaining momentum as it came. Between the racket of men using pickaxes on the rock, the din of the crusher, and carts being filled, and the sheer exhaustion of working long hours with little rest, Joe did not hear the cart barreling toward him. The men were expected to work nearly around the clock until the freighter was fully loaded. As his horrifying screech ricocheted off the cliff work paused, machinery ground to a halt.

High above the accident, William wiped the sweat from his brow, pushing his shovel into a mound of finely crushed limestone. The sun beat unmercifully on his shoulders as he lifted yet another shovelful. Beside him Phil pushed a full cart, rolling it on the rails toward the tunnel where it would be taken by conveyor belt to the waiting freighter. Both men froze in place and looked to one another for answers nobody yet had. Phil's worried gaze locked momentarily with William's, communicating their shared concern; it was the first day of work for their younger brother, Jack, and the brothers knew well the hazards involved. William swore and mumbled something about not borrowing trouble. Jack had turned twelve the previous winter and was anxious to pull his weight, to add his earnings to that of his father and brothers in the family pot. It would be another hour before the bell would clang, summoning the men to a much-needed meal and where answers to their many questions might be had.

Word spread quickly and a thunderous voice could be heard shouting for a horse and wagon to take the wounded man up to the surgery.

Grey-faced, Charlie worked alongside the other men to empty the overturned cart in order to free the pinned man. Blood pooled and ran freely along the track mixing with the limestone dust that sat inches deep on both sides of the track. The men could smell its odor, and the sight of it struck fear into every heart. Exhaustion left them and an adrenaline rush had them working feverishly. Charlie's solemn demeanor leant urgency to the work. Serious and quiet, Charlie was known to keep to himself, but he was also known to spend a fair bit of time up at Joe's place. A silent repetitive and plaintive prayer kept looping through his thoughts: *Hang on, Joe, please, God, help him, hang on b'y, hang on. Don't give up, Joe, don't ye give up. Oh, God, please, please ...Please, God, help him...* Charlie numbly pressed on. Silently and grimly shovel after shovel of stone was tossed aside. Joe's body was buried in limestone spilled from the heavy cart that had him trapped, fortunately one shoulder and his head were visible from the get go. It was Joe's salt and pepper cap that lay on the ground close by that Charlie had first recognized, lending urgency to his efforts.

"Heave! Ho," Charlie cried as the men rocked the cart off the inert body. Charlie dropped to his knees and carefully slid his arm under the shoulders of the injured man. Vic kneeled across from him; his expression mirrored that of Charlie's. Unsaid words formed thick lumps in their throats as they considered Joe's chances. It didn't look good. Both of Joe's legs had been crushed, but the right looked to be the worst, and blood continued to spurt freely from his wounds. "Wait!" Charlie commanded and quickly removed his belt for use as a tourniquet, pulling it as tightly as his strength allowed mid-way up Joe's right thigh, bringing the blood that had been gushing freely to a slow trickle.

"Make way! Make way!" the cry rang out as the driver of a horse and wagon maneuvered his way through the crowd. A wide plank normally used as a bridge across a nearby stream was put to use as a stretcher to carry the injured man to the wagon. Charlie cautiously rolled Joe onto his side as Vic and another man slipped the make shift stretcher under him. Two coworkers helped to hoist the inert body and carefully slide it into the wagon. The driver lost no time urging the horse forward. Charlie stood watching, heaving a great sigh and silent prayers heavenward. Walking back to the overturned cart he bent and retrieved Joe's tweed cap, shoving it into his back pocket.

Joe was well-known and well-liked in the tiny community where they lived. Vic stood next to Charlie, breathing hard and allowing memories to wash over him, like a slow-motion picture film he'd once seen: The time when Joe had, with infinite patience, taught him how to whittle a fine slingshot. Years later Vic used that same slingshot to bring down a duck. *Elsie and Joe come for supper that night and it was wonderful to see him eat. Did any man enjoy his food as much as Joe did?* Vic wondered to himself. Joe loved to dance a jig, leaping and stomping and having a time. He also loved to tramp across the fields and was teased about the flowers he'd often collected for his wife.

3

Joe and Elsie had no living children and to all the youth they were known as Aunt and Uncle, even those who were no blood relation. It was Joe who had taught Vic how to fish for cod and many times they had sat in companionable silence as the waves lapped softly against the dory. Memories collided with the shock of seeing his friend sprawled flat upon the ground, his life blood pouring out. Vic felt like he was losing his grip on reality. Thoughts incoherent and making no sense at all were free-falling through his mind. *Why would I remember the damned duck at a time like this?* He asked himself. Vic came out of his reverie when Charlie spoke, "Jesus, Mary, and Joseph what a going on. We best get back at it b'y, ye knows the mining captain will be screeching for us to make up the lost time." Silently Vic picked up his shovel and trudged slowly back with Charlie. Charlie moved like an automaton; thoughts and feelings tamped down until such time as he was free to examine them. The work was far from done and the men knew from experience that no accident would keep the powers that be from demanding a full day's work. Harry, the man who had been working alongside Joe, was in the midst of the group of men looking on as Charlie, Vic, and others worked to free the hurt man from the overturned cart.

God damned place, Harry thought to himself, he remembered Joe's cheerful demeanor that morning despite being as weary as the rest. *Then the bloody wheels wouldn't turn and I left to go get more grease. Why the dickens didn't ye wait fer me, Joe? Why'd ye try to budge that god damned cart all by yerself?* Harry was sickened by the whole business. He turned and walked away, away from the quarry, toward home. *There's work to be 'ad out to in the logging camps. I ain't sticking around 'ere to get 'urt and maybe killed. No sir, there's nuddin' to hold me 'ere.* Harry thought as he marched out of the quarry, breath hitching as he climbed the steep hill. *Aw, Joe, we bin buddies since we was just little lads. Leastwise til ye up and married and I went me own way. I 'opes ye pulls through this – but ye will. I knows ye will. As fer me, I ain't sticking round 'ere. Logging might be 'ard work, but it's damn sight better than 'eaving up rocks. . .*

Harry's thoughts tumbled one upon another as he made plans. He walked quickly, trying to outpace his thoughts and the images of Joe's crushed body.

4

Chapter

2

Doc was used to caring for the work horses, and he was frequently called upon to deal with broken fingers, cuts, head wounds, and various medical emergencies that were suffered by the men who labored in the quarry for eleven cents an hour. Injuries were common, but he felt ill-prepared to deal with dire emergencies, such as that facing him today. Luckily, he had a helper, if the injuries were as serious as he feared he would need help. It had been nearly an hour since a messenger had brought news of the accident. Doc looked up to see the horse and wagon coming at a fast clip up the hill.

"Make haste Ben," Doc ordered. The two men were outside waiting when the driver pulled up. One look at his face told Doc it was every bit as bad as he'd feared. "Come on man, lend a hand," Doc called as he strode to the back of the wagon. Carefully the three men lifted their bloodied burden and hustled the hurt man inside.

Hours later Doc dropped heavily into a chair. Ben moved about cleaning up and placing the blood-soaked linens in a tub of water. Minutes ticked slowly by as Doc reflected on his gruesome work. He'd had to amputate Joe's right leg. Gruffly he said, "Well b'y, I done me best but it's a true doctor he'll be needing". Ben hesitated a moment before asking, "Will we be leaving him be?" "Yes lad. Let him rest and we'll figure out where to lay him later. I'll not be moving him just yet. I will stay here and keep an eye on him," Doc answered.

"Would you like me to fetch ye something to eat from the cookhouse?" Ben asked.

"Ben, my son, I sure could use a cup of tea, that would be good," Doc replied.

Quietly Ben left the surgery and made his way downhill to the cookhouse. The quarry employed over a hundred men and accidents were bound to happen, but in the years that Ben had been employed there nothing this bad had ever happened. Entering the cookhouse Ben was met with anxious expressions. He'd come just as the men were having a much-deserved break. Joe's brother, Mick, sat with his sons, William and Phil, at the end of a bench a few feet from the door. Jack, their younger brother was with them. Phil was first to voice the question, "Well, then, how's he faring?" Steel-gray eyes bored into Ben's blue ones. Tall, lean, and gangly Ben stood awkwardly; shoulders stooped as he held the larger man's gaze. "Doc had to take off his right leg, and the left is in bad shape. He's out cold up in the surgery, but he's alive, at least for now," Ben answered bluntly. Around the dining hall the men reacted with grim acceptance. Only Jack, the youngest, allowed his emotions to show, jumping up from the table he burst out: "No, no, no! – poor Uncle Joe!" the boy turned away, embarrassed by his tears. Mick stood up behind Jack gripping his son's shoulder. Charlie also stood, taking Joe's cap from his back pocket he handed it to Jack. He'd had a notion to return it to Joe, hoping for a miracle. His eyes regarded the boy, remembering how Joe would go on about his nephew. "Hold onto this for yer uncle. It's yer first day so let this be a lesson to ye. Always be careful, you don't want to be dying here in this quarry," he growled, his gruffness masking his deep worry, "and ye don't want to be responsible for harm to nobody else neither".

Jack's fingers reached out for the cap, his eyes downcast, unable to meet Charlie's gaze, or anyone's. He swiped the snot that threatened to drip onto his shirt with his elbow while his other hand held the cap over his heart like a sacred talisman.

Ben shuffled his feet, one hand nervously squeezing the fingers of the other. "Mick, I'm thinking someone should go get Joe's missus," he said.

Phil glanced at his younger brother and thought of how he could race, often outpacing both his older brothers. "Jackie-boy, how fast do you think you could run to Uncle Joe's place?" He asked.

Jack's face turned a shade whiter, even as he pulled his shoulders back and considered his answer. This was no small thing, he knew, but he answered quickly: "Sure, Phil, you knows I am the fastest runner around. I'll go right now!"

"Finish yer food first, b'y, you've put in long hours up there and need yer strength," Mick told his son, but Jack was a ball of nerves and anxious to do something for his Uncle Joe – anything at all.

"No, Da, I'll be alright," he replied.

"Go on then, I'll make it right with the captain," Mick answered, "Go on."

Elsie was hanging clothes on the clothesline when she seen Jack racing toward her little clapboard cabin. Jack's mother stood rocking an infant in her arms close by. Jack gripped something tightly in his hand as he ran and Elsie's heart skipped a beat. She waited patiently when he reached them as he tried to catch his breath.

"Calm down now, son, tell us what happened?" She asked. Jack looked into Elsie's kind but troubled eyes and words failed him. It took a bit before he could force the words past the huge lump in his throat. "Tis Uncle Joe, ma'am," and with that Jack's tears flowed once more. "You gotta come quick. There's been an accident," Jack blubbered. "He's up at the surgery and it don't look good."

Elsie dropped the wet pillow case she'd been holding into the basket; her blood ran cold and she felt weak. "Oh my God, what's happened?" She questioned him. Fanny moved forward quickly, shunting the infant to one arm as she reached to grip her friend's hand.

"It's his legs. They got crushed by the carts and he had to be taken to the surgery. I don't know more than that. Come! Quick!" Jack begged, not wanting to tell her his deepest fear: that his Uncle Joe might die.

Elsie's eyes dropped to the object clenched in Jack's hand – Joe's tweed cap – and moved on legs that suddenly felt made of jelly toward the cabin door, the wind tangling her long skirts about her as she moved. Grabbing a shawl, she pulled it around her shoulders, "Let's go," she said.

"Oh, Elsie, I'll be here praying for him," Fanny whispered, "Jack, take good care of yer aunt, mind." Fanny reached out to brush wisps of hair from her son's forehead. Jack impatiently waved her away. "We gotta go, Ma," he choked out as he turned away.

7

The pair walked quickly through the fields, taking a shortcut to the rough path that led uphill to the surgery. It was a fine day. The sun shone brightly on the bay and the breeze carried the sea's briny odor, but Elsie and Jack were both quiet as they trudged up the hill, their inner worlds as dark as night. Words seemed frozen in throats tight with pain. Fear gripped them both in a stranglehold. Elsie did her best to pray as they mounted the sloping hill to the rough structure known as the surgery, but all she could manage was 'please, God' and 'help us'. Ben watched them approach from his perch on the stool just outside the door.

"Where's Joe?" Elsie blurted out as soon as she came within hearing distance. Ben rose slowly to his feet, not relishing the news he had to give. He waited while the twosome hurried the last few yards to him.

"Missus, I am so sorry for your troubles," he began, "Doc's done the best he can for him, t'is prayers he'll be needing now."

"Please, tell me what's happened," Elsie demanded.

Ben's blue eyes were troubled and he prayed silently for help as he mentally tried to form the words that would change this woman's life forevermore. "I can't say with certainty, but I heard 'em say that Joe was crushed between two fully loaded limestone carts early this morning. I think it'd be best if you hear the rest from Doc – he can explain everything better than I can," Ben softly answered.

"Can I see him now?" Asked Elsie.

"Will ya wait just a moment while I check with Doc?" Ben answered.

Elsie peered anxiously through the door as Ben entered. But Joe was not to be seen and she grabbed helplessly for Jack's hand.

"Do yer want I should go in with ya?" Jack wanted to know.

Elsie shook her head. She wanted time alone with Joe. And she was very afraid of what she might see, and her reaction to it. Seconds seemed to slow to a standstill while they waited. Elsie held her breath, the suspense almost more than she could bear, wanting only to be at Joe's side; to see for herself and to hold him once more. Jack gripped her hand tightly, squeezing it now and then as time seemed to crawl. He had no words, but did his best to comfort her with his presence. Finally, the door opened and Ben ushered her

8

inside. Jack clung to her hand for a moment, unwilling to let go, fearing to be alone with his thoughts. Gently Elsie extracted her fingers from his grasp, "Wait for me," she whispered and turned to face whatever may come.

Doc stood inside waiting for her. His face was grim indicating the serious nature of Joe's injuries. He gestured into another room and Elsie's step faltered for a moment as she approached the doorway. Reaching the opening Elsie's gaze fell upon the pallet where Joe lay pale and wrapped with bandages. Her step quickened and she dropped in a heap by his bedside. She let her gaze fall first upon the face she loved so well and for so long. 'He's so pale and still,' were her first thoughts.

Joe was not a man to sit still for long, always at something and their little farm was well kept. She lifted his limp hand to her lips and the pain of seeing him immobile brought tears to her eyes. She fell forward sobbing quietly on Joe's chest allowing her fear to trickle out onto his body. It was a momentary thing, steeling herself she sat up and allowed her gaze to travel the length of him. One leg, the right leg, was severed and only a stump remained. Both were heavily bandaged. Joe moaned softly in his stupor snapping her back from her shock.

"Joe?" Elsie called quietly. She stroked the face she cherished more than any other. "Oh God, please, help him," she whispered. Elsie had no idea how long she'd sat by his side when she heard Doc gently clearing his throat. Turning her head, she saw him motion her outside. Reluctant to leave Joe she tenderly kissed his brow before rising to follow Doc into the outer room.

"It's pretty bad," Doc admitted with a grimace. "I ain't no doctor. I just take care of the horses here and the odd bump, broken bones, or minor injuries. I ain't never had to take care of such a badly hurt man before. I did my best, Missus, I did."

"I am grateful you were here, Doc," Elsie replied. "What do you think his chances are?"

"Well, I have put down horses for a lot less," Doc began.

"Joe ain't no horse," the sudden rage surprising them both. Elsie's face burned with embarrassment and indignation.

"Oh me nerves, I am sorry," Doc avowed, "Sorrier than you could know. I'm not much of a speaking man. Joe lost a lot of blood and then I had to take off the leg – it was crushed worse than anything I've ever seen." Doc paused for a moment before continuing: "But Joe, he's a strong man, so it's hard to know how things'll turn out. You keep the faith, now. We can't move him to the hospital – it's too far away and I fear the jostling would make his leg start ta bleeding bad again..." Doc trailed off.

"So, what more can we do?" she asked.

"Nothing more we can do, Missus, but pray and leave him in God's hands," Doc offered.

Elsie nodded her head. She had expected as much.

"Is there aught I can do for you, Missus?" Doc asked.

Elsie frowned, the only one who needed 'doing for' in her mind was Joe. Dear, sweet, Joe. With mighty resolve Elsie pushed her pain and fear down deep inside. "No, nothing," she replied.

"Young Jack is still waiting outside," Doc noted. "Should I send him on home?"

"Jack's still here? No, I better have a word with him," Elsie said. She'd forgotten she'd asked him to wait. She walked to the door and looked outside. She was surprised to see the sun low in the sky, it didn't seem like she'd been there that long. Jack sat on the stool earlier occupied by Ben. He looked up when the door opened "Aunt Elsie?" Jack's eyes betrayed his worry and fear.

"Aw, Jack. Thank you so much for coming to get me and for waiting. Joe is still asleep, and likely will be for quite some time. You can go on home now. I will be staying the night to see to him. But please, will you pray for my Joe?"

"Aunt Elsie, you have no need to thank me, and yes, ma'am, I will pray for Uncle Joe," Jack answered.

Abruptly he threw himself at Elsie and her arms wrapped around him in a hard hug. Jack was not usually given to such displays, but it did not surprise her. She knew Jack had a special fondness for Joe. He had a close bond with his uncle. He was more like a son to them both.

"Jack, will you do one thing more for us?" Elsie asked

"I'd do anything for you and Uncle Joe," Jack assured, "Anything!"

"I left my laundry basket in the yard, and a pot of stew on the wood stove," Elsie explained. "Would you kindly move the stew pot off the stove and put the basket inside?"

"Of course, I will," Jack answered. "Would you like me to bring you food or anything?"

"No, I don't feel like eating and I'm sure Doc can manage to give me a bit of water or a cup of tea. You go on home now. Your mother will be worrying. Please don't forget to pray."

"I won't ferget," Jack responded and turned to leave.

Jack was true to his promise. On his way home, he dropped to his knees on the sandy shore to offer up his petitions for Joe. Jack was not much given to prayer. Oh, he went to the church with the rest of his family, his mother insisted on it, but he didn't give much thought to God once he exited the church on Sundays. He worked hard and he played hard but none would say he prayed hard. Now, however, he poured every bit of passion into his plea on Joe's behalf, begging and bargaining with God in the hope his uncle's life would be spared. Feeling slightly better Jack rose and continued walking homeward.

Jack was surprised to see his mother sitting on the huge boulder at the edge of their field waiting for him with his four-year-old sister, Rose, by her side. His mother waved as he came into view. Jack felt his heart lift a little. She had been concerned about him starting work at the quarry at such a young age, but as his father had pointed out, it was time for him to leave child-like activities behind and 'learn to pull his own weight'. His mother slipped off the rock and rushed to meet him, her concern for him obvious on her face.

"How did you know I'd be coming?" Jack asked her.

"Do ye not know how important ye are to me? To yer father and yer aunt and uncle, too? I been watching fer ye since not long after ye left with Aunt Elsie," she responded.

"So, how bad is he?" she asked him.

"Aw, Ma, he got caught between two full cartloads of limestone and both his legs were crushed," Jack told her and swiped angrily at the unmanly tears that rushed unbidden to his eyes.

Fanny put her arm around his shoulder, wanting to comfort him as she did when he was a little lad. "Oh, Jack, I was so afraid for you, and when Elsie come over telling me about the scream she'd heard…." Fanny's words trailed off

"I was fine. At least until I heard what happened," Jack told her. "But, Ma, what if he dies?"

Fanny swung around in front of him and grabbed his shoulders. "Now you listen to me, Jackie-boy," she ordered. "We will not be borrowing trouble; besides we don't know how bad it is yet, now do we?"

"When I went up to the surgery with Aunt Elsie Doc said it was bad, Ma. It's really, really bad. They don't know if he will make it. Doc had to take off his leg," Jack reported.

Rose began to cry and Fanny's face went white at this news. "Oh, dear Lord," she exclaimed, scooping Rose up in her arms.

Jack waited for the shock to ease somewhat before filling her in on what he knew. By this time, they had reached the covered porch where his younger sister, Sarah, was sitting rocking their infant brother, Jimmy.

"Here", Fanny said, setting Rose on the stoop and taking the baby from her arms, "take Rose inside and play with her".

"What's the matter, Mama?" Sarah asked worriedly as Rose, still sniffling, clung to her side.

"I'll come to talk to you and yer sister in a minute. Just take her inside, Sarah, right now!" Fanny ordered.

Joe and Elsie lived a stone's throw away in the neighboring field. They were frequent visitors and often helped out with child care and work on their small farm. In turn, Jack and his brothers were often called upon to help their uncle with chopping firewood for the winter; getting hay into their small barn, hauling water, and dozens of other chores. The path between the two cottages was packed down, the soil hard as rock. Jack spent almost as much time at Joe's as he did at home. All of this, and more, went through Fanny's mind as she fought to accept the awful news. The infant began to fuss in her arms and Fanny was unable to question Jack any further.

"Aw, Ma, I almost forgot. Aunt Elsie asked me to take care of a couple of things at their place. I'll run over there now," Jack said.

"I looked after the stew already. The laundry is inside. It will keep. Why don't you come have a cuppa tea?" Fanny asked. Jack nodded silently and followed his mother into the little cabin.

Fanny watched Jack as he sipped his tea, jiggling the baby in her arms. Her son's face was solemn and he spoke little. 'Mick and the boys will be home soon,' she spoke softly to comfort herself, 'I best see to the girls and get supper underway'.

"Ma, I'm just gonna go for a bit of a walk before supper," Jack spoke quietly, eyes somber as he waited for his mother's assent. At his mother's nod Jack let himself out the kitchen door.

Fanny found her daughters in the front room. Sarah was sitting in the big chair with Rose cuddled up beside her. Sarah's eyes were large in her small oval face. Fanny dropped onto the sofa across from them and sighed. She chose her words carefully as she told them about the accident. She didn't want to alarm them, but felt she must prepare them somewhat for she had a terrible feeling.

Much later Jack entered the little house where his parents and older brothers were gathered around the kitchen table. His younger sisters were sitting on the floor by the woodstove playing while the baby slept soundly in the cradle beside them. Heads turned as Jack entered the room. His father had a deep scowl on his face, while his mother's countenance betrayed her worry.

"Sit down here Jackie-boy, I'll fetch you a cup of tea. Can you eat, lad?" Fanny enquired. "I made pea soup, if you'd like some."

"Yes, I s'pose so," Jack answered.

"I spoke with the captain about sending you off to get Aunt Elsie," Mick spoke up, "He didn't like it, but said considering the situation and all he'd let it go this time."

"Thanks, Da," Jack responded. "Will I be at the same post tomorrow then?"

"Report to Josiah, the pit boss, in the morning. I expect you will be, but I didn't think to ask," came the answer. "If I find out who let that cart go with no warning," Mick, growled. "And what was Joe doing standing on the track?" He banged his fist loudly on the table making Fanny jump and the baby howl.

"Michael Kelly! Calm yourself!" Fanny exclaimed. "You'll frighten the little ones," she said as she rushed to lift the crying baby from his cradle. Sarah grabbed Rose's hand and followed their mother into the living room.

William reached over to grip his father's shoulder as the others gazed down at the tabletop. "We'll know soon enough," he told his dad.

Phil had been sipping his tea and brooding about this same question when Jack arrived. Soon talk turned to conditions at the quarry and the deplorable long hours that often led to mishaps, but none as serious as this. Joe figured strongly in the conversation as the family tried to come to grips with the tragedy. One question burned in all their minds: *Would Joe make it?* At least the bloody freighter was loaded and was sailing out to deep sea even while Mick and his sons considered the personal cost of the cargo it carried. The men had worked even harder to get it underway so Joe's relatives could get home. Jack silently ate the soup his mother brought and sipped the welcome tea. His mother had put the girls to bed and now sat quietly rocking little Jimmy and listening to the men talk. She knew her husband was angry. It was his way. And his right. After all, it was such an avoidable accident. But Fanny was a believer in waiting for all sides of a story to come to light before passing any judgements. Finally, it was time for bed and each shuffled off, too weary and disheartened to talk any longer.

Chapter

3

J ack opened his eyes and slowly the events of the day before filtered through his morning haze. Quickly he popped out of bed and hauled on the clothes he had carelessly discarded on the floor the night before. The house was silent. His brothers slumbered on in the bunk beds across the room. Quietly Jack tiptoed to the door and gently closed it behind him. He hoped to have a moment alone before the rest of the family made an appearance. Fanny sat in the living room calmly rocking beside the wood stove, upon which a kettle of water was steaming. *I should have known better,* he thought, *nobody can beat Ma out of bed.* Jack nodded at his mother's whispered good morning and crossed to the back door to make his way to the outhouse to relieve himself. When he returned Mick had joined his wife and the two were talking very quietly.

"Do you think I have time to slip over to Uncle Joe's to feed the animals before we leave for work?" He asked his father.

Mick nodded, Fanny smiled her encouragement and Jack quickly retraced his steps outside. He looked up at the soft dawn just beginning to lighten the sky and sent up an earnest prayer for his Uncle Joe. Thoughts of his aunt and uncle were constant as he went about the business of feeding the animals. The hens clucked softly and the pig made joyful grunting noises as Jack filled its trough with vegetable peelings and table scraps. Afterward he turned the cow out of the barn and then went into the little cabin to grab the laundry his aunt had started the day before. He wasn't a good hand at hanging clothes, but he did his best.

"Yer doing it all wrong," Sarah piped up. She had been watching his efforts with consternation and quickly stepped in to help.

"Does Ma know yer over here?" Jack asked, handing her another pillow case from the laundry basket.

"Yep, she sent me to keep ye company," Sarah retorted. Jack frowned at his little sister, "Hang on a minute," he told her, noticing the difficulty she was having reaching the clothesline, "Here, ye go," he plunked the stool down in front of her.

"Thanks, Jack," Sarah smiled at her brother and stepped up onto the stool.

He watched as Sarah capably dealt with the remaining garments. "C'mon, let's go home," he lifted the stool to replace it by the door. Sarah skipped beside him as they made their way across the field, chattering about all kinds of nonsense that Jack let go in one ear and out the other. Sarah missed her brother yesterday. Jack could be counted on to show her all kinds of interesting things, like how to catch trout in the stream that cut across the fields before emptying into the ocean; how to skip stones across the calm water of the little bay; how to blow into long blades of grass to make them whistle, among many other things. Sarah loved playing with Rose and minding the baby while their mother worked around the house, but spending time with Jack was the best.

Their mother was stirring a huge pot of porridge by the time Jack and Sarah returned home. Their father and brothers sat at the kitchen table waiting for breakfast and discussing the happenings of the previous day. Sarah set about putting spoons and bowls on the table while the youngest members of the family slept on. There was tension in the air and all faces wore glum expressions. Sarah knew something was afoot, but had yet to be told any more. An energetic but patient child, she knew her Ma would tell her eventually.

The walk to work was vastly different from the day before when his father, uncle, and brothers had alternately teased and advised him about his first day of work. Today William and Mick walked ahead of Phil and Jack, their strides markedly shortened. They were just a quarter of the way there when Mick asked Jack if he would run ahead to the surgery to see if there was any news, Jack fairly flew the distance, his feet seeming to have grown wings overnight. Jack had always been a fast runner, but adding purpose to his race made him even swifter. He huffed and puffed outside the surgery, waiting to catch his breath before he timidly knocked on the door. It was Ben who answered the door.

"Hey, Ben. My father and brothers and me are on our way to work. I ran ahead to see if there was any news about Uncle Joe. How is he? Has he woken up? Has there been any improvement? Will he be okay?" Jack barely drew breath as he questioned Ben.

"He has not awakened. At least, not that I'm aware of," Ben answered him. "There's naught a difference since yesterday. His missus is still here with him. She's refusing to leave his side."

"Might I come in just for a moment?" Jack asked. He was resolved to see his beloved relations before he faced the work day ahead of him.

"Wait right here and I'll ask," Ben told him.

Like the day before time stood stubbornly still while Jack waited impatiently for an answer. It was Elsie who opened the door. Her face was drawn and a sleepless night was in evidence. Disheveled clothes and wisps of hair that had escaped the bun she wore gave further witness to the long night she had passed.

"Aw, Jackie-boy," she breathed, "Ben says you want to see Joe, but I don't know if that's wise," she said.

"Please, Aunt Elsie, please," Jack begged. "I promise I will be quick. I just need to see him, only for a minute,"

Elsie regarded the young man for a moment, thinking again of how much he loved Joe. "Are you sure, Jack, are you sure?" She asked. "He's still not awake. He won't be chatting with ye, or even know you're here."

"I need to see him," Jack pleaded.

Elsie sighed deeply and looked into the distance, her gaze troubled, before she finally answered. "Jackie-boy, we have to be very, very brave," she barely whispered, and, looking into Jack's face said, "All right, then, but only for a moment."

Jack nodded quickly and pushed the door open. Floorboards squeaked as the pair made their way to the little room where Joe lay.

Jack's breath caught in his throat as his glance fell upon the still figure. His step quickened until he stood beside Joe's pallet. Tears filled his eyes once again. Dropping to the stool beside the bed, Jack folded his hands as if to pray. In truth, he was trying desperately not to strike out in frustration and desperation as he regarded the unmoving form before him. He wanted badly to hit something – he was hard pressed for what to do with the emotions that threatened to be his undoing. Breathing deeply Jack fought to maintain composure and to rid himself of the anxiety that had plagued him for the past twenty-four hours. A quiet rage consumed him as he considered the pain and suffering his uncle had endured, and had yet to endure – if he made it! Leaning forward Jack placed a hand on Joe's wide shoulder. "You get better, ye hear," he told him. "We need ye here," and with that Jack choked up again. Abruptly he stood up, glancing at his aunt, he turned and bolted for the door. Elsie let him go, understanding his grief and pain better than any other. Joe softly moaned again in his sleep and she turned to minister to him.

Jack's headlong dash took him outside and his feet carried him at a furious pace to the path. He could see his father and brothers far ahead of him, and he hurried to catch up. The men heard his footfall and paused to wait for him. Jack's gaze met his father's steady stare.

"Well? What news," Mick asked gruffly.

"Naught to speak of," Jack puffed, "he's about the same as yesterday – been no change."

Quick nods met Jack's response. The foursome stood quietly on the path while Jack caught his breath until Mick rasped, "Well, nothing can be done for it and we best get going afore we're late ta work".

When they reached the work site Mick grasped Jack by the shoulder, telling his older sons to carry on. "Come with me," he ordered.

Jack followed his father into the rough shed where the mining captain was drinking from a tin mug. He looked up as Mick entered the shack. His bushy eyebrows were raised in surprise and he grimaced at the boy who shuffled nervously behind his father. "What do ye want?" he asked.

"I come to give ye a report about me brother, Joe. You remember Joe? The one that was nearly killed yesterday, and may yet die?" Mick growled.

The mining captain moved slowly, his great bulk defying years of hard, strenuous work. "Well, out with it, then." He spat.

"Jack here stopped by the surgery and I thought you'd want to know ye'll be a man short today, and for some time to come." Mick's anger was obvious in his demeanor and tightly held control.

The mining captain looked to Jack for more information. "You got anything to add?" He asked Jack.

"Well, sir, Uncle Joe is in an awful way. They had to cut his leg off and he hasn't awakened since the accident yesterday," Jack quietly responded.

"What good is a one-legged man 'ere?" The mining captain wanted to know.

"You'd fire him for that?" Mick's voice rose in anger and disbelief. "It was because of ye he lies there, near death, if he makes it a'tall".

"Don't be blaming me," the mining captain barked back. "T'is not me fault…"

"Whose fault, then?" Mick cut him off. "Forcing men to labor well past endurance to fill your precious freighter and to make gains for yerself. Ye think we don't see how ye lick the boots of the uppity ups? We knows what yer about. Beasts are treated better!"

"Ye best 'old yer tongue if ye wants to keep yer job 'ere," the mining captain threatened.

Mick stood stock still. Quietly he repeated, "Are ye going ta fire Joe?"

"Look, man, some things are beyond me own control," the mining captain began, "there ain't gonna be no decision today. Leave it be for now. Ye're a good worker, Mick. I knows that. And Joe is a good worker too. Let it be and I'll see what I can do. That's the best I can tell ye right now. I 'ave to go see the agent about this, but I got no time for that today. But I will, and soon."

Mick stood staring at his boss for several seconds before turning on his heel to stomp away. Jack followed and waited silently for his father's instructions. Mick stood quietly for a moment wrestling with his thoughts before he admonished him, "Don't ever expect fairness from the likes of them," he said, "just do yer job, do as they tell ye, but watch out for yerself and fer the men around ye" Mick paused, his brown eyes considering his young son, "go on now, I'll see ye at the break."

Jack nodded his assent and quietly they parted ways. Jack went to see the pit boss, who had assigned him work the day before. As before Jack was stationed next to the rock crusher, but the work was not as hurried or intense as it had been yesterday, though equally as heavy and as loud. Jack's job was to empty heavy cart loads of rock into piles to be fed into the crusher by other men. It was hard, grueling work and soon his shoulders and back were in agony once again. Mindlessly, ignoring the fire burning in his back and triceps, Jack worked on. The manual labor helping to dissipate the anxiety and stress he'd been enduring thinking of his uncle and what the future may bring. A soft breeze ruffled his curly hair and helped cool his slick-with-sweat brow. Slowly the morning passed and next he knew the crusher stopped and he heard the bell clanging, calling them to the cookhouse for lunch. Stretching his back, Jack looked about, searching for his brothers and father. Spying them on the path below, Jack scrambled down the hill.

The cookhouse was relatively quiet when he entered. The men were hungrily shoveling plates of beans into their mouths. A few murmured quietly to one another. Jack made his way to the bench to sit with his father and brothers. The air fairly crackled with tension left over from the day before. It was a small community and word of Joe's accident had spread like wildfire. All hands knew of Joe's state of health and all waited for news.

The sound of a bench scraping against the floorboards and the crack of a punch landed on a bony jaw made the men turn their heads and crane their necks to see what had happened. Charlie was on his feet standing over the sprawled body of a co-worker, while Vic did his best to wrestle him away.

"Get up, ye son of a bitch, get up!" Charlie grated out as he tried to fling off the arms that pinned his own behind his back.

"Give it up, mate, give it up," Vic ordered his friend.

"I'll kill the son of a bitch," Charlie responded, gasping raggedly with anger.

Other men jumped to Vic's aid and wrestled the livid man outside. All around him men stood or sat anxiously at the edge of their seat. Jack looked to Phil, wondering what was going on. Soon the cookhouse emptied with men making their way outdoors to find out what was happening. They were standing around in small groups when Jack came outside. A knot of men surrounded Charlie and Vic, who continued to talk quietly. Jack inched his way to the outer rim to listen to what was being said.

"T'was his doing," Charlie was saying, "He deserves everything he gets."

"I allow yer right," Vic tried to pacify him, "but, let's just hear his side of it, alright?"

"I tell ya, it was naught else but a horrible accident," another man reasoned, raising Charlie's hackles once again.

"That t'was no accident" Charlie barked, "T'was pure stupidity and naught else. Are ye gonna tell Joe's missus, it t'was 'just an accident'?"

The man made as if to say something and changed his mind. He hung his head balefully, like a shamed dog. Charlie seemed to be calming down and Vic released the arm he had been holding fast as his friend's ire rose again. Charlie waved the men away, noticing Jack for the first time. Vic followed Charlie's glance to where Jack stood. Unknown to Jack, his brother, Phil, was standing behind him.

"What do you know about this business?" Phil softly questioned, his burning eyes a contrast to the tone of his voice.

Charlie's gaze never left Jack's face as he answered, "Heard that buddy over there," he waved, gesturing toward the man he'd hit, "didn't apply the brake on the cart that hit Joe".

"We don't know that for fact," Vic quickly interrupted. "But that's what they're saying. Maybe Harry might know something, but nobody's seen him since it happened."

On the other side of the yard the accused man stood rubbing his jaw. His shoulders were slumped, as though he carried a heavy load and his rejection by the others obvious – only one man stood by his side. Just then the bell clanged again, summoning the men back to work.

On the way home at the end of the day the allegations were topmost on the minds of the brothers and their father. They discussed the ramifications as they trudged along. Ominously, Mick had little to say, responding only with grunts as Phil relayed what he learned. It added to their anger, grief, and distress. As they neared the surgery Mick announced he'd meet them at home, having made the decision to check on his brother's condition. His sons nodded agreement, but Jack asked to accompany their dad.

"Jackie-boy, I know what yer uncle means to ye, but I need to do this alone," Mick answered his query. "Besides, ye need to help yer brothers. I need ye three to chop some wood for the morrow".

"But, Da, there's wood enough for a fortnight. Can it not wait 'til tomorrow?" Jack implored.

"Jack! Not another word," Mick replied. "Go on home with yer brothers. Tell yer Mum I will be along shortly," and with that Mick swung away toward the surgery.

Phil dropped his arm across Jack's shoulder, "Maybe ye can stop by Uncle Joe's, make sure the animals are fed and they have firewood and enough water for when he gets home," he comforted. Jack nodded his agreement and the three continued on their way.

Across the bay a flock of gulls swooped and skimmed over the water's surface. Their piercing cries echoing mournfully across the waves. Jack watched the birds, reminded of the sick gull he'd found and brought to his Uncle Joe when he was just a bit of a lad. The bird's leg seemed broken and his uncle had held the bird firmly under his arm while he examined it. The gull had not made a single sound while Uncle Joe gently checked it over. In the end he'd fashioned a box for it from an old, broken lobster trap. Jack had been about five or six at the time and Joe had instructed him to feed the bird and give it fresh water every day. "I don't know how badly he's hurt, but his leg seems broke to me," he'd told the boy, "We'll just have to wait and let nature take its course". Jack had visited his uncle's place every day, bringing scraps of food to feed the gull, until finally the day came when his uncle felt it was healed well enough to be set free. They had walked down to the bank with the box in Joe's arms, but it was Jack who was given the honor of releasing the bird. They stood on the green bank and watched the gull wheel above them in the sky, before finally taking its leave and flying out to sea. It was a magical moment in the young boy's life. As he remembered it now, Jack thought of how his uncle had taught him a deep respect for all life. William broke his reverie when he spoke suddenly.

"I been thinking, maybe we ought to take up a collection for Uncle Joe and Aunt Elsie," he said, "I mean, I hope he pulls through, and if and when he does, he won't be able to work no more at that quarry. And he won't be able to fish neither, or go logging for the paper mill. I allow he'll be laid up for a long time, I knows the b'ys will chip in whatever they can".

"That's a great plan we'll put it to them tomorrow, eh?" Phil answered.

"Da won't like it. He detests taking charity," William responded.

"T'is true enough," Phil replied, "but I think we can bring him 'round".

"Perhaps it's a good thing he stopped off at the surgery – give us a bit o' time to talk it over with Ma," William answered, "She can make him see the sense in it".

The three remained quiet as they walked the well-worn path home, each lost in his own thoughts.

Phil looked thoughtfully at his brother. William, at nineteen, was the eldest of their clan and was given to consider the practicalities of life. Normally he was taciturn, speaking very little. Phil, was also down to earth, but was a bit of a dreamer. He longed for the day when they could buy another dory or two and make fishing a more lucrative venture than it had been thus far. He loved being out on the ocean jigging for cod or dropping the lobster pots into the sea and waiting for a good haul. He hated the work at the quarry and though fishing also had its hazards he knew the quarry represented the greater risk. There'd been talk of another lobster cannery coming, which would make fishing for lobster profitable.

As they neared their home, Jack left the path and headed once again to look after his uncle's animals, calling over his shoulder that he'd be there shortly.

"He's a good lad, our Jack," Phil remarked, "I sure hope Uncle Joe can pull through this. It will go hard on Jack if he doesn't"

"Yes, it will, but, Uncle Joe – he's as strong as an ox," William replied.

Fanny was jiggling their infant brother in one arm as she stirred something on the stove with her other hand. She turned as her eldest sons entered the room. "Where's yer Da and Jack?" She asked.

"Jack's feeding the animals, milking the cow, and checking on the firewood over at Uncle Joe's. He'll be here soon. And Da stopped by the surgery to see how Uncle Joe's doing," Phil said.

"I been praying for them both all day. I sure missed your aunt's help today, God bless her. Sarah tries her best, but she's such a small girl....aw Joe, poor Joe – I don't know what she'd do without him ..." Fanny became lost in thought, considering.

"Don't fret, Ma. What is it yer always telling us? Don't borrow trouble, leave it in God's hands," Phil gently reminded her.

"Yer right, me son, yer right," Fanny spoke so lowly Phil had to strain to hear her. "Here, Ma, give 'im to me," Phil said as he reached to take his tiny brother from his mother's arm.

"Ma? There's something we want to talk with ye about," William began, "Something we need help with concerning Da."

Fanny listened intently as William told her of the plan to raise money for Joe and Elsie and revealed his worry about Mick's stubborn pride and views regarding charity.

"Yer Da believes in hard work and taking care of yer own," Elsie told them, "But Joe did a lot for folks around here and there's many who will want to return a kindness. Your da has to see that and understand it would be cruel to keep 'em from doing what they can. Don't ye worry. Ye let me handle yer father."

William stood and planted a kiss on his mother's cheek, pleasing her with his seldom displayed affection. He then turned and walked outside.

Phil was still cradling Jimmy in his arms. "Hand 'im over," Fanny told him, "Go wash the grime off ye. Supper will be ready in a few minutes. Will ye take a gander and see if yer Da's coming? But wash away that grime first. Sarah, oh, there ye be – here take the baby for a bit".

William was sitting on the steps when Phil walked outside. "Do ye see Da coming?" Phil asked his brother as he looked out across the field.

"Ain't seen hide nor hair of him yet, but he should be along soon," William answered. Both men turned when they heard Jack's shrill whistle, and saw his wild gestures beckoning them to come. Far across the fields they could see the miniscule figures of a man and a woman walking slowly down the hill. Phil marched across the yard to meet Jack.

"I think that's da coming with Aunt Elsie," Jack was saying as he ran toward Phil. "Can we harness up the buggy and go meet them?"

24

"Jackie-boy, the time it'd take to do that they'll be here," Phil responded.

"I already have it done," Jack admitted guiltily, "I figured Da would be some tired after all the long days at work and all. I thought I'd ask you or William to drive up to the surgery to get him...."

Phil was moved by his younger brother's thoughtfulness. The buggy was saved for special occasions and for going to church on Sundays. Mick didn't want it soiled by their grimy work clothes, and besides, it wasn't very big, just large enough for three at most. Mick sometimes took Fanny out for a ride on a Sunday afternoon, but since Jimmy's arrival a few weeks back the buggy had mostly sat safely stored in the small shed. The old work horse neighed as the brothers reached the vehicle and Phil noticed Jack had thrown an old blanket across the seat to protect it from the limestone dust that Mick was sure to be covered in.

"Ye're something else, ye are," Phil told his younger brother as he climbed aboard. "Will ye let Ma know I'm gone to get Da?"

"I will," Jack replied and stood back as Phil flicked the reins and the buggy began rolling out of the yard.

Phil was glad Jack had the foresight to ready the buggy when he observed his father and aunt's wearied faces. Elsie's face looked wretched with grief as Mick helped her climb into the buggy. Neither said a word as Phil turned the buggy around to head back home. Mick didn't even ask why he'd come, but sat stiffly beside his sister-in-law, tense and somber.

Jack was waiting by the shed when Phil pulled into the yard, ready to remove the harness and take care of the horse. Mick jumped lightly to the ground and turned to aid Elsie. They kept their silence, neither one speaking a word as they made their way to the house.

Fanny was standing cutting thick slabs of bread when Mick entered with Elsie. She dropped the knife and rushed to embrace her sister-in-law.

"Oh, Elsie, I've thought of naught else but you and Joe since we got the news," Fanny began. Elsie clung tightly to her for a moment before stepping back to look Fanny in the eye. Quietly she shook her head, her own eyes bright with unshed tears as she gazed into Fanny's.

25

"Joe?" Fanny breathed. Elsie shook her head once more; her grief stealing her voice and preventing any comment.

Fanny turned her head to look at her husband. Her face held the question her heart would not let her ask.

"Joe's gone," Mick announced gravely. With that Elsie crumpled and would have fallen had she not been held in Fanny's strong arms.

"Come," Fanny said and led the distraught woman to a chair. Fanny dropped to her knees in front of Elsie and tightly grasped her hands. The women were sitting silently when Jack burst through the door. One look told him all he needed to know, confirming his deepest fear. He paused for a moment before making a head-long dash out the door.

Chapter

4

William had remained sitting on the steps when Phil drove the buggy into the yard. The brothers had assumed there was bad news and lingered outside to give their aunt a bit of privacy and to allow their parents time to speak with her. The pair were now leaning over the log fence, gazes on the hills, far off in the horizon when Jack rushed back outside. "Jackie-boy?" William let the endearment fall unanswered and watched as Jack made a bee-line for Joe and Elsie's place. "Let him be for now," Phil muttered as they watched Jack run across the fields.

It was Mick who found the boy huddled in a corner of Joe's barn about an hour later. Quietly he sat down beside him, saying nothing he grasped his son's shoulder and waited for Jack to speak.

"It just ain't fair, Da," Jack whispered. Mick had to lean in to hear him. Jack's head was dropped low, eyes cast down upon the rough boards of the floor. Mick's grasp tightened as he replied, "No, it ain't. Life ain't fair, my son," he hesitated a moment, "But, somehow we gotta go on".

"I didn't even say good-bye," Jack mumbled, "I couldn't say it. I didn't want him to die…"

"I know, son. Joe, he thought the world of you," Mick said. "He appreciated all the ways you helped him and Elsie. He'd understand. I think, somehow, he knew you were there…." Mick paused. "What's that ye got there?" he asked, noticing the cap Jack had tightly clenched in his hands.

"Charlie gave it to me. It's his cap. He was wearing it when it happened…" Jack turned the tweed cap in his hands, smoothing the fabric as he did so.

"T'was his favorite cap," Mick noted. "Elsie gave him that cap years ago".

"Do ye think she'd let me keep it?" Jack asked. For some reason that cap had become symbolic of everything Joe stood for in Jack's mind. It was a little piece of Joe he could keep with him, always – tangible proof that his uncle had existed.

"I think so," Mick answered. "But let's not ask just yet. She's hurting pretty bad right now," Mick hesitated once again, "It might make her feel a tad better if ye would come in and see her," he suggested.

Jack nodded and slowly climbed to his feet. Mick stood up also, and, keeping an arm about Jack's shoulder led him back across the field to home.

"Ye have to keep up yer strength," Fanny was telling Elsie as Mick and Jack re-entered the house. The women were sitting at the table, a bowl of soup on the table in front of Elsie. She held a spoon loosely in her hand and her eyes were downcast. Sarah and Rose were sitting wide-eyed on the bench behind the trestle table.

Jack stood awkwardly at the foot of the table while Mick took his seat at the head of it. Elsie looked up and smiled weakly at Jack, "I hear ye been taking care of the animals. Thank ye," she said.

"T'was nothing. I just wanted to help however I could," Jack responded.

"I knew I could count on all of ye," Elsie glanced around the room. "I know my Joe would appreciate everything you've done".

"We ain't done much," Mick replied, "And, of course, ye knows we'll be here to help with the farm and whatever ye may need," he gently continued. "We have much to discuss, once all these young'uns are abed".

"I am much obliged..." Elsie started to say, but Mick cut her off.

"None of that, now. Yer family, and family takes care of their own," Mick gruffly intoned.

Fanny reached over and embraced her sister-in-law. "Try to eat a bit more of that soup," she told her. "I'm just going ta see to the rest of supper".

Later, after the table had been cleared and dishes had been done, Fanny put the girls to bed and laid the baby back in his cradle, placing it near the wood stove for warmth and to keep an eye on the child, while the boys, Mick, and Elsie sat back down at the kitchen table. Fanny bustled about the kitchen and filled the kettle to put on the stove for tea.

"Now, Elsie, I think ye should spend the night here with us," Fanny began, "and we can think on what to do ta morrow, make plans ... for the funeral ..."

Mick nodded, "There's two sets of bunks in the boys' room. I can sleep in there tonight. Ye women can share the bed in our room," he asserted. "Phil, yer to go to the mining captain and let him know about Joe. I won't be going ta work ta morrow and neither will William – tell the captain so. I need to be here, and William, I'll be needing yer help ta build a coffin and to fetch Joe's body home".

At this point Elsie covered her face with her hands and softly wept. Jack jumped up from the table to comfort her, putting an arm across her shoulders. All was quiet and for several minutes no one spoke. All hands jumped at the knock on the door. Fanny hastened to open it. Charlie stood there with cap in hand.

"I am sorry to bother ye, I heard the news and..."

"Charlie!" Mick butted in. "C'mon in b'y".

Charlie entered the room and seeing Elsie so distraught dropped his eyes. "I am mighty sorry for your troubles, Missus," he said. Elsie nodded her thanks, not trusting to speech.

"Mick, may I have a word with ye outdoors?" Charlie asked.

"Sure thing," Mick replied and followed him outside. The men walked around to the back of the house before Charlie revealed the reasons for his visit. He had crossed paths with the parson and gave him the sad news. The parson had promised to visit the family the next day, but that was not the real purpose for his visit.

"I s'pose ye knows I've been spending time with Constance from over on the head," he shyly began, "we've been talking 'bout getting married".

Mick nodded assent – nothing much got by folks in the village and he'd heard the rumors.

"I bought some nice oak lumber, had it brought in from the mainland," Charlie continued, "in any case it's not quite enough to build the table I wanted fer a wedding gift fer her..."

Mick waited patiently. "I just thought, well, it's nice lumber. I shaved and sanded it meself. It'd make a mighty fine casket for Joe and I'd consider it an honor if ye'd use it," Charlie finished.

"Well," Mick said, "That would surely be a time saver. Would ye be willing to let me pay fer it?"

"Please, Mick, Joe was a good friend, a wonderful friend," Charlie pleaded, "and this is the last thing I can ever do fer him. I'd consider it a kindness if ye would just accept it as a gift, fer him and fer his missus".

Mick looked into Charlie's solemn eyes and nodded. Charlie released a deep breath; one he didn't know he'd been holding. "Okay, good. I borrowed Vic's wagon to bring it. I was hoping ye'd let me give it. It's over by the barn. D'ye think yer boys would help me unload it?"

Mick turned to shout out for his sons to come help. Together they all walked to the barn.

"That's fine wood," Mick remarked as he ran his fingers over the smooth lumber. Charlie nodded. The men made short work of stacking it inside the corner of the small barn. Mick wiped his brow and stood regarding Charlie. Mick's sons thanked him for the gift and left the two men talking.

"Oh, almost fergot these," he said handing Mick a sack he retrieved from the wagon seat. Mick looked inside and poured brass fittings into his hand: handles, nails, hinges – everything he'd need to build his brother's coffin. Mick was not given to emotion and Charlie was embarrassed to witness it, but Mick was quick to tamp down his feelings as he held out a hand for Charlie to shake.

"I'm gonna go on home now. Please tell Elsie I would be happy to help in any way ..." Charlie said.

"Yer a good man, Charlie, we're much beholden to ye," Mick began, but Charlie waved his thanks away and as he moved to leave said, "One more thing, if it pleases all of ye...I'd consider it a real honor to carry his casket...if ye would let his widow know..."

"I will, Charlie, I will," said Mick.

He watched as Charlie drove the wagon across the field to take the road up to Vic's. The sun was setting, the end of another long, painful day, and life wasn't finished with them yet, Mick thought to himself and kicked a small stone out of his way.

He entered the house to expectant glances from his family. "Charlie has supplied the lumber for Joe's casket," he said bluntly. He looked at Elsie and became gentler, "T'is fine oak. Joe will have the best, the very best, even brass fittings."

"That's so kind of him," Elsie answered, overcome.

Mick turned to his sons, "Why don't you lads take a walk?" he suggested.

After the boys had gone outdoors Mick sat at the table once again and looked at his sister-in-law. "How ye holding up Elsie?" He asked.

Elsie shrugged her shoulders in response. Fanny reached across the table to hold her hand.

"I was just wondering about Joe's body. D'yer want to care for it yerself or should we find someone to do it fer ye?" Mick carefully asked.

Elsie straightened her spine. "Joe's my husband. T'is my duty and no one else's. I will look after my Joe!"

Fanny gentled patted her hand. "I'll help ye, if ye wants," she offered.

"Please," Elsie whispered. Looking at Mick she asked, "And will ye get the parson?"

"Charlie ran into the parson on his way here," Mick told her, "He'll be here tomorrow to talk with ye".

Elsie nodded; her relief evident in the sudden lifting of her shoulders. She sat straight and her shoulders no longer slumped, 'Good', she thought, 'things are being looked after...'

'Mick, will ye ask the boys if one of 'em will go up the road and ask Hilda if her girl can come sit with the little ones tomorrow? There's a lot to do and I'll be needing her help," Fanny told Mick. Mick grunted and rose to do her bidding.

William was quick to volunteer, stating he had need of a good, long walk. With that detail taken care of Mick returned inside. Phil was studying Jack and considering how he could best help him.

"Hey, Jackie-boy, shall we take a walk down to the beach?" He asked.

Jack, who had been sitting quietly with his thoughts, looked at his older brother. Phil was only seventeen, but wise beyond his years. Jack nodded assent and the two moved away in a relaxed stroll toward the front of the house. It wasn't long before Jack was confiding in his brother and releasing some of his pent-up pain. Once they reached the beach, they searched for rocks to skip out into the waves. A while later, the calm of the bay coupled with listening to the waves lap softly upon the shore, seemed to have the desired effect on Jack and the brothers retraced their steps back to the little house. As they turned the corner of the house Phil spied William coming across the field and the pair waited for him to join them. "She coming?" Phil addressed William. He suspected his brother was sweet on the maiden, who was close in age to William's. He inwardly smiled at William's quickness in volunteering to visit the homestead that lay a couple of miles away. William glanced quickly at Phil's face, attempting to figure out if his brother was teasing him once again. Satisfied he wasn't he answered, "Of course she is, said she'd be happy to do it".

"Do yer think it's safe to go inside yet." Jack piped up, not noticing the undercurrents between his elder brothers.

"Only one way to find out," Phil suggested, "you go first Jackie-boy".

The trio made their way to the back door, pausing under the window for a moment to see if they could overhear anything. When nothing seemed to be amiss Phil pushed Jack toward the door.

Fanny was replacing the kettle on the stovetop when the boys entered the room. "I am just making tea, if ye'd like a cup," she said. She turned to William, "Will Ginny be able to lend a hand tomorrow?" she asked.

"Yes, Ma. She said she'd be here right after she helps her ma do the cleaning up after breakfast," William replied. "Is the tea ready?" At his mother's nod he reached into the sideboard and grabbed a cup.

William poured tea and sat beside his father. Phil and Jack decided to go on to bed as they had to return to the quarry in the early morning. William sat and listened as his parents and Elsie continued talking over their tea, until finally all the details of the funeral were worked out.

Chapter

5

Wearily Jack swung his legs off the bunk. Light was beginning to filter through the small window. He was later rising this morning. The bunk his father had slept in was empty and his brothers were also waking up. The floor boards were cold on his feet and he hurried to pull on socks and clothing. He could hear the women softly talking out in the kitchen and the memory of his uncle's death caught him like a sledge hammer to his chest. Jack fought off the heavy grief with great difficulty. He didn't want to upset his aunt by appearing in the kitchen all teary-eyed. He cursed his sensitive nature, wishing once again he was tougher. He had to get past his mother and aunt without breaking down, and Jack knew any hint of sympathy would be his undoing. He screwed up his courage and opened the door. Softly he padded across the kitchen to the back door, he was picking up his boots when he heard his mother wish him a good morning. He muttered a response and rushed out the door. Feeling like he'd run a gauntlet, Jack sat to pull on his boots before making his way to Joe's field, stopping at the outhouse on the way.

Mick was in the process of feeding the chickens when Jack appeared. "Morning, Da," Jack said. Mick turned, the bucket of chickenfeed in one hand, "Morning, son, how're ye holding up?"

"Ah, I'm alright," Jack replied. "Didn't know you were over here".

"Thought I'd save ye the trouble this morning," Mick responded, "wanted ye to have a bit of time before ye head off to the quarry".

"Thanks, Da," Jack spoke quietly as he surveyed the yard and the chicken coop. "I'll shovel out the coop this evening…"

"It can wait a bit," Mick gruffly replied, as he continued to toss chickenfeed around the yard. The hens clucked and raced after the food.

There was an uneasy silence as father and son tried to avoid the subject of Joe's death and upcoming funeral.

"Jackie-boy, ye gonna be all right today?" Mick finally broke the awkward stillness between them.

Jack pulled his shoulders back and looked quietly at his father. "I'll be alright …. It's never going to be the same around here ever again, is it, Da?" He asked.

"No, that's a certainty," Mick began, and regarded his son thoughtfully, "Jack, I want ye to know your Ma and me are both mighty proud of ye. I know it's a hard row to hoe, and maybe hardest on ye. But, ye knows yer aunt is going to have ta depend on all of us now more than ever. Can ye be strong fer her sake?".

"Yes, sir, I knows I can," Jack's worried eyes met his father's. "She's gonna be lost without him".

"That's a fact, he will be sorely missed," Mick nodded his agreement.

Father and son stood mutely considering the change Joe's death had wrought, and the changes yet to come. After a while Mick spoke again, "Well, my son, I guess we better get back to the house. Ye need to eat and get yerself out the door ta work".

Together they tramped back across the field. By the time they arrived everyone was awake and Fanny had a large bowl of scrambled eggs on the table along with a mound of toast. Elsie was rocking Jimmy in the chair beside the wood stove. She looked up as Mick and Jack came in.

"Did ye rest a'tall?" Mick asked, noting her pallor and the dark shadows under her eyes.

"I did, a little," Elsie replied. "I slept a deal more than I did up at the surgery," with the reminder of her husband Elsie's face paled further, making her dark eyes seem even darker in her pale face.

"The pig is coming along well," Mick said to change the subject. "And once the weather warms a bit more, we'll hitch old Flossie up to the plow and turn over that field again so's it's ready for planting…" Mick continued in this vein for some time before he eventually trailed off.

Elsie smiled weakly at his attempts to distract her. "Yer a good brother, Mick", she told him.

"Well, Jackie-boy, we'd best shove off," Phil said as he wiped his mouth and stood up from the table. Jack had been listening to his father and Elsie. He nodded at Phil and gulped his last mouthful of tea, hurrying to join his brother for another day of work.

"Take good care," their mother admonished as they reached the door. Fanny had yet to fully come to terms with her menfolk working at that ghastly place. Since Joe's accident her worries had multiplied. Yet she said no more as she bade them good-bye and turned her attention to her daughters once more. Life was hard, as she well knew, and she prayed a silent prayer her sons would return safe and sound in the evening. She called the girls to her to braid their hair and get them ready to go outside to play.

Phil and Jack marched across the fields matching strides as they went along. Phil put anxious thoughts aside and dreamed of the day they would no longer make the daily journey to the quarry and instead be up even earlier to row dories out to check their own lobster pots. Uncle Joe had encouraged his dreams and Phil promised himself he'd make the dream come true. It would be a far healthier life to breathe in salt air instead of the limestone dust that seemed to be ingrained in his skin and made breath itself a challenge at times. Uncle Joe would like that, he thought and his memories turned to the last time he was out in the dory with his uncle.

Jack was lost in his own thoughts, remembering his uncle and wondering what the wake would be like. He'd never been to a wake before and he wasn't sure what to expect. He knew his uncle's body would be laid out for visiting that very night. Worry about bawling in front of people plagued him. He was also a bit nervous about what the captain would say about his father's and William's absence. He hated the quarry, his once exuberant enthusiasm now completely vanished. Jack was strong, but piling rock for a living was not something he wanted to spend his life at. Yet he welcomed the distraction from his maudlin thoughts and the grief that sat like a ten-ton weight on his shoulders. He wished his father could be with him and help with his adjustment to all these new experiences.

Soon the pair were climbing the hill that led to the quarry. Jack accompanied Phil to the captain's shack to deliver their father's message. It was accepted better than Jack had envisioned it would be and the captain surprised them both by informing them the employees would be permitted to leave early the day of the funeral – just a day away.

Much later Jack was relieved when the crusher finally came to a grinding stop indicating break time. It had been more than six hours since breakfast and Jack's stomach rumbled loudly. He was surprised to see Phil, Charlie, and Vic waiting for him as he scrambled downhill. Whatever they'd been discussing came to a stop with Jack's approach. Jack could think of nothing more than his empty stomach and missed the furtive glances between the older men. He looked forward to the baked beans and hard tack that were a mainstay at the cookhouse, not because they were good, but because they filled his stomach.

The rough shelter was nearly full when the men entered and a line-up snaked along one side of the room where tin plates were filled and each man given a mug of strong tea. The four joined the line and before long were seated at their favorite table near the door. Conversation was not to be had as the men quickly consumed their humble meal. Jack was spooning beans into his mouth when the captain strode through the door. There was a clatter of cutlery dropping as the men halted eating in shock and varying degrees of surprise. The captain made his way to the front of the room before turning to address the workers.

"Ye all know we lost one of our own this week," the captain began. "Many of ye knew Joe well, and there's many 'ere a relation in one way or another. So, as a tribute to a fine man, the owners 'ave agreed to let ye 'ave a 'alf day off – without pay, mind – so ye can attend the funeral. That's all I come to say". And with that he turned on his heel and left.

There was a quiet murmur, like the drone of a beehive, as the men made comments on the announcement. At Jack's table Charlie frowned, and Vic's face betrayed his consternation.

"Fine tribute, that," Charlie growled, "T'is no kindness to be sure. The bloody swine are hoping to keep us quiet by throwing us a bone".

36

Vic nodded his agreement. "They're worried we won't be worked to exhaustion the next time they want a shipment to go out faster".

"No doubt they have reasons that have naught to do with our health or happiness – or any respect for Joe," a red-headed man piped in.

"Did ye know anything about this," another labourer questioned Phil.

"Yeah, he told us this morning, before we started our shift," Phil answered. "We had stopped by the shack to let him know Da and William would not be here today".

Phil turned to Charlie, "And the business about the brake that wasn't applied, did ye learn any more of that?" Charlie glanced at Jack. "If he's old enough to risk life and limb at this damned quarry, he's old enough to hear the truth," Phil stated.

Charlie shrugged and replied, "That's what I hear. We'll ferret out the truth, ye can be sure of that. Harry didn't turn up again today, be good to have a word with him,"

Vic, seated beside Phil, grasped his forearm. "Let it lie for now, my buddy. Charlie and me, we've been asking around and we'll find out the truth of the matter. Yer family got enough on yer plates getting ready for the funeral. There's a time fer everything and there will be justice for Joe, I promise ye that."

Back at the house Mick and William were busy hitching the horse to a small wagon that was normally used for farm chores. Today they would use it for their sad trip to the surgery to collect Joe's remains. Mick noticed William's sudden fascination with something out in the field. Looking up he noticed Ginny making her way across the pasture. William quickly coughed and looked away when he saw that Mick had caught him staring at the maiden. "She's a pretty slip of a girl," his father noted. "Yeah, I guess so," William replied.

William refocused his attention on the wagon and the work at hand, keeping his head lowered and his thoughts to himself. Once the horse was hitched and the wagon ready to go Mick went back to the house to speak with his wife and Elsie. He returned with blankets in his arms. "Alright, son, let's go," he muttered.

Ben was nowhere to be seen when they reached the surgery, but Doc was keeping vigil with Joe's body inside the structure. He was quick to answer the knock at the door and ushered his visitors inside.

"Tis a sad business," Doc said as he shook Mick's hand. "He's in here," he added, leading the men to the small room where Joe still laid on the makeshift cot. William's face paled a little as his gaze fell upon his uncle's body. His face had been washed and his thick head of dark hair had been combed, but limestone dust still clung to his shirt. William pulled his gaze away to look at his father. "We're grateful for all ye did," his father was saying to Doc.

"Wish it could have been more," Doc sighed. "T'is a crying shame".

"Well, t'is all said and done, now," Mick replied and looked at William, wanting only to get home, "Are ye ready, son?"

Together they lifted the man who had once been larger than life and walking slowly made their way to the waiting wagon laying Joe's body down on the blanket they had spread out in the back. Mick carefully covered his brother's body and replaced the back board to ensure the safety of his precious cargo.

Doc had followed them outside and stretched out his hand yet again. "Thanks again, Doc," Mick said shaking the proffered hand.

"I'll be by tonight for the viewing," Doc told him "See you then".

William scrambled up onto the seat of the wagon and Mick flicked the reins. Neither man spoke and Mick took extra care to avoid any bumps on the journey home. William kept glancing back to make sure nothing untoward happened to the body. It was a tense and unsettling trip over familiar hills and fields, but finally Mick was guiding the wagon into Joe's yard and then near the door to the little cabin. Fanny and Elsie had been waiting for them inside and Fanny was opening the door wide. "Just lay him there on the table," she instructed the men. The pine table was a long one, with benches on either side, a wedding gift from Elsie's sister and husband. It filled the center of the oblong room. The kitchen had been tidied. A pot-belly wood stove sat in the corner and a sideboard sat below open shelving on one wall. The tiny living quarters were cozy and comfortable. Joe's big chair sat next to Elsie's more delicate rocker while a settee took pride of place under the window next to the front door.

The women stood back as William and Mick carried Joe's body inside and laid it carefully on the surface. Fanny was once again gripping Elsie's hand. The women had a large kettle of water on the stove, in preparation for their ministrations. Mick and William left them to their labor returning to the barn to start work on the casket.

Late in the afternoon William and Mick wrestled the finished box onto the wagon and returned to Elsie's cabin. The women were sitting on a bench outside when the wagon pulled up to the back door. Elsie's eyes were red from weeping and Fanny held her hand lightly in her own. Standing she laid a hand on her sister's shoulder before going to inspect the handiwork. "Oh, Mick, ye have done a fine job," Fanny told her husband. William had jumped off the wagon seat and was standing awkwardly waiting to be told what to do. Mick climbed down and joined his wife at the back of the wagon. "Is everything ready?" he asked gingerly, not wanting to know the details of preparing a body for burial. Fanny intuitively knew what Mick was referring to and answered instead: "We need a few pieces of furniture moved around," his wife replied. Hearing that Elsie stood up. "No, Elsie, dear, you stay put. Mick and William can move things about," Fanny gently ordered. "I'll show them where things are to go". Elsie gratefully sank back down, the events of the last two days beginning to catch up with her.

William followed his parents into the cabin and listened while his mother explained how she wanted things set up. First, they had to move the body into the bedroom. William was grateful to see his uncle dressed in his best clothes. He'd been worried about what he'd see. He helped his father haul the settee and chairs outside and to move the table to the far end of the room by the front door. The casket was to rest on it for the wake that evening. Elsie remained seated outside while Fanny arranged everything, including laying Joe's body out in the casket. She had brought a pillow covered in a fine white linen case and sheets to match to line the casket. Mick had fashioned the lid in two pieces so only Joe's upper body would be on view. Once, all was ready Fanny called Elsie inside to examine her work.

"Ah, Fanny, dear, you are an angel," Elsie whispered. She stood in front of the casket and gazed down on the man she had loved for almost all of her life. Thoughts and memories swirled making her dizzy and threatening to overwhelm her. One hand stroked Joe's hair while the other rested on top of his folded ones. Mick touched Fanny's shoulder and together they exited the room, leaving Elsie to have this last bit of time alone with her beloved.

The parson was entering the yard just as Mick and Fanny came out. The couple stood waiting to greet him. William had elected earlier to go back home to check on his sisters and Ginny and to get a much-needed bite to eat.

"Everything is ready for the wake tonight," Mick told the clergyman. "Do ye have men to dig the grave, or should we make arrangements?"

"No need to worry on that count," the parson answered, "Charlie, Ben and Vic have already been to the graveyard with a few other men and it's all ready".

Mick breathed a sigh of relief. He hadn't forgotten this one detail, but hadn't yet found time to round up enough men to do it.

"Thanks be to God," Fanny answered. "It's been a mite busy 'round here and we are grateful for that".

"Aye, no doubt about that a'tall. And Elsie, how is she faring?" The parson wanted to know.

"She's heart broken, of course," Fanny replied. "I don't think it's all sunk in just yet. She isn't sleeping or eating much. Still in shock, I expect".

Fanny stood and talked with the minister while Mick excused himself to return home to eat and clean up a little. Elsie was still standing in front of the casket when Fanny brought the minister inside.

"Elsie," Fanny called softly, "look who's here".

Elsie turned and waited for the parson to cross the room, not moving from her place by the coffin. "Let me make ye both a cup of tea, and then I'll be leaving ye alone for a bit," Fanny told them.

Fanny bustled about making the tea while Elsie spoke with the clergyman in low tones. "Here ye are," Fanny interrupted, passing the cups into their hands. "Why don't ye sit a spell and have yer tea. I am going to slip over to the house and make sure all is well. I will be back in a bit". Fanny untied the apron and folded it over her arm. Quietly she opened the door and left. She had barely got in the door of her own home when there was a light tap on the door. Opening it she was pleased to see Rebecca, Vic's wife, balancing a large basket on her hip. Rebecca came from a big family and lived nearer quarry hill, a fair distance up the road. "Why, Rebecca, come in, come in," Fanny invited. Rebecca was a short, stout woman and did not visit much, as a rule. She was kept too busy with her own brood to get out much. Rebecca's generous, wide mouth smiled in answer.

"Fanny, dear, we are all so sorry to hear about Joe. I was going to take this over to Elsie, but yer house is a bit closer, so I thought I'd stop in here first," she informed her. "I brought 'er some sweet bread and salt cod as well as bottled caribou she can warm later."

"That's very kind," Fanny answered. "The wake is tonight and I think they're planning ta have the funeral tomorrow afternoon. We'll know better this evening. The preacher is with her now."

"Perhaps it was a lucky thing I stopped here first, then, I don't want to intrude at a time like this," Rebecca said.

"It's been a busy day. I was just going to have a drop of tea. Would you like to join me?" Fanny asked.

Rebecca nodded her acceptance and laid the basket at the end of the table. She looked around the cozy room and complimented Fanny on the pretty white curtains hanging over the window. "Elsie made those," Fanny told her. "She is a much better hand at sewing than I am".

Rebecca sat on the bench and waited for Fanny to join her. "Where are yer little ones?" She asked.

"Likely down on the beach with Ginny, Hilda's girl," Fanny answered. I was just going to call out to them when you knocked".

The two women chatted about the funeral, about their growing families, and catching up on news. Presently, Ginny returned carrying the baby in her arms while Rose and Sarah danced and skipped beside her.

"Thank ye fer the tea. I need to get going now," Rebecca told Fanny after greeting Ginny and the girls. "I will try to come back this evening with Vic."

"Thank ye again for yer kindness. I know Elsie will appreciate it," Fanny answered and said her farewells.

"I am so glad fer yer help today," Fanny said, turning to Ginny, "Do ye think you can come again tomorrow?"

"I am happy to help," Ginny answered. "I can stay and help with the little ones this evening, and anything else ye can think of. And yes, I'll be back again in the morn," she promised.

Fanny studied Ginny's pretty face and slim build. Her eyes were a startling green and suited her fair skin and blonde hair. She wondered if it were true that William was smitten with the girl. He could do worse, Fanny thought, Ginny was more than pretty. She had her mother's generous ways and kind spirit. "We'd be much obliged," she said aloud and smiled at the girl.

Ginny put the baby down in his basket and turned to the older woman. "I like watching the girls and minding the baby. Sarah was a big help and Rose is so sweet. Jimmy is no trouble at all," she added.

Fanny was still sitting chatting with Ginny while her small daughters sat and listened when Mick appeared.

"What's fer supper?" he asked.

"Ginny made a nice stew," Fanny replied. "Phil and Jack should be home soon. Where's William?"

"He's out in the barn milking the cow. We filled the water cans fer ye, and the rain barrels as well. There's not been enough rain to fill a cup lately and I figured ye'd want us all ta have a bath afore the funeral." Mick answered.

"Ye're a dear, thanks," Fanny smiled, appreciating her husband's thoughtfulness. She knew it was hard work hauling buckets of water from the brook at the edge of the farm.

All but one of the family were sitting down to eat supper together. Mick was missing. He had eaten quickly so he could relieve his sister-in-law. He had gone over to sit with Joe's body, sending Elsie back to the house for a much-needed meal and a break. The body would not be left alone for a second throughout the long night, as was the custom.

It was a quiet meal without the usual chatter and camaraderie, except for the two little girls who were chatting about their day with Ginny and the fun they'd had on the beach. They had been told about their Uncle Joe and about the funeral the next day, but Fanny felt they were both too young to attend the wake. Fanny had decided to keep the baby with her at Elsie's, knowing it was a comfort to her sister-in-law to hold and rock the infant. Sarah and Rose would not be left alone either. The boys would have to go to work in the morning, so they would attend the early evening portion of the wake.

Ginny had stayed to help with the clearing up and to get Rose and Sarah off to bed. William stole glances at her whenever he thought nobody was looking. Fanny had noticed and it filled her with a secret delight. It was impossible not to like the girl. She had a sneaking suspicion that Ginny returned William's interest – she had given him the biggest slice of pie and had lingered a bit longer than necessary as she served it to him. Considering Ginny as a possible addition to the family was the one ray of sunshine in an otherwise dark and somber day.

When Jack's turn came to sit with the body Mick decided to go back over with him. He was concerned about his son and his first real experience of death. Jack had been a small child when Mick's mother died, and had no real memory of it. Elsie was already at the cabin when father and son entered. She had moved her rocker close to the head of the coffin and was sitting quietly when they came in. The cabin was softly lit by the one hurricane lamp. All windows had been covered, as was the norm for a wake. One bench had been lined up against the wall, while the other separated the kitchen and living room area, providing seating areas for the mourners.

"C'mon, Jack," Mick said, keeping a hand on his shoulder as he led him into the room.

Jack nervously approached the casket, glad of his father's hand upon his shoulder. Elsie stood up to move to Jack's side. Jack reached out and lightly placed his hands on the edge of the coffin willing himself to be strong as he allowed his gaze to settle on the face of the uncle who was like a second father to him.

"He looks like he's asleep," he finally spoke in a tremulous voice.

"Aye, he does that," Mick replied. Elsie reached out and laid a hand over Jack's.

"He loved you so much, Jack. Always remember that," she told him. "Ye were like a son to him".

Jack gulped, trying to swallow the lump that made it so difficult to speak. "I am so sorry, Aunt Elsie, so sorry," he finally managed, still looking down at Joe. He breathed deeply. "I sure am going to miss him a lot".

"I know ye will. We all will," Elsie answered pensively. Neither spoke but remained standing quietly for some time as they each thought of the huge hole that Joe's death had wrought. Presently they heard footsteps and turned as Phil and William entered.

"We're here," Phil greeted them uneasily, at a loss for words and not knowing quite what to say. Jack and Mick stepped aside to allow them to view the body. Elsie stayed beside them and patted Phil's shoulder as he paid his last respects to his uncle. Like Jack, William had difficulty speaking. Finally, he gave up and turning embraced his aunt quickly before moving away. He crossed the floor to sit on the bench not knowing what to do with himself. Jack was quick to join his brother, relieved to have his company. Mick had stepped outside, needing a moment to himself. The weight of the day sat heavily on his heart and he feared revealing his feelings. After a short reprieve he took a deep breath and returned.

Phil was still standing at her side when Elsie turned toward them, "I have a great favor to ask of all ye," she said. "I need six strong men to carry Joe's body tomorrow. I was wanting to ask ye to be pall bearers for yer uncle."

"It would be an honor," Phil instantly replied. "But, there's only four of us ..."

"I plan to ask Charlie and Vic as well," Elsie hastened to reassure him.

"I know they will be well pleased," William chimed in.

"Well, that's settled then," Elsie sighed. She had had many details to work out and time seemed to be going both fast and slow at once. Part of her felt frozen, numb, and incapable of all the tasks at hand. She was grateful for Mick and Fanny and all the help they'd been. The two couples had become close over the years and Elsie did not even want to imagine how'd she'd handle all this without them. Phil's head turned at the sound of wagon wheels outside. Mick went to see who it was. Opening the door, he peered outside. "Ye won't have long to wait, Elsie. Vic and Rebecca are here, and Charlie's with them," he said. Other men were seated in the bed of the wagon, including Doc and Ben. Phil and Jack got up as people began to make their way inside.

Elsie moved to stand at the head of the casket as Mick greeted the newcomers at the door. The little room seemed crowded with people and Jack began to feel uncomfortable. Phil leaned toward him whispering, "We can go now, Jack, if ye want".

Jack nodded and the pair waited to catch their father's eye, gesturing they were leaving. Mick gave one nod, indicating his assent and the two young men made their way outside.

Neither spoke as they tramped back across the field. In the distance they could see another small wagon rolling down the road toward Elsie's cabin.

"There's more people coming," Phil remarked. "I daresay the chapel will be full-up tomorrow".

"Uncle Joe, he is …was … the best," Jack responded. He was relieved he had avoided most of the mourners, still unsure of his ability to rein in emotion.

Phil squeezed Jack's shoulder. "He was."

Fanny and Ginny were sitting at the kitchen table when the boys reached the house. "Oh, good, yer back," Fanny said. "I'll be taking the baby along with me, but ye will have to keep a sharp ear out fer yer little sisters. They're both in bed, sound asleep, I hope, but don't be leaving them alone here," she admonished.

"No worries, Ma. We won't be going anywhere," Phil answered her.

"Da may be back later," she continued as she untied her apron, "It will be a long night, Ginny wants to pay her respects, so she's coming with me. I am hoping William will walk her home. I will see ye both in the morn". Fanny lifted the baby in his basket and accompanied Ginny out the door.

As Fanny had predicted, the evening was long. Many came to pay their last respects and out of deference for Joe's widow not one person brought up the reason for his untimely demise, nor pointed a finger of blame, but most were aware of the undercurrent of tension throughout the evening.

Ginny's visit was short, as she needed to get home to help her mother before returning in the morning. William had been quick to agree to walking the girl home, but both were quiet and self-conscious as they trudged along. Finally, William ventured to break the ice. "T'was mighty kind of ye to come help me Ma," he said.

Ginny blushed. "Oh, it was nothing," she shyly replied.

"D'yer think ye'll be coming for the funeral?" He asked.

"Oh, yer Ma asked me to come again in the morn to help with the girls and the baby and we will definitely be there for the funeral. Ma was saying last evening how it was yer uncle who made my cradle when I was born. She's used it for every babe since. Ma and Da, they're very fond of yer aunt and uncle…" Ginny answered.

"Good. I will look forward to seeing ye," William responded, and, not knowing what else to say fell silent once again.

William waited while Ginny climbed the final few yards up the hill to her home and after returning her wave turned to start back. He was a ball of confusion as he strode back home. On one hand he was glad to have had the time with Ginny, on the other he was a mixture of hurt and anger over his uncle's death. Emotions tangled and twisted leaving him filled with turmoil. The fact that the quarry manager expected them to show up to work the very day of the funeral rankled. The injustice continued to fester as he walked home. By the time he was nearing the cabin William had decided he would have a long talk with Phil, when all was said and done. They had to know the circumstances that led to Joe's death. He let go a deep sigh, after the funeral, he told himself.

He stopped at the cabin on his way home. People were sitting on the bench or standing about in the small kitchen. It gladdened his heart to see many familiar faces, even while it made him a little squeamish and wanting to make his escape as soon as possible. Grief, anger, mourning, and the morass of feelings were something he preferred to work out privately, without witnesses. Still, he knew how much it would mean to his aunt and to his parents. Charlie was the first to notice him and stepped forward to greet him.

"Ye made a wonderful job of the casket," he said "it's mighty fine".

William gave a brief nod, "Helped having fine materials to work with," he grunted. "T'was good of ye".

Charlie shrugged away his thanks. "Elsie tells me the funeral will be at four o'clock. I already spoke with Vic, and seeing how we're to be pallbearers we'll be here early so's we can help ye get the casket over to the chapel," he said. William nodded his agreement. "Guess I'll see ye tomorrow," he answered and moved away to find Mick.

After pulling his father aside for a brief word and to let him know he'd delivered Ginny safely home William made his exit.

It made him angry when his father had told him the captain had stopped by. He didn't want to make small talk with his neighbors. He just wanted to go home. He sighed. He'd be glad to have it all over with, 'this is hard, too hard', he thought to himself as he walked the worn path back across the field.

Phil and Jack were sitting at the table when William came in. "Da says he won't be going to the quarry in the morning. Says he spoke with the mining captain when he showed his face over ta the wake," William told his brothers.

Phil's face hardened, "Got some nerve, that does," he said in reference to his boss. "Surprised he showed up a'tall".

William frowned, thoughts of the quarry and Joe's death weighed heavily on his mind. "He got some gall alright," he agreed. "I don't know about the two of ye, but I'm going to turn in now. It's been a long day and tomorrow will be even longer." With that William crossed to the bedroom he shared with his brothers. He needed time alone; time to think.

Jack glanced at Phil. They'd been having a good heart-to-heart right before William had come in, all about death and life and trading stories about the good times spent with their uncle. But William was right, they had to be up again at first light and the hour was growing late. In silent assent they stood up from the table. Phil crossed to the girls' room and peeked inside, both little girls were sound asleep. Satisfied that all was well Phil turned to follow Jack into their room.

Chapter

6

Dawn was barely breaking when Jack opened his eyes. He felt like he had not slept at all. Visions of his uncle laying in the coffin had haunted his sleep. He'd spent a fitful night tossing and turning. Across the room William's bunk was empty, but Phil slept on. Jack could hear murmuring outside his room. He stood and pulled on his trousers. He shivered. It was a damp morning and the wood stove must have burned out during the night. With so much on their minds the boys had forgotten to stock it with birchwood before heading to bed. The dampness left a chill in the house that only a good fire would fix.

Jack crept quietly into the kitchen, doing his utmost to avoid waking his little sisters. Mick and William were there. William was feeding firewood into the stove where kindling was already blazing. It would not take long before the little house was toasty warm. Mick sat at the table watching. He turned his head when he heard Jack.

"Morning, son," Mick said. "How're ye faring?"

"Alright, I guess. How did it go last night?" Jack asked his father.

"T'was hard, as ye might expect," Mick answered. "Not much ta tell, really. Yer Ma sent over breakfast for ye boys." Jack glanced at the basket on the table. "Boiled eggs and biscuits," Mick told him. "Rebecca makes fine biscuits. She brought 'em to Elsie last night. There's a ton of food over there and yer aunt figured ye'd enjoy 'em with the eggs."

Jack frowned. He didn't feel much like eating, but he knew he'd need the fuel. "Thanks, Da."

"I already fed the animals and milked the cow so ye don't have ta go over ta Elsie's this morning. But will ye grab the bathtub when yer coming back in? Ma said she needs it filled and put on the stove to heat the water. She's planning on giving the girls a bath this morning."

Jack nodded groggily and headed to the door. After a trip to the outhouse Jack went to retrieve the galvanized steel tub from the barn. Flossie neighed in greeting and Jack stopped to rub the horse's nose. He spent a few moments patting and stroking the mare before turning to go back to the house. He looked across the field to the little cabin and whispered, "Ain't going ta be the same, Uncle Joe, ain't never going ta be the same." He dashed away the tears that came to his eyes and angrily slashed at the long grass with the steel tub, swinging it wildly and with all his strength. Unknown to Jack Phil had just come outside and witnessed his brother's show of emotion.

"Ain't going ta be able to cut hay with that thing," he lightly teased as he met Jack on the pathway. "Maybe this summer Da will teach ye how to use the scythe".

Jack turned his frustrated gaze on his brother. He didn't want his older brothers to think him a sissy and he was embarrassed with his behavior. Phil smiled gently at his younger brother, "It will be alright, Jackie-boy, it'll be alright".

Jack stood still and hung his head. When he was sure the tears were gone, he looked up at his brother. "I prayed for God to heal him. He didn't."

"Not all prayers are answered the way we want," Phil countered. He was uncomfortable with God-talk and wasn't sure he was the best person to speak of such things. He bided his time waiting to see what Jack would say next.

Jack stared earnestly at Phil, "Do ye believe in God? Do ye believe Uncle Joe is in heaven now?"

Phil calmly took the tub from Jack's white-knuckled grasp and placed it on the ground. "Yer not the first to question the Almighty, and ye won't be the last, I'm sure. It's natural when people die. All I know is that God always knows best and it's not for us to ask why. Yes, I do believe in God. And a better man ye'll never meet than our Uncle Joe. He was a fine man. The kind of man I hope to be. The kind of man I hope ye'll be too. Of course, he's in heaven – where else could he be?"

Jack held Phil's gaze for a second before he bobbed his head in agreement. "I sure wish he were still here with us," he muttered.

"He will always be with us in our memories. As long as we remember him, he will live on in us. That I can promise ye," Phil softly said.

Jack stood quietly for a moment digesting Phil's words. "Thanks, Phil. I guess I better get back ta the house. Da wants to fill this thing so Ma can bathe the girls." Suddenly he grinned, "Ye best not take too long, or me and William will eat up all the biscuits," he warned and grabbing the tub ran off toward the house.

William was nowhere to be seen, but Mick was sitting at the table sipping a cup of tea when Jack re-entered the room. "I left the tub by the door, Da," Jack told him.

"Thanks, son. Ye may as well sit and eat, the eggs are cold, but the biscuits are nice and fresh," Mick answered.

"Where did William go?" Jack asked.

"I suspect he's looking to see if Ginny is coming yet," Mick said dryly.

"Well. He best not take too long if he wants any biscuits," Jack replied around a mouthful, "these are some good".

Mick stood to take the teapot off the stove where it was steaming merrily away. "Tea?" he asked.

Jack nodded his head quickly up and down. Mick moved to place cups and saucers on the table. A small jug of cream sat in the center. Jack watched as his father filled cups for him and his brothers. Phil came in the door with a smirk on his face. "I think William's all soft on Ginny," he announced.

"Aw, no, not that," Jack piped up, genuinely disturbed.

Mick smiled, relieved at the first bit of family normalcy. "And what makes ye say that?" he asked Phil, with a twinkle in his eye.

"Why else is he making a show of splitting kindling out in the yard?" Phil enquired. "I noticed Ginny coming across the field and high tailed it in here. William has never been keen to split wood so early in the morn before.

Mick chuckled. "Ye may well be right, but don't be tormenting him about it.

"Sorry, Da, can't make no promises in that regard," Phil retorted.

The next they knew Ginny was coming through the door with the bathtub. William was right behind her. "I'll haul some buckets of water in so it can start to heat," he was saying to Ginny.

"William, b'y, ye better come eat," Mick interrupted. "Morning, Ginny. I'll fetch the water, ye need not be worrying about that, son. Come eat, before these gluttons have it all gone".

"Thank ye, anyway, William," Ginny said with a blush.

William bowed his head and muttered a response that nobody quite heard. His neck and ears turned red as he busied himself with the food. William was saved from further comment when their little sister, Rose, appeared in the doorway. Mick scooped her up in his arms laying a kiss on her cheek. The child rubbed her eyes sleepily and wanted to know where her mama was and if Ginny would take her to the beach. The questions continued fast and furious as the boys made ready to leave for work. The trio said their good-byes with a promise to hurry home in plenty of time to get ready for the funeral.

William walked quickly, trying to put space between himself and his brothers. He suspected Phil would not be able to resist teasing and tormenting him about Ginny. He was right.

"Hey, William, what's yer hurry?" Phil called after him.

Jack took up the teasing tone, "William, will yer fetch water fer me, if I needs it?"

"Ye did a fine job of piling the kindling nice and tidy-like," Phil added. "Wonder why ye took such extra care?" The light teasing dogged William's steps. He ignored them and walked even faster, but Phil and Jack were not willing to let him get off so easily. Soon the three brothers were playfully punching one another and their jostling match continued to the road. Phil and Jack kept up their litany of playful questioning as they went.

"Give it up, ye hear," William grumbled. "Yer gonna make us late ta work C'mon, now".

As they rounded the bend in the road the surgery loomed ahead dousing any light-hearted banter. The high hill seemed to cast a dark shadow over them and grief grasped their hearts in icy fingers. They would never pass this way again without thoughts of death intruding on their peace. Almost as quickly as it had begun the light banter dissipated in the air like mist when the sun rises and warms the earth. Wordlessly the brothers climbed until they reached their place of employment. William and Phil left Jack to climb to the wide outcrop further downhill where the rock crusher was installed. Soon the racket of pickaxes and shovels created a din that defied any conversation, which was a blessing to Jack. He didn't want to answer any question his coworkers might put to him. When the crusher was started up it was impossible to hear a thing.

The heavy work was mind-numbing, which was a relief to the young man who wanted nothing more than not to think. He poured his energies into piling the rocks nearby. Another worker cracked the rocks with a pickaxe, cutting them down to size to fit the crusher where another man lifted the smaller pieces into its mouth. The machine sat on its wheels with four heavy railway ties making a platform around it. Every precaution had been taken to make sure the machine was installed in such a way to prevent it rolling away or sustaining any damage. It was the pride and joy of its owners and evidence of the industry's growing business.

Jack worked hard all morning, barely taking a breather as he made small piles of rock to be fed into the crusher. He was used to working hard and had developed muscles equal to the task from the many chores he labored at around the family farm. Hauling pails of water from the brook and helping to chop wood had strengthened his upper arms and shoulders. Still, it was back breaking work and while his muscles were solid, they still complained. Jack was glad to finish for the day.

He was covered in limestone dust and sweat had made white streaks down his face when quitting time finally came. Jack stretched and rubbed his upper arms as he moved to leave. He stopped to drink a dipper of water from the pail just beyond the work site before climbing the hill up to the path. Several men nodded a solemn greeting as he made his way past them. Without waiting for his brothers Jack scrambled down the path to the road. He stopped to rest taking in the familiar surroundings. On his right the little bay was quiet with the waves making barely a ripple on the surface. On his left the hills sloped gently upwards forming peaks and valleys. Straight in front of him the roadway followed the coastline and wound like a river through the small community.

His thoughts were somber as he considered what the rest of the day might bring. He was startled when Phil laid a hand on his shoulder, and chuckled at Jack's response.

"Jackie-boy, how ye holding up?" his brother asked.

"I'm all right," Jack answered. "Where's William?"

"He'll be along. He stopped to have a word with Charlie and Vic. C'mon, let's go home," Phil responded.

"About the accident and Uncle Joe?" Jack asked.

"Yeah, we need to know what happened, and not just for our own sake, but for the sake of the safety of all the men," Phil answered.

Jack considered this as he moved to follow his brother. It had been the first bad accident in the quarry in many years and he didn't want to see a repeat. It got him thinking again about his uncle, which led to thoughts of the funeral.

"Phil, I am a bit worried about carrying the casket. What if I drop it?" he asked.

"Nothing to worry about, Jackie-boy – there are six of us, so there will be two at each end and two in the middle. It will be okay," Phil told him.

"What if I break down and start bawling?" Jack wanted to know.

"I am going to stay right by your side through it all. Ye start bawling, I'll give ye a little smack." Phil smiled at him.

Jack grinned, "And I'll smack ye right back,".

"Look, Jack, ye will be okay. And if ye don't think ye can keep from bawling then ye will just have to take off down to the beach or somewhere private. Okay?" Phil replied. "But it won't be so bad as ye think."

Feeling a bit better Jack bent to pick up a stone. He threw it as hard as he could hoping it would make it to the water several yards away. He was delighted when he heard the splash.

"Look at ye," Phil retorted, "Ye're getting some strong. I won't be begging ye to arm wrestle me any time soon."

The boys turned around at the sound of footsteps. William had caught up with them.

"Any news?" Phil asked him.

"Nah, nothing worth speaking of," William replied. "We might all meet up after the funeral is over to discuss it".

The three boys walked the rest of the way in silence, each busy with their own thoughts. Soon they were strolling into the yard. William stopped to splash water on his face from the rain barrel by the door. Phil and Jack grinned at each other from behind his back, knowing the reason for William's sudden concern with his appearance. Once inside the young men were gratified to spy a plate piled high with sandwiches in the center of the table. Ginny came timidly from the living room where she had been telling the girls stories and singing songs. Their parents were nowhere to be seen.

"I got the tea ready," she began, "and yer Ma sent yer Da over with all them sandwiches. Yer Ma sent a message that yer to eat and then get yer baths straight away." As she told them this, she moved about the kitchen putting cups and saucers on the table and filling them with tea.

"Thank ye," William answered while Phil and Jack elbowed one another and grinned cheekily.

William glared at his brothers, "Where's yer manners?" He asked.

Jack and Phil both mumbled their thanks and reached for the food. The bread was soft and thickly sliced and their mouths watered before the first bite was taken.

Sarah came into the kitchen pulling little Rose by the hand. They sat across the table from their brothers and kept up a stream of chatter about the stories Ginny told; about the beach yesterday, and about the funeral to come. Sarah did most of the talking, though Rose chimed in from time to time. Their hair had been washed and braided and they were almost ready for the funeral service. The boys grunted in reply as they ate and listened to their sisters.

Ginny stood aside and listened to her charges, glad to have them as a shield between herself and the young men.

"Da said to tell ye that ye can set the tub up in the barn for privacy. He said Ma will be back over before the funeral. Ginny put pails of water on the stove to heat fer ye," Sarah told them. "But Da said the water in the rain barrel is not so cold, and ye can use that."

Phil grinned at his little sister and her matter-of-fact speech, knowing it was embarrassing William. He slid his eyes over his older brother and winked, making him even more uncomfortable. The undertones went unnoticed by Jack, who was still battling his fear of losing his composure during the funeral.

"Who wants to go first?" Phil asked his brothers.

"I will," William announced, wanting only to get away from the house and his brother's silent teasing. He stood up, and reddening, made his exit.

The tub was overturned on the grass and William righted it. He wondered about the wisdom of using the thing that was no more than four feet long and had a depth of two, at most. Finally, he shrugged to himself and carried it to the barn.

Jack looked at Phil, "I dare ye to come down to the beach for a swim," He challenged him. Phil thought for a moment, before reaching over to ruffle Jack's hair. "I'm game if ye are".

Ginny was relieved. The thought of the boys bathing made her uncomfortable and made her cheeks flush pink.

Jack and Phil went to their room to grab clean clothes before leaving to carry out their plan of washing in the cold water of the bay. It was still early spring and the temperature was sure to be freezing, but having laid down the gauntlet neither one would back off. They joshed and tormented each other all the way out the door and to the seashore.

Jack gasped as the icy water trickled over his feet. He didn't see Phil's approach from behind him but felt cold water splatter over him as Phil charged, his pumping feet and legs causing a great splash. Jack quickly dove underneath the waves to avoid the cool breeze on his bare skin. The shock of icy water was almost too much. Jack remembered his mother's admonishment never to go swimming right after a meal. However, he wasn't there to have a swim, but to wash the hated limestone dust from his skin and hair – or so he rationalized. It wasn't long before the pair stood shivering on the sand. They rushed to towel off and don dry clothes.

"Not the best idea I ever had," Jack's teeth chattered as he tried to speak. "Perhaps not," Phil agreed, "But it beats sitting in that frigging tub".

The sun had warmed the long, flat slabs of shale that jutted out into the bay and the boys lounged there to warm themselves. It was a comfort to watch the gulls and seabirds wheeling above the water in search of fish and the pair sat idly watching them.

"Well, b'y, I guess we better get back," Phil spoke aloud.

Jack nodded and stood up, still watching the flocks of birds. He took a deep breath and tried to banish the paralyzing fear of the funeral and the underlying worry of embarrassing himself.

Fanny was in the kitchen when they returned. She'd obviously bathed and washed her auburn hair, which was attractively styled high on her crown. "I sent William and Ginny over to sit with Joe so's yer aunt could come over here to get ready," she told them. "She should be here any minute". She examined her sons for any sign of dirt or grime before pronouncing them passable. The breeze had played with Jack's curls and lent a bit of color to his cheeks. "Yer aunt will need yer strength and support," she reminded them both, but her gaze was on Jack as she spoke.

"She will have it, Ma," Jack answered. "I promise".

Jack heard his father calling to someone outside. Sarah had been sitting out on the porch with Rose. Now she came running inside, "Jack, Da's looking for ye and Phil. The men are over ta Aunt Elsie's ta take the casket to the chapel and Da wants ye to help," she finished breathlessly.

Phil and Jack waved to Vic who was standing at the back of his wagon as they made their way over. It was nearly two hours before the funeral service was to start. It was enough time to do what they had to do before getting dressed for the services. They met Elsie part way across the field. She still looked very wan but resigned. Jack stopped for a minute to talk to her before going on to the cabin. The men stood in the little cabin and waited for instructions. The lid on his uncle's casket had been closed after Elsie left. That helped, at least a little. Charlie and Vic were speaking in quiet tones with his father while Phil stood listening. William was outside saying good-bye to Ginny. It seemed their relationship had grown a little closer during their time together. But the moment was too solemn for any jovial teasing of their brother.

"Okay, Jackie-boy, here's how it's gonna go," Mick interrupted his thoughts. Me and William will take the head of the casket. You and Phil will be in the middle and Charlie and Vic will take the foot."

Jack nodded, feeling relieved with the plan. William came in the door in enough time to hear what his father had said. "All right, William, come on over here," Mick commanded. "This will be a bit of a trial run before church".

The men took their places and lifted the casket off the table and slowly swung it around to take it out the door. Once it was in place on the back of the wagon Mick jumped up on the seat beside Vic while Charlie joined Jack and his brothers in the back. The four of them would keep the casket steady as they drove to the little chapel. It wasn't far to go. The chapel was located in the center of the community within walking distance of Mick's home. It was less than half the distance they usually walked to work. The white steeple could be seen easily from the crest of any of the little hills nearby. Jack noticed the mound of earth in the churchyard as they approached. The grave was ready. It brought home to him the solemnity of the day. The pastor was waiting for them on the little covered porch and moved to open the double doors to make entry easier. Vic pulled the wagon up as close to the entryway as he could. There were four wide steps up to the doorway, but Vic had maneuvered the wagon so that they would not have to lift it up the stairs. Mick, Charlie, and Vic moved to the front of the casket and slid it smoothly onto the top step until only a third of it rested on the wagon bed. William, Phil, and Jack waited while Vic jumped back onto the seat of the wagon to move it out of the way. Finally, the six men lifted the casket and carried it into the vestibule where it would rest until the service. Mick stopped to chat for a few minutes with the pastor and get any last-minute instructions before joining the rest of the pall bearers in the yard.

"Much obliged, Charlie, Vic," he thanked them, "I guess it's time we all go get ready for the funeral. The boys and me will meet ye here 'bout an hour before the service, it that suits ye both".

"Yis, that's fine," Vic answered while Charlie simply nodded. Mick turned to his sons, "Let's go lads," he said.

"Are ye sure ye don't want a lift back to the house?" Vic asked.

"No, a walk will do us good, but thanks. Besides, it will give the women a bit more time alone," Mick replied and turned to start walking back, his sons keeping stride with him.

Father and sons turned and headed for home, each one felt the heaviness of the day press against them as if death itself were a leaden weight crushing their hearts and souls. It was a quiet walk with little to say as each were preoccupied with their own thoughts.

Chapter

7

Fanny had the girls clothed in their Sunday best and was dressing the baby when the men returned. Sarah was sitting cuddled up beside Elsie in the living room when she heard the door and scrambled off the couch to greet them.

"Is it time to go yet?" she asked her father. "We're all ready. Doesn't Ma look pretty?"

Elsie stood in the doorway and smiled weakly at the child's questions.

Mick glanced at Sarah before taking in all the females in the room. "Ye all look very fine," he told her. "It won't take us long – two shakes of a lamb's tail and we'll be right out".

The boys were already in their room donning the freshly ironed shirts and trousers Fanny had laid out for them. Mick hurried into his room to do the same as Fanny tied a red ribbon in Rose's dark hair. Soon the boys reappeared. "What's this fer, Ma?" Jack asked, holding a black ribbon in one hand.

"It's an arm band. It's traditional for the pall bearers to wear one. It's a sign of respect, and of mourning," Fanny explained. "Come here. Ye need to comb yer hair".

Jack stood impatiently as his mother tied the black band around his upper left arm. Elsie stepped forward to assist Phil and William with theirs. Fanny lifted the hair brush to tidy Jack's unruly locks but placed it instead in his outstretched palm. Her son was growing up and she would not embarrass him by treating him like a child. Moments later Mick reappeared and the family made ready to leave. They had already discussed travel arrangements and the buggy was readied for the short ride to the chapel. Jack was to take especial care of Sarah as there was no room for everyone to ride. It was decided that she would walk to the church with her brothers while Rose would sit on Elsie's lap. Naturally, the baby would be carried in his mother's arms.

Sarah felt quite grown up as she walked with her brothers along the path to the roadway. Before Jimmy came along, she had ridden in the buggy with her sister and mother. She chatted about Ginny and how much she liked her and did her best to distract Jack as they walked along. She had overheard the adults talking about how he would handle the funeral and caught the concern in their conversation. She had loved her Uncle Joe too and she was sad that he died. She thought of how gentle he always was with her and how he never talked down to her the way some men did. Most, in fact, shooed her away as if she were a bother. But Joe was always interested in her stories and daydreams and asked lots of questions. Jack was a lot like their uncle. He, too, was gentle and kind.

Jack listened to Sarah's rambling chatter with half an ear. Sarah had been his constant playmate when they were very little and he loved her dearly, but his mind was on the funeral and he was praying earnestly for help to keep his emotions in check. Still, he was glad to have Sarah's company as they trod the winding road to the chapel. Phil and William walked a little distance ahead of them, forgetting about Sarah's shorter stride and preoccupied with their own private thoughts. Soon they reached the churchyard where they could see Vic's wagon pulled up alongside of the little building. Vic and Charlie stood on the steps waiting their arrival.

"Da will be here any minute," Phil told the men. We left earlier as we had to walk. Da was hitching up the horse, but that won't take long".

Charlie nodded curtly. "Rebecca is inside if ye'd like to sit with her," Vic told Sarah.

Sarah bobbed her head and entered the church to await her parents' arrival.

The men were standing in the yard when Mick arrived, driving his buggy up beside the little chapel. Charlie walked over to help. He lifted Rose down, then turned to offer his hand to Elsie. Mick was greeting the men after helping Fanny when he heard the parson's footfall on the wooden steps. Heads turned to watch the preacher's approach. Reverend McGrath was solemn as he greeted them. "Why don't ye all come wait inside," he invited them and guided the parishioners to the door. Sarah had heard the buggy through the open door and was waiting for them in the doorway of the vestibule. The little waiting room was just large enough to house the casket and the chairs and benches for the bereaved to sit on while they waited to take part in the funeral procession.

"Pastor, will ye please ask Ginny to come in when she gets here?" Fanny asked the preacher. "She has promised to sit with my girls," she explained.

"Yes, of course," he answered and went on to explain the details of the service.

Mick had the foresight to bring arm bands for Charlie and Vic and now he took them out of his pocket and handed them to the men. The little group spoke little as they waited, each caught up in the finality of the day.

When Ginny arrived, Fanny sent Rose and Sarah to sit with her in the front pew. She embraced the young woman with one arm before handing the baby to her.

The little chapel soon filled up with mourners and, as they'd been instructed, they rose with the sound of the opening hymn. The men stood ready to lift the casket and the funeral began.

Jack kept his eyes downcast as they walked slowly up the aisle to the front of the church. He didn't want to be unnerved by a sympathetic glance and he did his best to ignore the quiet sniffling that seemed to be all around him. It all seemed so surreal and it felt like he was walking though quicksand, but soon they were placing the coffin in front of the altar.

Fanny had linked arms with Elsie as they followed the casket to the front of the chapel. She could feel Elsie's trembling and the tension in her stiff back and shoulders. It was a great relief to finally sit when they reached their pew. Rose moved to sit between the two women and Elsie was grateful to hold a small hand in hers. Sarah sat on Elsie's other side and leaned against her shoulder.

"Dear God," Elsie silently prayed, "Please receive my Joe, and help me through this day. I beg of you, give me strength".

Across the aisle Jack sat beside his father and tried to pray, but was lost in a quagmire of feelings and grief threatened to overwhelm his resolve to be strong. When the preacher spoke of God's love Jack's thoughts turned bitter. *How could God let this happen? Is there a God? Why? Why did He take my Uncle Joe?* His questions burned his heart and fueled his anger. His anger gave him strength to sit through the rest of the prayers and soon the services were over. Jack stood with the rest of the pall bearers to carry his uncle out of the church and to his final resting place.

The mourners stood in a knot around the family while Joseph Kelly's coffin was slowly lowered into the grave.

Elsie tightly grasped Fanny's hand and willed it to be over. The pastor was standing in front of the gathering giving the final prayers and benedictions.

Elsie could not concentrate. Her grief mocked the proceedings and made it impossible to take any comfort in the prayers or hymns. Her heart, like an iceberg lodged in her chest, was completely frozen. The numbness served to keep her from weeping, but simultaneously blocked any solace the prayers might offer. Like a traumatized child Elsie felt lost, as though Joe had abandoned her and left her in a vast wilderness of overwhelming heartbreak and agony.

Mick touched her shoulder and gestured toward the coffin. Slowly she walked forward and bending over picked up a bit of soil in her hand. Wordlessly she let the soil trickle through her fingers to fall upon the coffin below her. One by one each family member did the same. Each thud of dirt hitting the wooden surface was like a dagger in the widow's heart.

Mick glanced at his sister-in-law. She would find the days to come even harder, he knew. The past few days they had been kept busy with funeral arrangements. He promised himself he would do all he could to make life bearable for his brother's wife. *Aw, Joe,* he thought, *she will be so lost without ye – as will we all. A better brother and friend no man could have.*

Mick was not the only one thinking of the impact the tragedy would have. Charlie had done his best to keep from thinking how much he'd miss Joe. Thoughts of his friend flooded his mind: *he never made fun of folks the way some did; never pushed or pried into my business. Joe's fair with everybody. He is someone a fella can trust, someone who can be counted on to help wherever it is needed…. Joe, the brother I never had…more like family than me own.* Charlie caught himself, realizing he would never be able to turn to his friend for help or support again. The pain of it lodged deep in his heart.

Elsie stood with Mick and Fanny and their children at the edge of the graveyard and accepted the condolences of her friends and relations. *I know they mean well. I know they do, and I am grateful, but I will be glad when this day is over,* she thought as she embraced one after another. Finally, it was time to leave and Elsie shuddered at the sound of men filling the grave with earth as they drove away. It wasn't over quite yet as people gathered at Mick and Fanny's home to pay their respects to the family and offer what comfort they could.

The day dragged on as Elsie did her best to respond to the kindnesses of so many people. She was depending on Fanny to help her remember all the favors, big and small, that had been bestowed. *It was a real comfort to listen as people regaled us with stories of Joe,* Elsie thought, *and so kind of people to bring casseroles – so many foods of all kinds so I won't have to give a thought to cooking for quite a while.* Tears filled her eyes as she thought of the meals she had cooked for Joe and the way he ate them with such gusto and with gratitude. *Joe appreciated every little thing I ever did fer him,* Elsie remembered. She shook her head and tried to cast off thoughts of tomorrow and the empty days to come. *I hope I don't wear out my welcome here. I allow I'll be visiting more often than ever.*

Elsie snapped out of her reverie when she felt the small hand tugging at her skirts. "Auntie, may I have a drink?" Rose asked. Fanny was busy with hostess duties and the children had been playing in the yard. Rose's face was flushed and her blue eyes large in her little face. Elsie stood up to see to the child, glad for the distraction from her thoughts.

Jack sought comfort at the beach. He needed time alone – time to grieve and say good-bye to his uncle on his own terms, in his own way. He had retrieved his uncle's tweed cap from his room where he had left it - the night he learned that Joe had passed away. Now he sat, as he had then, twirling the cap in his hands and watching the waves crash on the shore. *Thanks, Uncle Joe, for lending me yer strength like I asked. I didn't break down today. I kept remembering how ye told me 'bout when ye had to go to yer mother's funeral and how it were just you and Da there and how crushed ye were. So, when I was walking down that church aisle, I did what ye did and imagined all the ancestors helping me lift the casket. It did seem lighter ... and I imagined how happy ye all were, now ye didn't have to work any more; or have any of the troubles of this world to carry. And I imagined how happy ye were to finally hold yer wee baby in yer arms. That made me happy too, so I didn't cry or embarrass meself. Ye've always helped me, Uncle Joe and I thank ye for that and for helping me today. I will miss ye so much....* Jack's heart hitched up in his throat and the pain of losing his uncle nearly overwhelmed him again. *I just wanted to come down here and talk with ye again, like we used to... it's not the same... but I promise ye I will look after Aunt Elsie, you can count on that.... That's my solemn vow ... Just send me a sign sometimes that ye hear me alright? Let me know yer okay. Cuz I am sure gonna miss ye ...*

Suddenly a gust of wind tore the cap out of Jack's hands and sent it tumbling over the sand. Jack raced after it and catching it stood and smiled. He remembered his uncle doing the exact same thing with the exact same cap on this exact stretch of beach. As suddenly as the gust came up it was gone again. "I'll take that as a sign, Uncle Joe," he whispered.

"Jackie-boy?" Phil called out, "Is that ye?"

Jack turned and waved at his brother, "Course it's me, who'd ye think it was?" he asked.

Phil didn't answer but continued to walk toward him. "Figured ye'd be here," he told Jack when he reached him. "Ye used to come to this very spot with Uncle Joe. So, how are ye holding up?"

Jack turned a calm face to his brother. "I'm all right. Just needed time alone – to say my good-byes ..." he trailed off. Phil nodded and bent over to pick up a rock to skip on the water. Their father had sent him to look for Jack, but now he felt he was intruding. He kept quiet as he waited for Jack to speak.

"Hey, Phil, is there any food left up ta the house?" Jack asked. Phil turned with a wide grin. "Ye hungry? Too bad ye stayed down here so long," Phil teased. "But, I s'pose Ma will find something for ye. C'mon let's go see".

Men were standing in little groups around the yard when Jack and Phil returned. Children of various ages were chasing one another around the house or playing games in the yard. They didn't stop but headed straight for the kitchen. Women were sitting at the table or standing around the living room once all the seats were taken. Phil noticed Ginny sitting with her mother, Hilda, and Rebecca and wondered if William was close by. He grinned to himself at the thought. Jack grabbed a plate and helped himself, piling it high with food. Phil vied with him for the last thick slice of ham and the two pushed and elbowed each other for other choice morsels before heading outside to sit on the bench beside the door to eat. Phil was shoveling the last bite into his mouth when he noticed their father motioning for them to come. Mick was standing with Vic, Charlie, William and a few other men speaking in low tones as Phil approached with Jack.

"Good, ye found him," Mick said to Phil. "We've been discussing the 'accident'," Mick spat the word with contempt, "and it seems it weren't no accident. Lou was working near the new man and seen that cart move off on its own – it wasn't finished being loaded, but t'was heavy enough to gain momentum once it started moving. The load was not spread out right – it was mostly all on one end and that brake was never applied". Mick looked directly at Jack. "Now, I called ye over because I knows ye'll be hearing stories once we get back to work tomorrow. I don't want any of ye saying or doing nothing 'til I talks with Lou, I'd like a word with Harry too, but nobody's seen hide nor hair of 'im since it happened". Mick let his eyes rest on each face as he spoke, but his gaze lingered on Charlie's. "Joe's my brother. I want ye all to leave it in my hands for the time being. Is that understood?" The men all gave solemn nods of assent, though Charlie hesitated a second. "Tomorrow is Saturday and we'll have a day of rest on Sunday. I was thinking we could meet in the evening. How's that sound?" Mick asked. One by one the men nodded their agreement and slowly they dispersed, some to collect their families and say their farewells.

Mick and Fanny insisted Elsie stay at least one more night with them and she was grateful for that. The past few days had been so hard and she was not quite ready to face her lonely cabin. She had been immensely relieved when the last of the mourners bid them good evening and were on their way. *Tomorrow*, she promised herself, *I will go home tomorrow.*

William was standing at the gate post when Ginny was leaving with her parents and siblings. William cleared his throat and nervously walked toward them. Ginny noticed and bowed her head as he approached. "Thank ye all fer coming," he spoke in a low voice. "Ma sure appreciated yer help, Ginny". At the sound of her name the young woman lifted her head and smiled timidly at William. "T'was no trouble," she said. William mustered his courage and looked at her father. "Sir, I was wondering if I might have yer permission to call on Ginny?" William asked anxiously.

Hank and Hilda glanced knowingly at one another before he asked: "Ginny, how do ye feel about that?"

Ginny had dropped her head once again, but quickly looked up at William. "Sure, that would be alright," she answered her father, while darting a quick look into William's brown-black eyes.

"Well, there ye have it," Hank replied to William, "but ye take real care to stay close by so's we can keep an eye on ye".

William flushed a bright red and nodded quickly. "See ye soon, then," he said and turned on his heels and left.

Phil had watched the little scene with amusement. It was a welcome diversion from the solemnity of the day. He waited until his brother was mere steps away before crowing with delight and throwing his first barb at William.

"Now I wonder what ye were up to over there chatting up Ginny and her folks," Phil remarked. "I am beginning to think there is more going on in that head of yers than ye let on. Ye're sweet on 'er, ain't ye?"

William shoved Phil aside and continued on his way to the house. "Go on with ya," he retorted, "Ye don't know nothing!"

"C'mon, William, ye knows yer going ta tell me sooner or later," Phil continued. "What's going on with ye and Ginny?"

"Nuddin's going on b'y," William grated out, "Jus let it be".

"Aw, but ye likes the girl, don't ye?" Phil kept it up, "Ye think she's pretty".

"Lay off, Phil," William growled, "I ain't gonna talk to ye about it!"

Sarah came running up to her older brothers and brought an end to Phil's taunting.

"I need yer help! Right now! Rose followed me up into the hayloft and now she's scared to climb down," Sarah huffed and puffed as she tried to get the words out.

"Ye know ye ain't s'posed to be up in the hayloft," William scolded, his annoyance with Phil making him gruffer than he intended.

"Please don't tell Da," Sarah begged, her soft dark eyes tearing up as she searched William's for mercy.

"I ain't gonna tell Da, but ye keep out of that hayloft, ye mind," William answered.

Sarah nodded quickly but kept turning her head back to the barn, obviously upset.

"I'll come with ye," Phil told her and the two sprinted off to the barn.

Rose was clinging to the ladder for dear life when the pair entered the barn. She had only stepped down one rung when fear had overwhelmed her. Bits of straw stuck out of her braids and the ribbons had come untied. She was frozen with fright and dared not turn her head to look at her sister and brother. Phil climbed the ladder while crooning softly to her that she would be okay. A grateful Rose kept her arms tightly wound around his neck as he climbed down, holding her in one arm. She continued to cling to her brother, even after they were safely on the ground.

"I told ye not to follow me," Sarah rebuked the little girl. "Ye're always on my heels, never give me a minute to myself. Why didn't ye go play with Martha? I told ye to go play with her!"

Rose's eyes filled with tears. "Don't like Martha. She's mean."

Sarah's demeanor underwent a rapid change as she studied her sister's face. Martha was mean and at times downright cruel. Still, Sarah had not realized Rose had followed her into the barn and not being able to help her safely descend the ladder had given her a scare. She had been truly terrified her little sister would fall. Sarah hated being scared. She wanted to be brave and strong like her brothers. Sarah reached up and patted Rose's back. "Just don't ever do that again, okay?"

A fat tear rolled down her sister's cheek and Phil took his time trying to cheer her up before leaving the barn. Soon they were playing her favorite game of 'ring around the rosie'. The trio fell to the ground and before long all three were giggling and grinning ear to ear.

Phil carried Rose back to the house while Sarah walked alongside them. The house was quiet when they went inside. All the visitors had left and the women sat chatting quietly in the kitchen, while Fanny rocked the baby in her arms.

"Where's Da?" Sarah asked her mother, worried lest William had decided to tell on her after all.

"He's with Jack and William taking care of the animals over ta Joe's…Elsie's place." Fanny answered with a quick look at her sister-in-law. "Phil, he wanted ye to go fetch the water fer the morning".

Phil set Rose down on the floor before answering. "Sure, Ma, I'll go now, as soon as I change out of these clothes".

Sarah and Phil exchanged a guilty look before he left to do the evening chores of getting water and wood for the fire. Neither wanted to tell their mother about the misadventure in the barn.

Before long all the family were gathered around the kitchen table once again. It was getting late and the men had to face another day at the quarry. Elsie helped Fanny dish up leftovers for their meal and the conversation swung from one topic to another as they each told tidbits about the day. Soon the adventure in the barn was forgotten as talk turned to the morrow and the work ahead.

"Okay, girls, time fer bed," Fanny announced with finality. Sarah went around the table hugging her father and brothers before turning her attention to her aunt. "I love you, Aunt Elsie. I hope you stay at our house forever," she said seriously. Rose was following Sarah's lead and now climbed into Elsie's lap. "Love you, you stay here?"

Elsie smiled tenderly at Rose, "Yes, dear, I will stay here, but just one more night". She turned her gaze to Sarah, "I can't stay here forever. I have to go back home. I have work to do there and the animals need to be cared for."

"But, Auntie, there's enough room for you here," Sarah began to argue.

"How about you and Rose come visit me every day?" Elsie asked.

Sarah looked at her mother. "Can we?" She asked.

"Ye're getting to be a big girl and I think ye could take yer sister over to visit," Fanny replied. "And Auntie can come here as often as she wants".

Mollified, if not entirely happy with the answers, Sarah grabbed Rose's hand to lead her to their bedroom, "Good night every one," she said. Rose parroted her as they went.

"I'll be there in a minute to hear yer prayers and tuck ye in," Fanny promised as she laid a tea towel over the pail of milk on the sideboard. She would skim the cream off the top in the morning to be saved for making butter once she had enough. Jimmy began to fuss and cry in his cradle and Elsie lifted him up putting him over her shoulder and gently patted his back. She turned as Mick came through the door.

Chapter

8

Elsie drew her shawl closer around her as she gazed out over the bay. It was early; So early that even Fanny, usually the first out of bed, slept on. The sun had yet to peek above the horizon, but the pre-dawn sky was light enough to see by. It had been long days. Grief was a frigid bedfellow and Elsie tired of its company, leaving her bed in search of comfort that never seemed to come. *Oh, Joe, how will I ever get used to life without you?* she asked herself. Thoughts tumbled one over the other. She knew Mick and a number of neighbours would be meeting that very evening to talk about Joe's death, and about working conditions at the quarry. She also knew Mick was very angry at the way Joe died. She knew he blamed the man who'd forgotten to engage the brake; angry at the powers that be that demanded so much of the men; angry that Harry had disappeared; angry with the unfairness of it all. She knew he wanted justice for Joe. *But what does it matter? Nothing will bring Joe back to us;* Elsie was heartsick at the talk of retribution. She wanted changes made so that this kind of tragedy would never happen again, but vengeance was far from her mind and heart. Empty days and nights spread out before her in a never-ending march of time – time that was interminably long, try as she might to keep herself occupied and distracted. Minutes passed as Elsie was lost in her thoughts and memories. A rooster crowed bringing her back to the present and she turned to walk back to her little cabin.

"Elsie, dear," Fanny called, "Why don't you come in, join us for breakfast?"

Elsie smiled and turned to walk across the field. She was in no great hurry to return to the emptiness of her little cottage. She was so very grateful to Fanny and Mick and their clan. Her family, if only by marriage, had become very dear to her over the years she and Joe had been married.

"Morning," Mick greeted her as Elsie closed the door to the cheery kitchen. Mick sat at the end of the table cradling his infant son in his arms. Elsie carefully searched his face for an indication of his mood. He seemed calm and pleasant. "Good morning," she answered as she tickled the infant's soft downy cheek. "May I?" she questioned gesturing to indicate her desire to hold the baby. "Of course," Mick replied, placing the infant in her arms. "I should get out to the barn; the cow needs milking". With a nod to his wife Mick shuffled out the door.

"Did you get any rest?" Fanny asked as she set a cup of tea on the table in front of her. "No, not much," Elsie replied. "It's so strange sleeping without Joe next to me ..." she trailed off. Fanny pulled out a chair and sat next to her friend.

"It will take some time, I think," She consoled Elsie, "It must be so hard. I hope you know you're always welcome here – any time, day or night!"

Elsie smiled at her and dashed away an errant tear. Their brief chat was interrupted by the sound of little feet as Rose appeared in the doorway. The small girl rubbed her eyes, yawning widely, and moved to crawl into her mother's lap. Elsie smiled at the little girl. Fanny hugged her daughter and said, "Okay, duck, I have to get breakfast started. You sit here with Aunt Elsie. Fanny settled the child next to her aunt and began bustling around the cozy kitchen. Rose sat swinging her legs under the table and quietly watched her mother. Before long the rest of the family made their way out of their bedrooms. Jack stopped on his way through the kitchen to rub his aunt's shoulder before going out to help his father with the morning chores. William and Phil followed; Phil tweaked his baby sister's nose as he went by. Fanny dropped several eggs into the pot of water that was boiling on the stove. Sarah collected utensils and dishes to set the table. Fanny set a glass of water on the table in front of Rose then turned to lift the lid on the sideboard taking out a loaf of bread to cut for breakfast.

"Sarah, honey, would you please get a fresh jar of partridgeberry jam from the pantry?" Fanny asked. "Oh, and the molasses as well."

Sarah, still not fully awake, nodded her assent and moved to collect the requested items. Before long the family was gathered once again around the kitchen table.

"All yer animals are fed," Mick told Elsie, "That pig is growing nicely. You'll have plenty of salt pork to get through the winter. Once the work quiets down at the quarry the boys and I will go out cod jigging. There will be plenty of fish for all of us come winter, that's a promise." Mick continued in this vein in an attempt to reassure his brother's wife that she would be well taken care of. Fanny reached across the table placing a hand over her husband's. "Everything will be alright," she whispered. Mick's gaze met his wife's in silent understanding. They had talked quietly in the night as the moon shone through the curtains of their bedroom window. Fanny understood his deep pain and the anger he wrestled with since Joe's untimely death. "Aye, and better than alright, once I've dealt with this business," Mick answered, breathing a deep sigh. Fanny smiled and gently patted his hand.

"Well, I best get this all cleared away. I need to get the little ones ready for church," Fanny absently moved away from the table. "Sarah, will you please brush Rose's hair and help her get dressed for church? And you boys, are the chores all done? Go, clean yerselves up. We'll meet you at the chapel." Fanny continued to give orders as Elsie sat quietly rocking the baby in her arms. "Oh, Jack, wait for Sarah. She can walk with you."

Jack kicked a pebble and shuffled his feet waiting for his little sister. William and Phil had already left and his father was in the barn harnessing the horse to the little buggy. Jack struggled with his feelings. His anger at a God who could take away his beloved uncle stalked him like a lion in the jungle. In turns quiet and brooding or roaring its rage until Jack thought he'd blow up from the intensity. His chats with Phil had helped a little, but Jack was still frothing inside whenever he had a quiet moment to think, like this. "C'mon, Sarah," he impatiently intoned to himself. "What's taking her so long?"

"Here I am," Sarah chirped as she stepped outside the door. Sarah came to a sudden stop as she seen the stormy look upon Jack's face. "What's wrong?" she asked.

"Nothing, never mind," Jack growled and stomped away. Sarah hurried to catch up with her brother. They were more than half-way to the chapel before Jack uttered another word. "Don't say nothing to Ma, Sarah," he ordered.

"Are you mad at me?" Sarah whispered.

"Naw, it's not you, Sarah. I just don't want to go to church," Jack told her.

"But, why, Jack? Why?" Sarah's curiosity overcame her.

"Look, I don't want to talk about it, okay?" Jack replied. "I just don't want Ma to worry or be questioning me about it."

Sarah still did not understand but she loved her brother. "Sure, Jack, okay. I won't say a word," she promised. The pair continued on their way. Jack stopped as they came to the graveyard beside the little chapel. "Will you be okay from here?" he asked Sarah. Sarah nodded and walked slowly away, but not before Jack noticed the look of hurt on her face. Jack mentally kicked himself and was relieved when he noticed Ginny on the church steps beckoning to his sister. Treading softly Jack opened the gate in the picket fence that surrounded the cemetery. Slowly he approached his uncle's grave. There was still no marker but the fresh mound of earth made it easy to find. Jack reached up and tore his cap off his head as he stood at the foot of the grave. "Hey there, Uncle Joe. I sure miss you," Jack whispered. He waited but received no answer. Jack didn't know how long he was standing there before his father's voice beckoned him to come. Jack left the grave site and joined his parents and his aunt. His father laid a hand on his shoulder, squeezing gently. "Are you okay?" Mick asked his son. Jack nodded and then looked up into his father's face. "Do I have to go to church today?" he begged. "Do I?" Mick glanced quickly at his wife, but it was Elsie who answered.

"Jack, it sure would be nice to have fresh flowers on Joe's grave. I don't think the good Lord will mind if you go gather some while we're at worship." Elsie looked to Fanny for approval. At Fanny's nod Jack tore off at a run, relieved to be set free, at least for the moment. He ran hard and fast through the village before pivoting to the right to continue up a gentle hill to a clearing where wild flowers grew in abundance. Jack dropped to his knees as heaving sobs overtook him and he tried to spit out the grief that strangled him. Slowly his heart beat less quickly and the tears that had poured like a torrent at last abated. Jack hiccupped, rubbed his eyes and glanced over the meadow. It was a place he knew well, having picked berries there last summer in the company of his uncle. Memories came unbidden, slowly at first and then like a quickening flash, a kaleidoscope of colorful scenes.

Slowly Jack began to collect his uncle's favourites, and as he did so a sense of peace enveloped him. He remembered his uncle's stories, jokes, and the way he'd celebrated life, no matter how hard things got. And he remembered his uncle's faith. "Tell God what yer feeling, Jackie-boy," his uncle seemed to say. It was as if he could feel his uncle's hand on his shoulder, guiding him, as he always had. Jack looked up into the blue sky and began to pray. His words did not come from any prayer book, but from the depths of his soul, his very being. Holding the wildflower bouquet in his hands, Jack told his God all he felt: about his anger; about his fears; about the horrible emptiness that seemed to be everywhere; about how much he missed his uncle; and he asked why. Again, and again he asked 'why'. In the end he got no answer to that question, but he left the meadow with a deep sense of peace. The anger, if not entirely gone, was at least lessened considerably. Jack could see groups of people standing outside the chapel as he made his way there. As he drew closer, he spied his aunt standing with his mother and a few other women. Elsie was the first to see him coming and lifted her hand in greeting.

"Oh, how beautiful," Elsie said once Jack reached her. "Will you come help me place them on Joe's grave?"

Fanny turned a worried gaze on her son, searching his face. "Are you okay, Jackie-boy?" she asked. Jack nodded at his mother and turned towards Elsie. "Just me and you?" he asked her. Elsie held out her hand, nodding as she did so. I ain't a baby any more, he thought to himself, but shrugged and gripped his aunt's hand as they moved toward the small cemetery. Neither spoke as they approached the gave. Jack handed the flowers to Elsie and watched as she leaned down to place them on the centre of the mound. "All your favourite colors, Joe," she whispered. "Aren't they beautiful?"

Jack stood respectfully silent, allowing his aunt a few moments to compose herself. After a few minutes Elsie turned to Jack, "Did you know those blue ones are called forget-me-nots?" She asked him.

"No, I didn't. I just picked them because I remembered Uncle Joe picking them for you and that blue was yer favourite color," Jack replied. Elsie smiled. "Well, you did a great job," she answered. They remained at the grave site for some time until Elsie noticed people were moving away from the churchyard to make their way home.

At home Fanny and Elsie were kept busy making dinner for the family while Mick stayed outside to inform his sons about the meeting he'd arranged for that evening.

"The pastor agreed to let us use the church hall for the meeting," Mick told his boys. "I figure it will last at least a couple of hours. I had to talk a few of the men into coming. They got the idea Joe's death was nothing more than a terrible accident. Still and all, it was an "accident" that would never have happened were it not for the long hours we'd all been working and I pointed that out to 'em. Anyhow, there's not much to tell, 'cept we will be talking about how it happened and what we can do about it," Mick told his sons. "Now, for this meeting we can't all be talking at once or we won't get nothing done. So, I asked Charlie to lead it. He's a man of few words and he has the respect of the men," Mick added.

"What time, Da?" Phil asked.

"Right after supper we'll head over," Mick replied.

Chapter

9

Charlie stood speaking quietly with Mick as the room slowly filled with coworkers.

"Had a chat with Lou," Mick told Charlie, "Weren't much help though. He didn't see much of anything, just noticed Jake was working that cart all on 'is own. Ain't nobody seen Harry, neither. I'd like to know where he got to."

Charlie cursed and rubbed the back of his neck. "I dunno how this might help but I was talking with Hank earlier today," he told Mick. "He was telling me about a cousin of his in St. John's. He says the fellow was involved with starting an association to protect the men working at Belle Island. I think it might be good to have him explain how that works."

"Something has ta give," Mick replied. "There's Elsie now with no man to help her and no means of providing for herself. It just ain't right."

Charlie nodded grimly, "first thing to do is find out how this happened tis too bad nuddin' panned out with Lou and still no sign of Harry."

Mick nodded. Their anger had abated somewhat since the funeral, but both men wanted to do something to make a change on how the quarry operated. Neither wanted to see such a tragedy ever happen again.

"Hank here yet?" Mick asked.

Charlie searched the room. Finally, he laid eyes on their friend. Charlie waved to get Hank's attention gesturing him to come over. He was gratified to see Hank making his way toward them. The room was filling quickly and a soft buzz of conversation surrounded them.

"Hey b'ys, how ye getting on?" Hank greeted them.

"I was just telling Mick about that cousin of yers but I thinks ye can explain it better," Charlie told Hank.

Hank turned toward Mick. "Well, I don't know an awful lot about it, but the gist of it is it's a movement that helps widows when they suffer the death of their husbands." Hank began. "As I understands it, it gives widows a small sum of money. It also gives families a bit of help if a man gets hurt too bad to work – like sick pay," Hank explained.

"Do ye think we might be able to find a man that knows about all this who can explain it to the men?" Mick asked.

"Peter, my cousin, left a couple of days ago, but he's coming back. I can have a chat with him if ye wants." Hank responded.

"That would be wonderful, Hank. Let me know, will ya?" Mick said.

The trio continued their discussion while men continued to fill the hall. Charlie moved to the front of the room once it seemed nobody else was coming.

"Well, mates, I'd say it's time we got started with this," Charlie told his friends. Charlie had a strong voice, which carried well, making it easy to hear him, even from across the hall. He gave a sharp whistle to get the men's attention before he started talking.

"B'ys, ye all knows why we're here," He began. "First things first. We need to know exactly what happened to Joe that day."

The sound of shuffling boots greeted him and a few of the men murmured quietly.

Vic was the first to address them all. "I heard the new man, Jake's his name, fergot to lock up the brakes on his cart."

"It wasn't done on purpose," Paddy spoke up. "Look, I knows Jake, and this here is killing him. The man is falling all apart."

"The bastard needs it done to him. So's he can see what agony he put Joe through," another joined in.

"Did ye notice the son of a bitch hasn't showed his face since it happened? If it weren't done a purpose why hasn't he spoke up for hisself?" another voice rang out.

Paddy's voice rang out loud and clear, "Leave off Jake. He's been at the quarry. He just wouldn't come to the cookhouse. Do ye think he's stupid? He knows what ye all think of 'im. My God, try to walk a moment in 'is shoes. He's beating himself up worst than anythin' ye all can do to 'im. He's ashamed and full of guilt. Any man here wants to make it worst fer 'im will have to get past me first."

"Simmer down, everyone," Charlie barked. "Look, Joe was a good buddy of mine and nobody wants to see justice done any more than I do, but first we needs the facts. We needs to know exactly what happened that day."

Paddy spoke again: "Look here, Jake is a good man. You may not know this but his wife just had a set of twins. The babies are up crying half the night most nights. Me aunt thinks they have the croup, so the pair of them have been worried sick as well as making do on next to no sleep."

"Fair enough," the second man piped up again, "but there's many here been in the same sort of situation and never got nobody killed".

"Has anyone seen Harry or know where he got to?" Charlie asked. His question had the men looking to one another and several shook their heads.

Mick's sons were standing in the middle of the hall and listening to what was being said.

"Uncle Joe was a fair man," Phil spoke quietly and slowly. "He wouldn't want vengeance on this man, Jake, was it?" He paused for a moment before continuing. "Correct me if I'm wrong, but didn't Uncle Joe make the cradles for those little ones? They live out on the point, right? Uncle Joe was telling me about the family and all the struggles they've had. I knows they ain't had it easy" . . . Phil trailed off.

"They ain't from around here," Jake's defender began. "Jake, he ain't used to quarry work. He's a carpenter and he's farmed and fished some. He may be a stranger, but he is a good man. I grew up with the man and I'm here to tell ye, he ain't one to cause trouble. And yes, Phil, yer uncle bought a mess of mackerel and cod from 'im last year and they worked something out to do with them cradles. Joe felt bad for the young couple, I expect."

"Joe was like that," Charlie butted in, "What we needs to know right now is if anybody seen what happened." He turned to address Vic. "Who told you about the way the cart was loaded and all the rest of it?"

Vic stood gazing into the eyes of Jake's defender. "T'was Jake told it to Lou, right after it happened. Seems he was mighty shaken up and blaming hisself. Like ye would," Vick answered.

"Lou?" Charlie spoke directly to him, "You know any more about this?"

"Yeah. It's like Vic says. After the accident I seen Jake bent over throwing his guts up. I give 'im a cup of water. I didn't know it was his cart 'til he told me so. He was pretty upset, but he owned up to it straight off," Lou told the room full of men. "He didn't realize 'til it was too late that he'd forgotten to set the brake. Like Paddy says, he hadn't done this type of work afore. He only started the day before, and then he was on the crusher."

"Nobody show him what to do or how to do it?" Charlie wanted to know.

"I don't know, but probably not," Lou replied. "You knows they hired another dozen men to get that shipment out, Jake was one of 'em. T'was all they cared about, getting the freighter loaded."

"Ye got that right," Vic grated out. "Bloody bastards don't give a damn about the men, only about lining their pockets."

"I'm thinking we ain't going be risking life or limb fer the likes of 'em any longer," Mick joined in. "We can't have me brother's life be in vain. If nothing else I thinks we should honor his memory by making sure this ain't never gonna happen agin."

Charlie took up Mick's unspoken thoughts. "Hank here was telling us about some sort of association where we can come together to deal with such tragedies." Turning, he asked, "Hank, you want to tell the men what you know about it?"

Hank scratched his head. "I ain't no expert, but me cousin was telling me about an association he helped set up over on Bell Island. It gives the widow a bit of money, or if a man gets hurt, gives him a bit of sick pay until he's back on his feet and back to work," Hank repeated everything he'd told his friends earlier.

"How's that gonna make a difference at the quarry?" Lou asked.

"No shipment is going to get out without us working like dogs," Charlie began. "I say we stick together and not let 'em push us around no more. Just do our work, but refuse long hours. But we all have to stick together on this."

"I cain't afford to get fired," one man worriedly put in.

"They can't fire all of us," Charlie advised. "If we stick together, what are they gonna do?"

"Charlie's got a good point," Vic answered. "They need the shipments to go out. And we'll get them out, but by God, on our terms, not theirs!"

"I'm mighty interested in this association thing," Lou added. "How can we find out more about it?"

Charlie looked at Hank, "Do you think your cousin'd be willing to come meet with us, tell us all more about it?"

"I think he'd be willing," Hank responded. "I will ask him first chance I get."

"In the meanwhile, don't be chatting on about this when we're at the quarry. We don't want the mining captain to get wind of it. It's getting late and we all have to be up and at 'er in the morning. What do ye say we meet again next Sunday evening? Would ye all be willing to do that," Charlie asked the gathering. "We needs to figure out what we wants and the best ways to go about it."

As the men nodded solemnly or shouted out a 'yeah' a general assent was given and Charlie turned to leave.

Chapter

10

M ary worriedly watched Jake. He was never one for idle chit
chat, yet he was quieter than usual the past few days. He'd
told her what happened in the quarry and his part in it. She
knew he was beating himself up something terrible over it. It stung
even more knowing the man who had reached out to them both
when they'd first arrived was the one fatally injured in the accident
and it made it that much more painful. Nothing she said made
a difference. Jake was somber and remorseful and was pushing
himself to exhaustion with work around their small farm. Not even
the dog he loved could move him from his morbid thoughts. Mary
had watched while the German Shepherd went through all her
usual tricks to get her master's attention – to no avail. She gazed out
the window watching as the dog sat back on her haunches looking
pleadingly up at Jake and whining softly.

"Smokey! Go lay down," Jake snarled roughly at the dog. Mary
turned from the window, her heart breaking, feeling helpless to help
her husband. *Will he ever get over this?* She asked herself and wished
they had never moved to the little community. *Well, there's naught to
do but get through it, somehow,* her inner dialogue continued. *We done
spent all we had to buy this cottage and land.* She remembered the nights
of rocks thrown through the windows and what had brought them
to move so far away. She sighed. It seemed their lives were wrought
with troubles. She turned to their small bedroom where the twins,
finally asleep, slumbered on in the cradles Joe had crafted for them.
She leaned over the little beds placed side by side and watched them
sleep. Fine downy hair crowned the little heads and she gave thanks

once again that they seemed to be on the mend from the croup – *if it was croup*, she thought. Mary watched and prayed softly to herself, begging the Lord to help them both and for comfort and help for Joe's widow and his family.

Out in the yard Jake rose from the stump he'd been resting on. The accident at the quarry had been torturing him ever since it happened. And it didn't matter how hard he swung the axe while chopping wood or how long he pushed the plow churning up the small garden, nothing seemed to tire him out enough to sleep through the night. He'd rest for an hour or two and then the nightmare would begin anew – the cart careening down the track away from him; the sound of Joe's scream; the cookhouse and the accusing expression on the faces of his coworkers. On and on it went in a never-ending loop. Memories of meeting Joe when they'd first settled here figured into his dreams as well and made his guilt and shame that much harder to bear. *He was a good man,* Jake thought. *And, it wouldn't matter even if he wasn't, nobody deserves to die like that.* And off he went again on his circular loop of self condemnation. Jake was so lost in his thoughts that he did not hear the horse and cart enter the yard; didn't notice his dog's sudden sharp bark.

"Whoa, girl, whoa," the man called to the horse and gently pulled up on the reins. Patrick, known to his friends as Paddy, climbed down from the high perch above the wagon. Still, Jake was unaware of his visitor. It wasn't until the dog's frantic barking and leaping that Jake realized he was no longer alone.

"Jake, b'y, you look a sight," Paddy said. "How ye keeping?"

Jake looked over Paddy's shoulder and out over the bay. "I'm good," he answered.

"Yer face don't look it," Paddy remarked. "Look, I don't mean to be a busybody, but I knows you been taking this hard."

"Is there some other way to take it?" Jake said quietly. "It's my fault, nobody's but mine."

"Ye made a mistake – an awful mistake – but a mistake none the less," Paddy told him.

Jake's stormy eyes and blank face was his only response.

"Look, man," Paddy continued. "Did ye purposely leave off the brake? Well, did ye?"

Jake continued to look out to sea, giving no answer to Paddy's question.

"Did ye want Joe dead?" Paddy continued to force the issue.

"Leave off, will ya," Jake shoved at Paddy trying to find a way past his burly friend.

Paddy planted his feet and grabbed Jake roughly by his upper arms. "I ain't leaving here 'til ye talks to me," he warned.

"No! Okay? No! Of course not!" Jake's voice rose in volume.

"Did ye do it on purpose?" Paddy pushed on.

"I said no!" Jake pushed back, trying to disengage himself from the bigger man's grip.

"Then why are ye punishing yerself?" Paddy wanted to know.

"Look, ye don't understand. Nobody can understand. I took a man's life. Don't ye get it? I killed him meself, whether by accident or no don't matter. He ain't ever coming back," Jake was shouting now, bringing Mary back to the window once again.

"It was naught but an accident. Do ye hear me? T'was a horrific, terrible, awful accident!" Paddy insisted. "Ye still have a wife and family to think about. Ye can't be wallowing in self-pity!"

Jake took a step back in shock. "Self-pity, is it? Wallowing, is it? Ye don't know shite!"

Paddy's face paled. He'd known Jake since they were small lads and he was sorry as hell about what happened. He considered the man more like a brother than a friend, and was fighting to get through to him.

"My buddy," he spoke slowly, "ye knows I don't mean it like that. But ye have to get a hold of yerself, for Mary's sake, and fer those two wee babies in there."

"Jake?" Mary called from the doorway, "is everything alright?"

Paddy dropped his hands, balling them at his sides. The last thing he wanted was to bring more grief to the little cottage. He watched Jake's face, waiting.

Jake turned his face toward the door, "Everything's fine," he tried to reassure her, even as his body language said otherwise. His shoulders were hunched, his face tight and tense. "Go on back inside. I'm just gonna have a word with Paddy here," he told her. Mary paused in the doorway looking askance toward Paddy.

"There's nothing to worry about, Mary," Paddy spoke quietly, loosening the fists at his sides. "Just a few things I needs to discuss with yer man."

Mary gave a small nod before disappearing inside the cottage.

Paddy turned back to Jake. "I knows ye blame yerself, and I can't say I'd be any different," he told his friend. "But ye can't go on this way. People who know ye well knows the difference. They knows it t'was an accident, and the rest don't matter."

Jake sank down on the stump he'd abandoned earlier. All the wind seemed to go out of his sails. All the fight was gone, vanished like fog in the sun. "I knows ye mean well, Paddy. I do. I just have to figure it out," he spoke so quietly Paddy could just barely hear him. Paddy grasped Jake's shoulder and squeezed. "Just don't let it eat ye alive. What's done is done. Ye gotta find a way to forgive yerself," Paddy responded. Jake nodded curtly. "Alright then, guess I'll shove off. Will ye be back at the quarry in the morning? The captain was none too pleased when ye didn't finish yer shift yesterday."

Jake was so still Paddy wondered if he'd been heard. "Jake?" He paused a moment. "Look, I knows it won't be easy to show yer face, but things 'ave calmed down some. Ye won't be lynched, if that's what's worrying ye," Paddy gave a forced laugh and elbowed Jake in the side, "There was a meetin' last night. I was there and stood up fer ye. Tis true there's men who blame ye, but there's more that don't."

"I deserve to be lynched, or leastwise punished somehow," Jake retorted.

"Man, methinks ye been punishing yerself quite enough," Paddy answered. "So, what's it going to be?"

Jake raised his eyes to his friend's face, "I s'pose I ain't got much choice," he replied, "as ye just said I have a wife and family to look after."

Paddy clapped a hand on Jake's shoulder. "Ye knows I will stand behind ye, no matter what. And there's others that will too."

Jake gave a single nod and Paddy turned to leave. Jake watched as the horse and wagon carried his friend out of his field and wondered how he would face the men. Still, he was no quitter and didn't shy away from facing the consequences of his actions. Yet, it would take every ounce of courage he possessed to take himself to work on the morrow.

Chapter

11

The morning dawned misty with fog. It hung over the fields and skimmed the shores of the bay giving the illusion of clouds hovering just above the surface of the water. Jake shivered as he set out on the long walk to the quarry. The dampness seemed to seep into his bones, chilling him thoroughly. The threadbare jacket he wore was little comfort as he put one foot determinedly after the other. Despite what he'd told Mary earlier he was jumpy with nerves. He had decided to take a shortcut to avoid meeting any coworkers on his way. The narrow path cut through the woods and a wet tree branch brushed his face as he shuffled along. He swiped at it cursing quietly to himself. "Ye gots to face up to what ye did," his father had often said, usually after some hijinks or other he and his brother had got up to, like the time the pair had thrown rocks through the church window. His father had marched the two of them straight to the rectory to apologize and make amends.

But how can I ever make amends for this? Jake asked himself. Again, the wretched image of the runaway cart plagued his thoughts and Jake was stopped in his tracks. *How am I going to face the men?* he thought before moving on. Jake's thoughts continued to castigate and torment him as he trudged onward. The shortcut petered out opening onto a meadow above the quarry. From there a stony pathway wound downhill to the work site. The sun had burned off the fog during Jake's journey and warmed his back as he reached the small cabin that was the headquarters for the big boss. Jake pushed the door open peering inside. "Captain?" he searched the low-lit room for the man in charge.

"Well come on in man, don't stand there dawdling at the door," came the retort.

Jake stepped up into the rough-hewn structure. "I was told to come see ye, sir," He began. "T'was me that were responsible for Joe's death." Words failed him after this confession. Jake stood holding his breath waiting for a response that seemed long in coming.

The captain pushed back his chair and standing looked angrily into Jake's eyes. "So, t'was ye that caused all this, was it? Do ye 'ave any idea the trouble ye 'ave caused. It ain't only the death of a good man. Ye 'ave caused a 'eap of problems for this operation. I 'ad to tell the owners. And by law, the death 'ad to be reported. That means the bloody government will be sending an inspector out 'ere," the captain ran his fingers through his hair and turned frustrated eyes on Jake. Jake did not breathe a word but stood waiting for the axe to fall. "Tell me in yer own words 'ow this 'appened," the captain ordered.

Jake pulled his cap off his head and nodded briefly. "Well, sir, I don't rightly know exactly how it happened. One minute I was shoveling limestone into the cart and the next minute it was rolling away" . . . Jake's boss interrupted him. "Did ye not apply the brakes on yer cart?" he asked.

Jake gave a short shake of his head and continued, "No, sir, I didn't. I didn't know there was a brake, and the cart moved off so fast I couldn't catch it. I made a grab for it but it was too heavy with stone and got away from me." Jake paused again.

"And was there any man nearby to witness all this?" the captain questioned, an idea beginning to taking shape. Jake frowned. "Think, man, think, was there a soul to witness this? Was there not anyone 'elping ye? Rules state workers must work in pairs. Who was paired with ye?"

Jake shook his head. "No, sir, I was working alone."

The captain took a deep breath and turned his back on Jake, looking out the small window that overlooked the quarry. Jake stood quietly waiting for whatever was to come next. His worry reached ever deeper depths as the seconds ticked by and he wrung the cap in his hands. Eventually the Captain turned around to face him.

"There will be repercussions to all this and I don't rightly know what the outcome will be. By rights I should fire ye right 'ere and now, not only 'ave ye caused a 'eap of misery, ye 'aven't bin workin' up to par. I 'ave to talk to the pit boss and we needs all 'ands for the duration," he glanced at Jake and paused momentarily. "Ye are not to speak a word of this to anybody, do ye understand me?" At Jake's nod he turned away again. "Go on then, go about yer work," he tersely ordered. "But I wants ye on the crusher, tell the man on it to come see me."

Jake noticed the grim expressions on his coworkers' faces as he made his way uphill to where the crusher was located. Some gave him dirty looks and spat in his direction, but not one said a word. He delivered the message he'd been given and began the gruelling work of filling the crusher with rock. The din made it impossible to give any more thought to his situation and he focused on the task at hand.

Later Jake paused at the door of the cook house screwing up his courage to step inside. Sighing heavily, he pushed open the door. He stood stock still for a moment as all conversation came to an abrupt stop. The silence was deafening as he made his way to the canteen. Paddy stood up as well and made his way across the room to his friend. Clasping a hand on Jake's shoulder, he said, "Good on ye, mate. I am glad to see ye." Jake made no response as he waited for his plate of beans. His shoulders were stiff with tension as he turned to follow Paddy back to his table. He kept his eyes down as he walked and it wasn't until he was sitting next to his friend that he released the breath he'd been holding.

"Son of a bitch," came a low voice meant to be heard. Jake heard other such slights and ignored them all as he wolfed down the plate of food. Paddy sat straight up and gazed around the room daring anyone to challenge him as he swept the room with his eyes. The two men remained at the table waiting while the room emptied out as fellow workers made their way back to work.

"Thanks, Paddy. T'was kind of ye. . ." Jake started to say.

"Jake, don't be thanking me," Paddy answered. "Let's just get on with it, b'y. And don't let the b'ys get to ye. Like I told ye afore, there are good folks that know the difference. The folks that don't and wanna judge ye – well, there's naught we can do about that."

Paddy was first to exit the cookhouse and was surprised to see Mick waiting for them. A small group of men stood watching from a short distance away. Paddy stood ready to fight any or all who came after Jake.

"Paddy," Mick nodded at him. Paddy kept his eyes on the group of men as Mick walked toward him and Jake. Without a glance he said, "We don't want no trouble, Mick."

"I ain't looking fer trouble b'y," Mick told the pair. "I just wants a word with ye."

Jake stood worriedly glancing from Mick to the knot of men. "Paddy, this ain't yer fight," he began. "I can speak fer meself."

Mick stood taking the measure of the man who had caused so much sorrow. "We ain't met yet. The name's Mick. It was my brother that was killed," he spoke softly to Jake. "I ain't here to cast blame. I just wanted to know if ye'd be willing to come speak to me and my family about what happened."

Across the yard men were straining to hear what was being said. Paddy continued to watch them as Mick conversed with Jake. Jake gulped. He wasn't keen on meeting with Joe's kinfolk, but he also knew he'd have to face them, much as he'd had to face his coworkers and putting it off wouldn't make it any easier. "When?" he asked.

"Was thinking after church on Sunday, if that suits ye," Mick responded.

Jake gave one short nod and held his hand out to Mick to shake. Mick paused for a moment before gripping the outstretched hand. "I can't begin to say how sorry I am ..." Jake faltered in his apology.

Looking at Paddy, Mick answered, "So we've been told."

Jake nodded again and the trio turned at the clanging bell summoning them all back to work. Unbeknown to Jake the knot of men nearby included Phil, William, and Jack as well as Charlie and Vic. It was Charlie who had been watching the exchange so intently. Jake remembered Charlie as the man who had struck him after the accident. Jake warred with his memories as he made his way back to the crusher.

"So, what did he have to say?" Charlie asked Mick when he joined them.

"Not much, an apology, and an agreement to come to the house to speak with us," Mick told him.

Charlie kept his thoughts to himself as the men made their way back to their positions. None of the men had much to say, each digesting the news and ruminating on the meeting to come and none relishing the prospect.

The week passed quickly and Sunday dawned clear and bright. Mick stood in the yard beside his home watching the gulls sweeping low over the bay. His thoughts were consumed by memories of Joe and the unfairness of his passing. He'd held many a conversation with Fanny as he struggled to come to terms with it. The anger that held sway in the days following Joe's accident still had not burned itself out and Mick worried about how he would handle speaking again with the man who was the cause of so much anguish. Still, he knew his brother would not want him taking vengeance on his behalf. Joe had always been the fairest man he'd ever known. "Just hear him out," Joe's spirit seemed to say. "Aye, I will hear him out," Mick told him, "And I will get to the bottom of this affair, I promise ye that, Joe".

It was Paddy, running interference once again, that came up to Mick and his family following the church service. "Jake will be along soon," he told them. "His wife needed him to do a few things before he left. She's worried about him, and frankly, so am I. Should we be?"

Mick answered softly, "No need at all. We aren't looking for revenge, just some answers that only Jake can give."

Paddy studied each man's face before turning to walk away.

The family were back at their cabin when Phil, looking out a window, spied a man climbing the bank at the back of the property. "Be right back," Phil told his father and walked to meet the solitary figure. Fanny had taken the three littlest ones to Elsie's, leaving the men to talk it out. Charlie and Vic sat at the table with Mick and his sons. Each of them tense and quiet as they waited.

"Hullo, Jake," Phil greeted their visitor. "Phil's the name. I'm Mick's son."

"Morning," Jake replied, surprised and uncomfortable he said nothing more.

"What do ye have there?" Phil asked gesturing to the bulky package wrapped in burlap sacks that Jake carried beneath his arm.

"I'd rather not say just now. Let's just say it's a peace offering of sorts…. not that there's anything I can do to make up fer what I done," he answered awkwardly.

Phil's curiosity was aroused but he simply nodded and the two men continued to tramp down the long grass as they crossed the field to the house.

Phil shoved the door open but Jake stood timidly on the threshold blinking nervously at the men seated around the kitchen table. Opening the door wider Phil stood gesturing for Jake to enter. Jake lay his bundle on the stoop and straightened. His heart thumped loudly in his chest and he was sure these men would hear it. He straightened his shoulders, his back stiff as he entered the room. Phil spoke softly as he made the introductions. Jack's knee bounced nervously under the table. His emotions were in a whirl as he stared at the man, he considered him to be his uncle's killer. Taking his cue from his father Jack sat quietly listening and trying to still his inner voice, which was screaming silently.

William surprised everyone by initiating the discussion. "Let's just cut to the chase. We all want to know what happened that day," he began. "Why don't ye tell us yer side of it?"

Jake's face went white as he considered how to begin. His throat went dry and he swallowed to dislodge the lump that formed there. He fixed his gaze on Phil's face and kept it there as he tried to get words out. His tongue felt hopelessly thick and for a moment panic set in and his only thought was to escape the room. It was Jack's whispered 'please' that moved him to begin. *This family has a right to know,* he thought to himself, and finally the words began to slip off his tongue without much forethought on his part.

"I was supposed to be operating the crusher," he began, "I had gotten used to it the day before. But the pit boss said he needed me loading carts; that he was gonna run the crusher hisself and he sent me down to get started. I'd seen men filling carts and I thought it would be easy. It weren't." Jake took a long pause and his eyes took on a faraway look. "I kept shoveling limestone into the cart. I never looked inside I just kept shoveling" . . .Jake stopped speaking finding it difficult to go on. His hands covered his face and he shuddered.

"Go on, man, go on," Mick spoke gruffly.

Jake began pacing the room. He paced for several minutes before he could continue. "The cart began to move. I made a grab fer it. My fingertips brushed the edge, I was off balance and I fell. . . and it was gone." Jake seemed to choke for a moment and the men looked askance at one another.

"The brake, man, the brake. Did ye not set the brake?" Mick questioned.

Jake could not respond. The lump was a hard core that he was having trouble clearing. He stood still but nodded slowly.

"Ye did set the brake?" Mick, confused, asked again.

Jake shook his head and got out a ragged "no" and rushed toward the door. The nightmare was on him once again, tearing him up inside. Phil's hand came down on top of Jake's on the doorknob. "Wait! Don't go!"

Phil paused. The expression of desperate panic on Jake's face was unsettling.

"Take it easy, mate, take it easy," he murmured.

Mick's anger warred with his pity for the man. Pity won out.

"Please, don't leave," Mick began, causing Jake to stop in his tracks.

Jake stood, his head hanging down in shame. Guilt consumed him and he wearily turned toward Mick. "T'was all my fault. Yer brother's dead and 'tis my fault, only mine. I am mightily sorry fer what I did," he half-whispered in reply.

Mick stood observing the man he'd held responsible for Joe's death. Seconds ticked by as Mick tried to put into words his growing suspicions.

"Ye may have made mistakes – fatal mistakes, but I be thinking t'was not yer fault alone," Mick began.

Jake stood staring stupidly at Mick. "Whadda ye getting at?"

"That there is more blame to go 'round than we first thought," Mick replied. "That's why we needs ye to tell us everything ye knows."

The men had sat quietly taking it all in but now Vic spoke: "Who showed ye how to set the brake?" he asked.

Jake gave no answer, the words of the big boss flashed suddenly in his memory: *Don't say a word to nobody* ... he stood shaking his head as if to work the memory loose; to overcome the implied threat as he remembered the intensity of his eyes, the tone of his voice. Vic and Charlie looked at one another in confusion as Jake remained silent.

"Who was working with ye?" Charlie asked. Still there was no response. Jack looked from one face to another trying to figure it all out and in the end his gaze settled on Jake and stayed there. Jake's confusion, remorse, and his guilt and shame were written all over his face revealing his inner torment.

"I gots to git home," Jake finally rasped and turned again to the door. This time nobody stopped him and he was out and gone before anyone could react. Not a word was spoken as each individual tried to digest the sparse information Jake had given them. A chair scraped along the floor boards as William got up from the table. Mick was still standing where he'd been when Jake made his sudden departure. "There's a lot more to all this than we knows," he said. William stood beside his father watching Jake's quick strides across the field through the kitchen window.

"Dad?" Jack piped up, "What are we gonna do now?"

Mick looked at his youngest son and seemed lost in thought for a few moments.

"I dunno yet, Jackie-boy, but we are gonna get to the bottom of this. That I promise ye," he said.

"Was it just me or did he seem a mite scared to ye?" Phil wanted to know.

"Something smells bad to me," Charlie replied. "There's something about this business that is rotten to the core."

The men continued to discuss Jake's reactions to their questioning until Vic reminded them time was growing short and he had to get back home for supper before the meeting that evening. Charlie and Vic left together and Jack was sent to Elsie's for Fanny.

Chapter

12

As Mick stood outside with his eldest sons, he noticed the burlap-covered parcel propped up against the railing. "What's this?" he asked absently.

"Aw, Jake brought that with him, said it was a peace offering or something," Phil answered.

Mick walked over and picked the package up. Walking back to his sons he slowly unwrapped the burlap covering revealing the wooden cross carved with Joe's name. "Well, I'll be!" he exclaimed. "Where the heck did Jake get this?"

William read the epitaph out loud, "Joseph Kelly, Beloved husband to Elsie, May he R.I.P." His throat closed and he could speak no more.

It was wonderfully carved with intricate decoration and bevel work. The mitred corners were the work of a master carpenter and Joe's name and particulars were meticulously chiseled out. Jack noted the Easter lily that was carved above Joe's name on the horizontal bar while the carver had worked tiny forget-me-nots all along the edges of the vertical cross-piece. Jack knew the small blue flowers were Elsie's favorite flower. Each flower was painted blue while the epitaph was stained a dark green, as was the outline of stem and leaves on the lily. Elsie and Joe had lost a wee babe on Easter Sunday the year after Jack was born. Joe had once told Jack the sad story. Mick gave his head a shake and looked at his sons, "Well now, I don't know what to think. But one thing I know fer sure, Elsie will be mighty touched by this". Whomever had made the grave marker must have known the couple well. The cross was truly a thing of beauty. Mick stood up, mesmerized. It was a mystery that would have to wait.

"I've a feeling that might be Jake's handiwork," Phil thoughtfully replied. "He did say it was a peace offering of sorts".

At the sound of his wife's voice chatting with Elsie Mick quickly rewrapped the bundle and strode toward the barn, calling back to his sons: "I am just going to put this away for the time being. Don't be saying nothing about it, mind".

"If the weather holds, I'd like to get the sheets washed and on the line in the morning," Fanny was telling Elsie as the women approached. Rose was skipping happily along next to Sarah. It made for a pretty picture as the men watched them approach. Jack was nowhere to be seen. Elsie hadn't responded as she studied the faces of her nephews alighting on Phil's and staying there.

"Phil? Is something wrong?" Elsie asked with concern in her voice.

Phil swiped at the hair that had fallen over his eyes. "No, nothing," he answered, but his grave expression gave him away.

Elsie exchanged a quick glance with Fanny. "Are ye sure, son?" Fanny enquired. "Sure, looks to me like something ain't right."

"Everything's alright," William cut in. "Phil's just worried about all the water we're gonna have to haul if ye go washing sheets," William grinned at the women and gave Phil a light punch on the shoulder. Elsie gazed knowingly at William, her look telling him she knew he wasn't being truthful.

"Thanks for helping me," she said, smiling at Sarah as she spoke, "I'll bring over some bread tomorrow, and maybe some lassy buns." Elsie was well aware of Sarah's weakness for sweets. Sarah smiled and began chatting about the morning's doings as she followed her mother and Aunt inside.

Fanny turned to admonish her sons not to go far before disappearing into the cabin. Elsie glanced around and asked, "Where is Jack," before following Fanny inside.

"I'll go hunt him down," Phil answered.

As before Phil found Jack on the shore staring out to sea.

"Whaddya up to?" he asked as he reached Jack's side.

"Just thinking about that fella, Jake." Jack answered. "What do ye make of 'im?"

"He seemed pretty shook up to me, which is only natural I s'pose," Phil replied. Phil shook his head. "I sure wouldn't want to be in his shoes."

"I been so angry. I wanted so much to hit him," Jack admitted. "But now, well, it would like kicking a puppy he's so woe begone."

"Life is never simple. There ain't no black and white," Phil began. "No clear line between right and wrong in all this. I think Da is right. There's more here than meets the eye."

Jack's face turned red as he thought about his uncle's death and the plight that his aunt was now in. "I wanted to hurt him," he confessed. "I wanted to hurt him bad, maybe even kill him." Jack looked quickly at Phil to gauge his reaction.

"Vengeance is mine, saith the Lord," Phil quoted. He shrugged. "I dunno, Jackie-boy. T'is hard stuff. I wanted to hurt him too," he went on, "but I never thought how he was feeling, or how hard all this has been on him and his family."

"I don't wanna feel sorry fer him," Jack whispered, "but I kinda do. Is that wrong?"

"No, it's not wrong," Phil replied. "I feel sorry fer him too. I guess maybe we'll find out more about the accident at the meeting. Maybe."

"Uncle Joe wouldn't want us to hurt him, would he?" Jack questioned.

"Naw. Uncle Joe didn't believe in 'an eye for an eye'," Phil responded.

"He was so kind and so understanding," Jack reminisced, remembering again the hurt sea gull, "What do ye think he'd want us to do?"

"I can't say as I know," Phil replied. "Ain't never been a situation like this that I knows of, but Uncle Joe was not a violent man."

"No, that's fer sure," Jack answered. "I sure miss him."

"We all do, Jackie-boy. We all do," Phil said. "Well, we best be getting home. Supper should be 'bout ready."

Jack nodded his agreement and the brothers headed back.

Once inside the small cottage the two women were careful not to speak of their concerns in front of the two small girls. Fanny knew

Sarah worshipped her brothers. She also knew it would cause her endless worry and incur a long list of questions that Fanny simply had no time for just then. Fanny laid her sleeping infant in his cradle and sent the girls off to play outside.

"What do ye think that was all about?" Elsie asked with a toss of her head toward the door.

"I think the men are trying to protect us," Fanny stated, "but we'll hear soon enough. Mick always needs to chew things over in his mind before he talks about it."

Fanny paused. She knew her friend was grieving quietly, that Joe's death had hit her very hard. "Aw, ye know – men!" she exclaimed. "It is Jack's first job, no doubt Mick's worrying over it and more so now since …" Fanny bit her lip. She really did not want to add to Elsie's distress and mentally gave herself a kick.

"Fanny, dear, there's no need of ye trying to protect me. The idea of anything happening to Jack," … she trailed off. "All your children are precious to me, but Jack, well he's Jack, if there's something wrong, I want to know." She told Fanny.

Fanny put down the paring knife she was using to peel vegetables and looked into her friend's eyes, "I'm sorry. I didn't mean to upset ye. Jack's doing better handling Joe's death than we thought he would but he is a worry wart. Always has been, as ye knows. I think he's worrying about the accident and something happening to someone else. He's afraid. He don't say it, but I knows he is." Fanny answered.

"Are ye gonna let him go to that meeting again?" Elsie wanted to know. "I knows he went to the last one and I knows Mick feels he needs to learn but …"

Fanny did not answer right away but continued with the peeling. Glancing quickly at Elsie she said, "I wish he wouldn't go. I think all this has been too heavy a burden fer a young boy. But he does have to learn. He has to grow up and know what's what in this life. He is a bit too gentle. Mick thinks it will toughen him up a bit to hear the men talk and hear different points of view. I hope he's right. I fear more for Jack than any of the others."

Elsie was slicing onions and Fanny was unsure if the tears in her eyes were due to this or other causes. *God knows she has enough on her plate*, Fanny thought.

"He's so much like Joe," Elsie said, "He wears his heart on his sleeve. There's never any trouble to know when something's upsetting him."

Fanny nodded and Elsie continued, "Mick knows best, I'm sure. And I know he'd never put him in harm's way. Perhaps, in the long run this is all for the best."

"God willing, it will all come out right in the end," Fanny replied. "We just have to leave Jack in God's hands."

Elsie nodded her agreement and the two women were silent and lost in thought as they considered all that had happened and what the future might hold.

The women were not alone in their concern about the future. William had followed his father into the barn to discuss the meeting and to share his concerns about Jack.

Meanwhile Phil had meandered over the fields to find Jack. On the way he spied his sisters in the field picking wildflowers.

"Hey, don't wander too far," Phil yelled. Sarah stood up shielding her eyes from the sun. "We won't", she answered and taking Rose's hand started walking closer to the cabin to a new patch of brightly colored blossoms.

Spying Jack on the beach Phil waved to the girls and made his way down to the shore.

"That was delicious, Fan," Mick complimented his wife as he pushed his chair away from the table.

"It really was a fine meal, Ma," William agreed, as he too stood up from the table.

Fanny smiled and reached out a hand to grasp her husband's wrist. "Might I have a word with ye before ye go off to the meeting?" she asked. Fanny stood and began walking to their bedroom before Mick had a chance to deny her. Mick glanced around the table at the faces of his children.

What on earth is the woman up to he wondered as he followed her into the room.

"What's this all about?" he asked as he closed the bedroom door.

"T'is about Jack. Do ye really think it's good fer him to go to these meetins?"

"Fan, ye knows how hard a life it can be. Is Joe not evidence enough of it? Yes. The boy has to come. It will do him good to learn what's going on, and," he stressed," to see what we might be able to do about it. If we can find a way to make the work safer, well it would relieve him a bit, I think"

Fanny was quiet momentarily. "Well, then, so be it," she answered. "But please, Mick, keep a close eye on him."

Mick crossed the room taking Fanny in his arms. "Don't ye be worrying. I'll look after the lad," Mick promised. "Now we got to git going. I wants ta have a chat with this man, Paddy. He knows Jake better than anybody. I wants to see if he knows anything more about what happened."

Fanny nodded and hugged Mick hard before turning to open the door.

"God help us all," she whispered, half turning back to Mick she said: "I hope ye men can do something to make the work safer. I'll be praying fer ye all." Mick gave a quick nod and calling his sons left the house.

Chapter

13

Mick was surprised to see Paddy waiting outside the church hall. The door was open and the men could hear the voices of the coworkers already gathered inside.

"Go on in," Mick told his sons, "I'll be there directly." Paddy was staring him in the face as they'd approached and Mick wondered why the man seemed to be waiting for him, even while he was grateful to be able to have a chance to speak with him.

"Mick," Paddy nodded, "I'd like a word with ye."

"What's on yer mind?" Mick asked.

"Ye knows Jake is a friend of mine," Paddy began, searching Mick's face to gauge Mick's reaction to his words. "He ain't got many in these parts being new to the area and all. He really is a good man," Paddy began. "And I'm sorry as hell fer what happened to Joe. I really am."

"Nobody's looking to do Jake any harm," Mick answered.

"Why the meeting then?" Paddy wanted to know.

"Look, what happened to Joe could happen to any of us," Mick replied. "This isn't about Jake. It's about finding out the truth of the matter. What exactly happened that day? If ye knows any more I'd be grateful to hear it. I was hoping Jake would shed more light on the matter, but he left my place without really telling us much more than we already knew, and Harry, the man who was working with Joe that day seems to be gone missing." Mick studied the face of the man in front of him. "Has Jake told ye anything?"

Paddy allowed himself to relax somewhat. Letting out the breath he'd been holding he said, "Jake's not saying much to anybody. He's blaming himself and keeping pretty much to hisself, which is not out of the ordinary. If ye knew Jake ye'd know what I mean. But this is different, he's beating himself up pretty bad. And not talking about the accident at all. It'd probably do him some good if he did."

"I have a feeling that there is more to this than meets the eye," Mick responded. "I just want to get to the bottom of it. That's what this meeting is all about."

"Fair enough, I'd like to know too, to tell ye the truth," Paddy answered.

"We're in agreement, then," Mick said. "Why don't we go in, meetin's about to start?" Paddy nodded his agreement and the two men walked to the door.

Inside the room was buzzing with conversation as men grappled with the reality of their precarious positions at the quarry and the very real possibility that harm could come to any one of them. As at the prior meeting Charlie had been asked to act as their leader and to keep control of the meeting.

"I guess it's time to start the meeting," Charlie strong voice rang out. He waited a moment before he continued. "First off, is there a man among ye that saw what happened the day Joe was killed? Has anyone heard anything of Harry and where he might have got to?"

The men looked at one another each of them shrugging or otherwise indicating their ignorance. Charlie stared pointedly at Lou, whom he knew was close by when the cart that struck Joe got away from Jake.

Lou shuffled his feet hating to be put on the spot like this. "Fer Christ sakes b'y, you knows how late we were at it the day before. I was beat to a snot, like the rest of ye, and what with the rush to get that stone out I wasn't paying much attention."

"What about afterwards then, after it hit Joe, did ye see anything?" Charlie asked.

"Yeah, I seen Jake bent over throwing up his guts," Lou replied, "like I tole ye afore."

"Who was helping him fill the cart?" Charlie wanted to know.

"Wasn't nobody else there," Lou replied. "At least, I didn't see anyone, but I wasn't paying much attention, like I said."

"Are ye sure about that?" Charlie raised his voice slightly as the buzz of conversation met this remark.

"Pretty sure," Lou responded. "I was busy filling me own cart, me and Billy. Like I said, I was beat to a snot and weren't paying a lot of attention. Look, b'y, why ain't ye asking Harry? T'was he what was working alongside Joe that morning."

"Nobody's seen hide nor hair of Harry since Joe got hurt that day," Charlie answered. "T'would help a lot to have a word with 'im, too."

Charlie glanced around the room looking for Billy, another of the new hires. He was a distant cousin of Charlie's and had recently returned from the mainland. "Anybody seen Billy here tonight?" Murmurs traveled around the hall as the men repeated the query.

"I'm right here," Billy pushed through a knot of men. "Yeah, I was there working by Lou filling that God-dammed cart. I didn't see nothing though. Like Lou says, we was working like madmen and plum wore out. Tis the worst job I ever had."

Charlie gazed for a moment at his young cousin. "Remind me, Bill, when did ye start work here?"

"Bout a fortnight ago, never worked so bloody hard in me life," he answered.

"Did you get told the rules? Cuz I knows ye never worked in the quarry before," Charlie remarked.

"Rules? This outfit don't care about rules. They don't care about the men!" A voice called from the back of the room. A murmur of assent rippled through the room.

Charlie glanced at Billy before responding. "That is true, but they still gotta tell new men what's what," he replied. "Well, Bill, what did they tell ye when they hired ye?"

"I don't remember them telling me no rules. The boss man just seemed to want us to get to it," Billy answered.

"No man is supposed to work them carts alone. Did they not tell ye that?" Charlie asked. "Did he show ye how to set the brake, or the importance of keeping the load balanced?"

"Nah, he didn't, but Lou did," Billy responded.

Men begin commenting to one another about how the company ignored rules set out to keep them safe and about the recent rush to get the freighter underway; about the conditions that were fraught with danger; about the peril all around them. Charlie had to raise his voice to restore quiet.

"Listen! Listen!" He roared. "What I want to know is who was working alongside Jake?"

No answer came. "They can't expect a man to fill a cart by hisself," Charlie remarked. "Look, we gotta get to the bottom of this. Find out what all happened that morning. Find out why Joe lays dead and buried. We needs to know who's at fault here," Charlie's eyes swept the room as silence descended. "God damn it! Somebody's got to know how this happened!"

Again, he was answered by silence. "All right, look, if any of ye hear anything or remember anything come see me. There ain't no point in continuing with this meeting like this. But we will call another one, once we learns more. This ain't just about justice for Joe, it's about justice for all of us. We all have families to look after. We got to stick together. What say ye?"

"Hear, hear!" a man shouted, and the sentiment was echoed by many.

Charlie moved away to where Mick and his sons were standing. Men continued to talk in pairs and small groups.

"Well, that's that for now," he told Mick, "There's something mighty peculiar in all this, wouldn't ye say?"

Mick's eyes were guarded but he met Charlie's gaze without answering at first. "Something stinks, that's a fact," he finally answered.

"Not much more we can do or say until we find out more," Charlie continued. "Somebody needs to talk to Jake again." Charlie thought about the punch he'd landed the day Joe got hurt. "I don't think I'm the one to do it."

"I can try," Phil offered. Charlie nodded and looked to Mick for his opinion.

Jake was not at the meeting, which was no surprise to those gathered. Mick's hand came to rest on Phil's shoulder. "Yes, have a word with Paddy. Perhaps he'd be wiling to help," he told his son, "He seems like a good sort."

Phil lost no time but approached Paddy just as he was going out the door. "Paddy, hey, Paddy," he called out as he crossed the room. Paddy stopped, his hand holding the door ajar as he waited. His eyebrows rose in silent query as he wondered what Phil wanted with him. Phil gestured outside and followed Paddy out the door.

Few men were present, most had already started the trek home. A few stragglers were chatting to one another by the gate. "Me wagon's over there," Paddy pointed a finger to where an old nag and work wagon waited for his return. The men strolled toward it while they talked. "Da thinks it would be a good idea if one of us had a chat with Jake. Like he said, we didn't learn much more when he came to the house and he left kind of quick-like," Phil began. "We was hoping maybe you'd help."

"Not sure if I can do much. Like I told yer Da, Jake keeps things pretty close to his chest. He ain't been saying nothin' to nobody," Paddy replied.

"I was just thinking he might be a mite more agreeable to talking to me if you was there too," Phil answered.

Paddy was watching Phil and could determine not one whit of antagonism in his expression. He continued to size Phil up as he formed his opinions. Phil stood, becoming more uncomfortable as he waited. He shuffled his feet and began to think perhaps it was a mistake to try and enlist Paddy's help. His answer seemed to take forever. "And just when do ye figure on having this conversation?" Paddy asked him.

"Whatever time is good for ye and Jake," Phil answered. "Of course, it'd have to be after work. Don't think it'd be wise to try and have a talk at the quarry, too many eyes and ears there."

Paddy's smile was bitter as he turned toward the wagon. "I'll talk to Jake and let ye know," he said over his shoulder as he climbed into the wagon. "But, don't count on it. Like I told yer dad, Jake keeps pretty much to hisself. But I will see what I can do."

"Thanks, Paddy, much obliged," Phil responded. He stood and watched as Paddy turned the wagon and headed homeward. His emotions were jumbled as he thought of his uncle and of Jake's behaviour when he came to their home. He knew without a doubt that Joe would have been the first to offer forgiveness to the man, had somebody else been killed. A squawking crow interrupted his thoughts and he turned to go back to the hall to rejoin his father and brothers.

Mick was still standing talking to Charlie and Vic when Phil entered the building. Jack was taking in every word, his expression somber while William seemed impatient to leave.

"Well, what did Paddy have to say?" Mick questioned Phil when he reached them.

"He's gonna talk to Jake and make arrangements, or try to," Phil said.

Mick nodded gravely. "I sure hope he can convince Jake to talk with ye." Mick considered Phil a good choice. He'd noticed how quick Phil was to defend the man, much like Joe would have. "Well, tis getting late," Mick told them, "We best be heading home."

"Before ye go I got something fer ye," Charlie reached into his pocket and pulled out a small sack, coins clinked together as he passed it to Mick. "It ain't much but it's something. Tell Elsie it's from the men at the quarry. They all thought a lot of Joe."

Mick nodded. "It's appreciated. I'll make sure she gets it."

The group separated at the gate with promises to discuss the situation further on the morrow. William surprised them all by turning off the road telling his father he had something to do before going home. Mick walked beside his younger sons fully knowing what that something was.

"Wonder what he's up to?" Jack queried out loud.

"I bet he's gone off to call on Ginny," Phil grinned.

"Might be," Mick replied. "He does seem smitten with 'er. So, ye think ye can get this man, Jake, to talk to ye?" Mick asked, changing the subject. "I'd do it myself, but he seemed to be more comfortable with ye," he told Phil.

"Time will tell, Da," Phil answered. "I guess we just have to wait and see if he's willing. Paddy didn't really hold out much hope but we'll see."

"How we gonna learn anything if he won't talk and with Harry gone?" Jack wanted to know.

"God doesn't always move instantly. Sometimes he gives us the time we need to work things out," Mick answered. "Leave it with the almighty, like Joe and yer mother would say."

"If God is good why'd he let Uncle Joe die?" Jack asked his father.

Mick noticed the tremor in his young son's voice and said nothing for a spell as the trio continued their walk home.

"It was just his time, Jack. It's not for us to question the Almighty, son. Joe, he was a good brother, a good friend, a good man. He was always kind to everyone he knew." Mick remembered Joe telling him about the young couple who had bought the old Simon place. It was a bit run-down and needed work. He remembered Joe telling him about the hard-working young man who'd taken it on. He remembered helping Joe sand down the cradles he'd made for their twins and the high regard he'd had for these young people. "And he was kind to strangers as well," Mick continued. "But when it's yer time, it's yer time. It's not fer us to question why. We just have to trust the Almighty knows what he's about."

Jack listened to his father's words but they failed to comfort him. He still couldn't understand how a good God allowed people like his uncle to die. Maybe he never would. Phil reached out and ruffled his brother's hair, "Bet I can beat you to the house," he challenged.

Mick's grin was wide as he watched his sons race one another to their little cottage. His heart swelled with pride in his family and, in the moment, particularly with Phil. *He's so much like his mother*, he thought as he crossed the field to their homestead. If any of us can get through to Jake, it's Phil.

Fanny was lifting a heavy kettle of water onto the wood stove when Jack and Phil nearly stumbled over one another coming through the door. "What a racket you're making," she scolded, "if you wake the baby one of ye will be minding him."

"Sorry, Ma," Jack responded without the smallest degree of contrition. He looked at Phil and grinned, "Beat ye again."

"Huh! I let ye win. I wasn't trying at all," Phil answered with a smile.

"Oh yeah? We'll see about that. Want to try again on the way to work tomorrow? Just to the churchyard, wouldn't want to tire ye out too bad before work." Jack protested.

"Yer on!" Phil exclaimed, happy that he'd been able to distract his brother from his morbid thoughts.

Mick entered the cabin just as Fanny was telling Jack to bring in kindling to start the morning's fire and Phil was bouncing his littlest sister on his knee. Rose was giggling softly and Sarah sat rocking in the corner.

"So, how did it go," Fanny asked her husband. "Did ye learn anything more? And where's William?"

"William, I expect, is calling on Ginny, though he didn't say that's where he was going," Mick replied. "And no, we didn't learn anything new. These things take time, I s'pose." Mick's eyes bored into Fanny's in an unspoken message to leave it until later, when they could be alone. Jack entered with his arms full of kindling sticks. He stacked the split wood neatly in the box. "Here ye go, Ma. Mind if I run over to see Aunt Elsie?"

He was quick to turn to leave when Fanny gave her assent but Mick stopped him at the door. "Don't mention that money just yet, I'll give it to 'er at the right time," he said. "The men took up a collection fer Elsie," he told Fanny. "I wants to wait a bit, see if there's any to add to it before I gives it to 'er." Fanny nodded but said nothing.

William entered an hour later and Phil was quick to pounce, teasing and ribbing his brother without mercy. Fanny smiled as her sons engaged in this ritual and was content with the normalcy after so many days dogged with the heavy pall of grief.

Over at Elsie's cottage Jack was engaged in an earnest conversation with his aunt about God and death and trading stories of his uncle.

"It's normal to have these feelings," Elsie told Jack. "It's not easy to accept. I miss him something terrible. We will have the answers when God calls us home."

Jack sat in brooding silence for a time.

"Well, it ain't fair and it ain't right," he finally retorted. "Uncle Joe was the best."

"Yes, my son, yes he was," Elsie replied softly. "And he wouldn't want ye to go on so, he'd want ye to keep going, keep living."

Jack angrily dashed the tears from his face. Elsie smiled at the stubborn refusal to accept what seemed impossible.

"You're only young now, but one day, soon, I hope, it won't be so painful and hard."

Jack stood up. "I dunno, Aunt Elsie, I just dunno. I best get back home," he said as his eyes travelled again to the comfortable old chair where his uncle once sat telling him stories of his youth on a night much like this. The sight of the empty chair caused spasms of pain in his heart. He strode toward the door before fresh tears could add to his shame. He wanted to be strong for his aunt, but here he was asking for comfort when he felt it was he who should be offering that to her. Jack mentally kicked himself as he considered this. "Will ye be okay here tonight?" he asked his aunt for the umpteenth time.

Elsie smiled at the youth, seeing in his scowls and in his smile the man she had married. *He's so much like Joe,* she thought to herself.

Out loud she said, "I will be fine, Jack, I promise you. I am going to go off to bed once ye leave. I am weary beyond belief."

Jack noted the pallor in her face and the wisps of hair that had come loose from the bun she wore high on her head.

"Are ye sure?" he asked. "Sure, as sure can be," she answered. "I'll be over in the morning to milk the cow fer ye and feed the chickens. Do ye have wood for the morning? Have ye got enough water? Do ye need more kindling?"

Elsie smiled as she regarded the overflowing wood box. "I don't think we could fit another stick in there," she told him. "Go on now, ye have work in the morning and needs yer rest. Thank ye for all yer help, Jack." The boy nodded and went out the door.

Chapter

14

The man sat looking out of the brine-coated window. The responsibilities of overseeing the mining operation at the quarry had always sat heavy on his shoulders but since Joe's death the mining captain had been having trouble sleeping. It was a precarious situation he was in. On one hand he had to follow the rules laid out in the *Handbook of Regulations*. On the other, his job was on the line if the operation did not return a fair profit for its owners. The pressure to fill freighters as quickly as possible to get the product to market was always challenging. Sometimes he had to throw caution to the wind. It wasn't right, he knew that. He wasn't the first to ignore regulations and wouldn't be the last. *Damned if I do, damned if I don't*, he thought to himself, *and now investigators are sure to come. This ain't anything I can 'ide. Too many knows about it . . .and it 'ad to be reported . . .*

A knock on the door interrupted the captain's thoughts. Jake stood outside the door shifting his weight from one foot to the other but stood stock still when the captain opened the door. "Sorry to bother ye, Captain. I couldn't find the pit boss and was just wanting to know where you want me today, should I operate the crusher? Or load carts?" Jake asked, his voice soft so that the captain had difficulty hearing him.

"Speak up, man," the captain growled, impatient with the poor sod who stood nervously in front of him. Then a suspicious thought entered his head and he eyed Jake more closely. "You been talking about the accident?" he asked.

Jake's face paled as he remembered his visit to the Kelly farm. He gulped as he looked at his boss. "I, um, I talked a bit with Mick Kelly and his family," he began.

"You did what?" the captain interrupted. "I told ye not to be talking about all this to nobody. What part of that did ye not understand?"

Jake gulped again. "They deserve to know what happened," he began. The captain cut him off. "And what exactly 'ave ye been telling 'em?"

Jake's face reddened, "Not much, just that it was all me own fault." Jake's heart quickened as the stress and the shame of causing the death of another threatened to overcome his emotions.

The captain noticed the barely contained emotion and the fear that had sprung to the young man's eyes. "Did ye tell 'em ye was working alone? That ye didn't apply the brakes? That ye 'ad not balanced the cart?"

Jake reacted as if stung by the rapid-fire questions. "No, Sir, I only told 'em it t'was all me fault, that's all I said." Jake gulped again expecting to be fired and his heart plummeted, with the twins and a wife to support he needed this job.

The captain studied Jake for several minutes before he spoke again, "Ye best not be causing any more trouble around 'ere," he told Jake, "It won't go well with ye if ye do." Jake merely nodded. "Go on, then. Yer on the crusher, where 'opefully ye won't be killing nobody else," he continued, "Think ye can manage that?" Jake nodded again and began to turn away when he felt a heavy hand on his shoulder. "I am gonna give ye this last warning: keep yer mouth shut."

Jake's face was ashen as he lumbered down the hill to the rock crusher. Guilt, fear, sorrow, and more wreaked havoc in his head and in his heart. He walked like a man about to be fed to the lions, which maybe he was.

In the shed the captain grinned maliciously. *I gots something on ye, boy,* he thought to himself. *Ah yis, my son. Ye best not step out of line. Not even a toe. I knows about yer Micmac grandmother and I can make it so ye never get work again in these parts.* He rubbed his hands together, cheered by the thought. And set about his plan to make sure Jake shouldered all the blame for the mishap. *Why wait?* He asked himself and walked quickly to the door to call Jake back to deliver his threats. He had to walk downhill a short way before he spied Jake climbing down to the crusher. "Hey, Jake" he called.

Jake stopped and turned back toward his boss. "I fergot to tell ye something important. Come on back up 'ere." Jake hesitated only a fraction of a moment before climbing back up the hill to the captain's quarters. Once again fear clawed at his heart, sure the boss was about to fire him. *How will we manage without these wages? Oh, dear God, what are we gonna do?* Jake thought as he climbed. A short time later, the threat delivered, Jake retraced his steps down to the crusher. He was despondent and worried. He'd met men like the captain before. It was because of men like him that he'd had to move away. Once folk knew he carried Indian blood life would get even harder than it already was. Mary knew, but only Mary, and Jake trusted his wife to keep it a secret, their livelihood depended on it. She understood that. She'd grown up in a small community that was heavily populated by Mi'kmaq people. She knew well the hardships faced when men could not find work.

He hadn't had to work very hard to convince her to buy the homestead. They could grow vegetables at least and keep animals for meat, a cow for milk, and chickens for eggs. With that and a bit of fishing and berry-picking they wouldn't starve. They had made a good start, but it was only a start. Jake had thought they were safe here. *We'll never be safe anywhere!* Bitterness welled up within him as he considered their precarious position. He needed the wages for clothing, shoes, and other items they could not make or grow themselves.

Jake allowed himself to remember the money he'd made building furniture. He had a talent for woodworking. He wasn't vain about it, seeing it as just a fact. Everybody was good at something. At least, that's what his parents said. And folks had paid well for his tables, chairs, and chests of drawers. He'd even made a grandfather clock for one of the richer clients he'd met. People were pleased with his work and that was gratifying. He'd had to leave all that behind when folks learned of his Indian blood. Poor Johnny had not meant to cause trouble. His little brother was too trusting and he'd trusted the wrong feller. And he, too, would have to leave for work when the time came for him to leave school. Jake sighed. Thoughts of the past had tumbled one upon another, but now he had to start the crusher and at least the racket would put a stop to his runaway thoughts, or at least he hoped so.

Chapter

15

J ake watched as fellow workers made their way to the cookhouse. He hadn't heard the whistle blow, intent as he was on his work and focused on closing his mind to the past with all its turmoil and pain. He switched the machine off and began the climb down the hill. His arms ached. He moved slowly, not wanting to be noticed, or pulled into a conversation that would, no doubt, lead back to Joe's death. Paddy stood waiting and Jake dropped his head, ignoring the hand raised in greeting. *Paddy's a good man, but he'd never understand.* Jake cursed silently to himself wondering how best to avoid his friend's overtures. If he wasn't so ravenous, he'd skip dinner altogether. Jake groaned inwardly as he sensed Paddy's approach. He didn't want to talk, not to Paddy, not to anybody.

"Jake, been waiting fer ya," Paddy began, pausing at the guarded look and stiffening of Jake's shoulders. Following his gut instinct not to push Paddy continued, "Wanted to let ya know I been talking to Mick and his sons. Nobody's gonna bother ye. Just wanted to let ye know that,"

"Don't need ye butting in or speaking up fer me," Jake growled. "Just let it be."

"Look here, mate, I ain't trying to butt in. But fair is fair and I didn't want ye taking a beating, or worst," Paddy responded.

"Yeah, well, maybe I do deserve it," he replied. "Look, just stay outta my business," Jake choked as he sputtered out the words, stress, anger, and worry stealing his voice. He wanted badly to strike out at someone or something and at that moment Paddy made a good target. Paddy stood for a moment regarding Jake's antagonistic glare before shrugging and turning to enter the cookhouse. Men formed a line waiting for their plates to be filled. Paddy joined the line thinking about his short exchange with Jake and knowing Phil would be wanting to know the outcome. *It really is none of my concern. Can't force the man to talk to me if he don't wanna,* he thought to himself. Frustrated, Paddy bunched his hands into fists. He knew Jake fairly well – well enough to know he didn't have a snowball's chance in hell in getting him to talk once he dug his heels in, and Jake was definitely digging his heels in. Paddy flexed his fingers, clenching and unclenching his fists as he thought about Jake, Joe, and the whole sorry situation. Reaching the front of the line he took his full plate and turned to go sit and eat his meal, in peace, if at all possible.

Jake watched through hooded eyes as Paddy made his way to the counter for his food. The tin plates and eating utensils made a racket as the men filed from the counter to the tables and benches. There was a low buzz of conversation around him but Jake did not notice, intent on getting food and avoiding Paddy, in that order. Paddy watched as Jake crossed the room to an empty table, and then as Jake went to work hungrily on the plate of food in front of him. Jake never looked up and Paddy sighed thinking of the pressure Jake must be under, having no idea how much weightier that pressure had become since the work day had began.

Hours later, after the work day had finally come to a close, Phil approached Paddy as he was about to climb into his wagon for the drive home. He noticed the older man's reserve at his greeting. Paddy was abrupt in his answer: "Look, Phil, I told ye, it would take time. Like I said before, Jake's no open book. He ain't talking, not to me, and not to anybody that I can figure. When and if I do get him to talk to me, I'll do me best to convince him to talk to ye. Let it rest for now. Okay?"

"Alright, Paddy. I ain't trying to push ye, we just needs to know what's what, that's all. Aunt Elsie deserves to know what happened, and so do all me family." Disappointed, Phil turned away.

"These things take time," Paddy called to Phil's retreating back. "They just takes time. I will let ye know, if I ever manages to get through to him. Ye are just going to have to trust me with it, that's all."

Phil stopped, turned, and gave a nod as Paddy climbed into his wagon and made ready to leave.

Chapter

16

Over a month had passed when the mining inspector visited the quarry. It was a cursory inspection at best. Fred Johnstone had not wanted to visit this far-flung coastal community. In his view, deaths were to be expected when men worked in mines of any kind, this one was no different. He was satisfied it was nothing more than a tragic accident. It was the price one paid for employment. The Company paid him well to look the other way. His was a plum position, he well knew. Unrest in the city as well as the outports was growing.

Johnstone knew his days of easy existence may well come to an end, perhaps sooner than later. He cursed out loud as he thought about the Industrial Workers Association that had formed in the city and hoped it would not spread further afield. The damned association had made his work there harder and more intense. Companies like Dominion Limestone no longer held the upper hand. Investigations such as this, with no witnesses to whatever had caused the incident, was cut and dried in his opinion. He saw no need to make changes in how the quarry operated and that is what he recommended in his report, much to the chagrin to the men employed there.

The company, however, was well pleased. The status quo would be upheld and the company would not have to shell out any funds for the man's widow. Johnstone smiled to himself. He'd soon be able to make his way back to the city and away from this God-forsaken outback.

Vic lifted yet another heavy load of limestone and dumped it into the cart. As before he worked alongside Charlie. Both men had heard news of the report regarding Joe's death and neither were too happy about it. Word had spread about a meeting to discuss just that. Vic pushed his shovel into the pile of limestone and thought again of the captain's announcement after the inspector had gone. He'd made his little speech down in the cookhouse the week before. *Damn the man. His empty words mean nothing. That bunch don't care about the men who work like dogs and they gots no intention of improving our lot.* Vic leaned his shovel against the cart and using a handkerchief already stained with dirt he wiped the sweat from his brow.

"Hey, Charlie? Were ye able to get word out about another meeting?" he asked. Charlie paused in his work and glanced around before answering. "Best not to be discussing that here, mate. Words going 'round and I am waiting to hear when Peter will be here so we can learn more about this association business they got going in the city. We can talk about it later. It might be better to hold off til he's here to advise us like." Vic nodded in agreement.

"Just sticks in my craw that ain't no changes gonna be made. That report was a sham, nuddin but a sham," he retorted.

"We all knows that, b'y. Which is why we needs to do something to force 'em to take us seriously." Charlie replied softly. "Just let it lie fer now. Don't ye worry, I'll be letting ye know once we gots a plan in place". Vic nodded at his friend and the two resumed their labours.

Jake automatically made his way to the crusher. The mining captain, thankfully, nowhere in sight. The man had dogged him for the past few weeks, ensuring his threats would guarantee Jake's silence, always waiting each morning before the work day began. Jake shuddered picturing his nemesis in his mind's eye. The bully had even dared to visit his home on the pretence of needing to talk to him about mining business. Jake's wife had bought the lies without question. Jake felt trapped. He could see no way out of his troubles. He thought about his brief conversation with Paddy over a week ago. *What does Phil's family want with me? I can't take back what I done, much as I wish I could. I told Paddy so. There ain't no use going over and over it. I caused Joe's death. Me, only me. I ain't gonna talk to 'em, No sir! I can't!*

Jake tried his best to shake off morose thoughts once again. The frequent appearance of the mining captain guaranteed he kept his promise to stay quiet on the matter, even as his conscience tormented him and the need to make restitution continued to plague him. He was grateful for Paddy's friendship, not that he deserved it. He'd been willfully stubborn and taciturn towards the man ever since Joe died. *I don't deserve friendship.*

His thoughts turned to his wife and twin babies. I have to look after me own. That's all there is to it. I gots to! With that Jake climbed up to start the machine even as he tried to turn off the thoughts that roared constantly in his head.

Paddy lifted the heavy pickaxe and swung it into the cliffside, loosening rock and stepping aside quickly as larger chucks fell. He had an intuition on just where to strike into the rock face and had yet to be hit by falling limestone. He watched as the dust began to settle and lifted the pickaxe once more. Not far from where he worked Phil and William were loading carts as usual. Paddy could not help but see them from his vantage point on the ledge where he stood.

As he swung the pickaxe his thoughts went over the situation in the quarry once again and Jake's part in it. Paddy sighed heavily. He'd known Jake forever, it seemed, and knew how easy if was for him to take on all the blame for Joe's death. He thought of Jake's wife, Mary. When he'd heard what had happened to Jake back in Robertson's, he convinced him to take a look at the old Simon homestead. He'd looked forward to having family, of a sort, nearby when Jake and Mary moved here, for Jake's clan were connected to Paddy's, though he could not remember exactly how. Paddy pictured the small homestead the pair had bought. It was a pretty little place with black soil, perfect for growing vegetables, and plenty of animals to hunt for meat. Now and then he was able to borrow a dory to go out for a few cod, mackerel, and other fish. It was a good place to make a life, or so he'd thought.

Poor bastard is still torn up with shame and guilt. I done me best to help him, but he ain't making it easy. Something's gotta give. The man's going to blow a gasket if he don't let off the pressure on hisself. It could be a good life. A hard life, yes, but a good one. But he's got to give up on punishing hisself. Paddy swung the pickaxe once again and vowed to try one last time to convince Jake to tell what he knew. *Hopefully before Charlie has that meetin' set up,* he thought to himself.

Chapter

17

The shepherd was barking causing Jake to look up. He groaned inwardly at the sight of Paddy's wagon coming across the yard. He had thought that Paddy had given up on talking to him about Joe and all that had happened. He knew he couldn't evade him this time, already Paddy was waving at him as he guided the wagon toward where Jake stood. Jake took the handkerchief out of his back pocket and wiped his forehead. The shepherd whined softly and pulled at the rope that confined her.

"How are ye getting on?" Paddy greeted him after stopping the wagon and jumping from the seat.

"Fine as kind," Jake returned, "and ye?"

Paddy pushed his hat back on his head and looked up at the blue sky.

"Can't complain, b'y, can't complain," he answered.

"So, what brings ye here?" Jake wanted to know.

"Me aunt wants a bunk bed made fer their young'uns. I thought maybe ye'd be interested. She's willing to pay ye good money." Paddy replied.

Jake looked around his yard and the garden that was growing well, and thought of all the work he had yet to do. He raked his fingers through his hair as he considered the request. "I don't know as I've time fer it just now," he began, noticing the pile of rough lumber piled in the wagon.

"I'd be willing to lend a hand," Paddy replied, and with a smirk continued, "Fer one of Mary's partridgeberry pies."

Jake's answering grin was a welcome sight to Paddy. He wasn't sure if his visit would be exactly welcome after all the conflict of the past weeks. He promised himself he would not speak one word about the quarry but would let Jake bring it up, if he'd a mind to.

"Well, the money sure wouldn't go astray," Jake pondered the offer. "Are ye sure ye got time to help with that? I wouldn't want ye to go putting yerself out."

"I got all the time in the world," Paddy retorted, "I ain't got no wife or children to worry about. When do ye want to get started? I'm free fer the rest of the day."

"Hold up there now, I ain't agreed to do it yet," Jake rebuffed him. "I have this here wood to finish chopping up fer the stove, the garden needs weeding, and I gots to haul water and a million other chores to do ..." Jake trailed off as he thought about the long list of chores that never seemed to end.

Paddy walked over to the dog and rubbed her ears as he waited for Jake to come to a decision.

"Two hands make short work," Paddy pointed out.

Jake nodded; his mind made up. "Well, if yer sure."

Soon the two men were unloading the lumber near the open barn door.

"Ye were pretty sure of yerself," Jake said as they dropped the last of the lumber on the ground. "C'mon, then, lend me a hand. I needs to make room in the barn to get to work on this."

Paddy followed Jake into the small barn. The upper level was filled with the last of the hay from the previous summer. A hen coop took up space in one corner, boarded off from the rest of the structure with a small door for access to gather eggs. Paddy glanced about, taking in the scythe that hung neatly along with other tools on the back wall. A small plow sat in the middle of the floor and another stack of logs off to the right of it.

"Think we can get all this stacked behind the barn?" Jake asked. "I want to bring that lumber in here where I can work on them beds rain or shine."

"Let's get to it," Paddy responded. Soon the logs for the wood stove were stacked neatly on the lee side of the barn and the lumber piled along one wall ready to use. Paddy and Jake kept up a light banter as they worked and the quarry was forgotten during their labour.

"Would ye like to come in for a bite to eat?" Jake asked.

"I could eat," Paddy answered with a grin. "Only a fool would say no to Mary's cooking."

Mary sat rocking her twins when the men came into the room. She made to rise from the chair when Jake stopped her.

"No, me love, you stay right where you're at. I can get us a bowl of stew," Jake told her.

Paddy stood near the door. "Hello, Mary. Ye're looking good. How're the little ones doing?"

Mary smiled, "Much better now, Paddy. T'was a worry for a while, but they're coming along just fine now. C'mon in and have a seat," she answered, gesturing with her head toward the table. "Jake, are ye sure ye don't want me to do that?"

Jake was busily pulling bowls out of the sideboard and searching the buffet for spoons. "Naw, it's fine, Mary. Would ye like a bit of stew?" he asked.

"Let me just change these two and put them for a nap. Yeah, I could do with a bite. I'll be back in a bit." She answered.

A little while later the trio were sitting at the table dining on the stew Jake had dished up.

"This is some good, Mary," Paddy said while reaching for yet another thick slice of bread.

"I'm glad you like it. That's nice moose meat, not grousy at all," she smiled at her husband. "Jake brought that one down hisself, butchered it, too. He's a good hand at it."

Jake's face reddened at the compliment. "Aw, go on, Mary," he mumbled.

"Paddy, I got some bottled, if ye'd like a bit to take home," Marry offered.

"I won't say no to that," Paddy answered. "Thanks a lot."

Conversation turned to the bunk beds Jake would be making and small talk about the weather before turning to news from back home in Robertson and their mutual relations there. After they'd finished eating Mary rose to clear the table. Paddy stood up, "Well, thanks again for that fine meal. Guess we better get to it," he looked to Jake.

"Y'is b'y, time's wasting," Jake agreed.

The men were in the barn working on sanding the rough lumber when Jake brought up the quarry.

"I wants to tell ye how sorry I am fer the way I been acting," he began.

"Nothing to be sorry fer, as far as I'm concerned," Paddy replied.

"Ye've been a good friend, always have been, and I been a horse's ass" Jake rebutted. "It's just been a lot of things on me mind ..." he trailed off.

Paddy waited in silence to see where this talk would lead. Moments passed as they continued to plane the wood.

"Do ye remember the time that Missus caught us jumping the ice pans out in the bay back home?" Jake asked.

Paddy nodded wondering where this was going.

"She was right upset. Mind?" Jake reminisced.

"She sure was. Madder than a wet hen," Paddy retorted. He smiled ruefully, "She boxed our ears but good, didn't she?"

Jake grinned. "She sure did, but at least she didn't tattle on us to our parents. The old man woulda given me some trimming."

"That's a fact. I know mine would probably have had me cutting switches to tan me arse," Paddy answered. The men chuckled.

"Ain't many can keep things to themselves," Jake spoke softly, weighing in his mind whether or not to speak of his problems with the mining Captain.

Paddy waited, sensing Jake was about to impart something of importance. Jake stopped planing wood to look into his friend's eyes.

"I wants to tell ye something, but it can't be spoken to another soul. It could cost me my job at the quarry . . ." He began.

"I hopes ye know by now ye can trust me," Paddy began. "I hopes ye knows I wouldn't ever do a thing to bring harm to ye or yer family."

Paddy waited again as Jake went back to the job at hand. The men worked in silence as Jake worked out how much he would share and what.

"It's just been so hard," Jake began. "That day that it happened," he paused, "I never meant . . ."

"It was an accident, just an accident," Paddy put in, stopping when Jake stood again, his hand gesturing for Paddy to stop talking.

Jake took a deep breath and swallowed noisily. "I was all by meself, working like a dog to fill the damned cart. I was beat to a snot, the babies were up most of the night afore, crying and miserable. Mary and me was scared to death. I was thinking about 'em and Mary when the cart got away from me. I made a grab fer it, but I slipped and fell. The cart was more than half full and went speeding away . . ."

Tears filled Jake's eyes as he spoke and Paddy moved to put a hand on his friend's shoulder. He didn't speak but waited for Jake to continue.

"I heard the screech. I was sick to my stomach with the suspicion someone'd been hit . . . It was all me fault," Jake covered his face with his hands as remorse and guilt filled him yet again. Paddy didn't say a word but patted him roughly on the back.

"Jesus, Mary, and Joseph," Jake cursed…. "And now, the captain, he has something on me and has threatened to fire me and make sure I can't gets any work around here if I speaks about it to anyone at all," he finished.

Paddy's anger at the gross unfairness exploded. "He be threatening ye? That arrogant, pompous, useless son of a bitch."

Jake's fear was obvious as his gaze met Paddy's.

"Fer Jesus' sake b'y, ye can't be telling a single soul what I just told ye," Jake implored.

"I ain't gonna say a word to nobody," Paddy hastened to reassure his friend. "Look, me and ye has been buddies fer a very long time. Yer words are safe with me. But yer gots to know. First off, nobody is supposed to be filling them carts alone. Them's the rules. Secondly, ye were supposed to be told how to set the brake," Paddy paused. "Did ye know to set the brake?"

Jake shook his head. "No, I didn't set the brake. I shoulda known that."

Paddy stared at Jake a moment before continuing, "And just how were ye supposed to know that? Ye never worked in no quarry in yer life!"

Jake stared worriedly at his friend. "It just be common sense."

Paddy cursed and spat into the dirt. "I knows this, my buddy, that son of a bitch is happy to have ye take the brunt of the blame. It ain't yer fault, I'm telling ye. Were ye not told that the stone has to be balanced to keep the cart from moving away from ye once the brake's released?"

Jake shook his head once again. "I weren't told nothing. I was just told to get up there and start filling the carts."

Paddy blew out a breath of exasperation. "T'wouldn't have taken more than a few minutes to explain it to ye. It ain't hard. Three things: first, set the brake, second, mind the load is balanced so it don't shift and overturn the cart when ye sets it going and so it don't get so heavy in one end it goes rolling away without ye. Third, ye are never to work a cart alone, just in case anything were to happen, like a cart jumping the track and causing an accident. It'd take at least two men to muscle even an empty cart back onto the track."

Jake said nothing as he absorbed all Paddy was telling him. "I weren't told," he repeated.

"Now, do ye see. It weren't yer fault. It weren't ever yer fault," Paddy insisted.

"Well it's said and done now. Joe's dead," Jake began, rubbing his forehead. "I just don't know what to do. That Captain is watching me like a hawk. He even stopped by the house here."

"He did what?" Paddy voice was soft and menacing.

"Look here, Paddy, I don't want ye getting involved. I'll lose me job if he finds out I spoke to ye," Jake pleaded. "Please, b'y, ye can't say nothing."

Paddy's anger and frustration were easy to see and Jake worried he'd made a mistake in taking him into his confidence.

"What the hell does he have on ye?" Paddy wanted to know but Jake shook his head once again and refused to answer. Paddy threw the plane he was holding across the barn then immediately stomped over to retrieve it. He stood heaving with emotion as he thought about the grave injustices visited upon his friend.

"Fine then! Fine! It's yer business and I won't be butting in. But ye should know this ain't right. It ain't right by a long shot," Paddy finally spoke.

Relieved, Jake returned to the board he was working on. He glanced up quickly at Paddy, "thanks, mate," he said quietly.

Paddy grabbed him roughly by the shoulder, "I said ye can trust me, and ye can. Let's get on with this, eh?" The men spent the rest of the morning shaving the rough lumber and sanding it to a smooth finish. Afterward Paddy helped Jake with other chores around the small farm. He refused Jake's offer of supper and the two made plans to work more on the bunkbeds the following weekend.

Mary noticed the difference in Jake when he entered the little cabin. He seemed lighter, somehow, a bit more at peace with himself

"T'was nice to see Paddy today," Mary said. "T'was good of him to help out with the chores."

"Paddy's a good man," Jake smiled. "Supper about ready? I sure could eat."

"T'will be on the table in two shakes of a lamb's tail, why don't ye go wash up?" Mary hummed to herself as she went about setting the table and getting supper. I don't know what happened today, but I will be sure to thank Paddy when next we see him. Mary's thoughts were happy as she thought about the change she sensed in Jake. It's nice to see him back to himself. Mary felt a great weight had been lifted and a shift in the dark clouds that had been plaguing them. The couple spent a quiet evening together, enjoying one another's company and making plans for further work on the house and farm.

Chapter

18

F anny smiled to herself as thoughts of William and Ginny warmed her heart. The weeks since Joe's untimely death had been difficult for the whole family. She suspected there would soon be news of an engagement it was a welcome thought and lent joy to her days. Her eyes caught sight of her girls through the kitchen window as they played. It was midmorning and the sun beat gently down on the rolling hills surrounding the small community.

Across the field Elsie was busy sweeping the floors of her little cabin and doing her best to keep thoughts of the future at arm's length. She'd spent yet another sleepless night as her grief pounced again and again like a starving wolf upon its prey. Thoughts turned to Jack and the many traits he shared with her beloved Joe. *T'was so thoughtful of Jack to make sure I have water and firewood. He's so much like Joe. I wonder what life would have held had our own sweet child lived? Would he have been like Jack?* Elsie's thoughts turned to that sad day when they'd laid their infant son to rest in the cemetery that now held all her most cherished dreams. *No more of that, she chastised herself, what's done is done and there ain't no changing it.* And with that admonishment she swept ever more furiously in an effort to keep dismal thoughts at bay.

Down at the shore Jack stood skipping rocks and thinking once again of his uncle. He wore his uncle's salt and pepper cap and the donning of it always gave him a small bit of comfort, as if in wearing it gave proof to the fact his uncle had lived. *Uncle Joe, if yer listening, please help me. I know ye believed with all yer might in God and an everlasting life beyond the here and now. I can't understand why God took ye from us.* He waited but no answer came. Jack thought again of the conversation he'd had with his aunt about life and death and God and the ever-present questions he had. Like, why? Why? Why? Elsie had not been able to give him an answer to that one. She advised him to accept what is and to make peace with the mysteries. He had yet to find a way to make that peace, but the pain was less cutting, less all-consuming than it had been initially.

Jack turned as rocks and pebbles rolled down the bank, evidence he was no longer alone. He raised a hand to greet his brother who seemed to always know where to find him. "Hey, Phil, what're ye doing here?" His brother grinned, "Come to fetch ye for dinner b'y. Ma sent me to find ye. Ma cooked yer favorite and wants ye to have it before it gets cold." Jack turned and skipped the stones he held in his hands before wiping them on his trousers in readiness to leave. "Rabbit stew?" He asked his brother. "Ye knows," came the answer.

The brothers were quiet and they climbed the bank each lost in their own thoughts and concerns. Some minutes later Phil nudged Jack's shoulder, "Seen William at all today? He disappeared after church and I ain't seen hide nor hair of him since." Jack smiled. "I think he went off to Ginny's place again," he answered with a twinkle in his eyes. "I asked where he was off to but he wouldn't answer, but I knows - we all knows," he laughed. "Yeah, he sure is smitten," Phil replied, "I hope he remembers we still have water to haul and wood to chop." He gave Jack a playful shove, "Guess we will have to put ye to work after ye eat yer stew." Jack shoved back and then took off running. "Ye'll have to catch me first," he called as he ran. Jack poured all his energy into outpacing his brother and did so, but not by much. Soon the two were bent over panting outside the door to their cabin. "Yer like that story of the gingerbread man Ma used to tell us," Phil told Jack. "Run, run as fast as ye can, ye can't catch me, I'm the gingerbread man. But I will catch ye one day." Jack's smirk betrayed his doubt and his confidence in his own ability to out run Phil any day, any time.

The two were still trading barbs and challenges as they pushed through the door. Mick sat cradling his infant son in his big calloused hands looking up as the brothers tumbled in the door still shoving and pushing one another. "Leave off that ruckus ye b'ys," he ordered but his eyes were filled with merriment as he spoke. It did his heart good to see the brotherly antics. It put him in mind of his youth and the days he and Joe behaved in much the same way. *Jack really could be Joe's son,* he thought as he watched his sons. *And not only does he look like Joe, he acts like 'im too,* his thoughts continued, out loud he said, "Ye best wash up afore ye come to the table."

Fanny lifted the small bundle from Mick's arms and turned to place him in the waiting basket beside the stove. The babe slept on as his mother laid him gently in the make-shift bed. The older boys moved to obey the order as their parents went about setting the table for the noon-time meal.

Fanny glanced at the door as Elsie came in. "That rabbit stew smells divine," she told Fanny as she walked to the basket to peer in at the sleeping babe.

"Da got two of 'em," Sarah piped up from her place on the bench where her little legs pumped energetically and her little face lit up with delight, for she loved her aunt and looked forward to her visits.

"Yes, I saw how plump they were when yer Da brought 'em in." Elsie answered.

"Them bad bunnies were eating Ma's garden vegetables," Rose solemnly announced. "I think they were hungry. Now, we're gonna eat them!"

Elsie smiled at her nieces. "That's what wild creatures do. They eat whatever they can, wherever they find it. That's just the way of things."

Rose nodded very seriously, "But they ain't gonna eat our food no more," she told her aunt. "Sarah drew a picture of a rabbit in a pot. We're gonna put it in the garden to warn other bunnies not to eat our carrots and potatoes."

"I think that's a fine idea," Elsie answered.

"Sarah's a fine hand for drawing," Jack put in with a grin for his sister. "Like as not that drawing will scare every rabbit silly enough to come near Ma's garden half to death." Jack's face went white at his slip of the tongue but Elsie merely smiled and nodded.

Phil elbowed his brother, "She draws better than ye ever could," he teased.

"May I please be excused, Ma? Just for a moment?" Sarah asked her mother. Fanny glanced at her daughter in surprise but nodded her assent. Within moments the little girl was back at the table excitedly waving a piece of paper above her head. "Here it is, Jack," she said pushing the paper into his hands.

"Look at them long ears," Jack began, "and that steam coming out of the pot ye drew him in. That there sends a clear message!" he exclaimed. "Look at this, Phil," Jack passed the drawing to his brother and one by one the family examined Sarah's art work and made their comments upon it. The meal continued, with most of the talk surrounding rabbits, gardens, and the best ways to deal with such pests. It also offered an opportunity for the adults to teach the younger ones the necessity of holding in tandem a respect for all life, even while feeding the family made it necessary to take life at times.

The family were chatting about these and other matters when William pushed open the door holding a furry bundle in his arms. Rose was the first to notice. "What's that you got there, William?" she asked. She hopped down from the bench to take a closer look. "Oooooh so sweet," she squealed as William bent down to let his little sister get a closer look. He held a small gray and white kitten in his arms. Sara was quick to join the twosome and reached out to stroke the soft fur.

"William, where did you get that kitten?" Fanny wanted to know. William blushed before answering.

"Well, I went up to Hilda and Hank's to call on Ginny and she was telling me about the litter of kittens her barn cat had a while back and what with the rabbits making a nuisance of themselves, I just thought maybe it's be a good idea for us to have a cat again," William held his breath. He knew his mother was not big on cats, which was why he wanted his sisters to see it. He knew once they set eyes on the little thing that Fanny would have a hard time saying no. Besides, having a cat would ensure her garden was safe from mice, rats, and rabbits.

"You should have talked to yer Da and me before ye brought one home," His mother replied coming closer to have a look. "It looks too small to be much help with the rabbits, but it will be grown in no time. Take it out to the barn. I don't want no animals in my kitchen," she went on. "And don't be thinking it can come in the house. It will have to stay outside. Who will look after it? I don't have time fer no kittens. Fer heaven's sake, William, what gets into yer head?"

William smiled as he watched his little sisters cuddle and pet the kitten. Lifting his head to look his mother in the eye he said, "I'm sorry, Ma. I know I should have asked ye before I brought it home. But Ginny says the mother is an excellent mouser and has been training her young to hunt too. Ye knows we had no trouble with rodents when Fluffy was here. She kept them mice and the likes away from the house and the garden," William said, having had practised his arguments on his way home.

Sara was quick to offer to take care of the kitten. "Please, Ma, please, we won't let 'er come inside the house and me and Rose will take good care of it. Ye won't even know it's here," Sara pleaded.

"Please, Ma, can we keep it?" Rose joined in. Fanny watched the two girls with the animal and pursed her lips while she considered. She couldn't help but smile when the kitten began to bat at Rose's hair ribbon. Fanny heaved a sigh and looked to Mick for his opinion.

"Don't be looking at me," Mick said. "It's up to ye. I knows ye don't much care fer cats, but it's a fact they do earn their keep. And the girls sure seem to like 'er".

"Oh, alright then," Fanny replied. She knelt down and took Rose's face in her hands. "That kitten is not allowed in this house, do ye hear? And Sarah, ye better make sure it has food and water. Take it out to the barn. I don't wanna lay eyes on it. William, see it has a safe place to sleep in the barn. And if it causes me any worry at all ye'll be taking it back where ye got it, mind?"

William grinned and his sisters whooped their joy. "If ye are finished yer dinner ye can come help me make a bed for 'er in the barn," William told his sisters.

"Can we, Ma?" Sara asked Fanny. "I ate all my stew, and so did Rose." Fanny nodded and the trio were quick to make their exit. William carried the kitten to the barn while his sisters danced beside him, excited at this new addition to the barn.

"I need a dish to put 'er food in to feed her," Sara exclaimed. "I'll be right back," she told her brother and turned to run back to the cabin to beg her mother for something to use. Fanny was seated at the table talking to Jack and Phil when she burst back through the door.

"Mama, please, I need a dish fer the kitten and something to feed 'er," Sara announced breathlessly.

"It's not here ten minutes and already it's a nuisance," Fanny retorted, but got up from the table to find a dish for the cat. "Here, ye go, child," she said handing Sara an old chipped bowl. "Ye can dish a bit of stew into it fer it. But, Sara, ye mind now, I don't wanna see that cat in this house," she warned once again. Sara was quick to make her promises and to hurry back out with the small dish of stew for her new charge. Sara had to walk slowly with the dish in her hands, not wanting to spill a precious drop on her way back to the barn. She was cheered to see the kitten chasing a bit of string that Rose dangled in front of her as William looked on, enjoying the antics of the kitten and his littlest sister's obvious fun. Sara stood for a few moments watching and laughing as the kitten played with Rose. "I got 'er some stew," Sara announced with a nod of her head. "But where shall I put it fer 'er?" She asked glancing around for a good spot to place it.

"Over here, Sara," William instructed, guiding Sara to a corner of the barn where he'd already set an old wooden crate that he'd stuffed with straw. Sara set the dish on the ground beside the crate and called Rose to bring the kitten over. Rose came running, dragging the string, which the kitten leapt after, pouncing continually when Rose pulled it away. "Here, kitty,"

Sara crooned and was gratified when the kitten came to investigate the dish of food. William hadn't forgotten the girls' misadventure in the barn the day of the funeral and was quick to remind them that the hayloft was off limits. Rose looked solemnly up at her big brother, "I won't go up there ever, ever again," she promised. Sara also looked up at her brother, "We won't go up in the loft unless either ye or Phil are with us," she nodded, the fright she'd had still not forgotten. The girls were quick to return their attention to the kitten and had great fun playing with the little ball of fur while their brother watched over them.

"She's gonna need a name," William pointed out. "What are ye gonna call 'er?"

Sara and Rose looked at one another and back at the kitten. "I dunno," Sara replied. The girls studied the kitten coming up with several names before settling on 'Mouser'. "Because she's gonna catch lots of mouses," Rose intoned seriously.

"Mice," William corrected her. "More than one mouse is called mice." The trio were still discussing Mouser's future when Phil appeared in the doorway with Jack.

"Come to see the great hunter," Jack began, leaning down to stroke the soft fur.

"We named her, 'Mouser'," Sara told her brothers. "Because she will catch lots of 'em. And rabbits too, but maybe not yet. She's too little, but when she gets big."

"Mouser, eh? Well that's as good a name as any," Jack answered her.

"Hey, William, I needs yer help filling the wood box," Phil told his brother. "Jack, are ye gonna stay here with the girls?"

"Yeah, I'll stay," Jack answered as he lowered himself to the ground to sit with his sisters. He didn't want to admit to wanting to play with the kitten, too. He didn't see the knowing look his older brothers exchanged.

"Don't stay out here too long," William told him. "There's plenty of chores yet to do. Ye're not going git out of 'em that easy." And with that William followed Phil out of the barn.

Mick and Fanny were sitting and talking when Elsie returned carrying a basket of fresh molasses buns "Thought ye might like some lassy buns fer a lunch before bed," she said as she entered the cheery kitchen. "I won't be able to eat 'em all and it seemed a shame to let 'em go to waste."

"They smell so good," Mick commented. "I'd like to eat one now but I'm so full," he rubbed his stomach as he spoke. "I guarantee ye, they won't be going to waste here."

Fanny rose to accept Elsie's gift. "Sit right down and have a spot of tea. The young ones are all outside at the moment and Jimmy's fast asleep," she told Elsie.

"This is a good time fer me to have a chat with ye about the quarry while the youngsters are not about," Mick told the women. The three adults made good use of their time alone to discuss the ongoing meetings and their hopes to make working conditions safer for all the men employed there. The afternoon soon flew by as the adults talked and the boys went about doing their chores. There was a lot of laughter and shrieks in the barn as Jack and his sisters watched the curious kitten explore her new home. Time passed quickly and before long they were called in for supper.

The girls were excitedly telling their stories about Mouser, and the antics she'd got up to in the barn, while the family ate supper. Mick watched them all with great pride and joy. It took some time for the little girls to wind down after the excitement of the afternoon. After supper Sara jumped up from the table, determined to save whatever scraps she could for the tiny bundle she was quickly becoming attached to. "Mama, may I take a little milk out to the barn for Mouser along with 'er supper after I help with the dishes?" Sarah asked.

"I suppose we can spare a drop or two," Fanny replied. "But first the chores, then you and Rose may go back to the barn, but not for too long." Sara wrapped her arms around her mother's legs, "Thank you, Mama, thank you. And you'll see, Mouser will make you glad to have 'er 'round here."

Fanny bit her lip, "Still not sure it was wise, but time will tell," she answered. The girls were quick to run out the door as soon as the last pot was washed and put away. Mick and his sons made plans for the meeting to be held that evening. Fanny and Elsie had raised questions that Mick planned to voice. He was glad they'd had a chance to discuss it. He held both women in the highest esteem. He had high hopes for the meeting even while he knew that certain men were very worried about losing their jobs were the company to get wind of their plans to form some sort of association.

The girls asked to go out to the barn to play with the kitten the next morning as soon as breakfast was over. They met Elsie on her way over to visit. Rose raced to meet her. "Aunt Elsie, come see our kitten," the little girl grasped her aunt's hand and was tugging hard, "please, come, she's so sweet and funny."

Elsie smiled down at her niece, "okay, okay, let's go," she said. Rose was swinging Elsie's hand in hers while Sara skipped happily ahead to open the barn door. The children raced across the floor calling for their pet and the kitten popped up from behind the crate William had set up for her. Sarah ran to scoop her up in her arms, "this is Mouser," she told her aunt. Elsie reached out to stroke the soft fur. The girls were chattering and dancing happily about as Mouser raced across the floor after making her escape from the fondling. Suddenly the kitten leaped upon a burlap wrapped bundle leaning against the wall. Her claws hooked and the burlap came undone revealing the top of the wooden cross. The girls raced one another across the barn to see what the kitten had found. Sarah, who had begun to learn to read, recited the wording out loud, "Joe Kelly," she began and instantly stopped when Elsie reached her side.

"What is this," Elsie questioned, lifting the burlap bundle and unwrapping it as she did so. "Oh my," she said so softly Sarah could barely hear her. Sarah became worried as tears filled Elsie's eyes. "This is beautiful," Elsie quietly said as her eyes travelled over the cross. "Where did this come from?", she wondered out loud. Lifting it, she carried it into the sunlight streaming through the door to examine it more carefully.

"Girls, you stay here, I have to go see yer Mama," Elsie ordered as she carried the cross out the door heading toward Fanny's house.

Elsie had barely made it through the door when Fanny gasped in surprise at the grave marker she was carrying. "What on earth? Where'd ye get that?" Fanny asked.

"T'was wrapped up in burlap out in yer barn," Elsie told her. "Did Mick make it? Why didn't he tell me? Why was it hidden?"

"No, Mick didn't make this," she answered, "I've never seen it before. What a beautiful job. Oh, Elsie, look at the lily and the forget-me-nots. I wonder who carved it? Tis a fine piece of craftsmanship. You said it was wrapped up and hidden in the barn?"

Elsie nodded her answer, still too overcome with emotion to speak. Fanny, looking up, hurried to embrace her friend. "We'll ask Mick when they gets home tonight," she continued. "Come, sit down now and I'll get us a cup of tea."

Mick knew right away by the look on his wife's face that something was up. He washed up quickly and faced her. "Whaddsa matter Fan?" He asked.

"Elsie found the cross in the barn," she answered. "Where'd it come from and why didn't ye tell me about it?" she asked him.

"Aw, no," Mick said as he wiped his hand over his face. "I fergot all about it with all this business with trying to find out what happened to Joe and then the meetings. I'm sorry, Fan. Jake made it and brought it here the day he came out to talk with us. I was a bit taken aback, wasn't sure how to tell Elsie. After all, t'was him that caused Joe's death and I didn't know how she'd take it," he finished. "So, I hid it in the barn until things calmed down, 'til I calmed down," he smiled ruefully at his wife. "How'd she come to be out in the barn?" He asked.

"The girls wanted her to see the kitten. She went in the barn with 'em and while they were in there the kitten crawled up on the sack and 'er talons got caught in the burlap and pulled it down," Fanny answered quietly. "She was in a bit of a state when she brought it in to show me and to ask where it come from. I couldn't tell 'er a thing. I didn't know." Fanny shook her head. "T'is a beautiful job he made of it. I think Elsie wants to see it placed on his grave. She'll be over this evening and you can explain it all to her," Fanny studied her husband's face for a minute. "Did ye notice the flowers carved into it? The lily and the forget-me-nots? Elsie was really touched by that. Not many know about their baby, born on Easter Sunday and died the same day. I wonder how Jake knew about that."

Mick was quiet as he considered. "Joe must've tole 'im. He did spend a fair bit of time with 'em when they moved out here. Ye knows what Joe was like, always welcoming and kind to everyone. He seemed to really like the young couple." Fanny smiled as she thought of Joe, *dear, gentle man, it should never be. Elsie so misses 'im.* Aloud she said, "Well, Mick, ye best give some thought to it now and have a talk with Elsie when she gets here." Mick took Fanny's hand for a moment, "I will and I am mighty sorry I hadn't told ye about it. T'would have put ye on the spot, no doubt." Fanny nodded.

"Well, what's done is done. We best get supper over with so we can spend time with Elsie," she said and turned to the sideboard, gathering dishes and flatware to set the table.

The family had finished their meal and were going about their chores when Elsie stepped through the door. The door was barely closed when Mick began his apologies to her. Elsie could see the sorrow on his face and crossed the room, grabbing his hand. "Don't worry, Mick, I'd just like to know who made it and where it came from," she hastened to reassure him.

"Well, ye best sit down. T'is a bit of a story," Mick answered. After she was seated Mick told her the story of how the grave marker came to be in the barn and who had carved it so beautifully.

"But how'd Jake know about the flowers and all they meant to ye and Joe?" Mick asked Elsie. Then it was Elsie's turn to explain. She told Mick a little more about Joe's dream to make a living lobster fishing and Jake's talent as a wood worker. "He'd hoped with Jake's help to build another dory or two to make lobster fishing something that would support us all," Elsie smiled. "My Joe, he was such a wonderful dreamer, but he was practical, too. He wouldn't make a move if he didn't think he could make it pay."

"Well, now, it might be we can make Joe's dream come true yet," Mick responded, "and speaking of making money, I have something fer ye." He stood and went into the bedroom he shared with Fanny, and returning he placed a sack of coins on the table in front of Elsie. "That's money each and every man down at the quarry gave to help ye out. There's many a man and many a family Joe helped out in one way or another. They wanted to return his kindnesses."

Elsie was overcome and did not speak but her facial expression spoke volumes. Finally, she said softly, "tell the men thanks a lot. I'm overcome."

Mick patted her shoulder, pulling out a chair he dropped into it. "I'll let 'em know," he said.

Elsie stayed visiting with Mick and Fanny and discussing the friendship Joe and Jake had been developing before the horrible tragedy.

"I know ye're having a hard time with forgiving Jake," Elsie told Mick, "I know it ain't been easy. But that cross tells me how closely Jake must've listened; how much he must've thought of Joe. It took a lot of courage for him to carve it and then to bring it here."

Mick thought back to Jake's demeanor the day he'd brought the grave marker to his house and grew uncomfortable.

"It sure would help a lot if he would just talk to me man to man," Mick told Elsie, "I may well 'ave been wrong about 'im, I dunno. I'd rather not talk 'bout it any more, if ye don't mind."

It was now Elsie's turn to offer solace and she reached out to lay a hand on Mick's shoulder. The discussion ended abruptly when the boys came through the door balancing pails of water.

"Where'd ye want this water, Ma?" Phil asked grunting as water sloshed and nearly flowed over the top of the pail.

"Aw, thanks, Phil, set 'em there by the door," Fanny answered. "I'll need a lot more to wash all them clothes tomorrow."

Phil grimaced and he and William set buckets of water where Fanny indicated. The evening passed, as most did, with chores to be done before the family could call it a day.

Chapter

19

The men were noisy as they discussed in pairs and in small groups the results of the mining inspector's report. None were happy with the lack of interest in their welfare or the fact that no recommendations were made to make changes to the operation of the quarry. Things were to remain just as they were if management had any say in it at all. Charlie had to shout to be heard over the din. It took several moments before the men quieted enough for him to be heard.

"Look, ye lot, ye knows we has to look out fer ourselves," Charlie began. "The mining captain, he made it pretty clear when he brought us the report that ain't nuddin gonna change around here. Peter Parsons, Hank's cousin from Sin John's, will come and explain what an association can do to help us and how it all works if we decides we wants to do that. So, that's what this here meeting is about, to make up our minds if we wants to form an association, or if we wants to keep on going like we have been."

"There ain't been no changes to the Code in fifty years. T'is high time something was done," a man called out from the back of the room. This remark was answered with agreement from the vast majority.

"Sure, me Da's brudder was killed in a mine back in England," the man spat, 'he weren't even ten years old when he died." There was a general murmur as the men began to talk among themselves once more.

"Listen up, ye men," Charlie's voice bellowed. "We all knows that mines and quarries have been the death of far too many. We needs to focus on the here and now. There's naught we can do about what happened over in England back in the day. But we all knew Joe, and he oughtn't to have died the way he did. The thing is, are we willing to take a chance on losing another of our own? Well, are we?"

A thunderous 'no' answered his question.

"Look here, I don't want nobody to get hurt or nuddin like that," Andrew, another labourer, spoke up, "but I got six children to feed and clothe. I can't risk losing me job. How do we know that this association yer talking about will help? How do we know we won't all get fired as soon as the captain and owners finds out what we're up to? Cuz I don't see no way of keeping it a secret." He looked around the room suspiciously. "There's always one who is willing to sell us out. There ain't no guarantee that everybody here will keep their mouths shut. But there is strength in numbers. They can't fire all of us. And if they fire one, then the rest of us refuse to work til they gives his job back. How about that?" Charlie asked the men.

"I can't afford to lose any pay," Andrew began, "I don't know about the rest of ye but I ain't got much laid aside fer them rainy days." Many men nodded in agreement while others seemed to be considering the possibilities.

"T'would be a day's pay at most," Charlie answered, "ye knows they wouldn't let the quarry sit unworked fer long. There's too big a need fer the limestone upalong."

"A day's pay!" Andrew glowered, "are ye not hearing what I'm telling ye? I can't afford to lose one red cent, never mind a full day's pay!"

"Can ye afford to lose yer life?" Charlie asked ominously. "Or be hurt so bad ye'd never work again? Can ye afford that?" Andrew glowered back at him.

"I hears what yer saying, Charlie, but ye ain't got no family to look after," another voice spoke up. "A day's pay is a lot to ask fer most of us." A general murmur of agreement was heard throughout the hall.

"I have a family," Mick quietly intoned, "and I knows I don't want 'em being left to do fer 'emselves if something happened to me. Ye all knows what can happen in the quarry – one slip and ye can be hurt bad, if not killed out right like what happened to me brother."

"No disrespect intended, Mick," Andrew answered, "but there ain't been any other deaths like that here, ever."

"True enough, mate," Mick turned to look the man in the eye, "but what about Mike, ye remember how he lost 'is finger and was out of work for months while his hand healed. Or Pat, remember how he dropped that pickaxe on his foot and was out fer a fortnight. He has limped around ever since, that foot never did heal right. Or there's George, remember how he threw his back out shovelling stone into the cart one day? He was off work fer a long time, too. We jist been lucky there ain't been more deaths – one rock dropping on a man's head is all's it would take."

"Them's the risks we take working the quarry," Andrew returned.

"That's what this meeting is about," Charlie cut in, "looking at the risks and figuring out if it ain't worth making an effort to make sure we have some kind of help if we do get hurt. I ain't sure what all it can do, but an association can give a man a bit of money to help him out if he gets hurt. It may even be able to make things a mite safer and better fer all of us. But we gots to stick together."

"That all sounds fine as kind," another man spoke up, "but who's gonna help feed our families if it takes more than a day to get our point across?"

"How many here can't afford to lose a few days pay?" Charlie asked

"Thought ye said t'wouldn't be more than a day," Andrew spat out.

"Look, I can't tell ye if it would mean losing one day's pay or three or more. I ain't got no crystal ball," Charlie rubbed the back of his neck in frustration. "All I can tell ye is that if we votes for an association it will improve the lot of each and every one of us; and not just us, but fer the youngsters who will eventually come here to work, too. We don't need to make that decision tonight, but Peter Parsons ain't coming all the way from Sin John's unless there's a good chance ye all will vote 'yes'. Are ye all willing to hear the man out? Are ye willing to consider voting yes fer an association? There has to be a majority on this, otherwise we might as well ferget it and have no more meetins."

The men took to chatting amongst themselves once more and Charlie waited a few moments before speaking again.

"Look, I knows this is all a lot to take in, and this is an important meeting. Why don't we all take a bit of time to discuss it before we puts it to a vote?"

"Before we does that," Mick interrupted, "give some thought to how we can all help one another out. Perhaps we can barter or trade things we need. Like maybe somebody's got extra grain fer to feed the chickens, or a bit more flour than is strictly needed. Things like that, perhaps we can trade goods to help us through if we do lose a bit of pay." Mick silently thanked his wife and sister-in-law whose input had given him that particular idea. "I knows we gots more moose meat than we can eat and I can go gets another before winter sets in again. I thinks we all got something extra we can share to make sure no family goes without . . ." Mick trailed off.

"Mick's right," Charlie said. "Whatever may come of this, we always have helped one another. Don't be too proud to ask fer a hand is all. In the end we can all benefit one another. I think ye all should talk among yerselves and then we'll put this to a vote." With that Charlie stepped away and the men continued their discussions. The room buzzed with conversation.

"I sure can see the sense in it," Lou told Hank, "What do ye think of it all?

"Well, see, it ain't just fer us. An association will help us, yes, but it will also help our sons and future generations too," Hank replied, thinking of his own boys. "If we can make things better, safer, then I think we should vote yes."

"Never thought about it like that," Lou said, "That's a mighty good point. I think we should, too."

Andrew was not easily swayed, "That's all good and all, but what about those of us who need cold, hard cash? Bartering goods is all fine and dandy but it won't pay fer a man's credit note up at the general store. It won't pay fer medicine if we needs it. What about cases like that?" he asked.

"We don't have all the answers, mate. Like Charlie says nobody got no crystal ball. This is all new to all of us. Look, if it's money ye needs maybe that's something we can discuss at another meeting. Ye knows this one is only to settle whether or not to even start the process of associating," Hank answered.

"I ain't saying it's me who needs cash," Andrew blustered, "I just happen to know someone in that situation. There's a lot to consider before we all agrees to forming an association."

"You make a good point," Lou replied. "But like Hank just said, that's something to bring up at the next meetin, if we decides to go ahead with all this. And once this Peter feller comes out, we can ask his advice about such matters."

The men continued to discuss the ramifications and the possibilities of being without work if the quarry owners found out about their plans. Many were in agreement with the need of some sort of protections, and how much better life could be if working conditions were improved and there was some sort of financial safety net in place if men were injured on the job. None could foresee another tragedy like Joe's happening again and none could guarantee it wouldn't. Phil had spied Paddy across the room and made his way over to talk to him.

"How's it going?" Phil asked him as he approached. Paddy was guarded as he looked at the younger man.

"All's well. Ye come to talk to me about all this?" Paddy asked.

"I think ye knows what I wants to talk to ye about. But that can wait til after the meetin," Phil answered. "Are ye willing to have a chat when this is all over with?"

Paddy took his time in answering, "Well, b'y ain't nuddin changed since I last saw ye. I don't suppose there's much to talk about," he said in answer. Phil nodded but remained standing in front of Paddy. "Still, and all, I'd like a word," he said. Paddy nodded curtly just as Charlie called the men to attention.

"Do any of ye have any other questions before we puts this matter to a vote?" Charlie asked the men. "Any other worries or concerns?" Charlie looked directly at Andrew as he asked that question.

"Yis, I do," Andrew responded, "But being as this is just to find out if the men are willing to form an association, it will keep."

"What say ye then, are ye willing to come hear Peter out and then make a decision?" Charlie asked the gathering. "With a show of hands, those of ye voting yeah, raise 'em up."

Charlie released a sigh of relief as hands shot up all over the room. "With a show of hands, who among ye vote nay?" Charlie noted there were only a handful who voted 'nay' and of those some seemed unsure with hands raised no more than halfway, as though they were not convinced to vote in the negative.

"Thank ye all fer coming out. We don't know yet when Peter will be able to meet with us. Ye will all be told, one way or another that meetin will be important fer ye all to attend. I guess that goes without saying. Peter will be able to answer yer questions and explain better how it works. I don't need to tell ye how vital it is to keep this quiet. No chatting on about it at work either. Come see me, Mick, or Hank if ye needs to ask questions, and make sure it's after work! See ye all at the quarry in the morning." Charlie turned away and the men began to disperse.

"Well, that went better than I hoped fer," Mick remarked as Charlie came to stand beside him. "Don't know that Andrew feller very well, but I guess he raised some fair points."

"Was glad when ye spoke up to address 'im," Charlie replied. "The man's right. I ain't got a family to look out fer, at least not yet."

"Did ye and Constance set a date yet?" Mick asked.

"Naw, she's got an obligation to look after her Ma and Pa, so it's not likely to happen fer a good while yet. Her folks offered to have us live there with them, but I think not. I'd rather have me own roof over me head," Charlie answered ruefully.

Mick regarded Charlie for a moment. He'd long been a good friend of Joe's and Mick had great respect for the man, though he didn't know the man as well as Joe had. He knew Charlie to be a bashful man where women were concerned and had been surprised when Joe told him about the engagement. "Lots of time, b'y, yer only a young man yet," Mick responded. "Lots of time."

Charlie blushed and agreed with a nod. "Still and all, I'm more than ready to settle down. Here comes Hank, maybe he has an idea when Peter can make it over to this side of the island."

Hank was making his way toward them, stopping here and there to shake a hand or catch up with his many relations. "That went better than I thought it t'would," he said to Charlie. "You did a good job leading the meetin'. We're all grateful that ye agreed to it."

"T'was glad to do it b'y. Not sure about some of the men. How well do ye know that man, Andrew? He seems set against it, don't he?"

"Can't say as I know him well, worked with him here and there. He ain't a bad sort, just very careful what he involves hisself in.

There's a few more are just as cautious and just as nervous," Hank replied. "We'll bring 'em around. Peter's got the gift of gab and can be pretty persuasive – the man ought to be in politics, sure."

"I hope it won't take 'im long to come meet with us," Charlie answered. "Better to strike while the iron's hot, if ye know what I mean."

"The man did make some good points," Mick replied. "A man has to be able to take care of 'is family, so I understand where he's coming from." William, Phil, and Jack stood with their father, listening as the men discussed the meeting. None made any remarks but took in all that was being said.

"Well, b'ys, I guess I'll be shoving off now, lots to think about, but we gots to be at the quarry in the morning and I don't know about all of ye but I'm beat out," Mick said. "I'll see ye all at work on the 'morrow," turning to his sons he asked, "Comin'?"

"I'll catch up with ye,' Phil answered. "I'm just gonna have a word with Paddy, Twon't take long". Mick nodded as he locked eyes on his son. "Hope ye have better luck this time 'round," he answered. With that Mick shook hands with Charlie and Hank and turned to leave. As before William took his leave to pay a visit to Ginny. Jack was glad to have his father to himself as he had wanted to confide in him. The pair were quiet until Jack piped up, "Da, what do ye think Uncle Joe would make of all this?" he asked his father.

"Joe would be leading the charge to get something done fer the men, had it been somebody else who'd died," Mick was quick to answer. "Joe, he had a sense of fairness about him and he'd not brook no injustices, nor out and out meanness, such as the company what owns the mine has done. No, sir, and that's a fact."

"But what about what that man said about us maybe getting fired?" Jack asked worriedly. He knew that his family, like all the rest, needed the wages the mine paid.

"That's not likely, if we all stand together," Mick replied. "But what if it does?" Jack pressed.

"Look, Jackie-boy, what else did yer uncle teach ye? Was he not a man of faith? Would he not tell ye to trust to God in all yer needs?" Mick responded. Jack was quiet as he considered this.

After some moments he spoke up again. "Da? I'm having a load of trouble trying to believe in God. I mean, since Uncle Joe died.

I don't understand how God would let that happen to 'im, or why Aunt Elsie has been left with nobody at all, even their baby died. Why'd God let their baby die? I don't understand," he confided.

"Elsie ain't alone, is she? She's got all of us and she has friends too, though she don't see 'em often," Mick replied. "As far as the baby is concerned, it's likely it wasn't strong enough to survive, so God took 'im home as a mercy. Besides, like Joe would say, some mysteries are too great fer a man to understand. It's times like these we have to rely on the mercy and the love of God. We can't know the answers. God's ways are too high above our ways. But, son, I knows that yer uncle is surely sitting up there in heaven and watching us all struggle fer an answer and likely smiling to hisself thinking, 'this is where faith comes in', yup, that's what he'd be thinking. Jackie-boy, if yer faith is being tested it also means it will come out stronger because of all this. And, ye can always ask fer the gift of faith, cuz faith is a gift from God," Mick finished. Jack looked up into his father's eyes. He was still unsure and he didn't answer but continued walking in silence. Soon the pair were climbing the few steps to the cabin door.

After a lunch of tea and molasses buns and more discussion about the meeting Jack went on to bed with questions continuing to make doubts arise and his struggle with faith rage on. He laid in his bed listening as Phil came in and the talk continued in the kitchen. Jack had wanted to be alone before his older brothers entered the bedroom they shared. He lay thinking over his father's answers about God and life and thinking of his uncle, as he had ever since the tragedy.

After a while his thoughts turned to the time he'd gone out in the dory with Joe. They had been sitting quietly watching the jiggers as they bounced up and down enticing the cod that swam along the ocean floor. "Jackie-boy, it's like this: we are sitting in this great big world that God holds in his hands. P'rhaps he's rocking us all gently in his hands, just like this dory is rocking us here while we wait fer the cod to bite. Or p'rhaps God is like that anchor that keeps us in one spot on the water, still and steady-like." Joe's voice had trailed off as he took in the beauty of the bay and the green hills that surrounded it. Jack smiled at the memory. *Yes,* he thought, *Uncle Joe sure was a man of faith. I want to be like that. I want to be like my Uncle Joe.* With that a sense of peace came over the boy and he turned toward the wall as sleep overtook him.

Paddy gave a sigh as he watched Phil cross the room at the end of the meeting. He came alone, as before. Paddy shoulders tensed as he considered the thorny issue of wanting to keep Jake's confidences while simultaneously wanting to give closure to Joe's family. He was growing to like and respect Phil. Despite wanting answers, the young man did not push. He liked that. He was growing to like the whole clan.

"Paddy," Phil greeted him. "Thanks, fer waiting. Ye knows I want to ask about Jake again. Has there been any movement a'tall? Is he willing to talk to me or me Da?"

"Well, ye ain't one to beat around the bush, are ye?" Paddy responded. "I hates to disappoint ye, but no, Jake ain't wanting to talk, not to nobody. Look, I knows ye want answers and I wish I could give 'im to ye . . ."

"Do ye think he might be more agreeable if I spoke to 'im direct-like?" Phil interrupted.

"No!" Paddy answered emphatically. "That would not be a good idea."

"But why? We ain't blaming 'im. We knows a lot more than we did at the beginning," Phil began, "We just wants to know how it happened, is all."

Paddy sighed again, gazing at Phil his eyes were filled with compassion. "I can't rightly say I knows what yer going through. But ye have to understand. Jake, well, he ain't ever been much fer talking, and he ain't now, 'cept to keep sayin' tis all his fault. That's all I been able to get outta him," he lied. "I told ye it would take time."

"How much frigging time?" Phil asked, exasperated. "Seems to me we give 'im more than enough time."

Paddy rubbed his forehead. "I knows that. And it's not like I disagree with ye. I just knows Jake and if he decides to keep something to hisself ain't heaven nor hell gonna budge him. And it ain't like he don't care. He's as sorry as sorry can be fer what happened. Try to be patient. I'll have another go at him but I can't promise nothing."

"Paddy, b'y, it's asking a lot. Da is getting impatient, as is the whole family," Phil answered. "I don't know how much longer we can wait. If ye can't get through to him, maybe one of us can."

"I can't stop ye from doing that," Paddy retorted, "and I ain't gonna try, but if ye can wait until I gives it one more crack, I'd appreciate it." Phil stared without responding for several moments. "I'll talk to Da, see what he wants to do. It ain't in my hands neither." With that Phil turned away, his disappointment obvious in his body language.

Chapter

20

The bunks were finished. It had taken Jake a few weeks, laboring after work and every spare moment in between, to complete the job, even with Paddy's help. Between his job at the quarry and keeping the animals looked after as well as the many chores on the small farm there were not many spare moments. He was wiping the sawdust off the wood when Paddy entered the barn. "Ye did a fine job, as ye always do," Paddy remarked as he ran his hand over the side rails. "Tis smooth as silk. Me Aunt is gonna love it."

Jake grinned, "And how is it ye knows what silk feels like? Burlap and denim's all ye knows." He continued wiping down the headboards as he spoke.

And I s'pose ye knows what silk feels like, eh?" Paddy returned.

"Actually, I do. Made a casket once fer a family in the city. They wanted it all fancy-like and sent silk to line it," Jake wrinkled his forehead, "felt kinda like a baby's skin, real smooth and soft." Jake paused. "funny thing was nobody had died yet, but they wanted it ready cuz their father, or maybe it was the grandfather, wasn't well and not expected to live long. T'was a tad morbid, but practical, know what I mean? Anyway, it paid well. Ain't many people want a fancy coffin so that was the one and only time I made anything like it.

Do ye have the wagon empty? It's ready to go, if ye wants to take it today." Jake stood back to look over his craftsmanship one more time.

"Naw, she isn't finished having me uncle knock down walls and getting the room ready. I will let ye know when I'm coming fer it," Paddy answered, "just stopped in to see how ye all are doing. And to fill ye in on the meetings, thought ye'd want to know what's happening with all that. Be better if ye'd just come along with me though, ye'd get a better understanding of what they're trying to do."

Jake shook his head, "I knows what they're trying to do and best of luck to 'em, but nothing's changed. That mining captain has his eyes peeled on me from the time I gets there 'til I leaves. At least he ain't paid me any more visits." Jake's face was grim as thoughts of the quarry and the mining captain crossed his mind. "I don't mean to give 'im any more cause to fire me. I still needs the work."

Paddy watched his friend with solemn eyes, all the banter and humor had vanished. "There's something else," Paddy slowly began, "The Kelly family ...".

"What about the Kelly family?" Jake asked, unconsciously his fists balled at his sides.

Paddy studied his friend's face for a moment before continuing, "Look, they just wants to know how Joe got hurt is all. They ain't looking for revenge or a comeuppance of any kind. T'would help his widow and the rest of his clan to know the truth," he spoke hesitantly, unsure of how his words would be received.

Jake's head dropped in shame. Paddy watched as the struggle to protect his own family wrestled with Jake's sense of fairness and justice played out across his face. "Ye knows why I can't tell 'em nuddin', ye knows," Jake sputtered.

"I do know and I wouldn't be raising it now 'cept they been asking me to talk to ye, to see if ye'd be willin' to come have another chat with 'em. They been asking fer weeks now and after the meeting that youngster, Phil, came to me again. I ain't said nuddin' to ye about it since last we spoke cuz I knew ye didn't want to talk about it..." Paddy pulled his cap from his head and raked his fingers roughly through his hair, "but now, well, they may very well approach ye themselves and I felt ye deserved a warning at least." Paddy replaced his cap and stood waiting to see what Jake would say.

Jake smacked his hand hard upon the headboard. "Jesus, Mary, and Joseph, what am I gonna do?" Jake cursed and turned his back to Paddy as he considered this new problem. He felt hemmed in on all sides with no answers coming to him to resolve a single thing.

He was well and truly trapped. If he told the Kelly family what he knew he risked losing his job. If he didn't, he'd have to continue living with the guilt and shame that came the instant that cart got away from him.

"Look, b'y, if ye can see yer way clear to trusting me maybe I can help ye," Paddy pointed out, "two heads are better than one; can ye just tell me what the captain has on ye?"

Jake began pacing back and forth the barn considering all the ramifications of confiding in his friend. Jake's desire to clear the air with the Kellys, and, by extension, the community, helped him decide.

He turned toward Paddy. "What do ye know of me Ma and Dad?" he asked. Paddy looked confused, "What does yer parents have to do with all this?" he asked. "Please, Paddy, I needs to know first, what do ye know about my family?"

Paddy's eyes bored into Jake's, "Yer fadder and me mudder are cousins, not close relations, but cousins none the less. Don't know nuddin about yer mudder," he answered. "Me family moved away when we was still young. It's not like our parents spent time together," Paddy's curiosity was aroused and his keen eyes watched Jake closely.

Jake took a deep breath and met Paddy's eyes with a straight-forward look of his own. "What I has to tell ye must stay between us," he began, "if word were to get out not only could I lose my job, but we could get run out of the community, or worst."

Paddy's surprise was evident on his face. "What the hell does this all mean?" he asked.

"Look, Paddy, I ain't saying another word til I has yer oath that what I tells ye will stay here between us and these here walls," Jake told him.

"Go on, then, ye have me promise, I'm all ears," Paddy countered, as he leaned in, listening earnestly. Paddy watched as Jake's Adam's apple bobbed as he gulped; as he sought to find his resolve

Jake studied Paddy's face as he spoke, "Did ye know all that happened fer us to have to leave Robertson's? Without waiting for an answer Jake hurried on. "I knew my grandparents were Mi'kmaq and I knew it had to be kept a secret if I wanted to work; if I wanted to keep a job. Folks don't like to hire Mi'kmaq. They think they're lazy and good fer nuddin'" Jake spat into the dirt before continuing. "I kept quiet about it, never told a single soul, 'cept fer Mary. I wouldn't marry 'er without telling 'er everything. Things was going good. People were buying our tables and such but then Johnny, well, he was just a kid, he didn't realize ..."

Jake paused a moment, remembering. "Johnny let the cat outta the bag, by accident, but afterwards the rumours started about how Indians can't be trusted; how Indians were thieves; how Indians are sneaky and conniving conmen and worse, heathen pagans. We started losing business and then the troubles started, rocks were thrown through our windows, people who we thought were friends snubbing us, threats of harm to our family. It just became unbearable. We were treated like rubbish, like we didn't deserve to live. Dogs are treated better than that. Me and Mary had already married and were looking fer a place to make our lives together and then suddenly everything I'd worked fer came to naught. Nobody wanted anything made by a 'filthy savage'. It was a blessing when we got yer letter telling about this here place. That's why we came. We had no choice left to us,"

Jake paused again, studying Paddy's face for judgement or any sign of distaste. "And that's what the captain has on ye," Paddy nodded, grasping the impossible situation Jake was in. "That son of a bitch!" Paddy cursed. The relief Jake felt was evident in the straight spine and shoulders and on his face.

"Nobody can know," Jake said again. "Me and Mary, we can't live through that again."

Paddy was quiet for a moment and then began to chuckle and that soon gave way to great belly laughs. His eyes watered and his whole body was shaking.

Jake was shocked. He didn't know what to think as he watched as his friend was wracked in waves of cackles and guffaws. Then Jake began to get angry. What a bloody nerve, he thought.

Paddy watched as the look in Jake's eyes turned stormy, it took Paddy a moment to regain his composure and his breath. "No, no, don't get mad," he told Jake, "Don't get mad, it's just that, well, I been keeping the same secret."

Jake's face revealed his consternation and confusion. "Yes! Ye thinks yer alone, yer not," Paddy's eyes twinkled with merriment.

"I don't see what's so funny," Jake growled.

"Well, ye will," Paddy replied while wiping his eyes, "My great-grandmudder was Mi'kmaq too. I only found out a few years ago and, like ye, was told to guard me tongue; to never, ever, let it slip, fer all the same reasons ye held yer tongue."

Jake silently studied Paddy's face for any sign he was pulling his leg, or outright lying, and could find no evidence of either. "Yer kidding me," Jake's voice was barely above a whisper, "All this time, I never suspected."

Paddy nodded. "So ye see, I knows how to keep a secret," he replied. Paddy slapped Jake on the back. "So, c'mon now, spill it. Is that what the captain's been blackmailing ye with?" Paddy didn't really need an answer, Jake's expression told all, but he nodded when Jake finally said 'yes'. "Alright then," Paddy said, "I guess we has to figure this thing out. Don't be worried, man. We'll sort it out between the two of us."

Jake continued to be quiet and Paddy waited, knowing his friend would need time to chew it all over. "By the way, Jake, nobody in these parts knows about me great grandparents, neither, so I am trusting you, too, to keep my secret."

"Fine pair the two of us makes," Jake grinned at his friend. "Two half-breeds in a sea of white men." Jake shook his head in amazement, then his face darkened once again as he remembered the look of terror on Mary's face that night that rocks rained terror through the windows, shattering glass and scaring the life out of everyone inside. Then his thoughts swung to memories of the sneering glance of the mining captain. He wasn't brought up to back down from a fight, but this was different and he had more than himself to consider.

People wondered why he kept to himself, didn't socialize and wasn't very friendly. *If they knew they sure wouldn't be inviting us to no garden parties or such.* Jake thought to himself bitterly. He thought of the stories his mother had told him about life in the Mi'kmaq village where she'd often visited. Many Mi'kmaq women had married white men, intrigued and seduced by their goods, language, culture, and overall way of life that was foreign, exciting and new. His Mother had cut herself off from her family when she married, not by choice but by necessity as her husband had moved her far away from kith and kin.

Paddy stood by quietly as Jake's thoughts took him far away from his surroundings. Jake's attention finally snapped back to the present and he regarded his friend seriously. "Still can't see no easy way outta this," he said. "To be honest, neither can I at the moment. Let's just leave it be fer tonight. I needs to give it a lot more thought but I still thinks we can find a way, you and me together will hash it out and come up with something," Paddy replied. "Not tonight, it's late, let's just let it stew fer now. We will figure it out though. Yes, by God, we will!" With that Paddy squeezed his friend's shoulder once again. "Just remember, ye ain't alone. I got yer back." Jake didn't answer, his face grave as he gave a single nod.

"What did Paddy think of them beds?" Mary asked Jake when he came into the house. She had her back turned folding the diapers she'd washed earlier in the day and didn't see the solemn look on her husband's face.

She turned toward him when no answer was forth coming. "Jake?" she asked softly, "whatever is the matter? Did he not like yer work?"

"Naw, Mary, he liked 'em just fine. We was just talking about the meetins that the men have been holding to talk about the quarry and ..." Mary waited while Jake walked over to the wash tub to clean his hands.

"And?" she asked. "And about Joe's death and working conditions," Jake's voice was slow and barely audible. "Look, Mary, I don't wanna talk about it, alright? I just want to git to bed and fergit about it all fer a while."

"Alright, Jake. Do ye want something to eat first?" Mary asked. She waited quietly while Jake dried his hands, his back to her. "Just a cuppa tea," he finally answered. Jake dropped heavily into a chair putting his face in his hands for a moment before raising his head to look at his wife. She was taking cups out of the cupboard and turned to bring them to the table. Their eyes met and one look at her husband's weary face told her enough. There'd be no cozy chat tonight. She went to him placing her arm around his shoulder to comfort him. Aw, Jake, how I wish I could help ye, she thought as she stood silently by his side. Jake glanced up catching the tender expression on his wife's face. "Don't ye be worrying 'bout me now," he told her. "Everything's gonna be just fine, ye'll see. I'm just tired is all."

Mary moved away to get the tea ready. "Ye need help. There's too much restin on yer shoulders and too much on yer mind," she said thinking about the meetings that Jake never attended and the weight of Joe's death that threatened to be Jake's undoing. *Back in Robertson's we would have had all the help we needed,* Mary thought as she spooned tea into the pot. She sighed as she worked, the silence heavy and she longed to have family around to help and to visit with. *It's such long days and so lonesome* her thoughts tumbled *I can't burden Jake with this, he's got too much on his plate as it is.* Mary's thoughts continued on their circuitous route while she automatically made the tea and brought it to the table.

Jake watched her idly as he made a determined effort to close the door on all thoughts of the quarry, the mining captain, and Joe's family. He studied Mary's face and remembered the first time he'd seen her and how he'd fallen hard for the small woman with the beautiful eyes, so incredibly blue, like the sea, and so unlike his own black-brown ones. He began to relax as he remembered their courtship and all the hopeful plans they'd laid. He glanced around the tiny kitchen appreciating how Mary had turned the roughshod place into a home.

She's lonesome. I know she is. She misses her sisters, and her parents and friends, she thinks I don't know, but I do, Jake thought to himself, out loud he said, "How were the twins today? Did they give ye any trouble? Do ye need me to haul in more water afore we turns in?"

Mary smiled at Jake's sudden burst of questions. "I will need a bucket or two. I finished the washing but I always needs water fer cooking and washing the babies. It's amazing how much water I go through since they came," she replied. "And they aren't a bit of trouble. They sleep a lot, still. But they're pink and healthy and I am so grateful fer that. They'll be waking up any minute fer a feeding," Mary was interrupted by the thin wail of an infant as if she'd been heard. She rose to get the one before it woke the other. Jake smiled at the perfect picture of his wife cradling their firstborn and stretched out his arms in invitation. Mary laid the child in her father's arms. "I'll fix yer tea and then I'll feed her," she told him. Jake's attention was all for his daughter and the tiny fingers gripping his finger but he nodded agreement. *No matter what comes,* he thought, *I will protect ye,* and he smiled down into the child's tiny face.

Jake sat admiring his infant daughter's soft skin and perfect face, the mere presence of the child helping him relax somewhat and he startled when Mary brought his tea. "I'll take 'er now. I wants ye to enjoy yer tea while it's hot," she smiled at her spouse. "When will Paddy be bringing the wagon to take them bunk beds?" She asked. The pair chatted softly while their infant daughter nursed hungrily. Before long her twin also stirred and Jake moved to pick her up. Although a tension seemed to cling to Jake like the limestone dust from the quarry, he was able to put his troubles aside and focus on his family.

151

Chapter

21

H is parents were sitting at the table when William entered. His face was flushed from the cold wind that blew in off the bay as he walked home from Ginny's. Each visit cemented his plans to ask the girl to marry him, when the time was right.

Phil, his mind still on the meeting and the chat he'd had with Paddy afterward, did not even tease his brother and William relaxed when no barbs or foolishness were forthcoming. "Tea?" his mother asked as William joined them at table. William reached out to take a molasses bun and nodded his head at Fanny. "Guess I'm lucky there's any of this left," he said tossing a look in Phil's direction. Accustomed to staving off his brother's tormenting he wondered why his younger brother was so quiet. It wasn't like him to forego a chance to torment William about his budding romance.

"Phil tried again to talk to Paddy," Mick told William, "Without any luck. We've just been talking about whether or not to pay Jake a visit ourselves". Mick pushed back his chair and stood looking down at William. "What do ye think of that?" He asked. William glanced at his mother and then at Phil before answering. "What did Paddy say about it? Did he give any hope at all of ever getting Jake to talk?" He asked his father and brother. "He says Jake ain't saying much a t'all, still," Phil replied. "So, I told him our patience was wearing thin, that we deserved to know exactly how Uncle Joe got hurt. T'was hard though, because he's in agreement that we deserve to know what happened that day," he finished. "We talked about the meetin' a bit then I left," he lied.

Phil didn't want to tell his folks of his visit to the cemetery before coming home. Phil had been supportive, especially of Jack, since his uncle's death but kept his own sorrow under wraps not wanting to burden his family any further. After a lengthy communion at the grave site Phil had felt somewhat better and less apt to lash out. His frustration with being unable to make any headway with Paddy, and by extension, Jake, ate at him. He knew his father thought he held the key to getting through to Jake after the man's visit shortly after the tragic death. *Da thinks I inherited Uncle Joe's gifts in being able to talk to people,* Phil thought absently, *I ain't so sure about that. Uncle Joe was special, so kind and understanding, and wise. Yes, very wise.*

Phil started when William spoke his name. "Sorry, b'y, I was wool-gathering. What did ye just say?" he asked his brother. William stared at Phil for a second before he responded. "I just asked how ye felt about going round Paddy direct to the man hisself? Would ye be okay with that?" He asked.

"I was just thinking about Uncle Joe and how he seemed to have a gift fer people, ye know? And wishing I had that same ability," Phil answered. "I just don't know if Jake would even speak with me, or with any of us . . ." he trailed off. "Paddy says it's his way, Jake's that is, that he ain't much fer talking on the best of days. It ain't anything personal. He just don't talk much, though I got the feeling there's more to it than that," Phil continued.

Mick, who had continued to lean on the wall studied Phil's face thoughtfully. "It's not just about Joe any more. We knows Jake was working alone that day, which should never be. We knows conditions at the quarry ain't safe and never have been. We knows something's gotta change. Maybe if it were presented that way. But then, Jake, he ain't been at any of the meetins, makes me wonder why? Is he still scared of being savaged? I knows Charlie gave him an awful smack in the lips right after it happened, but the men have pretty much ignored him ever since, 'cept fer Paddy." No one spoke as Mick seemed lost in thought once again. "No, Phil, we ain't gonna send ye to speak with Jake. Let it be a while longer. There's more to all this than meets the eye," Mick continued, "I guess we best be gitting to bed. Mornings come early and I am beat out."

Mick made it his business to be placed closer to where Jake worked running the crusher at the quarry the next morning. The pit boss didn't question why he asked for the change but simply shrugged and sent the other man to Mick's usual spot. From his place on the quarry wall Mick could plainly see Jake operating the crusher and Mick's gaze often wandered in that direction as he filled a cart with limestone. He worked steadily and easily pushing his shovel into the shale fragments and lifting his load to dump it into the cart in fluid movements. He didn't know the other man very well, but was glad he was a seasoned worker. The pair worked well together filling the carts and sending them on their way to the crusher where the stone would be transformed into the fine, almost dust-like material that was then shovelled into further carts to be loaded on the freighter waiting out in the bay.

It was part way through the morning when Mick noticed the mining captain taking a stroll toward the crusher. Mick took note of the fact that the boss slowed his gait to stare up at Jake in the crusher. *Not like him to show his face, he's usually inside his cabin paying little attention to the men,* Mick thought to himself. *Not sure what he does in there but he sure as hell ain't one to involve himself much in the actual workings of this place.* Mick's attention was on Jake's crusher and he didn't notice the captain noticing him. *Wonder what he's up to?* Mick thought to himself and dumping another shovel full of rock into the cart he looked up in time to lock eyes with the man. The captain was quick to look away. He hadn't been able to look Mick in the eye since his last visit to the cookhouse to inform the men of the results of the mining inspector's report.

How could Mick know that the mining captain had made it a habit to check on Jake regularly, but always at various times in order to keep Jake on his toes. *That's very peculiar,* Mick's thoughts continued, *yes, sir, mighty peculiar.* Mick dropped his shovel and moved as if to get a drink of water, all the while taking quick glances at the crusher and back to the captain. Suddenly the captain swung on his heels and made for his cabin. *Yer up to something, I knows yer are,* Mick thought to himself. Mick wondered just what that something could be as he drank the dipper of water and went back to shoveling limestone. Surreptitiously, he took note of the men who worked within view of the crusher.

Well now, Mick thought to himself, *I thinks it's time I had a chat with some of these b'ys.* Unknown to Mick, Paddy had also seen the captain's stroll through the quarry. He clenched his jaw as he watched, knowing this was one more warning to Jake. Paddy spat onto the ground. *We'll see about this,* he thought, *this shit is going to end. And it ain't going to go well fer you,* he nodded to himself as he watched the captain. Jake also had noticed his boss walking past the crusher and although the man made no eye contact, he knew his message had been delivered. Somehow, this particular warning did not hold as much fear for him as it had in the past. *Paddy, b'y, it sure would be good if we could put a stop to all this,* Jake thought. At the end of the day the three men went home with much on their minds.

Chapter

22

Hank was not a regular visitor at Charlie's place, but he felt it best to deliver his news in person and well away from the watchful eyes at the quarry. *If there's one thing me and Andrew agree on, there's good reason to play it safe. Don't need the wrong man knowing all our business,* Hank thought as he drove the wagon into the field where Charlie lived.

Charlie was outside sharpening the scythe. He was getting ready for cutting hay. He laid the blade against a saw horse and walked across the yard to meet him; eyebrows raised in silent query. "What brings ye by, Hank?" He asked the other man as he approached.

"I got word from Peter; he says he will be here in about a fortnight. That should give us more than enough time to get the word out to arrange another meetin'," Hank answered. "Didn't want to wait to tell ye. Ye knows how many busybodies there are at the quarry, thought it best I stop by with the news. It will be easy to let Mick know, that boy of his is up to my place nearly every other day," Hank folded his arms across his chest as he spoke.

Charlie grinned. "Seems ye ain't entirely happy with them developments. Mick's raised a fine family though and I think that's naught fer ye to worry about," he said. He was thinking of his Constance and the less than welcoming looks he often got from the girl's father and felt a certain sympathy for William. "In any case, that's none of my business. Glad to hear yer cousin is willing to come help us sort out this business. T'was good of ye to come out here to let me know."

Hank nodded and reached into his pocket to draw out the pipe that was a habit of his. His hand cupped the bowl as he drew a packet of tobacco our of his other pocket. He took time to fill the bowl before lighting it and drew several breaths of the smoke before speaking again. "Word is sure to have reached the ears of the mining captain by now. You and me both know there are a few boot lickers amongst the crew at the quarry," Hank replied.

"There's one or two in every bunch, not much to be done about that." Charlie regarded his fellow labourer, "T'is true enough," He responded. "And that pompous ass may already know something of what we've been discussin' but he won't know all. I knows the men yer worrying about and it might not be a bad idea if maybe we fergot to let 'im know about the next meetin'. What do ye think?" He asked.

"They'll have to be included by and by, but I have no objection to forgetting 'em fer this next meetin," Hank nodded in agreement. "T'would be no trouble to fill 'em in later, once we decides what we wants to do." Charlie looked out across the fields to the little bay in the background. He didn't like to do it, but it was important to keep a lid on things until they saw which way the wind blew. "How well do ye know that feller, Andrew?" He asked.

"Don't know 'im a'tall," Hank answered, "worked with 'im here and there over the years. He keeps pretty much to hisself. He ain't one fer mixing much with others. But I don't think he's one to go bawling to the captain about what we're doing," he finished. Charlie nodded. "Ain't no way to keep all this quiet fer much longer. No doubt there's been something said. Ain't against the law to have a meetin though. At any rate just about every man in this area already works fer the quarry. Who they gonna git to do this work? I'd say there's many who'd give it up if a better position presented itself."

Hank nodded again in agreement. "Heard any more about that lobster cannery they's planning on building in these parts?" He asked. Charlie studied the horizon while he spoke, "Most of the men don't have the equipment fer lobster fishing. There has to be enough lobster to make a cannery worth while, but there's some talk of the boom there'll be down the road a piece. Who knows? If we all works together, we could build the traps and whatnot to make it possible. I knows I'd much prefer the brine in my face to the bloody dust of the quarry. Even if I went to work with someone with a boat, two men

157

working sunup to sundown can catch a good haul." Charlie paused again, studying the horizon and thinking. "Ah, but it's naught but a pipe dream fer now," he said, "We needs to concentrate on getting something done at the quarry."

Hank finished his pipe and was shaking the ashes onto the ground, stomping on the small hot coals. "Dreams is all that keeps a man going at times," he replied. "Sooner or later, there will be a bit more choice as to what grind stone a man has to put his nose to," he remarked. "Fer myself, I hope that day comes sooner rather than later. Now, I ain't gonna keep ye, I have a few more stops to make. If ye do see any of the men, perhaps ye can let 'em know?" He asked. Charlie nodded his agreement and stuck out his hand toward Hank. The two men shook hands and Charlie turned to walk back to the waiting scythe as Hank made his exit. In the following days word passed quickly about the important meeting coming up. And before long Charlie was standing in front of a gathering once again.

Whistling to gain the attention of the men Charlie began: "If ye lot are ready to listen we have Peter here from Sin John's to talk to all of us 'bout how we can make things better fer ourselves and fer our families. Now don't be interrupting the man. Let him have his say and we can deal with questions afterward. Alright, then, Peter?"

The man strode over with shoulders straight and a look of confidence about him. The room was quiet as the men waited to hear what he had to say. The man who stood in front of them was of slim build, wore a battered hat and a neat beard and moustache.

Peter stood for a moment looking out at the men in front of him. Hooking his thumbs into his vest and rocking back on his heels he began to address the assemblage.

"If ye thinks fer one minute that ye're alone in facing harsh working conditions and the supreme disinterest of the powers that be ye ain't alone. Let me tell ye a little bit about associations and unions and how they came about here in the Dominion of Newfoundland," he began.

"Ye knows there is a handbook all mining companies has to follow. And ye also know the regulations ain't really followed," Peter paused as murmurs began around the room. "Hear me out now.

Ye ever hear of the sealers strike? Well, yeah or nay, do ye know of them?" He paused expectantly as murmurs rose again.

"What does the sealers have to do with us?" A man spoke out.

"Ye'll see in a minute, first I wants to know, do any of ye know about it?" Silence met him and he waited another moment before continuing.

"In the 1840s the merchants on the East coast decided they'd pay the sealers with credit notes good only in their own establishments instead of with cash. Now they were a crafty bunch, them merchants. If they could convince the sealers to agree they could charge more fer their wares and keep the men tied to them fer years to come. They'd never see the light of day, owing the merchants and never being able to pay off the debt. The men did not like this. Can ye blame 'em? Anyways, a bunch of 'em got together and decided it weren't good enough. They threw their gaffers and tools aboard ship and refused to go out on the ice fer the seals until the merchants agreed to pay 'em in cold, hard cash. Now do ye think they would have gotten that agreement if it'd been just a few men? No, sirs, that would never work," Peter paused for dramatic effect before continuing.

"But when a hundred or more men took up the cause and every jack among them threw down their gaffs and tow ropes and refused to go get the seals, what do ye think happened?" Peter waited but no response was forthcoming. "They won! Of course, they did! That was one of many times the common folk stood up to the establishments that paid their wages. But it wasn't the last.

"About twenty years later the sealers had to defend themselves again when the price of seal fat bottomed out and sealers were losing money. Over three thousand men refused to work until they were given a fair return on their labour." Peter looked out into the crowd and was pleased to see the men were hanging on his every word. "And it wasn't just sealers, or fishermen either, the Trade Union Act made working conditions a bit better, safer, and increased the wages of many a man and woman.

"The shipwrights were one of the first to form a union and they were followed by tradesmen of every stripe. Then came unions for paper mills, and several others. There's mechanics societies and many, many more that came together to address issues in the working place." Peter looked out into the crowd his gaze stopping now and then on individual faces. "There is power in numbers," he told the crowd. "Ye don't have to put up with unsafe working conditions, long hours, or lower pay than what's being paid at other quarries in the country. Ye can demand better pay, safer work, shorter hours. Ye can, if ye wants.

"Let me tell ye a little more about why an association would be well worth yer while. An association would bring in sick pay fer when a man is injured or too ill to work. It would bring in a program of death benefits if a man were to be killed while doing his job. And, it would make work better and safer by putting rules in place fer how long a man can work in a given day or week. Ye could demand hazard pay fer the more dangerous occupations. And ye could find out what other mining companies are paying and demand the same pay fer yer work," Peter stopped and looked out over the crowd who remained quiet, waiting for more. "That's about it in a nutshell. Now, I need to know if ye want to proceed. No doubt ye all have questions."

The room ignited with voices calling out questions until Charlie strode in front of the men and gave a short, shrill whistle. "Look, ye lot, we ain't gonna git anywhere like this. Tell ye what, I'll call out a name and that person can ask his question and we'll continue like that, sound good?" He asked. There was a general nod of approval and the meeting went on with the men questioning Peter, one after another.

"Just how would these death benefits or sick pay be paid fer?" Mick wanted to know.

"Well, it would have to be worked out but mostly it comes from a small fee each man would pay from their wages once a month and that total sum would have to be matched by the company. That's how it usually works," Peter answered.

"How do we find out what other quarries are paying?" Paddy inquired.

"I can find that out and get back to ye. I don't rightly know what the going rate is at the moment," Peter replied.

"How are we gonna make the company make work safer and the hours shorter?" Vic questioned.

"If ye make an agreement to associate or form a union all them details will have to be written out, all legal-like," Peter said.

"How about shorter work weeks? I ain't got near enough time to work the farm as it is now," Hank noted.

"Again, that's something we have to work out together and have written up. Keep in mind we have to get the company to agree to the changes we want and the only way to do that is to stop work until they do agree," Peter told the men.

"What happens if we get an agreement and then the company tries to go on as usual-like? I mean if they don't honor the agreement what do we do then?" another man queried.

"Then ye have what's called a grievance and there's several ways it can be handled. Remember t'will be a legal document. In the most drastic case ye call a strike and refuse to work until the problem is dealt with to yer satisfaction," Peter responded.

Excitement made many raise their voices and the meeting went on much longer than anyone expected. Charlie had to give another whistle to get the attention of the men.

"I want ye all to give this some serious thought and when we meet again next week ye will have to vote yeah or nay to forming an association. It's late and we all needs to git home. I just wants to thank Peter fer coming out and helping us with this," Charlie turned to shake Peter's hand as the men cheered.

The men left, all chatting to one another as they made their way out the door. Charlie was pleased to see the hope that was evident on each and every face, even those of which had been doubtful at previous meetings. Peter, Charlie, Vic, Hank, and Mick along with his sons were the last to leave.

"Ye will be able to stay fer that next meeting, right?" Charlie asked Peter.

"Yes, I have a few things I need to take care of out this way so I will be back next week fer yer meeting," Peter replied.

The men discussed the success of the evening before parting ways for their respective homes with lightened hearts and renewed hope.

Chapter

23

Jake walked quickly away from the building. He didn't think anybody had noticed him at the back of the room. He'd come late and left early so he could escape notice. The men were all so caught up in what Peter had to say no one noticed him, he was sure. He hadn't planned on coming but Mary would not hear of it, feeling it was important for him to hear first hand all that was said. None of it made a difference to Jake's situation though as much as he hoped for the men's sake that an association would be formed. He could see the wisdom in it.

He tramped through the woods much as he had before when wanting to avoid others. It wasn't long before he came upon the spot where he'd first met Joe near the end of winter two years previously.

Joe'd been bent over a rabbit snare and a small fox was yipping and snarling at him. *The man had no fear a'tall. He'd held that animal's leg that'd been caught in the snare as gently as I hold the twins,* Jake thought. Jake's memories took him back to that encounter and how he'd stepped forward to help the older man. *"T'isn't too bad, I think we will save the leg, though she may have to live with a limp,"* Jake remembered Joe telling him. It had taken them a bit of time with the fox in pain and the fear causing it to nip and squirm in every direction trying to escape the two men.

Jake remembered Joe crooning softly to the vixen as he worked on freeing her. He remembered Joe instructing him to hold her jaws closed so neither of them would end up with a bad bite and before long it was free and racing away from them. *I wonder what he'd of done if I hadn't happened along,* Jake thought.

He remembered the chat they'd had and how easy the man was to talk with. *He reminded me a lot of me old grandfather,* Jake thought and a pain pierced his heart once again. *He was the first friend I'd made in these parts, why did it have to be Joe?* Jake thought, and then, *'Not that I'd wish that on anyone'.*

Jake tried to steer his thoughts away from Joe, away from the accident, but they tumbled one upon another, Joe's kindness and wisdom, his respect for nature and for all life. They'd shared their love for the outdoors, for wood working, for many things. *Aw, Joe, how I wish I could change places with ye. I am so frigging sorry, b'y, truly sorry.*

Jake allowed the pain to wash over him as he walked and remembered. It seemed to him that some very awful cosmic curse had been visited upon him. To have caused a death was bad enough, but to cause the death of somebody he was so beholden to, someone he respected and really liked, seemed the ultimate insult.

Just as he was coming out of the woods near his home Jake noticed movement along the tree line. He stopped walking and watched; the moon shed light on the fields but was not bright enough for him to make out what was trotting leisurely along the tree line. Suddenly it turned as if sensing Jake's presence and loped across the clearing.

Jake watched in amazement and wondered if his eyes were deceiving him. *No, I ain't wrong, it does have a limp. It does.* Jake thought. Out of nowhere Jake heard a voice, but it wasn't audible. The voice seemed to come from somewhere deep within his spirit. *"Ye remember that fox, eh? And ain't ye been a lot like that fox? Yipping and snapping at those who would help ye if ye'd allow it. Listen to me good, son, hear me. T'was me own fault. I was beat out and instead of pushing that cart away from the side like usual I got on the track behind it. I was so beat out I didn't hear yer cart careening toward me, by the time I realized t'was too late. It weren't yer fault. And don't worry none 'bout the captain. Everything is gonna work out just fine. Hear me!"*

Jake shook his head and dropped to his knees. He didn't notice the dampness soaking through his trousers. He wept and afterward he didn't know how long he'd knelt there weeping the pain and guilt and shame onto the ground. He didn't remember rising up.

He didn't remember the rest of the walk home. When he got there, he was still locked in a daze and questioning his sanity.

Mary wondered at his behaviour. He seemed so bemused. *It's different than usual,* she thought, *Jake, he lives in his head more than most folk. I can chatter on for hours and he listens without complaint. And I know he's really listening, making all the right responses at the right moments.*

She smiled to herself. *Whatever it is, he'll tell me when the time is right.* She moved behind the chair where Jake was sitting, silent and withdrawn. "Did something happen at the meeting? Anything ye want to tell me?" She asked. Jake shook his head slowly. "I needs to give it all some thought," he told his wife. "There's naught to worry yerself about."

Mary rubbed his shoulders. "I made yer favorite while ye were at the meeting, it's still warm. Would ye like a bit of figgy duff with yer tea?" She asked. Jake patted the hand on his shoulder. "That's sounds wonderful," he answered. Jake shook his head once more to try to shake the strange events of the past hour or so.

A bit of normalcy that's what I need just now, he thought, *that and a good night's sleep.*

Mary moved away to prepare the tea and serve the steamed pudding. "Did ye see Paddy at the meeting tonight?" she asked.

"No, it was crowded and I left before anyone else did. He's sure to stop in again soon when he comes to pick up them beds. At least I hope it's soon, would like to get 'em out of the way," Jake replied.

"Here ye go," Mary said as she placed the figgy duff in front of him and moved to get the tea. "I hope ye like it. I'd planned to have it fer dessert today but the twins were fussing a lot and I didn't get 'round to it. They slept all evening though, thank God."

Jake pushed a spoon into the pudding, "Mmmm, some good," he told her. "How long have they been sleeping?" He asked.

"Just long enough for me to get that made and to clean up afterward, not that long," Mary answered. "No doubt they'll be waking up fer their feeding soon." She took a sip of her tea and her fingers played with the napkins she'd set on the table. "Jake? I been wondering how ye'd feel if I wrote and asked for my sister to come stay with us for a while? I could use a bit of help with the babies and the company would be so nice."

Jake's eyes glanced about their tiny quarters. "But where'd she sleep?" He asked. "I thought we could make a little pallet over in yonder corner. She ain't very big and she'd be no trouble a'tall," Mary entreated. Haldi was fourteen years old and Mary's second youngest sister.

Jake reached across the table and patted Mary's hand. "I don't mind a bit. I knows it's been lonely here fer ye. Do ye think yer parents would allow it?"

Mary's eyes gave away her longing and relief. "I hope so. I'm thinking the change might do her some good. I'll write a letter tomorrow, but how am I gonna get it to them?" She asked.

Jake patted her hand once again. "I'll ask Paddy tomorrow. I'll see him at dinner break. You just worry about writing that letter and I'll make sure they gets it," he answered. Just then the babies began to wake and Mary was quick to see to them.

Jake smiled as he watched his wife. Her step seemed lighter and he was glad to do anything to make her life a bit happier. *I sure hope her parents are agreeable to this,* he thought, *she'll be mighty disappointed if they ain't.*

Mary returned balancing a twin on each arm. "They're getting some big, Jake, soon I won't be able to hold more than one at a time," she said.

Jake rose to relieve her of one and she smiled up at him. "Let me feed Liza and then we can switch and I'll feed Lily. Once they're fed and cleaned up, we'll go to bed. Sound good to ye?"

Jake smiled and nodded; his attention completely diverted by Lily's trusting face. *They're growing so fast,* he thought, *dear God, help me do well by 'em.* He glanced over at his wife rocking and nursing the smaller of the twins and promised himself once again that he'd work hard for his family and give them the best life he could. Lily clutched his shirt in her tiny fingers while staring into his eyes. Jake's heart was overcome by emotion, not for the first time, and again came the deep feelings of satisfaction and pride.

In the early morning hours Jake was awakened by an insistent voice that was not a voice. He struggled to shake off the dregs of the deepest sleep he'd had in weeks. The voice that was not a voice came again more insistently. *"Help Elsie,"* it said. Jake pulled himself to his feet and blearily looked around the room searching for the source of the voice. *"Help Elsie,"* it said again. Jake's whole body was tense and his mind struggled to understand where the message was coming from. It was not audible but seemed to be speaking straight into his mind. He half staggered from the small room. He was sleep walking to the door, still in a daze he pulled his boots onto his feet and went outside to relieve his bladder.

The cool morning air helped him awaken more fully. *What the hell is going on?* He asked himself. *"Help Elsie"* came unbidden to his thoughts once again. Jake stood in the pre-dawn light and thought, *who's Elsie?* It was several moments before it hit him: Joe's wife. He'd never met her and only knew her name because of the stories Joe had told him. Funny stories, sad stories, and inspiring stories, for Joe was nothing if not a good story teller. He'd deeply loved his wife, Jake remembered.

He stood in the cool morning air and scratched his head. *How in the dickens am I supposed to help Elsie? I ain't ever met the woman,* Jake thought. He shrugged and turned to go back inside, deep in thought and very disconcerted.

"Paddy b'y, might I have a word with ye after we eat?" Jake asked his friend while they waited in line for their food. Paddy gave him a concerned look. "What's going on?" He asked. Jake shook his head and looked around at the men in line. "Nuddin I wants to talk about in here," he answered. "Good enough, but we best eat quick, ye knows we ain't got much time," Paddy responded, his curiosity peaked.

It was unlike Jake to want to chat at any time and he'd been so withdrawn since the tragedy that it made Paddy wonder just what Jake might want to discuss with him. As soon as they had cleaned their plates Jake was jumping to his feet. "C'mon b'y, let's take a walk," he said to Paddy, impatient to get out the door so he could have a word in private with his friend.

Paddy lumbered to his feet his large frame a contrast with Jake's slimmer, wirier one. He followed Jake out of the room and up the hill, well away from any ears that might overhear them. "What's with ye? Why all the secrecy?" he asked.

"I don't want nobody listening in," Jake replied. "First though, Mary wants to have her sister come and stay fer a spell. Would ye be able to get a letter to 'em?" Jake asked. "Sure, that'd be no problem a'tall," Paddy answered. "But ye could have asked me that back there," Paddy gestured with his head back toward the cookhouse.

"I knows that," Jake retorted, "that ain't why I asked ye to come out here. I just wanted yer opinion. I was walking back from the meetin last night . . ." "Ye were at the meeting"? How come I never saw ye?" Paddy interrupted. "I came late and left early and stayed at the back of the room. Didn't want anyone seeing me. Anyway, it ain't about the meeting.

"Paddy, b'y, I thinks I'm losing me marbles. There's weird stuff going on and I jist wants yer opinion," Jake burst out. "I'm scared I'm going crazy."

Paddy looked incredulously at his friend. "Hold on, hold on now. Let's start again. What the hell are ye going on about?"

"Last night, on me way back home I saw the fox, that one I told ye about, what me and Joe saved from the rabbit snare, remember? And afore ye ask, it was definitely the same fox, it had a limp on the hind leg what was caught in that snare. I knows that fer a fact."

"What the dickens, why does seeing that fox got yer all churned up?" Paddy interrupted again. "Paddy. Please, just hear me out. I needs to get this off me chest," Jake implored. "It wasn't just seeing the fox. I am certain I heard Joe's voice. And then this morning just as I was waking up I heard 'im again telling me to help Elsie. That's Joe's wife. Paddy, b'y, it was all so strange and I don't rightly know how to explain it all," Jake told Paddy. "Am I going mad?"

Paddy was quiet as he studied his friend's face. It was more animated than he'd ever seen and Jake was talking a mile a minute, which was so unlike him. "Are ye telling me yer hearing ghosts?" Paddy asked.

"I don't frigging knows what I'm hearing. All I know is that after I heard Joe talking to me in the woods, I felt like a big weight had been lifted off, ye know? And fer the first time since he died, I slept all night – no dreams about the accident; no dreams about the captain, nuddin. And it ain't like a voice ye hear with yer ears. It was like it was inside me, kind of. I don't know b'y. I jist don't know. I keeps thinking I'm losing me mind," Jake said. He took a deep breath and his eyes met Paddy's searching for his reaction to the tale.

"Wow! Man, I don't know what to tell ye. But if it's any comfort to ye I do know me folks talked about strange stuff like that there me grandmother used to get on about. Stories from her Mi'kmaq mother and other relations," Paddy responded very quietly.

Jake glanced around to make sure they were still alone. He was terrified of anybody else learning his secret. "Far as I can tell ye're just fine," Paddy reassured his friend. "Look this ain't the time or place. I'll come over after work tonight and we'll hash it out. If ye wants my opinion, no, ye ain't crazy, but ye're sure having some spooky stuff going on," Paddy grinned at his friend. "Ye're all right b'y. Ye're jist been under a heap of worry, and been through a lot, that can play tricks on a man's mind. Feel any better?" he asked. Jake stared at his friend for a spell before nodding his head. Then they heard the whistle blow. "Gotta get back to it," Paddy said, "sure ye're alright?" Jake nodded again and the pair separated each going to their perspective place in the quarry.

Jake went out to the barn as soon as supper was over, anxious to have a bit of time to mull things over before Paddy showed up. He took the dog into the barn with him, because he was still so spooked. He'd been in a bit of a strange way all day and was still trying to pick sense out of his experience the night before and the 'voice' he'd heard. Jake was moving around the barn tidying up when Paddy finally made an appearance.

"Hey, Jake, ye sure piqued my interest today. What's going on with ye?" Paddy asked.

Jake hauled a small bench out and motioned to Paddy to have a seat while he balanced on the side of the bunk bed. He blew out a breath. "I dunno where to start, b'y. T'was a strange night, and to hear Joe's voice once more this morning was spooky. I'd convinced myself I was imagining things 'til then," he began. "Before I starts, don't be telling all this to a soul. It's making me itch just to think 'bout it and I don't needs to make meself a laughing stock."

"I think ye knows me better than that," Paddy objected. "Ye knows I won't be telling anybody. Now, just start at the beginning."

"Well, like I told ye earlier, I was on my way back from the meeting. I noticed something moving along the tree line but couldn't make out what it was. Then she loped across the clearing and I knows it was that same fox what me and Joe freed from a rabbit snare last winter. I knows it was the same vixen by 'er limp," Jake looked up at Paddy for a reaction. When none was forthcoming, he continued, "that's when I first heard 'im – Joe, I mean. He was comparing the way I been acting with the way the fox was acting when we was trying to free 'er. We had a hard time fer a bit, cuz it was snapping and yipping and squirming like mad. And then he was telling me how the accident weren't my fault, that he shouldn't have been standing on the track."

Jake paused waiting for a response from his friend. Paddy's face was somber but he didn't speak but merely nodded for Jake to go on. But Jake did not, remembering how he'd dropped to his knees and wept. He didn't want to share that with Paddy.

"Well, b'y, that makes sense. I hadn't thought about why he was standing in the middle of the track. Now, see, what I been tellin ye. It weren't yer fault, like I been sayin all along," Paddy said. "that makes a pile of sense, b'y. Wonder why I didn't think of that," Paddy's voice trailed off.

"And then this morning his voice told me to help Elsie. It was strange. It wasn't like hearing yer voice now, it wasn't outside myself. It seemed like it was coming from somewhere inside me," Jake shook his head, "I can't pick sense of it well enough to explain it to ye."

"I dunno, b'y," Paddy answered, "but it sounds somewhat like the stories I heard 'em tell about my grandmother, the one who was Mi'kmaq, they says she had some kind of gift to speak with the ancestors. That's how they put it. Stranger things have happened I s'pose. Anyway, they said she wasn't at it all the time, but when there was some kind of trouble, off she'd go and commune with the spirit world. And she'd get answers every time. That's what they say. They say she was as steady as a rock, nuddin' wrong with the woman's mind a'tall. It's something that's more accepted among the Indians. We don't put much stock by it, raised in the white world like we were. But what if it's true? I ain't ever had no experience like it, that don't mean nothing though.

"I ain't ever seen the sun when it's behind the clouds but I knows it's there," Paddy grinned at Jake. "Look, b'y, whatever it was, it sure makes a lot of sense and I don't think yer losing yer mind. Fact is, ye're likely the most sensible person I knows."

"But what about that message to help Elsie. How am I s'posed to do that?" Jake asked earnestly.

"I ain't got the foggiest notion," Paddy replied, "but if it's anything like what used to happen with my grandmother, you'll be shown the way."

Jake's knee bounced up and down and he fidgeted with a bit of straw he held in his fingers. "I hope it don't take too long, then, cuz this is enough to drive a man mad," he told Paddy. "So, ye don't think I needs worry about it then?" He asked.

"Ye made it to work today. Ye did yer work. Ye came home. Far's I can tell yer acting pretty normal to me," Paddy grinned, "as normal as yer ever been."

"Thanks, I think," Jake responded sardonically. He was deep in thought for a moment before he said, "Nuddin' to do but wait fer Joe to give me more instruction."

Paddy stood up, "Ye have been through a lot b'y. Maybe Joe will tell ye more, and maybe he won't. I wouldn't worry meself any further."

Jake gave a nod and stood up stretching a hand out to Paddy. "Thanks, me buddy, really, thanks," he said as he shook Paddy's hand.

"Don't mention it," Paddy answered, "and if Mary's got 'er letter ready I can take it now. Me aunt is going into town this week some time and will bring it out to the post office there."

"Aw, that's wonderful," Jake replied. "She does, I'll go get it and bring it out to ye. Thanks, again, Paddy, t'is much appreciated."

Jake's dog stayed at his heels as he went to the house and back to the barn to deliver Mary's letter into his friend's hands. Paddy bent and rubbed Smokey's ears.

"Ye gots a beauty of a watch dog there," Paddy said before standing to take the letter. "See ye at work tomorrow, and don't give that no more thought. Ye're alright, b'y, ye worries too much but ye're alright. Go get some rest. Tomorrow's another day."

Jake said his good-byes and watched as Paddy drove his wagon our of the yard.

Chapter

24

Elsie had sat with Mick and Fanny a little longer than normal, the discovery of the cross had brought back the day Joe had died and all the anxieties that his death had given birth to.

She hung her shawl on the peg near the door and made her way into her bedroom. Joe's jacket hung on a peg behind it and Elsie took it down and buried her nose in it. The scent of her husband clung to it and she allowed her tears to soak into the fabric.

When will the sorrow lift? When will I ever feel like myself again? She thought as she sat rocking herself on the edge of her bed. Hours later Elsie awoke, she'd cried herself to sleep hugging Joe's jacket to her chest. She stood and hung the jacket back on its peg and turned to unpin her hair and change into her nightgown.

Wearily she climbed into bed pulling the quilts up under her chin. She'd been asleep a short while when the dream began. "Don't cry, love, please, don't cry," Joe's voice spoke into her dreams. "I'm so sorry. I never meant fer it to happen. I never meant to leave ye," Elsie moaned in her sleep and tears rolled down her face. In her dream Joe reached out for her hand. "Come with me, love, there's something ye needs to see," Joe took her hand in his and together they walked into the quarry.

Elsie watched as two men discussed how to get the cart moving. She recognized Joe. It was rather strange since he was standing beside her. "That's Harry, there with me," Joe told her. The two men tried to rock the cart but it held fast. Then with a man on either side, they tried to push it to get it going on the track, but it held stubbornly to the track, unmoving. Joe dropped to his knees looking underneath. "Them wheels needs grease. They're seized up but good," he told the other man. The man cursed and spat. "I'll go see the pit boss and git some. T'was s'posed to be greased up last night," he said. "Nuddin' fer it now but to go get some and do it ourselves. I'll be back," he said and turned to walk downhill.

Joe held Elsie's hand tightly and she watched as her husband continued to try to get the cart to move. Then she saw him stand in the middle of the track and push hard from behind the cart. The next thing she knew he was screaming in pain as a second cart careened into him from behind. Yet she remained calm as Joe stood beside her holding her hand tightly. She watched as men appeared, Charlie and Vic among them. She watched until the horse and cart came to take his body to the surgery. She watched the men disperse and Harry walk away from the job site.

"Tell, Jake, t'was never his fault. Tell Mick, too, he'll know what to do. Please, Elsie, help Jake," Joe whispered. "I'm so sorry, love, I never meant to leave ye."

Suddenly Joe no longer held her hand but was in front of her with their infant son in his arms. "I'll be lookin' after 'im til ye come, that I promise ye. And know I love ye, always and forever. You gots to go on living, but don't ferget me, remember I love you, always, always," he said so quietly that Elsie had to strain to hear him.

Elsie woke to tears rolling down her cheeks. Her hand brushed the hair from her eyes, and, rising, she splashed cold water from the water basin over her face. The dream felt so real. She could swear Joe had stood here just moments before. She wrapped her arms around herself.

"*Help Jake,*" Joe's voice came to her insistently. Elsie walked out into the kitchen. She'd stocked birch wood into the wood stove the night before but only embers remained. She moved like an automaton, gathering kindling from the box she opened the little door and placed the splits on the embers, blowing gently until the thin sticks of wood caught fire. Leaving the door open she moved back to the kindling box and lifted three small pieces of firewood and moved back to the stove. She knelt in front of the open door and watched as flames licked along the kindling until a small fire was going before placing the logs on top.

She thought about how many times she'd watched Joe at this morning ritual and felt closer to him. And she thought about how she could do as Joe asked and help Jake.

She was wide awake when she turned away from the wood stove and comforted by the dream. "I will never, ever forget you, my Joe," she whispered. She filled the kettle with water and went to get dressed to go outside and feed the chickens as was her habit.

She stepped out into the yard and her eyes went immediately to the skies admiring the fine morning and giving thanks. She glanced around the well tended fields and barnyard. *Aw, Joe, how could I ever forget you? You have left your mark on every inch of this place,* she thought to herself, *I hear ye, Joe, and I will figure out a way to help Jake.*

Later in the morning Elsie visited Fanny and told her of her dreams while Rose and Sara entertained themselves in the barn with the kitten.

"And it seemed so real," she told Fanny, "It was like I could feel his hand in mine." Elsie wiped away the tear that ran down her cheek. "I miss him so much. In the dream he was so insistent that I help Jake; that I tell Mick. And then after I was up and about, I sensed his voice again, telling me to help Jake, I don't know how I can do that. But Fanny, I have to try. I'd like to go visit him, perhaps after church on Sunday. I need to thank him for the cross. Do you think Mick would take me?" She asked.

Fanny reached across the table to take Elsie's hand in hers. "I am so sorry for all your troubles," she said, "I think Mick would be happy to do anything for ye; anything that would make you feel better. Come have supper with us tonight and we can have a chat with Mick about it all."

The day passed quickly as the women went about cooking, cleaning, gardening, and taking care of the children, among many other chores.

Elsie's dream was uppermost on her mind as she worked and before she knew it, she could see Mick and the boys crossing the field through the small window in her kitchen. Automatically she looked for Joe before the reality of his death pierced her heart yet again. *Oh, Joe, it's going to be a while before I remember,* she thought, *it's still seems so strange, so unreal.*

She removed the apron she wore and sat in the chair that Joe once occupied whenever he was at home. It was easier to do so than to sit in the rocker beside it. It seemed less lonesome that way. She didn't know how long she'd been sitting there, thinking again of the dream and holding the memory of Joe cradling their infant close to her heart. It was Jack's light tap on the door that brought her back to the present.

Jack opened the door and looked inside, "Aunt Elsie," he called, "Ma sent me over to get you. She said ye're gonna join us fer supper and it's almost ready."

Elsie smiled to herself. "Yes, I'm ready. How was yer day?" She asked. Jack filled her in on the doings of the quarry as they walked over to Fanny's.

"I'll be damned," Mick said later when Elsie told him about her dream and about Harry. "No wonder nobody's seen 'im. Well, he won't be gone forever, sooner or later he'll show his face and me and 'im is gonna have a talk, cuz if yer dream is true and them wheels were stuck fast . . . and if them wheels hadn't been greased ..."

Mick covered his face with his hands and the two women looked at one another in shock. Mick never, ever, showed his feelings this way. His shaking shoulders gave away his emotion and Fanny stood up, hurrying to his side. Mick allowed her arms to embrace him from behind, reaching up he patted her arm. The display was short-lived. Standing up Mick wiped his face and paced the floor while clearing his throat. Fanny stood still watching him.

"I'm so sorry, Mick. I didn't mean to upset ye," Elsie said quietly, her hands twisting in her lap. Mick turned to her and gently said, "No, me dear, don't ye worry. I'm okay now. I always knew there was something more to all this. Joe, he was always so careful, but my God, that was a hard go trying to get that freighter loaded and on its way. We was all so beat out." Mick paused, looking out the window at his brother's place so close by. "I'm gonna have to find Harry and get the story from him. I don't mean any offense, Elsie, but I needs something more than yer dream to go on, to bring to the men before we votes fer an association."

"That's not all, Mick, there's more to the dream. Can you sit and let Elsie finish?" Fanny asked. Mick nodded and returned to sit at the table.

"Joe was very insistent that I help Jake," Elsie's worried eyes bored into Mick's, "but I don't know how he means fer me to do that. Still and all, I need to go see him, to thank him fer the cross he carved fer Joe's grave, if nothing else. I don't know how that will help though."

"We thought maybe ye could take 'er to Jake's after church on Sunday," Fanny put in.

Mick glanced from Elsie to Fanny and blew out a breath. "It's not like I wouldn't do that fer ye, Elsie, ye knows I would. But his friend, Paddy, has been trying to get 'im to come talk to us again without any luck. We wanted to find out more about what happened that day but Paddy keeps tellin' us that Jake won't talk to nobody so I dunno how willing he'd be to have us visit 'em," Mick told the women.

"Perhaps he won't talk to ye men but he's going to talk to me," Elsie announced decidedly. "He won't turn Joe's widow away from his door. And from what Joe told me about 'em it may be just the thing to get 'im talking." Elsie smiled at Fanny, "Sometimes we women can get through where ye men can't."

Mick didn't argue the point and plans were made for the following Sunday.

Both babies were wailing while the harried young parents walked the floor each with a child held over their shoulders as they paced frantically, both ignored the barking dog out in the yard and neither noticed as the horse and buggy pulled into the yard.

Mick climbed down and reached up to help Elsie descend. Smokey continued to jump and bark a warning to her master, but he didn't appear. The pair made their way to the door and Elsie tapped nervously and stood back to wait. Nobody answered.

Elsie looked anxiously up at Mick, "Maybe this wasn't such a good idea," she said hesitantly.

"Well, we're here now, let me," Mick answered and reaching past her gave a hard, loud knock on the door. Both were surprised when Jake pulled the door open and the wailing of infants assaulted their ears.

The young father instantly recognized Mick from their meals in the cookhouse and he stood with door half-open, dumbfounded, his mouth dropping but not a word coming out. Behind him Mary said, "Jake, for heaven sakes, ask these good folks in."

Jake opened the door wider and stepped back for Mick and Elsie to enter. "Come in, come in," he said, still stupefied, and worriedly moved aside.

"Hello, I'm Mary, Jake's wife," Mary spoke above the din. "I'm sorry, but these wee ones are a mite upset," she apologized.

"May, I?" Elsie asked holding her arms out to take the infant Mary held. Mary glanced quickly at Jake and then held the child out to Elsie.

Elsie took the baby and rocked her gently, crooning as she did so. Within minutes the wailing stopped and the baby stared into Elsie's eyes trustingly. Her twin was also settling down, though she whimpered still.

"I am so sorry to intrude on yer afternoon. My name is Elsie Kelly and I just came to thank yer husband for the beautiful cross he carved for my Joe," Elsie smiled at Mary. "I guess I should have given ye fair warning of the visit."

Mary smiled at the older woman. "Ye just caught us at a bad time. You must have a gift for calming fussy babies. Will ye look at this, Jake?"

Jake still held the other twin who was now relaxed against his shoulder. He didn't know what to think or say and his confusion was evident on his face. "Ye're Joe's widow?" He asked quietly.

"I am. And I guess ye knows Mick here," Elsie answered. Jake nodded.

"Please, come, sit," Mary told her visitors. "Here, give 'er to me," Mary told Jake. "I'll just put 'er down fer a nap. I'll be back to take 'er," she said to Elsie, who continued to croon and rock the child in her arms.

"Please, take yer time," Elsie replied, "I love rocking babies." Looking at Jake she said, "I am sorry for intruding, but I really needed to talk to ye, if ye don't mind sparing me a little of yer time. I know ye must be busy."

Jake snuck a quick peek at Mick before responding. "Ye didn't need to take the trouble to come all the way out here. Yer husband, he was a mighty fine man, and I'm awful sorry fer what happened and fer my part in it," he told her bravely. Elsie nodded but did not respond.

"Elsie, if yer okay here, I think I'll take a ride up to Hank's. There's something I needs to talk to him about," Mick spoke up.

Elsie smiled at Mick, "That'd be fine. If it's okay with Jake that I stay fer a while." She turned her gaze to Jake expectantly.

"Ye're welcome to visit, if yer wants to," Jake responded. "Mary will be back in a few minutes."

Elsie glanced down at the baby in her arms, "And who, might I ask, am I holding here?"

"That's Lily, she's a bit bigger than her twin, Liza, "We named 'em after their grandmothers," Jake answered.

"They're beautiful," Elsie answered, her gaze on the child's face. "How old are they?"

"Just two months," Jake replied, "they gave us a big surprise. We'd only been expecting the one."

"A nice surprise anyway, I'd bet," Elsie smiled.

"Ye looks right content, so I'll be shoving off," Mick said. "Shouldn't take too long, maybe an hour or so."

"Thanks for bringing me, Mick," Elsie replied.

"Ye're welcome, I'll be back fer ye soon," Mick answered.

As Mick rose to leave Mary appeared. "Ye ain't leavin' so soon, are ye?" She asked.

"Sorry, Ma'am, I just got a bit of business up the road, but Elsie here will be staying, if that's agreeable to ye," Mick answered.

"T'Is a pleasure to have a bit of company," Mary remarked. "Yer welcome to stay."

"Like I said, I got a bit of business to attend to, but perhaps I will stop fer a bit when I gets back," Mick blurted and reached for the door knob.

"I hope ye do," Mary said warmly. "And now, little Miss, it's time fer yer nap," she took the sleeping child from Elsie's arms and moved toward the bedroom. "Thank ye fer getting 'er to sleep. I'll be back in a bit."

"Would ye like some tea?" Jake asked awkwardly when he and Elsie were left alone.

"No, thank ye, I just wanted to have a word with ye," Elsie replied. "T'was a beautiful job you made of the cross fer Joe. How did ye know to carve an Easter lily, or the forget-me-nots?"

Jake rubbed his arm, "I spent some time with yer man last year. We got to talking and he'd tell me stories – lots of stories about ye, and forgive me, but also about the baby that died on Easter Sunday." Jake paused as the look of sadness crossed Elsie's face. He waited for a moment before he continued. "And he told about the wife he loved and the forget-me-nots he planned to plant in the spring," he finished quietly.

"But ye even knew the year he was born. Ye must have spent a lot of time with him to know that," she questioned.

"I can't rightly remember how that came up, but I remembered he was born the same year as my eldest brother," Jake replied. "I don't know why I remembered. I just did."

"I'm hoping to place it on his grave this week. It's been bothering me, his grave not being marked, proper like," she murmured. "He will have the most handsome marker in the cemetery." Elsie smiled at Jake.

"I'm so mighty sorry, Missus," Jake repeated his apology. "T'is my fault he died."

"That's something I wanted to talk to ye about, if yer willing," Elsie spoke so quietly Jake could just barely hear her. Just then Mary reappeared, and Jake breathed a sigh of relief.

"I am so sorry," Mary began, "she woke again just as I was about to put 'er down. It took a little bit to settle 'er. Would ye like some tea," she asked.

"Actually, I was just saying to Jake that I'd love fer him to show me around yer farm," Elsie said smoothly. "But a cup of tea afterward would be welcome." Elsie smiled sweetly up at the young woman.

Jake tried to hide his surprise. He hadn't expected that. "Of course, but there ain't much to see, just an old barn and the gardens," he blurted.

"Joe gushed on and on about what prime land ye have here and how much work ye've done," Elsie replied, "I'd truly love to see it."

Jake felt trapped and without a polite way to refuse he suddenly found himself leading the way outside and across the yard to the little barn.

Elsie gave a little cry of delight when she saw the bunk beds, yet to be delivered. 'These are beautiful. Ye made them?" She asked as she ran her hands over the bed rails. She stood back to admire them and her eyes traveled around the small structure, noticing how neat and tidy Jake kept everything.

"Yes, Ma'am. My friend, Paddy, well his aunt wanted 'em fer her young'uns," Jake replied. He stood rather stiffly waiting for Elsie to get to the reason for her sudden visit.

"My Joe, he was quite a carpenter. Well, I guess ye knows that. He made the cradles fer yer little ones," Elsie said.

"Yes, and I was grateful fer that. I'd of made 'em meself but between trying to make the house liveable and repairs to the barn and whatnot I didn't have a spare moment, and then the twins came early," Jake replied.

Elsie nodded, "Yes, Joe told me about all the work ye was doing. He was impressed with all ye got done with the old place, said ye were a hard worker.

"Ma'am, I don't mean to be rude, but why'd ye come here today?" Jake asked. "I knows it weren't just to size the place up."

Elsie smiled as she caressed the wood on the headboard. "Ye gets right to the point don't ye?" She paused, gathering her thoughts. "Do ye believe in dreams, in visions?" She asked.

Jake shuffled his feet uncomfortably. *There's no way she could know about all that*, he thought, aloud he said, "I don't rightly know."

"Joe and me, we were close, very close," Elsie began. "I don't want ye to think me crazy, but I had a dream about Joe. About the day he was hurt so bad." Elsie hesitated staring into the young man's eyes seeking to discover his reaction. When he simply held her gaze, she went on, "I don't know if I can explain it, but it seemed so real. He took me to the quarry to show me how it happened."

Tears welled up in her eyes and she swallowed before continuing. "There was a man working with him. Joe told me his name is Harry. The cart they were working was filled to the brim and when they tried to set it to rolling it was stuck fast and no matter how hard they pushed they couldn't get it to move. That man, Harry, went to get grease fer the wheels. Joe was alone, but my Joe, he was not one to sit idle. He got behind the cart and was heaving with all his might trying to get it moving. That's when it happened," Elsie's voice stopped as a lump in her throat refused to allow her to continue. Tears spilled down her cheeks. Jake stood silently watching her, words would not come as he watched the grieving widow struggle to regain her composure.

"Maybe, this was a mistake. I shouldn't have come," Elsie's voice was just above a whisper but Jake was listening intently.

"Missus, I can't tell ye how mighty sorry I am. T'is my fault yer husband died," Jake's voice was hoarse as he apologized again.

"No! T'is not yer fault." Suddenly Elsie understood why Joe had wanted her to tell Jake. "No!" she shook her head emphatically. "T'is not yer fault. I didn't understand at first but Joe, he was insistent I come here. He kept telling me to 'help Jake'," Elsie said. "He told me how he wasn't supposed to be on the track; about how worn out he'd been with all the long hours and how he wasn't thinking straight. So, ye see, it wasn't yer fault."

Suddenly, Jake dropped down on the little bench he'd left out after Paddy's visit. His face was white and it alarmed his visitor.

"Jake? Are ye alright?" Elsie asked worriedly. But Jake sat with his head down and his shoulders hunched. "Maybe I should leave," she whispered.

With that Jake looked up into the widow's eyes. "Joe talked a lot about ye," he began, "so much I feels almost like I already knew ye, even though we'd never met." He searched her face for a moment, "I woke up the other morn and kept hearing his voice telling me to 'help Elsie'," he told her seriously. "What are the odds we'd both hear 'im?"

Elsie shook her head in amazement. "That's so strange," she replied, "it's all so very strange."

"I thought I was losing me mind," Jake told her. "He was mighty insistent about it, too, but, I confess, I still have no idea what he meant."

"He talked about ye a lot, too. He talked about maybe seeing if ye might be interested in helping him craft a dory or two and lobster pots, said ye were a master carpenter. He had an idea maybe he could convince ye to go to work with him and the rest of the family. He wanted to go at lobster fishing. He had a lot of big plans and dreams, my Joe."

Jake said nothing concerning dories and lobster pots but tried to process all Elsie was telling him.

"Well, all this is mighty interesting. I needs to give it all some thought. Now, ye seen the barn, such as it is. Would ye care to see the gardens?" Elsie smiled and nodded and Jake held out his arm for her to take and guided her back outside. After a stroll around the property the two made their way back to the little cottage.

Mary was reaching up to take cups down from the open shelving above the sideboard when they entered. "Aw, here ye be, just in time, too, the tea's ready," she said as she half turned toward them. "I made figgy duff the other night, would ye like some?" She asked Elsie.

"I love figgy duff," Elsie answered. "I haven't had it in a long time."

"Mary makes the best figgy duff I ever ate," Jake put in, "best anywhere on the island, I allow."

"That is so good," Elsie agreed after her first taste. "Better than any I've made. What's yer secret?"

Soon the women were trading recipes and talking about gardening, babies, and the weather, among other things, while Jake sat listening quietly. Before they knew it, Mick was lightly knocking on the door. Jake rose to open the door.

"Here, let me fetch ye a cup of tea," Mary fairly sprang from her seat when Mick entered.

"If it's all the same to ye, I'll forego the tea this time," Mick answered. "As soon as ye're ready, I'd like to get going," Mick said to Elsie and he shifted uncomfortably on his feet. "I still got lots to do at home," he apologized to his hosts, "perhaps another time."

"Will ye come again?" Mary asked Elsie and then looked anxiously at Mick. "Ye're both welcome back any time. Ain't that right, Jake?" Jake nodded his agreement.

"I'd like that," Elsie replied. "What do ye think, Mick, could ye or one of the boys bring me back fer another visit?"

Mick nodded, "Sure, that could be arranged."

Elsie turned to Jake, "Thank ye fer showing me yer place. Ye sure have turned this old farm around," turning to Mary with a smile she said, "Thank ye so much for the tea and the figgy duff, it was delicious. I'd love to visit ye again. I'll give ye fair warning next time," she laughed. After saying their good-byes Mick and Elsie departed, both with much on their minds. The two spent the ride back home in comfortable silence, both lost in thought.

Chapter

25

While Elsie had visited Jake and Mary, Mick had spent the afternoon talking things over with Hank regarding the suspicious behaviour of the mining captain and his obvious surveillance of Jake. Hank was in agreement that something strange was going on.

"Sure, that's Billy, Charlie's cousin," Hank replied to Mick's description of one of the men who happened to be working near the crusher Jake was operating. "Ye should have a chat with Charlie, too. He knows pretty much every hand down to the quarry. Though I think he said something 'bout going up to see Constance today so he prob'ly ain't home."

"I'll see if I can have a private word with 'im tomorrow at work," Mick replied. "What do ye know of Harry's whereabouts? Have ye heard where he disappeared to?"

"Last I heard he was heading up the coast to go logging. It's a good few days away by horse and cart, a lot longer if ye walk it," Hank said, "and then who knows how long it'd take to find 'im out in the bush."

"I don't plan to go looking fer 'im, but maybe ye could help spread the word I needs to speak with 'im. T'was he that was working with Joe that day and he likely knows more about how it all happened," Mick told Hank. "I have a few questions only he can answer."

Hank nodded somberly. "I'll be sure to pass it along," he answered. "With a bit of luck, maybe he'll show up sooner rather than later."

"Yes, hopefully. I gots to get going. I have lots to do yet at home. See ye tomorrow," Mick replied.

Mick was thinking of the conversation with Hank as well as how to get at the truth of Harry's sudden disappearance after the accident. Elsie's dream made more sense the more he thought about it. It would explain why the mining inspector made such a slapdash inspection after Joe's death. If the captain knew more than he was letting on it would explain a lot of things. Jake's role in it all seemed to shrink more and more with each piece of information. All of this and more went through Mick's mind as he guided the horse and buggy over the hills to home. Elsie sensed Mick's preoccupation and sat quietly thinking over her visit with Jake and Mary and smiling at her memories of Joe's stories about the young couple. *It's easy to see why ye liked 'em both so much* Elsie thought as they bounced along. *They are good people. Aw, Joe, how I wish I could have been with ye when ye went to see 'em. T'would have made things simpler now.* Elsie smiled as she thought about the twins and Mary's obvious devotion to them and to her husband. Her thoughts turned again to the beautifully carved cross and Joe's yet unmarked grave.

"Mick, do ye think we could place that cross on Joe's gave next Sunday?" she asked.

Elsie's voice broke into Mick's thoughts. "What was that, Elsie?"

Elsie repeated her request. "I just thought, well, it's high time his grave had a proper marker," she spoke quietly, "and I'd like to have a small prayer when we place it."

Mick turned the buggy into their field. "I think that would be fine," he answered. "After the church service or before?"

"After church would work fine," she responded, "I was thinking I'd like to ask Jake and his wife to come, seeing as he carved it. Don't know how ye'd feel about that."

'I know I was awful mad at Jake. In fact, I blamed 'im fer Joe's death," Mick spoke slowly and carefully, "but there's things I learned since then, made me realize I was wrong to cast blame. If ye wants to have Jake and his wife there, that's fine by me."

Elsie placed a gloved hand on Mick's arm. "Thank ye, Mick, for everything. Ye're a good brother, always have been," she said.

"Aunt Elsie! Aunt Elsie!" Sarah called as they approached, "Come see Mouser, she caught a mouse and she's playing with it in the barn. Come see!"

Mick smiled as he watched his daughter excitedly take Elsie's hand to lead her into the barn and then turned his attention to removing harness and straps from the mare.

Hours later the family gathered for supper. Elsie had joined them, as had become her habit since Joe's death. After grace was said William surprised his family with an announcement.

"I went to see Hank last night," he began, "I asked his blessing and his permission to take Ginny as my wife." William glanced nervously at his father and then his mother. "Now, I'm asking fer yer blessing, too."

Fanny smiled widely at Mick and answered for them both, "We bin expecting it, and yer father and me couldn't be more pleased," she gushed. "When do ye plan to marry? It'll take time to cook all the food for the weddin'."

William blushed, "It ain't gonna be real soon. First off, I needs to build us a home. I ain't got money enough to take care of 'er, yet. I was thinking in another year, maybe longer," he answered.

"Have ye asked her yet?" Mick asked his son.

"Naw, I wanted to get 'er folks blessing, and yers as well," William replied.

"This is wonderful," Elsie piped up, "Ginny is such a sweet girl."

The meal continued with much laughter, teasing from the boys, and a lot of happiness. Mick's eyes sparkled with humor and pride as he watched and listened to the interchange. Phil and Jack offered their help in building a cabin for the young couple in between the usual tormenting and teasing. Sara and Rose were delighted that Ginny would soon be their sister for they had grown very fond of her. Even the baby was cooing as if he, too, celebrated the news. The meal was eaten and the chatter continued as plans were made.

"Well, William, what are ye waiting for? Go, ask the girl," Mick suddenly broke in with a grin.

In an unexpected and far from usual display, William jumped up and wrapped his arms around his father's neck, "Thanks, Da," he said. "I'm going now!" William glanced quickly at his mother and aunt and slipped quietly out the door.

Phil and Jack were making kissing sounds and hounding William like mad as they walked to work the next morning, but William no longer cared. Ginny had said 'yes' and he was happy enough to burst. His brother's taunts and teasing deflected off of him like water off a duck's back. Even the thoughts of the back-breaking labour ahead of him did nothing to sour his mood. His thoughts were dampened only when, turning at a bend in the road, the shadow of the surgery fell over them. *Sure wish Uncle Joe were here so's I could tell 'im,* William thought, *he would have loved Ginny, everybody does.* William allowed himself a few minutes of sadness before the future once again inserted itself and all the plans he was making took pride of place in his wonderings.

Chapter

26

Mick was quick to ask Charlie for a private word when he met him outside the cookhouse at the noon break. Nobody paid much attention, the two men were often seen going off to discuss something or other, many of the men assumed they were talking about the meetings.

"What's on yer mind?" Charlie asked when they'd walked a fair distance away.

"Well, b'y, it's like this, the other day I noticed the captain taking a walk around the crusher. He seemed mighty interested in Jake. I was talking with yer cousin, Billy. He tells me that the captain often takes a stroll by the crusher, sometimes more than once a day. He makes it a habit to glare at Jake when he gets close. Billy put it down to the fact that Jake's new, and is responsible fer Joe's death."

"Makes sense the boss would be keeping an eye on 'im," Charlie agreed, "I get the feeling you have other ideas."

"What if I tell ye that I was talking to someone who pointed out Harry's sudden departure after the accident, that maybe there's more reasons fer the captain to take an interest in Jake?" Mick asked. "Like maybe the equipment, the cart, in fact, was faulty?"

"What are ye saying, Mick?" Charlie asked.

"Look, man, I got no proof, but I was told the wheels on that there cart was seized up; that even with both Joe and Harry pushing with all their might they couldn't get the wheels to move," Mick said. "What would ye make of it? Do ye think it's possible?"

Charlie rubbed his chin as he considered the possibility. "Some of these carts are pretty old, brought out here from God knows where. Of course, it's possible, anything is possible."

"Look man, this has to stay between me and you, but if them wheels were seized it stands to reason that's why Joe was in the middle of the track. He was trying to push it to get it moving from behind. But where was Harry? And why'd he shove off so sudden-like? Nobody's seen him since Joe got killed. And why is the captain keeping such close tabs on Jake?" Mick rolled the questions quickly off his tongue as he watched Charlie's face closely for his reaction.

"Ye think Harry might be to blame fer Joe's death?" Charlie asked.

"No, that's not it. I ain't blaming nobody. I just would like a word with Harry, but he ain't around no more. Harry's a stand-up guy, if he'd had anything at all to do with Joe's getting hurt, he would have fessed up. I got no doubt about that. No, I ain't blaming Harry. I just wanted yer opinion and Hank mentioned ye would likely know the men working carts near the crusher Jake's on. It might be worthwhile to have a word with a few of 'em," Mick replied. "And that mining inspector's report was not too thorough, was it? If the cart was faulty, then the company is to blame, leastwise that's what I'm thinking. First off I'd like to know why the captain is so mighty interested in Jake."

Charlie's lips were pressed tight in a grim line. "Leave it with me, Mick. I'll find out who the men are. Who told ye about the cart? Could be we have a better case against the company if they'd come forward."

Mick shook his head, "I can't tell ye that. We ain't got no proof of it, not without Harry and he ain't here. But maybe Jake seen something, or one of the men. We gots to be careful how we handles it though."

"Fair enough. We'll get to the bottom of it one way or another. I promise ye that," Charlie replied. "Count on it!"

"It ain't good for us to be chatting 'bout it here," Mick said. "Do ye think ye could stop over to my place later, after work, or whenever it suits ye?"

"I'll find a reason to take a stroll over to Jake's crusher after we eat. I'll get the names of whoever works near 'im," Charlie answered. "I think I can stop by this evening, don't see why not."

"Thanks, Charlie, guess we best go eat before we gots to go back at it," Mick replied.

187

Charlie was as good as his word and made a display of himself 'accidentally' knocking over the pail of water set close by. "Vic, b'y, I'll be right back, just gonna refill this here bucket," he said. Grabbing the pail, he walked uphill to the stream to refill it. He stopped where he could easily see the crusher and the men who worked closest to it, taking note of who they were he filled the pail and returned to the cart he was working with Vic.

Mick and his family had just finished supper when Charlie drove his wagon into the field by their house.

"That'll be Charlie, Mick told them as he rose from the table. I asked 'im to come, I needs to have a chat with 'im." With that Mick left the house to meet Charlie outside.

"Thanks fer coming," Mick greeted his visitor. "Care to take a stroll?"

Charlie hopped down from the wagon seat and joined Mick as he headed off down a path toward the beach. The men did not speak but matched each other's stride across the field and down to the seashore.

"Well, mate, what did ye find out?" Mick asked as he turned toward Charlie.

The younger man was looking out across the bay as he spoke. "Found it interesting that Jake's friend, Paddy, seemed to be keeping an eye on 'im from the ledge above. Didn't catch sight of the captain, but there's two men besides Billy who may have noticed the captain lurking around. T'was Bob and Jacob working a cart not far from the crusher. And I can have a word with Billy, see what else he knows," Charlie reported. "Do ye think maybe Jake seen Joe and Harry working that day?" He asked.

"I don't know what to be thinking. I'm mighty curious about the captain's interest in Jake. Might be there's a reason he won't talk to us," Mick answered. "I dearly wish I could have a word with Harry, seems like he could shed some light on what happened that day. Nobody seems to know why he left so sudden like."

"Mind telling me who it was that told ye about the cart?" Charlie asked.

"T'was told to me in confidence, I can't say any more than I already told ye," Mick replied. "There ain't no proof, just supposing is all, but it seems like them wheels were seized up. That's why Joe and Harry couldn't budge it. That's why Joe was standing in the middle of the track trying to push it from behind. I dunno where Harry was when it happened. T'is all I knows. I'm thinking maybe Jake saw something."

"Do ye want me to talk to Bob and Jacob? It's not far from where I lives, I can stop by on me way home," Charlie asked. "If they seen the captain paying any special attention to Jake, they'd take notice."

"I don't want to put ye out," Mick began.

"Ain't no trouble at'all," Charlie replied. "I'll have a word with 'em and we can talk about it tomorrow, after we eat this time, won't take but a minute to fill ye in on whatever I finds out."

"Well b'y, I'd be much beholden to ye," Mick replied.

"Ye have to know, Joe, he was my best buddy. I'll do whatever it takes to make sure we gets to the bottom of it. His death ain't gonna be in vain," Charlie responded tightly.

Mick's serious eyes met Charlie's as he nodded and stuck out his hand. "I appreciates it more than ye know," he said, "I hopes ye knows yer welcome here any time and if there's anything we can do fer ye, anything a'tall, ye lets me know. I means it, anything a'tall," Mick spoke gravely as the men shook hands. "We gots to stick together, it's what Joe would want."

Charlie simply nodded and turned to head back up the slope. The men did not speak again, each had Joe very much in mind as they climbed the bank and walked back over the field.

I can't tell 'im it was a dream Elsie had. Might be he'd think I'm off me rocker, Mick thought as he made his way back to his cabin. *But that dream rings true to me. If only we could have a chat with Harry. I sure hope Jake knows something 'bout it. Could be that's why he ain't been wanting to talk to us. Joe sure seemed to think a lot of 'im. Could be Jake don't wanna cast Harry in a bad light.* Mick's thoughts continued in that vein as the men strode across the field, puzzling over Elsie's dream, Jake's role in it all, Harry's sudden disappearance, and the odd behaviour of the captain.

Joe, b'y, yer were always a God-fearing man. I sure wish I could talk this over with ye. If ye could find a way let us know what happened that day. Charlie gave himself a mental shake, *I ain't much of a praying man, but it seems like we sure could use some help from the Almighty. Joe, he'd know what to do. He knew how to talk to the Almighty, unlike meself.*

189

Joe, b'y, if yer listening, we needs yer help. Charlie grinned sardonically at himself. *And that's as close to a prayer as I'm likely to get.* He thought.

"Would ye like to come in," Mick asked as they neared the cabin.

"No, b'y, I best get going up the road so I can have a chat with the b'ys before it gets much later," Charlie responded.

'Well, I sure appreciate ye comin'. See ye tomorrow then," Mick said.

He stood and watched as Charlie climbed onto the wagon and continued to watch as he drove out of the field and onto the road leading out of the community before turning to go in the house. From the yard he could see his sons working in the barn while his daughters played outside.

"Everything alright?" Fanny asked when he came in.

"All's well, just a bit of peculiar behaviour on the part of the captain I needed Charlie's help with," Mick told her. "There's naught fer ye to worry about."

"Elsie was telling me she'd like to place the cross on Joe's grave this Sunday after church. She said she'd already talked to ye 'bout it. Are ye okay with Jake being there?" Fanny asked.

"T'is fine by me, Fan, don't ye worry none 'bout that. We should tell the b'ys though. I haven't said nothing to 'em and they should be told. Phil and William will understand, but what about Jack?"

"He's been spending a lot of time with Elsie. I imagine she's helping him see things a mite more clearly," Fanny told him. "But it couldn't hurt fer ye to have a word with 'im too."

"Where is he now, I'll go see to it right away," Mick said.

"I believe he's out there mucking out Elsie's chicken coop," Fanny replied.

"I'll go see how he's making out," Mick told her. "I may just give 'im a hand."

The girls came running to their father as he strode across the yard.

"Da, our kitty caught another mouse," Sara excitedly told him. "That makes three just this week. Soon she'll be chasing off the rabbits, too." Rose was also nodding her head in agreement. "Well, that is good news," he replied.

Mick stooped down looking his youngest daughter in the eye. "Are ye helping yer sister look after that kitty?" He asked.

"Yes'm, Da. I helped feed 'er today." Rose nodded solemnly. "Hers getting bigger. Come see, Da, come see," the little girl tugged at his hand.

"Tell ye what, I gots to go help Jack over ta Elsie's. If yer both still out here when I get done ye can show me then, alright?" Mick stood and ruffled Rose's hair. "I'm some proud of ye girls," he said, looking at Sara. "Yer doing a great job with the kitten, and I'm some glad she ain't got into the house. Ma wouldn't like that."

Sara smiled up at her father, "I promised 'er Mouser wouldn't come inside. And she ain't." Mick smiled at his eldest daughter, "Well, go on and play, I won't be too long and then the two of ye can show me yer cat." Sara grabbed her sister's hand, "Alright, Da, but please, please, come see 'er when yer all done." Mick smiled and nodded then stood to walk the short distance to Elsie's barn.

"Jack?" Mick called out as he entered the small structure. "You in here?" Mick's eyes took a few minutes to adjust to the dimly lit space.

"Hey, Da, I'm over here," Jack answered from the corner of the barn where he was piling the manure he'd shoveled out of the coop. "Just piling the hen poop over here. Aunt Elsie wants me to spread it over her garden when there's enough."

"Are ye about finished? Do ye need a hand?" Mick asked.

"I gots the coop all cleaned out," Jack replied. "I just needs to scrape all this back into the corner like Uncle Joe always did. Almost done."

"Whew, smells some sweet don't it?" Mick laughed and leaned against the barn door. "I needs to talk to ye. I'll wait."

Jack wrinkled his nose, "Sweet, it ain't," he returned, "but it does make fer good fertilizer."

"That it does," Mick agreed, watching as his son worked. "Elsie appreciates all yer help, too. And yer Ma and me are mighty proud of ya."

"Anything wrong, Da? What is it ye wants to talk to me about?" Jack asked.

"It will keep til yer finished," Mick replied. "We don't often get a chance to talk, man to man. Just wanted to have a chat is all. Nuddin fer ye to worry over."

Jack hurried to finish off his chore and hung the shovel back on the pegs Joe had pounded into the wall. "Got a minute to come have a look at the pig, Da? He sure is getting big." Jack walked out into the yard with Mick following to the pig stye attached to the back of the barn. Jack had shoveled fresh hay into the pen and cleaned out the manure as well.

"Well, Elsie will have more pork than she can eat," Mick remarked as he looked at the animal. "Ye weren't kidding, that pig is twice the size he was a month back."

"What do ye want to talk to me about, Da?" Jack asked, his curiosity getting the better of him.

"No beating 'round the bush, eh." Mick said as he nudged Jack's shoulder with his own. "Well, it's like this, ye knows Elsie found that cross that Jake made and she's fixing to have it put on yer Uncle's grave after church on Sunday. She'd like all the family to be there with 'er."

"Sure, Da, that ain't no trouble," Jack answered, "is that all ye wanted me fer?"

"Well, Jackie-boy, there's a mite more to it than that. She'd like fer Jake and his wife to come as well and I didn't know how ye'd feel 'bout that." Mick said slowly. "So, what do ye think?"

"Da, I was pretty mad at Jake. I thought he killed Uncle Joe, ye know? Then, when he come here, I felt kinda sorry fer 'im," Jack began. "I been talking a lot 'bout it all with Aunt Elsie. She doesn't believe Jake killed 'im, at least not on purpose. She says it was a horrible accident and I should forgive 'im. I didn't think I could, but now, well, Aunt Elsie says there's much more to it than that. She didn't want to tell me any more. She says it wasn't ever Jake's fault. She was very firm 'bout that. Then she told me stories Uncle Joe had told 'er 'bout Jake and his wife and their babies. So, now, well, if Aunt Elsie wants 'em there that's all that matters. Ain't that right?" Jack finished.

Mick's hand squeezed Jack's shoulder, "Yer a better man than many twice yer age," he told his son. "Now, it might be that they don't even come, I dunno if they will or not."

"Is there anyone else gonna be there?" Jack asked.

"No, my son, it will just be our family besides Jake and Mary and maybe their babies. I s'pose they can't leave babies all alone, can they?"

"Aunt Elsie told me 'bout the babies, and about how nice Mary is," Jack replied, "and of course them babies can't be left alone. They're much too small fer that."

"Alright, then, so she also wants some prayers said at the grave when we puts the marker up. But it ain't gonna be like the funeral, it will be short.

I expect it may be a bit hard on yer aunt though. Are ye gonna be strong enough to face that?" Mick questioned his son.

Jack stood quietly, not answering right away. "I kinda wish it'd be just us, but if Aunt Elsie wants Jake there, well it's up to 'er. Yes, Da, I'll be fine. I ain't no baby," Jack straightened his shoulders and his spine as he spoke.

Mick patted his son's back, "That's good, son, that's good. Now, I better get over to our barn cuz yer little sisters wants me to see that cat of theirs. Why don't ye come with me?" Jack nodded and they walked back across the yard to their own little barn.

Chapter

27

Paddy and Jake were surprised the next day when Mick approached their table at the cookhouse.

"I come to invite ye to join us at the cemetery after church next Sunday. Elsie would like ye and yer wife to be there when we place that cross ye made," Mick said gazing at Jake.

"Well, b'y, I don't have no way of getting the wife there. I ain't got no buggy or wagon of any sort," Jake's surprise was evident on his face and he stuttered over the words.

"If ye wants to go, I can come get ye with me wagon," Paddy put in. "if ye wants to."

Jake didn't answer. He was thrown by the sudden friendliness Mick displayed. He paused for a few moments before he replied, "Well now, I will have to talk to the wife. I will let ye know tomorrow, if that's all right."

Mick nodded and, the invitation extended, took his leave.

Paddy elbowed Jake, "What was that all about?"

"Well b'y, I told ye about Joe's wife visiting us. Mary was so taken with 'er. I made a cross fer Joe's grave and Elsie came to thank me fer it." Jake answered. "I dunno if I wants to spend any more time with the Kellys though, might be an excuse to question me and ye knows how that goes. I can't be seen talking to 'em, in case the captain finds out."

"It's just my opinion b'y, but I don't think that's likely as long as the women folk are with ye," Paddy replied. "And ye said yerself how Mary needs another woman to talk to, could be good fer 'er to have a friend. Elsie and Joe are both held in mighty high esteem round here."

"I dunno b'y, I dunno," Jake spoke quietly. "I'll have to give it some thought."

Paddy nodded, "I will be going to church anyway so if ye wants a lift in the wagon let me know. I needs time to clean out the back so ye can ride in it." Jake nodded but made no other comment.

At the end of the work day Jake was mulling over the invitation as he walked home. He hadn't yet been to the little church. For the first while he'd simply had too much work to do fixing up the little house and barn but he remembered Joe trying to convince him to join the community for worship. He'd had a built-in excuse, with Mary pregnant at the time and no conveyance of any kind it was just too far for her to walk. Since then, the twins had come and then Joe died. Mary had been after him about it, wanting to have the twins baptized. So far, he'd held her off, but if they went to the cemetery, they'd also have to go to church with Paddy. Jake wasn't sure he wanted to do that.

He had no love for church, his memories of it were not such as would encourage him to do so. He remembered telling Joe about his feelings once, about how he could see God in all of nature and how he felt the church saw it as sinful. *"Aw, Jake, b'y, there's naught that's sinful in it. There's a bit of the creator in the created, even trees and wildlife. How can ye look at all the beauty this land holds and not see the Creator in it?"* Jake remembered Joe saying.

Jake remembered the old pastor at the church he'd attended with his parents and the many fire and brimstone sermons the man had preached. Those sermons had done nothing to inspire him, or make him want to continue the practice once he'd grown up.

And then there's the worry 'bout the captain finding out I'd spent time with the Kellys. He was none too pleased when I told 'im I talked to them that one time, Jake thought. *No, best to steer clear of Elsie and the Kelly clan. I can't see any other way round it.* With a decision made Jake felt a bit better and he hastened his steps home to Mary and to his tiny daughters.

Jake was surprised to see Paddy's wagon outside the barn as he crossed the field to his home, and even more so to find Paddy sitting at the kitchen table visiting with Mary.

"Hey, Jake, sorry, if I'd known I was coming here I would've offered to bring ye home," Paddy began, "I no sooner got in the door than me aunt was insisting I come right over and get them bunks."

Mary was beaming at Jake, "Paddy tells me we're going to church on Sunday," she said.

Jake glared at his friend, none too pleased he'd let the cat out of the bag. "I don't want to go to no church. Paddy shouldn't a been filling yer head with that nonsense," Jake gruffly replied. "What the hell are ye at?" He asked turning on his friend.

"Mary wants to have yer little ones baptized. She was just telling me," Paddy started to say.

"It ain't none of yer business," Jake growled, cutting Paddy off.

Paddy grinned unrepentantly, "Be that as it may, I think ye'd better talk to yer wife afore ye goes biting me head off."

"If Paddy is willing to come get us, we will be going," Mary broke in stubbornly. "I have not set foot inside a church since ye brung me out here and I miss it. And, ye, Jake Fitzgerald, will be comin' with me!"

"I didn't mean to cause no trouble," Paddy interrupted. "Let me just get them bunks and I'll clear out of here."

"Ye sit right there, Paddy, ye ain't going nowhere," Mary commanded. "I gots supper ready and by God, the two of ye are gonna have it now while it's hot. I ain't finished with either one of ye!"

Jake and Paddy exchanged a look as Mary moved around the kitchen banging plates and pans and letting them know how angry she'd grown. Neither dared to make a peep while Mary stomped back and forth putting dishes and cutlery on the table. Finally, she moved the huge pot of soup from the stove onto the table and began to ladle it out into bowls.

"Go, wash yer hands," she barked at the men, "and don't be long!"

Mary took a deep breath as she settled herself at the table and waited for the men to come back in. She willed herself to be calm and said a prayer to the angels for help. *Angels of God*, her thoughts whispered, *give me patience and please, give me the right words.*

She was sitting quietly when Jake walked gingerly through the door, followed by Paddy. Mary didn't speak as Jake pulled out the chair at the head of the table. Paddy climbed behind the table to sit on the bench there. Neither man spoke but waited to see what came next.

"Bow yer heads," Mary instructed them. "Dear Father of all," Mary began the blessing, "we thank ye fer this food. May it give strength to our bodies as ye give strength to our spirits. Amen."

Mary lifted a spoon and looked at the two men who awkwardly sat waiting. "Well, go on. Eat!"

"I'm sorry fer causing ye trouble," Paddy hesitantly began, "I didn't mean to cause any grief."

Mary turned toward him, "Ye ain't done nuddin' wrong. Ye just eat yer soup. Have some bread. It's fresh, I made it this morning."

Another quiet lull descended as the trio ate in awkward silence. Paddy shifted his feet under the table willing the meal to be over quickly so he could make his escape.

Jake cleared his throat, "I'm sorry, too, Mary. We will talk about church later."

"No, Jake, me mind is made up. Them girls are going to be raised right, and that means taking 'em to church. I ain't discussin' it. I am tellin' ye. We are going to church on Sunday with Paddy."

"Thanks a lot, Paddy. Now, look what ye done," Jake growled.

"Jake Fitzgerald, ye leave off Paddy," Mary spoke quietly, but determinedly. "This ain't got nuddin' to do with Paddy. I been after ye to take me to church fer a while now. We can talk about it, as long as ye knows me mind is made up. It ain't Paddy's fault he offered to take us in his wagon. How could he know yer feelins on the matter? Ye don't talk."

Mary then turned to Paddy. "Did he ever tell ye his feelings on church and God and such?" She asked.

Paddy looked from Mary to Jake and back again. "Well, ma'am, the subject ain't ever come up, truth be told."

"She's right, it ain't yer fault," Jake told Paddy. "I guess we'll be joining ye on Sunday."

Satisfied, Mary sat back in her chair. "Now, that's sorted, do ye want tea?"

After supper Paddy followed Jake out to the barn to load the bunk beds onto the back of the wagon.

"I am sorry, Jake. I didn't realize church was a sore spot with ye," Paddy apologized.

"What's done is done. I would'a had to deal with it sooner or later," Jake replied. "I wish ye hadn't mentioned it, but t'is done, so . . ."

"I ain't much of a man fer talking 'bout God and stuff," Paddy said, "I wondered why ye never seemed to be at church but didn't give it a lot of thought. Knew ye were busy fixing the place up, then the twins came, then all this with Joe . . ." Paddy's voice trailed off.

"It's been hard going, that's fer sure," Jake answered. "I just worry 'bout the captain finding out if I spends any time at'all with Joe's family."

"He ain't ever stepped foot in the church, far as I know," Paddy responded, "Like as not he won't hear nuddin' 'bout it."

"Hope yer right, b'y," Jake said, "It will cost me job if he does, and maybe more if he tells folks 'bout my Mi'kmaq blood."

"Ye ever notice how many folk 'round here keeps to 'emselves?" Paddy asked. "Could be there's reason fer that. Maybe there's more with Indian blood than we knows about."

"Could be," Jake replied, "Ma always said there were a lot more than just us, but not many would let it be known."

"Fer good reason, too," Paddy said. "Well, let's get these beds on here and I'll shove off. Morning will come afore we knows it."

The week passed by quickly and before he knew it Jake was donning his best shirt for church. He was nervous, but Mary was happy as a lark singing in spring.

"Paddy's here," Jake called to his wife.

"Here, take Liza," Mary ordered. "I just have to get my hat."

"Morning," Paddy greeted. "I fixed up the back fer ye, Jake, thought Mary could sit up here with me."

Jake balanced Liza on one arm and passed a basket up to Paddy to place on the seat. "Put that in the middle so's Mary can lay one of the babies in it," he instructed. "She can't hold 'em both at once."

Paddy did as he was told and then jumped down to help Mary up onto the wagon seat.

"Morning, Paddy," Mary greeted him, turning to Jake she said, "Can ye hold 'em both 'til I get settled?" She asked.

Jake held a twin in each arm as Paddy helped Mary climb aboard the wagon. She reached down for one of her infants and settled Lily in the basket and covered her with a blanket then held her arms out for Liza. Before long they were on their way with Jake sitting on clean hay and holding tight to the wagon sides. Paddy eased the horse along at a slow trot, being careful to keep a close watch on Mary and her children as they clopped along. Mary looked eagerly around her. "It's such a beautiful morning," she commented as they drove over the rough roads, "Doesn't the bay look lovely?"

"It does, indeed," Paddy answered. "It sure is pretty country."

Conversation was sparse as they went. Jake was very nervous and Mary, lost in the beauty of the shoreline, was content to drink it all in. Paddy concentrated on avoiding the worse bumps in the road and was preoccupied with making sure no harm came to the woman beside him, or her little ones.

It seemed to Jake like all eyes were on him and his family as they entered the little church. It made him uncomfortable as heads turned to look. Mary simply nodded and smiled and seemed for all the world to be in her element, in Jake's eyes at least. They found a pew near the back and seated themselves. Jake's eyes were downcast and he didn't notice Elsie, Fanny and Mick and all their children coming into the chapel. Elsie paused to greet Mary as they went by and smiled at Jake when he lifted his eyes. It made Jake feel a little less conspicuous as they waited for the service to begin.

The service was not near as bad as Jake had been dreading and soon the last hymn was sung and people were standing, getting ready to leave. The morning was fine and people visited in little groups in the churchyard. Jake was standing with Mary, each holding an infant, when Elsie brought the pastor over to meet them. Jake spoke little but listened as Mary made plans to have their daughters baptized.

"What you do ye think of that?" Pastor McGrath asked Jake.

Jake was embarrassed to be caught day dreaming. "Sorry, what do I think about what?" He asked.

He was surprised when the Pastor began to laugh. "Not much interested in church things, are ye? I was asking what ye think of having yer children baptized? Are ye willing to go along with yer wife? Are ye willing to start coming to services and raise them young'uns in the church?"

Jake looked at the pastor and could swear the man had winked when Mary wasn't looking. He could definitely detect some merriment in the man's eyes.

"Well, sir, if that's what Mary has 'er heart set on, I ain't about to stand in 'er way," Jake answered. "If I can find a way to get us here fer services, we'll be here."

"That's fine then, ye ain't unlike a lot of young men," the cleric remarked. Smiling at Mary he said, "Maybe ye can make a God-fearing man out of 'im yet."

Mary smiled back. "We'll have to talk over who we wants to ask to be Godparents to the girls. We ain't discussed it yet. Can we see ye after worship next week to set a date fer them to be baptized?"

"I'll look forward to it," the pastor answered. "I need to have a word with yer friend, Mrs. Kelly. See ye next week."

While they'd talked the churchyard had emptied and only the Kelly family remained. Jake and Mary remained where they were as the minister met with Elsie and her family. Paddy joined them and teased Jake about his new position in the congregation.

"Ye can leave off tormenting Jake, Mister," Mary scolded him good-naturedly, "Or we ain't gonna ask ye to be Godfather to our girls! Ain't that right, Jake?" Mary asked as she turned to her husband.

"Well, aren't ye full of surprises?" Jake asked in turn. "I ain't given any thought to any of it. But seeing as we ain't got nobody but Paddy to thank fer being here in the first place, I guess he'll do, that is, if he wants to."

Paddy face was a picture of consternation. "I ain't never been good round small ones. Don't know if I'd make much of a Godfather, but I'm honoured to be considered," he blustered.

Mary laughed; happy everything was working out as she'd hoped. "I guess ye will do. But we needs an answer," she said.

"Answer's, yes, of course. I'd be honoured," Paddy replied, blushing.

Jake glanced across the churchyard where Elsie was talking earnestly with the Reverend McGrath and he grew somber. He recognized the burlap-covered bundle Mick held.

"Paddy, b'y, if it ain't too much of an imposition, would ye mind waiting fer us? The Kellys want us to join 'em while they place a marker on Joe's grave," Jake explained.

"Don't mind a'tall, a'tall," Paddy answered. Jake had already explained the reason for the invitation.

"Mind if I lay the babies in the basket in yer wagon? They sure are growing fast, and getting heavy," Mary remarked as she repositioned the sleeping babe in her arms.

"Sure thing," Paddy replied. "Why don't I just go bring the wagon over so's it's closer to the cemetery?"

Jake nodded and Paddy strode off just as Mick was walking over to talk to Jake and Mary.

"If yer about ready," Mick said, "we're about to go visit Joe's grave and place the cross ye made."

"I was just about to settle the twins in their basket," Mary answered, "we'll be right there."

Jake took Mary's hand as they followed Mick into the graveyard. They paused long enough for introductions to Mick's wife and family before the little group walked over to stand in a circle around the grave.

"Mick, if yer ready," the pastor began. Mick unwrapped the wooden cross and moved to place it at the head of Joe's grave. "If ye'll all bow yer heads," he continued. Elsie grasped Fanny's hand tightly as the prayer began:

"God, creator of all, as we mark Joe's grave with this cross, we remember how ye marked his soul fer all eternity. Joe was a good man, a good husband, brother, uncle, neighbour, and friend. His untimely death reminds us all of how short life can be and how we are not privy to know when or how our end might come. In yer mercy, help us remember our days are numbered and only ye know when the last one will be. As we mark Joe's grave with this cross, symbol of the great sacrifice ye made fer all yer people, let us remember that we, too, are marked in baptism. Let us live our lives in such a way as all will know we are people of God, just as yer servant, Joseph Kelly, was observed to be. Amen."

"Amen!" came the answer from each of the people gathered.

"Thank ye, Pastor," Elsie said quietly. The minister nodded and made his exit as the men in the family each took a turn pounding the marker into the ground. Once the cross was firmly in place the family stood again in a circle around the grave. "Thank ye, Jake, Mary, fer coming," Elsie said. "Does anyone have anything they want to say?" She asked.

"I miss ye, Uncle Joe," Sara piped up, surprising her family, "ye were the best uncle, ever."

One after another made similar remarks, praising the man they knew and loved so well. Jake shifted uncomfortably as Elsie turned her attention to him.

"There's a reason I asked Jake and Mary to join us here. Firstly, it was because it was Jake that carved this beautiful cross to mark 'is grave. But more importantly, Joe considered Jake a friend. I know that first when this tragedy happened many held Jake to blame for Joe's death. That was wrong. It was an accident, a terrible and tragic accident. So, I would like us all to offer Jake our hands in peace and forgiveness. It's what my Joe wants and more than that, I know he'd like us to welcome Jake and Mary and their family into our homes and into our hearts as friends, just as Joe befriended them." Elsie finished her short speech and turned her gaze on each of her family members one by one.

Jake was saved from a response by the sudden wailing of the babies laying nearby in Paddy's wagon. Mary hurried to the wagon with Jake and Elsie following on her heels.

Paddy was quick to hand a screaming child down to her mother while Jake climbed up onto the wagon to retrieve the second twin.

"Please, may I hold her?" Elsie asked and Jake handed the child down to her. The women were crooning and rocking the babies and the rest of the Kelly clan slowly followed them, Fanny holding her own little son as they stood near the wagon.

Elsie smiled at the little face and the eyes that stared trustingly up at her. "Aren't they just the sweetest?" She asked Fanny.

"Yes, they are precious," Fanny answered.

Elsie turned to Mary, "Please, won't ye come have tea with us, and a bite of dinner?" She asked.

Mary looked at Jake and then Paddy, unsure of how to answer.

"I've been planning this all week and I'd greatly appreciate if ye all would join us. You, too, Paddy," Elsie pleaded.

"I could eat," Paddy replied, "but I'll leave that up to Jake."

"Please, Jake?" Elsie turned imploring eyes to the young man.

"We really ought to get home," Jake replied but the look of disappointment in Mary's eyes changed his mind. "Well, we can't stay too long, but I guess it would be all right. Yes, thanks."

"Well, then, let's go," Elsie enthused. "I don't know about ye lot but I am famished!"

"Lots of room in the back of me wagon, if anyone wants a lift," Paddy invited.

"Don't mind if I do," Phil responded, "Sooner we gets back, the sooner I can eat. C'mon Jack, William, let's go."

"I don't wanna walk back all alone," Sara put it.

"Well, c'mon over here, then," Phil laughed. "It'll be fun." He lifted his little sister into the back of the wagon before climbing in behind her.

Jake was overcome by a great wave of shyness as the Kelly boys, along with their sister, joined him in the back of the wagon.

"My name is Sara," the little girl introduced herself, "May I see yer babies? I'm good with babies. I help Ma with Jimmy all the time."

Jake smiled at the little girl. "I'm Jake, and this here is Liza," he told her as he lifted a corner of the blanket, "and that one is Lily," he said nodding toward the basket next to Mary.

Jake was grateful for Sara's chatter as they rode over the field to Elsie's small cottage. He was very much a homebody and not given to visiting much. Like many in the village, he was in the habit of keeping to himself, and he was worried about being questioned by the Kelly menfolk. He was counting on Paddy to run interference during their unplanned visit.

It wasn't long before Paddy was circling his wagon to leave it where Mick indicated. It seemed Jake and Mary were not the only ones to be surprised as Elsie and Fanny ushered the family and their guests into Elsie's little yard. Apparently, the women had planned this all week and the only other one to know was Mick.

"William, Phil, I needs ye to go to the house and haul over a bench," Fanny ordered her sons. "And don't be long, dinner is about ready."

The men stood outside while Fanny and Elsie went inside, taking Mary with them. Fanny popped her head outside, "Jack will ye bring over Jimmy's cradle? And Paddy, we'll likely need that basket fer Mary's little ones," she said.

Jack raced to catch up with his brothers while Paddy strode to the wagon to get the required basket.

Mick was pointing out various features of the little farm, including his own place and barn. Jake made few comments and simply nodded as Mick spoke. He was obviously ill at ease and Mick did his best to help the younger man relax.

"What a pretty little place," Mary complimented as she looked around the little house.

"Joe was handy and liked his comforts," Elsie smiled. "Come, have a seat," she said gesturing to the settee.

Mary sat balancing a twin on each arm and watched as the two women worked.

"Here ye go, Mary," Paddy said as he stood in the doorway with the basket in his arms. "Where'd ye like me to set it?"

"Put it right here by me," Mary replied, "thanks, Paddy."

Paddy made a hasty retreat as Mary settled the babies in the large basket. "Can I do something to help?" She asked after the babies were settled.

"Would ye mind slicing this bread?" Elsie asked, Mary moved to the sideboard to cut the bread while the women worked to set food and dishes on the table.

"I thought William and Phil could sit there on the settee to eat. Is that all right, Fan?"

"That'll work," Fanny answered. "Once the boys get here with that bench there'll be room at the table fer the rest of us."

"What about Jimmy? Where we gonna put him?" Sara asked. She was sitting in the rocker with her baby brother in her arms with Rose beside her. "Jack's bringing his cradle over, he'll be here in a minute," Fanny answered.

Soon the little dinner party was underway and the younger children were regaling their visitors with stories of Mouser and her stellar performance at keeping rodents away from barn and gardens. Rose had been shy at the start but was quick to follow Sara's lead and made many observations that kept the meal light and amusing. Jake, Paddy, and Mary were entertained by the girls' stories and the family's responses. Jake watched Mary and thought how it was the right decision to come after all. *She seems right in 'er glory,* Jake thought, and looking at Paddy, *and he seems right at home, too.*

"Aunt Elsie, Ma, that was some good," William said, "But if ye don't mind, I think I'll shove off now. I wants to go see Ginny, if ye don't need me fer anything else."

Mick and Fanny shared knowing looks. "Go on, b'y, just be back in time to do yer chores," Mick answered.

"William and Ginny recently became engaged," Fanny told Mary, "They're hoping to be married in a year or so."

William accepted well wishes and congratulations as he made his escape.

"Ma, can we go outside and play now?" Sara asked.

"Yes, go on and play, but mind ye go change into yer play clothes first," Fanny replied.

The group continued to sit at table trading stories and getting to know one another. Jake was rather quiet, as was his nature, but the welcoming generosity helped him relax. He answered the questions put to him and breathed a sigh of relief when the tragic circumstances surrounding Joe's death were never raised. Mary mentioned the letter asking for her sister to come and Elsie was delighted to learn her family was acquainted with Mary's.

"Perhaps, if Eleanor and Edward come for a visit, they could bring Haldi with them," she suggested. "I don't know if they can come. They have six children of their own and Edward runs a saw mill and is busy most of the time, but it can't hurt to ask. I will write to them."

"That would be a Godsend," Mary smiled back at her new friend, "and a comfort if she could travel with an escort. I'm sure Ma and Pa would feel better about letting 'er come if that were the case."

"I can't promise anything, but it's worth the attempt," Elsie replied.

"I understand you're quite a hand at carpentry," Mick said to Jake, "Elsie was telling us what a fine job ye did of a set of bunk beds. I remember Joe going on about yer workmanship. Joe, he liked woodworking too. He made most everything in here."

"Y'is, we had many a chat about wood workin'," Jake replied. "I woulda liked to have built somethin' with 'im."

"Joe had a talent, that's fer sure. I ain't as handy, but I knows my way around a hammer and saw," Mick retorted. "T'was wondering if ye ever did any boat building? Me and Joe and a few others were talking about maybe making a few dories to go at lobster fishin."

"Yeah, me and Joe had talked some about that," Jake replied.

"Have ye ever made any boats?" Mick asked.

"Just the one and it was a canoe, not a dory," Jake answered. "Still, it can't be too hard. Have to shape the bow and that'd take a bit of effort, but I don't see why a few good men can't pull it off."

"How many dories are ye wanting to build?" Paddy asked.

"Well, there's me and me sons, Charlie, Vic, and yerselves, if yer interested," Mick replied. "I hear there's talk of opening a lobster cannery, and if that happens it'd be good to be ready, to have the boats and lobster traps we needs to make a decent living at it. I'd say we'd need at least four good dories. Joe and me had one that we shared, used it to go jiggin' fer cod, and other fish. I knows a good bit about lobster fishin'. Me father and grandfather used to go lobster fishin'. Whadda 'bout ye, Paddy? Would ye be interested?"

"I think that's a mighty fine idea, y'is, b'y, ye knows I'd be mighty interested. Would beat slogging rocks at the quarry, eh?" said Paddy.

"The other thing is, have either of ye ever fished fer lobster?" Mick wanted to know.

"Mostly just fer the table, to feed the family," Jake put in, "And me and Paddy used to go out now and then when we was lads."

"We'd need an awful pile of lumber to make boats and lobster pots, too," Mick said thoughtfully. "Could be something to put food on the table and clothes on our backs. We should all get together to figure out how we might get started."

"Sounds mighty fine to me," Paddy replied, "whadda ye think, Jake?"

"I needs to give it some thought. I am kept mighty busy as it is between the quarry and work I needs to get done at home."

"Well, let's let it be fer now, I ain't expectin' to get right to it, but t'would be good to have plans," Mick answered. "Let us know what ye decides."

"We sure will," Paddy answered for them both, "But, I needs to get going. Thank ye fer the dinner, t'was some good," he told Elsie.

"Y'is, thanks very much," Jake nodded at his hosts, "Ready, Mary?"

Mary added her thanks and the trio stood to leave. "Come visit any time," Elsie answered. "I'm so glad ye came."

"T'was nice to meet ye all," Fanny said. "Hope ye will come again."

"The pleasure was all ours," Mary answered, "t'would be nice to have ye come to our place. "Ain't that right, Jake?"

"Sure, maybe we can have ye all fer supper one day soon," Jake replied.

"Sounds good," Fanny smiled back at the young couple, "Let us know when."

"We will. Thanks again," Mary said, "We better get going though, I have supper to get ready."

"Wait, wait," Rose came running, "I gots some flowers fer ye," she said holding a bunch of wildflowers tightly in her small fist.

"Aren't they some purdy? Thank ye so much, Rose," Mary responded.

"Are ye going to come visit us again?" Sara piped up from behind Rose.

"That would be very nice," Mary answered. "And perhaps ye can come to our house one day soon."

"When?" Rose wanted to know.

"I ain't sure exactly when, but soon," Mary told the little girl. "We have to go home now, so I can put these flowers in some water. We'll see you again, soon, I hope."

Mary handed the basket with the babies in it to her husband as Paddy helped her climb into the wagon. Jake carefully handed up the basket to Paddy and watched as Mary settled the blankets more snugly around the infants.

"Thanks again, Fanny, Elsie," she called as Paddy tapped the reins to get the horse moving.

Chapter

28

H arry fell backward as the tree he'd been sawing recoiled and snapped, trapping the bucksaw and slamming him to the ground.

"Oh, me gosh, are ye all right?" Harry's partner, Rob, asked rushing over to the fallen man. "Here grab me hand, I'll pull ye out."

Harry didn't answer as he lay winded on the ground with the heavy tree partly pinning him down.

"Harry, b'y, are ye all right," Rob's voice rose in fright. It took several minutes before he got an answer.

"God damned tree," Harry groaned. "Can ye lift this thing off me?"

Rob moved around Harry and grabbing the trunk he heaved and Harry was able to crawl out from under the giant spruce, before falling back again.

"Are ye all right, mate?" Rob asked again.

"Dunno yet, give me a second to catch me breath," Harry grumbled in return. He remained laying still for several minutes. He gave a great groan of pain as he tried to sit uprightand fell back again. "Somethin' ain't right," he told Rob, "I think maybe I broke something, can't breathe," he wheezed. "It 'urts to breathe."

"Think ye can stand if I helps ye?" Rob asked. Harry's gray eyes were filled with pain as he stared at his partner.

"Won't know 'til I tries," he answered.

Rob leaned down grasping Harry's left arm, "Ready?" he asked. At Harry's nod Rob hauled Harry to his feet. Harry stood gasping heavily as he stood stock-still waiting to see if his legs would hold him.

"Where's it hurting?" Rob asked.

"T'is in me chest. Legs are all right, I think," Harry answered. "But me goddamn chest feels like it's on fire."

"Can ye walk?" Rob asked.

Harry took a step forward, both arms hugging his chest. "It 'urts like a son of a bitch," he told Rob, "Like someone swung a frigging sledge hammer at me chest."

"Here, lean on me, mate," Rob grabbed Harry's arm and pulled it over his shoulders. "Let's just go slow, over there by that pile of logs." Rob helped the hurt man until he could walk. Finally, he was leaning against the wood pile.

"How are ye doing?" Rob asked.

"Jist 'urts something awful, 'ard to breathe," Harry told him.

"Are ye hurt anywhere else?" Rob wanted to know.

Harry laughed, then groaned again, "Besides me chest, just me pride. Now 'ow in the devil did that 'appen?" Harry asked.

"Sometimes these buggers have a mind of their own," Rob answered. "It should have fallen due East, not to the frigging North. Let's just rest here fer a spell then we'll get ye down to the camp." Harry nodded his agreement. "It 'urts to breathe, 'ard to talk," he told Rob.

"Let's just wait here fer a bit, ye don't need to talk. I thinks maybe ye have either a broken rib, or maybe it's just cracked," Rob replied. "I had a cracked rib once, hurt like the devil. I fell on the rocks comin' up from tying off me boat. Stupid, eh?"

"No more stupid than what I just did," Harry answered slowly with pauses between each word.

"That weren't no fault of yers," Rob replied, "T'was just dumb luck."

"If it weren't fer bad luck," Harry answered in a whisper, "I'd have no luck a'tall".

"Don't try to talk now, just try to stay quiet," Rob advised, "I remember how it hurt to talk, or even just to take a breath." Harry nodded again.

Slowly the two men made their way downhill to the logging camp. The cook was the only man present; all the rest of the men were busy falling trees in the forest surrounding the camp. Rob left

Harry leaning against one of the bunk houses and went ahead to find help.

"Ernie! Ernie!" Rob called as he ran across the camp's yard. A burly man in a dirty apron came out of the mess hall.

"What's going on?" Ernie shouted back.

"C'mon! I needs yer help. Harry's hurt and we needs to get him back to 'is bunk house."

Ernie quickly ran toward Rob and followed him back to where he'd left Harry. The two men helped the injured man back to his bunk and urged him to lay down. Rob did all the talking as Harry laboured for breath after the long walk back to camp.

"Ye ain't gonna be able to finish out the season," Ernie told Harry, "Ye can't work like this. We needs to get ye to a doctor."

"I ain't going to no doctor," Harry wheezed out, "I just needs to rest a day or two. I'll be all right."

Rob and Ernie exchanged looks as they considered Harry's gray face and difficulty breathing. "We'll see about that," Ernie told the hurt man. "Ye just rest here. C'mon, Rob, ain't much more ye can do here. Ye want anything, Harry? I got a bottle of whiskey in me cabin, I can bring it to ye, might help some with the pain."

Harry grinned and then winced, "I won't say 'no'," he replied. Rob followed Ernie out of the bunk house.

"What happened to 'im?" Ernie asked Rob once they were outside. Rob explained the incident and his suspicions that Harry had either cracked or broken a rib bone or two. "Do ye think he's gonna be all right?" Rob asked the cook. "Hard to say," Ernie answered, "I ain't no doctor, but he's a stubborn kind of man, ain't he?"

"Harry's as tough as they come," Rob responded "But I did that once and let me tell ye, it ain't no picnic. Ain't no way he can go chopping down trees in his condition. If he thinks it hurts now it's nothing compared to how he'll feel tomorrow and the next day."

"As luck would have it, I needs more supplies. I was gonna ask the boss if he could spare a man to take a wagon into town fer 'em. Could be Harry could get a ride in the wagon that far anyway. Where's his home?" Ernie asked.

"I believe he lives in one of the communities down the coast, he don't live nowhere close to here," Rob answered.

"And ye have lost a partner, at least until the boss finds somebody to go back in with ye," Ernie commented. "The boss man should be here around sundown, guess it t'will all get sorted then. Let's go get a coffee, whadda ye say?"

"Coffee sure sounds good," Rob replied.

"Hang on 'til I gets that whiskey I promised 'im," Ernie responded, "Go on in the mess hall, I'll be there in a sec."

"Here ye go, mate," Ernie said handing Harry a flask of whiskey, "don't overdo it, you may needs that to help with the pain."

"No worries, mate, I ain't about to drain it in one go," Harry spoke slowly, gasping between words.

"Take a shot or two and then try to sleep, it'd do ye good," Ernie advised. "I'll come back to check or ye, or else Rob will."

"Thanks, Ernie, much obliged," Harry whispered and took a mouthful of the whiskey.

"That's strong stuff, only keep it around fer just such an emergency," Ernie advised, "I ain't much of a whiskey man meself."

Harry simply nodded, not trusting himself to speak. He placed the bottle beside his bunk and laid back down.

"Take it easy now, I'll be back" Ernie told him. Harry grunted as Ernie turned to leave and gingerly returned to his bed.

"How's he doing?" Rob asked when Ernie returned to the mess hall.

"Oh, he's hurting something bad, even if he don't wanna admit it," Ernie said in reply, "I don't think he'll be here long."

"I feels bad," Rob reacted, "didn't see that frigging tree coming. First time I ever seen the like."

"I've heard all kinds of stories about what can 'appen out in the bush," Ernie remarked, "There's times ye expect 'em to fall one way and they falls the dead opposite. I wouldn't blame meself if I were ye."

"Scared the ever-lovin' outta me," Rob replied, "thought fer a second 'e was dead."

"He was mighty lucky," Ernie replied, "Mighty lucky! Could've been much worst."

"Don't I know it," Rob agreed.

"Well, how about that coffee? Did ye want somethin' to eat while I'm at it?"

"Whadda yer offering?" Rob queried.

"Got some hard tack, but ye'd probably like a bit of cake better, eh?" Ernie chuckled as he put the choices to Rob.

"Yeah, ye can keep the hard tack. I'd take cake any day," Rob retorted.

"All right then, c'mon back to the kitchen. I ain't servin' ye," Ernie ordered.

The men spent the next hour drinking coffee and chatting about the logging operation as they waited for the return of the boss-man and the rest of the lumberjacks.

"How many cord did ye manage to cut afore Harry got hurt?" the foreman, Jim, asked Rob.

"I daresay we got a good many, I wouldn't hazard a guess but there's plenty to be hauled out this winter" Rob told him. "We worked most of the day, t'was getting late in the afternoon when it happened. If Harry can't work I'll be needing a partner to help me finish the chance me and Harry were working," Rob replied.

"If he's as bad as yer telling me he won't be able to go at it fer a while, if at all," Jim said thoughtfully, "We'll see how he is in the morning and go from there."

"Good enough," Rob replied, "I'll see ye in the morning then."

"Ye can bring Harry some food, if ye wants, man's gotta eat, hurt or no," Jim said, "if ye don't mind, that is."

"Harry? Hey Harry, are ye awake? Brought ye some grub." Rob stood in the doorway of the dimly lighted bunkhouse calling to his partner.

Harry groaned as he tried to swing his legs off the bed. "What time is it now?" He asked.

"Just getting on early evening, not sure what time it is, but ye missed supper. Jim sent me to bring ye this," Rob answered. "How are ye feeling now?"

"Feels like I got kicked by a mule," Harry replied, struggling for air.

"Ye was out like a light," Rob noted, "We's all wondering if ye can go back into the woods, if ye can work. Ernie says there's gonna be a supply wagon going back into town soon, in the next day or two. Might be something to consider if ye needs to go home. Whaada ye think? Are ye going to be able to go on loggin'?"

Harry reached for the plate of food with one hand while the other pressed against his ribs. "Pains like a son of a bitch," he told Rob.

Rob sat on the bunk across the aisle and watched as Harry attempted to eat the food he'd brought.

"Jesus, Mary, and Joseph," Harry cursed as he fought to balance the plate on his knee while one arm clamped tightly around his rib cage, "I dunno, b'y, I dunno. Boss say anythin'?"

"Said we should wait and see how ye are in the morn," Rob replied.

"Jumpin' dyin' what a goin' on," Harry rasped, "It 'urts to breathe, b'y."

"If ye can't breathe, I don't see how ye'd be able to handle the bucksaw. T'is hard work, that, and I can't see how ye'll be any better in the morn. Like I told ye, I had cracked ribs once, took a while to heal, and I knows I wouldn't have been able to push and pull no bucksaw," Rob said. "Good thing, the scaler was here the other day, at least ye got most of yer pay already. I'd say we cut at least three cord since then and if ye has to go I'll get the rest of yer money to ye somehow. You don't has to worry 'bout that."

"Money is the least of me worries," Harry remarked, "How long will I be laid up with this, I wonder."

"Like I told ye, when it happened to me I was laid up fer weeks, maybe a month or more," Rob told him, "and ye knows the company ain't gonna feed ye if ye can't work, best bet t'would be to make yer way home. Is it far from here?"

"Far enough," Harry replied, "took me almost a week to get out here, and that was with getting lucky enough to hitch a ride part of the way."

"Sorry fer ye, mate," Rob commiserated, "I thinks ye should take a ride in the supply wagon, least it'll get ye into town and maybe with a bit of luck ye'll find somebody headed yer way."

Harry laid the plate on the bed beside him as a spasm of pain caused him to wrap both arms around his midsection. After it passed he looked up at Rob with watery eyes, "No, b'y, I can't work like this, much as I wishes I could, better let Jim know so he can figure out who to send back in with ye," he said.

"If yer finished with yer plate I'll take it back to the cookhouse and let Jim know afore I turns in meself," Rob answered him. "I'm sorry fer ye, I really am. Is there naught else I can do fer ye?"

"Naw, b'y, thanks fer bringing me the grub," Harry replied, "I 'ates to leave like this, but it's all I can do. I'll like as not see ye in the morning. I'm gonna 'ave another pull on that there whiskey and turn in."

"Good enough, Harry, I'll let Jim know and maybe I'll see ye in the morn," Rob answered. Harry nodded and Robb turned away, *poor bastard,* he thought as he let himself out, *I knows he's sufferin' and it may be his ribs broke not just cracked and that'll put 'im out of commission fer a good while.*

The noise of over twenty men moving about at first light woke Harry. He'd spent a miserable night tossing and turning on the spruce boughs that made up his bed unable to get comfortable enough to sleep well, despite the day's hard labour. Slowly he swung his legs off the bed and stood. The pain would not subside. Harry cursed as he moved toward the door. He had to relieve himself and made his way outside and across the yard to the bushes. *Well, ain't this a fine kettle of fish,* he thought, *nuddin' fer it but to make me way back 'ome.*

Harry spoke with Jim before making his way to the mess hall. *T'was good of 'im to let me stay until the wagon goes out,* Harry thought as he walked to the mess hall, *Jim's a good sort, good thing he knows me pretty well. Wonder if I'll get to work with 'im again. Well no use dwellin' on it, what's done is done.*

Men were scraping back chairs as they made ready to go back into the woods surrounding the camp when Harry entered. A few, including Rob, stopped to wish him well as he gingerly sat on a bench after collecting his plate of beans. It was plain fare but filled a man's belly and Harry was grateful for it as he watched the loggers file through the door. He listened to Ernie washing tin plates as he ate and thought of how he could keep himself occupied until he could leave for home. He'd just finished scraping the last of the beans from his plate when Ernie sauntered over.

"How ye feelin'?" Ernie asked him while he reached to take the empty plate.

"I've 'ad better days," Harry grimaced, "Thanks fer the whiskey, it 'elped somewhat."

"Glad to hear it," Ernie replied, "heard yer gonna be leaving."

"Yeah, Jim said I could hitch a ride on the supply wagon," Harry replied. "Can't work like this, 'urts somethin' awful."

"Supply wagon ain't going out 'til the day after tomorrow," Ernie advised, "why don't ye stay here in the mess with me? Could use a hand peeling spuds, if yer up to it."

"I think I could manage that," Harry answered, "It sure beats sitting in the bunkhouse twiddling me thumbs."

"C'mon back to the kitchen after yer done yer coffee and I'll put ye to work," Ernie grinned.

"Good enough," Harry replied, "won't be long."

Ernie nodded and walked away. The mess hall seemed eerily quiet as Harry gulped down the bitter beverage and followed Ernie to the kitchen where he sat on a high stool drying plates.

"George will be taking ye to town on the supply wagon," Ernie told Harry. "He's a good man, not much of one fer talking so that will be a help to ye. I allows it ain't easy fer ye to talk much what with busted ribs and all."

Harry grunted his assent as he peeled a potato. He was glad he didn't have to do much more than grunt or nod as Ernie kept up a steady stream of chatter. Harry helped out with other kitchen chores as Ernie got supper ready for the hordes of hungry men. It seemed no time before the day was done and the men began to return.

Two days later Harry had his backpack ready and made his way back to the mess hall for a final meal before pushing off for home. He stopped to visit Ernie in the kitchen to thank him for the whiskey and for the bundle of food Ernic had made up for him, mainly hardtack and beans, but Harry was grateful.

215

Harry's arms were frequently wrapped around his ribs as the wagon ran over bumps and lumps in the road as they drove into town. It felt like the most torturous ride Harry had ever taken and true to Ernie's description the driver rarely spoke. The four hours seemed indeterminably long as the hurt man was jostled on his seat but at last, they were driving down the relatively smooth road into town.

"I can't thank ye enough," Harry told the driver as he wearily climbed down from the wagon seat. "I'm much beholden to ye."

"No trouble fer me, had to come in anyway and t'was good to have a bit of company," the driver waved away his thanks, "take care of yerself and good luck to ye."

Harry nodded and heaved his backpack out of the wagon, a great moan of pain escaping his lips as he did so.

"Ye sure yer gonna be all right?" the driver asked.

"I'll manage, thanks," Harry answered quietly, somewhat embarrassed. "I'll likely stay put 'ere in town fer a day or two afore I push on. Thanks again fer the ride."

The driver stood examining Harry's face for a minute before nodding and turning away.

Harry grasped his backpack in one hand and grimacing, turned to walk to the center of town where a small rooming house that had sheltered him once before was located.

Chapter

29

"**D**id ye hear, Harry's back. He's staying at his brother's place," Charlie told Mick.

"Well, that's good news, just in time, too, when did he get back?" Mick asked.

"Just a couple of days ago, apparently he busted up his ribs up north in a logging camp," Charlie replied.

"Care to come with me later to pay 'im a visit?" Mick asked. "We needs to have a chat with the man afore we meets with Peter on Sunday."

"Sounds good to me. Right after work, or would ye like to go home and have supper first?" Charlie wanted to know.

"After work is fine, me sons can tell Fanny," Mick replied, "Just as well to get it done so's we knows where we stands. But can ye give me a lift home afterward?"

"Sure thing, b'y, wouldn't expect ye to walk back. See ye after work then," Charlie grinned at Mick before turning away to go back to work.

The day passed quickly enough and soon the two men were in Charlie's wagon heading to see Harry.

"Was he hurt bad, do ye know?" Mick asked.

"All's I knows is that he busted up his ribs bad enough that he was forced to come back 'ere," Charlie said.

"Timing couldn't be better," Mick reflected, "sorry to hear he's been hurt, but I knows he can shed light on what happened that day and with a bit of luck maybe we can convince him to come to the meetin' to tell what he knows."

"That would be a help," Charlie agreed, "have to wait and see how bad he is, I s'pose."

The two men continued to discuss the upcoming meeting as well as their hopes for the future as they traveled the distance to see Harry.

"Ye set a date yet fer yer weddin' yet?" Mick asked.

"Naw, not as yet," Charlie said, "Constance wants to wait a bit. She's hoping maybe 'er sister will come look after 'er parents. They're too old to be left alone and I have no intention of livin' in that house with 'em."

"Are they all that bad?" Mick wanted to know.

"Naw, it ain't that they're hard to get along with. I'd just be more comfortable under me own roof," Charlie answered. "Sides, ye knows how small their place is. We'd be tripping over each other all the time, and the old man is kinda set in 'is ways. Know what I mean? What 'bout William? Is he fixin' to tie the knot soon?"

"Not at all, he wants to have his house built and a bit of a nest egg saved up first," Mick replied. "They're sensible youngsters, the both of 'em."

Charlie nodded and urged the horse to a faster trot. "Sounds mighty sensible to me. William is still a young feller yet; he's got lots of time. Me, I'm gonna be one of the oldest bridegrooms in these parts." Charlie laughed. "Maybe that's why I'm so stubborn, perhaps I'm set in my ways too."

"Ye ain't that old, still gotta lot of life ahead of ye yet." Mick answered, "once we gets these meetin's done with we'll have to start getting' together to figure out how best to go about building dories so we can leave that damned quarry behind us."

"Yup, one thing at a time," Charlie agreed, "but I thinks it's a mighty fine plan. A few good boats and some hardworking men can make a go of lobster fishing."

"I won't be sorry to shake the limestone dust off me boots fer good," Mick told him. "Lobster fishin' is hard work, but not near as hard as shoveling rock."

"Here we are," Charlie said as he turned the horse onto a field. A small cottage sat near the bank overlooking the bay. Neither man spoke again as Charlie drove the horse across the pasture to the house. Mick jumped down first and waited while Charlie turned the wagon. The men walked to the door of the little cabin and knocked loudly. A small woman answered the door. "Who are ye and whaddya ye want here?" She asked gruffly, her small beady eyes sizing up her guests.

"We're looking fer Harry. We was told he's staying here," Mick told her. "He used to work at the quarry with me brother. Name's Mick Kelly and this here is Charlie Samms."

The woman stepped back, "Yes, he's here, c'mon in," she grudgingly invited.

The men stood just inside the doorway while their hostess called out for Harry.

"He'll be here in a moment. He ain't moving too fast these days," she told her company. "Why don't ye pull up a chair," she nodded to the small table placed in front of the one window. "Harry won't be long. If ye don't mind, I've got things to do. Sit down and wait right here."

Mick glanced at Charlie. *She's a mite unfriendly*, he thought as he pulled out a chair. The men heard Harry as he made his way from the back of the house.

"Well, Mick Kelly, I'd know ye anywhere," Harry crowed as he came into the room. "What brings ye 'ere?"

"Ye knows Charlie, don't ye?" Mick asked as Harry approached the table.

"Yes, I knows 'im all to pieces," Harry exclaimed. "Charlie, 'ullo b'y! Well don't this beat all! What are ye doing out this way?"

"Are ye feelin' fit enough fer a little visit?" Mick asked. "Heard ye busted up yer ribs in a loggin' camp."

"Yissir, that's true," Harry answered. "Still 'urts like a son of a bitch, but not near as bad as it did at first. Couldn't 'ardly talk or breathe a couple of weeks back. But t'is getting better every day. What can I do ye fer?"

"S'pose ye knows Joe died?" Mick asked.

"Just 'eard about it a couple of days ago. Mighty sorry fer yer loss," Harry answered gravely. "Joe was a good man. Didn't think he was 'urt so bad as that when I left."

"Doc had to take 'is leg off," Mick told Harry, "But it didn't work. Maybe he lost too much blood. In either case, he didn't make it.

That's kinda why we're here, to tell ye the truth. We're hoping you can tell us what happened that day."

"I weren't planning on working the quarry this year. I was gonna 'ead out to the loggin' camp fer the spring drive but me brother talked me into staying," Harry began. "Listen, ye men wants a cup of tea or somethin'?"

"No, I'm good, do ye, Charlie?" Mick asked.

"Naw, thanks, just wants to hear how Joe got hurt," Charlie answered.

Harry lowered himself carefully into a chair. "T'was an awful fright I got when I came back with da grease and dere's Joe flat on the ground and blood everywhere. I tried like 'ell to move it off 'im but that cart t'was too 'eavy for just one man," Harry began, 'them wheels on the cart what we was working was seized up fast. Joe and me tried over and over to get 'er moving but there was no way that cart was going anywhere, no matter 'ow 'ard we threw our weight against it." Harry paused, "Sorry, mates, me ribs are still making it 'ard to breathe, 'ard to talk, too."

"Take yer time my son, just take yer time. Sorry to bother ye with it when yer still not up to snuff," Mick said, "there's good reason we needs to know right now, or I'd let it be 'til yer feelin' better."

"Naw, I'll be alright," Harry proclaimed, "Like I were sayin', them wheels were stuck fast so I went to get grease to try and work 'em loose, when I got back, well ye knows the rest."

"Them carts should have been in good workin' order," Charlie put in, "I'd like to know why that cart was seized up so hard."

"That's a good question, one Joe and I were chewing over," Harry answered, "It was like that god damned cart was stuck fast to the rails. T'wouldn't budge no matter what we did."

"That's one of many questions we needs to deal with," Mick said thoughtfully. "Were ye gone long, Harry? And why the hell did ye disappear right afterward?"

"Can't say 'ow long I was gone, not longer than it took to walk down to talk to the pitboss and tell 'im what was going on and get a can of grease fer them wheels," Harry responded. "And then seeing Joe dere like dat, after working our guts out fer so long, it t'was just the final straw. I got it in me mind to get the 'ell out of it; to go logging like I'd been planning all winter."

The men sat in silence for several moments before Harry began again. "Joe and me, well, ye knows, Mick, we been buddies since we were knee 'igh back 'ome. Didn't get together much after he got married so I was right glad to be partnered with 'im at the quarry, t'was the only good thing 'bout the friggin' place. To see 'im lying dere, badly 'urt, blood everywhere made me want to throw me guts up. I had to get out of dere, so I left, made up me mind I weren't coming back, neither. At the time I thought Joe'd be alright. He was a tough son of a bitch. Ye could've knocked me over with a feather when I learned Joe'd died."

The men sat in silence for a while before Mick began to explain why they'd needed to talk to him and about the association the men were hoping would make the quarry a safer place to work.

"Anyway, Harry, we'll be meetin' again come Sunday night, was hoping maybe ye'd come to the meetin' and tell the men what happened to Joe," Mick explained. "T'would make a big difference if ye would."

"I dunno, b'y. I ain't much fer talking to a crowd. Couldn't ye just tell 'im?" Harry asked.

"I can do the talkin', if ye wants, but ye would have to be there to say it's truth I'm tellin', not somethin' I made up meself," Charlie offered. "All ye'd have to do is nod. Can ye do that much?"

"I s'pose I could do dat," Harry agreed. "But I ain't got no way of getting' dere. I did a great deal of walkin' to get 'ome, but I ain't goin' too far 'til these ribs of mine are 'ealed up."

"That's not a problem. I'll come get ye," Charlie replied.

"I gots one more question fer ye, Harry," Mick interrupted. "Do ye know that new man, Jake, lives over yonder?" Mick gestured with his head, "He bought the old Simon place. T'was his cart that hit Joe from behind. I guess Joe was trying to move that cart on his own while ye were gone to get that grease."

"Can't say as I do," Harry answered. "That was one 'ell of a day, we was all working like dogs. Well, ye knows dat."

"Do ye remember who was working carts near ye?' Mick asked.

"Naw, can't say as I do," Harry replied. "I was beat out, we all were, and I weren't payin' much attention to who was working alongside us."

"Alright, Harry, thanks," Mick said, "guess we should shove off, I ain't had me supper yet and Fanny will be wonderin' where I got to. I hope yer feelin' better real soon. Appreciate ye talking to us, so we'll see ye on Sunday then?"

"As long as Charlie 'ere don't mind 'auling me to the meetin' and 'ome again, I'll be there," Harry promised.

"Thanks, Harry, I means it, thanks so much," Mick responded, "see ye Sunday then."

"See ye Sunday, Harry," Charlie parroted.

The men stood up and each of them in turn shook Harry's hand before making their exit.

Neither man said much as Charlie drove Mick back to his home. Grief sat heavily like a dark ghost between them. Neither man wanted to speak of it. Each mulled over what they'd heard from Harry, the totally preventable tragedy, and what it would mean regarding their attempts to form an association.

Chapter

30

Fanny was rocking their infant son when Mick walked into the little cottage. She was alone in the little kitchen. She rose to put the baby down as Mick dropped heavily into a chair at the table.

"Kept yer supper warm, won't take a minute," Fanny told him as her worried gaze swept his face and she moved toward the stove.

"Sounds good, I'm frigging famished," Mick replied.

"Care to tell me what was so important ye didn't come straight home?" Fanny asked as she carried a plate of food to the table. "Where did ye go with Charlie?"

"Went up to the head. Harry's back," Mick told her, "And we wanted to have a word with 'im afore he disappeared again. He tends to make up 'is mind sudden like to do whatever comes in 'is head."

Fanny nodded. "I knew it had to be of some importance fer ye to go off like that right after work. So, did ye learn anything new?"

Mick lifted a forkful to his mouth and, closing his eyes, savored the food before answering. "It's pretty much as Elsie told us happened in 'er dreams. Harry said the cart would not budge and he'd left to go get grease fer the wheels when it happened."

Fanny nodded her head once more but her face paled, "So strange that Elsie would dream something so real, so true to life. It's a bit spooky, ain't it?"

"Stranger things have happened, I s'pose," Mick remarked. "T'is a bit spooky, but Elsie and Joe were close. Stands to reason that he'd find a way to get a message to 'er and a way to say good-bye."

"If it t'were anyone else I'd have a heap of doubt, but Elsie is as down to earth as they come. She ain't ever been given to superstition or ghost stories," Fanny remarked. "Did Harry have anything to add? Did he say why he left so sudden like?"

"He didn't say it, but I 'spect it was the shock of seeing Joe like that – laying in 'is own blood and hurt so bad," Mick told his wife. "He said he'd been planning to go loggin' and it was only because of 'is brother that he came back to work at the quarry. He told us after Joe was hurt, he couldn't see his way clear to staying on, so he left fer the loggin' camps."

"He ain't married or got no family?" Fanny asked.

"Naw, Harry, he's what ye call a confirmed bachelor," Mick retorted.

Fanny nodded once again, "So, what happens now?" She asked.

"Well, that's a good question alright," Mick answered, "We have a meetin' planned fer Sunday. Peter's gonna be there. I'm hoping to trash it all out with 'im at some point. There're so many points to bring up. It ain't no simple accident no more."

Fanny nodded gravely, "Finish yer supper, we can talk more when yer done. I'll get yer tea."

Mick took her at her word and dived gustily into his meal while Fanny bustled around the kitchen making tea and ruminating on what her husband had told her. Placing a cup of tea on the table she seated herself and watched him eat. He seemed more at peace since having had the opportunity to question Harry and she was grateful for that. She knew how his brother's untimely death had eaten at him and how the unanswered questions had cost him many a night's sleep. Mick sopped the remaining gravy up with a thick slice of bread and reached for his tea when the last morsel had been swallowed.

"Aw, thanks, love," Mick sighed as he pushed the plate away, "that was some good. I needed that!"

Fanny smiled gently at him; her fingers entwined in her lap as if to stop herself from moving. She waited quietly while Mick sipped his tea. *My, he looks so very tired*, she thought as she watched him, *how I wish he didn't have to work so hard. Glad I am that he's finally gotten a few of his questions answered, but what next, I wonder.*

"Charlie and me were talking, wondering if Jake saw Harry go fer the grease, if he saw the pair of them trying to get that cart to moving. Could be why the captain is acting so queer," Mick continued. "He's been keeping an awful close eye on Jake. Billy says he makes it a habit to walk around the crusher where Jake's to, and that he glares at the boy when he can catch 'is eye.

"No doubt Jake did leave the brake off 'is cart that morning, no doubt in my mind at all. But that's only part of the story – only part of the reason Joe's up there in that cemetery," Mick said. "Would be nice if we could get 'im to talk to us so we could see the full picture of how it all happened."

Fanny reached for Mick's hand, laying her own over top, but said nothing.

"He seems a good sort, don't he?" Mick asked.

"He certainly seemed like a good man to me, a troubled man, but a good one," Fanny quietly agreed. "And Joe seemed to think a lot of 'im, and so does Elsie since she met with them at their place."

"It's an awful burden to carry, a man's death," Mick reflected, "especially a man who'd befriended ye."

Fanny's eyes were focused on the window and the little cottage across the field where Elsie and Joe had once enjoyed a simple but happy life and she said nothing. For several minutes the pair were quiet as they reflected on a life snatched away too soon.

"If ye don't mind, Fan, I wants to go over and have a word with Elsie, let 'er know I've talked with Harry," Mick said as he stood up from the table. "There's still a few days afore we has that meetin' with Peter 'bout the association. Time enough to figure out how to handle it all."

Fanny also stood up and placing her hand on Mick's upper arm said, "It will do Elsie good to hear there's truth to 'er dreams about Joe and how he died. Maybe it will bring 'er a small bit of comfort. Ye go on. I'll be right here when ye get back," with that she placed a kiss on Mick's cheek and turned to clear the table.

Mick heard shrieks of laughter coming from the barnyard as he strode across the yard to Elsie's and stopped to watch Phil who was tossing a delighted Rose into the air as Jack and Sarah sat watching on an overturned stump. Sarah waved excitedly at her father when she caught sight of him. Mick waved back and called, "All the chores done?" He asked.

"Yissir," Jack answered, "Just having a bit of fun before we have to turn in."

"Yes, I see that," Mick smiled his answer, "Don't stay out too long, it's near time fer them girls to get to bed."

"We won't, Da," Phil replied. "We're having a contest to see who can throw Rose higher. Sara is the judge. I think she's favoring Jack, though, she's not an impartial judge at all!" Phil grinned at his sister.

"Don't let 'em throw 'er too high. Don't want nobody getting hurt," Mick told Sara. "I needs to have a chat with yer Aunt, I'll be home in a bit."

Mick turned back onto the path to Elsie's as the laughter continued.

Elsie was sitting on the small porch watching the sun set and listening to the antics of her nephews and nieces when Mick appeared.

"Hullo, Mick, what brings ye by?" she greeted her brother-in-law.

"I have something I wants to tell ye, didn't want it to wait," Mick replied.

"Did ye want to come inside?" Elsie asked.

"Naw, this is perfect, right here," Mick told her pulling a stool over to sit with her. "T'is a nice evening and we might just as well enjoy it, Lord, knows it will be blowing snow afore we knows it."

Elsie smiled and settled her back against the wall as she waited to see what Mick had come to tell her.

"So, ye knows Harry's come back, right? Went up to the head to see 'im after work. Charlie came with me," Mick began.

Elsie turned toward him her attention riveted on his face as he spoke. "And what did he have to say?" She asked.

"It was pretty much as you described in yer dream. The wheels on the cart were stuck. Harry went to see the pit boss to get grease to see if that might work. He wasn't there when it happened, just like ye saw in yer dream."

Elsie's eyes filled with tears as Mick spoke and he wondered if he'd done the right thing in coming to tell her.

226

"And if that part was true, then it stands to reason, so was the rest of it. Joe really did come to me," Elsie whispered. "Aw, Mick, I was wondering if the grief were making me imagine things. I was wondering if maybe I was losing my marbles."

Mick reached out and awkwardly patted Elsie's hand. "Like Fanny said when I told her, 'ain't nobody as down to earth as our Elsie'. I never questioned yer sanity, no, not fer one minute. It made every bit of sense to me. But I am glad to have a witness, so to speak. Harry can testify to the faulty cart and that will make a difference to us forming an association to keep the men safe. I knew ye weren't making up a story. Just needed something a bit more concrete to offer at the meetin'," he said. "If ye hadn't told me about the dream I'd of never known the right questions to put to Harry. I am mighty grateful you did."

Elsie's arms hugged her thin frame as she looked out at the setting sun. "He told me how sorry he was to leave me," she spoke slowly, quietly, "he was holding our baby and promising to take care of him until I came. Did I tell ye that?"

"No, ye didn't tell me that part," Mick answered solemnly. "Joe, he loved ye so much. Ye was everything to him. Hold onto that, Elsie, don't ever ferget how much he loved ye. And he loved yer wee son, too."

Elsie wiped her eyes and smiled forlornly at Mick, "he said much the same in my dream. And like I told him, how can I ever ferget? Every bit of this little farm has his mark on it. Every single bit."

Mick nodded and sat quietly watching his brother's widow and said nothing more. The two sat in companionable silence as they remembered Joe. The sun had faded from the horizon when Elsie stood up.

"Ye need to get back over to Fanny and yer family. I thank ye for coming to tell me about yer conversation with Harry. It's more comforting than you can know," Elsie told Mick.

"Are ye going to be alright?" Mick asked.

"The nights have been hardest. In the daytime I am kept busy, but once I go to bed, well, it's just hard. I miss him so. But tonight, I will sleep better, I think," Elsie replied. "It helps a lot knowing Joe really did come to me. It's a comfort."

Mick studied Elsie's face a several seconds before taking his leave. "I hope ye knows if ye needs anything at all – anything – ye just come to me," Mick promised yet again. "Y'er family, Elsie, and yer cared for more than ye knows."

"I do know, Mick," she answered, "I truly do. And I thank ye. Go on home to yer family now. I'm just going to sit here fer a bit longer before I turn in. I'm fine, really I am."

Elsie watched as Mick walked away and waited until he was out of sight before she allowed the tears to flow. Yet, somehow these tears felt more healing to her than any of the billions of tears she'd wept since Joe died.

Chapter

31

J ake strode quickly into the house waving a letter. "It's come, Mary, it's come," he spoke animatedly and his excitement had Mary dropping the diaper she'd been folding. "It's the letter from yer folks ye 'ave been watching fer. Paddy give it to me today at work."

Mary nearly tripped over her skirts in her hurry to take the letter from her husband's hands. Jake pulled out a chair and Mary dropped gratefully onto it. She took the envelope and smoothed it slowly as she gazed down at the familiar handwriting. Jake sat beside her. "Open it!" He demanded impatiently. Mary slowly opened the envelope and eased the letter out. She unfolded the pages and glanced quickly over the missive. A smile lit up her face.

"Oh, Jake, she's coming. Haldi's coming!" her voice trembled with anticipation.

"When? When will she be here?" Jake wanted to know, as excited as his wife at this welcome news.

"Give me a moment to read it through," Mary laughed. Jake waited impatiently as he watched his wife's eyes travel slowly over the pages.

"Oh, my, Jake, she will be here within the fortnight!" Mary squealed and threw her arms around Jake, nearly knocking him off the chair in the process.

Mary sat upright and read a section of the letter aloud. When she finished she looked quickly around the little room.

"We need to get ready," she said, "Jake is the cot finished yet?"

"I just needs to sand the wood one more time and haul it in here to set up," Jake replied. "I'm some glad we kept that old straw mattress. And I found some hooks I can fix to the wall there for her to hang her things on. That won't take long to do. Aw, Mary, I'm so glad for ye. It will be good for ye to have company while I'm at work."

"I can't wait!" Mary smiled widely her excitement making her eyes dance with merriment. "And the twins will get to know at least one of their aunts," she enthused.

"One day soon I will add a couple of rooms to this place. If she decides to stay for a while, she'll need a room of 'er own," Jake said.

"It'll be fine. Haldi is a simple soul, she won't want fer much," Mary answered. "Oh, I am so glad Ma and Pa are going to let 'er come!"

"T'is good of 'em," Jake replied.

"Well, apparently there's some young buck been snooping around 'er, a feller my parents do not approve of, so the timing couldn't be better. Ma says Haldi is not interested in this young feller and is glad fer the chance to leave home just now."

"Will they send another letter to let us know when she will be in town so's I can arrange with Paddy to go get 'er?" Jake asked.

"No need to worry about it. Ma and Pa are sending 'er with a couple who are coming to visit Elsie. Now, ain't that somethin'?"

"I didn't know Elsie had folk out that way," Jake replied. "It's funny, she never mentioned it."

"Oh, but she did tell me," Mary retorted, "when we was at her house that day after church. I didn't get a chance to ask much about it we was so busy getting the dinner on the table and all. I fergot about it til now.

"Hey, Jake, maybe we could send her an invitation to come here fer dinner after church this Sunday? What do ye think?" she asked.

"Does that mean I have to go to church again?" Jake asked in turn.

"Give it a chance, Jake. The pastor seemed nice, didn't he? And he didn't preach no hell and damnation, did he?" Mary replied.

"True enough, but that was last time, don't mean he won't be at it this time around," Jake replied doubtfully.

"Yer not giving it a fair chance, Jake, ye knows yer not!" Mary exclaimed.

"Mary, ye knows I hates going to church – any church! But I will go, just to be fair. But if that preacher starts going on 'bout pagans and hell and all that stuff I'll up and leave! I'll just leave and wait fer ye outside!" Jake threatened.

Mary stared at him in dismay but an inner nudge had her answer before she could give it much thought: "Fine, then, as long as ye give it a fair chance. I mean, ye can't be getting up two minutes into the service. Ye has to listen and if he starts onto damnation talk, then fine, ye can leave." Mary compromised.

"Ye better mean that, Mary. I had enough of that kind of talk when I was a youngster. I don't mean to put up with it now." Jake retorted.

Mary took a deep breath. "Don't know what kind of preacher ye heard back then. I never did hear the like of it. But yes, I do mean it. Church shouldn't be a torture fer anybody. It should be a place where a body can find peace, not have their peace or their faith destroyed." She promised.

Now I done it, Jake thought as he considered the resolve in Mary's eyes. "I don't wanna be butting heads with ye," he told Mary, "But I feels just as strongly about it as ye do. And I don't want my children exposed to no Indian-hating hypocrite."

Mary's eyes softened as she considered her husband knowing the anguish he'd suffered as a result of his blood lines.

"Jake, I honestly think this pastor is a good man, I really do," she implored. "Please, don't make judgments based on one bad preacher, who should never 'ave bin behind a pulpit."

Jake thought about the merriment in the preacher's eyes and the way he'd winked at Jake when Mary wasn't looking.

"I will give 'im a chance, Mary, fer yer sake," Jake answered.

"Thank ye, kindly," Mary responded, "Now go wash up and I'll get supper on the table."

After the couple had eaten and the babies were fed, changed and tucked in for the night Mary returned to the subject of church.

"Jake, I'd like to talk some more about church and what your church was like when ye was growing up. We never really talked much about it and I just want to understand you better," she began. "We don't actually talk much about yer life when ye was growing up. I'd like to know more, if yer willing to tell me."

"Aw, Mary, what's the use of beating a dead horse? It's all said and done and so long ago," Jake answered.

"The use is that it would help me know me husband better," Mary spoke softly and her imploring blue eyes made it hard for Jake to refuse. "Besides, once Haldi gets here we won't have much private time. I mean, I am really looking forward to having 'er here, but life will be different once she is."

"What do ye want to know?" Jake asked.

"Well, we never talks much about yer past, about yer Mi'kmaq ancestors or any of that. Ye said that preacher ye didn't like was an Indian-hater. How do ye know that?" she asked.

'Aw, Mary, it's kind of hard to remember exactly what was said. He used to go on and on about pagans and how Indian people worshipped 'false images' he called 'em. He left no doubt about how he felt about natives, that's fer sure."

"That must 'ave been hard on ye," Mary sympathized. "I just bin trying real hard to imagine what it was like fer ye, fer yer family. It'd help if ye would just tell me."

"That preacher, he thought my ancestors prayed to trees and the sun and moon, stuff like that. Said it was pagan practice and against God's laws," Jake softly began, "made us feel like something dirty, something unwanted – like we was less than human."

"But, yer family never did pray to the moon or sun, or what not," Mary puzzled, "not that I ever seen."

"Naw, they didn't," Jake paused, remembering, "It never happened to me, but my parents told stories of how their parents would be beaten fer speaking their language, or fer missing church service, fer anything, basically, that was different from the white folk. They got made fun of a lot. That's why they moved away. T'was why we was never to speak about our grandparents being Mi'kmaq," Jake replied.

"So, why did that preacher bother ye so much, I don't understand," Mary responded.

"Because I could see the hatred in 'is eyes when he talked about Indians," Jake tried to explain, "it must 'ave bin the same look my grandparents seen in the eyes of so many white people. I don't remember them well, but I remember how gentle they was and how kind, even to people who were mean to 'em. That preacher, he made me ashamed to have any Indian blood a'tall. So, I understood how my grandparents must 'ave felt and it ain't right. Ye don't understand, Mary, how different people treated me when they found out I have Indian blood running in me veins. One day I was right as rain, accepted and befriended everywhere. The next I was tossed on the garbage heap like so much trash. That preacher, if he'd still bin there, would likely have burned me whole family at the stake, just fer having Indian blood in us," Jake shook his head as memories plagued him.

"Aw, Jake," Mary whispered, "I remember when they came fer ye. It scared the daylights outta me. It weren't right."

"I remember my Ma telling stories of when she was a girl and how happy they were afore they moved into town. How her parents told all kinds of stories explaining everything about nature. Some of the stories were pretty funny, the ones she remembered and told me," Jake mused, "and stories about the Creator and having respect for all life because all on earth came from the Creator, people, animals, plants, birds, fish – all of life. Made more sense to me than anything that preacher ever said."

"I don't see why there can't be room for all of it. Your grandparents were taught about the Creator. My grandparents were taught about God, which is another name for the Creator," Mary reflected. "In Genesis it talks about how each day God created the land and sea, then the fish and the animals and finally he created mankind. Isn't that sort of the same?"

"Aw, Mary, that's why I love you so. You see things in such a clear light. Wish more people were like ye." Jake spoke gently in answer. "But, ye see, most people don't see it that way. That preacher sure didn't."

"Well, I ain't learned like some preachers are, but I think he was wrong," Mary answered reaching for Jake's hand.

"That's what Joe said," Jake held Mary's hand in his own, "I wish ye could've come to know 'im. He sure was a gentle soul and a good man."

"I wish I could've, too," Mary squeezed Jake's hand, "I sure am glad yer finding some peace around 'im and remembering the good things."

"Elsie's helped a lot, and she weren't even trying," Jake smiled as he remembered Joe's message to them both to help the other. *Somehow, some way, I will find a way to help Elsie,* Jake thought to himself. "We can ask 'er fer supper soon, but not right now. I still 'ave things I needs to get done afore Haldi comes, and a fortnight ain't long. That's about all the jawing I wants to do fer one night," he squeezed Mary's hand once again, "Ye about ready fer bed?" He asked.

Mary smiled as she stood up. "T'is a mite early fer bed, ain't it?" she asked. She blushed as Jake's eyes roamed over her body.

"I never said nothin' about sleep," he grinned at his wife, "and with yer sister comin' and all . . ." Jake let his words trail off as he swung Mary off her feet.

"Now, Jake," Mary began but Jake's kiss stopped her in mid speech.

Chapter

32

H aldi sat on the hard seat of the wagon tightly grasping the handles of the valise in her hands. The small bag held foodstuffs her mother had prepared for her for the journey. Her few clothes and necessities were packed in the little trunk that was stored in the back of the wagon.

Haldi was nervous, but also excited. This was her first real trip away from home and she looked forward to seeing her sister again and meeting her little nieces at last. That alone was worth the price she'd paid for the weeks of anguish and anxiety caused by Ralph. The name caused a shadow to cross her face and her lips became set in a grim line as she thought about her tormentor. *No! I will not allow him to ruin this fer me*, she thought to herself and gazed determinedly at the hills stretching out before her.

The rough road had been beaten down by the many wagons that had traveled it over the years but the tall evergreens and rocky outcrops revealed an unspoiled and serene landscape. Haldi took a deep breath of the chill morning air and pulled her shawl tight around her shoulders.

"Are ye all right?" her companion, Elsie's sister, asked. "If yer cold I have a blanket ye can wrap up in."

"Oh, no, I'm fine, really I am," Haldi smiled at the gentle woman beside her. "T'was just a little chill suddenly."

"Yes, the hills do cast a shadow," Eleanor responded warmly. "T'is beautiful country, ain't it?"

"It surely is, and I am mighty grateful to have eyes to see it," Haldi replied. "I ain't ever been this way afore."

Haldi glanced around her appreciatively. They had left their little town far behind them and though she knew she'd miss her folks Haldi was looking forward to the adventures the future promised.

"Do ye travel out this way often?" Haldi asked.

"Edward has been out this way a time or two, mostly we stay close to home. I ain't much fer traveling so I ain't never been to see Elsie. I am so looking forward to our visit. I ain't seen 'er in fifteen years. Ye must be looking forward to seeing yer sister, too?" Eleanor asked.

"Oh my, yis, and to holding my two baby nieces," Haldi enthused. "Does yer sister have children?"

Eleanor shook her head sadly, "No, she had the one wee babe, but he died not long after he was born and Elsie's husband died this past spring. I wanted to go to her right after we heard the news, but this is the first chance I got," she said.

"That's so sad," Haldi replied and then sat quietly, not knowing what to say.

"Yes, it is sad. Elsie would have been such a good mother. She loves children, as did her husband. Joe was such a nice man, a good man! But that's life, ye never know what's around the corner," Eleanor carried on, "T'will be glad to see her. I hope our visit will be a comfort to her."

"Was he sick or somethin'?" Haldi asked.

"No, he died after an accident at the quarry where he was working," Eleanor's eyes were troubled as she answered. "Should never be, but life is hard and often we don't understand the reasons why people have to die. All we can do is put them in God's hands and carry on livin', what else can we do?"

"We heard about that," Haldi said, "Jake, my sister's husband, works at the quarry there, too."

"T'is a small place, much smaller than Robertson's. I imagine a lot of the menfolk work there," Eleanor told Haldi.

Haldi nodded and turned her gaze back to the rolling hills. Eleanor glanced at the young girl's profile. *She's so young still and no doubt has not seen much of life's hardships. I don't mean to make her uncomfortable,* she thought as she took in the stiff spine and hunched shoulders. "Are ye and yer sister close?" she asked to change the topic and to put the young girl at ease again.

"Me and Mary, we was always together when she was home. At least we was til she married Jake," Haldi answered. "Mary is the kindest, sweetest, person I knows."

"I bet she will be so happy to see ye," Eleanor replied with a smile. "And she has a set of twins, how old are they?" she asked.

"Only a few months old," Haldi wrinkled her forehead as she tried to remember their exact age, "they was born this past spring."

"Aw, they're just new babes, how exciting for ye to get to hold them and care fer 'em," Eleanor replied.

"I love babies," Haldi returned, "leastwise when they ain't throwing up on ye."

Eleanor laughed, "Yes, they do that now and again."

"I helped my Ma with the little ones," Haldi went on, "I'm second eldest in our family and when Mary married Jake it fell to me to help Ma around the house," she explained.

"Yer Ma must have been glad of yer help," Eleanor said.

"I dunno, but I like helping 'er. Now I'm on my way to help Mary," Haldi told her companion. "Ma will be okay, there's Debra next in line to me and she will be a help to Ma. Mary ain't got nobody there to help 'er and Ma says twins would be a heap of work." Haldi chattered on about her family and Eleanor enjoyed her prattle as the wagon rolled on.

Edward pulled gently on the reins as they reached the bottom of the hill. On the right a small meadow looked to be a good resting spot. He'd taken a break in this same spot during past trips to the peninsula.

"Time to stretch our legs," he told his wife, "Maybe have that lunch you made fer us. There's a spring over there where I can get us some water." He jumped lightly down to the ground and reached up to take Eleanor's hand to help her down from the high seat. Eleanor's hands went straight to her lower back and she stretched on her tiptoes while she gazed around her.

"What a pretty spot, and such a lovely day, too," she commented.

"I like this place. I'm gonna grab that jug and go fill it at that spring I was tellin' ye about. Ye two stay right here, I'll be back," he told the women.

Haldi had grabbed the hem of her skirts and jumped down from the wagon unaided and now stood next to Eleanor.

"Oh, my, how beautiful is this?" she asked as she came to stand beside Eleanor. Small rolling hills surrounded the little valley and a large pond reflected their greenery, clad as they were in evergreens and alders. Wildflowers grew in abundance in the meadow in bright yellows, white, pinks, and purple.

The two women stood admiring the view for several minutes before Eleanor moved to the back of the wagon to retrieve the basket of sandwiches she'd made for the journey. "Will ye take that blanket there to spread on the ground and we'll have a picnic?" she asked of Haldi. "It's nice to have a wee break from all that jostling. T'is hard on my bones."

"Nice spot, ain't it?" Edward called as he walked toward them swinging the water jug as he came.

"T'is absolutely beautiful," Haldi responded.

"T'is heavenly," Eleanor agreed.

Eleanor took the blanket Haldi was holding and spread it out over the soft grass and began unpacking the tin cups and sandwiches from the basket.

"Ma sent some lassy buns and sweet cakes. Should I go get 'em?"

"Aw, girl, lassy buns?" Edward asked with a grin, "Now yer talking, just the thing to 'ave right after I finish a sandwich or two."

Haldi ran to the wagon to retrieve her satchel and returned to drop onto the blanket beside Eleanor, grateful to have something to contribute to their repast.

"Ma makes the best lassy buns," she told her companions as she placed the valise beside her.

"Lookin' forward to trying 'em. After we eat, we won't be making any more stops fer a good long while. I wants to make it to the peninsula afore it gets dark," Edward warned them. "Better enjoy it while ye can."

"Will it take long to get there?" Eleanor asked.

"We're about halfway there," Edward answered. "That was why I wanted to leave so early. Didn't want to have to camp out overnight. Yup, we'll make it afore sundown. Glad the weather's stayed nice." Edward tilted his head back looking up at the bright skies.

"T'is a perfect day fer traveling," Eleanor agreed.

The trio ate in relative silence, each one savoring the beauty all around them and anticipating the reunions to come. Before long they were packing up the basket and returning things to the wagon.

It was dusk when Edward guided the horse and wagon down the steep hill to the peninsula and the travelers were weary, each looking forward to a soft bed and freedom from the constant jostling of the wagon seat.

"Won't be long now, Haldi, yer sister lives just around that next bend," Edward noted. "Once we gets there it won't be no time 'til we're to Elsie's."

"That's a relief," Eleanor replied, "was beginning to think this journey would never end."

The news made Haldi sit up a little straighter and she looked with interest all around her.

"T'won't be much longer," Edward said again.

Chapter

33

"She's here, she's here," Mary called excitedly to Jake when she spied the wagon coming into the yard. Smokey was leaping and barking and straining against the rope that kept her tethered to the stake Jake had driven into the ground. Mary shushed the animal as she ran out the door and into the yard to welcome her little sister to her home.

Eleanor had to grab Haldi's arm to stop her from jumping from the wagon when Mary appeared in the yard. "Be careful, my dear, just wait," she warned her young charge, "don't need ye to break yer neck!"

Edward pulled gently on the reins bringing the horse to a walk as he eased the wagon into the yard. Haldi, heedless of any danger in her excitement to hug her sister, jumped from the wagon as soon as the wheels stopped turning.

"Mary! Mary! I'm here! I'm here at last," Haldi sang out as she rushed toward her sister.

Mary met her halfway and caught her up in a hard hug, crushing her against her chest in her excitement and delight. Jake walked easily toward the wagon; hand outstretched in welcome to Edward who had dropped lightly onto the ground.

"Can't thank ye enough fer bringing 'er," Jake said as he approached the older man. "Name's Jake, pleased to meet ye!"

"I'm Edward and this here's Eleanor," he replied as he shook Jake's hand, "We ain't going to stop just now. Eleanor is anxious to see Elsie and to finish this journey."

"Are ye sure ye don't wanna come in fer a cup of tea?" Jake asked.

"Oh, I'm sure, b'y," Edward answered as he dragged Haldi's little trunk from the back of the wagon. "Per'aps another time. It's been a long day and we just wants to git to Elsie's."

Jake nodded, "We much appreciate ye taking care of our Haldi," he said.

"Yes," Mary said as she came to stand beside Jake, her arm still around Haldi's waist as they walked forward. "Thank ye both so much!"

"T'was a pleasure," Edward responded, "weren't a bit of trouble, we was comin' out this way anyways."

"Thank ye both," Haldi told the couple, "T'was so kind of ye."

"We'll be off then," Edward said as he climbed back onto the wagon, "have a good night," he nodded at Haldi, "Hope ye ain't too sore on the 'morrow."

"I'll be fine," Haldi retorted, "Drive safe and thanks again."

The trio stood and watched as Edward turned the horse and wagon and left the yard, waving at the couple until at last the wagon was out of sight.

"Come on, let's go in," Mary squeezed Haldi's waist and the sisters moved toward the little cabin.

"Where should I put this?" Jake asked Mary as he turned around the little room with Haldi's trunk in hand.

"Just lay it there, under the window. We'll sort it all out in the morning," Mary answered. All the excitement seemed to hum in the air and acted like an alarm clock for the babies and they soon let their presence be known.

"Seems like yer nieces are not gonna wait long fer an introduction," Mary told Haldi.

"Sit down and rest yer bones, I'll go git 'em," Jake said.

"We fixed up a bed fer ye," Mary said, pointing to the pallet in the corner, "It ain't much, but we tried to make things comfortable fer ye. T'is a small house, but Jake says he'll build ye a room all ye own, if ye decides to stay."

"T'is perfect," Haldi replied looking around the small cabin. "Besides I don't need much, just a place to lay me head. This is nice."

"Jake's been working like mad ever since we came out here," Mary told her sister, "We got lots of plans, but it's coming along. Here, sit down, ye must be tired."

"T'is funny, I was some tired just afore we got here. I thought the trip would never end. But now I'm here I don't feel one-bit tired at'all."

"Sit yerself down and I'll make us a tea," Mary ordered. "Are ye hungry? Got some left-over pea soup, did ye have supper?"

"Naw, not a bit hungry, just so happy to be here," Haldi told Mary.

"Look who's here," Jake said as he came into the room balancing a twin on each arm.

"Can I hold one of 'em?" Haldi asked, "I bin dying to meet 'em."

"This here's Liza," Jake told her as he placed the babe in her arms.

He tilted his arm so Haldi could see the face of Liza's twin, "And this is Lily."

Haldi looked back and forth from one to the other, "How do ye tell 'em apart?" she asked.

"Oh, ye'll be able to tell in no time," Mary grinned at her sister, "they do look alike, don't they?"

"They sure do," Haldi replied, "I don't know how ye don't get 'em mixed up."

"Ye'll see," Jake answered her, "Once ye gets to know 'em better."

The evening hours passed quickly as the trio caught up on news and fussed over the infants.

In Elsie's yard a similar scene played out as the sisters, separated for too long, made much of one another and expressed glad feelings at their reunion.

"How was yer trip," Elsie asked once she had them settled in her little home.

"Seemed too long," Eleanor answered, "I've been longing to be with you ever since news of Joe's death reached us."

Elsie reached across the table and held her sister's hand. "And I am so glad to have ye both here, so very glad. Ye must be so tired, though, was it a good trip?"

"Edward wouldn't let us take many breaks, just to eat and a couple of times to stretch our legs," Eleanor answered, with a quick look at her spouse.

"Well, ye wanted to get here as quickly as possible, didn't ye?" Edward defended himself, "and I got ye here in just one day, what kind of thanks is this?" he teased.

"I did! And I am grateful," Eleanor replied. Turning once again to Elsie she said, "I just wish we could've come sooner."

"Ye're here now and that's all that matters," Elsie told them.

"T'was a nice day fer a ride in the country," Edward replied.

"It is beautiful country 'round here," Eleanor said, "I can see why ye love it so."

"I do. I really do. I can't wait fer ye to meet Fanny and Mick. They have been so good to me. I don't know what I would have done without them after Joe died," Elsie said, "and their children too. They're wonderful people and they're my family, just as ye are."

"I am so glad they're been such a help to ye," Eleanor remarked. "When will we meet 'em?"

"Ye can meet Fanny and the younger children tomorrow, but Mick and the elder boys work at the quarry so they will be off at first light. Ye will meet 'em after they get home from work tomorrow," Elsie answered. "I was thinking to prepare a big supper on Sunday for all of us. Would ye like that?"

"Ye don't need to go through so much trouble on our account," Eleanor began but Edward cut her off.

"Don't be talking, woman," He put in, "Elsie, my dear, I'd be happy to have a big meal with all ye any day of the week."

Elsie laughed, "I will see to it, then."

Eleanor was shaking her head at Edward, "Man loves to eat," she said.

"It's always a joy to cook fer people who enjoy eating. I know my Joe did," Elsie responded.

"They musta bin cut from the same cloth," Eleanor smiled. "I sometimes think I ain't ever gonna be able to fill this one."

"I'm just gonna go grab our things, mebbe have a look around," Edward said, "If that's all right with ye, Elsie."

"Ye just make yerself at home," Elsie replied, "don't be long though, I'll have tea and a lunch ready in just a little while. Ye must be hungry."

"Edward is always hungry," Eleanor replied, "I must confess, a cup of tea sounds good."

"Be back in a bit," Edward said as he walked to the door, "Give ye ladies a chance to chat."

Elsie hugged her sister once again. "I really am so very glad yer here. Come, have a look in the pantry and see what ye'd like to have with yer tea."

"Don't be going to too much trouble. We had our supper, we're fine, really we are," Eleanor replied but followed Elsie to the small closet that served as a pantry.

"That gooseberry jam looks so good. Ye always did make the best. Edward would love to have that on a bit of bread," Eleanor told her.

"I have some left over stew. Do ye think he'd like some?" Elsie asked again. "Won't take long to heat it."

"No need to fuss. He'll be happy with a bite of bread and jam," Eleanor replied. "We don't want to put ye out."

"I'm so happy yer here," Elsie said. "Just want ye both to make yerself at home."

Eleanor glanced around the cabin. "Yer home is so nice, Elsie. We will be comfortable, I'm sure of it. Don't worry yerself about us."

Elsie moved to the table to lay out the food, "tell me, how are the children? They must be so grown up by now. It'd be so nice to see them."

"Isaac is a head taller than me and nearly as tall as his father already. Phoebe is quite the young lady. She made handkerchiefs for ye. They're in my bag. She embroidered them in tiny blue flowers, so pretty they are," Eleanor answered. "The youngest boys are growing as well, I wish they could all meet ye. Per'aps one day ye will come see us."

"Life is a funny thing," Elsie replied. "Ye never know, maybe one day. I remember Isaac's curls and those big brown eyes. Phoebe was such a tiny little thing when I left home. And Ma didn't mind comin' to stay with the children?"

"Not a bit," Eleanor replied, "Said she'd be keeping a close eye on all of 'em. Phoebe will help and the boys are all old enough now that she won't need to be toting little ones around. Isaac will look after the animals and firewood, and such. It's strange to be away from them all."

"Ye will miss them, and they will miss ye," Elsie answered. She filled the kettle and put it on the stove while they chatted.

"Elsie, dear, how have ye been doin'? I've been so worried about ye. I knows it got to be so hard," Eleanor sympathized.

"It is. It was such an awful shock when it happened," Elsie paused as she lifted cups and saucers from the cupboard. "I miss him so much. He was such a dear, dear man. I will take ye up to the cemetery tomorrow, if ye wants."

"Yes, of course," Eleanor answered. "We do want to pay our respects. If it isn't too hard for ye."

"Not a bit," Elsie returned to the table and sat beside her sister. "I've been fine, well, as fine as a body can be under the circumstances. Fanny and Mick have been wonderful and their children are often here, especially Jack. They all make sure I don't want for nothin'." Elsie's eyes filled with tears. "The only thing I want for nobody can give me and that's Joe back." She shrugged her shoulders and Eleanor stood to wrap her arms around her. The women were quiet for several minutes while Elsie collected herself again.

"Ye know, Ma would be delighted to have ye come back home," Eleanor began but Elsie shook her head violently.

"This is my home. This is where I feel close to Joe. I won't leave," Elsie said, passionately.

"Ye don't find it harder, being here with all the memories?" Eleanor asked.

"I don't expect ye to understand but having Joe's things around me, well, it gives me comfort," Elsie replied. "If I were to leave, I think it would be even harder than it has been. No, my place is here in this house Joe built fer us with 'is own two hands. Besides, I like to visit his grave and our little one's as well. I couldn't do that if I moved back home with Ma."

"T'is a fine place ye have here," Edward said as he came in the door carrying Eleanor's satchel. He stopped in mid-step as he took in the solemn expressions. "Guess I should go back out fer the trunk," he said.

"No, no, dear," Elsie answered. "Ye come right in and sit yerself down. Eleanor assures me ye love gooseberry jam and the tea will be ready in just a minute."

Edward looked to Eleanor for reassurance before lowering himself onto a chair. "Don't want to be interrupting yer talk," he told the women.

"We'll have plenty of time fer chatter," Eleanor replied. "We was just making plans to go up to the cemetery to visit Joe's grave, that's all."

"Did ye have a look at the barn and the animals?" Elsie asked. "We share the cow with Fanny and Mick and their crowd. It's worked out well fer all of us. Mick says the pig is growing nicely and will soon be ready to butcher. He's quite a size, eh?"

"Yes, I did have a look-see," Edward answered. "That pig is big enough to feed an army – my gosh, what a size. What are ye feeding it to get it so big?"

"Mostly table scraps and vegetable peelings is all," Elsie replied. "I can scarce believe it's the same piglet Joe brought home last fall. He was some proud of it, got 'im in trade fer a few chickens and ye wouldn't know but he roped the moon and brought it home to me." Elsie smiled at the memory of Joe holding that piglet under his arm as he pushed open the door calling for her to come see what he had. "He was some proud."

"Well, ye did a fine job raising it. Most people get a piglet in the spring and butcher it in the fall. Maybe that's how he got so big, all them extra months of eating." Edward retorted with a grin.

"Can't take all the credit, Mick and the boys have been helping a lot," Elsie replied. "Can't wait fer ye all to meet. Ye'll like them. They're a fine family."

Conversation continued on into the evening about the farm and sharing stories about Joe and the ongoing efforts Mick was undertaking to make sure changes came to the quarry to safeguard the men. Elsie heard all the recent news and caught up on the recent goings on with all her family before Edward's stifled yawns made her declare it time for bed.

Chapter
34

Haldi was already dressed and sitting on the cot with a blanket around her shoulders when Mary crept from her room the next morning.

"It's barely light, yet. What are ye doing up so early?" Mary asked her.

"T'was too excited to sleep," Haldi replied. "I remembered ye was always an early bird. I ain't been up long."

Mary smiled at her sister as she crossed the room to place more logs in the little wood stove. "Old habit," she agreed. "I love the early morning hours, especially here. Jake will be out any minute. He has to go to work. If yer alright I'll tend to him first. Do ye want tea? Ye look cold. Not warm enough fer ye?" She asked.

"I was fine. Blanket's too nice and toasty to give up," Haldi replied. "Do ye need any help?"

"Naw, I'm fine," Mary replied, "Just got to get the kettle on fer tea. What would ye like fer yer breakfast? I was gonna fix porridge fer Jake and a couple of boiled eggs, if ye'd like some."

"Porridge is fine," Haldi was answering when they heard the thin wail of a baby. Haldi hopped up off the bed. "Why don't ye see to yer little ones? I can start the porridge fer ye."

"Jake will pick 'er up," Mary replied. "He helps me with 'em afore he goes to work."

"Well, I'm here to help ye now," Haldi firmly replied, "Ye go see to 'em and I will do this."

Mary smiled at her sister. "If yer sure ye ain't too tired after the trip . . ."

"Sure am, I 'ad a good sleep. I'm fit as a fiddle ready to be played," Haldi told Mary, "Ye go on now. I come here to help not to lay about." With that Haldi gave her sister a friendly push toward the bedroom. Haldi was at the stove stirring the pot of porridge when Jake came out of the room.

"Morning, did ye 'ave a good rest?" He asked as he crossed the floor to pull on his boots.

"Slept like a baby," Haldi answered. "Where are ye off to already?"

"Gonna go look after the animals, that's all," Jake replied. "I'll be back in a little while."

Haldi nodded and turned back to the stove. "At least he'll have a bit more time to do whatever needs doing afore he heads off to work," she said to herself as she stirred. Moments later Mary returned with Liza in her arms.

"Where's 'er sister?" Haldi asked.

"Liza is an early riser like her Mama," Mary answered, "Lily will be waking up before long though."

Soon the little kitchen was abuzz with chatter and laughter as the sisters looked after the babies and got breakfast underway. Jake was whistling as he set out toward the quarry. Not even thoughts of the captain could dampen his spirits as he strode through the woods.

Around the bay Elsie was also up and doing many of the same kinds of chores as she waited for her company to awake from their slumber. She was at the sideboard cutting bread for their breakfast when Eleanor appeared.

"Sleep well?" Elsie asked, turning toward her.

"I did! Still feel bad about ye giving up yer bed fer us, but yes, slept like a log," Eleanor answered. "What about ye? Still don't like the idea of ye sleeping on that little settee."

"I had a wonderful sleep, best I had since Joe died," Elsie responded cheerfully, "had I known I would've slept there fer long ago."

"Ye ain't telling tales, are ye?" Eleanor's wrinkled brow betrayed her concern.

"Now would I do that?" Elsie grinned at her sister. "Come, have a seat. Kettle's about to boil and we'll make tea. Stop yer worrying. I'm fine."

"G'mornin' ladies," Edward greeted them as he stepped into the kitchen. "I just need to step outside, be right back,"

Edward had just finished using the outhouse and was heading back to Elsie's cabin when he noticed Jack coming from the barn.

"Morning, we ain't met yet, I'm Edward Ryan," he introduced himself.

Jack nodded shyly and held out his hand, "I'm Jack," he said.

"I hear ye all have to get off to the quarry this morning, thought I'd offer to make meself useful. If ye show me where ye keep the feed fer the animals I can help out."

"Da's already in the barn," Jack replied, "c'mon I'll introduce ye. Yer married to Aunt Elsie's sister, right?"

"That's me," Edward nodded and followed Jack into the barn.

"Da, hey, Da," Jack called out as they entered the small shelter.

Mick had been milking the cow but stood up as he heard Jack calling out to him. "What's going on?" He asked his son before he noticed Edward behind him.

"Da, I want ye to meet Edward, I mean Mister Ryan," Jack blustered through the introduction with a blush on his cheeks.

"Edward's fine," the newcomer hastened to add, "Elsie's me sister-in-law, which I guess ye knows." Edward stood ready to shake Mick's hand.

"She's mine as well," Mick grinned, "Opposite side of the family though. But any kin of Elsie's welcome here."

"Thank ye, kindly," Edward said as he shook Mick's hand. "Joe was yer brother, right? T'was sorry to hear that terrible news, sorry fer yer troubles," Edward paused, "I just wanted to make meself useful, like I was tellin yer son. I'd be happy to feed the animals or do anything might need doing while yer at work today."

"That's mighty good of ye," Mick replied. "I already looked after the animals. I can't think of anything at the moment, but I will give it some thought while I'm at the quarry. Do ye plan to stay long?"

"A fortnight's about all I can take from the sawmill," Edward answered, "and I know the wife will be wanting to get back to the family."

"Well, if I think of anything, I'll be sure to let ye know," Mick answered. "Why don't ye come over for a tea after supper? Say, do ye fish at'all? Dory's there if ye a mind to take 'er out."

"That's a grand idea. I just wants to give the women time to visit and catch up. Don't wanna be underfoot. Do ye have any gear I can use?" Edward asked.

"There's cod jiggers hanging up in the barn. Help yerself," Mick answered.

"I appreciate that. Was wonderin' what I'd be doing with meself," Edward replied.

"Well, we got to get going, but yer welcome to use whatever gear ye find and like I said, come on over this evening fer a visit, if ye wants."

"We may just do that," Edward answered, "see what the wife wants to do. Ye have a good day now. Pleased to meet ye both, and thanks again fer the lend of yer boat." With that Edward exited the barn to return to Elsie's cabin.

"Met yer kin, well, Mick and Jack anyway," Edward told Elsie as he sat at the table. "Seems like mighty fine folk. Offered me the use of a dory if I care to go fishing. What are yer plans fer the day?" He asked the sisters.

"Elsie and me were gonna to go visit the cemetery," Eleanor told him. "I want to pay my respects to Joe. Did ye want to come?"

"Sure, we can take the wagon. How far away is the cemetery?" He asked Elsie.

"Not far at all. We could walk, if ye like," Elsie replied.

"T'is a fine day," Edward answered. "Nice day fer a walk."

"I'd rather walk. I'm in no hurry to climb back on that wagon," Eleanor commented ruefully.

"Let me clear away the dishes and we'll do that, then," Elsie smiled.

Later that morning the trio were strolling toward the churchyard as Elsie pointed out various places she and Joe had visited frequently and filled them in on Mick's ongoing efforts to form an association and plans for the future.

That afternoon Edward went to check out the dory that was overturned on the bank. *Well now, she's in good condition, needs a coat of paint,* he thought, *if the weather holds, I think I'll have a go at catching a few cod on the morrow.* With that Edward decided to have a walk along the beach to give his wife and sister-in-law a chance to catch up.

It was a beautiful evening and Elsie paused to point out the osprey flying overhead as the trio walked across the yard to visit Mick and Fanny.

"They're such fantastic birds to watch but I am grateful Joe thought to make the chicken coop hawk-proof. These ones are known fishers and we haven't had any trouble but folk say they will kill chickens and small rodents and such. Some even say they will kill cats and small dogs," Elsie said, "I remember watching them back home as a girl. I get such a thrill when I see them . . . they kind of remind me of home."

"There's still plenty around home," Eleanor replied, "eagles, too. We've seen fights when an eagle was trying to make a fish hawk drop its catch."

"The eagle was bigger, but that hawk wasn't letting go of its supper easily," Edward continued the tale, "it was mighty feisty and that eagle finally gave up and flew off."

Elsie smiled, "I feel for birds of prey. Most folk try to kill them or at least drive them off the land. Joe felt there was plenty of food for people and birds and hated to see them hunted."

"I think most people have a fear of 'em. They do have wicked looking talons," Edward replied. The trio stood still watching the raptor until Elsie motioned toward Fanny's cottage. "Shall we?" she asked.

Elsie rapped lightly on the door and opened it, calling out softly as she did so, "We're here, Fan."

"Come in, come in and welcome," Fanny greeted her company. Mick sat in a chair he'd pulled out from the table cradling his infant son in his arms. "Ye made it, forgive me fer not standing, got me 'ands full," he apologized.

"Don't get up," Elsie told him, "I know ye met Edward and this here is my sister, Eleanor."

"Pleased to meet ye," Mick nodded, "Did ye take the dory out?" He asked Edward.

"Not today, I hope to do that on the morrow, if the day is fine," Edward replied.

"This is Fanny," Elsie finished her introductions, "my best friend and sister-in-law."

Fanny stepped forward; hand extended in welcome to her visitors. "So glad to finally meet ye," she told them, "Elsie speaks highly of ye both."

"Where're the boys? I assume the girls are already in bed," Elsie spoke to Fanny but her eyes settled on Mick and the baby he held in his arms.

"The boys are all out in the barn, doing chores, and yes, I just got the girls settled a few minutes ago," Fanny answered.

Elsie turned to her sister and Edward, "Ye will meet all the children soon. They are all so nice."

"Ye and Joe had a hand in that," Fanny told her, "Sure, ye helped raise 'em."

"And I hope to help raise this one, too," Elsie said as she walked across the kitchen, "May I?" she asked Mick, indicating the infant he held.

Mick stood and gave the baby to her, "He will love his aunt just as much as the others do," he told her as he laid the child in her arms.

After the small talk was over the group sat at the table sipping tea and getting acquainted.

The following Sunday Mick, Fanny, and their family crowded into Elsie's small yard.

"T'was a beautiful service," Eleanor remarked, referring to the church service they had taken part in, "yer pastor seems like a nice man."

"He's wonderful!" Fanny agreed, "we are fortunate to have him."

"He's a man of God, a true man of God," Elsie agreed, "Joe thought the world of him."

"Sarah, come rock Jimmy while I help yer aunt and Mrs. Ryan," Fanny ordered her daughter, "and Rose ye stay right here. Don't need ye getting into anything."

"They're fine, Fan, ye don't need to worry about Rose getting into mischief, she's a good child," Elsie defended her niece. Looking at Eleanor she said, "Rose and Sarah have been wonderful company and a big help, too."

Rose smiled shyly at her aunt as she crawled into the chair beside her sister. The men were still standing outside. Mick's sons were all quietly listening to Mick and Edward as they chatted about the quarry and the hoped-for protective association. Before long the families were gathered in Elsie's kitchen enjoying the meal and getting to know one another better.

Chapter
35

The men were milling about as they waited for the meeting to begin. Many were worried but many more were ready to fight for fair pay and decent hours, those were the men who had left the island and had enjoyed better pay and conditions on the mainland. These men worked hard to convince their comrades of the wisdom of an association, of the real strength in numbers.

"I'm sure it ain't just me can't afford to risk losing me job, or to be losing pay from refusing ta work," Andrew growled, "I ain't afeared to say it like it is; to call a spade a spade!"

"I knows what yer sayin'," Jacob began, "but we needs safer workin' conditions. Stuff that 'appens 'ere would never be up on the mainland. I tell ye we can win this fight if we sticks together."

"Them that owns the mine will make us pay fer our actions," Andrew argued, "ye knows they's gonna find a way to make life miserable. Either they'll not give us our jobs back or else make us work fer less pay, or fer longer 'ours. Mark my words, they's gonna make us pay fer it if'n we does this thing."

"And I'm tellin' ye they will give over," Jacob refuted, "I seen it 'appen afore. Like Charlie said, they wants the freighters filled and they don't want no work stoppage. Oh, they'll threaten and try to browbeat us but if we sticks by our guns ye'll see, they will back off. I promise ye that."

"Put it this way, mate, the few of ye who don't join us still ain't gonna have any work," a burly man spoke up, "if ye ain't with us then ye'll be on yer own. Won't be enough of ye to run the quarry so ye won't be working anyway. Then where will ye be? Yer better off joining us and try to make it better for the whole crew."

Andrew glared at the man. "Still would like to know 'ow long we'd be outta work."

"Sure, there's nobody can tell us that," Jacob retorted, "It depends on whether the company decides to dig their heels in. Peter should 'ave some idea. Let's just see what the man's found out and what he's got to say."

"I'll 'ear 'im out all right, but I ain't got a good feelin' 'bout this at'all," Andrew complained.

"I know yer worried. We all is," Jacob said as he grabbed Andrew's shoulder and gave it a squeeze, "Looks like they're 'bout ready to start. Just give it a fair 'earing."

"I'm here, ain't I?" Andrew asked. "I said I will give it a listen. That's alls I can promise."

"Fair enough," Jacob returned, "fair enough."

Charlie gave a sharp whistle and the murmuring fell quiet.

"Look here, men, there's something we learned that we wants to share with ye all afore we starts the meetin'. It could make a difference to how ye all vote. So, if I can have yer attention," Charlie began, "Harry, do ye mind comin' up here and standin' with me?"

"Ye tole me I wouldn't have ta talk," Harry answered.

"No, ye don't need to say nothin'," Charlie answered him, "Just come here alongside me while I tells yer story so's the men knows it's true."

Harry gave Charlie a glare but made his way to the front of the room to stand beside him.

"This here's Harry," Charlie told the room full of men, "T'was Harry that t'was working with Joe the day he got hit by that cart. This is important cuz it could've of bin any one of ye that got hit.

"That day Harry and Joe had filled their cart with limestone and it was ready to send down the line, but the cart wouldn't budge. That right, Harry?"

At Harry's nod Charlie continued, "They tried everything to get it rollin' but it was stuck fast." Charlie looked at Harry for confirmation. He nodded again. "So, Harry went to get grease, figuring the wheels on that cart was seized up. Is that right so far, Harry?"

"Yup, that's right," Harry agreed.

"Would ye say that maybe that cart was not in good working order?" Charlie asked Harry.

"The son of a bitch wouldn't budge, no matter what we tried," Harry answered.

"So, Harry went to see the pit boss to get grease to apply to them wheels. We can't know exactly what happened while he was gone. But it stands to reason that Joe got behind the cart intending to try again to push it along the track. He got caught between his cart and the one Jake had accidently set rolling down the track. Ye all knows what happened and now ye knows why," Charlie finished the story.

"Did I leave anything out?" he asked Harry.

"Nope. Nar a ting," Harry replied.

"Thanks, Harry, ye can go on back now, if ye wants," Charlie said. Harry nodded and moved away.

"The thing is, we knows Jake was working alone, which is against the regulations. We knows the new hires weren't being told all the rules. And now we knows the cart Joe was working when he got hurt was not in good working order," Charlie told the crowd. "Joe would be alive today if it weren't fer the fact this company only cares 'bout their money and not one whit about the men they hire to do the work. Now, I'm gonna turn this over to Peter, who has a few things he wants to tell ye afore we puts this to a vote. Peter, ye ready to take the floor?"

Men shuffled their feet and there was some mumbling as they waited for Peter to take the floor. Charlie gave another sharp whistle to get their attention as Peter stepped forward.

"Right! Well, now, it seems to me we got a very strong case that will make the company think twice about denying yer demands," Peter began. "Look, I knows yer worried about the response ye may get from the company, but I am here to tell ye that ye have a good, strong case, especially now with Harry's story, and if ye all sticks together we can make yer jobs safer and more profitable.

"But that report says it weren't the company's fault what 'appened to Joe," Andrew pointed out, "So 'ow can we prove it?"

"If men are willing to speak up, to stand up fer what's right, we can get justice fer Joe, but it takes courage. I don't think a one of ye are cowards. And, Harry, ye don't work fer the quarry no more so they can't threaten ye. Are ye willing to stand behind what ye told us?" Charlie responded.

"Joe was a good man. I considered 'im a friend, damned straight I will stand behind me story," Harry answered.

"It likely won't come to that," Peter replied, "It's enough to know that there are men that are willing to come forward. We just needs to lay it out to the captain when we gives him the terms of association."

"Just what are the terms?" one of the men spoke out.

"First things first," Peter responded, "We need to decide if ye wants to form a protective association or not. Let me explain a few things I found out as far as wages go, and fair work hours too. And remember what I told ye all before, about the sealers' association and how they stood up to the merchants. It all comes down to strength in numbers. If there's enough of ye that agree to forming an association we will draft a list of demands to bring to the captain. He will have to take it to the owners and wait for their answer. In the meanwhile, not a man works this quarry – not one! It will have an impact. I can promise ye that. In fact, the demand for limestone is such that the owners will not want to leave the quarry unworked, not even for a day. But it will take a day or two to bring it to the captain and for him to get an answer from the company.

"Look, b'ys, men at the limestone quarry on the mainland are being paid twenty cents an hour – that's nearly double the wages of what ye men are getting. That's one thing. And there's times ye men are working double the hours like when there's a rush to get a freighter out, like what happened when Joe got killed. The company can be forced to hire more labourers so's that won't happen ever again. And to pay overtime wages – that's time and a half, so your hourly wage and half that again – for whomever chooses to work over and beyond the hours normally worked.

"Quarries on the mainland work much the same as here but with one difference – they don't run sixty to eighty hours a week. No, sir, mining companies with protective associations run ten hours a day five days a week – five, mind you, not six! And as I already told ye, the men there are paid twenty cents an hour, not the eleven cents an hour ye lot are getting.

257

"I already answered most of yer questions at the last meetin' and there's been developments since then, like Harry comin' back and learning 'bout that cart not workin' right – and that's another thing we can put into the demands – tools and machinery have to be in good workin' order. There's more, of course but we got to get on with it,"

Peter laid out the terms of the association and the demands to be made upon the company. "Now, we needs to put it to a vote. I am calling a break so ye men can discuss it. But when we come back, I need an answer either yeah or nay to forming an association. All right, then, the time for talking is past. I will give ye a half hour, then I expect an answer." Peter finished his speech and walked across the hall where Charlie, Mick, and Harry were standing. "Guess I don't need to ask how ye three feel about all this, seeing as ye helped organize these meetings. What do ye think? Will the men vote for an association?"

"I think it stands a good chance. From what I'm hearin' the men will vote 'yes'," Mick answered. "at least, the majority of 'em will."

"That's my take on it, too," Charlie agreed. "Listen, Peter, we're all much obliged to ye fer all yer help with all this."

"Happy to help, b'y, happy to help," Peter replied. "T'is long past time ye lot got a fair shake, in my view."

"Will ye be able to stay and write it up to bring to the captain?" Mick wanted to know.

"I plan to give it my all," Peter promised, "This ain't my first go 'round at this. I know someone who is willing to write it up so it's legal and binding. Ye don't need to worry about that. And I can come with ye to present it to the captain, if ye wants me to."

"Don't know how we can ever repay ye fer all yer help," Mick said.

"Don't need no payment," Peter responded, "I have me own reasons for helping ye out. Remember too that Hank's my cousin, a distant cousin, but blood nonetheless. I will be satisfied to see the association in place and better lives fer ye all."

"It's mighty good of ye just the same," Charlie put in, "If we can bring pressure on the company, well, it will be justice, of a sort, fer Joe. Much as I'd like to see the captain and every last one of 'em put in jail fer what they done. I knows that ain't likely to ever happen."

"No, not likely a'tall. T'is a rich man's world and that's a fact," Mick replied.

Peter shuffled and seemed uncomfortable with the turn in conversation. "Be that as it may, this here's a step in the right direction," he told them. Hank, Vic, and Mick's sons joined the small group and the discussion continued around the injustices to be put right once an association was in place. Around the room men had broken into small groups and some had moved outside where the odd raised voice could be heard arguing for or against. Before long the time for discussion passed and Charlie was once again whistling for order.

"Okay, ye lot, what say ye? With a show of hands who among ye vote 'yeah'? Charlie's deep voice boomed out. Peter counted as men raised their hands.

"And who among ye vote 'nay'?" Charlie asked again. The number of hands were easily counted and many who had initially raised a hand quickly lowed their arms as they looked about the room seeing few in agreement.

"Gentlemen," Peter grinned widely. "I believe we have an association!"

Applause was thundering and the meeting erupted. Peter stayed to answer the questions that continued to fly. Excitement mounted and Mick was gratified as the meeting wound down to see the hope and satisfaction on many a face.

"All right, men," Peter said as he closed the meeting, "I will be back with the proper paperwork to present to the captain. Once these papers are delivered all work is to stop until we get an answer from the company. Until then, work will continue as usual. Give me a week to get this wrote up and delivered to the captain. Ye did a good thing here. I can promise ye, ye won't be sorry. Carry on and I will be seeing ye all soon."

"One more thing," Charlie called out, "I'd like ye all to show Peter here yer gratitude and appreciation fer all he's done fer us, by round of applause."

The room exploded with applause, whistling, and foot stomping as the men gave evidence of their gratitude.

"Thanks again, Peter," Mick said as he held out his hand to shake. Peter was surrounded as one after another came forward to do the same.

Chapter

36

eter shook the rain from his hat and placed it on the desk after entering the small law office. "Morning, Uncle John," he greeted the gray-haired man behind the desk. "I come to draw up them papers I asked ye about."

The barrister sighed deeply as he gazed at the younger man. "Guess you're determined to carry on with it, then? Despite all my recommendations and guidance to the contrary?" John asked as he wiped his spectacles with gaunt and bony fingers. "I can write it up for ye but I don't want my name associated with this business," he said.

"T'will be as we agreed," Peter nodded. "As far as anyone here in town knows, I am just here to visit my beloved uncle, that's all. Dominion Limestone will never catch wind of it. I give ye my solemn oath not to breathe a word of yer involvement."

"I wish to God ye had never started down this road," John replied. "But I will take ye at yer word. Ye knows I have to protect my name and the reputation of this establishment. If word of this were to get out it could spell trouble," he warned.

"Not a breath, not a word will ever pass my lips," Peter promised. "Besides, many will assume I wrote it up myself, even though I never finished my law studies."

"I hope yer right," John said, "It ain't just my own affairs would be affected. The family takes a dim view of your shenanigans, as they call it. Ye need to get over what happened all them years ago. Go into the business with yer father and brother, like they planned on ever since ye were a small lad."

"That's never going to happen, Uncle John," Peter answered firmly, "Never!"

John sighed again, "I won't harp on it again. Have ye been home at all in the last six months? Seems to me all ye do is travel back and forth across this island stirring folks up and trying to change how it's always been. Men have a right to make their fortunes however they see fit."

"No, Uncle John, not when making their fortunes means the death of good men or at the very least, severe crippling, so they cannot put food on the table for their families," Peter retorted. "I won't forget what happened, not now, not ever. Our family was to blame and I will spend my life making amends the best way I know how."

"It t'was just a stroke of bad luck, nothing more," John argued.

"That mine had been run down, ye knows that's true," Peter refuted, "and the men had been at it all hours. They were pulling iron ore out of it almost 'round the clock. That's how Luke's father got killed. They called it an accident. It wasn't an accident. I heard all the talk. I know that mine wasn't safe and I know how that section collapsed. Father and his partners owed the men better than they got. Ye can't treat people like animals – no, worse than animals! It ain't right, Uncle John, it just ain't right. And I intend to keep working toward making sure men are treated fairly, and paid fairly too, whether that's on sealing ships, in mills, or in mines!"

"My dear boy, we've been through this time and time again," his uncle responded, "I don't have a hope of ever convincing you otherwise. But still I try, for your father's sake." The elder gent gave another deep sigh as he regarded his nephew. "Blood is thicker than water. I know Luke was your friend and playmate when ye were little lads but we're talking family here, your blood and kin."

"And what about Luke's blood and kin? They were scattered far and wide, sent to beg and plead for their daily bread, at the mercy of hard-hearted task masters, much like my father," Peter passionately burst out. "Don't talk to me about blood and kin. I begged my father to help them. He would not. I was too young to do anything for Luke and his family. But I haven't forgotten and I will help those I can. I will!"

261

"Your father is neither hard-hearted or cruel. His hands were tied. You know that," John answered the outburst. "He was not the sole proprietor of that mine. He had partners to answer to. He couldn't have changed the working conditions without their agreement ..." John's words trailed off as he regarded the hardened expression on his nephew's face. He shook his head and sighed again. "I can see there's no moving ye. All right then, let's get to your bit of business."

Peter's face softened as he gazed at the face of his uncle. "Thank, you, Uncle. I mean that sincerely."

"You're fortunate, you know. That mine has allowed ye to be a man of means. Ye might consider that as ye go traveling back and forth across this land," John replied, mildly.

"I do consider it," Peter said bitterly, "every single day."

"Right, then, well, let's get to it. I have other business to attend to," John spoke gruffly as he pulled paper and pen from the wide drawer of his desk. The two men spent the rest of the morning drafting a legal document that Peter hoped would make life easier and better for the men of the quarry and for the generations that would follow.

"Right, then, I think we covered everything," John said as he pushed his chair back. Standing, he stretched, bony fingers kneading his lower back, "that document is air-tight, at least, as air-tight as I can make it. Ye'll have to make copies. I won't ask my clerk to do that. I don't need tongues wagging. Make sure ye dot every 'i' and cross every 't'."

"I will, Uncle, I will, I do appreciate your help. I really do," Peter stood as well and reached out to shake his uncle's thin hand.

"Give yer father some thought, my son," John answered as he shook Peter's hand, "things aren't so black and while as you may think. Life is never so simple as that."

Peter shook his head, "As long as conditions continue the same at the mine, I cannot abide his company," he answered.

"Be that as it may, he's still your father," John advised, "try, just try, to see it through his eyes".

"I cannot, Uncle John, I simply cannot do that. All I see are the worn-out bodies of men old before their time," Peter answered sadly. "But I do appreciate your kindness and your commitment to the family. I will see you again before I leave town. Perhaps we can have a meal, or a pint at least."

"I'd like that," John replied. "Since your aunt died, I usually dine alone. I would welcome your company."

"Shall we say a week from the morrow?" Peter enquired.

"That suits. Come to the house," John answered. "But let's have no more talk about the mine or of protective associations, ye hear?"

Peter smiled and nodded, "Sounds wonderful, Uncle. I look forward to it."

It was hours later when Peter laid the pen down. He had made one more copy and intended to make a second before he'd hand the documents over to the captain to take to Dominion Limestone. He stood up and gazed out the window of his place of lodging in the rooming house. The rain continued to pour; great sheets blown sideways by the high winds. His thoughts turned to his uncle and the summers he'd spent with him on the West coast of the island. *He was always more like a father to me than Papa ever was.* Peter allowed himself to reflect on the past until images of his friend, Luke, sprang to mind, as often happened when he allowed himself to wander back in time. *Enough of that,* he sternly told himself, *what's done is done. But I made myself a promise – a promise to Luke as well, I will use my family's money to make things better where I can and by God, I will.* Peter nodded to himself and pushed his chair away from the small table that served as his desk. The rain had finally stopped and he fancied a hot meal.

Chapter

37

"That's wonderful news," Fanny exclaimed when Mick had finished telling her about the meeting and the affirmative vote.

"It's a step in the right direction. We still have to wait for Peter to have the papers drawn up to give to the captain and then we'll see what the company has to say 'bout it all," Mick replied. "It ain't a done deal, but I believe the b'ys will stand by their vote and stay away from the quarry 'til we gits what we wants."

"So ye won't be workin' this week? How long will it take before the papers are ready?" Fanny asked.

"Naw, we'll be workin' until the papers are given to the capt'n. Peter figures he should have it all done up within the next few days. Then we'll hold a meetin' to go over it all. Peter says we needs somebody to represent the men on a day-to-day basis. I'm thinking Charlie would be a good man fer that," Mick responded. "Like I said, it ain't all said and done yet, but at least the ball's rollin'."

"That's wonderful," Fanny said again, "I'm right proud of ye, I am."

"Like as not we'll work this week, after that, well, guess we have to wait and see, so hold yer tongue, ain't nuddin' to be proud of just yet," Mick spoke gruffly but his face wore an expression of satisfaction giving lie to his words.

"I seen Elsie fer a few minutes today. She was telling me Eleanor and Edward are leaving in a couple of days," Fanny said. "I wonder if ye'd mind having them over before they leaves. I knows yer tired after working all day."

"Not a bit of it," Mick replied, "fact is I'd like a word with Edward about that saw mill of his. There's a bit of business I wants to talk with him about. It's too bad they're leaving so soon. I was hoping to get to know them better but all these goings on with the association has kept me hopping."

"I'll go over to see them tomorrow then, ask them to come fer a visit," Fanny replied. "Should I offer 'em supper, do ye think? Or would that be too much fer ye after working all day?"

"After supper might be better, by then I'll have my second wind," Mick answered, "right now I best be getting out to the barn, check on the animals."

Mick rose wearily from his chair and had his hand on the door when he turned back to his wife. "Fan, I knows I don't say it often but I appreciates all ye do," with that he was out the door leaving Fanny with a pleased look on her face.

It was a long day at the quarry the next day but Mick noticed how the men seemed to walk lighter, shoulders back, as though a burden had been lifted. After supper that evening Fanny put the older boys in charge as she gave them marching orders to make themselves busy outside while they visited with Elsie and her family.

"Keep a close eye on yer sisters and make sure all yer chores are done. I don't wanna see ye back here 'til yer called," she told them as she ushered them all out the door. "I don't want any of ye under foot while we're visiting."

William marched off ahead of his siblings, insulted at being barred from the conversation. Phil took it all in stride as he teased his sisters and Jack on their way to the barn. William grabbed a spade and was busily shoveling manure out of the chicken coop when his brothers and sisters entered the little structure.

"What's eating ya?" Phil asked him as he leaned against the door to the coop.

"Just don't like being treated like a child, here I am about to be a married man," William spat onto the dung and flung a spade full of the pungent stuff into a wheel barrow.

"Don't think Ma meant anything by it. House is too small to hold us all and company too," Phil remarked mildly, "she weren't meaning to insult ya."

William said nothing as he continued to work energetically at cleaning out the coop. It was a job the boys took turns doing. Phil gazed at his brother's back for a few seconds before turning away.

"Hey, Jack, want to give me a hand sawing a few logs fer the stove?" Phil called over to Jack who was sitting on the wood pile just outside the barn door. "And ye girls can help stack the junks of wood."

Phil turned to lift the buck saw from the wall without waiting for an answer and glanced again at William's back before turning to go back outside. The saw horse was standing not far from the wood pile and Phil strode toward it. Jack and his sisters joined him there. An axe was leaning against a large stump used for splitting the small logs into kindling for fire starter. The girls skipped over and were standing beside the stump while Jack stood waiting at the saw horse.

"Sarah, do ye know if Ma still has enough water fer the morrow?" Phil asked as he lifted the buck saw. The boys had hauled water the night before and Phil was not eager to haul more.

"I think so," Sarah answered. "There's still three full pails in the house."

"I'll go ask after we're done with this," Jack offered. Phil nodded at his brother and the two began the process of lifting a long log from the pile to set it on the saw horse. Sarah and Rose sat on the ground and watched their brother's work.

"Will ye take us down to the beach after the chores are done?" Sarah asked Phil.

Phil looked up and grinned at his little sister. "That's the plan. If ye two can help stack the junks of wood the job will get done faster, then we'll have time fer play."

Jack and Phil pushed and pulled the old buck saw back and forth until the small logs created a small mountain and then paused to pile it. With the four siblings working together it wasn't long before there was enough fire wood laid by for several days. Phil stood and stretched his back, rubbing the back of his neck. "I think that'll do," he told his brother and sisters. "Let's go. Hey, Jack wanna go let William know where we're going? Maybe he'll want to join us but chances are he'll want to be off to see Ginny, and take that saw with ya, hang it back up, if'n ye don't mind."

"Will do," Jack replied, "I'll catch up to ye."

The girls gave excited squeals as they danced beside their older brother. Walks on the beach were always fun, especially with Phil and Jack, who would point out interesting driftwood or seashells among other things. When the tide was out the shore often revealed mysteries which the girls had not yet seen. It was always a fun adventure for them. Jack was huffing when he caught up to them.

"William coming?" Phil asked.

"Naw, he's going off to see Ginny, like ye thought he would," Jack replied between breaths. "Said he'd see us at home later, and I didn't dare bother Ma while company's still there so we'll have to find out about hauling water after we gets back,"

"Good enough, t'is a nice evening," Phil remarked as he looked out over the bay, "there's barely a ripple on the water. Whaddaya say, shall we have a rock skipping contest?"

"What do I win if I beats ya?" Jack asked in turn.

"I'll do yer chores tomorrow night, but if I wins ye gotta do mine," Phil offered.

Jack grinned, "Ye're on!" He agreed.

"All right, Sarah, Rose, will ye help us look fer flat rocks for skipping?" Phil asked his sisters.

A pleasant hour passed as the four of them skipped rocks and collected seashells. Jack won but suspected his brother had thrown the game.

Back at their house Elsie had arrived with Edward and Eleanor in tow and conversation centered first around the planned association before Mick turned the conversation around to his cherished dreams.

"Joe and me had planned to build dories to go at lobster fishing," He was telling Edward, "Truth of the matter is I still want to do that. That quarry is dangerous work, even if we gets what we wants from the company. It ain't somethin' I wants to spend the rest of me life at."

"I heard somethin' 'bout a lobster cannery," Edward replied, "but fishing ain't an easy living either."

"Naw, it ain't," Mick replied, "But sure beats slogging yer guts out in that quarry and since Joe died it's a big worry to me wife and to Elsie, too."

Fanny shuddered, "That's the truth," she agreed.

267

"Have ye fished fer lobster before?" Edward asked.

"Joe and me used to fish fer lobster and all kind of fish," Mick responded, "but mostly fer the table. It weren't worth going at with no cannery nearby. Word is the cannery is comin' and expectation is it will be built soon. Trouble here is we only got the one dory. I'd like to have at least two more. And then there's lobster pots to be made. This is where ye come in."

"I don't know a blessed thing 'bout boat building, nor lobster pots either. Dunno how I can help ye," Edward replied.

"T'is wood we need, lumber fer the dories and slats fer lobster pots," Mick explained, "and seeing as how ye owns a saw mill I wanted to see if ye might be interested in a partnership of sorts."

"That would work if I lived nearby, but we're miles away," Edward pointed out, "don't see how that would work."

"Here's what I'm thinking," Mick began, "if ye can see yer way clear to supplying the lumber we could work something out where ye would have a share in the business. Like so much of every haul would be yers and ye wouldn't have to do a thing."

"Except supply the lumber," Edward nodded slowly, beginning to understand, "That might work but t'is a fair jaunt from here to home. How would ye get the lumber out here?"

"I have the work wagon and chances are I could borrow Vic's as well. I sure would like to see me sons set up in something better than a life working the quarry," Mick said, "since Joe died it weighs heavy on me mind."

"Yeah, I can see how it t'would," Edward answered. "We ain't leaving yet fer a couple of days. Why don't ye let me think it through? I needs to size it up, give it more thought. But it seems like a sound idea to me."

"Fair enough," Mick replied, "Do ye think ye might be able to give me an answer afore ye goes home?"

"Sure thing," Edward responded, "might not need that much time to chew it over. Let me sleep on it, maybe we can chat again tomorrow? I knows ye needs to be getting to bed."

"It's been a day," Mick admitted, "I appreciate y'all coming over. Thank ye. And, Edward, whatever ye decide, thanks fer hearing me out."

"Ain't nuddin' to thank me fer, as far as I'm concerned yer family and family takes care of their own," Edward replied, "I know we ain't blood, but we got connections through Elsie, here, and that makes ye family in my book."

Eleanor patted her husband's shoulder, "And ye have been good to Elsie. She's been telling us about all yer kindnesses," she pointed out, "me and Edward, we're both beholden to ye."

Mick glanced at Elsie, "she's family to us and like ye said, family takes care of their own."

"Exactly!" Edward retorted. "Well, ladies, shall we be off and let these good people get to bed?"

The trio rose and were saying their good-byes just as Fanny heard her children chattering to one another in the yard.

"Time to get the girls into bed," she smiled, "I wish ye were stayin' longer."

"Why don't ye come over tomorrow?" Elsie asked. "Edward mentioned taking the dory out again to catch a few cod to take home. It will just be me and Eleanor most of the day."

"Elsie's been tellin' me she's missin' the girls and minding the baby as well," Eleanor smiled at Fanny.

"Elsie is always such a big help," Fanny replied, "I don't know what I'd do without 'er. Yes, I will come, after I get the men off to work and the girls dressed and ready."

"Until the morrow then," Eleanor smiled.

"Thanks fer comin'," Fanny responded, "good night. Girls, come on in, it's past yer bedtime!"

"Ma, do ye need more water?" Jack asked.

"I think I have enough fer the morrow but ye will have to get more by t'morrow evening," Fanny answered. Mick followed his company out into the yard and the trio spent a further few minutes talking with him and the boys after Fanny had called her daughters inside.

Chapter

38

Sarah and Rose loved the attention that Elsie and her sister lavished upon them and were thrilled when Elsie allowed them to bring their cat in for Eleanor to pet and admire. After a while Fanny scooted them outside to play, with an admonition to stay in Elsie's yard. Before long the women were chatting about a multitude of things while intermittently taking turns holding baby Jimmy in their arms, cooing and ahhing over him.

Elsie and Fanny looked quickly at one another as Eleanor continued to talk about what a nice girl Haldi was, what a nice family she was from, and about the gossip she'd heard that Mary had married a half-breed.

"There are many families in these parts that have Indian blood," Elsie replied, "there's naught to be ashamed of and Jake is a fine young man."

"I met Jake when we brought Haldi to their house. He did seem like a good sort. But ye knows people love to talk, I heard he and Mary had to leave. The story goes that folk did not cotton to the idea of Indians living in their midst," Eleanor continued on, "I ain't got a thing against 'em, but lots of folks back home hold a grudge. I think they're jealous."

"Whatever for?" Elsie asked. "Jake is a hard worker and a good man. Joe thought highly of both Jake and Mary, as do I."

"He was making good money, getting' ahead, and certain folks didn't like it," Eleanor replied. "You know how folks can be."

"I never heard the like of it," Elsie retorted. "As my Joe would say, we're all the same in God's eyes."

"There was a preacher liked to give sermons about heathen ways, pagan ways," Eleanor replied, "it was no secret that he hated Mik'maq people. I think he had a good bit to do with it. He's bin gone fer years but the damage was done."

"A man of the cloth should rise above such things," Fanny opined, "Mick and Joe were of one mind in that and I fer one agrees with them."

"People are people," Elsie said, "there's good and bad in all, as Mother is fond of sayin'."

"Makes ye wonder what makes people act the way they do," Fanny pondered, "I mean, a man of the cloth really should know better than to go 'round stirring up hatred."

"But he did," Eleanor nodded solemnly, "it made both Edward and me uncomfortable. Now, I'm not sayin' that preacher was all to blame fer what happened but it sure didn't help. He fanned the flames, so to speak, sowed the poison seeds."

"It must have been somethin' serious to drive Jake and Mary so far away from home, from their family and kin," Fanny spoke aloud.

"I heard that a bad bunch from the area went to their house and caused a lot of damage," Eleanor said, "broke windows and threatened to burn 'em out."

"Oh, my goodness," Elsie exclaimed, "how horrible!"

"Yes. It was," Eleanor agreed. "Jake's whole family moved away, I heard they went to Nova Scotia."

"That's so sad," Fanny replied, shaking her head as she spoke.

"Mary and Jake are such kind and gentle people," Elsie spoke softly, "but I'm beginning to understand why Jake keeps so much to himself."

"That's such a sin," Fanny responded. "They are fine young people. Oh, Eleanor, you should see their twins. Such pretty little babies."

"I know Mary's mother, she's a good woman and so proud of all her children, and proud of them twins, too, even though she's not yet set eyes on 'em. She didn't know about Jake's family until after the fact," Eleanor confided. "She was mighty upset, let me tell ye, an she weren't long putting a stop to wagging tongues – well they stopped their wagging in her presence anyway. She stands up fer Jake and won't hear a word against him."

"Good for her!" Elsie exclaimed. "It's really quite shocking, isn't it?"

"Sadly, there are still some who would do the same again – witch hunters is what Edward calls 'em," Eleanor told them.

"Some people got nothing better to do than put their nose in where it don't belong," Fanny said indignantly.

"Ignorance is what that is," Eleanor replied, "people who got no learnin' at'all."

"Speakin' of learnin'," Fanny began, eager to change the subject, "Elsie, I was wonderin' if ye would consider setting up a school? I am so grateful to ye fer helpin' my youngsters learn their letters and 'rithmatic, but there are so many children here that have nobody to teach 'em. I bin thinking 'bout it a lot, especially since summer's nearly over and we got no teacher fer the fall. Now with Rose just about ready fer school and Sarah's so bright . . ." she trailed off.

"Oh, my!" Elsie exclaimed. "I hadn't given that any thought at'all."

"Well, just sitting here and talking brought it back to my mind," Fanny responded, "I think ye would be such a fine teacher. I had it in my mind fer a long while, but then, well, I didn't want to bring it up with all ye've had on yer plate."

"Elsie, she's right, ye have a gift fer explainin' in ways children would understand," Eleanor agreed, "I think that's a wonderful idea. Nobody loves children like ye do."

"And ye could teach more than writing and 'rithmatic," Fanny enthused.

"But I ain't got no training in that," Elsie disagreed.

"Ye know at least as much as that young'un who barely lasted the year," Fanny argued, "we still have the books from the mainland, ye can look through 'em if ye needs help."

"I don't know," Elsie began.

"Yer a natural," Fanny interrupted, "and it would be such a blessing not to have to go lookin' fer another school mistress."

"Ye've taken me by surprise," Elsie answered. "I would really need to think about it."

"It would be a way to fill yer time," Eleanor said gently, "I know ye miss Joe somethin' terrible. This might help ye as well as the children."

Elsie nodded slowly, "I promise to give it careful thought," she said.

"Please do," Fanny replied, "now, I best get going, I started bread this morning and it's sure to be risen by now. I enjoyed the visit and the tea. Thank you, both. I best call the girls and get on home."

Fanny was taking her leave just as Edward came through the door.

"Yer not leavin' on my account are ye?" He asked. "Sure, there's lots of time."

"Spoken just like a man," Eleanor laughed. "Sure, don't ye know a woman's work ain't ever done?"

"Yes, and I got plenty yet to do at home," Fanny grinned. "No, Edward, it ain't on yer account. I got bread that has to be kneaded and this little one needs a nap," Fanny nodded at the babe she held in her arms.

"Thank ye both fer the tea and company," Fanny said again turning toward the door, "and, Elsie, please be sure to give that more thought." On that note Fanny exited the little cabin calling the girls to her as she went.

"May I ask what it is ye must give more thought to," Edward asked Elsie.

"Fanny's got it in her head I should teach school," Elsie told him, "but I'm not sure I'm up fer the task."

"And I've been tellin' 'er she'd make an excellent teacher," Eleanor added.

"Why not," Edward asked, "ye do have a talent fer it."

"I need to give it a lot more thought. It's come as somethin' of a surprise," Elsie replied. "We don't even have a proper schoolhouse, just a little shack that's really not fit. It's always cold in the winter – too many cracks that let the wind in."

Edward stroked his chin thoughtfully, "Perhaps that's somethin' I might be able to help with, if ye decides ye wants to do it."

"Edward? What do ye have in mind?" Eleanor asked.

"It's just a thought but if I get enough help from the men around here it wouldn't take that long to build a schoolhouse – a one room schoolhouse. T'wouldn't take much at'all." Edward answered.

"Oh dear," Elsie responded, "I haven't had a chance to think it through yet. I do appreciate yer kindness, Edward, but I just don't know."

"Lots of time, you can always write to us and let us know yer plans," Edward reassured her, "there's no rush, is there?"

"Fanny says there's no school teacher here. The last one left rather abruptly," Eleanor told him.

"So, time is of the essence, then?" Edward asked.

"You could say that," Elsie answered.

"Well, my dear, if ye wants to teach and need a schoolhouse to do it in, I'm yer man," Edward promised.

"This is all happening a bit too fast," Elsie said, "I haven't even agreed to it yet. I will be sure to let ye know what I decide. Thank you, Edward, you are a dear."

"Now, would ye like to see the fine haul of cod I got fer ye?" Edward asked.

"Lead the way," Elsie answered. "C'mon, Eleanor, let's go see."

Chapter
39

Fanny and Mick were sitting with Elsie in their cabin. The boys were out doing chores and Fanny had already settled the littlest ones in their beds. Elsie had bid farewell to her sister and brother-in-law that morning. The story of Jake's treatment was weighing heavily on Fanny' heart. Soon Mick was listening as she related the story Eleanor had told them.

"Jumpin' dyin'!" Mick swore and was silent for several moments, "now, that I think about it everything begins to make a lot of sense," Mick said, "could be why the mining captain has been acting so strangely. He must've got wind of Jake's background. Could be why Jake has been reluctant to talk with us. Poor devil is likely afraid of anyone here learning of his Indian blood. Can't say I blame 'im, if there's any truth to the tale."

"Eleanor was not trying to make trouble, and she doesn't carry tales," Elsie replied, "she doesn't know that ye and Joe also have Mi'kmaq blood. She feels badly 'bout what happened to Jake and Mary and believes the tale to be true. It ain't right what happened. Why else would Jake up and leave a thriving wood working business?"

"I don't know," Mick paused while he digested the news. "It sure ain't right, not by a long shot," Mick continued. "Not many here knows that about me and Joe, sure it could cause a lot of trouble, even these days. I remember how often we was warned not to tell folks. People can be real mean-spirited."

"That's a sad truth," Elsie nodded, "Joe told me once that if people knew, it might mean he'd never get work."

"That's the truth," Mick replied, "and if the captain learned that 'bout Jake he might well have bin holding it over 'is head."

"Mick, is there anythin' ye can do to help Jake?" Fanny asked.

"I dunno, I have to give it a bit of thought." Mick answered, "might be time we had a visit with 'im. I can't just out and out ask 'im. But mebbe if he gets to know us better he might come to trust me."

"Ye did mention building a dory when they were last here," Fanny said, "perhaps that would be reason enough to ask 'em to come fer another visit."

"That's right," Mick agreed, "and Edward's agreed to provide enough lumber to get that project started." Mick told the women.

"That's wonderful," Fanny answered, "perhaps ye can use that to get through to Jake."

"He's pretty guarded," Mick responded, "I'll try, by God, yes, I will give it my best shot. We only have a couple of days before Peter brings them papers fer the association. I'll see Jake tomorrow at work and see if I can arrange to meet with 'im."

"Perhaps if ye trust him with yer background," Fanny began, "hear me out, Mick, I know you have guarded that family secret all yer life. Sure, our own children don't know. But perhaps, just perhaps, it will lead 'im to have a bit of trust in you in turn."

"And how do I know I can trust 'im?" Mick asked exasperatedly.

"Joe suspected Jake was part Mic'maq," Elsie broke in, "Ye knows Joe was a good judge of character, and he held Jake in the highest esteem. I think ye can trust 'im, Mick. I really do. I think Joe may have told 'im himself, had he lived."

"I ain't ever spoke of it to anyone but Joe," Mick replied, "don't know if it's a good idea to let it out now."

"But if it could help Jake and his family," Elsie responded, "I think Joe would want you to do that."

"Elsie, don't take this the wrong way, but yer still grieving, I dunno if ye can think straight right now. I mean, yer thinking with yer heart, not yer head," Mick spoke gently, "and Joe and me kept it a secret with good reason. If it got out it ain't just me would be affected but the whole family."

"Sometimes yer heart is a better judge than yer head," Elsie replied. "No, Mick, I've had this in mind ever since I had that dream of Joe, the dream where he told me to help Jake. I think maybe this is what he had in mind. I didn't know at the time that Jake has Indian blood, but I know now. And I know how careful the two of ye have been to protect yer secret. But don't ye think it might be good for ye, and fer Jake? Joe's gone and ye have nobody to share that burden with, but Jake would know and understand the importance of keeping it to yerself. He'd understand how heavy the burden can be."

"Ye make a good point, Elsie, and I don't mean ta hurt yer feelin's," Mick responded. "I will bear it in mind. Per'aps yer right. I needs time to think it over."

Elsie reached over and patted Mick's arm, "Ye didn't hurt my feelings, not one bit. I do understand. Joe and me had many a talk about it all. I know it's been hard, worrying all the time about who ye can trust and who ye can't."

"Fer what it's worth," Fanny said, "I ain't one bit worried about yer confiding in Jake. I got a good feeling 'bout that young man."

Mick nodded. "I will keep yer views in mind," he said to his wife, "and yers as well," he turned to Elsie, "leave it with me. It's a lot to consider."

Mick spent a restless night turning over in his mind the new information about Jake, thinking of the upcoming confrontation with the mining captain, and the idea of building dories to go lobster fishing. After a fitful night Mick was first to rise the next morning and was filling the wood stove with logs when Fanny appeared.

"Ye had a rough night," Fanny observed, "ye were mighty restless." Mick finished loading the wood stove before turning to his wife. "There's bin a lot going on. Would like to see William set up afore he marries Ginny, besides a whole parcel of other things."

"I hate to see ye so worried," Fanny told him.

"What is it yer always tellin' us? Oh, yeah, 'put it in God's hands'. Guess I ain't bin too good at that. I ain't Joe. Joe was the one always praying," Mick smiled at his wife, "but I made the Creator a promise after tossing and turning through the night. "I'm gonna leave it in His hands."

Fanny embraced him tightly, "I am glad to hear it," she said. "More things are wrought by faith . . ." she trailed off.

277

"Seeing as how ye seem to have the ear of the Creator," Mick replied, "mebbe ye can speak a good word fer me. I will have a word with Jake today, try to arrange a meetin'."

"I always speak to the Father about ye. I pray for ye, fer our children, fer Elsie, for all of us. I will add a special prayer fer yer talk with Jake." Fanny answered.

"Yer a good woman, Fanny Kelly," Mick said as he kissed the top of her head. "Everything will work out."

"Yes, it will, ye just keep the faith," Fanny responded and giving Mick another squeeze turned to the kitchen. "Now, what would ye like fer yer breakfast?"

On the way to the quarry that morning Mick filled his sons in on the progress he was making in getting their dream of lobster fishing off the ground.

"Plan was that Joe would build the dories, with my help," Mick told his sons, "But now he's gone I'm thinking of asking Jake. I 'appen to know he's a master craftsman."

"Will we all quit the quarry then?' Jack asked hopefully.

"Mebbe not right away, Jackie-boy," Mick answered, "it might take a year or two to start making money at it. My thoughts was that first me and William would go at it hard. Then mebbe once it's going good ye and Phil could join us. What do ye think b'ys?"

"I'd rather be out in a dory with ye than in this cursed quarry," William answered, "I bin talking to Ginny 'bout the prospects and she'd rather see me out at sea too."

"I am glad to do whatever ye think will help the family most," Phil put in, "but I sure will be glad to leave this quarry, the sooner the better."

"Another whole year of working the quarry?" Jack asked worriedly.

"Yes, Jack, but it may not be that long. It all depends how well we do at selling lobster. I can't say fer sure how long that might be," Mick told the boy. Mick and his sons talked about the prospects all the way to work and Mick warned them not to talk about it in the canteen. "T'is family business. Let's just keep it to ourselves fer now. And Jack, we're going have them papers to give the captain in the next day or two. It will make a difference once changes are made. Peter's confident we'll get better pay and shorter hours. The work will be safer, too. Things are looking up, my sons, yes, indeed. Go on now, I'll see ye at the break," Mick said.

It was several hours later when Mick spied Jake walking to the cookhouse.

"Jake, hey, Jake, wait up, will ye," Mick called.

Jake turned and waited while the older man hurried to catch up with him. "What can I do fer ye, Mick?" he asked.

"Remember when ye were at Elsie's we spoke about building dories to go at lobster fishing?"

"Yeah, what about it?" Jake asked.

"Well, this ain't the place, but I needs to talk to ye some more, looks like it could happen sooner than I expected." Mick answered.

"When do ye want to meet, and where?" Jake asked.

"Can ye come to my place after church on Sunday?" Mick asked. "There's another bit of business I wants to discuss with ye, but this is not a good place fer it."

"I'll have to ask the wife, and ye knows we'll be comin' with Paddy," Jake told him, "That's if we comes."

"That's fine, mebbe ye can let me know tomorrow?" Mick asked.

"Will do," Jake replied.

"Wonderful, that's great," Mick replied, "now, let's go get some food."

The rest of the day went by quickly and before long Mick was trudging home with his sons.

"Had a word with Jake," he told his sons, "I'm hoping he will come by after church on Sunday so's I can talk with 'im 'bout building dories."

"Do ye think he'll want to do that?" William asked.

"We'll know soon enough," Mick answered. "I sure hope so, can't see why not. Who'd want to keep on at this if ye have a chance to get out of it?"

The conversation continued as the foursome made their way home. Fanny was pleased to see her sons with spirits high when they returned. Mick seemed a lot less burdened as well. The evening passed with chores to do and the time passed quickly. Before they knew it was Sunday again and the family went to worship as per usual.

Chapter

40

Jake had given Mick his agreement to meet with him but unlike before Jake was alone when he visited the farm.

"Where's Paddy and yer family?" Mick asked when Jake came to the door.

"The babies were crying all through the service and Mary wanted to get them home so Paddy offered to take 'em," Jake replied. "I promised ye I'd come. Here I be."

"Would ye like a bite to eat first?" Mick offered.

"Naw, I needs to get home too, got lots to do," Jake replied.

"Fan, I'll be back. Just gonna take a walk with Jake," Mick told his wife. "Why don't ye come into the barn, wind's comin' up and it looks like rain," Mick said turning toward the building. Jake followed, his thoughts churning as he walked. *Sure hope he ain't gonna bring up Joe again,* he thought. Jake shuffled his feet anxious to get the conversation over with as Mick turned over old crates to use for seating.

"Take a seat, b'y," he told Jake.

"I'd rather stand, if it's all the same to ye," Jake replied.

"As ye wish," Mick answered and remained on his feet as well. "Here's the thing: Joe, he was the master carpenter. Me, I'm a jack of all trades and master of none," Mick began. "If yer willing, I'd like yer help with building two dories. One to start with, likely over the winter once the quarry shuts down. I got lumber comin' and I'd like to know if I can count on ye."

"I tole ye I ain't ever built a dory," Jake replied, "I've built all kinds of things, even a grandfather clock, but I ain't ever built no dory and only the one canoe."

"How hard can it be? Ain't much different than building anything else, 'cept it has to be water proof and sea-worthy." Mick asked, "And ye wouldn't be at it alone. I can help. I used to help Joe with all kinds of stuff: beds, tables, chairs, all kinds of things."

"Why me? Ain't there anyone else in these parts can build a dory?" Jake enquired.

"Because Joe told me yer good at it, that ye have a rare talent fer woodworking and I trust my brother's instinct," Mick answered, "and because Joe had told me he wanted to bring ye in on it. We had been planning on it a long time."

"But ye don't hardly know me," Jake pointed out, confused.

"No, but my brother did, and 'e had great respect fer ye," Mick told him.

"And I killed 'im," Jake spoke so lowly Mick barely heard him.

"No! I thought that once but I was wrong. The company what owns the quarry played a much bigger role in Joe's death. Ye knows that. Surely ye heard 'bout Harry comin' back, 'bout the wheels that were stuck fast, didn't ye?" Mick asked.

"I heard, but it were still my doin' that let that cart git away," Jake replied.

"As I understands it, that was yer first time workin' a cart. Ye weren't told nuddin' bout the brake, or nuddin' else." Mick answered, "and I knows ye fell when ye was reachin' out fer it when it started to roll. And we was all beat out from all the long hours. Joe, he shouldn't've bin standing in the middle of the track. T'was an awful accident. Ye ain't to blame. We all needs to go on. Can't keep harpin' back to things we can't change."

"I still feels awful guilty," Jake spoke softly, head hanging, eyes on his feet.

"And the captain, he's countin' on that," Mick observed, "wants to use ye to pin the blame on so's the company won't be held to account, but it ain't gonna work."

"That ain't all he's countin' on," Jake muttered bitterly.

"I noticed 'im watching ye mighty closely, was wonderin' what that was all about," Mick said.

Jake's head whipped up suddenly and Mick was moved by the fear he seen in the eyes of the younger man.

"I wants to tell ye a story," Mick said smoothly, "ye may not know this but my family ain't from these parts. Now, before I go on, I have to have yer word that ye won't breathe a word about what I'm 'bout to tell ye. Not to anyone, not even yer wife. Understand?"

"I ain't ever kept anything from me wife," Jake retorted, hestitantly.

"Ye will understand once I tell ye the rest, but first I have to have yer word," Mick insisted. "This ain't got nuddin' to do with yer wife and could cause my family no end of grief if it got out."

Jake nodded slowly, "Ye have my word, I promise it will stay between just between us."

Mick took a long breath while he studied Jake's face. "Fine, then, that's fine. Joe was the younger of the two of us. We have relations back home, sisters, brothers, our parents died but we still have lots of relations back home. We had to leave to find work. We couldn't get work back home. So, Joe and me, we struck out to find our own way," Mick paused again and studied Jake again for several moments before continuing. "We couldn't get work cuz we have Mi'kmaq blood." He finished and watched Jake carefully, "Now ye know why I need to keep this between us."

"Is that true?" Jake asked, incredulous, "Really true?"

"Why would I lie 'bout that?" Mick asked in turn.

Jake turned away from Mick and paced back and forth the barn, thoughts tumbling like pebbles in a landslide within him. Finally, he turned back to Mick.

"Do ye know what brought me and Mary to these parts?" He asked.

"I heard a story," Mick admitted, "bout a young man who was doing well for hisself until word got out about Indian blood and then townsfolk turned on 'im. Is that true?"

Jake sank down onto the overturned crate, his face in his hands. "I shoulda known. I shoulda known," he said desperately.

"Is that what the captain 'as on ye?" Mick asked quietly.

Jake didn't answer but his head nodded once.

Mick blew out a breath, "and that's why ye wouldn't talk with us 'bout what happened to Joe?"

Jake nodded again, wiping his face with his hands he looked up at Mick. "He told me he'd make sure I wouldn't get work anywhere 'round here. Mary and me spent every cent we had buying the Simon place. We couldn't go home. We had nowhere to go, nowhere to turn. I had to keep quiet. I had no choice," he told Mick, "I wanted to tell yer family how it happened, how the cart got away from me but the captain threatened me, told me not to speak to nobody about it."

Mick nodded, "His kind are everywhere," he said, "it's why I have to keep my background to myself. Well, ye ain't alone, my son, ye ain't alone. I'd guess there's more like us than most people know. Ye won't have to worry 'bout that captain any longer. Hear me? I got friends in these parts, more than the captain, fer sure. Ye'll find more folks are willin' to stand up fer ye than ye would guess. Not all 'round 'ere are mean-spirited. Fact is most folk are good, decent people. Now, son, I'm askin' again. Would ye consider building dories with me?"

Jake stood up, his back straight and his eyes met Mick's, "I needs to talk it over with the wife but I can't see why not," he smiled as he held a hand out for Mick to shake.

Mick shook his hand then slapped Jake on the back, "Well, that's a start, a mighty fine start," he said. "We'll have to work it all out later, right now I have enough on me plate getting' this protective association past the gate. We'll get together again and work out the details."

"I don't know how to thank ye," Jake said.

Mick waved his thanks away. "Just remember what I tole ye and keep it to yerself," he warned.

"Believe me, I will, but mind if I ask how ye learned about me and Mary?"

"Eleanor tole Elsie and Fanny," Mick answered. "But ye got nuddin' to worry about. It ain't going any further. We knows how important it is to keep mum on that subject."

Jake nodded. "But what about Eleanor, can I trust she won't be tellin' it to others?"

"No need to worry 'bout that, they left the other day and ain't no way Elsie or Fanny would breathe a word of it. Ye have my promise. I don't know Eleanor well, but if she's anything like Elsie she ain't given to gossip, though ye might think otherwise. No, my son, ain't nuddin' to worry over." Mick replied.

Jake sighed and nodded again. "I hope ye're right. I guess I best get on home," Jake responded, "Haldi is here helping Mary with the twins but I want to make sure they're alright."

Mick clapped him on the back once again. "Yes, sir, I understand that. Are ye walking home?"

"Yessir, got no other way to get there," Jake answered.

"Why don't you hold up a second? The mare's not had a good outing all week. I think she could use a good stretch. Let me ask Phil to harness 'er up and take ye home." Mick replied.

"I don't want to put nobody out," Jake objected.

"Ye need to get back to yer family and the mare needs exercise, it ain't no trouble," Mick answered. He strode to the house and called for Phil when he got there.

Not long afterward Phil was guiding the horse and buggy through the field. The pair did not speak much as the mare clopped along. Jake was not given to chatter although Phil was friendly enough. In addition, Jake's mind was filled with the secret Mick had entrusted him with and the excitement over partnering with the older man. Phil's was also much occupied with the prospects for a brighter future away from the quarry and wondering how the man beside him would figure into that future.

Haldi was sitting on a bench in the yard, scratching Smokey's ears when they pulled into Jake's yard. The dog's tail wagged furiously and she barked joyfully.

Jake jumped down from the buggy and turned to thank Phil. He grinned to himself when he noticed Phil only had eyes for his young sister-in-law.

"Haldi, why don't ye come meet my buddy?" He called to the young girl.

Haldi stood shyly looking up at Phil in the buggy. Jake made the introductions and then asked Haldi about the babies.

"They was both sound asleep when I come out. I ain't bin out 'ere long," Haldi replied.

"I best get inside. Thanks again fer the lift," Jake spoke to Phil, whose eyes were still on Haldi's face. Jake ruffled the dog's fur, "Comin' inside?" he asked Haldi.

"T'was nice to meet ye," Haldi said to Phil before she turned to follow Jake into the house.

"Hope to see ye again, maybe at church?" Phil called out.

"Maybe," Haldi shyly answered. "See, ye," she said and disappeared into the house.

"Thanks again," Jake grinned knowingly and waved his good-bye.

Phil turned the buggy and made for home, visions of Haldi's auburn curls and hazel eyes stayed with him as he drove. He had noticed Haldi at church, of course, but this was the first time he'd had a proper introduction. Suddenly Phil was very glad that Jake would be working with them to get the dreams of fishing for a living off the ground. Phil was still daydreaming about the freckles across Haldi's nose and the girl's shy demeanor when he realized he was just about home. Phil had never minded going to church but now he looked forward eagerly to next Sunday.

Chapter

41

T he mining captain paced the floor. It was long past time that the men should be at their posts. A freighter was scheduled to be loaded any day. It was already sailing to the deep-water wharf nearby. *It's mighty strange that fifteen minutes 'as passed since the work day was to begin and not a single man 'as turned up. What the bloody 'ell is going on?* He asked himself. The quarry was eerily quiet and even his pit boss was missing. He went to the door and threw it open just in time to see Mick, Charlie, Hank, Vic, and a stranger walking toward his hut. The captain glared at the men suspiciously.

"Morning, Cap," Mick greeted him, "This here's Peter. He's representing the men of the quarry, including us."

The captain looked at the stranger in confusion. "What the 'ell are ye on about?"

"If we could step inside, I will explain," Peter spoke up.

The captain looked bemusedly at the man, taking in his expensive leather boots and the fine cloth of his jacket. He stood aside to allow the men to enter. The group stepped inside and stood aside while the captain turned a questioning gaze on each in turn.

"What's this?" the captain asked when Peter dropped the sheaf of papers on the table in front of him.

"This, sir, is a legal document outlining the demands that the Limestone Quarry Protective Association want you to bring to Dominion Limestone before any work can continue here," Peter replied. "In point of fact, until these demands are met there will be no limestone mined at all."

"Demands? Protective Association?" the captain asked stupidly, "just what is this all about?"

"It's about fair wages and safer working conditions," Peter told him. "It's about shorter work weeks and shorter days. It's about the men that work here getting a fair shake. That's what it's about."

"It's about us not risking life or limb fer little pay," Mick spoke softly.

The captain's gaze swung to Mick's face. "I knows what this is about. It's about Joe, ain't it?"

"No, not entirely," Peter answered, "But what happened to Joe Kelly was the last straw. Ye lot ain't going to get away with the unsafe conditions these men have been exposed to any longer."

"What 'appened to Joe were an accident," the captain protested, "the mining inspector wrote a report that says just that."

"That report was a farce, we knows it, and ye knows it, too," Charlie's voice was dangerously calm, while his eyes were alight with fiery anger.

"It t'were an accident," the captain blustered, "t'was that 'alf-breed's fault. Jake admitted that to me right 'ere in this cabin."

"What did ye call him?" Mick's voice held a menacing note that the captain did not catch.

"He's a 'alf-breed! Ye didn't know that, did ye? And ye knows them kind can't be trusted," he continued to bluster.

"And just what 'kind' is that? The hard-working 'kind'? The 'kind' the likes of ye like to push around? Is that the 'kind' ye means?" Mick's voice was dangerously calm.

"Look 'ere, Mick, 'e stood right 'ere in this shack and admitted to leavin' off the brake on 'is cart – the cart what struck Joe," the captain spoke gruffly, angrily, defensively.

"I believe the regulations state that no man is to work a cart alone," Peter spoke calmly, "it's my understanding that nobody was working on that cart with Jake. Ain't that right?"

"Weren't nobody to put wit 'im," the captain defended himself, "we 'ad a freighter to get loaded an' t'weren't time to waste. I was runnin' the place short-handed, not near enough men to get the job done as quick as was wanted. I 'ad to haul Jake off the crusher and put 'im to loading carts. T'is done all the time."

"Against regulations," Peter said again.

"Ain't no mine or quarry anywheres that sticks to them regulations," the captain insisted, "I weren't doin' nuddin' that every mine on this island don't do."

"But that wasn't in the report – not the one I read. Not one line about how the accident actually happened," Peter pointed out.

"What's it matter anyway? Jake said it was his fault, Joe getting' 'it that day. Said it were all 'is fault. He stood right 'ere sniveling like the 'alf-breed 'e 'is," the captain continued to sputter and reach for excuses.

"I'd be mighty careful with the name-calling," Mick's voice continued to hold a menacing note that the captain in his attempt to place blame elsewhere still did not notice.

"Look, mate, the company wanted that freighter loaded as quick as possible," the captain said, "I was just doin' me job, that's all."

"And the equipment - the faulty equipment – I suppose ye know nothing of that either?" Peter asked quietly.

"What are ye going on wit?" the captain asked, "all the equipment was workin' just fine, until that 'alf-breed fergot to engage the brake on 'is cart."

Mick's fist drew back. Hank was quick to grab his arm before he could land a blow and it took both Charlie and Vic to wrestle him back to the door. His companions worked to calm Mick down before the discussion continued. The captain rocked back and forth on his heels while he glared at Mick and the others.

"What if I were to tell ye that I have it on good authority that the cart that Joe was working with Harry was not in good working condition. In fact, the wheels were seized and the men could not get it to move along the track," Peter told the captain, who was now watching Mick nervously.

"That ain't true!" the captain exploded, "that's a bald-faced lie!"

"Lies, is it?" Charlie roared back, "Harry has told us that the wheels were seized up and that cart would not budge."

The captain's face was pale as he regarded the five men. He remembered the conversation he'd had with his pit boss about those carts, newly acquired from the mainland, and how rusted the wheels were after sitting for years, unused. He knew that Harry had been to see the pit boss asking for grease moments before Joe was struck.

"That man, 'arry ain't workin' fer the quarry any longer. The man 'as an axe to grind, that's what. He's makin' it all up," the captain lied.

"That could be, but fact is your pit boss told me much the same tale," Peter informed him, "so I'd be careful what ye say next."

"I ain't got time fer all this," the captain retorted, "I gots a freighter on its way to be loaded with limestone. I needs the men to get back to work. If ye knows where they all are ye best tell 'em to get their arses 'ere."

"Perhaps I wasn't clear enough," Peter replied, "this quarry will not be worked until the company agrees to all the demands laid out in these documents. I suggest if ye want to get that freighter loaded ye bring them papers to yer bosses. Now!"

"The company ain't gonna agree to pay ye more. They thinks yer all getting' paid too much already," the captain guffawed, "fat chance ye gots fer any of the rest of it!"

"That is not up to ye to decide. Take the papers to yer boss," Peter ordered, "there will not be a man here to work the quarry until ye do, and until we have an agreement."

"It'll take me most of a day to git up to town, and then wait fer an answer from the company," the captain complained, "might take two or three days and I gots that freighter on the way 'ere even as we speak!"

"Then ye best get on yer way," Charlie responded.

"The sooner, the better," Peter agreed, "let's go, men, we came and did what we set out to do." He turned toward the captain, "I am staying at Ruby's Boarding House, I suppose ye've heard of it?"

"Yis," the captain answered sullenly.

"Ye can reach me there once ye get an answer from Dominion Limestone. I'll be needing that in writing. The men have appointed me as their spokesman," Peter informed him, "once I am satisfied that the demands will be met the men will return to work – not until then!"

Peter gestured to his companions and the five filed out leaving the captain glaring at their backs as they left.

Chapter

42

"Can ye believe the nerve of that frigger? What bald-faced lies!" Mick's anger was still near a boil as the men walked away from the hut. He blew out a breath as he tamped down his rage and continued, "Now that business is looked after, whatcha got planned; how long do ye think afore we hears an answer from the company?" Mick asked Peter.

"I have no idea how long that will take but, like I told ye at the meeting, there is a high demand for limestone right now so I figure it won't be long at all," Peter answered. "Once I have the written response from the company, I will go over it and then be back to give ye the news."

"Was mighty good of ye to help us out wit it," Mick responded.

"Why did ye? Just askin' out of curiosity," Charlie asked.

"Let's just say I don't like to see men treated so unjustly," Peter hedged, "and Hank, here, he's blood and made a good case for ye all. Didn't want to see another man die before his time either."

"Can't thank ye enough fer all ye done," Mick repeated, "I knows I thanked ye already, but ye don't know what a difference it's made having someone speak up fer us all."

"Let's just hope my efforts won't be in vain, though, like I keep telling ye, there's strength in numbers and the company will not want that quarry to sit idle for long," Peter replied, "it's dumb luck that a freighter is underway to be loaded, that will bring a good bit of pressure to bear on 'em."

The men continued their discussion as they walked toward the roadway where horse and wagons stood in wait.

"Will ye come have a bite to eat afore ye heads back to town?" Hank asked.

"I sure will, Hilda's cooking is not something I'd pass up," Peter agreed, "sure beats what they serve up at Ruby's. I mean the food's good but would never hold a candle to Hilda's."

By this time the men had reached the wagons and each were heading back to their homes to await the outcome of their gamble.

"Mick, why don't you climb on up 'ere, I'll give ye a ride home," Charlie invited.

"Don't mind if I do," Mick replied, "needs to talk to ye 'bout somethin' anyways."

Charlie and Mick said their good-byes to the others and were first on the road toward home.

"First things first," Mick began, "Ye knows we need somebody 'ere at the quarry to keep that friggin' captain on 'is toes. Bin discussin' it with the others and we thinks yer the man fer the job. Will ye take it on?"

"Sure, there's others who could do it just as well," Charlie replied.

"That may be so, but we thinks yer the best one fer it," Mick answered.

"Won't say 'no'," Charlie responded, "truth is I'd take a real pleasure in it, 'specially after what they did to Joe and to 'is Missus makin' sure they wouldn't have to pay 'er any compensation."

"Was hoping ye'd feel that way," Mick told him. "Yes, there's others could do it, but ye have a better reason to take it on."

"Won't be a man injured on my watch," Charlie swore, "been too much of it over the years. Joe gettin' killed, well, that put a different face to it altogether."

"Ye got that right," Mick answered, "I hope that somehow he knows what we bin doin'."

"I gets the feelin' he does," Charlie replied. The two men were both quiet for a time as they each considered the events of the past weeks.

"Ye said ye had somethin' ye wanted to talk with me about, besides this quarry business," Charlie said.

"Yes, well, I wants to talk to ye about the lobster cannery. "Have ye heard any more?" Mick asked.

"Yes, I have," Charlie answered, "I heard they already got a site picked out and there's been workmen there starting on building 'er. Heard it will be up and operational by the spring."

"I wonder how many are going to be out fishin'?" Mick asked, "that's what I wants to chat wit ye about. I can get lumber fer building the dories and a man to help build 'em." Mick paused a minute or two before he continued. "T'is Jake O'Quinn. Ye knows Joe was spendin' time wit 'im last year. Joe was impressed wit 'is craftmanship and spoke with me a couple of times 'bout getting' 'im to help with building the boats and the traps we'll need. I already had a chat wit Jake 'bout it and he's agreeable. Turns out he's much like Joe was always tellin' me – a hard worker and an honest man."

"He weren't honest enough to come talk wit ye 'bout what happened to Joe," Charlie spoke very softly.

"He had good reason fer that," Mick told him, "I can't tell ye more than that but trust me, he had good reason."

"I noticed ye comin' to his defense back there," Charlie noted, "Was wonderin' why."

"Ye knows we met wit 'im a few times," Mick explained, "and Elsie as well. Let's just say we got a few things cleared up."

"Captain was callin' 'im a half-breed," Charlie pondered, "any truth to that?"

"Do it matter much?' Mick asked in turn, "ye got me word he's a good man, one I believe I can count on. And so did Joe."

"Naw, don't matter at'all," Charlie replied, "Guess I was just busy-nosing."

"Ye got any problem workin' wit the man?" Mick asked, still smarting from the captain. "Don't know 'im well at all, but I'll take yer word fer it. If ye says he's a good man, that's good enough fer me," Charlie replied.

"That's good to hear, because he's likely going to be workin' the boats wit me and my b'ys," Mick told Charlie.

"So, why did ye want to talk to me 'bout it? How do I figure into it?" Charlie asked.

"Well, b'y, it's like this: I'm thinkin' that lobster cannery's gonna need an awful lot of lobster and it will take more than just me and mine to keep 'em supplied," Mick explained. "I figures if we can get enough equipment and enough men we can supply that cannery with most of what they'll need."

"And there's strength in numbers, like Peter says," Charlie responded, "And if we all bands together we gots a better chance of getting a fair price. Is that what yer gettin' at?"

"Ye gots that right," Mick agreed, "I figures if we gots a half dozen dories, a couple of hundred traps and men to work 'em we could make a decent livin', and we could expand over time."

"Who else would be in on this?" Charlie asked.

"Beside me and my sons and ye," Mick answered, "I'm thinkin' Hank, Vic, Jake, and Paddy fer a start. Four dories, two men apiece, should be a very good start. I ain't talked to 'em all yet but I knows most men at the quarry would jump at the chance to make a livin' off the sea. I wants to give me buddies a chance at it first off."

"How would it work, though?" Charlie wondered, "when it comes down to brass tacks, how would ye share out the money when we gets paid fer the lobster?"

"I was thinkin' of askin' Peter fer 'is help in gettin' it sorted," Mick began, "but well, the lumber would have to be paid fer and the man supplying it is willin' to take a small share in the profits in exchange. After that we put a small amount aside to pay fer upkeep of the boats, rigging, and traps and then the rest would be split evenly. Now, that's what I come up wit. Peter might have better advice on how best to sort it all out.

"Have ye talked to Peter already?" Charlie asked, surprise in his voice.

"No, I ain't gonna get ahead of meself," Mick replied, "First I needs to talk to the rest of the men, see if they wants to do it. I heard men can get fifty cents fer every hundred lobster. Two men working hard can get at least that every day. Dere's thousands upon thousands of lobster out dere, enough to make it more than worth the effort."

"I sure wants a piece of it," Charlie spoke firmly, "Constance's bin at me, worried 'bout me gettin' hurt at the quarry. Bin wantin' me to find safer work."

"Can't say as fishin' is safe," Mick retorted, "but t'is a damn site safer than the bloody quarry."

"If a man has a bit of sense in his head, he'd be safe enough," Charlie replied, "just gots to mind the skies and to come in at the first sign of bad weather."

"That's why I'm thinkin' of ye five," Mick pointed out, "I knows ye all have good heads on yer shoulders. Yer all sensible. My sons don't have much experience so if they were out on the water with any one of ye I wouldn't worry so much and ye could teach 'em."

"Sounds reasonable to me," Charlie nodded, "could work."

"Won't be 'til the spring," Mick told him, "I figure we can get them dories built over the winter while the mine is closed and then go at it hard."

"Ye sure have given this all a lot of thought," Charlie replied.

"Joe and me have bin doin' nuddin' but talk of it fer years now," Mick said, "and when we heard a lobster cannery was gonna be built 'ere, well then, that seemed to be all we talked about."

"Ye ain't going about it all hare-brained, that's fer sure," Charlie responded. "Ye can count be in."

"Lots of details to be ironed out," Mick noted, "But glad to hear yer in agreement."

The men continued their discussion while Charlie guided the horse in a slow walk until they reached Mick's house.

"Want ta come in fer a bite?" Mick asked.

"Naw, not this time," Charlie grinned as he answered, "ain't often I get a day or two away from the quarry at the beginning of the week. I'm gonna go call on Constance, mebbe take 'er out in the wagon fer a little break from the house."

"Good enough," Mick replied, "see ya later. And thanks fer the ride home."

Chapter

43

The captain was none too pleased as he saddled his mare for the long ride into town. He was used to all the privileges and comforts that came with his position: a well-appointed house, a full larder, and a pay check that was many times that of the average wage-earner at the quarry.

He thought of his humble beginnings as he threw the saddle over the horse's back and placed the bit between her teeth. He swung into the saddle and kicked the horse into a trot, pushing her to a gallop once he reached the roadway. *Ain't a one of them rabble-rousers gonna cost me my job, he thought as he raced the mare along the bay.*

He was particularly incensed at the way Peter had spoken to him as if he were an underling not fit to scrape the mud from his boots. *We'll see about this, Peter Parsons,* he grumbled to himself as he rode. *I knows yer kind, all soft 'ands and fed wit the silver spoon. Ye don't know what yer up against,* he blustered to himself. He thought back to his own beginnings in the company. He'd had just enough education to fool the previous mining captain into believing in him. But it took many years of hard labor and a lot of boot licking before he reached the position he now held.

They thinks I don't know what 'ard work is. They gots no idea, the captain continued his inner dialogue. I ain't no fool. I knows who butters me bread. He nodded to himself. It had taken him many years of betraying the trust of his coworkers and bringing certain malicious titbits to his boss that enabled him to climb the ladder to his position at the quarry. Then he'd found out something about the agent that propelled him into the position much quicker than he'd anticipated.

They don't know and they ain't ever gonna know, he continued his self-evaluation. *I knows what to keep to meself and what bits of knowledge might come in 'andy. Thought finding out 'bout Jake's injun grandmudder would pay off. It ain't gonna 'elp like the last time.* The captain thought hard as he rode on how to tell the story in a way that would reflect favorably on himself. *Ain't me fault that dang uppity-up found 'is way to the quarry. First thing I gotta do is find out more bout this Peter Parsons, right after I brings the agent the damned papers.* The captain began his scheming as he rode. *Said 'e was staying at the Ruby. That's my next stop after I goes to see the agent.* He promised himself.

The sun was bright and the bay calm and peaceful as the captain made his way to town, but he did not notice any of this as his thoughts tumbled one upon another. He remembered other sticky spots he'd found himself in and re-examined the lessons he'd learned.

That other young buck what thought he'd git one over on me, well 'e soon learned the difference, he thought, *and if this blasted fool thinks 'e can interfere without comeuppance, well, Parsons will soon learn the difference. Ye don't cross the captain, no, sir!*

Memories of past injustices continued to feed his rage as he rode. Several hours later he tied the mare to the post outside the agent's office. He'd made one stop to refresh himself when he'd reached town and now, he removed his cap and smoothed back his hair in preparation. He knocked on the door before entering.

"I needs to see Mr. Langley right away. Tell 'im I'm 'ere on urgent business," he told the young clerk at the desk, "it's of utmost importance that I speak with 'im right now!"

"Yes sir," the clerk replied, "but I needs yer name."

The captain drew himself up to stand as straight as possible, "Ye may tell 'im Mr. Gallo, the captain at the quarry, is 'ere to see 'im."

The clerk disappeared behind a thick wooden door. The captain looked around him. He'd only been in that office once before, when he'd been hired to oversee the work at the quarry several years before. At that time another agent had approved him for the job, with a little bit of arm twisting. He noted that very little had changed in the building, except the clerk. *Old geezer who was clerk 'ere probly died,* he thought. A minute later the clerk reappeared. "Ye can go right in," he told him.

Langley stood, an expression of distaste on his face as he studied the cringing creature in front of him. He knew the type: the sneaky, conniving sort that he preferred to have little to no dealings with. He'd heard a fair bit of gossip about the man, most of it unsavory. The captain took note of that expression and pushed down the rage that threatened to overwhelm him.

"What brings ye here? Shouldn't ye be doing yer job at the quarry? Why are ye here?" Langley asked.

"Sir, there's trouble at the quarry," the captain wrung his cap in his hands, clearly discomforted.

"What trouble?" Langley asked. "Spit it out, man." He said impatiently.

"There's a man, Peter Parsons, came to see me early this morning. There was several men what work the quarry wit 'im," the captain said, "'e give me these papers to give ye, said there won't be no men to work the quarry until ye meet their demands."

At the mention of Peter's name Langley's face paled, "Did ye say Parsons? Peter Parsons?" He asked.

"Yis, that's right," the captain replied, taking a hidden glee with Langley's obvious distress. The agent had jumped to his feet and stood behind his desk. His knuckles were white as his fingers squeezed the back of his chair.

"Give me the papers," Langley ordered.

Langley dropped back into his chair and quickly scanned the paperwork. Finishing he eyed the captain. "And ye didn't see fit to come to me when this Peter Parsons first came to the community?"

"I swear I didn't know naught about it, sir," the captain stuttered, "not til this very day."

"Yer paid to oversee the quarry. That means knowing what yer men are doing at all times, before, during, and after work as well," Langley spoke sternly, "Ye should have had wind of this trouble long before it came to this."

"No, sir," the captain replied, "'tis a community that's spread out over a wide rural area – most of 'em 'ave small farms they runs – none of 'em lives nearby; 'ow was I s'posed to know they was getting' up to this?"

"It's yer job to keep tabs on all goings on – inside and outside the quarry," Langley retorted, "This is not going to look good for you."

"What, I'm s'posed to 'old the 'and of each and every man what works fer ye?" the captain asked, indignantly.

"Yer supposed to know what yer men are doing, outside of work as well, that's where they made their plans," Langley sneered, "especially since one of 'em died on yer watch. Did ye not think it prudent to keep a closer eye on 'em? Men generally take unkindly to the sudden death of one of their own. Do ye not know basic human nature?"

"I bin keepin' a very close eye on the man what done confessed to causing Joe's death," the captain defended himself. "And I knows the men did not take kindly to that report. And that ain't me fault."

Langley's dark eyes roamed over the captain's body, taking in his unkempt hair and clothing. He shook his head. "Go away, man. I need time to read these through more carefully. Come back in an hour," he ordered. Langley pulled the sheaf of papers toward him, head bent, he gave no further instruction nor farewell.

The captain pulled his cap onto his head as he turned to leave the office. He ignored the clerk as he stomped from the room, slamming the door behind him as he left the building.

What does the likes of that know about running a quarry? He asked himself as he strode toward the tavern down the street. He'd had a long, hard ride into town and very little to eat that morning, suffering as he was from a bit too much rum the night before.

He entered the establishment and dropped himself into a chair at one of the rough-hewn tables. It wasn't a fancy place but the food was plentiful and good. His mood was not improved by his audience with the agent. He resented his treatment deeply and his thoughts leaped from anger toward Peter Parsons, whom he blamed for his present predicament, to resentment toward Langley.

I gots to figure this out. 'Ow come I was not told about this Peter Parsons? He wondered. *I needs to have a word wit the pit boss when I gets back. He was s'posed to let me know if he overheard any grumbling or complaints of any sort. Damn the man.*

The captain's mind worked overtime trying to find a way to deflect blame from himself and onto one of his underlings – of which there were few – the pit boss and a couple of foremen. The captain stabbed his food furiously as his mind worked to devise a scheme. Before he knew it, the hour had passed and he was once again standing outside Langley's office, waiting for admittance. Langley had him cool his heels an extra thirty minutes before admitting him.

"I had the clerk send a telegram to the owner," Langley bit the words off as he glared at the captain, "He won't be pleased that all work in the quarry has come to a full stop. I have to wait for his decision. Parsons wants it in writing so ye will have to wait for it. It's not likely I will have an answer today, ye'll have to wait in town."

"I ain't got no lodgings in town," the captain protested, "where do ye expect me to wait?"

"I have a bunk my groom uses out in the horse barn. He's away picking up a steed I've bought," Langley said, "ye can stay there overnight. Come back in two hours and ye can follow me home."

"In yer barn?" the captain asked, incredulously, "out with the livestock, eh? I sees what ye thinks of me!"

"Yer lucky I don't take a horsewhip to ye," Langley angrily exploded. "Do ye have any idea at all what trouble ye've caused? Or how much money it will cost this company to meet the demands of the men? I ought to cut yer pay, or better yet, fire yer frigging arse."

"Ye 'ave more than a fair share of blame in this," the captain erupted, "yer the one that picked out that inspector and sent 'im to the quarry. I'd say yer share is equal, if not greater than me own."

Langley smiled grimly, "But ye see, my dear man, that's not how the owners will see it. They will see it as I do: dereliction of duty."

"No, sir, it ain't my fault," the captain said again.

"Ye can stand there and argue as long as ye like," Langley said softly, "it won't change the fact that the owner thinks ye are to blame. If I were ye, I'd be praying not to be fired."

The captain stood silently glaring at the agent. He remained silent.

"Now, get out," Langley continued, "I can put ye up in the barn, otherwise, find yer own lodging."

"I ain't got enough money wit me," the captain said, "I rushed up 'ere to give ye them papers. I didn't stop fer nuddin'."

"I can offer ye a bunk in the barn," Langley said again, coldly, "yer lucky I'm offering even that. Now, leave me. If ye wants the bunk be back here in two hours."

The captain stood glaring at Langley for another full minute before turning on his heels to leave. He made his way immediately to Ruby's rooming house to see if he could learn more about the man who had caused him so much grief.

"I am sorry, sir. We do not release information regarding our patrons," the tight-lipped proprietor informed him. "I am not privy to what business Mr. Parsons may have in the area."

The captain was in no mood to be gracious and though he tried his best to wheedle information from the woman he was unsuccessful, adding to the bitterness that was swiftly filling his heart.

"I must speak with Parsons on urgent business," he tried again.

"Mr. Parsons is not available at this time," the owner of the rooming house replied, "if you care to leave a message, I will give it to the gentleman."

"No, I do not care to leave a message," the captain spat out, "this business is urgent and of a delicate nature."

"I am sorry, sir," the proprietor said with emphasis, "I cannot help you."

"I cannot 'elp you," the captain repeated in a singsong voice, "Tell 'im I was enquiring after 'im."

"Very good, sir," the woman replied coolly, "if he should return, I will inform him of your visit."

The captain stared at the woman, venom in his gaze. Without another word he turned and left.

Langley sat brooding silently after reading the documents through several times. *Parsons, that's the man came to see me about Fred Johnstone a couple of days ago. He's connected – very well-connected. Damn the man! If only I'd had wind he was in these parts, and for quite a while it seems.* Langley's thoughts took him back to his brief meeting with Peter, one he did not enjoy remembering. His mental meandering also caused further bitterness toward the captain. *How the devil did that man ever get hired to oversee the quarry?* He asked himself.

The captain spent a miserable night in Langley's barn, which did nothing to improve his mood the next morning. Angry and resentful he followed Langley back into town. Once again, he was summarily dismissed to wait until Langley received word from the owner. It was past mid-morning before he returned.

"Well, thanks to ye, the company have decided to meet the demands. Ye can bet on it, Parsons knew he had us over a barrel. And thanks to ye, I had to spend valuable time crafting paperwork for ye to give the blasted man," Langley spoke so contemptuously that the captain could feel the blood rush to his face, "take this and get out of my sight." Langley passed a sealed envelope to him and waved his hand in dismissal.

The captain did not trust himself to speak, grabbing the envelope he turned on his heels to leave.

"Gallo," Langley stopped him, "ye best be very careful, yer on very thin ice. Make sure there's not a single thing that will give me further reason to terminate yer employment in this company."

The captain did not turn but opened the door and left very quietly.

Chapter

44

Charlie's sharp whistle once again brought the men to attention. Peter stood beaming with pride as he looked out over the room full of men. He waved a paper in the air. "Ye did it!" He proclaimed happily. "Now, the company is not offering the increase in wages ye asked fer. They're offering eighteen cents an hour, which is not equal to what limestone quarries are paying elsewhere. Yet, it is a full seven cents more per hour than before. The good news is that they're offering a bonus of ten dollars per man if ye accepts this offer. And," he continued, "they're offering twenty-five cents an hour for every hour worked over the fifty we stipulated."

There was a cheer and several questions spoken at once. Charlie had to whistle again.

"There's more," Peter announced, "the company agrees to regular maintenance of all equipment and has ordered an inspection for the equipment yer currently using. Besides that, if any man gets hurt, he will receive sick pay and if anybody were to meet his death here, like Joe, his widow will receive a death benefit equal to a year's wages."

Hooting and hollering met this announcement and the ruckus was such that Charlie had to whistle several times before the tumult died down.

"Work hours have been reduced to not more than ten hours per day and five days a week. Any hours worked beyond that have to be agreed upon and extra wages for those hours paid as stipulated in the agreement," Peter went on, "that means any man can refuse to work more than four hours in overtime," as the hooting began again, he held up his hand for silence. "We have a few other pieces of business," he said, "ye need a man to speak fer ye. Someone ye all can go to if something's not right or if the company is not holding up their side of the bargain. We need to vote on whether or not ye want to accept this agreement and we need to elect a few men to act fer ye in the case of a grievance."

"What's a grievance?" one of the men called out.

"A grievance is when the owners do not hold up their end of the agreement. For example, if ye get yer pay and it's not what it's supposed to be; or if equipment is not in good condition," Peter explained, "it's anything that goes directly against what ye have agreed to and it's legal so the owners have to keep up their side of it. It also means ye men also have to keep yer end up: to work the hours yer supposed to work, except fer sickness or injury."

Peter continued to answer questions for the next hour, as one after another brought up questions and had items explained or clarified.

"I looked it all over carefully and now all we need is an answer. Before we get to the rest of it, why don't ye all talk it over. Go on and chat amongst yerselves and then we'll vote on it. Half an hour enough time?" Peter asked. A chorus of voices called out their agreement and Peter ordered a break.

"Mick, may I have a word?" Peter asked as he approached Mick and his sons, "in private, if ye don't mind?"

The two men walked outside and away from the building until Peter felt secure that no ears would hear him.

"I need to apologize to ye," he started, "I took something on myself without asking for yer go ahead."

Mick looked at the younger man, puzzled. "What's that, now?" He asked.

"Well, I didn't think it was right that the report filed by the mining inspector made it so the company didn't have to pay Joe's widow a red cent," he began, "so I poked around a bit and found out that the inspector who wrote the report is a relative of the agent. He paid him off to write the report so it favored the company. He had no right to do that. So, I went to see him and had a word with the man. Name's Langley, by the way, in case ye should ever need to know it. I let him know we had witnesses that were willing to tell a court of law the real circumstances that led to Joe's death."

"Don't see what good it would do," Mick began, but Peter held up a hand to silence him.

"Let me finish," Peter said, "It has to be kept secret but if yer family is willing to sign papers saying ye won't try to bring the company to the law, they are willing to pay a death benefit to Joe's widow. It ain't a lot of money, but it's equal to a year's wages, enough to give 'er a nest egg."

Mick looked confused and Peter sought to explain it further.

"It's up to ye, and to Joe's widow, of course," Peter continued, But I needs ye to know if she signs it ye can never go after the company again."

"I thought the report made it so the company would never have to pay 'er a cent," Mick replied, "I don't understand."

"The agent was doing something crooked and underhanded on behalf of the company," Peter explained, "the law don't take well to that kind of thing. The agent and the company know it. All I did was point out those facts."

"And if we decides not to sign 'em, if we say no, what then?" Mick asked.

"Then ye would have to get yerself a lawyer and go to court," Peter said.

"And that would take a lot of money and a lot of time," Mick said, grasping what Peter was telling him.

"Yes, that's right," Peter answered, "I had to promise 'em it would remain between us. If ye would talk to Joe's wife and let me know what ye want to do she would likely see the money before the month's out. I know I stepped out of line doing that. I hope ye will forgive me."

"Nuddin' to forgive," Mick replied, "ye've really gone to so much trouble fer all of us in the quarry. But this, this is more than I can ever thank ye fer."

"I just wanted to make it right. I can't bring Joe back to ye," Peter responded, "this was the next best thing."

"Well, I need ye to know how much it's all appreciated," Mick replied, "I needs to talk it over with Elsie. I can let ye know in a day or two. Better yet, would ye do us the honour of comin' to supper so we can thank ye proper-like?"

"I'd be happy to eat supper with ye all, but no more thanks are needed," Peter responded. "Now, back to this business, what do ye think? Are ye satisfied with the offer the company has given?"

"Eighteen cents an hour is a good bit more than we bin gettin' and if men will be looked after if they gits hurt, or, God forbid, they dies like Joe did," Mick replied, "I'd say we got what we set out to get. And glad fer the reduced work hours, too."

"I guess we best get back inside and see if the men feel the same," Peter remarked.

"Mind if I asks ye, why are ye doin' all this fer us?"

"I'd rather not get into all that right now. It's kind of a long story," Peter answered. "Let's just say I have my reasons."

Mick gazed at Peter for a moment before grunting, "Alright, then, wasn't trying to busy-nose."

"I know ye weren't," Peter replied, "Like I said, it's a long story and one I haven't got time to go into just now. Maybe someday I'll tell ye all about it."

"Good enough," Mick responded, "guess we best git back at it."

The men were still chatting among themselves when Mick and Peter re-entered the room.

"All good?" Charlie asked looking from one to the other.

"Yis, everything's fine," Mick answered, "will ye git the attention of this lot?"

Charlie's familiar sharp whistle had the men turning around to where Peter stood waiting for their answer.

"Let's get to it ye men," Peter called out, "All in favor of accepting this agreement raise yer hands."

A sea of hands waved in the air. "All who vote 'nay' raise yer hands," Peter called again. No hands were raised. "I guess we got an agreement! Now fer other business," he continued. "We need to have men that can take any grievances to the captain if need be."

"Charlie Samms," Mick suggested, "He knows what's what and most of ye men know 'im."

"Charlie, are ye willing to do it?" Peter asked.

"I s'pose I could handle it," Charlie replied.

"Are ye men happy to have Charlie speak fer ye?" Peter asked. A general chorus of approval met his question. "Good. I think ye should have at least three men capable of dealing with the company and to deal with grievances. Ye can sort that all out at yer next meetin' as well as any other business ye think of. I will see the captain tomorrow so ye can all get back to work. That's all, folks, ye can all get back to yer homes now."

"One minute, ye lot," Charlie called out, "Just wants to thank Peter here once again fer all 'is help with all of this. We wouldn't of bin able to git this far without ye," he told Peter, "So, on behalf of all the men here, thanks a lot!"

The men applauded once again with several calling out their appreciation or whistling or hooting once again.

"Let's call it a night," Charlie shouted, "we'll have one more meetin' to sort out who ye wants representing ye and to tie up any loose ends. Thank ye all fer comin' and fer helpin' make this association a real thing."

The men slowly began making their way outside as the meeting broke up.

Chapter

45

M ick and his family were all up bright and early the next
morning, even though they did not have to work the quarry.
Fanny was relieved that her husband and sons were to finally
have a bit more leisure time.

"William, yer Ma and me got somethin' to discuss wit ye," Mick
told his eldest son as they ate breakfast. "Phil, Jack, can ye take the
girls out to the barn wit ye while yer doin' yer chores?"

"Sure, we can, Da," Phil answered, "are we goin' to get at cuttin'
hay today?" He asked his father.

"That's the plan, as soon as the rest of the chores are done," Mick
answered. "Charlie and Vic are comin' with their scythes as well so
it shouldn't take long to get the fields done. If yer all finished eating
ye might as well get to it."

Jack wiped his mouth with the back of his sleeve and stood up,
"I'm ready if ye are," he told Phil. "Ma where's the basket? The girls
can collect the eggs while we're out there."

"Right where it always is," Fanny replied, "why can ye men never
see what's right in front of yer eyes?" Fanny shook her head as she
handed the basket to Jack who grinned at her unapologetically.

"Comin?" Phil asked Jack and the girls. The foursome trooped
out the door amid good natured kidding and strict orders from
Fanny to keep an eye on Rose and Sarah.

"What on yer minds?" William asked as soon as his siblings were
out the door.

"Bin thinking of yer future with Ginny and needs to know
what yer planning to do. Have ye decided where ye want to build a
house?" Mick asked.

"Not really," William answered. "Ye knows we won't be marryin' til I have enough money to build a place and then we needs furnishin's – a bed, table, chairs and the like. I figures at least another year."

"What if we tole ye that we bin savin' up part of yer wages? It may be enough to give ye a start," Mick told his son.

"I thought that money was to help start our lobster fishin'," William said.

"That's where the rest of yer wages will be goin'," Mick replied, "tis money that will be well-spent if all goes well. Now, this here's important: do ye want to go at lobster fishin'? Yer 'bout to be a married man so ye need to make up yer mind what ye wants to do."

"We bin talkin' 'bout lobster fishin' almost as long as I can remember," William answered, "I don't need to think about it. Yes, I wants to fish wit ye and Phil and Jack. Jimmy, too, once he's big enough. I ain't got one bit of doubt in me mind. That's somethin' me and Ginny have talked about a lot."

"Yer Da and me have been talkin' and we think we have enough to help ye build a place," Fanny told William, "But where do ye think ye wants to build? Ginny may want to stay close to her family."

"We ain't really talked much 'bout that," William confessed, "it seemed too far in the future."

"We knows yer itchin' to start a life wit 'er," Mick said dryly, "and I think mebbe Edward can help us out with lumber fer a cottage and a few sticks of furniture."

"I don't know what to say," William answered, surprise evident in his voice.

"I thought mebbe it would take the year," Mick admitted, "but now wit the deal with the quarry there will be more money comin' in and if ye works as much overtime as ye can handle it's like as not it can be done much sooner than ye expected. Once Peter brings the agreement back to that agent we each will get ten dollars – that will be a good help to ye. It will go a long ways to helping ye build yer own place."

"I'd like to see ye build close by," Fanny put in, "but ye have Ginny's wants to consider."

"Ye give it some thought. Talk to Ginny first off, then let us know what yer plans are," Mick said.

"I didn't know ye was savin' money fer me," Wiliam replied, "I thought it was all fer the fishin' we plan to do; to pay fer lumber to build the dories and whatnot."

"T'is true, that was the plan, but me and Edward have worked it all out," Mick revealed, "and I plan to talk to 'im 'bout lumber fer yer place when we go out to get the first lot of wood to build them dories."

"Is that why ye sent us all off when they were here? I was a bit insulted, thought ye were treating me like a child and not a man grown and 'bout to be married," William told his parents.

"Didn't want ye to get yer hopes up if we couldn't work somethin' out," Fanny responded. She reached out across the table and patted her son's hand. "Wasn't meant to make ye feel small."

William nodded, "S'pose I'll go see Ginny once we're done cutting the hay. She's goin' to be so pleased. Leastwise, I hope so."

"I rather figured ye would," Mick replied, "well, guess we best get at it."

"Thank ye, Ma, Pa," William spoke quietly, earnestly, "Yer the best, really the best."

"Ye always made us proud," Fanny told him, "Yer a hard worker and yer goin' to be a good provider. I hope ye and Ginny will be very happy together."

William blushed, unused to the praise, though he always knew his parents thought highly of him. "Aw, go on, Ma," he said shyly.

"Lots more plans to make and things to chat about," Mick responded. "Before we know it Phil will be comin' tellin' us he wants to marry, but not fer a good long while, I hope."

"Bin watchin' 'im watching Haldi, Mary's young sister," Fanny told them, "Won't be that long, I don't think."

"Just what we need, another love-struck lad," Mick said gruffly.

William laughed, "He had such fun teasing me 'bout Ginny. I thinks I'm 'bout to give 'im a taste of 'is own medicine."

"He say anything 'bout 'er to ye?" Fanny asked.

"Not a word, but I did notice 'im lookin' all moony and in a big hurry to get to church last week," William answered with a grin. "Kind of suspected it might be a girl." He chuckled.

"William, don't ye be at that, now," Fanny warned, "could be it don't lead nowhere."

"Can't make no promises, Ma," William grinned, "I owes 'im a bit of tormenting, don't ye think?"

"Boy's got a point," Mick told his wife, "Ye didn't see the tormenting poor William was dealing with every day on the way to work and home again. And Phil egged Jack on, the two of 'em ganging up on poor ole Will."

"Ye boys are always at it," Fanny said, "William gives as good as he gets. That's one thing I'm sure of." She smiled at her son. "Have a bit of mercy fer yer brother."

"I tole ye, Ma," William retorted, "I ain't makin' no promises."

"Well enough of all this," Mick put it, "we gots to get at the hay."

"Did ye think to ask Vic or Charlie to bring along a couple of pitchforks?" William asked. "We only got the two."

"What do ye think?" Mick asked in turn, "of course I did, ain't the first time we 'ad help with cuttin' hay."

"Go on," Fanny ordered, "The two of ye, get out of my kitchen. I gots work to do as well."

Chapter
46

Peter rode his small mare into his uncle's yard and noted the well-kept yard was beginning to look a bit run down. His uncle was kept busy at his law office and without his wife to oversee the house and grounds it was beginning to be neglected. Peter looked with sadness at the wild roses beginning to overtake the fine entrance way. His aunt had always loved the wild flowers and had worked hard to keep them trimmed and well-manicured. This late in the season the flowers were all gone and only seed pods were left to give evidence of the beauty that once was there.

He walked his mare up the laneway, his thoughts on the past and the many summers he'd spent here. Moments later he was chatting with the groom/groundskeeper his uncle had hired decades ago.

"How are ye doing, Benjamin?" he greeted the older man, as he dismounted.

"I am well, Sir, or as well as can be expected," he replied, "getting old and achy but better than many."

"It's good to see ye," Peter replied, "You're looking good."

"Thanks to yer uncle," Benjamin told him, "Many are not as fortunate in their employers."

"He's a good man," Peter agreed, "glad there's some that know how to treat their fellow man."

"Tis true," Benjamin replied, "There's many that have a much harder life than I."

"That's a sad fact of life," Peter responded.

"I knows yer doin' yer best to change all that," Benjamin said, "and many owe their very existence to yer help."

"I wouldn't go as far as that," Peter chuckled.

"Aw, but I knows. I hears things," Benjamin retorted.

"Well, it's likely best not to believe everything ye hear," Peter denied.

"Not goin' ta argue wit ye. Here now, let me take care of yer mare. Yer uncle is lookin' forward to yer visit, no doubt," Benjamin replied, "why don't ye go on in."

"Thank ye, Benjamin. I know she'll be in good hands," Peter said handing over the reins.

Peter walked toward the big house taking note of the moss beginning to grow over the stepping stones, evidence of a seldom used walkway that led to a side door. Reaching the top of the steps he stopped to look out over the bay in the distance. It was a cool day in late August and a scent of autumn was in the air. Peter stayed outside for several moments enjoying the view and remembering. Suddenly the door swung open.

"Well, ain't ye a sight fer sore eyes," Mildred exclaimed. She had been employed as the cook there for many years. Peter remembering sneaking cookies from her kitchen when he was a lad and the warmth and kindness of this good lady. Peter was at once enfolded in her embrace which he returned with much affection.

"Hello, Missus," he said once he was relinquished from her arms. "Sorry it's taken so long for me to get back here."

"I bin 'earing all 'bout yer goings on," Mildred told him, "Yer bin doin' a lot of good and glad am I to 'ear of it."

"Ye sound just like Benjamin," Peter retorted, "and like I told him, it's best not to believe everything ye hear."

"Stuff and nonsense," Mildred responded, "I won't keep on 'bout it, but yer makin me some proud, b'y, some proud!"

"Never mind all that, do ye have any of those cakes I used to love?" Peter asked to change the subject.

"Soon as Mr. John tole me ye were comin' I got busy preparin'," Mildred replied, "think I wouldn't know to 'ave 'em ready fer yer visit? How long ye stayin' this time? I hope ye'll be 'ere fer a good while."

"No, I won't be staying long," Peter told her, "I have a bit of business to finish up and then I will be heading back to the city."

"No doubt with stops all along the way to 'elp this one and that one," Mildred retorted. "Tis a shame, was 'oping ye'd spend the winter this year. Mr. John would like that. I think he's mighty lonesome since 'is missus died."

"Wish I could, but there are things I need to be at in other places," Peter answered. "And he has ye and Benjamin. I know ye're both taking good care of him."

"We do our best, but we ain't family," Mildred replied.

"Sometimes family isn't everything," Peter spoke solemnly.

"Family is what's most important in this life," Mildred scolded, "and don't ye ferget it!"

"Where are those cakes, I've been looking forward to 'em?" Peter asked to distract her from yet another sermon on family.

"Sit yerself down at the table," Mildred replied, "And don't think I don't know what yer doin'. I knows yer avoiding the subject."

"I would never be able to pull the wool over yer eyes," Peter grinned as he said this, "never could, even as hard as I tried."

"Ye were a little rascal, that's fer sure," Mildred answered, "but a loveable little rascal. Yer still givin' the powers what be a dickens of a time, ain't ye? I knows yer are. I 'ears lots of things when I has to go to the market."

"I do my best to help the people that need my help," Peter replied mildly, "nothing more."

"I 'eard 'bout ye putting yer oars in down at the quarry," Mildred answered, "I weren't goin' to say nuddin' to nobody 'bout it. But I 'eard."

Peter shook his head, "Not much gets past ye, does it?"

"I 'ave me ways," Mildred answered, "and I'm mighty glad ye was able to 'elp 'em. A good man died cuz of the way that quarry's bin run. And it ain't right."

"Uncle John would likely not agree with ye," Peter said, "He wants me to go back home and work in the family business, which I cannot do."

"Yer uncle, he's a good man," Mildred replied, "family is important to 'im. And 'e worries about ye, though 'e don't say a whole lot. It made a big difference to 'im that ye were comin' to visit."

"I will make an effort to visit more often," Peter promised, "Uncle is a very good man but he doesn't understand why I cannot go back to work with Father."

"Neither do I, truth be known," Mildred replied.

"Missus, ye knows what happened in the mine and how Luke's father was killed," Peter began.

"Yis, I knows," Mildred responded, "but ain't it time to bury the hatchet, to let bygones be bygones?"

"This is a conversation I don't want to have," Peter answered.

"Peter, I knows ye since ye were a little lad. Ye can be curse-ed stubborn," Mildred replied, "don't wait until it's too late. Life is short b'y and I don't want to see ye living wit regrets."

"I regret my best friend had to grow up without his father," Peter responded, "I regret that his family was torn apart, each having to go their separate ways because their main means of support was gone. I regret that people have to scrounge out a living while merchants and the owners of mines, quarries, logging camps, and fishing vessels are living the high life. I regret the unfairness of it all. That's what I regret."

"Ye have a big heart – a huge heart, Peter," Mildred replied, "and yer doin' all kinds of good fer people, but family is family. There comes a time to forgive and forget."

Peter shook his head slowly, "I don't think ye can really understand, Missus. Ye don't know what it's like. Luke was like a brother to me. I didn't even get to say good-bye to him. And I've seen the kind of places he would have been sent to, to work fer little all his life long. I was too young and didn't know how to find him after the mine collapsed.

"I was there when they dug his father's body out. I seen how broken the spirits were of the men and their families. I begged my father to help Luke's family. He wouldn't, because to him it would have been an admission of guilt. Don't ask me to forgive and forget. Not when the same things keep happening: good men dying or worn out by hard work for too many years. Don't ask me to do that. Perhaps one day when there is change, real change, especially at the mine my family owns. Until then I cannot, I simply cannot."

Mildred shook her head sadly. "T'was a sad time in yer life, I remember. I was glad when yer father sent ye out to us. He's a good man, yer father. He may have made mistakes, but he's a good man."

"Let's not continue in this vein," Peter entreated, "I'd rather hear the local news. Tell me all that's been happening here since I left."

Mildred set out the little cakes that were Peter's favorite and changed the topic to local news even while she prayed in her heart for Peter and his family.

"Has Peter arrived?" John called cheerfully as he walked down the long hallway to the kitchen.

"I'm here, Uncle John," Peter called back.

"Might've known I'd find ye back here," John replied as he entered the large kitchen.

"Had to partake of my favorite little cakes," Peter retorted as he rose to greet his uncle. "Mildred makes the best cakes on the island!"

"That's a fact," John agreed, "The best anywhere in the country, I allow."

"Yer right," Peter grinned, bowing to Mildred, "Forgive my insult, good lady."

Mildred laughed, "Go on, the two of ye, as me mudder would say, ye must 'ave kissed the blarney stone."

"No blarney at all," Peter retorted licking his fingers, "these are like food for the angels – so heavenly good!"

Mildred laughed again, "Take yerselves into the parlor and I will bring yer tea."

After teasing Mildred for a few minutes more Peter followed his uncle as he led the way to the parlor.

"Any trouble with those documents I helped ye with?" John asked Peter once they were seated.

"No trouble at all, Uncle," Peter answered, "the company was quick to agree to the demands. I didn't know but there was a freighter heading to the quarry while we were busily crafting the agreement. It helped to bring it to a quick closure."

"Lady Luck was with ye then," John responded, "that could not have gone over very well."

"The captain, a Mr. George Gallo, was none too happy, nor welcoming," Peter smiled as he told his uncle of the interchange.

"So, yer work here is done?" John asked.

"I just have one or two more small details to sew up, then I will make my way back East," Peter answered.

"And that man, Langley, has no hint I was involved in drawing up the documents ye needed?" John queried.

"No idea whatsoever," came Peter's confident reply. "I have let it be known that I had studied law for several years. Do not fear, Uncle, if there are to be any repercussions, I will bear them."

"I hope ye're right, not that I wish any harm to befall ye," John sighed, "I am hoping Jeremiah will soon be ready to take over the law firm. He's in his last year of studies and is doing quite well, as I understand it."

"My cousin will make a fine barrister," Peter answered, "he has his father's keen mind and his mother's kind heart."

"He asks about ye in his letters," John replied, "I well remember some of the hijinks ye two got up to back in the day. Jeremiah idolized ye."

"I was two years older," Peter pointed out, "just enough older to be the leader, and the instigator of pranks and such."

"Oh, I well remember all the pranks," John spoke sternly but the merriment in his eyes was at odds with his tone of voice.

"Aunt Jane was very patient," Peter remembered.

"She was. Quite often she kept yer shenanigans to herself, or I would have had to discipline ye both," John reminisced. "She was a good woman."

"I wish I could have been here with ye when she died, Uncle," Peter said quietly, "the storms came one after another and made travel impossible."

"I know this, Peter," John comforted, "I know ye would have been here if the roads had been passable."

"I think of her often. She was like a second mother to me," Peter remarked.

"Enough of this somber talk," John interjected, "tell me, what projects are ye planning to take on as ye head East?"

The two men launched into a discussion of Peter's unpaid work and long-term plans. John tried once again to convince his nephew to return to the family fold and take up his place in the family business.

"Have ye considered ye might do more good inside the company where ye would have considerable influence?" John asked.

"Ye know my brother thinks much as Father does," Peter replied, "my 'influence' would be next to nil. And Father, understandably, plans on having Michael take over his share in the company one day."

"Still, if ye were there day by day, ye may eventually bring them around to yer ways," John insisted.

"I'm sorry, Uncle," Peter replied, "I don't see there being much chance of that. Michael is as stubborn in his viewpoint as I am."

"At least go see them," John entreated, "I know my brother misses his son."

"Aw, Uncle, ye have been making peace between myself and Father all of my life," Peter sighed, "perhaps it's time ye left well enough alone."

"I often wish ye'd never gotten mixed up with that priest. Priests and ministers ought to stay out of the affairs of commerce," John proclaimed.

"Father Williams felt that human endeavors should lead to a man being able to provide for himself and his family. The merchants were unjust, in his view, one I must say I agree with. Men were reduced to unacceptable levels of poverty while the merchant class became richer," Peter began, "that priest made certain that men could at the very least provide for the necessities of life. The church was none too pleased with him but that didn't stop him. William Croaker was another. You see, Uncle John, I am not alone in my views. There has to be better ways. We cannot continue to grow rich on the backs of the poor and the ignorant."

"Ye have preached yer sermons so often I almost know them by heart," John sighed, "why can't ye leave well enough alone?"

"Because there is no wellness, except for the rich," Peter argued.

John held his hands up, "I give up. Ye should have been a lawyer, a politician, no, yer were always best suited to be a preacher in some quiet church, preferably somewhere in the country when ye could do no harm."

"I am doing no harm," Peter disagreed, "shaking up the powers that be is no crime. Who would speak for the poor, the dispossessed, and the unlearned?"

"T'is a mission best suited to priests and ministers," John repeated, "not to a lay man unversed in the study of theology."

"There is a new world coming, Uncle," Peter replied, "and one I am happy to build with the help of others."

"Ye will be the death of yer poor father," John replied, "It is all well and good to take care of yer own; yer wives, sons, daughters, servants, and such, but ye are reaching into society itself. There are many who will not take kindly to it, nor to yer ideas of a new world. Take good care, Peter, I fear for ye. I truly do."

"Fear not, Uncle, I do take care," Peter comforted, "I am not without friends and supporters."

"I am well aware of that," John retorted, "t'would be best if they kept their noses out of it, too."

"Ye cannot be too strongly averse to my activities, else ye would never have helped me out with those documents," Peter noted. "And grateful I am that ye did."

"Yer father would not take kindly to my doing so," John said soberly.

"My father possesses neither yer wisdom nor yer compassion," Peter retorted, "He need not know of it."

"It so happens I have heard stories of how the men working the quarry have been treated," John related, "It was a small thing to help ye with, and something that will reap benefits for the families out there. Still, I am not given to interfering with such commerce, as a rule. Heaven help me, it may be that some of yer fine talk is rubbing off on me."

"T'was yer doing that I grew up with a sense of responsibility for those that others feel are beneath us," Peter countered.

"T'is true I took up the law as a way to make their burdens less weighty," John admitted, "But I do not make it a habit to put my oar in where it doesn't belong."

"Yer a good man, Uncle," Peter complimented the older man, "I like to think I am following yer example in some small way."

"I know ye care about yer fellow man, and I do not fault ye for that," John answered. "I just wish ye would have found a different path for yer passions."

"I am happy with what I'm doing, but sorry it causes you grief," Peter responded.

"My son, there are thugs in this world more than glad to fill their coffers with ill-gotten gains," John began, "Lord knows I see my share of them through my work. I hope you will be very careful. Sure, just last year I heard of one such ne'er-do-well, hired by a rich man to teach another a lesson. Of course, the rich have ways to keep out of jail, the ignorant are not so fortunate. It worries me that one day ye will cross the wrong man."

"I am not without resources, nor help from high places," Peter rejoined, "Perhaps I have ye to thank for that."

"Yer family name has offered much protection," John replied, "but it isn't fool-proof. God knows there's too many fools in this life."

"I will make sure to give the fools a wide berth, then," Peter reassured him, "I know how to defend myself. Don't worry yerself, Uncle."

"Worry will come, no matter what ye say," John answered, "but enough of this dismal talk now. Let us turn to more pleasant topics. Tell me yer plans. Where will ye be off to next?"

The two men spent the remainder of the evening in general conversation and sharing their political views, of which they were mainly in agreement.

Early the next morning Peter said his farewells to his uncle and his household, aiming to bring the agreement back to the agent before heading back to the quarry to see the men once again.

Chapter

47

"There ye have it, Langley," Peter said, dropping the sheaf of papers onto the agent's desk. "I don't have the widow's agreement just yet, but will be back with it before much longer."

Langley turned a burning glare in Peter's direction. "And ye made sure the men of the quarry know that the ten dollars is a one-time thing. They best not expect to receive that ever again," he growled.

"I explained it all carefully to the men and they know they have to keep up their side of the bargain. There won't be another work stoppage unless the company doesn't hold up their side of it," Peter spoke smoothly, unruffled by Langley's apparent displeasure, "if that's what worrying ye."

"Ye knows damn well that ain't all that's worrying me," Langley retorted, "thought ye'd have the widow's agreement to give me as well."

"I take it Dominion Limestone knows nothing of yer little side deal with Johnstone," Peter replied.

"That's none of yer concern," Langley spoke gruffly and huffed as he drew the agreement closer to examine.

"As ye wish," Peter spoke softly, "and as long as the men are treated right and the widow receives her money in a timely fashion, we will have no need to speak of it ever again."

"I will put the funds into yer grasping hands as soon as I have the signed agreement," Langley spat out. "I expect a receipt fer the amount specified when ye return."

Peter nodded, watching the man carefully. "I trust there will be no further reason to meet with ye after this business is done with, but I give ye fair warning, I have relations that work that quarry so I will be sure to hear of any further problems."

"Are ye threatening me?" Langley asked, his face darkening.

"No, not at all," Peter answered, "as I said, just a fair warning."

"There will be no further reason fer ye to visit this establishment," Langley bit the words off, "why don't ye take yerself off now, see to that agreement with the widow."

"T'will be my great pleasure," Peter retorted, "I will give the men yer respects when I let them know they can return to work." Peter grinned and turned to exit the office. He heard the man's fist come crashing down on the wooden desk as the door closed and he smiled to himself.

Peter took his time riding back to the quarry, enjoying the late summer sun, the peaks of the hills, and the blue bay that the roadway followed. He was whistling to himself as the mare jogged along and did not notice the man hidden among the bushes and trees he was passing by. Lost in thought he did not hear the footsteps hurrying toward him, nor did he feel the blow across his back after the mare reared, throwing him from the saddle. He fell heavily, striking his head in the fall.

It was only dumb luck that Vic found him, bloodied and dazed and half hidden by the bushes where his attacker had left him. Peter's mare had been standing not far away, Vic had recognized her. The sight of the mare caused him to look carefully around him as he searched for Peter. It didn't take him long to notice the boots poking out from the brush.

Victor brought his workhorse to a standstill and jumped down, hurrying to the hurt man. "Peter! Jumpin' dyin'," Vic cradled Peter's head, "what the dickens 'appened 'ere?"

Peter groaned and reached a hand up to touch the back of his head.

"Speak to me, man, are ye all right?" Vic's urgent tone reached through the hammering in Peter's head.

"That hurts," Peter stammered out.

"I daresay it t'would," Vic replied, relieved that he was getting a response, "ye gave me a scare, thought ye was dead fer a moment there. Can ye stand?"

"Not sure," Peter groggily replied. "Give me a minute."

Peter sat up slowly, Vic's arm continuing to support his upper body.

"What the 'ell 'appened to ye?" Vic asked as he helped Peter to his feet.

"I dunno," Peter answered, his hand reaching up to touch the back of his head. His hair was stiff with dried blood and his fingers found a good-sized lump. Peter spoke slowly, the pain making speech difficult. "I was riding along, admiring the scenery and then . . . My horse reared and I fell, something spooked her."

Vic looked suspiciously around him. Around a bend in the road the captain's house stood on the crest of the hill. "Something? Or mebbe someone." Vic muttered as he tried his best to steady the younger man.

"How are ye doing now?" Vic asked Peter.

"Where's my horse?" Peter asked, disoriented.

"She's up the road a piece," Vic replied, "I'll git 'er in a minute. C'mon, sit down 'ere fer a minute, 'til ye feels more yerself." Vic guided him to a large boulder sitting near the side of the roadway. "Yer lucky ye weren't killed. Ye could 'ave broke yer neck."

Peter gasped as stabbing pain overwhelmed him. "Kind of wish I had been. Jaysus, that hurts."

"Yer not going to be able to saddle up in yer condition," Vic told him. "When yer ready we'll git ye up onto the wagon and I'll drive ye to Hanks. That's where ye were 'eaded, right?"

"Yeah, that's right," Peter agreed. "But ye don't need to be at that. I can ride." Peter made to stand up and groaning sank back down onto the boulder."

"No, b'y", Vic retorted, "Ye ain't gonna be able to ride fer a day or two. I'll get the wagon, ye can lie down in the back of 'er, if ye needs to."

"Yer not going to haul me around like a sack of potatoes," Peter refused, "I'll sit up on the wagon seat beside ye."

"Right, then, we'll give 'er a try," Vic said, "do ye think ye can stand?"

It took Vic some time to maneuver Peter up onto the wagon seat and to tie his mare to the back before they could set off. Peter tried his best to suppress the moans and groans that threatened to unman him as they jounced along the bumpy cart track. Thankfully, Hank's home was not far away and soon they were driving into his yard.

"Ye just stay right 'ere," Vic commanded the hurt man, "Don't ye dare move. I'll be back with Hank in two shakes."

Vic strode quickly to the door and without knocking opened the door, calling to Hank to come help him.

"Vic, b'y, what in the name of all that's holy is goin' on?" Hank asked when he appeared in the doorway.

"T'is, Peter, e's bin 'urt," Vic said tersely as he headed back to the wagon where Peter waited as ordered. Vic explained about finding Peter on the road as they approached the wagon. "T'was not far from where the captain lives," Vic spoke grimly and quietly to his friend. Hank was quick to pick up on the unsaid accusation.

"How bad is he?" Hank asked.

"Can't tell fer sure," Vic replied, "e took an awful blow to the back of 'is 'ead."

Hank climbed up on the wagon and helped Peter descend. Vic stood below to ensure he didn't fall. The two men helped the injured man into Hank's house.

Hilda was standing anxiously in the doorway, watching as the trio approached. Peter's arms were stretched across his friends' shoulders. The trio came slowly with frequent pauses when Peter's legs threatened to buckle under him.

"Oh my God, what's happened?" Hilda cried out.

"Peter's hurt," Hank said needlessly, "We needs to get 'im in the parlour."

Hilda stood back as the men eased Peter into the house and to the parlour. Gingerly the men lowered Peter into a chair.

"How are ye doing, mate?" Hank asked.

Peter's eyes were closed but he mumbled his thanks and assurances he'd be all right.

"Can ye get 'im a bit of water?" Hank asked Hilda. Hilda bustled off to get it without another word, even as questions tumbled one after another through her mind. Bringing the water, she watched as Peter held the glass in trembling fingers and sipped it slowly.

"Ginny," Hilda called, "get me a bucket of water and some cloths. I needs to clean up 'is 'ead so I can see 'ow bad it is."

Vic stood back with Hank, both men studying their benefactor's face as Hilda buzzed around the room grabbing a footstool to make the hurt man more comfortable.

"Why don't ye men see to 'is 'orse," Hilda suggested, "I'll wash 'is 'ead and look after 'im."

"Thank ye, kindly," Peter whispered.

Vic and Hank left Peter in Hilda's care and went outside. Hank questioned Vic about what had happened and their suspicions of the captain featured heavily in their conversation.

"He didn't see nuddin'," Vic told his friend, "Tole me he was enjoying the view when 'is mare suddenly reared. He was thrown from the saddle and hit the road, 'ard."

"Mebbe after he has a good night's sleep, he'll be able to tell us more," Hank said, "it rained last night, mebbe we can go back up there, see if there's tracks or anythin' that can tell the tale."

"It's dumb luck I found 'im," Vic related, "was just 'eadin' 'ome after 'elping Mick with cutting hay. If I 'adn't found 'im it's fair to say 'e wouldn't have lasted the night."

"Do ye think it's as bad as that?" Hank asked.

"Don't know fer sure, but there was blood on the road where 'e 'it 'is 'ead when he fell off 'is 'orse," Vic said solemnly, "a lot of blood."

Hank nodded, "All the more reason to go check if we can find any signs. Let me go saddle up and I will follow ye to yer place. Not anything more ye can do 'ere."

Vic nodded, "Might as well, if it rains agin all signs will be washed away. And ye won't 'ave to come all the way to my place, mebbe 'alf-way or a bit better."

Hank nodded. "Let's go," he said. Vic followed Hank into the barn and helped him saddle his mount. Minutes later Hank was climbing off his horse as Vic pointed out the flattened brush where he'd found Peter. The two men walked all around the area, finding nothing incriminating, until Vic found a man's footprint in the soft mud several feet away from where he'd found Peter. Flattened foliage and broken twigs and branches as well as a trail of blood gave evidence that Peter's body had been dragged to where Vic had found him.

"At least we knows it wasn't that boulder what caused the bump on 'is 'ead," Hank pointed out. The men followed the blood trail several yards to where Peter had been knocked from his horse.

"There!" Vic exclaimed pointing to the spot on the road where blood had congealed and the blood trail ended.

The men stooped down to get a closer look at where Peter's head had hit the ground. "That's where e must've banged 'is 'ead," Vic said, pointing to the rocky ground."

"Sure looks that way," Hank agreed, "That's so hard-packed, t'was lucky he weren't killed. Like as not 'e was knocked out, but good."

"Yup, and somebody dragged 'im back there and left 'im in the bushes," Vic agreed, "Left 'im dere to die. T'was dumb luck I seen 'is 'orse and decided to look fer 'im."

"He's a lucky man, that's fer sure," Hank replied, "didn't mark the cap'n fer a violent man."

"Don't see who else coulda done it," Vic responded, "Seems mighty likely seeing as 'ow 'e lives so close by."

"Let's go see how far we can follow them footprints," Hank suggested.

The men returned to where Vic had found Peter's body but though they followed the boot tracks they had no luck. The tracks wound back to the hard-packed earth of the roadway and they lost the trail.

"Well, mate, nuddin' else we can do," Hank told Vic, "We might just as well head back home. We'll have to wait til Peter's feelin' more 'imself, maybe we'll learn more then."

Vic stroked his beard as he pondered the sinister thoughts gathering in his mind. "Never would 'ave suspected the cap'n could do such a thing," he said. "Course, we gots no proof, but it's mighty fishy that Peter should 'ave such a thing 'appen so close to where the cap'n lives."

"I hope Peter will be able to shed light on the matter," Hank responded, "can't do any more 'til then."

"I'll 'ead on 'ome then," Vic replied, "I will stop by yer place tomorrow. I promised Mick I'd lend 'em a 'and agin on the morrow with 'is 'ay. T'is near finished."

"And ye will let Mick know about all this," Hank asked as his arm swept the area.

"I sure will," Vic answered, "Not that 'e can do anythin' 'bout it, but 'e should know. I'll be by not much after noontime."

"Thanks, fer yer help, bud," Hank replied, "take care going home. I suspect the capt'n is likely the scoundrel who did this, but we can't know fer sure."

"I ain't much worried," Vic responded, "but I will keep me eyes peeled. See ye da morrow."

Chapter

48

The captain brooded as he sat at his kitchen table. The events of the past few days had left him bitter and frustrated. Between Langley's threats and Peter Parsons' obvious distaste, the captain's mood was black indeed.

Didn't mean fer any 'arm to come to 'im. Just meant to give 'im a scare, mebbe run 'im off. Wouldn't've done it if 'e 'adn't bin such a snot, actin' all uppity when I give 'im them papers.

The captain's hands rubbed his face as he considered his rash deed. He replayed the scene of the day before. He had been out walking the fields near his house, slingshot in hand to frighten off the crows that had been robbing his garden. He'd seen Peter riding on the road below him, his pure white mare easily identifying him. The captain hurried through a shortcut in the woods to stop him and have it out. He was out of breath when he reached the road and the mare was several yards ahead of him. There was little chance he could catch up.

It was pure impulse to bring the slingshot up and let go the rock aimed at the haunches of Peter's mare. *Always was a good 'and with a slingshot.* He grabbed the bottle of rum and took another swig. *Get a 'old of yerself, man*, he told himself as he swallowed the fiery liquid.

But images of Peter as he dragged him from the road, blood flowing freely from the wound on his head, haunted his thoughts, as they had all through the night. *Bastard 'ad it comin', 'e 'ad no business stickin' 'is nose in where it don't belong. Can't be dead. No b'y, 'e was breathin' when I left 'im.* The captain tried to console himself.

Thought 'e was a goner when 'e 'it the road. Scared the bejesus outta me. He took another swig from the bottle as he replayed the scene.

The bastard was some 'eavy to move, 'ad to do it b'y. Thought 'e was dead. Just made sense to 'ide 'is body. The captain chortled to himself. *Just knocked out. I was some glad when 'e got to groanin', least I knew 'e was still alive. Mabbe I should go check, see if 'e's still where I left 'im.* The captain considered this for a moment before deciding not to. *Sure, somebody would 'ave seen 'is boots sticking out.*

Nah, I don't needs to check. No doubt 'e's long gone. I seen a couple of wagons 'eadin' away from the quarry, woulda 'ad to pass 'im. Yis, b'y, somebody found the son of a bitch. He chortled to himself once again. *Didn't even know what 'it 'im.* The captain took an evil glee in the memory of the horse rearing and throwing Peter to the ground. *That'll teach ya,* he thought to himself. In his mind's eye he swept the area, searching for any possible witness. *Nah, nobody saw nuddin',* he reassured himself as he took yet another mouthful from the bottle. *Best be puttin' this away,* he thought as he screwed the lid back on the bottle, *back to the grind on the morrow.*

The captain's face darkened as he thought of facing the men. *Dem arseholes will git what's comin' to dem, too.* His memories turned especially bitter as he thought of Jake. *I ain't finished wit that 'alf-breed neither, no, b'y, not by a long shot.* He couldn't understand why Mick seemed to be coming to Jake's defense the day Peter had appeared to tell him about the decision of the men to stop work. *Ain't no sweat off me back. Let the company go broke payin' 'em all. Mabbe tis time I was movin' on.*

The captain glanced around the warm and cozy kitchen. Memories of Langley's threat to fire him caused his face to darken once again. *And that's one more arsehole gonna pay fer treatin' the captain like trash,* he promised himself. *Yis b'y, could be time to pull up stakes and move along. I've about 'ad it wit this outfit anyway. But not afore I settles a score or two.* With that the captain stood up, his mind spinning as he formulated plans for his future.

Unknown to the captain there was someone who had seen his movements the day before. Jake had been in the woods tracking caribou when he'd seen the captain striding past. He'd been quick to duck behind a cluster of pine trees and held his breath as the captain passed by, unaware of his presence. Jake did not follow but quickly made an about turn and headed home, caribou all but forgotten. *That was a close call,* Jake thought as he hurried away, *last man I wants to see today, or ever again, truth be told.* He knew the captain lived nearby but his concentration had been focused on the caribou tracks that had led him onto the captain's land, a mistake he vowed never to repeat.

Down in the valley Vic was helping Mick and his sons finish off the hay fields.

"Is Peter alright?" Mick questioned Vic after he'd told his story.

"I 'aven't seen 'im since I left 'im at Hank's yesterday," Vic replied, "gonna stop by there after I leaves 'ere."

Mick spoke gravely as they discussed the event. "Peter's got the calmest mare I ever did see. Can't see 'er rearing up fer no good reason. And ye says Peter was in no shape to talk 'bout what happened?"

"Peter was in a bad way," Vic answered. "I'm 'oping 'e's in better shape today."

"T'won't take more than a couple of 'ours to finish cuttin' them fields," Mick responded, "I think I will come with ye to see 'im. I needs to satisfy meself 'e's alright."

"Let's get at 'er," Vic replied, "sooner t'is done the sooner we can go see Peter and mabbe find out what 'appened."

The men spent the morning swinging scythes as Mick's sons used pitchforks to load the hay onto Vic's wagon. Normally they would let it dry in the sun for several days but Mick needed a wagon full for the cow that they expected to birth her calf any day. Mick had tethered her in the barn so he wouldn't have to search for her after she had her young. Fresh hay was always needed for bedding for the hens as well as the sow. The rest would be left to dry in the sun until Mick was ready to store it in the haylofts of the two barns.

"What do ye say we call it a day?" Mick asked as he wiped his forehead with the handkerchief, he'd pulled from his back pocket.

"Ye don't have to ask me twice," Vic retorted.

"Ye b'ys, get busy emptying the wagon," Mick told his sons, "there's somethin' I needs to talk to Vic about. Don't be comin' in the house til ye have it all done."

"Sure, da," Phil replied, "t'won't take long." Mick nodded at his sons and turned back to Vic.

"C'mon in the house fer a bite afore we goes," Mick invited his friend.

Vic agreed and the men were soon sitting at Fanny's kitchen table enjoying a much-needed lunch. Mick filled her in on Peter's misadventure as they ate and soon the men were getting ready to go visit Hank.

"I sure would like to know what 'appened to Peter," Vic said as they rode along and discussed the incident.

"I could tell the cap'n was riled up when Peter gave 'im the news 'bout the association," Mick replied, "But never thought he'd stoop to this."

The two men continued in this vein, both trying to puzzle out what could have caused Peter's mare to rear so suddenly.

"T'is true, it may have been nuddin more than a bee sting or some such thing," Vic agreed, "but t'is awful fishy that it 'appened so near the captain's place."

"Hopefully Peter will be up to talking wit us," Mick replied.

"We'll find out soon enough, 'ere we be," Vic replied as he guided the horse and wagon into Hank's yard. Ginny was outdoors minding the younger children. When Mick asked for her father, she left to let him know they had company.

"How's Peter doing?" Mick asked when Hank came outside.

"A damned sight better than yesterday," Hank replied, "Why don't ye come in and see fer yerselves."

The men dismounted from the wagon and followed Hank into the cottage. Peter was sitting at the kitchen table. He was very pale and Hilda had wrapped his head in wide strips torn from an old sheet. He smiled weakly at the men as they entered.

"Come to make sure ye're all right," Mick told him.

"I've had better days," Peter responded.

"Do ye remember anythin' at'all 'bout what 'appened?" Vic asked.

"Only that my mare suddenly reared up out of the blue," Peter answered. "I had no idea why she should. She's a good mare, not easily spooked."

"I was just tellin' 'im I checked 'er all over," Hank told the men, "She has a small cut on her right haunch, like she was struck by somethin'."

"And ye didn't see or hear anything?" Mick asked Peter.

"Not a blessed thing," Peter replied.

"Me and Hank went back to where it 'appened," Vic told Peter, "I 'magine 'e told ye. Yer lucky ye weren't killed in that fall. The road is hard-packed earth, lots of small stones, too. It looked like ye bled quite a bit."

Peter reached a hand up to gingerly touch the back of his head. "Ma always said I was hard-headed, guess that turned out to be a good thing," he said, trying to make light of it.

"T'weren't no accident," Hank put in, "somebody dragged 'im from the road and left 'im in the bushes."

"Shockin', that's what it is," Mick declared, "and it happened close by to where the captain lives. Seems mighty shady to me."

"I'd like to keep it just between us," Peter said softly, "Sooner or later whoever was involved will hang himself with his own rope. Can't be making any accusations, though I do agree. The captain had good reason to be angry with me."

"Hangin' t'would be too good fer 'im," Hank snarled.

"And there's no chance it may've been a robbery?" Mick asked.

"Nope! I went through 'is saddlebags," Hank answered, "Peter says nuddin' is missin'."

"Had to ask," Mick commented, "Ain't ever heard of anyone getting' robbed 'round 'ere, but there's always that chance."

"First thing Peter asked as well," Hank noted.

"Best stay put fer a few days," Mick told Peter, "Until yer feelin' stronger. Yer not in a hurry to get back to the city, are ye?"

"I do need to go, but I can spare a few days," Peter answered, "truth be known, I ain't feeling up to a long ride just yet. Besides, I still have paperwork to finish up in another matter. I have one more visit to pay to Langley so I wasn't planning on setting out right away."

"Hilda will feed ye up and get ye back on yer feet," Hank promised, "I know yer not one to 'ave women fussin' over ye, but it's fer the best, at least until yer back to yerself."

"Ye men need a woman lookin' after ye when ye go git yerselves 'urt," Hilda proclaimed from the far side of the room, "worse than children ye are, don't know what's good fer ye at the best of times."

"It won't be no hardship to stay a while with you and your family," Peter grinned at Hilda before turning back to Hank, "I will keep 'em company while yer at the quarry, breaking yer back."

"Won't be at that much longer," Hank retorted, "Mick's got a plan to get us outta that racket."

"Yes, we spoke a little about all of ye forming a fishing partnership," Peter answered. "If there's anything I can do to help I'd be happy to."

"We'll 'ave to get together to talk it over afore ye leaves fer the city," Mick said, "But that can keep until yer feelin' better."

"I'll be fine in a day or two," Peter vowed, "It's nothing more than a bad headache."

"Hilda heard ye puking yer guts up during the night," Hank disputed, "seems to be a bit more than just a headache."

"We should get going," Mick commented, "Let ye get yer rest."

"Ye do look better than ye did when I left 'ere yesterday," Vic replied, "but rest will do ye good." With that the visitors stood up to leave.

"Thank ye for coming," Peter replied, "T'was good of ye."

"See ye ta morrow," Hank said as he walked them out the door.

Chapter

49

There was a marked difference in the demeanor of the men at the quarry the next morning. Their manner was upbeat and the men stood straighter and walked with a spring in their step due to the guarantee of better wages and safer working conditions; It led to a brighter outlook for all. It had rained during the night and even the awful limestone dust had been tamped down in the deluge.

In the captain's hut the pit boss was being raked over the coals for not informing his overseer of Peter's presence in the community or of the meetings that had led to the protective association.

Josiah Picton hung his head while the captain took out his rage and frustration on him. He waited while the captain stormed and cursed him out. Finally, he'd had enough.

"Now, see here," he argued, his eyes blazing "I ain't seen no benefit to being yer pitboss. I sure don't get paid nuddin' extra fer the 'eadaches. I don't owe ye nuddin'. I ain't 'ere to be yer scapegoat or yer patsy. I works as 'ard as any man 'ere but all ye sees is a lackey – someone to kiss yer arse. Well! Peter Parsons sure fixed that, now didn't 'e?"

"Ye best mind yer tongue if ye wants to keep yer job," the captain roared.

"Well, see, ye don't 'ave that power no more," Josiah shouted back, "I listened good to what Mr. Parsons told us. Ye can go ahead and fire me and I can bring a grievance a'gin the company."

"So, ye was part of all this," the captain growled.

"Let's just say I took a page outta yer book," Josiah growled back, "I'll be watchin' me own back."

"Get out!" the captain jumped up from his seat screaming at the man, "get back ta work. And know this, ye will rue the day ye crossed the captain!"

Josiah stood gaping at his boss momentarily before turning and slamming out of the little shack.

Jake noticed the angry exit as he was about to climb onto the crusher, *wonder what's going on there?* He asked himself. *I ain't about to go askin'. Best I keep to meself as much as possible.* Jake started the machine and kept his focus on the job at hand.

Hank made a show of filling the water pail from the nearby stream as he looked down at the captain's shed. *Soon as I get a chance I'm going down there, see if them boot prints are the same,* he thought as he filled the pail. He didn't have long to wait, before the pail was three quarters filled, the captain stomped off away from the hut, heading toward the cookhouse.

Hank glanced around him. The men around him were all busily shoveling limestone into carts. Nobody seemed to be paying him any heed. Leaving the pail where it was, he quickly hurried downhill. Reaching the shack, Hank carefully examined the boot prints in the muck surrounding the building. *Just like I figured. Son of a bitch!*

Hank stood for a moment, taking deep breaths and trying to rein in the rage that threatened to consume him. Turning, he climbed back up the hill to the stream. He retrieved the pail and put it back in its place. *T'will have to keep. It ain't proof, but it's damned close. Not gonna let the bastard get away with this, no sir!* Hank thought. He returned to the job of shoveling limestone into carts even as his brain worked overtime trying to process what he'd suspected all along. The bell calling the men to lunch surprised him, caught up in his thoughts as he was.

Mick and his sons were sitting on their bench in the cookhouse when Hank approached. "Mick, when yer finished eatin' I needs to see ye fer a minute," he said, "Outside!"

Mick's sons looked at their father curiously, "Sure thing, Hank," Mick answered.

"Da?" William asked worriedly, "What do ye think he wants?"

"It's naught to do with ye, or Ginny," Mick remarked, mildly, "I'll tell ye all by and by. T'is not somethin' I can speak of here."

Mick hurried to finish his food and then went outside to meet Hank. Charlie and Vic were already there when Mick appeared.

"I knows Peter asked fer us to keep it to ourselves, but I figured it was alright to tell Charlie," Vic told them. "I already told 'im the awful goings on. All of it. If it were the cap'n what 'urt Peter, could be we're all in danger."

"We don't 'ave much time," Hank began, "Member them boot prints where ye found Peter?" he asked Vic, "Well, I took it on meself to check the captain's and they're the same. I knows it don't prove nuddin' but it's enough fer me."

"After the way he acted the other day when Peter gave him the papers, I ain't surprised a'tall," Charlie added.

"B'ys we needs to tell Peter, and decide what to do about it," Hank concluded. "I know yer probably sick to death of meetin's, but can ye come to my place after work?"

"Don't see as we got a choice," Mick replied, "We needs to hash this out, figure out what can be done."

"After work, then," Hank responded, "Charlie, Vic, are ye comin'?"

"Ye knows, I'll be there," Vic answered.

"Count me in," Charlie agreed, "the bastard can't git away with this."

"Vic, if ye gets a chance, have a look-see at the boot prints outside the captain's shack," Hank said, "it t'would be good if ye seen 'em, too. Just to back me up. T'was only the two of us saw them boot prints up where Peter was thrown from 'is horse."

"I'll do me best," Vic promised.

Hours later the foursome stood in Hank's barn with Peter in their midst. Hank had filled Peter in regarding the captain's boot prints.

"I took a chance and snuck down to 'is shack after work," Vic added, "captain was nowhere to be seen, but them tracks 'is boots made was the same as what me and Hank saw up the road from where ye was thrown from yer 'orse."

Peter stood quietly, his uncle's warnings resounding in his mind.

"Peter? What do ye want to do?" Hank asked.

"We aren't going to do a thing, not yet," Peter replied. "Ye may not know but I went to law school – didn't finish, but I picked up enough to know we need more than boot prints before we go making accusations."

"Jaysus, Mary, and Joseph," Charlie swore, "we can't let 'im away with this. Ye could have been killed!"

"Charlie's right," Vic agreed.

"Listen, ye men, just listen," Peter entreated, holding up a hand, "I know enough of the law that a boot print alone won't convict him. Just keep yer eyes and ears open. Ye may hear something that might help bring the coward to justice. I need to think this over. Just let it be for now."

"Peter, b'y, yer askin' a lot. He not only nearly killed ye. He also bears the brunt of responsibility fer Joe's death," Mick pointed out.

"We're grateful, truly grateful to ye fer helping us with the association business," Charlie put in, "But this is personal."

"I understand how ye feel," Peter insisted, "I'm just asking for ye to let it be. I have no intention of letting him away with anything. It's my experience that people like him eventually seal their own fate. So, if ye would be so good as to do as I ask: keep yer eyes and ears open. Could be somebody seen something that will help our case."

"Who works close by the captain's shed?" Vic asked.

"I can arrange it so at least a couple of us are posted nearby," Charlie answered, "I'll have a word with Josiah. Hank, no offense, but mabbe it'd be best if it weren't ye. Yer related to Peter, and may not be able to control yerself. Mick, same goes fer ye, if ye sees somethin' ye may be tempted to land a blow."

Mick thought back to their meeting with the captain when he tried to pin the blame on Jake for Joe's death. If it weren't for Charlie, he would have landed a punch or two.

"So that leaves ye and Vic," Mick pointed out.

"Is that agreeable to ye?" Charlie asked.

"I mean no offence neither, Charlie, but it t'was ye that swung at Jake right after Joe died," Hank challenged.

"T'is true, I did," Charlie admitted, "but it wouldn't be so strange fer me and Vic to work together. We usually do anyway. Wouldn't raise no suspicions."

"Man's got a point," Mick conceded.

"Fair enough," Hank relented, "Vic and Charlie then. I knows I can trust the two of ye."

"Thank ye all," Peter told the men, "I owe ye all a debt of gratitude, especially Vic, who may well have saved my life."

Vic flushed red, "I didn't do nuddin'. Anyone would 'ave done the same. I'm just glad I 'appened by when I did."

"And after everythin' ye did fer all the men at the quarry, it's us needs to be thankin' ye," Mick declared, "and if it weren't fer all that the cap'n wouldn't be aiming to do ye harm."

"We could stand here arguing all evening," Peter refuted, "but I am still feeling the effects of that fall. And I'm sure ye men want to be getting on home."

Mick suddenly noticed the pallor on Peter's face, "Sorry, b'y, ye best get inside where ye can rest. C'mon b'ys, let's get going."

The group broke up, each going on their own way.

Chapter
50

Peter woke, disoriented and confused. It took some time before he remembered where he was. Then the events of the past week came flooding back. He sat up slowly.

Don't need Uncle John to get wind of this, he thought, his uncle's warning about thugs and ne'er-do-wells flooding his memories. *Still, I thought the captain more a bully and a blustering fool than one to take matters into his own hands. Would not have taken him for a coward, either.*

Peter heard the sounds of footsteps and the creak of the door on the wood stove opening. Carefully he got to his feet. He felt his head. Hilda's make-shift bandaging was still in place and no dizziness arose. When everything seemed to be all right Peter sat to pull on his boots and straighten up his shirt and trousers. He'd slept in his clothes on the chesterfield in the parlour, his usual bed when he stayed with Hank. He attempted to undo Hilda's handiwork, but the bandaging stayed stubbornly in place. Giving up, Peter rose to go outside to relieve himself.

"Feelin' better?" Hank asked as Peter appeared in the little kitchen. "Got to say, yer lookin' a sight better."

"Yes," Peter answered, "A lot better. Hilda's a fine nurse – too good, maybe, I can't get this blasted bandaging undone!"

"Better leave it fer 'er to remove," Hank advised.

"I'll be back, shortly. Just got to use yer outhouse," Peter replied, "Is Hilda awake yet?"

"She will be out in a minute. She's getting' dressed," Hank answered.

Peter nodded as he opened the door, "Back in a bit," he replied.

His guest was standing in the yard, head tilted back, examining the early morning skies when Hank stepped outside. "Sure yer okay?" He asked Peter.

"Fit as a fiddle," Peter lied. "And grateful to ye and Hilda fer looking after me."

"Yer family," Hank waved away the thanks, "and like the b'ys said, ye done an awful lot, helpin' us set up that association. It will make a big difference to folks 'round 'ere. One good turn deserves another. What are ye thinkin' 'bout doin' as far as the cap'n is concerned?"

"I don't really know, not yet anyway," Peter replied. "I'm hoping someone hears something more. Does the man have any friends in these parts?"

"Not unless ye count a bottle of rum as a friend," Hank snorted. "I heard tell 'e only managed to get 'is position by hateful means. The man's a snake, nobody trusts 'em so 'e spends most of 'is time alone – even in the quarry."

"No wife or sweetheart either?" Peter questioned.

"Not as far as I can tell, leastwise I ain't never heard of one," Hank replied. "The man is not from these parts and keeps to himself."

"Would ye happen to know where he came from?" Peter asked.

"No idea whatsoever," Hank answered. "Don't know what rock he crawled out from under."

"A man like that is sure to have a history," Peter mused, "I need to find out what that history is." Peter thought of Langley and wondered if the agent may be forthcoming about his employee's past. He ain't fond of me, but I got the impression he's none too pleased with his mining captain, either. Perhaps there's a chance the man will talk to me. Peter's thoughts ran busily though his head as he pondered. *Perhaps if I bring a bit of pressure on the agent, I will learn a thing or two.* He thought.

"Do ye think, mabbe he did somethin' of this sort afore?" Hank asked.

"A man like him, well, he's usually done something less than noble," Peter said sardonically, "Can't say for sure but it bears looking into."

Hank shuffled his feet uncomfortably, "Ye will take care," he worried, "if he was willin' to leave ye in a bush to die there's no sayin' what the man is capable of."

"Ye sounds like Uncle John," Peter chuckled, "yes, I will be more careful. Once bitten, twice shy, I'll be keeping a sharp eye out."

"I best be getting' goin'," Hank replied, "Need to feed the animals and get meself to work. Will ye be 'ere tonight?"

"If ye don't mind putting up with me for another night, I don't wish to overstay my welcome," Peter answered, "I need to go see yer minister, have a word with him. Preachers tend to know more than most folk in a community."

"Then, come, keep me company while I check on the animals," Hank invited, "an ye knows yer welcome, any time, b'y, any time." The two men strode off to the sturdy barn across the field.

"Never seen the man's shadow cross the threshold at church," the preacher was telling Peter hours later, "but his reputation is, let's say, somewhat spotty."

"How do ye mean?" Peter asked.

"It ain't Christian to gossip, or to tarnish a man's name," the preacher hedged, "But I have to say I was worried when I learned who he was."

"Why were ye worried?" Peter asked.

"Tis not really something I can tell ye," the preacher answered, "just something a visiting minister told to me. In confidence. He wanted me to be aware."

"I told ye my story and my suspicions," Peter remarked, "If the man is a danger to his fellow man, then he should be removed. There's got to be consequences for his actions."

"It's not that I disagree with you," the preacher said carefully, "But we need proof that it was he who caused yer fall."

"If yer not willing to tell me what ye knows," Peter began, "will ye at least point me in the direction of where I may get some answers about this man's character?"

"Rumor has it he has a taste for the rum," the preacher said hesitantly, "he spends a bit of time at the pub up in town on a Saturday night. Stays at the Ruby, or so I've been told. I shouldn't be telling ye that and I wouldn't, only for the fact the man is a menace.

That much I can tell ye. Watch yer back, if what I've been told is true, he's not to be trusted," he advised.

"So I am beginning to learn," Peter conceded. "I thank ye for talking with me, much appreciated."

"This is a good community," the preacher commented, "I don't like to think of anyone getting hurt or worst. I also don't like to condemn a man I hardly know. Ye said ye studied law, and I know the good ye have done for the men that work the quarry. I am counting on yer good sense. I trust ye will heed my advice and take care."

"If it was the captain that caused my horse to rear and for me to take a spill, well, he's shown his hand and given me warning," Peter remarked. "I will be cautious, that I do promise." The preacher stood and clasped Peter's outstretched hand.

"I'll be praying fer ye, and fer the captain as well," he said, "his soul may be lost, but miracles can and do happen."

Peter nodded once and took his farewell without further comment.

Mick was swinging his pickaxe when he was struck by a thought. So much had been happening he'd forgotten about the way the captain had been watching Jake so closely. He had a feeling that the irksome man had it in for Jake. It had been over a week since they'd had their man to man and Jake had admitted to being blackmailed by the captain. *Time for another chat with Jake,* Mick thought. as his pickaxe found its mark and a hail of large stone fell. Later, as luck would have it, Mick was walking down the hill to the cookhouse when he spied Jake a few yards ahead of him.

"Jake! Hey, Jake!" he called as he hurried downhill.

Jake stopped and turned toward him, "Hey, Mick," he answered.

"I needs a word wit ye," Mick said as he walked toward him.

Jake hurriedly glanced around, looking for the captain. He worried about what his employer might do if he saw him conversing with Mick.

"He ain't here," Mick said as he noticed Jake's tense frame and furtive glances. "Ye gots nuddin' to worry about."

"What can I do fer ye?" Jake asked when Mick was beside him.

"I was just wonderin' if the cap'n is still botherin' ye," Mick answered.

"He ain't circling the crusher no more," Jake replied, "at least not lately."

Mick blew out a breath, "well, that's good. I'd say he's got more on his mind just now, what with the new association and all."

"He gave me a start the other day. I was tracking caribou and accidently wandered onto his land," Jake confided. "T'was afraid he'd seen me, but I was able to hide before he did."

"What day was that?" Mick asked, deeply interested.

"Day before yesterday, I think," Jake replied. "At least I think it t'was."

"Sunday?" Mick pressed.

Jake looked closely at his new friend, "Naw, not Sunday, the Missus is right particular about what I can and cannot do on the Lord's day."

"So, Saturday then?" Mick asked again.

"Mick, what's this all about? What difference does it make?" Jake asked in turn.

"Look, I can't get into it right now, but it's important," Mick disclosed, "I can tell ye more later, maybe. Tell me, what was the cap'n doin'?"

"I don't rightly know, hunting, mabbe?" Jake responded, "He had a slingshot sticking outta 'is back pocket. Mabbe to take down a bird or two?"

Mick's face was grave as he stared blankly out toward the bay. Jake waited and wondered where the conversation was leading.

"Yer sure it was a slingshot ye saw," He interrogated Jake.

"Yeah, I'm sure," Jake replied, "I was hidden among the trees and he was walking away from me. I remember thinking it was a fine piece of workmanship, the woodwork, ye know? Thought mabbe it would be good to make one just like it. Could use one to scare the birds away from Mary's garden."

Mick laughed and clapped a hand on Jake's shoulder. "Yer attention to that slingshot may just be the ticket to keep that cap'n away from ye fer good."

"Whadda ye mean?" Jake asked, thoroughly confused.

"I can explain it all after work," Mick answered, "Would ye mind comin' wit me to pay a visit to Peter? He's staying at Hanks, not far from here. I can promise ye, ye will be glad ye did."

"I dunno, Mick," Jake said, "I have an awful lot of work to do at home, was hoping to get another bit of hay cut while the weather's good."

"Tell ye what, if ye can come help me and my sons get ours into the barns, my sons and me will come help ye wit yers," Mick offered.

"Wasn't complainin' or nuddin'" Jake replied, "Just tellin' ye what I gots to do. But that would be some good. I'd appreciate the help."

"So, ye will come wit me to Hank's after work then?" Mick asked again.

"Yes," Jake answered, "and ye will tell me what this is all about?"

"That's a promise," Mick vowed.

Chapter

51

Jake was nervous as he waited for Mick. He hadn't seen the captain all afternoon, but his warnings about talking to any of the Kelly clan had not been far from his mind ever since Mick had approached him earlier in the day. Still, Mick's offer to help with bringing in the hay was welcome. It was getting harder to keep all the chores on his farm done, though the few days off had helped considerably. Finally, he spied Mick walking toward him.

"Thanks fer waiting fer me," Mick told him, "I had to have a word with my sons, let 'em know to go on home without me."

"Ye got me all mystified," Jake told him, "What's going on that ye needs me to come with ye?"

Mick took a careful look around before speaking. "Let's just say the cap'n has shown 'is true colors," he began, "and may have sealed 'is own fate as far the quarry is concerned."

"I don't understand," Jake shook his head, Ye gots me all confused."

"Let's just get up the road a piece," Mick answered, "don't want nobody else to hear what I gots to tell ye."

Jake shrugged and matched his pace to Mick's as they strode away. It wasn't until they were a fair distance from the quarry that Mick began to explain Peter's misadventure on his way to Hank's.

"So, I needs ye to tell Peter and the b'ys about seeing the cap'n and the slingshot ye noticed he had," Mick told Jake.

Jake's turned a very pale face toward his companion. "I knew he was a black-hearted man; that he was dangerous," he began, slowly, "could see it in 'is eyes when he was threatening me, but didn't figure on 'im being capable of causing a man's death."

"Men like that, they're capable of most anything," Mick replied, "especially if they feels cornered."

"Do ye thinks we have to worry about 'im. I mean will he try anything against any of ye men that worked to set up the association?" Jake asked, "I mean, I knows he has it in fer me, wouldn't put nuddin' past 'im."

"It'd pay to keep tabs on 'im," Mick confided, "I just don't trust 'im, 'specially after what happened to Peter."

"Do the other men know about 'im keepin' after me?" Jake fretted.

"Naw, I promised ye I wouldn't say a word to nobody, and I haven't," Mick reassured him. "I just needs ye to tell 'em 'bout the slingshot ye saw."

"I can't afford to aggravate the cap'n," Jake began, "ye knows he's already threatened to fire me and make sure I can't work anywhere in these parts."

"The thing is," Mick explained, "If we can prove the cap'n is responsible fer Peter's injuries; that he left 'im there to bleed out, mabbe die, well, stands to reason it'd be a case fer the law. Mabbe end up wit 'im losing 'is job at the quarry. Mabbe even land 'im in jail where he would never be able to bother ye agin."

Jake didn't answer but took it all in. Mick watched Jake's face as he gave it all his consideration. He gave him several minutes to chew it over before he spoke again.

"I knows yer worried 'bout losing yer job," Mick continued, "this might just be a way to make sure he can't ever cause ye any trouble ever agin."

"And if he finds out I saw 'im in the woods that day, that I spoke to this Parsons fella 'bout it," Jake paused before continuing, "that could make matters worst fer me."

"There's always a chance, but I don't take ye fer the kind of man that could let something like this go," Mick told Jake, "That ye could let the cap'n get away with causing harm to anyone."

"No, no I couldn't," Jake agreed, "I'd just like to keep me name out of it, if I could."

"Peter's actually bin to law school," Mick replied, "could be there's a way around it. Couldn't hurt to ask 'im."

Jake took a deep breath, "Seen the cap'n slam outta 'is shack yesterday, right after the pit boss left. Seemed like he was pretty worked up 'bout somethin'. He was right riled up, he was."

"Like as not he's learning he can't keep throwing 'is weight around," Mick observed, "Josiah ain't a man given to lickin' 'is boots. Cap'n never much liked that 'bout 'im. Josiah's bin pit boss since long afore the cap'n came to work the quarry. No doubt Josiah put 'im in 'is place and the cap'n wouldn't like that."

"No, I daresay he wouldn't," Jake agreed, "Sure would like to know what that was all about though."

"Yeah, so would I. That's Hank's place, right there," Mick pointed as the duo rounded a curve in the roadway. Jake nodded but fell silent as they approached the property. "Hank said fer us to come to the barn," Mick said as they entered the yard. The other men were already there and each wore a questioning expression as Mick entered the barn with Jake.

"Jake here has somethin' mighty interestin' to tell ye all," Mick told them, "somethin' that makes a lot of sense as far as Peter's mishap is concerned."

"Ye told 'im what 'appened to Peter?" Hank asked in surprise.

"I did. Just let the man speak and ye will see why," Mick retorted.

"I don't believe we've met," Peter stepped forward holding out a hand, "Name's Parsons, Peter Parsons."

Jake nodded as he grasped the man's hand, "Jake O'Quinn."

"Jake, ye have something that has bearing on my misadventure?" Peter asked.

Jake proceeded to explain how he happened to be tracking caribou when he came across the captain. When he finished his tale, the men had varied responses of outrage.

"That frigging snake," Hank exclaimed, "and yer sure 'e didn't see ye?"

"Yes, I am," Jake answered, "but I am worried 'bout him finding out I did. I have my wife and family to worry about. I don't need 'im comin' after me, and mabbe hurtin' one of 'em."

"I don't think ye need to worry about that," Peter tried to reassure Jake, "tis me that he wants revenge on, not any of ye."

"Look, I can't go into it, but he's already threatened to fire me and make sure I never finds work in these parts," Jake added by way of explanation, "and that was not long after Joe died. I know most of ye blamed me fer that. I did play a big part in causing his death, but the cap'n, well, he wants me to take full blame."

"That why ye never came to any of the meetin's?" Vic asked.

"He told me not to talk to any of ye and especially not to Mick, here, or any of his family," Jake admitted.

"I ain't ever apologized for that smack I give ye," Charlie confessed, "it weren't right. Joe was my good friend and I was pretty mad when it happened. But I never should've hit ye."

Jake shrugged off Charlie's apology, "I felt I had it comin'," he said, "I don't have any hard feelin's."

Charlie nodded, his respect for Jake going up a few notches.

"What are we gonna do now?" Hank asked turning to Peter.

"This makes a big difference," Peter said as he gazed at Jake, "My uncle is a barrister in town and I spent many years in law school myself. If ye would be willing to testify to what ye saw it could mean the captain will face time in jail."

"If the cap'n finds out what I know he will come after me," Jake responded, "I don't want to put my family in jeopardy. Is there not a way of keepin' my name out of it?"

"He ain't going to know," Peter promised, "Thank ye fer telling us about it. I give ye my word, the captain will not know anything about ye seeing him that day. At least not until he's in the bowels of some ship bound fer England."

"I need all ye men to promise to keep this between us," Jake entreated, "if he can do that to Peter, he will do that and worst to me. He hates me. He really hates me."

"Jake, I can tell ye, I've known all these men for years," Mick consoled, "Ye can trust 'em. Ye really can. I promise ye that not a breath of what ye just told us will leave this barn."

"Mick's bin tellin' us 'bout yer friendship wit Joe," Charlie piped up, "Joe, he was a good friend to everyone here. Well, 'cept fer Peter, he never met Peter. I knows ye spent a fair bit of time wit Joe; we all knows that. Guess what I'm tryin' to say is any friend of Joe's is a friend of ours. We'll have yer back!"

"Ye can count on that," Hank agreed, as Vic nodded his consensus.

"In the meanwhile, leave this with me," Peter told the men, "I have more investigating to do and the less said to anyone about the cap'n, the better. Now, I know ye all want to get home to yer suppers. I will let ye know what I find out. Let's call it a day.

"Jake, thanks again," Peter held out a hand once again, "Ye have my promise, and the promise of all the men here. Ye got nothing to worry over."

A general murmur of agreement met Peter's declaration as Jake shook hands with Peter.

"Ye lives up on the point, ain't that right?" Charlie asked Jake.

"Yes, that's right," Jake replied.

"My place ain't far from yers, I can give ye a lift, if ye wants," Charlie offered. At Jake's obvious hesitation he added, "I'd like a chance to bury the hatchet wit ye. Whadda ye say, let bygones be bygones?"

Jake blew out a long breath. "I'd appreciate that," he said as he accepted the offer, "bin a long day and I gots lots to do at home."

"I hear that. There's no end to the work when ye got a family farm, no matter how big or small it tis," Charlie replied.

The men said their farewells as the group broke up with each of the men going their separate ways.

Chapter

52

"Are the girls asleep?" Mick asked Fanny later that evening. "Wouldn't want 'em to overhear us talkin'."

"I looked in on 'em just before ye came in," Fanny answered. "They're both tuckered out. Ye don't 'ave to worry 'bout that."

"Good, good," Mick breathed a sigh of relief, the information Jake had shared sat heavily on his mind.

"What do ye need to tell us, Mick" Fanny probed.

"I told yer Ma about an incident that could well have ended with a man's death," Mick began as he looked around the table at his three eldest sons. "Now, I want ye all to just listen and don't be butting in wit yer questions til I'm done. This is serious and the only reason I wants to tell ye all is so ye keep a sharp eye out, especially when yer at work."

William and Phil looked at one another in stunned surprise while Jack leaned in to hear every word his father said.

"Now, this has to stay right 'ere between us fer now. Sooner or later the whole community will learn of it, but ye has to keep it quiet. Do ye understand?" Mick scrutinized his sons' faces as he spoke, satisfied at the solemn nods each gave.

"Ye knows Peter Parsons, the man what helped us set up the association. Well, a couple of days ago he was heading back to Hank's place when somebody caused his horse to rear, unseating 'im and landing 'im on 'is head in the road. The man was hurt bad, but worst than that the culprit dragged 'im off into the bushes, 'is head was bleedin' bad and 'e was left there in the bushes where 'e might have died if not fer the fact that someone found 'im there," Mick related the story solemnly.

"We found out today one of the men what works in the quarry happened to be in the woods tracking caribou when he seen the cap'n," Mick went on, "the cap'n had a slingshot pokin' out of 'is pocket.

"Now, Peter's horse had a small wound in its back flanks. We figures the cap'n shot a rock at the mare and made it rear up, tossing Peter off."

"Why would the cap'n do such a thing?" Fanny, shocked, wanted to know.

"I can't say why he would do such a thing," Mick answered. "But Peter was thrown from 'is mare not far from where the cap'n lives. The fact he was seen that same day with a slingshot in 'is pocket don't look good."

"What's this got to do with us, with our family?" William wondered.

"I don't think we got anythin' to be worried about, but it pays to keep an eye out fer anythin' suspicious ye might see down in the quarry," Mick warned, "I just don't trust 'im. He knew 'bout the wheels on Joe's cart. He knew new hires should be told how to set the brakes on them carts and the rules 'bout workin' the quarry. He didn't tell 'em nuddin'. It all goes to show how little he cares fer any of our lives. And now, he is directly responsible for nearly killin' another man. The man's come unhinged, I'd say, and that makes 'im dangerous to everyone. Ye b'ys, keep yer eyes peeled and yer ears wide open. If ye sees or 'ears anythin' at all ye keep it to yerselves til we gets home and steer clear of the cap'n. Keep yer noses to the grindstone, but watch yer backs. I just don't like this business not one little bit."

"Is he mad cuz we got an association now?" Jack asked quietly.

"I'd say he ain't pleased," Mick admitted, "looks bad on 'im and he don't like that."

"But what can he do to any of us?" Phil asked, "He ain't ever around. He stays in his shack fer the most part. I hardly ever sees him around the mine."

"I have no idea," Mick responded, "I just have a gut feelin' that until he ain't workin' the quarry no more we all have to be a mite more careful. Just do yer jobs, don't do nuddin' to call 'is attention to any of ye."

"Ye're scaring me, Mick," Fanny worried, "mabbe it'd be better if none of ye went back to work there."

"Now, Fanny, ye knows we gots to go ta work, ain't got a choice," Mick reproached her, "I just wanted our sons to use a bit more caution, especially if they happen to see the cap'n hangin' 'round. We can't afford to quit the quarry, not yet, but that time is comin'."

"It can't come fast enough fer me," Fanny retorted, "t'was bad enough worrying about yer safety afore, now I will worry twice as much."

"Don't be at that," Mick tried to comfort her, "Peter's going into town to do a bit more investigating, see what more he can find out 'bout the cap'n. The man's not from around these parts and nobody knows much about 'im. Peter's a smart man, he may find a way to get 'im thrown in jail fer tryin' to kill 'im."

"Tis hard to believe that anyone would stoop so low," Fanny confided, "tis shockin' is what it is."

"If ye could've seen 'is face when we went to give 'im the association papers," Mick said, remembering the captain's reactions, "ye wouldn't be a bit surprised."

"When will we be able to get that lumber so we can start on building the dories?" Phil asked.

"Yeah, Da, when?" Jack parroted his brother.

"Some time this fall, soon as work at the quarry dries up fer the year," Mick answered.

"Have ye talked to Peter 'bout setting up the partnership?" Fanny asked.

"Was about to invite 'im 'ere to do just that when I heard 'bout 'is accident," Mick remarked, "now wit all this goin' on I will have to wait a bit longer. The man has more than enough on 'is plate."

"I sure will be glad to see ye all finished with that bloody quarry," Fanny told him, "I hate that ye all have to work there."

Mick reached across the table and patted her hand. "I know ye worry 'bout us and I knows this ain't gonna help ye any. Would it be better if I didn't tell ye?"

"Ignorance may be bliss, but I'd rather know the truth of it," Fanny replied. "Ye all better look out fer one another," she admonished her sons, "and ye, too," she said turning to Mick.

"Nuddin' bad is goin' ta happen," Mick promised, "fact is, now the cap'n has shown 'is true colors there's more than enough reason to s'pose he will not be at the quarry much longer."

"I hope yer right, Mick," Fanny exclaimed passionately, "I truly do!"

"Ye b'ys have any more questions?"

"Da, who was it that saw the cap'n in the woods?" Jack asked.

"Jackie-boy, that ain't somethin' I'm at liberty to say, t'was tole to me in confidence. Ye wouldn't want me to break me word now would ye?" Mick asked in turn.

"Naw, Pa, it ain't that important, was just wonderin' is all," Jack answered.

"Ye b'ys know I always taught ye to keep yer word and by rights I shouldn't have tole ye all 'bout Peter either. Fact is, I just wants to keep ye all as safe as possible, otherwise I wouldn't have. So, I needs ye to keep this between these four walls. Ye understand?" Mick warned.

"We won't say nuddin' about it," William answered for them all but looked to his brothers for confirmation, both of whom nodded their agreement.

"Da, is there anything in particular we should be on the watch for?" Phil asked.

"Naw, not at all, just anythin' that seems odd or out of sorts, anythin' that just don't seem right," he told them. Mick looked at Jack, "Will ye be okay? I know there's bin a lot goin' on ever since yer uncle died. If ye'd rather not go back to the quarry ye don't have to."

Jack blushed. He knew his family were concerned about his sensitive nature and sometimes he really hated that, especially now when he'd felt they were beginning to treat him more like a grown-up than a child.

"I'm fine, Da, really I am. I will keep a look out fer the cap'n and I'll tell ye if I sees anythin' that seems wrong in any way," Jack straightened his back and shoulders as he spoke.

Mick clapped a hand on his son's shoulder. "We all bin noticing how much ye have grown up these past months. We're all mighty proud of ye." Mick glanced around the table, "yer Ma and me are proud of all ye b'ys. Mighty proud.

"So, Phil, what's going on wit ye and that young Haldi?" Mick asked to change the topic and lighten the somber mood. Now it was Phil's turn to blush.

"Ain't nuddin' goin' on," Phil spluttered.

"I don't know, b'y," William teased, "saw ye makin' moon eyes at 'er after church on Sunday."

"Yeah, Phil, ain't it bad enough to have William makin' a fool of hisself with Ginny now ye gots to go all soft on Haldi," Jack picked up the teasing tone, glad to have the attention shifted away from him.

"Jumpin' dyin', Mick, now ye done it," Fanny complained, "them boys are gonna be tormenting the life outta Phil from here on out."

Mick merely grinned, pleased with himself that his distraction worked.

"I gots a few digs to get in after all the tormenting he dished out to me over Ginny," William crowed.

"Aint nuddin' going on between me and Haldi," Phil denied.

"I seen ye watchin' her like she was a plate of cake or somethin' and ye was starvin'," Jack guffawed, "like ye wanted to eat 'er all up."

"She is a tasty-lookin' little morsel," William observed.

"Haldi is a lovely young woman, not a sweet to be drooled over," Fanny admonished, "How would ye all feel if some young man were to refer to Sarah or Rose that way?"

"Aw, gosh, Ma, that's just plain wrong," Jack complained. "They're our sisters! And they're just little girls!"

"They won't be little forever. Some day young men may take a fancy to them. How would ye feel then? I don't want to ever hear word that any of my sons treated a young woman with anything less that the utmost respect," Fanny warned. "When ye do court a young lady ye best remember to treat her the way ye'd want yer sisters to be treated!"

"Aw, we're just having a bit of fun wit Phil, Ma," William defended himself, "ain't meanin' any disrespect."

"Be that as it may," Fanny retorted, "I trust that ye will all be perfect gentlemen when yer in the company of any woman, and be well-behaved in general!"

"Fanny, b'y," Mick remonstrated, "Ye ain't got a thing to worry about. Our sons are all as grand as their old man, now aint they?' Mick's eyes twinkled as he spoke.

"Huh, ye thinks highly of yerself, now don't ye?" Fanny returned sportingly, a gleam in her own eye, "grand, indeed!" Fanny turned her attention to Phil, "Haldi really is lovely, but more importantly she seems like a good soul. I have watched how helpful she is with Jake and Mary's twins and how kind she is to others as well."

Phil blushed even more furiously, "I keep tellin' ye, there ain't nuddin' going on between me and Haldi!"

"But mabbe ye'd like there to be one day," William chuckled. "Yer denials don't add up to nuddin'. Yer face is giving ye away – again!"

"Aw. Leave off, will ya," Phil stood up, "I'm gonna go check on the animals."

"Do ye want some help?" William asked.

"No! I don't want yer help," Phil rejected the offer, "I just wants to be alone."

Phil stormed out of the door and his brothers sniggered after he'd left.

"All right, ye two, that's enough," Fanny warned, "Ye are to leave Phil alone, do ye hear me?"

"Can't do that, Ma," William insisted, "Ye saw how he tormented me when I first started showing an interest in Ginny. I owes him a few licks yet."

"It takes a bigger man not to seek revenge, son," Fanny preached.

"Ma, I ain't that big and I ain't that kind of man," William laughed.

"Mick, please, do somethin'," Fanny begged her husband.

"Nope, not gonna do a thing. Phil's got it comin'. Ye knows it. I knows it. Phil knows it, too," Mick countered. "Ye didn't see what a hard time them two gave William. And, Jack, ye better consider this fair warning, if ye gangs up on Phil the way the two of ye ganged up on William, well, this is what ye can look forward to one day."

"I ain't ever gonna be mooning around over some girl," Jack scorned the thought, "it aint ever gonna happen."

"Aw, we'll see about that," William jibed, "I thought that once, too."

"So did I," Mick enjoined merrily, "then I laid eyes on yer mudder, prettiest girl in all the land."

Fanny swatted Mick's hand, "And yer still just as full of blather as ye were then," she told him.

"That's enough of this," Jack proclaimed, standing up, "I'm going to go find Phil."

"Wait fer me, I'm comin'," William added.

"Leave yer brother alone," Fanny called out.

"No promises, Ma," William's sing-song voice called out as the door closed.

"Mick Kelly!" Fanny exclaimed, "Ye ought to be ashamed of yerself. Yer egging them on!"

William and Jack could hear Mick's laughter as they crossed the yard.

Chapter

53

Ruby was sitting quietly in the little room she'd made into her own personal parlour when Peter rapped lightly on the door frame.

"Evening, Missus, was wondering if I might have a word with ye?" Peter stood respectfully in the doorway waiting for an invitation to join her.

"Yes, of course. Please, come in," Ruby responded.

"Quiet evening," Peter remarked as he sat in the chair across from her.

"Yes, the house is nearly empty of guests tonight," Ruby agreed. "The men from the railway won't be returning for a fortnight and Mr. Smidt retires early. It's just the two of ye for the remainder of the month."

"I forgot to tell ye, I may be leaving sooner than I first thought," Peter informed the landlady, "I will be sure to let ye know."

'I will be sorry to see ye go. Have ye had yer supper, then? It's rather late, but I can rustle up something for ye to eat, if yer hungry." Ruby inquired.

"No, no," Peter denied, "I'm fine. I ate with my cousin and his family. I just needed to speak with ye about a man I've heard stays here on a regular basis."

"Oh, and who would that be?' Ruby asked.

"His name's Gallo. He's the mining captain down at the quarry," Peter began.

Ruby's face froze and Peter noted the sudden stiffening of her back and shoulders. "Yes, I know the captain," Ruby croaked, her throat suddenly dry. "He stays here once or twice a month, usually on a Saturday night."

"I just need to find out a bit about the man. It has to do with my work," Peter explained.

"I am not one to divulge information about my patrons," Ruby said apologetically, "I run a boarding house that I like to think has a respectable reputation."

"Indeed, it does," Peter agreed, "It came highly recommended when I needed a place to stay here in town."

"So, you understand that gossiping would do nothing for my business," Ruby rejoined.

"Madam, I am not one to jabber away about others," Peter defended himself, "But this is an important matter, else I would not be bothering ye."

"Tell me what it is ye need to know," Ruby conceded, "and if I can help ye, I will, But I need ye to know I'd prefer ye did not involve me in any shady business to do with the captain."

Peter's sharp ears took note of the term 'shady' and tucked it away for later consideration. "I just need to know where the man came from, first off," Peter said.

"I have no idea where he's from exactly," Ruby countered, "word has it he's from somewhere out east, St. John's, maybe."

"It's said a man's reputation can precede him," Peter carefully probed, "Can ye speak fer the man's character? How well do ye know him?"

"I do not like to tarnish a man's reputation," Ruby began, "yet, the man has done himself enough damage without any aid from me. He has a taste for the bottle and the only reason he stays here is because he likes to visit the tavern up the road a piece. Often, he overindulges in the rum and cannot ride his horse home. It's always on a Saturday night, right after he gets his pay."

"And he has not caused ye reason to refuse him a room?" Peter asked.

"I would refuse, if I could, but the house is rarely full," Ruby replied, "I run a business. It takes money to keep up the house, ye understand."

"Yes, I do," Peter responded quietly, "Are ye willing to share the reason why ye'd like to refuse him?"

Ruby sighed, twisting the handkerchief she held in her hands. "He's not the most genial of guests," she spoke slowly, "to be frank, the man is often rude and has little care for others who may be occupying rooms near his."

"Have ye had many conversations with the man?" Peter asked, "do ye know his views on the quarry or the people he works for?'

"He's a bully and a brute! I would not lower myself to converse with the man fer any reason," Ruby stated emphatically.

"Has he been less than respectful toward ye?' Peter asked gingerly.

"I let it be known I have friends in high places," Ruby admitted, "I was worried about letting him a room. I wanted him to know there would be repercussions were he to act in any way that could be perceived to be untoward, or ungentlemanly."

"And has he been ungentlemanly?" Peter continued his gentle questioning.

"No, not at all," Ruby began, "but he seems to be of the opinion that he can bully me into divulging information on certain guests, like yerself."

"He's asked ye questions regarding me?" Peter asked, surprised.

"Yes, he tried to elicit information about ye," Ruby advised, "he was less than pleased when I would offer him no information. I refused."

"I appreciate that," Peter smiled, "It seems the man has been making inquiries about me while I remain in ignorance of his character."

"I know ye to be a good man, at least as far as I can tell. Yet, I am a good judge of character, I'm told. Ye have to be in this business," Ruby explained, "which is why I'd rather not have the captain under my roof. Quite frankly, I dislike the man. I do not trust him. There is something quite unsavory about him."

"Do ye have any factual reasons for yer opinion?" Peter queried.

"No, just my own feelings," Ruby admitted, "but if ye visit the tavern ye may learn more."

"Thank you for being so forthright," Peter stood up and offered his hand, "I appreciate your assistance."

Ruby remained sitting but gently shook the outstretched hand, "I'm afraid I was not much help. The barkeep down at the tavern may have more information. As I've said, I limit any verbal exchanges with that man," Ruby shuddered, "I find him repulsive."

"I will try that, thank you," Peter replied, "I will require the use of the room for a few more nights at least. I will be sure to let you know once my plans are made."

"The room is yours for as long as you have need of it," Ruby told him.

"I will take my leave now, but will return. I think I will pay a visit to that tavern," Peter said, "Good evening."

Ruby nodded, "Good evening to ye, Sir."

Peter turned his collar up against the cool air as he exited the house and began walking toward the tavern located at the end of the street. The street was empty, not another soul in sight as Peter made his way. There was a single customer seated at the bar when he entered and a few others at tables throughout the room. Peter glanced about and chose a seat at the end of the bar.

"Evening, sir," the burly barkeep greeted him, "What can I get fer ye?"

"Just a mug of port," Peter replied, "quiet night in town, eh?"

"Don't usually do much business this early in the week," the barkeep told him, "It can get a bit rowdy when the men get their pay."

"It doesn't look like that kind of place," Peter observed. "Much trouble, then?"

"Not too bad," the man answered, "there's one or two I gots to keep an eye on, but most are just tryin' to have a bit of fun."

"One of them happen to be a man name of Gallo? He works in the quarry down on the peninsula," Peter questioned.

"The mining cap'n? Yes, b'y, he can be . . . well, cantankerous at times," the barkeep confided. "It's not like it's unknown. Most of the men who come here have seen him when he's had a few too many."

Peter nodded. "I've heard that about 'im. Where's he from anyway? Gallo is not a usual name round these parts."

"He likes to brag he's from Sin John's," the man answered, "looks down his nose at this place. I once tole 'im to find another place to drink his rum if he didn't like it here."

Peter glanced around the dimly lit room, "Why? What's wrong with this place? It's clean and rum is rum no matter where ye buy it, and I know the food's good. I've eaten here many a time."

"Cap'n likes to put on airs, figures he's better than the likes of us from around here," the barkeep's face revealed his dislike of the man.

"Is he royalty or something?" Peter asked with a smirk.

"A royal pain is what he is," the man grinned, "Name's Fargo, by the way, don't believe I've had the pleasure."

"Parsons," Peter replied and stretched out his hand.

"Don't believe yer from around here, neither. I seen ye around, but I knows ye don't live here," Fargo pointed out, "what brings ye here?"

"Was here visiting my cousin on the peninsula," Peter replied, "helping out with a little matter down at the quarry."

"Aw, t'was ye that did that association thing," Fargo's grin got wider, "nice to hear of someone sticking up fer the workin' man."

"As I said, my cousin lives down on the peninsula, works at the quarry, too," Peter replied, "he asked me to take a look into an incident there. That led to the association, was happy to help."

"I heard about the man that died," Fargo's smile vanished, "I didn't know him myself, but he had a reputation for helping people out. A real good man from what I hear."

"Yes. That's what I hear as well," Peter agreed, "shame fer his wife; couldn't be easy fer her."

"I heard rumors it was the cap' n's fault that man died. Any truth to that?" Fargo queried.

"Now, I can't attest to that," Peter responded, "I wasn't here when it happened and the inspector filed a report clearing the cap'n and the company of any wrong-doing."

"That ain't right," Fargo confided, speaking lowly, "I have relations that work in that mine and I hear there was lots of things not included in that report. Cap'n wasn't following the rule book at'all."

"I am not at liberty to discuss that," Peter remarked, "but the men have formed an association so incidents like that won't happen. And if something were to happen the men have protections they didn't have before."

"Don't see how the cap'n got that job in the first place," Fargo continued, "I heard he likes to gather dirt on his higher ups and uses it to line his own pockets and promote himself."

"And who told ye this?" Peter quizzed.

"Can't say fer sure. T'was just idle gossip," Fargo admitted, "wouldn't place no wagers on the truth of it. But like they say, where there's smoke there's fire."

"There is a grain of truth in that," Peter agreed. Does the cap'n come here often?"

"More often than I'd like, truth be tole," Fargo replied, "more often when the weather's good, not so much in winter or foul weather."

"He comes alone? No cronies or pals?" Peter persisted.

"Now and then there's a fella joins 'im, most often he's by hisself," Fargo answered, "like I said, he looks down his nose, figures he's too good fer the likes of us."

"Would ye happen to know the fella that associates with him?" Peter asked.

"Naw, he ain't from around these parts, likely from Sin John's," Fargo responded.

"Can't make for much of a life," Peter observed, "No friends and I heard he isn't married either, must be a lonesome kind of life."

Fargo snorted, "No woman worth 'er salt would take up wit a man like that. The man's got a nasty temper, and a taste fer the rum. Not the makin's fer a family man in my book."

"I take it he isn't one to pass the time with," Peter said, "He sounds like a rather disagreeable sort."

"That's one way of puttin' it," Fargo agreed, "most folk steer clear of 'im."

"Hmmm, thought maybe he'd be in the company of the agent, Langley, now and then, seeing as he works for the man," Peter wondered aloud.

"Like chalk and cheese, them two," Fargo's tone was derisive, "Langley ain't real friendly, but he don't look down 'is nose at folk like the cap'n does. He keeps to hisself and to 'is own circle. He comes in here now and then for a bite to eat, not much fer tipping the cup, if ye know what I mean."

"Some men seem to have a taste fer the hard stuff right from the cradle," Peter remarked, "perhaps that's the case with the cap'n."

"He can hold his liquor," Fargo agreed, "it ain't often he overdoes it, but when he does, look out!"

"Given to violence, is he?" Peter asked.

"Ye could say that," Fargo muttered, "Had to put him out a time or two when he was picking a fight with a couple of my regulars. I ain't about to put up with that."

"Has he caused much trouble here in town?" Peter wanted to know.

"Heard he busted up a man's nose. Poor frigger didn't know him and made the mistake of crossin' the man's path," Fargo reported, "that's all he done. Cap'n had one too many and was in a black mood. Didn't help his frame of mind when I threw him out of here. When he gets like that all a fella has to do is look at 'im the wrong way."

"He sounds like a piece of work," Peter responded.

"Why all the interest in the cap'n, if ye don't mind my askin'," Fargo replied.

"Just trying to get a handle on the man's character," Peter answered, "I'd rather this didn't get out but I am concerned he may try to get even with the men for forming that protective association. Just between me and ye, he wasn't too pleased when I presented him with the documents."

"I wouldn't put nuddin' past the cap'n," Fargo remarked, "He's got a big chip on his shoulder. No sir, wouldn't trust 'im as far as I can spit."

"That's the impression I've gotten as well," Peter said.

Just then two men entered and seated themselves close to Peter, putting an end to their talk. Peter drained his glass and hopped down from the bar stool.

"Thanks again, Fargo," Peter said when the barkeep had finished with his new customers. "I'll see ye again some time. Have a good night."

"Drop in any time," Fargo returned, "if I hears anything related to our discussion I'll let ye know. Good night."

Peter was thinking over his conversations with Ruby and with the bar tender as he strode back to the rooming house. *Looks like I need to visit Langley next, see what else I can find out. The cap'n sure is not well-liked. Could be there is more I need to learn,* he thought. *Langley may not be forthcoming, but it's worth the try and while I'm here I'll go see Uncle John as well, could be he's heard a thing or two about the captain.*

Peter stopped to retch in a small alley-way on his way back to his rooming house. The headache had returned and seemed to be growing worst. He laid on the narrow bed and closed his eyes as soon as he reached his room. *I will rest up once I see to this business,* he told himself wearily as exhaustion overcame him.

Chapter

54

Elsie's eyes filled with tears. She had met Peter Parsons briefly and couldn't believe he would take steps to help her. "Why, Mick, why did he do this for me? He doesn't know me and didn't know Joe, either. It's more than I ever expected," she blurted when the lump in her throat finally dissolved.

"He's a good man," Mick told her, "He felt it was wrong fer ye to have to do fer yerself since Joe died. The man has a strong sense of right and wrong and he felt it was wrong what the company did to ye. He wanted to make it right, as much as he could. It's a small amount when ye consider ye have a lot of years yet to live, but it's a nest egg against any kind of emergency.

"Now, Elsie, if ye chooses to sign them papers it will mean ye can never seek any further help from the company. Ye needs to understand that," Mick explained.

"I had no intention of trying to get money from the company. I have all I need right here," Elsie murmured as she glanced around her little cottage. "I am not wanting fer a single thing."

"Ye say that now, but remember if ye gets sick and needs a doctor, or some such thing as that, money will come in mighty handy," Mick retorted, "Ye knows we will take care of ye and will help with the farm and any repairs ye may need with the house or barn. But a good warm cloak fer the winter wouldn't go astray or if ye need anything else we can't raise or make, well, then ye'll need a bit of money."

"God has always provided everything we needed, one way or another," Elsie remarked, "Joe and me never lacked fer nothing."

"Per'aps this is another way the Almighty is watching out fer ye," Mick responded. So, what do ye think? If yer satisfied ye can go ahead and sign 'em and ye will have the money afore the month is out, Peter says. He just wanted me to explain it all to ye."

"Oh, Mick, it just feels like blood money," Elsie agonized, "like I'm getting' rich off Joe's death. It doesn't seem right."

"I'll tell ye what's not right," Mick disagreed, "the inspector makin' that report that was not truthful in the least. It was a way to keep the company from having to own up to their responsibilities as far as yer concerned. It weren't right a'tall. That bit of money won't make ye rich, that's a fact. Peter, he's educated and could explain it all better. Do ye want me to have 'im come talk to ye?"

"No, I do understand," Elsie replied. "If I sign these papers, it means I am releasing the company from all blame and cannot go back on them at a later date. Right?"

"That about sums it up," Mick agreed.

"It still feels wrong fer me to profit by Joe's death," Elsie sighed.

"What was wrong was 'ow he died," Mick argued, "if he had lived ye wouldn't have to worry none 'bout yer future. Ye deserve a bit of help, Elsie. It ain't a lot of money, really – one year's wages against how many years Joe should 'ave had."

"Can I take a bit of time to think about this?" Elsie asked. "I need time to pray over it."

"Take yer time, my dear," Mick comforted, "but in my view ye should take the money. Ye deserve that and a whole lot more. Like I said ye have a lot more years ahead of ye and ye don't know what life has in store. Don't think of it as profiting by Joe's death. Think of it fer what it is: a cushion to help ye should ye fall on hard times – a cushion ye wouldn't need if Joe were still 'ere to provide fer ye! I knows my brother would want ye to have it."

Elsie's eyes filled with tears once again, "I'd much rather have my Joe back here with me. No amount of money can ever replace him."

"No, of course not," Mick agreed, "but it is a small bit of justice to have the company pay fer causing 'is death."

"I leave the meting out of justice to the Almighty. I am not interested in justice. Joe's gone and no amount of justice can change that," Elsie's voice quavered as she spoke.

"Yer right, but we have to carry on livin' and ye have to be practical," Mick advised, "like I said, it could be the Almighty's way of providin' fer ye."

"I've been thinking a lot about Fanny's suggestion to teach," Elsie replied, "I know it won't bring in much money, but it would be enough to pay fer little incidentals."

"Ye have a lot on yer plate since Joe died," Mick answered, "and this is one more thing fer ye to consider. Whatever ye decide to do is fine by me. I do think ye should accept the offer from Langley. Like I said, ye have a lot of years ahead of ye yet. Teachin' would be good to keep ye occupied and we do needs a teacher 'ere."

"I will consider it," Elsie replied, "when do ye need to know my answer?"

"Peter should be back in a day or two," Mick replied, "He'll need the signed papers to take back to Langley, if ye decides to accept. Will that be enough time fer ye to make yer decision?"

"It will have to be, won't it?' Elsie asked in turn, a sad smile on her face. "I'd like to talk it over with Fanny. Is that alright? I know I'm not to speak of it otherwise."

"Yes, that's fine," Mick replied, "I tole Fanny about it. Fer what it's worth, we're of the same mind."

"Ye have both been so good to me," Elsie murmured, "ye all have been."

"Ye're family, and family takes care of their own," Mick said gruffly, "we don't need yer thanks."

"Be that as it may, I am grateful," Elsie insisted.

"I will take meself off now," Mick replied, "ye can let me know whenever it suits ye. If it's any comfort to ye, the association's agreement with the company says if a man were to die at work 'is widow will receive a year's wages. If that agreement 'ad been in place afore Joe died ye would have received that money as a matter of course. So, ye see, it ain't blood money."

"Thank ye, Mick," Elsie nodded, "and please convey my appreciation to Mr. Parsons as well." Mick nodded and took his leave.

It was early the next morning when Mick looked out the kitchen window to see Jake striding across his field.

"Ye b'ys 'bout finished eatin'? he asked his sons, "Jake's 'ere to help wit getting the hay into the barns."

William stood up, "I'll go git the horse hitched up to the wagon."

"He's here early, ain't he?" Phil asked as he gulped down the rest of his tea.

"I did tell 'im we'd be at it first thing this mornin'," Mick replied, "guess he took me at me word."

"And we're going up to his place to help cut his hay afterward?" Phil asked.

"That t'was the bargain we struck," Mick told him.

Jack grinned at his brother, "That should make ye happy, another chance to lock eyes with Haldi," he crowed.

"Don't even start," Phil warned him.

"Just don't be cuttin' off a leg with the scythe while yer makin' googley eyes at 'er," Jack continued to tease.

"Stop yer foolishness and go get the pitchforks," Mick ordered, "We got work to get done."

"Fer heaven's sakes, don't be foolin' around out there," Fanny added, "it ain't no joking matter, them scythes are sharp and can easily take off a limb!"

"Won't need the scythe this mornin', Ma," Phil answered, "we're just gathering the hay into the barns. It's all cut and dried already."

"All right, smart aleck, but remember them pitch forks can do a bit of damage as well," Fanny retorted. "Don't be carryin' on! Jack, you mind me!"

"Yes, Ma," Jack replied, suitably chastened by the stern look his mother was giving him.

"C'mon then, let's go," Mick told his sons. "Won't take too long," he said as turned toward Fanny, "We'll stop fer dinner afore we heads up to Jake's placc."

"I'll have it ready for ye," Fanny promised as she pecked her husband's cheek.

"Can we come help spread the straw in the hayloft?' Sarah asked her father.

"Not this time," Mick answered, "We'll be too busy and ye will just get in the way."

"Aw, but Da, we're gettin' big and we can help," Sarah begged.

"Sarah! Yer father said no, now let it be," Fanny reprimanded. "Why don't ye girls go gather eggs fer me? There's a job ye can do and t'will be a help."

Sarah looked sad as she nodded her head at her mother. Spreading the straw in the hay loft was a lot more fun and the chicken coop would stink. Fanny looked at her daughters sympathetically, "When yer done ye can come help me, could be I have something fun fer ye to do." Fanny smiled to herself as the house emptied and turned to clear the table, remembering as she did so the fun her girls had helping her knead the bread. She made a game of it with them and knew they would enjoy helping her again.

"Mornin', Jake," Mick greeted his friend.

"Mornin', am I too early?" Jake asked. "The babies had me up afore the birds, got me chores all done at home and figured I may as well come on over."

"Early is good," Mick answered, "should be able to get the hay in and then head to yer place to get yer fields cut."

"I sure am grateful to have ye all help with it," Jake replied, "Could do it by myself, but t'would take a fair while to get it all done."

"That's what neighbours are fer,' Mick retorted, "we all help each other 'round 'ere. I thought if we divides it up – three down below, pitching it into the wagon, one to drive, another to rake it back into the wagon bed, that oughta work. We have to fill both barns, but wit the five of us it will be no time at'all to get 'er done."

"Let's go," Jake replied, "I'm ready if ye are."

William had guided the horse and wagon over to the house. Phil and Jack were sitting in the wagon bed where the rakes and pitch forks were laid. Jake climbed onto the bed beside them while Mick climbed up on the seat, taking over the reins. The morning passed quickly as the men worked to bring in the hay.

Phil was relieved that Jake's presence meant his brothers made no mention of Haldi or his attraction to her. Jake enjoyed working with the family and was glad he had agreed to help out. He'd had a great fondness for Joe and found the rest of the Kelly men were a lot like him. There was lots of good-natured tormenting and teasing between the brothers making for a pleasant morning. Before long

Mick was closing the door on Elsie's barn, both hay lofts were filled and even the lower level on Mick's was filled half-way.

"That should be enough to see us through the winter," Mick remarked to Jake as he hauled the door closed. "Let's go eat!"

As the family ate the food Fanny had prepared Jake quietly enjoyed the continued banter. Sarah and Rose remembered him, Mary, and their twins and peppered him with questions throughout the meal.

"Well, if yer all finished, might as well get on up to Jake's place," Mick said.

"Thanks, fer the dinner, Missus Kelly," Jake remarked as he stood up, "t'was mighty tasty."

"Yer welcome, glad ye liked it," Fanny responded, "ye boys mind what I said, don't be carrying on when yer using them scythes. Those things can take off a foot like a hot knife through butter."

"Aw, Ma, we ain't little lads no more," Jack complained, "we knows how sharp them tools are."

"It has nuddin' to do with how little or big ye are," Fanny admonished, "I had an uncle lost his lower leg and he was a grown man – just one moment of carelessness was all it took!"

"We'll all be very careful, Fan, don't fret," Mick consoled, "ye may have to hold supper though. I ain't sure 'ow long this will take and I wants to git all Jake's fields done today, if we can."

"It's just stew, it will be ready whenever ye git home," Fanny replied. "Jake, t'was good to see ye again. Say hello to Mary, mabbe one day ye will bring 'er fer another visit."

"Sure thing," Jake responded, "she'd like that."

"We best git goin', them fields ain't gonna cut themselves," Mick remarked.

Jake was a lot more at ease as he climbed into the back of the wagon with Phil and Jack. He was remembering how different things had been between himself and the Kelly family just a couple short months ago. *Life's a funny thing,* he thought as the wagon jounced along.

Between the five of them they had three scythes and a couple of rakes but the fields were not as large as those on the Kelly farm and before long Mick, Jake, and William were taking wide swings with scythes while Jack and Phil raked it into little haystacks to dry in the sun. Small field mice raced away as the blades did their work. Jake's dog was entertained by chasing, catching, and releasing the little rodents. Jack was first to notice when Haldi appeared walking toward them carrying buckets of water.

"Don't look now but here comes yer sweetie," he told Phil.

Phil blushed and turned an angry face toward his younger brother, "She ain't my sweetheart and ye just be quiet or ye'll be sorry."

Jack, used to Phil's good-natured character, was taken back.

Mick also turned a stern face toward Jack, "That'll be enough of that. Yer lucky she's too far off to hear ye. I mean it, Jackie-boy, don't be at yer tormentin'. Ye will make Haldi uncomfortable and that ain't right."

Phil glanced at their father, much relieved that he was restraining Jack. William was walking toward them with Jake as Haldi drew closer, but Phil knew his older brother would have sense enough not to put the girl on the spot.

"Phil, why don't ye go help the girl with them buckets," Mick suggested.

Phil did not say a word but quickly pivoted to go meet Haldi.

"Here, let me give ye a hand," he said when he reached her, taking the pails she relinquished without a word. "That's heavy work fer a girl."

"I don't mind a'tall," Haldi responded and ducked her head to hide the blush that was creeping up her neck to her face.

"Do ye haul water often, then?" Phil asked.

"Someone has to do it," Haldi explained, "at home there's only Da, and he can't do it all. I'm used to helping wherever I'm needed. My sister, Debra, will help out and my brother, Zack, is getting big enough to do some of the chores," Haldi replied.

"Me and my brothers help Da do the heavy work," Phil commented, "my sisters are both too young, but Sarah helps Ma around the house."

"I seen yer sisters at church," Haldi said shyly, "Sarah must be the oldest?'

"Yep, she is," Phil answered, "Well, here we be. Where do ye wants these, Jake?"

"Right there's fine," Jake replied, "Thanks, Haldi. Tis hot work," Jake remarked as he wiped the sweat from his face and neck. He tilted his head back, gazing up at the sun that beamed down on them all. "Time fer a little break, whadda ye think?" He asked Mick.

"We got lots of time," Mick agreed, "Got a good start on 'er. Should be finished by the end of the day."

Jake looked across his fields. The men had already cut a good third or more of the hay. "I am thankful fer yer help," Jake told them, "Doing this on me own would have taken me a couple of weeks, fer sure. Paddy said he'd come give me a hand but he's helping his uncle with their spread and they gots a big farm. Guess I could've waited, but I wanted to git it done."

"Best not to wait," Mick agreed, "now it'll have time to dry out good afore ye have to git all in the barn." Mick took a dipper and filled it from one of the pails. "Thanks fer bringing us a drink," he told Haldi.

Haldi bowed her head and mumbled her response, clearly shy in the midst of the all-male company.

"If ye don't mind waiting a bit ye can take them pails back to the house," Jake suggested.

"This is fine, Haldi," Mick assured the girl, he took lifted the dipper and swallowed a much-needed mouthful. "Tis thirsty work," he smiled at Haldi as he dropped the dipper back in the pail. "Do ye like it here in these parts?" he asked trying to put the girl at ease.

"I do," Haldi responded, careful to avoid Phil's gaze, "Tis real pretty country and it's wonderful staying here with Jake and Mary. The twins are so sweet and I like helping Mary."

"Babies are a pile of work," Mick commented, "I'd bet Mary is right glad to have ye."

"She's been worth her weight in gold," Jake told Mick, "She not only helps Mary around the house, she comes out and gives me a hand in the barn as well."

"I likes to work," Haldi replied, blushing once again, "I'm used to it. My brothers are only now getting' big enough to help Da. Me and Mary used to help him all the time."

"Yer a good, strong girl," Mick commented, "not every man is lucky enough to have sons straight off. No reason why a girl can't do as well. Yer father must miss ye both."

"He still has Debra and now Zack is getting' big enough to help," Haldi repeated, "he was happy fer me to come out here to help Mary and Jake."

"He's a lucky man," Mick commented.

"Tis a fine family," Jake joined in, "None better, that's a fact."

Haldi smiled at her brother-in-law but made no response.

"Guess we better get back at it," Mick remarked, "can't be lolly gaggin' while the sun still shines."

Phil picked up an empty pail and offered it to Haldi, "Thanks again," he said.

"I'll just keep the other right here, in case we needs another drink," Jake told her, "tell Mary we'll be a while yet."

Haldi nodded and turned away. Phil watched her as she made her way back across the field. "Phil?" Mick tried to call his attention back to the job at hand. "If yer ready, there's more hay yet to be cut."

"Comin' Da," Phil said quietly.

Chapter

55

"I told ye to be careful. This is just what I feared may happen," John's fingers tapped on his desk as his eyes studied Peter's face. "Gallo is a ne'er-do-well. I've heard talk 'bout him blackmailing the former agent of the quarry. There is no proof, of course, Gallo is good at coverin' his tracks. Talk is, that's how he got his job at the quarry."

"The man's a coward," Peter conceded, "comin' at a man from behind is about as far from honest and upright as he could get. Now that I know more about him, I will be much more careful. Though, really, Uncle, who would suspect he'd lay in wait for me in the woods?"

"Tis the mark of ne'er-do-wells and scallywags, isn't it?" John retorted, "to perform such sneaky and underhanded acts."

"Uncle, ye know the law, I need yer advice," Peter replied, "from what I understand the man is unsavoury and has no friends here. It's been intimated that he has lived a rather shady existence and now, this. What proofs would I need to have the man sent back to England? Attempted murder is a felony, and if I remember correctly King William's Act clearly states that any suspected felon is to be judged in England. We do not have the gaols or the courts here to handle such cases and it's beyond the authority of the fishing admiral."

"You're quite correct. The fishing admiral does not have the legal background to hear such serious cases as this. Oh, they can hear cases dealing with simple mischief, drunkenness and the like, but that is all. There are gaols in the city, but even there, serious crimes are to be handled in England so the rascals are bound over to the admirals to arrange their voyage back to Britain." John explained. "As ye know the law has been served less than adequately on this island. Too often the fishing admirals are biased and many a poor innocent sod landed in the bowels of a ship on the say-so of nefarious individuals. Which is why I'm here."

"If ye were to judge the legality of sending the cap'n back to face charges, what would ye need?" Peter asked.

"Depositions from witnesses, clearly written," John answered, "are the men you mentioned literate? Can they provide a written statement of what they know?"

"I believe they have the bare rudiments. They can sign their names, other than that I am not entirely sure," Peter replied.

"They would have to be interviewed and their answers recorded," John said, thoughtfully, "but as ye would be the complainant someone else would have to take their testimony in order fer it to stand up in a court of law."

"I thought as much," Peter sighed, "and I cannot think of a single soul on the peninsula who could provide that service."

"Is there not an educated churchman in the area?" John asked.

"There is!" Peter exclaimed, "I actually spoke with him regarding the cap'n. And he would not be biased. That could work, if he is willing to do so."

"Just remember, if he does agree to take their statements, the documents will need to be dated, signed, and witnessed," John advised, "ye want the documents to be as strong as possible. If ye can get the evidence ye needs we will also need to find somebody willing to safeguard the documents on the voyage back to England. Though yer father does not have dealings in the fishery, he will know many of the naval commanders. Ye will need his help in this initiative if yer determined to bring that man to justice."

Peter folded his hands and rested his chin on them as he considered his uncle's input. "Father is not the only man of influence," Peter informed his uncle, "there is a gentleman in the city whom I can rely on in this matter."

It was John's turn to sigh as he regarded his nephew. "Yer father would be more than happy to help ye. Ye must know that!"

"I do," Peter confirmed, "I also know it would require a visit, which is what yer hoping for, Uncle. I am not ready to return to my father's house just yet. I am not without connections. I refuse to go crawling back to my father, begging assistance."

"Ye're a proud man," John observed, "ye come by that natural enough. I hope ye don't wait too long before ye go to see yer father and bury the hatchet."

"Let's not discuss father," Peter begged, "I have enough on my plate with this business with the cap'n. I have no time to waste on ruminating on the past."

"Go to that preacher then," John changed the subject, "he may well be willing to help ye in this matter."

"I thank ye for yer good advice and your help," Peter said as he stood up, proffering his hand to his uncle, "This matter will keep me in these parts longer than I'd planned. If yer willing to put me up, I will come spend a few days with ye before I leave fer the city."

"Ye know ye're always welcome, my door will always be open to ye," John said as he shook hands. "Just take extra care, my son. This Gallo creature is proving more dangerous than I'd first thought. If he was willin' to leave ye fer dead, he may well have another go at ye."

"I plan to visit Langley to let it be known I am well aware of Gallo's attempt," Peter responded, "once Gallo knows I am aware of his cowardice he may think twice before trying anything else."

"Or make him more determined to finish the job," John worried, "do not be cavalier in this matter. The less said the better, in my view."

"I am hoping Langley will fire the man, which may make him more dangerous," Peter admitted, "it may also make him show his true colors and reveal the depths of which he is capable. The man is a snake in the grass, but not a fool. He has been careful to cover his tracks, but more pressure brought to bear may force him to reveal himself."

"I fear for ye, Peter," John brooded, "ye will have to keep yer eyes peeled."

"I will, Uncle," Peter replied, "I promise ye, I have no intention of making myself a target for that man's rage."

"Whether ye intend it or not, the man obviously feels he has an axe to grind as far as ye're concerned." John fretted.

"I have a half dozen men keeping tabs on him down in the quarry," Peter revealed, "I will be forewarned of his movements and therefore forearmed."

"I am glad to hear that," John replied. "Let me know how ye fare in this matter."

"Look for me toward the end of next week," Peter vowed, "ye will see me then if not before."

"I look forward to yer visit," John told him, "And I will pray no harm comes to ye."

"Thank ye, Uncle," Peter answered, "Ye will be seeing me soon, that's a promise."

Langley's clerk recognized Peter instantly when he entered the office. "I will let Mr. Langley know ye're here," he said as he scurried across the room. A moment later the clerk ushered Peter into Langley's inner sanctum.

"Parsons, what brings ye here?" Langley queried with a frown. "Is it the widow's paperwork ye bring?"

"No, in point of fact I'm here in a matter concerning yer mining captain," Peter remarked smoothly. "I suspect ye were expecting me."

"I was not!" Langley denied, "When we last spoke ye indicated it would take time to get the widow's signature to them papers."

"No, I do not yet have those papers, but there will be papers that will be a bigger concern to ye," Peter declared.

"Speak plainly, man," Langley said gruffly, "what exactly is this all about?"

Peter dropped into the chair across from the agent and crossed his leg across his knee insolently. He allowed his gaze to hold Langley's as he took his time answering.

"I suppose ye know nothing of yer captain's attempt on my life?" Peter's tone was affable while his eyes narrowed slightly.

"What are ye talking about?" Langley rebuffed him, "I don't have the foggiest idea what yer gettin' at."

"Last time we met ye told me ye never wanted to see me again," Peter pointed out, "I didn't take that to heart at the time. Maybe I should have."

"Ye're a thorn in my side and I admit I'd not be lookin' forward to yer company," Langley defended himself, "truth be told, I wouldn't look to spend time with the cap'n neither. What are ye accusing me of – spit it out, man."

"I was on my way back to my cousin's place," Peter reported, "the captain was laying in wait for me in the woods. He shot a stone at my horse, causing it to rear and throw me off. I was knocked out. Gallo hauled me into the brush. I was bleeding heavily from a head wound. He left me there to die." Peter studied Langley's face as he divulged this information, searching for a clue that Langley was in cahoots with Gallo. The expression on Langley's face made Peter believe this was not the case.

Langley stood up abruptly, "I assure ye, sir, I had nothing to do with this! I may have done deeds that are less than honorable, but I would never stoop to such a thing as this!" The color had leached from the agent's face and his expression was one of anger, not guilt, Peter noted.

"Just how well do ye know this man in yer employ?" Peter questioned him.

"My only dealings with the man are purely related to the quarry," Langley insisted, "I would no more socialize with that creature than I would a wild boar. The man is crude, uncouth, and unsavory."

"Ye must have had some indication of his levels of experience; of his character; if he is a trustworthy employee," Peter inquired.

"The former agent hired the man," Langley replied, "I cannot speak to his character nor his honor, or the lack thereof."

"I have been conducting a little investigation into the man's character," Peter disclosed, "it is obvious the man has been involved in shady business dealings in the past. Do ye know anything about that?"

"As I've already stated, it was the former agent who hired the man, not I," Langley retorted, "I know nothing of his previous affairs."

"And ye know nothing of his attempts to get rid of me?" Peter asked again.

"I give ye my solemn word," Langley bit off angrily, "I had no knowledge of yer mishap. This is the first I've heard of it. How do ye know it was Gallo's doing? I am no admirer of the man but ye must have some proof to make such a heinous accusation."

"There is a witness," Peter said quietly.

"Who?" Langley demanded to know.

"I will not reveal that information,' Peter responded, "As I'm sure ye'll understand, the witness is fearful of the cap'n learning his identity, with good reason I might add."

"I will deal with this matter immediately!" Langley vowed, "I will not keep such a felon employed here to sully the good name of the company and mine as well."

Peter stood up, "Just what do ye plan to do?" he asked.

"If ye care to accompany me to the quarry ye will see fer yerself!" Langley exclaimed.

Peter followed the agent as he burst from his office snarling at his clerk that he'd be gone for the remainder of the day. Peter's mare was tied to a hitching post out front of the office, Langley turned to him, "My steed is at the livery stable. If ye care to come, meet me there," he ordered before striding away.

Peter's mare had trouble keeping up with Langley's steed as it galloped over the roadway heading to the peninsula. Upon reaching the quarry, men paused in their work when the two men came thundering through. Langley seldom made an appearance there and the men were staring in wonder at his sudden arrival. Josiah recognized the agent and hurried toward Gallo's crude shack wondering as he went what was going on. Langley noticed Josiah trotting toward the captain's hut and called out to him, "Ye there, take care of the horses," he ordered. The captain stood up as Langley came crashing through his door.

"What the devil is this?" the cap'n demanded as he took in Langley's angry countenance.

"Ye can clear out of here right this minute," Langley barked, "Yer fired! And get up to the company house and pack yer things. I ain't keeping the likes of ye employed one second longer."

"I demand an explanation," Gallo blustered, "what grounds do ye 'ave fer firing me?"

"Ye tried to kill this man," Langley shouted, his hand gesturing toward Peter, "and I ain't keepin' no criminals or felons employed here. Ye're a blot on the company's good name and I will not tolerate yer presence one more second."

"What? No! I did no such thing," Gallo denied.

"Ye were seen when ye aimed that slingshot at my mare," Peter spoke quietly, "and the men that found me where ye left me can testify it was yer boot prints there – the same boot prints right outside yer shack here."

Gallo looked from Peter's face to Langley's, "That's a lie," he insisted, "I did no such thing."

"I don't believe ye," Langley bit the words off as he worked to restrain his rage, a rage that had grown substantially as he'd made the journey to the quarry.

"Sir, I'm tellin' ye, it ain't true," Gallo grovelled as he pleaded with his superior.

"I ain't listening to yer lies," Langley replied tightly, "Now, get out! Ye have the rest of the day to clear yer belongings out of the company house. Go!"

The captain glared at the two men and turned to leave, "Ye'll be sorry fer this," he warned, "ye can't treat the cap'n this way. I'm leavin' but this ain't the last ye'll 'ear of me."

The captain brushed past Josiah who was waiting outside with the reins of both horses held fast in his bunched fist.

Langley took a deep breath and dropped heavily into the chair the captain had so recently vacated.

"I am telling ye this one last time," he said as his gaze locked with Peter's, "I had nothing to do with that despicable attempt on your life. I may be many things, but I am not a murderer."

"I believe ye," Peter replied, "now, what about the men? Ye fired the captain. Who will take his place?"

Langley was momentarily shocked, "Yer right! I was so enraged I didn't think. I will need to find a replacement! That freighter will be sailing into the harbour here any day now. Damn it all!"

"If ye don't mind a bit of free advice," Peter replied, "might be a good idea to hire somebody who knows the work here well. Somebody with a bit of intelligence and who will look out both for the men and for the company."

"Ye have somebody in mind," Langley responded, "Just what do ye know of runnin' a mine?"

"A good deal more than I did six months ago," Peter quipped, "I've spent a good bit of time with these men and with researching quarries. If ye have a mind to, ye can leave the pit boss in charge until ye gets it all figured out."

"And the man ye thinks will make a good mining captain?" Langley asked.

"He may not be interested, but his name's Charlie Samms," Peter answered him, "He's smart, he's honest, and he would make a good captain, that's if he's interested."

"Tell the man to come see me, if he's interested," Langley tore off his cap in frustration, "it won't solve the present dilemma though!" He got quickly to his feet and strode to the door, throwing it open. "You, man," he called to Josiah, "get somebody over here to take care of our horses and then get in here."

Josiah started when he heard the agent's call. He still clutched the reins of both animals tightly in his hand. "Yes, sir! Right away, sir!" He cast a look around him, nobody was near enough to hear or answer his call. His eyes fell on the crusher where Jake was working. Leading the horses Josiah walked over to the machine. Jake did not notice him at first, occupied as he was with the job at hand. It was the sight he caught out of the corner of his eye of Peter's white mare that got his attention. Jake threw the levers to bring the machine to a stop.

"Yes, sir?" he asked as he jumped down from the machine, "Is somethin' wrong?"

"Leave the machine for a bit. I wants ye to take these horses and tether 'em by the cookhouse," Josiah ordered, "then get back to work."

"Yes, sir," Jake took the reins from Josiah's grasp, "I'll take care of 'em." Jake led the animals away as Josiah hurried back to the captain's shack.

Josiah tapped nervously on the door. He'd seen the captain rush away from the hut and wondered what the hell was going on. It was Peter who opened the door to him and Josiah wondered about his presence there.

"Don't just stand there ogling," Langley growled, "Come in, man, come in!"

Josiah stepped inside and nervously pulled his cap from his head, "Sir?" he asked, confused.

"Yer the pit boss, are ye not?" Langley questioned him.

"Yes, sir, that's right," Josiah replied.

"What's yer name?" Langley enquired. "Do ye know the ins and outs of what the captain did here?" Langley asked.

"Name's Picton, Josiah Picton. I knows he took care of the bills of lading, dealt with the ships what came to load the limestone, kept records and that sort of thing," Josiah answered.

"Do ye think ye could do the same?" Langley wanted to know.

"But the cap'n takes care of all that," Josiah objected, "it ain't part of me job a'tall."

"The captain will no longer be employed here," Langley bit off, "I'll ask ye again, are ye capable of doing some of his work?"

"I can do some, but not all," Josiah gulped, "I ain't ever learned how to keep records or anything of the sort."

"Tell me, Picton, what exactly can ye do?" Langley pushed on.

Josiah twisted his cap in his hands as he tried to explain what he knew of the captain's duties, which was not a lot. Langley interrupted him to ask further questions.

"Do ye know the jobs the men do here? If one fell behind or could not do his task for any reason, would ye be able to step in and take over?" Langley asked.

"Yes, sir, for the most part," Josiah answered, "I bin a workman here for many a year and done just about every job there is."

"So ye can do manual labor, but ye don't know naught about bookkeeping and such, is that right?" Langley inquired.

"Yes, sir, that's right," Josiah admitted, "never was no call to learn how to do books."

"Gallo will not be returning to this position," Langley said, "I will have to take his place until we find another man. I will need to count on ye. If there's anything I should know; if there's trouble with any of the machinery or any of the men, ye come see me. Understand?"

"Yes, sir," Josiah bobbed his head, "May I ask, sir, why will the cap'n no longer be workin' here?"

"No! You may not!" Langley growled, "Ye can get back out there and do what yer paid to do. One more thing, where's my horse?"

"I sent Jake to take care of 'em, sir. I told 'im to tie 'em up down at the cookhouse," Josiah replied, his face red.

"All right, then, yer dismissed," Langley ordered, "go on back to work."

Josiah hurried to do the man's bidding, as the door closed behind him Langley looked at Peter. "Well, this is a fine kettle of fish," he remarked. "I am in need of a cup of tea. Care to join me?"

Peter looked at the man he'd assumed was every bit as unsavory as Gallo. His opinion had changed somewhat during the exchange he'd witnessed with the mining captain and the way Langley took charge of the quarry.

"I could do with a cup," Peter replied, "and to see to my mare."

Peter matched the taller man's stride as they walked to the cookhouse. He noted the stunned look of surprise on the faces of the men they passed filling carts with limestone. "I take it ye're not a frequent visitor down here," he remarked to his companion as they walked.

"Seems I've been remiss in not overseeing the captain more closely," Langley admitted, "ye can be assured that is about to change."

"Change can be good," Peter replied carefully, "perhaps ye're beginning to see why the men needed a protective association."

"As I told ye afore, Gallo was hired by the previous agent," Langley repeated, "I suspect he got the position by foul means. I dislike the man, but I never took him for an out and out criminal."

"I underestimated his penchant for violence," Peter confided, "I knew he was none too pleased about the men forming an association. I knew he took an immense dislike to me fer my part in it. Yet I never would have guessed he'd stoop so low as to try to attack my person."

"Tis good riddance to bad rubbish," Langley spoke bitterly, "the quarry will be better off without him."

"I have to agree with ye on that point," Peter replied.

By this point the two men had reached the cookhouse. As Josiah had said, both horses were tethered nearby. Langley pushed open the door. The room was empty but the racket of pots and pans from the kitchen gave evidence of workers busily preparing for the noon break. Langley strode behind the counter where the men were served into the back room. Peter stayed in the main room, seated at table while he waited.

He took a deep breath. The day had taken a lot out of him and he felt the headache building once more.

The man in charge of the cookhouse looked up, surprised, nobody but the scullery staff ever crossed the threshold to his kitchen.

"Sir? 'Ow can I 'elp ye?" he asked deferentially, recognizing the agent more by his bearing and superior attitude as someone of importance.

"There are changes coming to the quarry," Langley announced, "Gallo is no longer the mining captain here. I will be overseeing the operation personally. Right now, all I want is a pot of tea. Ye can have some one bring it out to us. Two cups, if ye please." As he spoke Langley's sharp eyes took note of the supplies stored on the open shelving. One more thing to look into he thought as he gazed around him at the inferior foodstuffs stocked there, more evidence of Gallo's mismanagement, or worst.

Langley was sitting conversing with Peter when the same man brought the tea. "Sorry, sirs, we have naught else to offer ye, but yer welcome to some hard tack if ye wish," the cook offered.

Langley declined, the look of utter contempt on his face making obvious his distaste for such fare. "No, that will be all," he dismissed the man.

"Ye're a man of action," Peter remarked when the cook had moved away, "tis quite a ride into town, do ye plan on making that trip daily?"

Langley ran a hand through his hair, "I hadn't given any of it any thought. It's all happened too fast. No, I won't be riding back and forth, it's too great a distance. Do ye happen to know of a lodge or such where I might stay until I get it all sorted out?"

"Tis all small farms 'round abouts here," Peter told him, "Most of the men work for ye, or they're fishermen. There's no idle visitors and no reason for a man to set up a lodge of any kind. Yer best bet is maybe the parsonage. The minister is a kindly man and would likely take ye in."

Langley nodded, "I will look into it. We do have a small bunkhouse here. I believe the men call it the 'surgery'. I will visit it after we're finished our tea. There may be room for me to lay my head there. Once Gallo clears out of the company house, I can stay there. I just need a bed for a night or two while I have the company house cleaned."

"Ye surprises me," Peter remarked, "I'd taken ye for a spoiled dandy. I was wrong."

'Nothing surprises me about ye," Langley retorted, "I've heard all about yer travels back and forth across this island starting protective associations in this place and that," he waved indiscriminately. "I know yer father owns a mine and I know ye have shunned the family business."

"Ye knows a good deal more about me that I do ye," Peter commented, "ye have me at a disadvantage."

"It could be some the assumptions ye've made about me are wrong," Langley said, tersely.

"That could be," Peter admitted, "I'd watch my back if I were ye, if Gallo'd make an attempt on my life it's likely he may do it again. Right about now I'd guess he'd have ye in his sights. The man is dangerous, more dangerous than ye know."

"I cannot argue with that," Langley agreed, "I had to fire him, if he's capable of trying to kill ye, he's capable of anything. I fear I may find more of his wrong doings here in the quarry. I need to stay to check on a number of things. I won't be returning to town until I'm satisfied the mine is secure."

"Might be safer to post a man or two to act as guards," Peter suggested, "as ye say, he's capable of most anything."

"That's a thought, one worth considering," Langley nodded, "do ye mind tellin' me what-all ye have uncovered about Gallo?

Peter proceeded to fill the agent in on the few scraps of information he had gathered. "The man's reputation is one of a base and loathsome character and that seems to be common knowledge in the city. Tis no wonder he had to look further afield for employment, preferably far away from his roots," he finished.

"I hope ye're beginning to understand I do not share Gallo's penchant for mischief and trouble. There are certain pressures the company has brought to bear, which I am not at liberty to discuss,"

Langley revealed, "as the son of a mine owner ye know well the main objective of any company is profit. Dominion Limestone is no different, which is why I was forced to make a deal with Johnstone, the mining inspector. There are certain considerations I must keep in mind as an agent for the company, many times my hands are tied."

Peter thought back to his friend, Luke, and did not reply immediately, finally he said: "As long as those considerations do not lead to unnecessary risks that could cause deaths."

"I am aware of the mine collapse when ye were a lad and the cost in terms of human life," Langley rejoined, "it's been said that collapse is the reason fer ye never joining yer father in the family business."

"I do not wish to discuss my father, nor my family's business interests," Peter cautioned, "my personal relationships do not bear any influence on the matter at hand."

"I suspect yer past has played a pivotal role in yer efforts on behalf of the working men on this island," Langley observed, "but I will not press the point."

"I would appreciate yer discretion in the matter," Peter replied, "my reasons fer helping working men are my own and I have no interest in them becoming public knowledge."

"And that business about the report Johnstone made, are ye still willin' to keep that to yerself?" Langley asked.

"As long as the men are looked after and Joe Kelly's wife gets all ye promised," Peter replied, "I will keep my part of the bargain."

"I was frustrated when Gallo brought them documents about the protective association to me," Langley confessed, "in the beginning I could only see how it would adversely affect the company's profits – profits I was hired to protect. I see now that a content work force is more productive and that will equal out to better profits, in the end. I did not arrive at that opinion until I had had an opportunity to study the pros and cons of the arrangement. I hope ye will forgive my harsh treatment in our initial meetings."

"Business is business," Peter shrugged, "ye had a job to do as did I. I take nothing personally, except being left to bleed to death in the brush. That I do take personally!"

"As ye would," Langley agreed, "I should, perhaps, have bided my time. I was impulsive in relieving the man of his post. Gallo needs to be brought to justice. Now he may well disappear and avoid his well-deserved consequences."

"He may," Peter agreed, "but it's not a big place, sooner or later he will make an appearance and when he does, I will be ready. The scoundrel will learn I have friends in all walks of life; Friends willing to help me see this rascal brought to justice."

"Well, Parsons, I never thought I'd see the day we'd be united in any purpose, but we see eye to eye in this matter," Langley remarked, "I must get on with my inspection of the quarry. I have a lot of work to do so I best get at it."

"Thank ye for taking my word regarding Gallo's despicable activities," Peter said as he stood up, offering his hand to Langley to shake, "I meant what I said, watch yer back, the man is cunning and dangerous. Worst yet, he has a taste for revenge, despite the fact he brings ill fortune on himself."

"I will be on guard," Langley responded, shaking Peter's hand, "ye have no need to be concerned on my behalf."

"I have other business to see to, now that I am here on the peninsula," Peter remarked, "If ye need any further help I will be staying with my cousin, Hank. He works here at the quarry. If ye let Josiah know ye needs to see me he can get a message to me through Hank. I'll see myself out. Farewell."

Chapter

56

Gallo rode his horse hard back to the company house, cursing while he rode and planning his vengeance. Bitter thoughts filled his mind and poisoned his soul. His anger rose like swells on the ocean as his horse's hooves pounded the hardened earth. Callously, he whipped his mount unmercifully, disregarding the foam flying out of the animal's mouth as he rode. Trees rushed by in a green blur as he rode and the blue of the bay was no more than a flickering streak in the corner of his eye.

Reaching his house, he threw the reins over the neck of the creature after leaping to the ground. The animal's sides heaved and it pawed nervously at the earth taking deep gasps of air. The captain did not stop to wipe the sweat from the horse's hide but rushed inside the dwelling. The animal's flanks trembled, muscles rippling as she attempted to cool off by moving side to side, walking in place to relieve the sustained burst of energy she'd been enforced to endure. Trained by frequent brutality and harsh punishments, the mare stayed where she'd been left, not daring to move away to where fresh water beckoned, despite her thirst.

Gallo threw the door open and stomped to the table where the flask of rum stood where he'd left it the night before. Grabbing the bottle, he quickly removed the lid and stood, head tilted back, gulping down the liquid like it was an elixir. Emptying the bottle, he tossed it aside, searching for another. In his maddened state it took him several minutes of looking before he located a replacement. Again, he downed the bottle until there was a scant quarter left over. Carefully he set it down and surveyed his surroundings.

Hatred of the agent had him grabbing a chair, swinging it over his head he brought it crashing down against the sideboard, the legs splintered and the crockery on the buffet came with it causing a din of breaking porcelain and broken wood. Unsatisfied, Gallo continued with his destruction of the kitchen, hurling items at walls and windows. Swinging a chair leg indiscriminately, jars, plates, and various implements added to the piles of broken pieces on the floors of the once serviceable room.

Gallo stood heaving, much like his mare after her brutal workout. His glance fell on the kerosene lantern hanging on its hook on the wall and a vile thought occurred to him. Hoisting it from its place he took it with him as he moved through the domicile, splashing kerosene liberally on furniture and walls as he went. He moved quickly, blinded by his rage. Satisfied, he returned to the kitchen and searched for the flint to strike a spark that would set the place ablaze. He grinned to himself as his hand caught up the tool. *Langley will pay fer treatin' the cap'n like one of 'is servants. I will clear out this house just like he tole me to, until dere ain't nuddin' left,* he promised himself. Laying the flint on the table next to the near empty bottle Gallo moved to the bedroom where he proceeded to toss his few items of clothing and his purse into a satchel. That finished he strode to the door and tossed the bag out onto the grass. Returning to the kitchen he grasped the bottle and swallowed the remainder of the liquid and pocketed the flint. Lifting the lamp, he made his way outside dripping kerosene as he went. He splashed the remaining fuel on the door and steps.

His mare scented the rum and kerosene and whinnied nervously. Gallo tied his satchel to the saddle and reaching down picked up a small rock from the ground. He bounced it gently from hand to hand as he stood gazing up at the company house. *All good things must come to an end but I'll be damned if I go out like a dog wit its tail between his legs,* he thought grimly. Reaching into his pocket he pulled out the piece of flint.

The captain did not vacate the premises immediately. Instead, he stood watching as the flames licked the doorway and began to race along the floorboards of the house. Once he was satisfied the place would soon be engulfed in flames Gallo swung up into the saddle. The horse pranced as its nostrils caught the scent of smoke in the air. She eagerly leaped away when the captain touched her neck lightly with the reins. Soon they were bounding away; away from the burning building; away from the quarry.

Jake had accepted a ride home in Paddy's wagon at the end of the long work day. The plan had been for Paddy to help him load hay into the wagon and then transfer it into the barn. The pair were gossiping about the sudden dismissal of the captain and what that would mean to the men when Jake noticed the plumes of smoke. "Look, there," he said as he pointed to the smoke above the tree tops.

"Looks like it's comin' from the cap'n's house," Paddy commented. "Think we should have a look-see?"

Jake hesitated. He had no desire to run into the captain, but fire was something he feared. If it spread it could easily burn out other farms in the area. In a matter of seconds, he'd made up his mind. "Let's go," he said.

Paddy took the road to the right and snapped the reins to encourage his horse to a faster pace. Both men felt their anxiety rise as they hurried toward the fire. They reached the inferno moments before Charlie also arrived, slowing his horse to a walk as he neared the burning building.

"Any sign of the cap'n?" Charlie asked as he slipped from his saddle.

"If he's inside he ain't got much of a chance," Paddy responded. The men looked about wildly for buckets or containers they could fill with water to fight the blaze.

"The barn," Jake suggested, "there's got to be buckets or something in there." He ran toward the structure with Paddy close on his heels.

"Over there," Paddy pointed, rushing toward the back wall where several pails were stacked one inside the other. Paddy grabbed them up and handed one to Jake. "There's a couple of rain barrels outside," he cried as he ran.

Quickly the two men filled buckets and raced back to the burning house where Charlie was busily using a spade to knock pieces of fallen beams from the door where the fire had nearly burned itself out. Other men were racing into the yard as Jake and

Paddy threw the buckets of water at the front of the house where the tongues of fire continued to lick upwards toward the roof. Vic had arrived with buckets and tools to fight the blaze along with Hank and Mick and his sons.

Down in the quarry Josiah had rushed back to find Langley when he'd noticed the plumes of smoke and guessed correctly where it was coming from. He knew the captain well enough to have well-founded fears. He rushed from building to building until he finally found Langley seated at the captain's desk going through papers.

"Come on, man, spit it out," Langley orderly brusquely, impatiently waiting for the pit boss to catch his breath.

"A fire! Looks like it's comin' from the cap'n's house," Josiah panted as he spoke, "Ye better come see."

Langley jumped up from the desk, dropping the sheaves of paper he'd been studying. Quickly they rushed outside and down the hill where the pit boss pointed in the direction of the thick, black smoke billowing upwards.

"Get my horse," Langley ordered, "and if ye see anyone tell 'em I need all hands to fight a fire."

Josiah rushed away to do his boss's bidding as Langley turned back to the shack. Langley's thoughts were as black as the smoke that was curling into the skies. He gathered the paperwork and stuffed it into the desk. *Parsons was right, that scallywag's capable of anything,* he thought. *I can't leave this place unguarded. What in the name of God am I going to do?* Langley's thoughts tumbled one upon another as he paced around the shack trying to decide how best to handle this newest crisis. Before long Josiah was back, leading Langley's horse and in the company of the cook as well as Doc and Ben. Doc was leading his own mount.

"I need a few men to guard the quarry," Langley demanded, "and, Doc, I need ye to come with me, just in case anyone gets injured fighting that fire. Ye, there, go back to the cookhouse and stay there," he told the cook. "I have reason to fear Gallo may come back. I don't want any building left unguarded. Understood?"

"Ben, ye may as well head back up to the surgery," Doc said.

"I was going to come help fight the blaze," Ben argued.

"Stay here, watch the barns and the surgery," Doc ordered, "there will be men enough to handle the fire."

"Picton," Langley broke in, "I need ye to guard the shack in case the captain returns. I doubt he will, it's likely he's miles away by now, yet I don't want to take any chances." Turning to Doc he asked, "Are ye sure there will be men enough to fight that blaze?"

"Ye ain't from around here," Doc replied, "in these parts a fire means every man will turn up to help battle it. No doubt there are men already there and more will come."

Langley nodded, "Alright, ye men, ye have yer orders," turning back to Doc he replied, "we best be off."

Langley and Doc reached the site of the company house in time to join the men fighting the fire. The men joined the line forming a bucket brigade leading to the small creek that ran through the property near the house. Jake filled the pails, handing them to the man next in line and the crew worked tirelessly in an attempt to save the structure and to keep the fire from spreading. Finally, only thin wisps of smoke and burning embers were all that remained.

Charlie stood back and pulled the cap from his head, swiping at the sweat that carried rivulets of black soot into his eyes. Around him men muttered and cursed or conversely stood grimly silent surveying the remains of the structure.

"One of us has to look inside, could be the cap'n met his end in there," Charlie solemnly spoke the fear each man struggled to face. Not a one had any fondness for the man, yet neither would they wish anyone such a gruesome death. "Who wants to go in first?"

The men looked around at one another, no one wanted to confront the possibility of grisly finds.

Vic was first to speak up, "I'll go in there, if somebody comes along wit me," he said softly.

"I'll come along," Charlie offered, "Just didn't want to go in by meself, neither."

Charlie led the way, pushing open the scorched door. "Careful," he told Vic, "Floorboards are half gone so watch yer step."

"What a friggin' mess," Vic remarked as his eyes fell on blackened walls and the broken and burnt furniture.

"It's an awful stench," Charlie replied as he pulled his jacket up to cover his nose.

The two men walked slowly and carefully through the structure but discovered nothing but fire damage, to their great relief.

"Well?" Langley demanded when Charlie reappeared.

"He ain't in there," Charlie replied, "Nuddin' left in there but burnt furniture and walls."

Men had been milling around outside as they waited for news of the captain. Now they began to depart while a few stayed to gossip about the cause of the fire and the captain's whereabouts, watching Langley's reactions carefully.

"Tis awful fishy," Hank commented, "He gets fired and suddenly the house he's been livin' in goes up in flames?"

"I don't like to point fingers, but it is mighty suspicious," Charlie agreed.

"It ain't even his 'ouse," Vic replied, "it belongs to the company, don't it?"

"Yes, it does," Langley confirmed, "and Gallo will pay for this, mark my words. Is there one among ye who might know where he'd go?"

"The cap'n wasn't one to make friends with the likes of us," Mick told him, "Josiah, the pit boss, prob'ly knows 'im best and he ain't 'ere."

"We could try to track 'im," Paddy suggested, "Jake is a fine hand at trackin'."

Langley spun around, "Where is this man, Jake?" he asked.

Jake stepped forward but not without first throwing an accusing glare at his friend. "I'm Jake," he responded.

"Do ye think ye could find him?" Langley wanted to know.

"Can't make no promises," Jake replied, "I'm willin' to give it a go. There's been rain off and on this past week so the ground will be soft. There may be a chance of pickin' up his trail."

"It would be best to take a few men along, just in case ye do find 'im," Mick suggested.

Langley nodded and searched the faces of the men, "Any volunteers?" he asked.

"I'll come," Paddy said stepping forward, not wanting his friend to be alone in the endeavor.

"It will be slow going," Jake commented, "tracking takes time."

Langley cast his eyes over the rest of the group, "Anyone else?"

"I can lend a hand," Charlie offered.

"Count me in," Hank answered.

"And me," Vic added.

"I'd like to join ye," Doc spoke up, "Ye never know, ye might need me."

Langley nodded curtly, "That ought to be enough," he observed, "Let's go!"

"Wait," Mick spoke up, "Ye might need a length of rope and maybe a gun. If it was the cap'n done this he will be dangerous. It ain't likely he will come along all peaceful-like."

The men looked at one another worriedly. None were given to carrying weapons.

"I have my hunting rifle," Charlie told them, "I wasn't sure what I'd find when I came. I was alone and wasn't going to take any chances. I've heard the cap'n goes right off his head when he gets riled up. I'd say he was right riled to do this."

Langley nodded, "At least one of us was thinking," he replied.

"Let's have a look-see in the barn fer anythin' else we might need," Paddy suggested and strode off to do just that. Jake and Hank followed him into the structure and returned carrying rope, lanterns, a jug of kerosene, and a host of other paraphernalia.

"Mick, could ye let Mary know what's happened?" Jake asked when they came back, "I'd be much obliged."

"Yes, I will do that," Mick promised, "wouldn't do to have 'er worryin' 'bout ye. I'll let yer womenfolk know, too," he told Vic and Hank.

Mick stood back watching as the make-shift posse headed out across the fields, *watch over 'em, Lord, keep 'em safe,* he prayed silently. He turned back to his sons, "that's about enough excitement fer a while. C'mon let's go home."

Chapter

57

F anny looked up when she heard the wagon and the sound of
voices, quickly she laid Jimmy in his cradle and hurried to the
door. She had spent anxious hours waiting after Mick left with
their sons to fight the fire. "Sarah," she called to her daughter who
was outside with Rose playing, "come inside, watch Jimmy, Rose,
stay with yer sister. I'll be right back."

Sarah and Rose had watched the smoke curling into the sky
in the distance and had become alarmed when their father and
brothers rushed away in the wagon to help battle the fire. It was very
frightening for the two little girls. Elsie had done her best to help
Fanny ease their fears and had only minutes before returned to her
cabin. Sarah was relieved to see Mick and her brothers return. She
grabbed her sister's hand at her mother's beckoning, "Come with
me, Rose," she said and the two girls went inside.

Fanny hurried straight to the barn to satisfy herself that her
menfolk were all safe and unhurt. Fire terrified her more than any
other danger they'd ever faced.

"Mick, oh Mick," she sobbed as she hugged him hard, "I was so
afraid."

Mick enfolded her in his arms, holding her for several moments
before he broke the embrace. "I'm black with soot and covered in
limestone dust. I'll get ye all dirty," he protested, "we're alright,
lassy, don't ye cry." His hands remained on her shoulders as he held
her away from him. "We're all fine. Nobody got hurt," he told her.

"We're all fine, Ma, really," Jack echoed, reaching out to place a
comforting hand on his mother's back.

William shuffled uncomfortably. Phil was already removing the tools from the back of the wagon and William moved to unhitch the horse. Fanny scrubbed the tears from her face with her hands. She was not often given to tears but the past hours had been fraught with fear and anxiety.

"Ye didn't even get to have yer supper," she smiled weakly at her husband. "I'll go get it on the table."

Mick patted her shoulder, "Fighting fires sure builds up an appetite. I'm famished. We all are. We'll be right in," he promised.

Fanny paused staring into Mick's blue eyes, "I am so glad yer home, so glad yer alright." With that Fanny pivoted and walked quickly away.

"Is the fire out?" Sarah's pleading eyes struck a chord in Fanny's heart.

"Yes, dear one. It's out and cannot do any more harm," Fanny answered quietly.

"Did somebody get burned up?" Sarah's panic rose.

"No! No! I meant no more harm to houses or farms," Fanny was quick to correct the girl. She hurried to embrace her daughter. "I know, fire is scary. But it's all right now. Da and yer brothers and all the men put it out. Nobody got hurt. The house might be burned but houses can be rebuilt. Come, help me get supper on the table," she said.

"Mama? Why did the fire come?" Rose wanted to know.

"I don't know," Fanny whispered, "but it's gone now," she said more firmly, "Why don't you help Sarah set the table?"

Out in the barn Mick was warning his sons not to scare their sisters by going into any detail concerning the fire. "They're too little and won't understand," Mick told his sons, "And we don't need 'em to be having bad dreams."

"Sarah will ask a million questions," Jack pointed out, "and Rose will follow her lead, like she always does."

"And we'll do our best to answer 'em and put their minds at ease," Mick replied. "It ain't that I'm askin' ye not to talk about the fire, just don't scare 'em wit yer talk is all."

"We'll be careful, Da," Phil promised, "ain't that right b'ys?" William and Jack nodded their agreement.

"Go on and wash the grime off yer faces," Mick retorted, "Ye all look a sight, yer faces alone will scare the bejesus outta 'em."

Phil grinned, his teeth seeming even whiter in his soot-blackened face. "What are ye sayin', Da? Sarah and Rose sees us grimy and dirty all the time when we gets home from work."

"They ain't ever seen yer faces this black," Mick chuckled, "Wish ye could see yerselves!"

"Da, ye knows yer not lookin' any better," Phil laughed, taking in the dirty streaks across his father's face.

"Go on wit ye," Mick retorted, "Go wash yer face and hands. Yer enough to scare the bejeepers outta a fella."

The young men pushed and shoved one another as they left the shed, each vying to be first to use the pan of water Fanny had set on a low table outside the door.

Mick chose to dip water from the rain barrel into a bucket to wash away the grime. He stripped off the shirt that stank of smoke before entering the house. His daughters rushed to hug his legs and torso when he stepped into the kitchen. He picked Rose up in his arms, holding her with one arm, he wrapped the other around Sarah. "What's all this, now?" he chided them gently, "Did ye miss me that much?"

Rose leaned back to look into his eyes. Two little hands held his face, "I lub you, Daddy," she said, earnestly, unable to form the words her emotions evoked.

"We was scared," Sarah told him, "I don't like fire and neither does Rose. Right, Rosie?" Rose solemnly nodded her agreement. Both children remembered a fire that had burned much closer to their home the year before and the fear their mother had been unable to hide then and now.

Mick hastened to reassure his daughters, who were soon distracted as their brothers came into the room. Soon, the chatter and banter between the siblings made home a safe haven once again. Mick and Fanny steered the conversation away from the fire and distracted the younger children by talk of the school year ahead. Rose was turning five later in the fall and would be joining her sister this year. Later, Elsie joined them, after the two girls and their baby brother were all safely tucked in for the night.

"Do ye really think it t'was the cap'n that set the place afire?" Fanny asked Mick.

"Stands to reason, he was mighty riled 'bout losing 'is job from what I heard," Mick answered.

"What possesses a person to do such a thing?" Elsie wondered out loud.

"Anyone who'd leave a man to bleed to death is capable of most anythin'," Mick replied.

"He must be an awful bad man," Jack opined. "Do ye think they will find 'im?"

"I've no idea, son," Mick replied, "Paddy was certain Jake would be able to follow 'is trail. I know Jake and Joe were fine hands at trackin' caribou and other game, so I guess there's a good chance they'll catch up wit 'im."

"What makes a man so evil?" Jack questioned.

"Nobody is born evil," Fanny commented, "some are turned that way by life."

"What do ye mean, Ma?" Jack asked. There was a lull in conversation as Fanny marshalled her thoughts.

"Not everybody is given a fair shake in this life," Fanny began, "some are raised up right and become decent folk, others are dragged up with little to no guidance about what's right and wrong."

"And some know right from wrong but just don't care," Mick added, "there are folk who are just plain selfish and don't give a damn 'bout nobody but themselves."

"Watch yer language, Mick," Fanny rebuked mildly. "Jack, ye have a good family and good people 'round ye. Some are born into harshness. Some are hurt so bad when they're still so young that their hearts harden and turn to stone til they got no feelin' fer their fellow man. They might know right from wrong but all they care 'bout is lookin' out fer themselves." Fanny gazed around the table at her sons. "I hope ye will always do the right thing, no matter what."

"Can't see any of us ever settin' fires, or tryin' to do harm to man or beast," Phil commented. "Tis hard to understand how anybody could."

"What do ye think will happen to the cap'n when they catches 'im?" William asked. "We ain't got no jails or nothin' like that."

"Langley will know what to do," Mick replied. "there's men enough to hold 'im and take 'im wherever Langley figures they can lock 'im up until it gets sorted out."

"Hilda and Rebecca will be so worried and Mary, too," Elsie murmured.

"The women were all pretty calm when we told 'em," Mick related, "Mary was anxious, I could tell, but she took it pretty good."

"I know it's selfish but I am glad ye didn't join 'em," Fanny said.

"I knew ye'd be getting' yerself worked up wit the fire," Mick told her, "Didn't want to make it any worst by ridin' off after the scoundrel. I thought it best to git back home as quick as I could. Besides, Langley said he 'ad enough men to do the job."

"Do ye mind if I head up to see Ginny?" William asked his parents, "Might be I can relieve their worry a little."

"Ye knows we still has to git to work in the morn," Mick warned him, "and the hour grows late."

"I'll be fine," William replied, "I really need to do this."

"Go on, then," Mick told him, "But be quick about it."

"I will, Da," William replied, "they'll be wantin' to get to bed soon, I bet."

"Hilda won't be sleepin' til her man gets home," Fanny said drily, "bear in mind we'll likely be in bed when ye return so keep quiet!"

"I will, Ma. I promise," William answered reaching to open the door.

"He sure has it bad fer 'er," Mick remarked as the door closed behind his eldest, "I hope he makes it quick visit."

"He will do as he sees best," Fanny commented.

"He's a good lad," Elsie remarked, "Ye are raising them right."

"Having ye and Joe to help us made a difference," Fanny answered as she reached out to pat Elsie's hand. "We have been blessed."

"Da, do ye think the men will be back to work the quarry in the morn?" Phil asked.

"Dunno, son," Mick replied, "guess it depends on whether or not they catches up wit Gallo."

"Do ye think he did it on purpose, Da? Maybe it was an accident," Jack wondered.

"It's be nice to think so, Jackie-boy, but I have me doubts," Mick responded, "I fear 'is heart is as black as that there stove. I well remember 'is reaction when we give 'im them papers fer the association. He was dancin' he was so mad."

"I wonder who will be the mining cap'n now," Jack pondered aloud.

"We'll find out soon enough," Mick remarked, "fer the time being I'm guessing Josiah will be taking over, at least until Langley appoints a replacement."

"I hope he hires somebody nicer than the cap'n," Jack replied, "I didn't much like him."

"Bosses are generally not all that friendly," Mick told him, "They can't be, I guess. I'll be satisfied if it's somebody honest and fair."

"Hopefully the agent has learned a thing or too after all this," Fanny commented.

"Don't much matter who he puts in charge," Mick replied, "the men have that association now. Things will get better."

"The work will still be just as hard," Phil grimaced, "will be glad when we can quit the quarry fer good."

"Aye, son," Mick agreed, "t'will be good to leave it behind us."

"It is getting late," Elsie remarked, "I best be getting' home. I'll pray the men looking for the captain are safe and soon return to their homes. Fanny, I will come over first thing in the morning. Good night."

"I'll walk ye home," Jack offered as he stood up from the table. "I need some fresh air anyway."

"See ye in the morn," Fanny told her sister-in-law, "Good night."

"Aunt Elsie, do ye think Jake is as good a tracker as Uncle Joe was?' Jack asked as they walked.

"I don't know. I know Joe held him in the highest regard," Elsie answered. "Why, Jack, what's botherin' ye?"

"I heard the Da sayin' they might need a weapon," Jack confided, "I'm kind of scared of somebody getting' hurt."

"The men are all sensible people," Elsie tried to comfort the boy, "they won't take any chances."

"I don't know," Jack continued, "I remember how angry Charlie was when Uncle Joe died. He let his temper get the best of him. He punched Jake real hard."

"Charlie was a good friend of Joe's," Elsie replied, "sometimes when someone we love dies, we become angry, especially when it seems like it could have been prevented. Charlie shouldn't have hit Jake, but they're friends now, right?"

"I suppose," Jack's doubt was obvious in his tone.

"Charlie has a fine sense of justice. He does not take kindly to wrong-doing," Elsie quietly surmised, "but he also has a fine sense of fairness. He won't do anything foolhardy. It was different when Joe was killed. Charlie was so close to Joe. This is a different situation."

"But if he blames the cap'n fer Uncle Joe dying, he might," Jack worried.

"Try not to worry, Jack," Elsie advised, "ye know what yer uncle would do? He'd pray about it and ask God to guide the men; to guide Charlie. He'd ask fer divine protection for them all – even the cap'n. Then he would leave it all in God's hands. Why don't ye try that? And remember, Charlie's temper has had a while to cool off, so he will be level-headed. If yer worried it hasn't, put that in God's hands too. Ask him to help ye, to give ye faith so ye don't be worryin'."

"Thanks, Aunt Elsie," Jack nodded as they reached her door, "do ye need water or wood or anythin' afore I goes?"

"No, Jack," Elsie smiled and ruffled the boy's hair, "ye have been keepin' me well stocked up on everything I need."

"Yer sure? I don't mind bringing a pail of water or an armful of wood," Jack insisted.

"No, I'm fine, truly I am," Elsie answered, "ye best be getting to bed. I'll see ye all tomorrow. Good night."

Jack nodded, wishing his aunt a good night he turned away.

Chapter

58

P eter had left the cook house after his discussion with Langley and went directly to the minister's rectory. The cleric was surprised to see him again so soon after his previous visit.

"Come in, come in," the churchman greeted his visitor, "what bring ye back so soon?"

"I have a great favor to ask of ye," Peter began, "if ye have time I'd like to discuss it with ye."

"I was just workin' up my sermon fer Sunday but it will keep," the minister answered. "Would ye like a cup of tea?"

"I'm fine, really. I'd just like to get this matter dealt with," Peter replied as he followed his host into his parlour, "it's rather important."

The churchman gestured toward a chair as he settled himself upon a sofa. "Have a seat and tell me what's on yer mind," he invited.

"I've spoken to a few people who have had dealings with the cap'n," Peter began, "the man does have a disreputable character, by all accounts. As it turns out there was a man who saw Gallo in the woods with a slingshot the same day I was thrown from my horse. My mare has a small cut on her flank likely due to Gallo hitting her with a pebble or something. The man that found me also seen boot prints in the mud nearby that match the same prints he found right outside the captain's shack in the quarry. These men are willing to testify to what they saw."

"Forgive me, but what does all this have to do with me?" the preacher asked.

"I need someone to write up the men's testimonies," Peter explained, "it needs to be dated and witnessed as well. It has to be able to stand up in a court of law. As ye know, any serious crimes have to be tried back in England. The fishing admirals try petty crimes but they have no jurisdiction over crimes like murder or attempted murder."

"I see," said the minister, stroking his chin, "I've never done anything like it in me life. I don't have much education as far as the law goes."

"I do," Peter told him, "I was training to become an attorney but it didn't work out. Still, I know enough to be able to help make sure the document is legal."

"Then why can't ye write it up yerself?" the clergyman asked.

"Because I would be seen as the complainant and therefore need somebody free from any charge of duplicity or conflict of interest," Peter explained further.

"But can ye claim attempted murder? It's like as not any judge will think the incident could be seen as nothing more than an accident," the cleric pondered.

"There could be an argument for that, if he hadn't dragged me into the bushes with me noggin cracked open and bleeding profusely," Peter agreed. "As it is there are two men who can attest to that fact and to the fact he'd tried to hide my body."

McGrath nodded solemnly. "As long as ye can give me some guidance as to exactly how to do it I'm happy to help."

Peter released a breath he'd been unconsciously holding, "I'd greatly appreciate it," he told the preacher. "There are three men ye'd have to interview and record their testimony. When is the best time for ye so I can arrange it?"

"I'm always at the beck and call of my flock," the minister chuckled, "but earlier in the week and early in the evening, if possible. I take it these men work the quarry?"

"That's right," Peter confirmed. "It might not work if it's too early in the evening. The men work long days and many will want to go home first to eat and perhaps change their clothes."

"I thought as much, most men around here work the quarry," the preacher said thoughtfully, "it will take time to write it all up and to make sure I got it all straight. Why don't ye talk to these men first, see what time suits 'em? I am kept busy all the time but I will make time to meet with each of 'em. Let me know when."

Peter stood up, "I much appreciate this. Gallo poses a danger to any man who stands up to 'im. The sooner he's removed from the community the better off everyone will be."

"I hate to say it, but I think yer right," McGrath agreed, "tis sad to see men turn to crime and it never ends well fer 'em."

"I'll let ye get back to yer work," Peter replied as he shook the man's hand, "I'll do my best to let ye know, first chance I get. Thanks, again."

"Tis a sad state of affairs. I'm happy to help, even if it does mean certain imprisonment fer the cap'n," the minister responded solemnly as he followed Peter to the door.

"One more thing," Peter paused by the door, "do ye know of any educated man who could act as a witness to yer signature and those of the witnesses?"

"Is that all that is required, somebody to confirm the signatures? Does it have to be a person of substance?" the preacher asked.

"It just has to be someone who has discretion and can read and write themselves," Peter answered. "Preferably somebody from the community not related to ye or to any of the witnesses."

"I will give it some thought," the minister replied, "shouldn't be too hard to figure it out."

"I've taken up enough of yer time," Peter remarked, "I greatly appreciate yer assistance in this matter."

The cleric waved away Peter's thanks as he opened the door, "I'll be seeing ye."

Peter walked away from the rectory his thoughts forming concentric circles as he strode to his horse. It had been a week of adventure he'd much rather have done without. Again, his planned return to the East coast would have to be put off until the depositions were written up, signed, sealed, and delivered. *Delivered to whom?* Peter wondered as he swung up into the saddle. *Tis past time this island had a better system. There's still the problem of transporting Gallo across the island to a fishing admiral. First off, he will need to be detained. That won't come easily. One step at a time, Parsons,* he told himself as his thoughts flowed as quickly as water over a waterfall.

In his distraction Peter did not immediately register the black plumes of smoke in the distance. It was the sound of a galloping horse that caught Peter's attention. To his surprise it was one of the men from the quarry and although Peter did not know the rider's name, he did recognize his face. The rider slowed his mount as he came closer to Peter's.

"What's going on? What in the name of all that's holy is yer rush?" Peter asked the man, noting his serious expression.

"There's a fire, looks like it's comin' from the captain's place," the man reported, pointing in the direction of the smoke. "It will take every man available to fight it. Will ye come?"

Peter touched his head gingerly, although he hated to admit it, he didn't feel up to fighting a fire. "Mate, I had a bad wound to my head, I wouldn't be much use," Peter began, "I'm still weak and wobbly on my feet. Go on ahead, I'll do my best to catch up to ye."

"Don't give it another thought, Mr. Parsons, it's habit fer every man to show up to a fire," the man explained. "Are ye all right? I noticed ye were riding kinda slow."

"I'll be fine. Ye best get going," Peter said as he stared at the smoke curling into the air in the distance. The man nodded and his horse pranced, sensing the crisis and the need for action. No more was said as he urged his mount forward, galloping away from Peter in his hurry to reach the scene of the inferno.

Hilda was shaking out clothes she was unpinning from a clothesline when Peter rode up. "Hilda, is Hank home?" Peter called out as he slowed his mare to a walk into the yard.

"No, Peter, there's a fire and all the men in the area will be gone to fight it," Hilda told him. "Did ye see the smoke?"

"I did. How long ago did it start?" Peter queried. "Perhaps I should join them."

"I can't say 'ow long it's been burning, not long, just time enough to carry the smoke high enough for all to see," Hilda replied, "it's not often we 'ave to deal with fire but when we do it's all 'ands on deck, so to speak. But ye're not well enough to go at that! Besides, there'll be plenty of men to 'andle it. Don't ye be worrying yerself 'bout that."

Peter remained in his saddle watching the smoke in the distance and trying to decide whether or not to join the men to fight the blaze. "So, Hank didn't come home after work?" he asked.

"No, it must 'ave started just when the work day was ending," Hilda answered, "like I said there'll be plenty of men to fight it.

They would 'ave seen the smoke from the top of the 'ill at the quarry. Somebody would've sounded the alarm."

"I met a man headed up there," Peter commented, "he said it looked like it was comin' from the direction of the captain's place."

"It's in that area, I'd guess," Hilda agreed, "I can't say fer sure, but looks like. Why don't ye take care of yer mare and come in the 'ouse? It ain't long ago ye took that knock on the 'ead. Don't be undoing all my good work by riding out like some kind of 'ero. Ye won't do the situation any good if ye gets up there and passes out or worst. The men have enough to deal with, ye don't want to add to their worries, now do ye?"

Peter's pride wrestled with his good sense as he sat atop his mare, considering. He hadn't wanted to let any of the men know just how bad the headaches still were, or the weakness that came over him without warning. He knew Hilda was right, yet he felt obligated to join the men in battling the blaze.

"Pride goes afore the fall," Hilda said sternly. "Do what I tole ye and put yer mare in the barn and then come in the 'ouse. Yer color's not good and I won't have ye riding off in yer condition. C'mon now, yer face is grey and I can tell ye needs ta rest. Hank's been tellin' me all about the goings on of late. Tis no wonder yer feelin' all the effects. Hank wouldn't be 'appy wit me if I let ye ride out there."

Peter smiled at Hilda's stance, she stood with hands on hips as she chastised him. Nodding, he did as she ordered and walked his horse into the barn. *I fergot just how fierce that woman can be, wouldn't do to make 'er cross,* he told himself.

Chapter
59

"**D**o ye see that, over there?" Jake asked Paddy, "Pull up fer a moment."

Paddy slowed the horse's pace and raised a hand in the air to let the others know they were stopping. The trail they were following in single-file was nothing more than a well-used caribou path. Tree branches brushed against the sides of the wagon in many places.

Jake hopped down from the wagon seat and walked over to where the long grasses were folded as if a great hand had reached down to flatten them. He searched the ground for signs somebody or something had come this way. It looked to him like a rider had come this way, many of the trees bore evidence, broken twigs lay everywhere. He continued his search noting how the grasses were tramped down but could see no further evidence. Still, it was enough to convince him they were on the captain's trail.

"Ye find something?" Paddy asked as he climbed back onto the wagon seat.

"Nuddin' in particular. But it looks like a horse or maybe a deer has been through here," Jake replied, "let's keep movin'."

Paddy waved his hand at the others as he tapped the reins lightly. They moved slowly. Jake was scanning the trees and pathway ahead of them, searching for clues that would tell him if they were on the right track. They hadn't gone far when Jake saw the empty rum bottle tossed aside.

"Looks like the cap'n did come this way," he told Paddy, "Least-wise there ain't many men I knows who would be sucking back rum as they ride along."

"Should I stop so ye can collect that bottle?" Paddy asked.

"No need, it don't prove nuddin'," Jake responded, "let's keep going."

Paddy did not reply and the wagon rolled onwards, leading the small posse that hunted the captain. It was some time later before Jake again bid Paddy to stop. Like before, grasses were laying flat against the earth and when Jake hopped down, he took note of the wide swath of flattened hay, as if a large animal had lain there. Further on he found what he'd been searching for: boot prints in the mud on the pathway.

Paddy waited while Jake went forward on foot, head bent down as his eyes scanned for evidence. Three hoof prints, and a fourth barely visible, as if the animal was not bearing weight on one leg. That hoof was making a very light indentation in the mud every few feet.

"Ye see something?" Paddy asked as Jake turned to come back to the wagon.

"I think the poor animal has come up lame," Jake replied, "it's not placing weight on it's one leg, that's how it seems to me."

"If that's the case we may catch the rogue sooner than we thought we might," Paddy commented. Jake nodded but made no other reply. His eyes searched the ground ahead and his attention was wholly focused on the job at hand. Slowly the little band of men crept forward.

It wasn't much longer when Paddy and Jake spied the lame horse standing still among the pines. It held one leg up, confirming Jake's suspicion. The saddle had been removed but the bit and halter remained. Paddy stopped and Jake once again descended the wagon seat to look for tracks.

He approached and felt the mare's side and back. It was still warm from its exertions and it whinnied nervously. Jake spoke softly to the animal and reaching down felt along the mare's hurt leg examining its injury. The pathway was pitted with holes and he suspected she had unwittingly harmed herself in one of the many potholes. He walked back to the wagon reaching into the box he grasped the canteen of water and the bucket he'd thrown in there before they'd left. He poured water into the container and walked back to the mare.

"Jake?" Paddy called, "We ain't got time fer that."

"Won't take but a minute," Jake replied, "He's on foot now, we'll catch up to 'im soon enough." Ignoring the questions called to him he brought the bucket to the lame animal and waited while the mare drank deeply. When she was done, he tied her reins to a nearby tree, stroking and whispering softly to the animal as he did so.

The men muttered and complained to one another as they waited for Jake to finish administering to the creature, impatient to find their prey. Jake climbed up on the wagon seat and turned to speak to Langley who was right behind them.

"His horse came up lame. He's on foot so t'won't take long to find 'im," he informed him. "He tossed a rum bottle aside a little way back so I'm guessing he'll be feelin' it, maybe. Might make 'im more dangerous. Best to carry on with care."

Langley gave a curt nod in response and they proceeded. The sun was sinking lower and Jake hoped they'd find Gallo before sunset. His nerves twitched as the wagon rolled forward, worrying about the confrontation ahead. Neither man spoke as they cautiously made their way.

They had ridden for several minutes before Jake once again bid Paddy to stop. Something had caught his eye to the right and a few yards ahead of them. Once again Jake jumped off the wagon seat to investigate. He had to walk into the brush before he found the saddle. It had been emptied of everything and Jake manhandled it back to the wagon, tossing it into the wooden box.

"Must've been getting too heavy fer 'im to carry," he told Paddy, "I'm surprised he tried to take it in the first place."

"Who knows what's goin' on in the man's mind," Paddy retorted, "he ain't sensible, I'd say."

Once again, they paused while Jake conferred with Langley before setting off again. It felt like a long time before Paddy spied Gallo's faltering gait in the distance. The man stumbled often and seemed to be reaching the last of his strength. Gallo seemed unaware of the men who hunted him, or had too much rum to care. Paddy slowed the mare until the wagon came to a stop.

"That's him, ain't it?" he asked Jake, "it ain't likely that any man would be out fer a stroll in the middle of the woods this time of day."

"It's got to be," Jake agreed, "and I ain't in any hurry to confront 'im." Jake climbed slowly from the wagon seat and made his way back to Langley, lifting a finger to his lips to indicate the need for silence. "Gallo's on the path up ahead," he whispered to Langley when he'd reached him. "I think we best plan how we wants to handle this."

Langley nodded and gestured for the men behind him to dismount and come closer. The men gathered on the path around the agent moving as quietly as possible so as not to warn Gallo of their presence. Their hastily whispered plans made Jake even more anxious as Charlie was to take the lead, armed as he was with his hunting rifle. As much as he hated the captain for all the worry he'd laid at Jake's feet, he didn't wish him ill, or worst, dead. Men on horseback moved around the two wagons, Charlie in the lead with Langley close behind him. At Charlie's raised arm the troop began their slow movement forward.

Gallo was halfway across a small meadow when the sound of hoofbeats finally filtered through his rum-soaked brain. Glancing behind him he turned searching for a hiding place where none was to be found. He had left the protection of the woods and was now exposed! He began to run but his gait was off and he stumbled, falling face-down onto the spongy ground. Charlie's rifle was aimed as he came slowly toward the prostrate figure. Soon Gallo was surrounded and he whimpered as he lay where he'd fallen. Langley cast a look of disgust at his former mining captain.

"Get on yer feet, ye swine," Langley ordered. "Come on! Get up!

Gallo's ears heard the words but the rum made it hard for him to comply. Stupidly he tried to raise himself to his knees and fell sideways again. After a few attempts Gallo finally made it to his feet and stood swaying back and forth like a sapling in a hard wind.

"Whaddya want with me?" Gallo slurred. "I ain't done nuddin' wrong."

"I s'pose ye know nothing about the fire?" Langley spoke gruffly, his lip curled.

"I ... what fire?" Gallo stalled, trying to think of a way to exonerate himself.

"Ain't no point trying to pick sense outta anythin' he says," Charlie growled, "the man's drunk."

"I ain't no drunk," Gallo mumbled, slurring his words once again.

"Tie 'im up," Vic advised, "e ain't gonna ever admit to it but we all knows it was 'im."

Gallo's eyes looked from face to face until his gaze fell on Jake. "T'was that 'alf-breed, there," he jeered and almost fell again as he stumbled backward.

"Who're ye callin' a half-breed?" Paddy warned, fists closing tightly as he confronted the man. He'd long been dreaming of punishing the captain for his treatment of Jake, among other things.

"Every man here was hard at work in the quarry all day, "Langley said, coldly. "None would have had time to set that fire. Only ye!"

"I'm tellin' ye, it was that savage over yonder," Gallo insisted.

"The only savage I see round here is ye," Langley thundered, "Enough! Who has the rope?"

Gallo fell to his knees, fear caused his face to crumble and he begged, "Ye ain't gonna 'ang me, are ye? Please, don't 'ang me!"

Paddy stepped forward and grabbing Gallo's upper arm hauled him to his feet. "Hangin's too good fer the likes of ye," he told him as he pulled him upright. "Best ye don't tempt me."

Gallo struggled against Paddy's grip but soon found himself held firm as Vic grabbed his other arm.

Charlie stood, rifle aimed at Gallo's chest, while Hank strode forward, a length of rope held in his hands.

Gallo looked wildly from face to face but found no sympathy or compassion on any of them. "I didn't set no fire," he denied shaking his head from side to side. "I'm tellin' ye, it weren't me! Listen! Just ye listen to me!"

"That's enough!" Langley ordered and turning to Hank said, "Tie the bastard up." Vic roughly pulled Gallo's arms behind his back with Paddy's help and held him as Hank wound the rope tightly around his wrists, tying it securely.

Gallo's knees buckled once again and he began once again to beg. "I ain't done lit no fire!" he cried out as he tried to shake off the strong arms that held him.

"Put him in the back of one of them wagons," Langley instructed. "We'll throw him in the root cellar back at the house. At least that's not burned down."

"I'm tellin' ye, t'was that 'alf-breed what lit that fire," Gallo continued, "them kind can't be trusted. Listen to me!"

Paddy had had enough and cuffed the prisoner in the back of the head. "Simmer down and shut up, else I'll muzzle ye like the mad dog ye are," he warned.

"Do any of ye have a handkerchief we can shut him up with?" Langley asked.

Vic pulled a soot-stained bandana from his back pocket, "Will this do?" he asked.

"No! No! Please!" Gallo begged the men, "Will ye listen to me? I didn't start no fire."

"And I s'pose it wasn't ye who left Parsons fer dead, either," Langley answered him. "But we know the difference. There're witnesses. This isn't just about the fire. Ye're a scoundrel and a rogue and ye're going to face the music!"

"No, I didn't," Gallo denied, "I ain't done no such thing!"

"I've heard enough!" Langley's voice rose, "shut him up," he instructed the men.

Vic shook the bandanna out and rolled it into a gag to place in Gallo's mouth. Stepping toward his former boss Vic uttered a shout of surprised pain when Gallo kicked out, connecting with his shin. A scuffle commenced with Gallo using his head to butt the men and his feet to do as much damage as possible. His efforts proved useless and soon he was again laying face-down on the ground. Paddy sat on his back and Vic worked with another length of rope to tie his feet together. Lastly, they placed the gag in his mouth and stood back, chests heaving from their efforts.

"Get him in the wagon box," Langley ordered, "and let's get going, daylight's failing."

It took several men to lift Gallo and carry him to the wagon. Their prisoner struggled the whole way, making their task as difficult as he could. Tied as he was, Gallo was unable to do more than squirm, and the men threw him in the wagon.

It was Jake's misfortune that it was Paddy's wagon Gallo was placed in, making Jake very uncomfortable. He wanted nothing more than to wash his hands of the whole affair. He glanced at Paddy as he climbed up onto the seat. Paddy shook his head indicating to him to keep his silence as they drove back to the scene of the fire.

Charlie followed behind them, his rifle held easily in his right hand as they rode. Charlie had made certain Gallo had seen the weapon when he'd swung into the saddle as a warning to cause no further trouble. Jake was glad to make his exit when they came to the tree where he'd left Gallo's mare tethered.

"I will walk with 'er. The leg's too weak, she can't be ridden," Jake explained. "I'll meet ye back at the house."

"It's going to be slow going but I guess we can't just leave 'er here," Paddy commented.

"Tis not that far," Jake pointed out, "tis no further than my walk to work every day. I won't be far behind ye."

Paddy nodded, understanding too well Jake's hurry to be away from the captain. "I'll wait fer ye," he promised, "and give ye a ride back to yer place."

The men made the trip back in less than a quarter of the time it had taken to catch up with Gallo. Their prisoner spent a miserable time in the back of the wagon where his head bounced against the hard wood floor as the horse cantered along. Once they'd reached the scene of the blaze the men followed Langley to the field where the root cellar stood.

"Do ye really think this is a good place to hold 'im?" Charlie asked as he swung from the saddle.

"There's little chance of escape," Langley answered. "The cellar is deep enough and there aren't any windows. We can lock 'im in there 'til I can arrange to transport 'im."

"Still, there will need to be a guard and someone to give 'im food and water," Charlie pointed out.

"Let's get 'im inside and we'll sort it out afterward," Langley responded.

As before, Charlie kept his rifle trained on Gallo's torso after the men had hauled him out of the back of the wagon. It took four men to wrestle Gallo to the door of the cellar which now stood open.

Langley stepped inside to study the suitability of the structure to stand in as a jail of sorts. He lit the kerosene lamp that hung on a hook inside the door. The building was dark and he needed the light to search the place for any potential loose boards or weaknesses Gallo could take advantage of to make his escape. A ladder led down to the deep floor of the cellar which was covered in sand while hay lined several wooden boxes once used to store the harvest. Satisfied the structure would work for his purposes Langley returned to the men.

"Keep yer rifle on 'im," he told Charlie. "Untie his feet," Langley told the men, "But watch him closely. He ain't gonna get a chance to kick no one else," he turned back to Charlie, "if he gives us any trouble shoot 'im."

Gallo's head throbbed as much from the rum as from the ride back to the property he once called home. Once his feet were untied Vic and Hank each grabbed an arm. Gallo's shoulders slumped in an attitude of defeat. Vic looked him in the eye, "Try it again, I'll break yer frigging leg," he warned. Gallo could do nothing but mutter incomprehensible grunts. The gag remained in place.

The burly pair half-pulled and half-pushed him to the doorway. Charlie followed; his rifle remained trained on Gallo's mid-section. Hank had to step aside and it was Vic who pushed their prisoner through the narrow opening, Charlie was close behind.

"Unbind him," Langley ordered, "but keep him in yer sights, still," he said, speaking to Charlie. Vic took his time untying the ropes that were burning Gallo's wrists. He left the gag in place.

"Get down that ladder," Langley ordered the captain, "and remember that rifle is loaded. Yer life ain't worth nothing to me."

Gallo stood shakily rubbing his wrists but took a step toward the ladder. Langley held the lantern high as Gallo began his descent. Once he'd reached the bottom Langley had Vic grab the ladder and pull it out. Langley dropped the hatch door in place and shoved the bolt closed.

In the cellar, Gallo pulled the gag from his mouth and spat onto the floor. Wearily he dropped to the floor. All fight had left him and he wanted nothing more than to weep.

Langley slammed the wood door closed on the shed that housed the cellar and laid the cross beam in place. He turned back to the men. "Seems sturdy enough to hold him," he remarked, "but Charlie made a good point. Much as I'd like to leave 'im down there to rot I suppose someone will have to bring him food and water. So, is there anyone willing to guard the place and feed the bastard?"

"How're we supposed to do that? The house is destroyed. There's nowhere to sleep and the kitchen is gutted," Hank responded.

413

"There's a stream fer water. If somebody could bring food," Paddy pointed out.

"Tis only fer tonight," Langley replied, "I plan to go into town on the morrow. I need to let the owners know what's happened here and work out what to do with 'im. If any of ye can spend a night here ye won't have to come to the quarry to work tomorrow. I need a man here until this time tomorrow."

"The barn is still standing, I could sleep in there," Paddy offered, "I'm a light sleeper and will hear if Gallo makes any attempt to escape and most of ye men have wives and families to think about, but Charlie, I'd appreciate the lend of yer rifle if I stays here. I need to wait fer Jake anyway."

"Where did Jake get to?" Langley asked.

"He's walking Gallo's mare back. She came up lame and could not be ridden," Paddy reminded him, "he should be here soon."

No sooner had the words left Paddy's mouth when he spied his friend across the field. "Here he comes now," Paddy pointed.

Jake did not come directly to the cellar but turned into the barn leading the lame horse.

"Can one of ye men bring Paddy some supper?" Langley asked, "least we can do if he's willing to spend the night out here. Charlie, will ye leave him yer rifle?"

"I can do that," Charlie replied, "and I can bring ye something to eat, too," he told Paddy. "My place ain't far from here."

With Gallo safely contained and plans made the men began to leave, only Langley stayed and was chatting easily with Paddy when Jake reached them. Paddy told Jake about the plan for him to guard Gallo and the three men chatted a little longer before Langley made his exit.

"I'm going to see to the mare and then I best get home to Mary," Jake told Paddy. "That mare's been ill-used and needs a bit of nursing."

"I pity any creature dependent on that rogue," Paddy replied. "Listen, it looks like I will be here until at least tomorrow evening. Why don't ye take my wagon back to yer place? Ye can use it to go to work in the morn."

"I won't say 'no'," Jake grinned at his friend, "truth is I am dead on me feet. It's been a long day."

"Go on and take care of that mare and then get yerself home," Paddy responded, "I'd look after 'er myself but ye have a way with hurt animals."

"Will ye be alright out here?" Jake asked his friend.

"I plan to sleep in the barn, once I'm sure there's no chance of Gallo making an escape," Paddy replied, "I'll be fine."

"Why don't we both have another look around the barn. I'll see to the mare and then I'll bid ye good night," Jake answered. "I doubt the cap'n will be giving ye any trouble tonight. Between the rum and his attempt to get away from Hank and Vic, I'd say he's done in. I will come back in the morn, afore I heads to the quarry and leave ye my dog to help guard 'im. I'll bring ye some food as well."

"Thanks, Jake, I'd appreciate that. I don't 'spect no trouble," Paddy answered, "but I dunno what the morrow might bring. The dog would be a help, if he gets outta that cellar, not that I can see much chance of that."

The men continued to chat about their adventures in tracking Gallo and his subsequent capture as Jake rubbed down the mare and put feed in her stall. He checked her leg and grunting, turned to Paddy, "I think she'll mend, like as not it ain't more than a bad sprain. I'll have a look at 'er again in the morning. She's a fine animal, wonder what will become of 'er."

"Ye might ask Langley if he'd be willin' to sell 'er to ye," Paddy commented, "saddle's still in the wagon, too. Could be ye could get 'er fer a fair price. Ye needs a horse, and a buggy, too."

"I don't see how I can afford 'er right now," Jake replied, "and it's Gallo's horse. I dunno if Langley would have the rights to 'er."

"Still, couldn't hurt to ask, he won't need 'er where he's goin'," Paddy replied.

"Worth thinking about," Jake agreed, giving the mare another pat before leaving the stall. "I'm gonna push off now, Mary will be worrying. I'll see ye in the morn, thanks fer letting me use yer wagon."

"Ye may want to take a bit of them oats," Paddy replied, "I knows ye got hay but mine will need to be fed too, once ye gets home."

"I'll need somethin' to put 'em in, wait, now, that bucket's still in the wagon." Jake went to the wagon where he lifted the saddle out of the box and made a second trip to grab the bucket that was there. He filled the bucket with oats for Paddy's work horse and then turned to bid his friend a good night.

"Yer sure ye'll be okay here?" he asked again.

"Gallo ain't going nowhere and I'm given to waking up through the night anyway. I'll check on 'im when I do. Don't ye worry 'bout me, I'll be fine. Get on home to Mary now."

Jake nodded and climbed upon the wagon seat. "Good night, then. See ye in the morn."

Chapter

60

Jake hurried home to his wife and family. The captain's words echoed in his mind and he worried if any of the men paid them much attention. *'Half-breed, savage', well I've been called worse. Still, I hope it won't cost me my job. I knew if I got near 'im he'd try to make good on his promise. Why does the man hate me so?* Jake worried as he rode along. *Yet, it seemed like the men were puttin' it down to 'is mean disposition. They didn't seem to put much stock in what he said.* Jake's thoughts continued in this vein, even the arrest of his nemesis did not relieve the worry or recriminations that had begun with Joe's death. Mary was waiting anxiously and jumped from her chair when she heard the shepherd's joyful bark and the sound of the wagon wheels as Jake rolled into the yard.

"Will ye keep an eye on the babies?" she asked her sister as she hurried through the door. Taking Haldi's agreement for granted she rushed outside. The dog was straining on its tether, as anxious to get to Jake as Mary was. The barn door stood open and Jake was already unhitching Paddy's horse when Mary reached him.

"Jake, oh Jake! Has somethin' happened ta Paddy? Why are ye all alone?" she asked as she came toward him.

"Paddy's fine, give me a minute and I'll tell ye everything," Jake answered as he worked to free the horse from the wagon. "Fire's out, that's the main thing."

"Yes, Mick Kelly stopped to let us know but he said ye were tracking the cap'n or whoever set the house ablaze," Mary replied, "oh, Jake, I've been so worried."

"We caught the culprit," Jake told her as he led the horse into a stall, "let me feed and water Paddy's horse. Won't take long."

Mary stood wringing her hands as she watched Jake, impatient to hear what had happened and nerves on edge from the hours of waiting and worrying. Finally, Jake was closing the barn doors and folding Mary in his arms.

"I'm fine, Mary, sorry I worried ye," Jake said, "I had to go. We had to find 'im."

"Oh, Jake, I was so scared fer ye," Mary mumbled into her husband's shoulder. She was shaking with relief and Jake rubbed her back, trying to comfort her. "Was it the cap'n set the fire?" she asked.

"Yes, it t'was," Jake replied, "can we go in the house now? I'm famished and wore right out. I'll tell ye all about it. Let's just go in. I just wants to eat and get to bed."

Mary released him from her hold. "Ye knows ye must be. Yes, let's go."

Jake stopped to ruffle Smokey's fur on the way, his heart lightened by the welcome of wife and being home. Once inside Mary's eyes fell on Jake's soot-covered clothing and exhausted expression. "Aw, Jake, ye look so tired."

"I am that," Jake admitted and looked ruefully down at his soot-covered clothing, "and will be glad to get out of these clothes. Sorry, Mary, they stink, and I likely got soot all over ye as well."

"It'll come out in the wash," Mary responded, "just sit down and eat, don't worry yerself about that right now."

Haldi was setting Jake's supper on the table for him the minute they stepped through the doorway. "We kept yer supper warm, come, eat," she told him.

Mary watched as Jake dug in, "Ye poor man, t'was an awful long day fer ye," she commented.

"T'was!" Jake agreed between mouthfuls of food, "Glad to be home."

"I made tea, put the kettle on as soon as we heard the wagon," Haldi told him, "And me and Mary made raisin buns today. They turned out some good." Haldi bustled about putting cups and teapot on the table as Mary sat quietly watching her husband eat. "Is there any more of this soup?" he asked Haldi, "I could eat a whole potful!"

Haldi took his bowl and refilled it. "I daresay ye are. That t'was a very long day fer ye, and more excitement than anybody wants." Jake simply nodded. In no time Jake had devoured his second bowl. "I really needed that," he said, smiling at the women. He reached out for a raisin bun and bit into it gratefully, "some, good!" He relished his meal as Mary waited impatiently to hear about what happened. Pushing the plate away Jake turned toward his wife.

"I was comin' home with Paddy in his wagon when we seen the smoke. Ye know with fire ye can't take no chances. It can spread so fast. So, Paddy and I headed right over there to try to put it out. There were more men than I could count came to help fight the blaze," he began, "when we got it put out the agent, Langley's his name, wanted to track down the culprit that lit it. We all figured it was the cap'n cuz Langley fired 'im this morning. Paddy tole 'em I was good at tracking and next thing I knows I'm with the small band of men tracking 'im into the woods.

"It took a while but we got 'im. He'd had a good bit to drink and kept denying it was him what done it. Nobody believed 'im. So, we got 'im trussed up and thrown into the back of Paddy's wagon.

"Langley's got 'im locked up in the root cellar not far from the house he tried to burn down and Paddy's staying there guarding 'im. He told me to use his wagon to get home and fer work tomorrow. I tole 'im I'd bring the dog to help him guard the prisoner afore I go to work, so I will have to leave earlier. Mary, do ye think ye could rustle up somethin' I could bring Paddy fer breakfast?"

"Yes, of course, but Jake, why'd did ye have to track the cap'n? How do ye know fer sure it was the cap'n who set the fire? Why was he fired? He's the man who came to see ye a while back to chat to ye 'bout yer job, right?" Mary's questions came fast and furious.

"Yes, that was him," Jake agreed, "Dunno why he got fired. It just stands to reason t'was 'im what set the fire. Leastwise, that was what most of the men believed, with good reason. He ain't a very nice man. He has a real mean streak, Mary, and it was Paddy who told 'em I was good at trackin'. I didn't even think, there wasn't much time."

"Mick didn't say much when he stopped by, just that the fire was out but ye were helping find the culprit who set it," Mary told him.

"He likely was in a hurry to get home," Jake replied, "we'd all worked all day and the fire was set just afore we left the quarry. We all rushed there from the quarry. We were all tuckered right out, Mick too."

"Did the house burn down? Is there anything left of it?" Mary queried.

"No, not completely, but there ain't much left of 'er," Jake responded, "I didn't see the inside, but the porch's gone. Roof's pretty scorched as well; it's still standing though."

"Why would a person do such a thing? It's awful is what it is!" Mary remarked.

"Like I said, he's as mean and nasty as they come," Jake answered, "and no doubt he was riled up. In fact, a few of the men were talking 'bout how riled up he was when he left the quarry after Langley fired 'im."

"And ye locked 'im the root cellar? I hope he don't get out," Mary said.

"Langley made sure there was no way of 'im escaping and Charlie gave Paddy his rifle, just in case," Jake told her.

"I hope not," Mary shuddered, "He didn't seem so bad when he was here, but I only seen 'im fer a few minutes."

Jake did not reply. Mary had no idea of the bullying Jake had suffered at the captain's hands and he had no wish to tell her about it.

"Mary, I really am exhausted. I needs to get to bed, especially since I gots to leave earlier in the morning to go make sure Paddy's all right afore I goes to work," Jake yawned in mid-sentence, "we can talk more about it after work ta morrow, all right?"

Mary nodded, "Ye go on in to bed, I needs to feed the twins again. I'll be in after I take care of 'em." The twins lay sleeping in their bassinet near the wood stove. Rising, Jake kissed Mary's cheek and wished the two sisters a good night. He glanced into the basket on his way and stood a moment admiring his infant daughters.

"Poor Jake," Haldi murmured when the door to the bedroom closed, "He really is dead on his feet."

"He is that," Mary agreed, "he works so hard. Wish there was more I could do to help him. I know it's been easier on him since ye came. I hope ye know how much we appreciate all yer help. Yer a Godsend, ye really are."

"I likes helping out around the farm. Them chicks are lookin' more like hens now." Haldi replied, "And the garden's comin' along good. It's nice to be out in the sun. Tis no hardship a'tall."

"Yer a hard worker," Mary commented, "ye always were. Sure, I remember when ye was dragging firewood into the house fer Ma when ye weren't very big. Some of them junks of wood was bigger than ye! I dunno how we managed afore ye came. I thank the good Lord fer ye every morning and every night."

"Aw, go on wit ye," Haldi blushed at the compliments, "I'm happy to be here."

Just then the babies began to stir and Mary moved quickly to tend to them before they could disturb Jake. It was not much later when the sisters followed suit and went to bed as well.

At every home around the bay husbands were greeted by worried wives while single men answered the many questions anxious parents and family members plied them with. Around several bends down the road a similar scene was enacted at Hank's home. Peter was sitting with Hilda and was anxiously waiting news about the fire when Hank arrived. After Peter had sat quietly waiting while Hank reassured Hilda and answered her many queries, he began to fire off a few of his own.

"I spoke with yer minister today," Peter told Hank. "It seems I may have to speak with him one more time. This fire will be added to the charges against 'im. Since the scoundrel is being safely held, I plan to speak to Langley about having him moved to the city. Then we need to see a fishing admiral to arrange to have 'im shipped back to England to face all the charges we will be bringing against him.

"Here's the thing though, I need ye and the other men to meet with the minister. He's going to write up depositions of yer testimony regarding Gallo's attempt on my life," Peter told Hank while Hilda hung on every word. "The minister says early in the week would work best fer him. I know yer all busy with work and yer farms but could ye make time to meet with the minister to tell him everything ye knows about how Gallo knocked me from my horse and then dragged me into the bushes?"

"What good will that do?" Hank asked, "It was done to ye, not me."

"It's to make sure all the legalities are covered," Peter explained, "yer a witness, so to speak, even if ye weren't there when it happened ye can testify to the amount of my blood on the road and the boot prints, and all. Ye needs to tell 'im everything ye told me so he can write it all down."

"Will that take long?" Hank wanted to know.

"Yers shouldn't take that long. There ain't a lot fer ye to tell," Peter answered, "If the courts over in England find 'im guilty he will go to gaol fer a good long time, maybe the rest of his life."

"And 'e wouldn't ever come back 'ere?" Hilda asked.

"No, not if he's found guilty," Peter replied, "but Hank's testimony as well as Vic's and especially Jake's would make the difference between an innocent or guilty verdict."

"And now there'll be more charges, because of the fire," Hank commented.

"I'd say Gallo has sealed his own fate," Peter agreed.

"Yes, of course, I can do that," Hank consented, "I need a day or two to get over fighting that fire and I'll be ready."

"Sorry I couldn't be there to help with fighting that fire, I feel rather useless right about now. I know ye must be beat right out. I think it's time we all got to bed," Peter remarked, "we can discuss all this again tomorrow. I hope ye don't mind my staying another day or two."

"Ye ain't in no shape fer fightin' fires and I told ye afore," Hank replied, "ye're always welcome to stay as long as ye want. I am beat out. Bed sounds good. See ye in the morn."

Chapter

61

Paddy was up and sitting on a boulder not far from the root cellar when Jake drove his wagon into the field. "Mornin', Jake," he greeted when Jake had drawn the wagon up beside him.

"Mornin', he didn't give ye any trouble?" Jake asked as he hopped down from the wagon seat. As promised Jake had brought his dog and the shepherd bounded forward, jumping up on Paddy.

"Not a bit," Paddy replied as he rubbed the dog's ears, "truth is I ain't heard a sound and I've been sittin' here a fair while. S'pose I better bring 'im some water. Can ye stay fer a bit? I don't trust 'im, don't wanna take a chance on opening the cellar door without someone to hold this weapon on 'im."

"Sure, I can do that," Jake replied, "Let me just unload this basket of food Mary sent fer ye. Did ye have yer supper? Charlie did come, did he?"

"Yes, he did," Paddy answered, "he ain't much of a cook but he brought me some hard tack and beans. It weren't much better than what they serve at the quarry but it filled the hole in me gut."

Jake hauled a large basket from the wagon box, "No fear of ye starvin' if Mary has anythin' to say about it. She sent enough food fer a small army." Jake reached back into the wagon to retrieve a length of rope with which he planned to tether the dog. "Ye may have trouble keepin' Smokey outta it though, she will rob it if ye give 'er half a chance."

Paddy grabbed the dog's collar, "I likes ye, Smokey, I really do but I ain't about to share me breakfast with ye," he said as he led her away to where a sapling stood. Jake threw him the rope and the dog was soon fastened to it.

"Let's get this over with," Jake said, "I don't have a lot of time. I gots to get to work."

Paddy left the basket of food balanced on the boulder. He lifted a bucket of water from where he'd left it next to the rock as well as a dipper.

"Grab the rifle," he told Jake, "Let's get this over with."

"Do we need to feed 'im too?" Jake asked.

"Me and Charlie gave 'im some hard tack last night. He won't starve," Paddy replied, "I'd sooner share me breakfast with yer dog than give that bastard any of it."

Jake made no response and followed Paddy to the root cellar. Paddy removed the cross beam and sunlight flooded the small shack. Paddy undid the bolt lifted the hatch door slightly, "Got some water fer ye," he called out, "My buddy's here and got a rifle trained to take yer to yer maker if ye give us any trouble," he warned.

Gallo stood as the hatch door opened wider. He had a terrible thirst but he said nothing as Paddy handed down the bucket of water. It splashed over his front as he grabbed the handle. "Here," Paddy growled and dropped the dipper down into the hole.

"I needs to use the outhouse," Gallo announced, glaring up at them. His gaze had taken in Jake's presence and his eyes narrowed. His hatred for Jake was unmistakeable.

"Ye can use any corner ye wants down there," Paddy retorted, "ye ain't gonna see the light of day til Langley gets here. Ye can ask him to let ye use the outhouse if ye wants. Until then use a corner or hold it, makes no difference to me." With that Paddy let the hatch door drop and bolted it.

Jake shuddered, even though he knew there the captain could not escape being so close made him nervous. He was glad when they began walking away from the root cellar.

"Do ye think the men made anything of 'im callin' me a half-breed?' Jake asked Paddy, the slur had dogged him ever since they'd captured Gallo.

"I doubt it. Can't say fer sure but the men were all pretty angry, and pretty tired," Paddy replied, "he ain't made a friend of anyone in the quarry so even if they noticed they wouldn't pay it much heed. I don't think ye have any fear of losing yer job no more."

"I sure hope not," Jake remarked, "I won't rest easy until the likes of that is far, far away."

Paddy's big hand gripped Jake's shoulder, "I think the worst of it is behind ye now. I know ye've been carrying an awful heavy load."

"He don't even know me. Did ye see that look he just gave me? I can't figure out why he hates me so much," Jake said.

"There's no figuring the likes of that," Paddy replied, "Don't let it worry ye. He ain't worth it."

"He reminds me of the bunch back home, the ones that ran us outta town," Jake replied, "ye could see the hatred in their eyes."

"They're all cut from the same cloth," Paddy agreed, "there's some that are just jealous, hates to see anyone get ahead."

"But that's not the case with the cap'n," Jake answered, "it's not like I had anythin' he'd want, or anythin' to be jealous of."

"B'y, what can I tell ye," Paddy shrugged, "he was likely raised on hate."

"That could be, I gots to get going. Should I come back here right after work?" Jake wanted to know.

"I guess so. I dunno when Langley will come, like as not after the work day is done, I'd say," Paddy replied.

"Good enough," Jake answered, "I'll see ye this evening then. If ye have to go back in there make sure ye bring Smokey with ye. She's right smart and if ye tell 'er to guard the door she will."

"I've seen how ye got 'er trained and I got to say I'm glad to have 'er here with me," Paddy remarked, "and she will make fer good company, too."

Jake climbed up onto the wagon seat and waved at Paddy, "See ye later," he said giving the reins a light tap.

Paddy stood and watched as Jake drove away. Then he eyed the basket. "Time to eat," he said and rubbed his hands together.

At Hank's house Peter had woken and eaten with the family. Hilda had fussed over him. It had been nearly a week since his fall from his mare but the headaches were not improving. Hilda had taken note of his pallor and had pointed it out to Hank.

If it were up to the woman, she'd wrap me in cotton and keep me on bedrest, Peter thought ruefully, *I got no time fer that. I need to meet with Langley, find out what he plans to do about Gallo. I sure could use his help.*

When Hank stood up to leave so did Peter, "I'm comin' with ye. I need to see Langley," he told them.

"Ye're not lookin' the best," Hank replied, "can't it wait til tomorrow?"

"No, it can't, and I'm fine," Peter replied, "Tis just a headache."

"A headache I 'spect he's had ever since his horse threw him," Hilda protested, "he really should rest."

"As soon as I arrange for Jake and Vic to meet with the minister I will be going to my uncle's," Peter told them, "I will rest there until I feel fit enough to travel."

"Ye can go with Hank to the quarry if ye must but I expect ye to come back here after ye do what ye need to do. Ye're in no shape to go very far," Hilda insisted.

"I wouldn't argue," Hank warned, "ye're better off to let 'er have her way, at least til she's satisfied ye're recovered."

"I've watched ye when ye think nobody's lookin', that 'eadache is worst than ye're lettin' on," Hilda told Peter, "I seen ye stumble more than once yesterday. If I didn't know better, I'd think ye'd 'ad a nip of whiskey, but I know better. Ye can't take no chances. Ye could easily fall from yer 'orse and get 'urt even worst. Ye listen to me and come back 'ere after ye're done at the quarry."

Peter held his hands up in submission, "Alright, Hilda, I'll come back. Don't look fer me for a while though. I have no idea how busy Langley will be. It may be hours before I even get a chance to talk with him."

Hilda looked at Hank, "is there somewhere he rest up there if Langley's busy?"

"There's the cookhouse, he can sit there while he waits," Hank replied.

"Ye knows the two of ye are treating me like one of yer youngsters," Peter complained.

"Stop actin' like a youngster and we won't 'ave to treat ye like one," Hilda retorted unrepentantly.

"I will take care," Peter promised, "I will sit and rest until Langley's available."

"Ye best keep that promise," Hilda threatened, "I'm not above locking ye in a room if I have to."

Peter laughed, "I will keep my promises and I will come back here to prove to ye I'm fine, if fer no other reason."

Hilda nodded, somewhat mollified, "Go on with ye then. I gots things to do. Just ye take care," she ordered Peter.

Hank chuckled after they were safely out of earshot, "She's a real mother hen but don't cross her. She's a handful if ye get 'er riled up."

"I should've begged room and board from yer minister," Peter replied balefully, "I'm pretty sure he has an empty room I could put to good use."

"Could be," Hank agreed, "but I bet the food wouldn't be so good."

"Ye make a fair point," Peter sighed, "I have to tell ye though, it may be a fair while afore I visit again."

Hank merely laughed as they entered the barn but watched Peter carefully as he saddled his mare. He hadn't wanted to question Peter but he'd also noticed times when he'd been shaky on his feet and he worried.

"Ready?" Peter asked as he swung himself up into the saddle.

"Yup, I'll follow ye," Hank replied.

It was a nice morning as they rode toward the quarry. Hank watched carefully but Peter seemed fine and they reached the quarry in good time. Hank rode his mount up to the cookhouse and tied her to the hitching post in the shade of the building.

"Langley should be in the cap'n's shack by now," Hank called out, "word is that freighter is on its way so he will be lookin' out for it."

"I will go see if he's there and I will meet ye at yer house later," Peter replied.

"Ye're sure ye're all right?" Hank questioned his friend.

"Right as rain," Peter confirmed, lying once again, "just itching to get this situation under control."

Hank nodded and waved, "See ye," he called.

Langley was sitting at the desk in the captain's hut when Peter rapped lightly on the door. "Come in," Langley said as Peter opened the door a crack.

"Mornin', heard ye had quite a night," Peter greeted as he entered.

"Ye could say that," Langley agreed, "bastard tried to burn down the company house. He's being held in the old root cellar, under guard."

"Hank told me," Peter responded, "that's partly why I'm here."

"I haven't time to chat much," Langley retorted, "I'm expecting that freighter at any time now and I have a deal of work to do here. Seems the captain was using his position to line his own pockets."

"His crimes seem to be mounting," Peter replied. "I know ye're a busy man, busier than ever these days. I'm at yer service, if I can be of any help a'tall."

Langley leaned back in his chair, "I don't know if the company would cotton to my embracing yer services, seeing as ye've cost 'em a pretty penny."

"Be that as it may I am willin' to help lessen yer burdens," Peter responded, "and the company doesn't need to know, do they?"

Langley's laughter rang out, surprising Peter. The agent wiped tears from his eyes when his mirth finally subsided.

"Ye do realize the irony, do ye not? T'was yer doing with setting up that protective association that lead to all these 'burdens'," Langley pointed out.

"I have to admit, we do make strange bedfellows," Peter grinned. "Yet, it's in both our interests to see Gallo is sent back to England to pay fer his sins. I must confess since I've come to know ye better I feel a certain commiseration fer yer present set of circumstances."

Langley eyed him for several moments before commenting. "If yer sincere, I could use another set of eyes to go over the books. It looks to me like Gallo was pocketing monies he made by working the men to death to get freight out quicker. No doubt the freighting company had certain inducements to ensure that Dominion Limestone knew nothing of Gallo's side deals."

"Like what?" Peter asked.

"Like charging fer extra freight that never materialized," Langley replied.

"Do ye mean the company was paying for tonnage that was overestimated?" Peter inquired.

"That's exactly what I mean. And more than that Gallo was buying inferior foodstuffs for the cookhouse but billing the company fer superior goods," Langley confided. "That's not all. The men were to be paid fourteen cents an hour, not the eleven cents Gallo was givin' 'em."

"So, he was stealing from the men as well as the company," Peter commented.

"He was. This," Langley waved at the papers that covered the desk, "is proof enough that the man is a liar and a cheat."

"And now an attempted murderer and an arsonist," Peter added.

"I need proof of everything, which is why I will accept yer help," Langley replied, "Perhaps between the two of us we can make certain Gallo never sees the light of day."

"What would ye have me do?" Peter asked.

"Start going through this paperwork," Langley answered, "I need a new mining captain, but I have to resolve this mess first."

The two men spent the morning combing through reams of paper work searching for Gallo's deceit. It was nearly noon when Peter stood up excitedly, "I think I've found something." He held two papers up to Langley. "Have a look at this."

Langley walked around the desk and scanned the papers, "It looks like the same shipment. It's the same date but different numerals. Could Gallo have been keeping two sets of books?"

"That's what it looks like to me," Peter agreed, "I've seen this before in the logging industry. It's not unheard of, this fixing of books. Corrupt practises are rampant in every industry."

"Yes, I am well aware," Langley spoke grimly, "but it ends here. The company hired me to prevent such excesses. It may well be my job on the line once they learn of it."

"Look again at those dates," Peter advised.

Langley bent his head studying the sheaves of paper and smiled grimly, "this was before my time!"

"It could be Gallo had made some kind of arrangement with the previous agent," Peter reasoned. "I know ye must be an honest man, else ye would not have had me going over these with ye."

"The company will not see it that way. All they will see is a mining captain that was robbing them blind and an incompetent agent," Langley said.

"Did ye have any reason to believe Gallo was lining his pockets?" Peter asked.

"I have only visited the quarry twice," Langley admitted, "each time everything seemed above board. He likely hid his duplicate books elsewhere."

"In my experience companies such as Dominion Limestone are well aware of the pitfalls of doing business," Peter tried to comfort him, "if ye present what ye've learned here I think ye will find they understand and respect ye're bringing this to their attention."

"I will clear up this mess first. I need to take care of Gallo and hire a new mining captain," Langley said, "then I will face the owners."

"Will these papers be enough for yer purposes?" Peter asked.

"It will be enough to justify my replacing Gallo," Langley replied, "and his attempt to burn down the company house will make the owners more willing to help me send him back to England for trial on the charge of attempted murder."

"I don't know about ye but I sure could use some sustenance," Peter suggested, "are beans and hard tack the only food choices at the cookhouse?"

"I had a word with the cook. I cannot stomach that fare. The menu will improve, not right away, perhaps, but it will improve," Langley replied, "I asked the cook to purchase eggs and bread from one of the farmers. How does an omelet sound?"

"Sounds mighty good," Peter grinned, "I can eat beans but eggs are much preferred."

"Let's go," Langley answered, "a break from this distasteful business will be welcome."

The two men were nearly finished eating when Josiah appeared, "That freighter's been sighted," he told Langley, "Should make the harbour within the next couple of hours."

"How're we fixed? Is there enough limestone down below to fill 'er?" Langley asked.

"We got enough to fill 'er at least half-full," Josiah replied, "this one don't look so large as the last one. Tis hard to tell from a distance if she'll take as much as the last one."

"Did ye ever stand with the captain to sign the paperwork once the job's done?" Langley's asked his pit boss.

"The cap'n didn't like me to hang around when he was dealing with the skippers," Josiah remarked, "only a time or two did he allow me to see that end of it. He was a might jealous of me learning much 'bout it."

Langley cast a knowing glance at Peter before answering, "I may need to depend on ye to sign off on the load of limestone. I can show ye later how's it done and what paperwork ye need to keep and which ye need to give the freighter's commander. Do ye think ye're up to the task?"

"If ye shows me what ye expects of me, I can," Josiah replied, "don't sound too hard."

"I have still to deal with Gallo, can't keep 'im locked up in that root cellar much longer. I need to be able to depend on ye today," Langley told Josiah as his gaze swept the man's face, judging his capabilities. "Ye seem smart enough to handle it. Chances are the freighter may have to sit overnight in the cove. In that case I will deal with it meself. We shall see what the day brings. Go on back to work now, and thanks fer letting me know."

Josiah nodded and turned on his heel to leave. "Wait," Langley called, "one more thing, I don't want the men worked to death. Many of 'em came to help fight that fire last evening, so ye just go easy on 'em today. The freighter will be loaded in good time." Josiah nodded again and left the building.

Peter had sat quietly through the exchange, his esteem for Langley growing.

"Looks like the examination of the quarry books will have to wait," Langley told him, "I will have my hands full training Picton to handle the paperwork fer that freighter. I need to get back to town this evening, see if I can arrange fer Gallo to be held somewhere until I can get him transported to the East coast."

"That's something else I wanted to discuss with ye," Peter responded, "I am making arrangements to have the testimony of the men recorded. There will be a charge of attempted murder fer 'im to answer once he's back in England."

"The man has caused no end of difficulties," Langley said exasperatedly. "If it were only the theft and fire the fishing admiral would have been able to handle it, I think, ye would know more about that than I."

"The fishing admiral only has limited powers to discipline petty crimes," Peter answered, "I know in the case of murder or attempted murder, or any other serious crimes have to be dealt with at the Queen's bench."

Langley rubbed his face in frustration. "It ain't so easy to have a prisoner delivered to the proper authorities in England. Gallo will be delivered none the less," he promised. "I best get back up to the shack. I need to go over everything with Picton. If ye're not otherwise engaged, I'd appreciate meeting with ye on the morrow, if that suits."

"I have business to take care of, but nothing pressing," Peter replied, "I can come back in the morning."

"I appreciate yer help," Langley said as he stood, "until the morrow, then."

Peter stood as well and the two men shook hands. Langley did not watch Peter as he walked away. Nobody saw him stagger as he made his way to his horse, nor see him as he laid his head against the mare's side before swinging himself into the saddle.

Chapter

62

"Ye're just in time fer dinner," Hilda told Peter when he reappeared at her house. "Ye look like ye could use a rest, too."

"A meal will fix me right up," Peter denied, "I'll be good as new as soon as I eat."

"We'll see about that," Hilda retorted, "sit ye down and tuck into that food. Ginny will keep the little ones quiet if ye needs to lay down in the parlour."

"I need to go see yer minister after I eat," Peter commented, "see if he can make time to take them depositions. In another month the naval ships will be sailing back to England. Time is of the essence if we want Gallo to be on one of 'em."

"Ye won't be seeing to nuddin' and nobody if ye don't take care of that 'ead of yers," Hilda replied. "Just eat yer food and we'll see 'ow ye be after dinner."

"Ye're a tough woman, Hilda," Peter responded, "as tough as they come."

"I don't mean fer ye to go riding off and p'haps 'avin another fall," Hilda retorted, "If that means I gots to be tough, so be it."

Peter made no replies but sat and quietly ate his dinner while Hilda bustled about the kitchen. Soon her brood joined him at the table and there was little opportunity for any more of Hilda's orders, or discussion of any kind. Peter enjoyed the interchange between all the siblings and was happy to note they kept Hilda rather occupied and soon he stood, hoping to make his escape without any further interference from Hilda.

"Don't be thinking ye can sneak off," Hilda warned as she whipped around as if she really did have eyes in the back of her head. "Let me 'ave a good look at ye first."

Peter hung his head like a school boy caught in a naughty act. "Aw, Hilda, I feel fine, I truly do," he argued. Hilda crossed the small room to stand in front of her patient. "Lift yer 'ead, let me see yer eyes," she commanded. Peter did as he was told, much to the amusement of the children.

"And ye're only going to the parson's 'ouse?" Hilda demanded.

"Only to see the Reverend," Peter promised, "and I will come right back here once I'm done."

Hilda searched the young man's face carefully, "All right, as long as ye come straight back 'ere," she ordered, "ye're in no shape to try to ride into town; Not sure if I should let ye go even as far as the rectory. Seems to me ye've overdone it the past few days. I ain't aiming to be an annoyance, I just don't want ye dropping dead on the road."

"Ye've been a wonderful nurse, Hilda, and I will abide yer rules. I will come straight back here after I've spoken with yer minister. I promise I will," Peter comforted. "I don't want ye to worry. I will not overdo it. Truth to tell, I know I am not quite up to snuff just yet, but I ain't needing to lay about the place neither."

"Go on then," Hilda said gruffly, "make sure ye do come straight back 'ere. I ain't above comin' lookin' fer ye if ye ain't back within a reasonable length of time."

Peter grinned boyishly, "Yes, Maw," he teased and was pleased to see the look of consternation on the woman's face. He hurried out the door and to the barn to get his mare before Hilda could stop him again. *She means well I know she does but Lord, jumping dying I shall be glad to get back to Uncle John's.* Peter's thoughts drifted to his uncle and the help he hoped to find there. Before long he was guiding his mare to the rectory and tying her to the post there.

Reverend McGrath opened the door and smiled widely when he saw his visitor. "Come in, come in," he welcomed Peter, "Ye're getting to be a frequent visitor here."

"I am sorry to bother ye again," Peter began, "I guess ye heard about the fire?"

"Yes, I did hear," McGrath agreed, "a sorry business, is that what brings ye here?"

"It is, I need to rely on yer good humour once again," Peter replied.

"Well, sit yerself down and tell me all about it. How can I be of service?" the cleric asked.

"Well, firstly, is there a chance ye'd be willing to take those depositions we spoke of later in the evening? You see, we need to have Gallo sent back to England and soon the navy ships will be sailing fer Britain and won't be back again until the spring. I'd rather not leave it that long," Peter explained. "Since the man was willing to set a fire – a fire that could well have spread to other farms in the area, well, I just don't trust what he may do next. I'd like to see him bound and shackled in the belly of a navy ship headed back to face a judge."

"As luck would have it, I just got word of a fellow minister who will be visiting me this week," McGrath replied, "he will be staying a fortnight or longer. It might be he will be able to witness signatures, mine included. That will make the process easier, and quicker as well. I know the men work long days, if it t'will help, yes I can do that."

"And would ye be willing to take depositions from Langley and others concerning the fire?" Peter asked. "I know it's more work than we originally discussed."

"I will do what needs to be done to bring the man to justice," McGrath answered. "Let the men know to come to me and we will make arrangements to get the task done. My colleague should arrive any day, matter of fact he's aboard a merchant ship that will be stopping at the port up near town any day now."

"That's wonderful news," Peter enthused, "perhaps this business can be tied up much sooner than I thought it t'would."

"'Tis a sad state of affairs, as I told ye afore, that man has a rather black reputation fer shady deals and an immoral character," McGrath replied. "Still, I would not have thought the man capable of any of this. A body never knows what's in the hearts and minds of people."

"No, I did not foresee him capable of such despicable behaviours," Peter agreed. "It will be troublesome to get the wretch back to

England, but it must be done. I am grateful you are willing to lend your assistance in the matter."

"Was the company house totally demolished, then?' McGrath asked.

"I have not been there, but Hank tells me the place is in ruins. Some of it may be saved, perhaps, but the kitchen and bedroom are totally destroyed," Peter answered.

McGrath shook his head, "That was a good position he had, good pay and a roof over his head to boot. I guess some people don't know how good they've got it."

"I suspect greed had a lot to do with it all," Peter commented, "Greed and a thirst fer power."

"I will pray for 'is soul. There's no time like the present. What say we start with yer deposition? We could do that now, if ye'd like," the cleric suggested.

"I can write it up myself, but I will need ye to witness it," Peter replied.

"Come on into me office, I will fix ye up with paper and quill, that is, if ye have time now?"

"T'would be best to get it done," Peter agreed, "I thank ye for yer help."

"I will leave ye to it," McGrath said once he had Peter seated at his desk, "I need to do a few more preparations afore my friend arrives. Now, is there anything else you'll be needing?"

"No, I think this is all," Peter answered glancing at the full bottle of ink and the paper laid out for him. "I appreciate ye thinkin' of this. May as well get it out of the way while I have the time."

"Give a shout if ye need me fer anythin' a'tall, I won't be far away," McGrath remarked. Peter nodded and unscrewed the lid on the pot of ink, suddenly he felt sick to his stomach and his head whirled as dizziness threatened to unseat him.

It was some while later that the minister popped his head into the room. There were several sheets of paper on the desk and Peter's head was bent as if he concentrated on his task.

"How are ye makin' out?" the minister inquired.

"I don't feel well. I may have to leave this for another day," Peter's replied hesitantly.

"I was just about to put water on the stove fer tea and was wonderin' if ye might like to join me?" McGrath invited, "per'aps a bite to eat and a drop of tea would help."

"Tea would be most welcome," Peter said, "this is more of a challenge than I supposed it t'would be."

"Just come on back to the kitchen, the missus who cooks fer me left a cake and we can enjoy a slice with our tea, if ye'd like," McGrath told his guest.

"Sounds wonderful," Peter smiled wanly, "I will be there in two shakes." McGrath nodded and moved away. He didn't see Peter wipe the sweat from his brow or the grimace of pain that crossed the younger man's face.

Chapter
63

L angley's head lifted from the paperwork he was studying when Josiah knocked on the door and peered inside.

"Sorry ta bother ye, boss, but that freighter's here. Tis being anchored now even as I speak," the pit boss announced.

Langley quickly arranged the papers into a semblance of order and rose from the desk. "Ye may as well come with me. I will need to receive the papers from the ship's commander and give instructions fer loading. Ye listen well and take note of all ye see and hear. I never asked, can ye read and write?" the agent inquired.

"I can, though I am not a great hand at it," Josiah shuffled his feet uncomfortably. He hated reminders of his lack of education and training.

"Ye don't have to be a scholar, b'y, as long as yer writing is legible and ye can understand what yer readin'," Langley spoke curtly, "this will be a bit of learnin' fer ye. It ain't all that hard, I promise ye. Don't look so worried. Ye're a smart man, ye'll get the gist of it."

Josiah gave a nod and followed the agent from the shack and down to the pier where the freighter was being made fast.

"Ye, there," Langley shouted as he neared the ship, "I need a word with yer skipper."

The sailor's hand came up to shield his eyes as he looked up the hill to where Langley came with Josiah beside him.

"Yis, sir, right away sir!" the crewmate called before turning away to seek out the captain of the vessel.

Josiah listened carefully to the exchange between Langley and the skipper of the freighter. It was not as fearsome as he'd imagined.

Gallo had made it seem such a difficult and troublesome task to receive the papers and explain the loading of limestone to the commander of each ship that docked at the quarry. *Seems pretty simple to me,* Josiah thought as he listened and nodded at Langley's instructions. *Gallo always made out like the agent was a difficult sort to deal with. He seems like a decent sort to me.* Josiah waited beside Langley while the agent shook hands with the skipper and then followed his boss back to the shack for further directions. By the time Langley had explained what was needed Josiah was confident in his ability to handle the task

"Just remember three things that's most important," Langley finished, "The date of arrival; the date of departure; and the total tonnage of limestone she's carrying. And make sure the skipper signs right here," Langley indicated the space for a signature, "and sign yer name beside it."

"Yeah, that seems pretty simple to me," Josiah commented.

"Not half so bad as ye feared, now, is it?" Langley clapped his pit boss on the back, "I need to get up to the house, check on Gallo and look over the damages. Can ye hold the fort til I get back?"

"Yes, sir. It's all pretty standard from here. I've loaded many a freighter over the years," Josiah said with confidence, "Ye can count on me."

"That ship was too late in comin' to get the load on today," Langley pointed out, "Like as not I will be here tomorrow in time to see to the departure. Ye know what to do if I don't make it back. Just remember what I told ye and ye'll be fine. In the meantime, ye can get started on getting 'er loaded. Go on and see to yer regular duties. I trust ye knows what yer about."

"Should I keep the men working late this evening, sir?" Josiah asked.

"No, that won't be necessary. Tis naught but a small order. No need of payin' overtime if we don't need to, tomorrow will be time enough to finish loading 'er," the agent replied.

"Very good, and sir, I thank ye for yer faith in me," Josiah mumbled, somewhat embarrassed. Langley simply nodded and waved him away. Langley retrieved the parcel of papers he'd been studying and locked them in the desk before making his exit. His thoughts turned dark as he thought about Gallo and the disagreeable task of seeing to his prisoner.

Paddy was sitting lazily on the boulder, facing the root cellar where Gallo languished when he heard the sound of hoof beats. Turning he watched as Langley's steed trotted toward the barn. He was still sitting there when Smokey's bark gave him warning of the agent's approach. He walked over to pet the dog and reassure her all was well.

"Good day, Paddy, where'd the dog come from?" Langley asked when he reached him.

"Tis Jake's dog. He brought 'er this mornin' in case Gallo gave me any trouble," Paddy explained.

"Has he? Given ye any trouble?" Langley inquired.

"Just that he wants to use the outhouse," Paddy remarked, "I told 'im he'd have to wait fer yer arrival. Didn't want to take no chances and as much as I dislike 'im I didn't want to waste a bullet on 'im neither."

"Ye gave him water and food?" Langley wanted to know.

"Gave 'im some hard tack that Charlie brought last evening and a bucket of water this morning, should've been enough to last the day," Paddy answered.

"This arrangement was meant to be temporary. I have to figure out what to do with 'im," Langley remarked. "How secure do ye figure it is? Could he be left here without a guard?"

"That cellar is at least eight feet deep and whoever made it, made it to last," Paddy replied, "them walls are solid rock. He won't be able to tunnel out of there, even if he was there a month of Sundays."

"Somebody would have to check on 'im, regular-like. Bring 'im water and food. We can leave a pail down there fer 'im to use 'is toilet," Langley was walking around the structure searching again for any weaknesses as he spoke. "It does seem pretty sturdy. It may serve the purpose pretty well, at least until we can move his sorry bones to the city."

"T'was meant to keep vermin out, not in," Paddy said sardonically, "It t'will hold that rat but good!"

"Problem is I got no time to keep checkin' on the scoundrel," Langley pondered aloud. "It might be best to move 'im into town, surely, they have a place to keep prisoners there, somewhere with a gaoler to keep watch over 'em."

"I got no idea, boss," Paddy replied, "never had no occasion to know what they do up in town in such a case."

"I best make a trip into town, see what's what," Langley commented. "Are ye able to stay here with 'im until tomorrow? I hate to ask but I will return as soon as I am able. There are several pieces of business I need to attend to, not least of which is letting the company know about these circumstances, and the fire, of course."

"I s'pose I could," Paddy began hesitantly, "I'd like to go home fer a short visit, explain what's going on over here. Maybe get some food and a blanket."

"There's no reason why you can't. Like ye pointed out, he's secure enough where he is," Langley agreed. "I promise ye, I will make it quick as possible. I came away without a change of clothes or anything so I also need to go home for supplies. I'd much appreciate yer help."

"As long as ye don't mind my taking a quick trip to my place, that's fine," Paddy agreed.

"I got no problem with that. Mind taking a stroll through the house with me? I need to assess the damages so I can inform the company," Langley invited, "and then we'll have a look, see how the prisoner is faring."

"Don't mind a'tall," Paddy responded, "I'd say there's a fair bit of damage though. Might be easier to tear it down and build a brand-new place."

"Have ye been inside?" Langley asked.

"Nope. Wasn't going to take a chance being all on me own here. If I went through the floor or hurt myself it would make fer a bad situation," Paddy remarked as they walked toward the remains of the house.

"Yeah, that's smart of ye," Langley replied, "I wouldn't want to go in there alone either. Do ye know of a carpenter nearby? It's going to need a few sticks of furniture as well."

"As a matter of fact, I do. Jake's a mighty fine craftsman. Anything ye need, Jake's yer man," Paddy told him, "He can make just about anything ye can imagine, even grandfather clocks."

"Jake's the man that tracked Gallo fer us, right?" Langley inquired.

"One and the same," Paddy agreed. "Ye won't go wrong with Jake. Like I said, he's a master carpenter."

"Can he build houses as well?" Langley asked.

"Like I said, ye name it, he can build it, no matter how big or small," Paddy bragged about his friend.

"Let's have a look, see what might be required," Langley said as he stepped gingerly on the charred stairs to the door.

The two men entered the burned-out structure. The smell of creosote was strong in the air and a faint stench of kerosene remained. Langley pulled his shirt collar up in an attempt to cover his mouth and nose as they ventured deeper inside. Parts of the wood ceiling were hanging down and the walls of the hallway were burned nearly to the floor. The floor itself was gone in several places and the men had to pick their way carefully over debris. The back side of the home was heavily damaged and little remained of the kitchen and Gallo's former bedroom. At the front, which overlooked the stream and forest, the parlour and front bedroom remained intact, thanks in no small part to the quick response from neighbors and the men of the quarry. Langley stood in what was once the kitchen doorway and surveyed the mess of burned wood and broken crockery. Oddly, the north wall still stood, mainly undamaged except for the scorch marks which gave evidence of the movement of the flames. Neither man spoke as they picked their way carefully back outside.

"Tis a bloody shame," Paddy spoke quietly, "that house would have lasted a good long time. Still, it's possible to tear off the back of 'er and rebuild. I'd say it's worth savin'."

Langley was looking out across the fields and did not speak for a while. "I could take a horse whip to that son of a bitch," he cursed. "The man has caused more aggravation and trouble than enough! The house will be rebuilt and the next man to inhabit it will be worthy of the station. I will make sure of that!" Langley spit out the words bitterly. "Gallo has signed his own death sentence with that action," Langley gestured wildly at the burned-out building, "I have no doubt a'tall that the company will spare no cost to bring the rascal to justice." Paddy made no response but stood waiting to see what Langley would have him do.

"Let's see to the prisoner and then I must be off," Langley growled while striding toward the root cellar. Neither man spoke again until they were standing at the door to the make-shift prison.

"Do ye want to hold the gun on 'im or shall I?" Paddy asked.

"Ye hold the rifle, I may be too tempted to use it," Langley swore, "are ye ready?"

Paddy nodded and Langley swung the board upward, allowing them entrance.

"Gallo!" Langley shouted, "We got a weapon on ye so don't try nothin'. Pass up that bucket and we'll see ye have water."

"I needs the out'ouse," Gallo whined, "I ain't been outta 'ere since ye left me."

"Yer lucky to still be drawing breath," Langley growled, "Pass up the bucket if ye don't want to die of thirst and consider yerself lucky we don't leave ye there to rot to death."

"Is that ye, Mr. Langley?" Gallo wheedled, "I'm right sorry 'bout the 'ouse, but I ain't the one what set it afire. I promise it weren't me!"

"So ye keep sayin'. I don't believe ye," Langley rebutted, "Now, pass up the bucket or we'll leave ye without a drop of water, do ye hear?"

Gallo moved within view holding the water bucket as high as he could above his head. Langley reached down and grabbed it.

"Please, Mr. Langley, 'ow long do ye plan to 'old me down 'ere? I never set no fire. I didn't," he begged. "Sir, listen to me, just listen. I gots money. I can pay fer the damages. Just get me out of 'ere and I'll give ye every penny I got."

"Money ye hoarded by stealing from yer men and from the company," Langley retorted, "it was never truly yours, was it?"

"Sir, no, sir, that ain't true," Gallo denied. "I ain't stole one tin dime from nobody."

Langley dropped the hatch door without responding, his face was white with anger that Gallo did not see. Paddy reached out and took the bucket from his hand. "I'll just go fill this. Be right back," Paddy told him. Langley leaned against the doorway and watched as Paddy walked to the stream and filled the bucket with water.

"Can ye believe the nerve?" Langley asked rhetorically when Paddy returned. The men delivered the water while Gallo continued to profess his innocence and beg for release. Neither spoke as the hatch door was dropped once again and the root cellar locked back up. Paddy followed the agent to the barn before another word was spoken.

"I will be back tomorrow at the first opportunity," Langley said as he swung up into his saddle, "Ye will be paid fer every hour ye spend here. Don't open that cellar unless ye have someone with ye. He has water enough to last the night and then some."

"What about giving him supper? I don't have much of anything here," Paddy asked.

Langley shrugged, "He has meat enough on his bones, a bit of fasting won't hurt him none." With that the agent swung his horse away and Paddy was left watching him ride away.

It seemed no time had passed when Jake came into the yard, driving Paddy's horse and wagon. Smokey began dancing at the end of her rope and barking joyfully.

"Hey, Jake, Good to see ye," Paddy greeted his friend, "It's been an interesting day."

"Wish I could say the same," Jake grinned, "bet ye can't guess what I've been at."

Paddy chuckled as Jake climbed down from the wagon, "I've got it pretty easy, have to admit."

"Ye didn't have any trouble with 'im, did ye? The cap'n, I mean," Jake asked as he scratched his dog's ears.

"Naw, he ain't gonna cause no trouble as long as he's locked in there," Paddy replied, gesturing toward the root cellar.

"What made yer day so interesting, then?" Jake asked.

"Langley was here. We poked around inside the house. He has to let the company know about the damages and the cost of repairs, I guess," Paddy divulged, his eyes twinkling, "could be work fer ye if ye wants it."

"What are ye getting on with?" Jake wondered as he watched Paddy's dancing eyes.

"He asked if I knew any carpenters so I told him about ye," Paddy confided, "the house will need to be rebuilt and furniture will be needed as well. Could mean a pretty penny fer ye."

"Where would I find the time? Between the quarry, my farm, and my family I'm flat out as it is," Jake remarked, shaking his head.

"Langley seems like a good sort. I've a feelin' he'd work somethin' out with ye," Paddy predicted. "Winter's comin' so the quarry won't be worked then anyhow."

"That's true enough," Jake answered. "Seems like even my winter will be busy," he said thinking about Mick and the promise of a place for him fishing lobster.

"Somethin' fer ye to think about, in case he asks ye," Paddy retorted.

"Well thank ye for that," Jake replied, "and what about Gallo? Is Langley moving 'im or is he goin' ta keep 'im here?"

"He asked me to spend another night here, and tomorrow as well," Paddy answered. "He's gone up into town to find out if there's a gaol where he can be kept. I hope there is, I really don't want to be 'is keeper much longer."

"What about yer family? They'll be lookin' fer ye and ye need to eat, too," Jake inquired.

"Langley feels it's safe enough to leave 'im here alone while I go to the house fer food. Here's yer basket. Tell Mary I sure am grateful fer the chow, t'was some good!" Paddy replied.

"What about feedin' the cap'n? Did Langley bring anythin' fer 'im?" asked Jake.

"He weren't too willin' to do more than give 'im a bucket of water," Paddy related, "said he could do with a bit of fasting."

"That don't seem right to me," Jake replied, "I mean I don't have no love fer 'im but it's just wrong to starve the man."

Paddy shrugged, "Makes no difference to me. After the way he treated ye I'd think ye wouldn't care one way or the other."

"I don't like it," Jake confessed, "Part of me'd like to see 'im starved or worst but that ain't how I was raised."

"Ain't got nuddin' to give 'im," Paddy retorted, "I did share a bit with yer dog but Mary's cookin's too good to waste on the likes of that."

"Ye won't get an argument from me," Jake grinned, "she is a mean cook and knows 'er way around a kitchen, that's fer sure."

"Tell ye what, if ye can give me a ride back to my place I'll see what I can find to give him. Ye'll have to bring me back here and then ye can keep the wagon until tomorrow after yer finished work," Paddy suggested. "Truth be known, much as I'm tempted to let 'im starve, I can't let 'im go another night without a proper meal neither."

"Let's go. Smokey can stay here with ye until the job's done and Langley's made other arrangements," Jake answered, "Do ye think ye got a bone or two fer the dog?"

"I'll find 'er somethin'," Paddy replied as he climbed aboard the wagon. "I'd sooner starve Gallo than yer dog any day!"

As they drove Paddy told Jake more about his visit with Langley while Jake, in turn, told Paddy about the differences in the quarry with Josiah in charge.

Chapter

64

T he clerk jumped to attention when Langley appeared at his office. He'd been wondering what was keeping his boss away for so long. Langley gave his clerk barely a nod before hurrying into his office. Once inside the agent quickly wrote a telegram to send to the company and reappeared in the doorway.

"Dawe, come, take this right away to the telegraph office and be quick about it. It's of the utmost importance," Langley ordered his clerk, "and wait there until ye receive a reply."

"Yes, sir," the clerk nearly tripped over his own feet in his hurry to do Langley's bidding.

Langley returned to his desk and set about writing a lengthy explanation of the recent developments at the quarry including a plea for help to send his former mining captain back to England to face charges of attempted murder, larceny, and arson. He wrote furiously and was still deeply preoccupied when his clerk returned a couple of hours later waving a telegram as he knocked on the open doorway.

"Here ye are, Sir," Dawe stammered in his effort to catch his breath after his quick walk back to the office. "Tis an answer to the telegram ye sent."

"Thank ye, Dawe, just leave it there," Langley gestured at the one empty spot on his paper-covered desk. "Close the door on yer way out."

Dawe dropped the telegram on the desk and turned quickly to return to his own desk.

Langley reached for the first page of the missive he'd written and carefully read over his letter. He nodded, satisfied he'd struck the right balance of justifiable anger and righteousness. He blew softly on the ink to hasten drying and dropped it on the desk. Picking up the return telegram he scanned it quickly. His face was grim as he read the terse response but now, he had the authorization he required to move forward. "Dawe!" he called out, "I need ye in here."

Once again, the clerk entered the room and stood expectantly waiting for instruction.

Langley gathered the pages together. "I need ye to take this, place it in a sealed packet and bring it to the post master immediately. It's to be addressed to Dominion Limestone and needs to go out with extreme haste. Explain to the post master it is vital that it gets to the company as quickly as possible. Tell him I am willing to pay any extra it may cost. There has been trouble at the quarry so I will not be in the office fer a few days. I need ye to oversee anything that needs immediate attention here. I don't expect there will be anything but the usual business. Do ye have any questions?"

"No sir, there is nothing that cannot wait," Dawe answered, "I will take care of this straight away."

Langley grunted and stood up. "I will return as soon as I take care of a few things down in the quarry. In the meanwhile, I am entrusting this office to yer good care." Langley nodded and left without further explanations.

The agent made his way to the tavern where he hoped to get the information he needed. He'd never had cause to look into gaols or gaolers. The area was normally quiet except for the occasional shenanigans and petty thievery. He figured the tavern was a good place to make his enquiries. Barkeeps usually had knowledge about such facilities as gaols, meeting folk of every stripe as they did in their line of work. It was early evening and Fargo was on duty behind the bar. Langley sat at a table and ordered his supper. It wasn't until he'd finished every last morsel that he moved to sit at the bar where he could more easily question the barkeep. It was early in the evening and Langley was the sole occupant at the bar.

"I was wonderin' if ye could give me some information," Langley said without preamble.

"Happy to help, if I can," Fargo said, carefully.

"I am interested in whatever form of law enforcement there may be here in town," Langley began, "I have a prisoner I need kept under lock and key."

"Don't know much about that," Fargo rubbed his chin as he spoke. "There ain't been much call fer it in these parts. It's pretty peaceful all in all."

"Is there no naval officer or someone to keep the peace?" Langley inquired.

"We're pretty far from the beaten path," Fargo apologized, "it ain't a big place, not like the city."

"It's as I feared," Langley nodded. "In the city I'd know where to go but I am mystified as to how to handle this here."

"Perhaps if ye tell me a bit more about yer situation I may be able to make a suggestion," Fargo offered.

"Tis not something I want to make public knowledge," Langley said as he studied the man.

Fargo spread his hands wide, "Can't be of much help if I don't know what it is ye needs."

Langley sat quietly, not speaking for a few minutes as he weighed the pros and cons. Finally, he decided to take the risk and confide in the man. Slowly he filled him in on the goings on at the quarry and the subsequent imprisonment of the captain in the root cellar.

"That was right smart of ye," Fargo commented, "them root cellars are solidly built, no chance of 'im getting' outta there."

"Trouble is, I haven't the time to keep a watch on 'im, which is why I was hopin' there's be a gaol here in town and somebody to guard 'im," Langley lamented.

"Ye may have to hire a man to guard 'im until ye can get 'im aboard a ship bound fer England," Fargo remarked.

"Yes, that's my only other choice," Langley sighed, "I best get back down there. Now I know what I have to do I best get to it."

"I wish ye the best of luck with it," Fargo replied, "Wish I could've been of more help to ye."

Langley shrugged and said his farewell. Outside the bar Langley tilted his head back to study the skies. *Tis getting late, looks like I will have to spend the night at home and ride out at first light,* he told himself as he walked back toward the office to retrieve his horse. As he walked, he made plans of what he'd need to pack for his continued absence.

Langley woke and stretched luxuriously. He'd had a good rest in his own comfortable bed after spending the previous night on the hard bunk at the surgery. He grimaced as he remembered it would be more than one more night ensconced at the quarry. *Damn the man,* he thought again as he remembered the reasons for his less than stellar accommodations. Then he recalled his appointment with Peter and hurried to get ready to leave. Striding into the kitchen he opened the door and shouted for his groom, ordering the man to saddle his horse. After hastily eating his breakfast, he left instructions with his housekeeper and left. Entering the stable, he gave further orders to his groom as he fastened his saddle bags to his mount. The steed danced impatiently and Langley gave the animal its head as he rode away. The agent enjoyed the animal's spirit as the horse galloped over the rocky ground and allowed himself to feel pleasure in the ride, ignoring the distasteful reasons for it.

Before long the steed had given way to a quick canter and Langley was able to take in his surroundings. The early morning air was crisp and fresh and the sunrise painted the skies a rosy hue as he rode along. The agent allowed himself to take pleasure in nature's glory, putting the trials of the days ahead on a back burner in his mind. A good night's sleep and a decent breakfast had put him in a slightly better humour, even as the challenges confronting him danced merrily on the periphery, threatening to destroy his peace. The thought of spending too many more nights at the quarry gave him the impetus to meet those challenges as quickly as humanly possible. Langley noted the freighter still anchored in the bay as he rode into the quarry. He had barely seated himself at the desk in the captain's hut when Josiah appeared.

"We should be finished loading that freighter later today," the pit boss reported, "just thought I'd check in with ye to see if ye had any further orders."

"Ye can carry on. I would like ye to take care of the paperwork when it's loaded. I will be here if ye have any questions. It t'will be good to have ye trained in case yer needed in future," Langley replied. "Tis always good to be prepared for any eventuality. Gallo should have taught ye the rudiments long ago. Ye can go about yer business. I'll be here if ye need further instruction."

"I'll take care of it, sir," Josiah promised, "It ain't near as difficult as I'd been given to think." His head bobbed and he turned on his heel to leave.

Mere minutes later Peter appeared and Langley waved him to the chair in front of the desk. "The papers can wait," he told him, "There is more urgent business to handle and that is finding a more suitable arrangement to keep Gallo in hand until I can arrange his one-way voyage to England." Langley then told Peter about his visit to town and his fruitless mission to find gaol and gaoler to hold his prisoner.

"There is a man ye may be able to hire to act as guard," Peter informed him. "He was once employed here at the quarry. He's rather limited as to what work he can do due to an injury he sustained at a logging camp. He seems like a good choice for a guard. The man seems honest and has no great love fer Gallo. Harry White's his name. I don't know where he lives but several of the men do. But that doesn't solve the issue of where to hold 'im. Ye may have to keep 'im locked in that root cellar until he can be transported."

"Trouble is the house is in ruins and with the weather getting colder there is no suitable place for a guard to stay," Langley replied. "There's the barn but it isn't weather-tight."

"The man was staying in a loggin' camp. I don't know if ye have ever visited one but I have. The accommodations are sparse at best. I bet ye could fix up a spot in the barn that would meet the man's needs," Peter answered. "As far as I can see, that would be the best solution to the problem."

"It needs to be done forthwith," Langley spoke thoughtfully, "That man, Paddy, has been watching 'im but we need 'im back at the quarry. He told me that Jake is a talented woodworker. Could be he could fix up a place in the barn for a guard to lay his head."

"I know the man. He operates the crusher," Peter nodded, "No doubt he's hard at it with that freighter being loaded."

Langley stood suddenly, "One moment," he said and hurried through the door. "Picton!" He shouted out, "I need ye here fer a moment."

Josiah hurried over, "Yes, boss, what is it?" he asked.

"Tell that man, Jake, to come see me. Take over on the crusher while I have a word with him," Langley ordered.

Jake was surprised to be summoned to the captain's shack. Nerves were jumping as he wondered what it could mean. He tapped timidly on the door before opening it to peer inside. "Ye sent fer me?" he asked as he stood in the open doorway.

"Yes, man, come in, come in," Langley barked impatiently. "I have a project I need to discuss with ye. Can ye accompany me to the top of the hill to the company house at day's end?"

"Yes, but what's going on? What do ye want with me there?" Jake questioned.

"There's a couple of things. I've been told ye have a talent fer woodworking and building. I need ye to look over the damages to the house and tell me if ye can do repairs there. But there's something I need done right away. I need ye to have a look at the barn and tell me if ye can create a makeshift place for a body to eat and sleep," Langley responded, "It won't have to be fancy, just something to keep the wind and rain out. I'd like ye to start on it right away. It has to be habitable tonight, if possible."

Jake nodded slowly; relief was evident in his face as he considered. "Ye want to go right after work? Tis my friend, Paddy up there with the cap'n. I had to go there anyway to return his horse and wagon," Jake divulged.

"That's fine, then. I will meet ye there. Ye can go on back to work now," Langley dismissed him.

Jake was taken aback at the agent's abrupt manner and gave a quick nod before turning to go back to his job.

Peter regarded Langley through hooded eyes, "Well, ye are decisive, ain't ye?"

"I haven't the time to be dealing with guards and guard houses. The sooner this is settled to my satisfaction, the better," Langley retorted. "Now, to find someone to hunt down this White fellow and set him up in the barn. I will rest easier once that bit of business is taken care of."

"I am at yer disposal," Peter commented, "Ye have yer hands full, I can see. If you give me leave to have a word with a couple of the men, I will get directions to Harry's place and bring him back here, if I find him."

"That would be an immense help," Langley remarked, "It seems I will be indebted to ye on many levels."

"It is rather ironic how our paths seem to continue crossing" Peter said wryly. "I'll be off then and hopefully will return with Harry."

"I thank you, sincerely, for your assistance," Langley rejoined, "I am in yer debt."

"It is also in my interest to see Gallo is kept contained until he can be sent back to face charges," Peter replied, waving away the agents' thanks, "Hopefully my mission will be successful."

Peter left the shack and walked slowly toward the quarry's center where men labored away. It wasn't long before he spied Charlie and walked quickly to where he worked to fill yet another cart with limestone. The din was such Charlie did not hear Peter hailing him until he stood nearly at his elbow.

"Hullo! Strange to see ye here!" Charlie exclaimed as he stuck the spade into the pile of limestone.

Peter explained his mission and need to locate Harry and after receiving directions made his way back to the cookhouse where he'd tied his mare. Within minutes he was mounted and riding away.

Peter followed Charlie's directions and was soon knocking on the door of the little cottage where Harry was living. He was confident he would find the man at home at this midmorning hour. Harry came to the door where Peter had been left to wait. He wore a perplexed expression as he greeted the man he'd only met briefly once before.

"What brings ye 'ere? I thought yer business with the association was done," Harry remarked.

"It is. I came to see if I might interest ye in a position that needs filling immediately," Peter replied. "I suppose ye heard about the fire in the company house?"

"Yis, it was more excitement than we've 'ad round 'ere in some time," Harry countered. "What type of work is it? Me ribs are not entirely mended. I can't do no manual labour."

"I think ye'd be able to handle this. It only requires sharp eyes and ears and the ability to handle a weapon, if need be," Peter replied. "Why don't ye step outside and I can explain."

Harry nodded and stepped out onto the open porch.

"T'would be easy money," Peter remarked when he finished explaining, "Ye need to come with me to see the company's agent if yer interested. I don't know how much he plans to pay ye. Ye will have to work that out with Langley. I think the job is yers fer the taking if ye want it."

"Seems like an answer to a prayer," Harry confided, "But I have neither way to get there 'cept me own two legs."

"Are ye well enough to walk it? Ye worked at the quarry before. Ye know where to go?" Peter questioned.

"Yis, I can walk it and I knows it only too well," Harry retorted.

"Come to the captain's shack when ye arrive. I will let the agent know ye're on yer way," Peter told him.

"Thank ye fer comin' and fer thinkin' of me fer the job," Harry said as he offered his hand to shake.

"All I did was offer yer name, the rest is up to ye and Langley," Peter remarked as they shook hands.

"All the same, I am much obliged," Harry replied.

Peter nodded and turned away to mount his mare. He took his time as he walked the mare through the field and around a bend in the road. There, he dismounted and bending over vomited into the grass. He had to wait several moments before the dizziness allowed him to continue his mission.

Langley was gratified to learn Peter had arranged for Harry to come and he rubbed his hands in anticipation.

"I know I asked ye to come help me go over these books," he said, "that dang man has caused me more trouble than enough. Now I need to see the cook to make up a food hamper to feed guard and guarded. I'm afraid I will have to leave the rest of it until I get all this straightened out," he apologized. "I'd hoped to have Gallo brought into town but there is no gaol there to imprison him so it looks like he will have to stay in the root cellar until I arrange to move him to the city. It's more worry than he's worth."

"Will the company help make all the arrangements?" Peter asked.

"That is my hope," Langley confided, "I've sent letters outlining the events here in the quarry as well as Gallo's attempt on yer life. I could not list the depth of thievery he's committed here in the quarry but I intimated my suspicions. Once I have searched through the paperwork, I will be able to give the owners a more complete report. The fact that he tried to burn down the company house should be enough reason for them to them to do what is necessary to bring him to the city. The telegram I received said as much."

"Let's hope they move quickly," Peter replied. "I have spoken with Reverend McGrath and he is willing to write up testimony and witness signatures, including yers."

"I forget ye have training in the law," Langley remarked, "I see ye have given much consideration to what is legally required."

"I have indeed," Peter agreed, "the man does not deserve to live in polite society."

"I suppose I will have to make myself available to the churchman," Langley sighed, "one more task to be completed."

"All that is needed is for ye to write yer testimony, date it, and have the minister witness yer signature," Peter explained. "Ye can write yer testimony at yer leisure but the sooner the better so all documents can be sent together in one packet. I need all the men who were involved in hunting and arresting Gallo to give their testimony as well. Reverend McGrath is willing to record their words. Would ye be willing to allow each of them to leave work early to get it done? It would only mean one man at a time so it shouldn't leave the quarry short-handed."

Langley rubbed his face as he considered. "I will let Picton know I have given certain men leave to finish work early. It won't be today. That freighter has to be loaded first. It should be finished by end of day."

"That's fine, I think," Peter agreed, "the pastor cannot write more than one at a time and if the men could leave here soon after the noon break that should serve well."

"I will write a list of the men's names and see that the pit boss takes care of it," Langley said. "Which men were involved with yer incident?"

"Hank, Vic, and Jake," Peter told him.

"That's the same men who helped capture Gallo after the fire," Langley replied, "and a few others. It's not so long a list as I'd feared."

"I had hoped to speak with ye about it and then the fire had ye hoppin'," Peter replied. "I took it on myself to ask the minister

455

to write all testimony, including those to do with the fire. Initially it was only the three depositions but Gallo's made the list longer."

"Gallo is a huge thorn in my side. I will be relieved to wash my hands of 'im," Langley spat venomously.

"Ye have my sympathy," Peter empathized, "He has made life difficult for many and has been doing so fer years, what with stealing the wages of hard-working men."

"He will pay fer all his crimes. Ye can count on that," Langley vowed, "I have to ask ye pardon now, I do have to get other, practical, arrangements made."

Peter stood, "Remember, I also have men of high station I can call upon. If ye run into any difficulty arranging Gallo's transport to the city please call on me."

"It wouldn't hurt fer ye to write those letters now," Langley responded, "the sooner the wheels of justice begin to roll the better. I cannot be certain the company will act swiftly and speed is of the essence if we want him on a ship bound fer England."

"It will be my pleasure," Peter said grimly, "I will leave ye to yer tasks, then. As I've told ye before, if ye need me give Hank a message. He will see I get it."

"Good day to ye, sir. Thank ye fer all yer assistance. I best get down to the cookhouse before that man, Harry, arrives."

"I will walk with ye, I tied my mare to the post there," Peter replied.

Chapter

65

Jake was waiting at the gate when Langley appeared on horseback with Harry walking by his side.

"Jake, this here's Harry White," Langley introduced the stranger, "he will be taking over guarding the prisoner. Would ye mind giving him a lift in yer wagon? I'm sure Paddy will be happy to be relieved of his burden."

"Yis, of course," Jake stammered, surprised at the sudden change in plans.

"One more thing," the agent continued, "There are food hampers at the cookhouse I need delivered up to the house. Do ye mind putting 'em aboard yer wagon?"

"Not at all, boss," Jake responded, "Hop on up here, Harry. Meet ye up on the hill?" Jake asked the agent. At Langley's nod Jake turned the wagon toward the cookhouse.

Conversation was sparse between the two men as Jake headed toward the remains of the company house. Jake was worn out from the long work day and secretly musing about Langley's expectations of him and Harry likewise was deep in thought. Paddy had been busy and there was a pile of burned lumber outside the house. Smokey took to straining on the rope that tethered her, leaping and barking her excited welcome to Jake as he drove the wagon toward the barn. Langley's steed had galloped ahead and was already in a stable when Jake arrived. He dropped down from the wagon and walked over to the dog, patting her head and sternly commanding her to be quiet. Paddy and the agent were inside the house and Jake and Harry followed their voices to the building. Jake tapped on the side of the burned-out doorway calling, "We're here, boss."

"Come on in here, Jake," Langley invited, "Ye may as well have a look at this first."

Jake stepped carefully over the floorboards, being cautious to avoid spots where the floor boards were burned badly; the earth beneath was easily in view. Harry waited outside.

"Paddy was just tellin' me how ye did all the repairs on yer own home and the wonderful job ye made of it," the agent reported.

"It ain't much but it's comfortable and warm," Jake replied, modestly.

"Now ain't a time to be humble," Paddy retorted, "the man wants a skilled craftsman, not a rough carpenter."

Jake made no answer as his keen eyes took in the damages all around him. He walked slowly through the wreck Gallo had made of the home, his eyes taking in every nook and cranny.

"Well, what do ye think? Must it all be torn down or can ye make repairs?" Langley asked.

"'Tis not so bad as I feared. The old kitchen and bedroom will need to be torn off and rebuilt but the rest of 'er is sound," Jake replied.

"Yer friend here has also been bragging about yer fine furniture," Langley remarked, "the place will need work benches fer the kitchen, a sideboard, shelves and such, as well as furniture."

"I can make anythin' ye may want or need," Jake said confidently, "I can make it plain or as fancy as ye'd like. That's up to ye."

"Let's see what ye can do with the barn first. That will give me something to judge yer work by," Langley suggested. "Come, see."

Langley led the way back outside and over to the barn. Harry followed, waiting for the agent to give him instructions.

"I tole 'im ye could do somethin' in that corner, there," Paddy suggested, pointing.

"That would be the best spot, the boards are closer together and not so much wind can get in," Jake agreed.

"Can ye make it sound enough fer Harry to keep warm?" Langley asked.

Jake looked around the building, "We could use hay to make a bed but I'd need to go home fer a few tools. Could use some of them boards that ain't so badly scorched to cover any cracks, help keep the wind out, and to make a bed frame. It'd be rough but it would keep 'im off the ground, away from the chill."

"Harry? How does all that sound to ye?" Langley asked turning to his new employee.

"I slept in much worst in the loggin' camp," Harry admitted, "A few pine boughs on top of the bunk would make a fine bed. Only other thing I needs is a blanket or two. Per'aps a pot to make tea and somethin' to drink it out of."

"There's sure to be blankets in the house. We'll have a look before I leave, as fer cups and stuff, I had the cook pack anything ye may need to make meals." the agent answered.

Langley turned suddenly when Gallo's mare neighed, "Where the devil did that horse come from?"

"Tis Gallo's mare," Paddy reminded him, "I've been feeding 'er but she could do with a bit of exercise. Jake said she came up lame when the cap'n was trying to get away after he set that fire."

"I'd completely forgotten fer a moment," Langley said as he walked to the stable that held her. "She's a fine animal. Jake, ye're a man of many talents. Have ye checked her over since?"

Jake shook his head as he approached, "No, she needed a good rest. I figure she hurt 'er leg steppin' in a hole on that caribou trail. The cap'n had ridden 'er hard and no doubt took little notice she'd been hurt until she couldn't go on."

"Paddy was tellin' me how ye have neither horse nor wagon," Langley replied, "Gallo never deserved so fine a beast. Could be we could work something out in trade. Is she lame? Might be she's not worth much."

Jake pushed the mare away as he opened the stall door, "She's a beauty." He stroked the mare's nose and head before moving along her side to the leg she'd injured. He gently felt along the mare's knee and foreleg, searching for signs of swelling. "She's a site better than she was but she shouldn't be saddled up for at least another week. Tis hard to know how bad it is until the swelling's all gone."

"I took 'er out and walked 'er around a bit this morning," Paddy told Jake, "She's still favoring that leg a little."

"It will take a while to heal," Jake said again, "can't say how long or even if it will heal."

"Would ye be willin' to look after 'er for a while, until I figure out what to do with 'er?" Langley asked Jake, "Ye have a barn don't ye?"

"Yes, I do," Jake replied, still stroking the mare's forelock. "Taking care of 'er t'would be a joy."

"Good. That's settled then," Langley replied. "And ye can fix things up fer Harry, here, tonight?"

"If ye don't mind if I go home first to eat and attend to my animals," Jake answered, "I need to fetch a few tools anyway."

"Seems fair to me," Langley replied. He walked over to his steed and reaching into his saddle bag retrieved a pistol he'd stored there. "Gallo's been locked in that cellar fer a couple of days. Guess I should let 'im out to use the outhouse and fer a bit of air. Ye two can go on," he told Jake and Paddy, but first off, get them food hampers off the wagon." The agent then turned toward his new employee. "Harry, I need to talk to ye about guarding the prisoner.

Paddy and Jake wrestled the heavy hampers off the wagon and placed them in the barn as Harry followed the agent to the root cellar. Jake placed bit and halter on the mare and led her outside where he tied her to the back of the wagon.

"Ye don't mind giving me a lift home do ye?" he smirked as he turned toward Paddy.

"Not if I can snag a supper from Mary," Paddy grinned in return. "May as well take the saddle as well," Paddy said lifting it from the side of the stall.

"I don't know about that," Jake worried, "Mr. Langley didn't mention anything about that."

"I mentioned it when we were chatting earlier," Paddy grinned again, "he'd tell ye to take it if he were here." Jake's face betrayed his worry. "Look, if ye're that bothered we can wait til he comes back, or ye can go see him yerself tomorrow and tell him ye 'ave it to exercise 'er once 'er leg's well enough. He did ask ye to take care of 'er and ye'll need a saddle if ye wants to ride 'er."

"Yis, okay, that makes sense, I guess," Jake said, doubtfully.

"Ye worries too much! Come on, let's go," Paddy replied, "if ye are coming back here to work on that bed fer Harry we need to get going."

Jake went to retrieve his dog before climbing onto the wagon seat, he sat Smokey beside him.

"She's some good dog," Paddy commented, ruffling the dog's fur before turning his attention to driving the wagon. "It will be good to see Mary and thank 'er myself for the chow."

"She'll be happy to see ye," Jake replied, "she was right worried about ye guarding the cap'n."

The two men had plenty to chat about as they made the short journey to Jake's house. Back at the company house Langley and Harry approached the root cellar.

"There's likely to be a stench, he's had to use a corner for his bathroom," Langley warned.

Harry said nothing as Langley removed the board that served as lock and key. The door swung open and Langley stepped inside, pistol in hand.

"Lift the hatch, ye'll need to put that ladder down to let 'im climb out," the agent ordered. "Gallo, ye can come up, just ye remember I have a pistol here and I ain't afraid to use it on ye!"

Gallo stepped back as Harry lowered the ladder. He eagerly grabbed the rough wood and began to climb. "Wait!" Langley ordered. "I am only going to tell ye once, I don't want to hear a word out of ye or this will be yer one and only outing. Ye understand me?" Gallo paused on the ladder; the agent's command coupled with the sunlight flooding the darkness made him feel disoriented.

"Did ye not hear me?" Langley growled again. He was satisfied to hear Gallo's sullen 'yes'.

Harry backed up through the door as Gallo ascended. Langley held his pistol on his prisoner and waited until Gallo reached the top before backing away and out the door. Gallo stood hesitantly, shading his eyes from the sun.

"Ye got two minutes to use the outhouse and then ye're going back in there," Langley's voice rasped out. "Come on, let's go," the agent waved his pistol in the direction he wanted Gallo to go. "Go open the door fer 'im," he ordered Harry. Harry hurried to do as Langley commanded, shocked at the dirty and disheveled appearance of the former captain. Gallo grasped the door and closed it in Langley's face with a sneer. Harry stepped away and picked up a short, thick stick laying in the grass.

"Just in case," he told Langley by way of explanation.

"Ye will need somebody with ye to take him to the outhouse, don't try this when ye're here alone with him," the agent warned, "the man can't be trusted."

"Per'aps I can find a bucket fer 'im to do 'is business in," Harry answered. "I'll 'ave a look around. I don't expect there will be many visits from ye."

"I will be stopping by to check on things," the agent answered, "but I can't promise it will be often."

"That's what ye got me 'ere fer," Harry replied, "to be 'is guard and make sure 'e is fed and whatnot."

Langley did not respond but stood gravely waiting for Gallo to finish his toilet. After waiting a few moments longer, the agent pounded on the door, "Time's up, come on out here," he said sternly.

"I ain't done," Gallo called back.

"I got this pistol and bullets will make it through wood easy enough," Langley spoke conversationally, "could be one hits ye in the leg, could be one hits a mite higher, can't tell where a bullet will meet with flesh, especially blind like I am."

"I'm comin' out now," Gallo cried, "don't be shootin' that thing." The door slowly creaked open and the captain took a hesitant step outside.

"Not another word, get going," Langley waved his pistol again and the trio marched quietly to the root cellar. "Once he's down there, pull the ladder out," he told Harry. "Be a good lad and we'll be back with water and food fer ye," he advised Gallo, "give us yer bucket fer water."

Harry pulled the ladder out of the hole and then leaned down to grasp the bucket Gallo held up. Langley continued to train his weapon on the captain until Harry dropped the hatch closing the captive in once again.

The two men were a fair distance from the root cellar before the agent spoke again. "Ye will have to bring him food and water twice a day, in the morning and again at supper time. Don't ever, ever let him talk ye into dropping that ladder down fer any reason. Is that clear?"

"Yes, I understand," Harry replied, "e don't seem dangerous to me but I won't take no chances."

Langley stopped walking and looked Harry in the eye, "I don't expect no trouble but ye must know, I will hold ye responsible if he were to escape. Ye have to be watching every move he makes. He's already tried to kill a man besides stealing from the company and burning down the house."

"Nobody told me nuddin' 'bout 'im trying to kill a man," Harry grunted, "I see why ye 'ave 'im locked in that cellar now."

"Make no mistake, if ye give him half a chance he will turn on ye," Langley warned again. "Are ye sure ye're up to the job?"

"I give ye me word, the cap'n will stay in that root cellar unless ye give orders otherwise," Harry vowed.

"Fine then. What say we have a look for blankets and anything else ye may need in the house?" Langley offered. "I'm sure ye're wanting yer supper as am I. Let's do that and then I will leave ye to it."

The two men rifled through the undamaged rooms searching for anything the agent thought would be of use. They entered the barn carrying blankets and assorted items, including a pail Harry deemed worthy of receiving Gallo's bodily fluids.

"I'd offer ye the use of the house," Langley told Harry, but I'd say the winds will rip through them open walls worst than through the walls of the barn."

"I'm fine with the barn, like I told ye, I slept in far worse in loggin' camps," Harry reassured his new boss. "At least in there it will be nice and quiet – no men snoring and keepin' me from me rest." He joked.

"I will try to return again tomorrow, but I cannot make any promises," Langley said, "the cook packed enough food fer ye fer several days. I will make sure to come back long before it runs out."

"Thanks, boss, that's fine, more than fine, really," Harry gushed.

"One more thing," Langley reached into his pocket and pulled out his pistol, "I will leave this with ye. Make sure Gallo knows yer armed any time ye have to enter the root cellar."

Harry reached out and took the weapon. "I ain't ever used one of these," he confessed, "tis a pretty little piece of iron, ain't it?"

"Pull the trigger all the way back," the agent instructed, "see, there, that's where the bullets go in." Langley spent a further few minutes making sure Harry knew how to use the weapon before striding to his horse to make his departure. "Ye can bring the prisoner some grub after ye've eaten yerself. Just make sure ye keep the pistol with ye."

Chapter

66

The cleric wiped the nib of his quill and laid it on the desk. *Do not judge, lest ye be judged,* he told himself and sighed. It had been a long week between taking depositions and dealing with his regular duties in the little parish. His work in writing out the men's testimony led him to return again and again to his early life in the ministry and caused a flood of memories. It had been his first position and he'd been sent to a very poor section of the city.

Nobody in the small community knew of McGrath's early ministry in the city where he'd first encountered the young trouble maker who would find his way to the quarry and fill such an important position. He had denied knowing the mining captain when Peter Parson had come calling and, in truth, he no longer knew the man but only the child he'd once been.

Suffer the little children and forbid them not, McGrath thought as reminisces took him back to the dirty hovel that was Gallo's home as a child. *That child seen more suffering and abuse than any body I've ever known,* McGrath thought, *and there's truth to the adage, as the twig is bent, so the tree's inclined.* The minister remembered sadly all the conditions of young Gallo's life: the cruel poverty; the absence of a father and a mother who was worn out by life and too sick and sad to give the lad any proper guidance.

Gallo was only seven years old when she died. *Tis not all so simple as that,* McGrath lectured himself, *there's many who have grown up in such states and did not turn to foul means to make a living.* The cleric allowed himself to indulge his memories a little longer. *Tis only the Almighty that knows a man's heart and what makes such a one turn so evil and dangerous. There's naught to do but leave them all in the Lord's hands, the good, the bad, and the indifferent.*

The minister knew that had he shared his knowledge of Gallo's youth and the stories he'd heard of him procuring young homeless boys for men with sick appetites it would go badly for the mining captain. He felt it was his duty to keep such knowledge to himself. He had intimated enough and felt guilty for divulging the little he had. *After all,* he told himself, *it t'was only gossip. Tis a mystery how some go astray and others rise above and become decent, hard-working folk. Ah well, all I can do is pray for his soul,* the churchman thought as he pushed his chair back.

His thoughts then flew to Peter, and Gallo's most recent victims. The men had come one by one to get their testimony recorded and, as McGrath had hoped, Samuel Brown, his friend and fellow cleric had arrived just in time to bear witness to the signatures, including McGrath's. Brown's arrival was a boon in many ways, not least of all the way he'd listened to all McGrath's worries and fears concerning the former mining captain. He was not at liberty to discuss Gallo's past wrongs nor his family life, if it could be called that. Brown could not know the horror stories he related to him were, in fact, stories of Gallo's early life. It had helped him a lot to get some of that man's history off his chest, though he never named him. *Time to see to my guest and leave such morbid thought aside!*

A knock on his door surprised the cleric. It was getting near his supper time and he hadn't expected anyone. He opened his door to a tall, well-dressed stranger who stood holding a sheaf of papers in his hand.

"How can I help ye?" he asked the hawk-nosed man.

The man shuffled his feet uncomfortably on the step, "Name's Langley, t'was told to bring ye my papers to witness and sign. Sorry to come unannounced, I hope it's not a bother to ye," the agent answered.

"No, not a'tall," McGrath replied, "I wasn't sure when to expect ye, but Parsons told me ye'd come by, so yer visit is not entirely unexpected. I wasn't sure the hour or the day is all. Why don't ye come on in to my study and we'll take care of it."

Langley followed the diminutive figure through the rectory, his eyes taking in the comfortable, if humble, surroundings.

"If ye will have a seat here I will return directly. I need to call my associate to witness both our signatures, won't take but a moment," the minister invited.

Langley poured his lanky form into the chair facing the large wooden desk and glanced about the room. It was rather sparse with nothing but a few chairs and crowded with the over-sized table that served as the cleric's desk. His fingers tapped impatiently on the wood surface as he waited. It wasn't long before McGrath returned with an average-looking man in tow. His collar announcing his position long before McGrath made his introductions.

"Let's get right to this business, shall we?' McGrath asked after introducing Brown, "I'm sure ye're a busy man and will be glad to get this taken care of."

Langley placed his pile of papers on the table and shuffled them until the final page was on top. "I believe all is in order. Peter described how it should be organized and now all that is left is to sign and date it," Langley explained.

The trio took care of all the legal requirements and allowed the ink to dry as they engaged in small talk about the weather and other incidental topics. Langley was not given to socializing with churchmen and was anxious to make his exit.

"Ye wouldn't be the son of Lawrence Langley by any chance?" Brown asked idly.

"No, but I am related. Lawrence Langley is my uncle," the agent revealed, "Do ye know him well?"

"Not at all, but the church in St. John's was his most fortunate beneficiary," Brown answered, "thanks to yer uncle the mission of the church was able to continue."

"Yes, my family has been great believers in supporting the church," Langley said warily, waiting for the sure to come entreaty for monies.

"I suppose you have all ye need now to send to the naval authority," McGrath said, changing the subject. It surprised Langley when no request for monetary aid was made.

"We do. All that is left is to have Gallo sent to the city to be transferred to England," Langley replied. "That is proving to be something of a challenge."

"I happen to know about a mission to oversee the medical and spiritual health of fishermen around this island," Brown announced, "there is a possibility your prisoner could be sent back to the city aboard one of their hospital ships. There should be one returning to the city in the near future. I could make enquiries if ye wish."

"Yes, the Royal National Mission, I wasn't aware they came this far south," Langley replied, "It was my understanding that these ships mainly sailed north-west up around the Northern Peninsula and along the coast of Labrador."

"That is true," Brown admitted, "but they have made exceptions and, if need be, will alter their route. I have sailed on several voyages with them."

"That would be a most welcome favor," Langley replied, "I have been waiting for Dominion Limestone to make arrangements but soon the last of the naval ships will be returning to England and time is passing quickly. We have been holding him in a root cellar on company property, but winter is coming and I would be most grateful to have him taken off my hands."

"I will write a letter to the church in St. John's, they have been instrumental in donating both financially and morally to the mission," Brown explained, "which is how I ended up sailing with them a time or two."

"Would he be kept secure until he can be handed over to the naval authority?" Langley enquired.

"The ships' main focus is to minister to fishermen," Brown explained, "I cannot speak to how they would secure a prisoner but I can testify to the goodwill and care for all souls."

"You will forgive me if I am reluctant to consider such a plan," Langley answered as he gathered up his papers, "Gallo's health, whether physical or spiritual is none of my concern. My only objective is to have the rascal tried at the Queen's bench for all his crimes."

"God works in mysterious ways," Brown responded, "it could be his voyage to the city will be an occasion for the Almighty to reach his troubled soul whilst at the same time relieving ye of yer burden."

"I will be more than happy to have him taken off my hands but ye must understand the company that employs me wants the man prosecuted to the fullest extent of the law, as do I. I cannot risk the scoundrel escaping in the process of having him moved," Langley argued.

"I do accept that the man must be held to account fer his wrong doings," Brown agreed, "I am not saying he will be loosely held, just that I do not know what accommodations they can make to keep him bound and secure. It depends on many variables such as the amount of room left in the hold of a ship that may be loaded with fish as well as medical supplies."

"It would be worthwhile to look into the possibility," McGrath pointed out, "After all, as ye say, winter is coming and the alternative would mean waiting for spring, which is long months away."

Langley nodded solemnly, "An enquiry cannot go astray. If it is even possible it must be considered. I would be most grateful for your assistance."

"I will write to my superiors in the city. Perhaps ye would be so kind as to send a telegram? That would be the quickest way to discover if there's even a hospital ship in the vicinity of the West coast," Brown asked.

"I would be happy to send a telegram, that is most wise of ye," Langley replied, "if ye wish to write it I will have my clerk bring it to the telegraph office as soon as I get to town."

McGrath went to a shelf where he kept his correspondence supplies and returned with a blank sheet of paper. "Here ye go," he said offering the paper to Brown.

Brown sat on the chair Langley had so recently vacated and dashed off the few lines enquiring about the location of the hospital ship and the possibility of it making port nearby to pick up a couple of passengers.

"Should it not include information regarding the prisoner?" Langley asked, reading over the cleric's shoulder.

"Let's first find out if there is even a remote possibility of it anchoring here," Brown replied, "it need not be detailed at this point."

"You make a fair point," Langley remarked, "I need to check on things at my office in town within the next day or two. If ye have the letter ready I can bring it to the post master while I am there. I do not mean to prevail upon yer kindness but as I've said time is of the essence."

"I will write it this very evening. If ye wish ye may stop by at any point on the morrow to pick it up and this telegram with it," Brown replied, "I am happy to be of assistance."

"I am in yer debt," Langley responded, "and yers as well," he said turning to Reverend McGrath holding out his hand.

McGrath enclosed the proffered hand in both of his, "I am glad to be of service. May I ask about the health and well-being of yer prisoner? After all, despite his many crimes he is still a child of God."

Langley gazed into the compassionate eyes of the preacher as he disengaged his hand, "He is well. I have seen that his needs for shelter, food and drink are met. I may appear to be hard-hearted, sir, but I will not abuse the prisoner in any way. You may rest easy in that regard." McGrath gave a simple nod of his head in understanding.

"I will have the letter ready for ye tomorrow," Brown promised again.

Langley tipped his hat to the two men, "I thank ye both and bid ye a good evening. Until the morrow, sirs," and with that farewell Langley made his exit.

Chapter

67

Peter had returned to further scolding from Hilda after his thwarted attempt to go through the paperwork with Langley. The agent had not commented on the younger man's pallor and Peter had not mentioned the dizziness that had assaulted him forcing him to lay his head on his mare's withers. His ride back through the community to his cousin's home had been slow and he'd been forced to stop twice to vomit and to wait for the dizziness to pass. Peter loathed to report any of this to Hilda, fearing she would hasten to curtail his activities.

"I knew ye were in no condition to go anywhere this morn," Hilda fretted, "I should have listened to my own good sense, seeing as ye seem to have none!"

Peter lifted a hand to his forehead, "Please, Hilda, if I might just lay down for a bit, I'm sure it will pass," he begged.

"Ye really are feelin' poorly. Come on into the parlour," Hilda ordered him, "I will close the curtains so ye can rest. The children are out picking berries with Ginny, thank the good Lord, so ye won't be disturbed. Honestly, ye men, worst than children, I swear!"

Peter did not utter a word while Hilda harangued him, he was too weak. He didn't notice the light blanket Hilda laid over him, nor did he see her softly tiptoe out of the room. He was asleep almost as soon as his head touched the pillow. He awoke to intense whispering in the kitchen.

"Hank, I'm tellin' ye, it's much like when my uncle died," Hilda was saying, "he wouldn't listen to sense neither and look where it got 'im!"

"I don't know what more we can do my dear, there ain't no doctor nearby," Hank worried, "and he's a man grown, ye can't be ordering 'im to do this and do that like he's a child."

"The man needs quiet and rest. 'E insisted on going to the quarry, against me own better judgement I let 'im, but, Hank, ye didn't see 'is face when 'e got back. I fear fer 'is life, I really do," Hilda's plaintive tone reached Peter's ears and he felt ashamed for worrying the woman.

Peter slowly sat up and listened to the couple's exchange. *This won't do, I need to get to Uncle John's where I won't be a burden on this family,* he thought. He felt intensely uncomfortable and embarrassed by his obvious weakness. Willing strength to his limbs he slowly stood and waited for the dizziness to return. When it didn't, he began to slowly walk to the kitchen.

"Ye're awake!" Hank's exclamation caused Hilda to stop talking in mid sentence.

"Are ye feelin' any better a'tall?" Hilda jumped from her chair as Peter entered the kitchen.

"I seem to be fine," Peter answered, "I think it's time I made my way to my Uncle's John's. I have overstayed as it is."

"Nonsense!" Hilda proclaimed, raising her voice, "It ain't wise fer ye to go ridin' off anywhere until ye're strong again. If ye would just rest fer a few days ye would regain yer strength."

"There are things that I must see to, not least of which is getting that scallywag moved to the city where he can be shipped off to England," Peter argued.

"I believe Langley has taken it on himself to make those arrangements," Hank pointed out, "Hilda is right, my son, ye needs to rest. A good long rest with no thinking on any of it. Ye won't be no use to no one if ye ends up six feet under."

Peter considered his relations' solemn faces and worried eyes before answering. "Ye cannot go repeating this but Langley asked my help in going over company records. It seems Gallo has been stealing from the company for some time. I promised I would assist him in going through the stacks of paper work."

Hilda shook her head. "Tell me the truth of it. 'Ave ye been 'aving a lot of 'eadaches? 'Ave ye been giddy, like ye could fall over?

'Ave ye felt like ye just consumed a whole bottle of spirits? "Ave ye been throwing up? The truth now," she demanded.

Peter hesitated just long enough that Hilda knew she'd struck the nail on the head. "It's just a bit of dizziness and it passes. I get tired, but it ain't nothing fer ye to be worried about."

"I know ye thinks I'm actin like a mother 'en. I'm tellin' ye, my uncle t'was much the same afore 'e died," Hilda scolded, "the man pushed 'imself too 'ard, too soon, and one day 'e just fell down dead. We knows it was the fall e'd took. We all knows that! Afore 'e took that spill e'd been 'ealthy as a 'orse. So don't ye be tellin' me it ain't serious!"

"Langley is expecting me to meet him at the quarry," Peter protested.

"Whatever the agent needs, it will keep," Hilda insisted, "them papers will still be there when ye're feelin' more yerself!"

"I hate to admit it, but Hilda's right," Hank agreed. "There ain't no use in arguing. I know it's not so quiet here as it t'would be at yer uncle's house, but ye're really in no shape to ride that distance. Tis better to take care and rest here fer just a few more days."

"I also have business to take care of in the city and need to arrange meetings there as soon as I possibly can. I should have been off after the association was formed. People are relying on me," Peter complained.

Hank stood and laid a hand on his shoulder, "If ye really mean to help 'em ye best do as Hilda says and rest a few days. Otherwise ye might not be around to help anyone."

"The blueberries are ripe as are the partridge berries," Hilda commented, "the children will be outside gatherin 'em fer me so they won't be here to make a commotion or bother ye any. Ye will be able to rest. I can promise ye that."

Peter's head dropped in submission. He hated laying about. He liked to use his mind to help others but his experiences earlier in the day gave credence to Hilda's concerns. Hilda sensed his capitulation and swooped in to force her advantage.

"If it tis a comfort to ye, ye can help me a bit around the house – nothing strenuous mind," she said, "no choppin' wood or nuddin' like that but there's plenty of light chores ye can do that t'will be a help."

"I don't want to be a burden to ye," Peter remarked.

"B'y, ye have done so much fer us and fer the men of the quarry," Hank replied earnestly, "ye have been far from a burden. If it weren't fer ye I wouldn't have that bonus and the increase in me wages. It is us who owes ye more than we can ever repay."

"I wanted to do that fer ye. It t'was no trouble a'tall," Peter tried to make light of his efforts on behalf of the quarry labourers.

"Be that as it may, we are beholden to ye," Hank spoke gently, "and this is one way we can give back to ye fer all yer hard work on our behalf."

"Listen to yer cousin," Hilda instructed, "let us take care of ye fer a change."

"I don't see as I've a choice in the matter," Peter admitted, "I will rest as ye want me to, but Hank, could ye let Langley know. Tell him I will come at the first opportunity, as soon as these damned dizzy spells let off."

"Ye need to have at least one full day with no headaches and no giddiness," Hilda warned, "afore ye think ye can go off anywhere."

"I will rest until I feel my strength has fully returned," Peter promised.

"I will take that as yer solemn vow," Hilda replied, "and don't be thinkin' ye can hide it from me. The pallor in yer face gives ye away."

"I will follow yer instructions and do what ye tell me. I do not want to a prolonged recovery. Ye were right, I should have listened to ye, Missus," Peter surrendered. He smiled at the look of relief on Hilda's face. "I am sorry fer worrying ye."

"Why don't ye men sit a spell out on the bridge? I need to get supper on the table without the two of ye underfoot," she spoke gruffly and did not notice the wink Hank gave Peter.

Chapter

68

Harry woke with the sun peeping in through cracks in the barn wall. The wind was up as well, judging by the racket all around him. He grunted and swung his legs off the bunk. He sat for a minute; arms wrapped around his ribs. *I'll be damned glad when this pain stops aggravating me,* he thought as he waited for the pain to subside before standing up.

After a few moments Harry made his way over to the food hampers he'd placed a few feet away. He lifted the lid and retrieved the tin tea pot. The evening before he'd made a fire pit and prepared it for the morning. *First things first,* he thought as he made his way to the outhouse. After using the rough facilities, he walked to the stream.

The wind was pushing him along, blowing through his thin clothing and chilling his bare head. Reaching the stream, he bent to fill the pot and walking against the wind made his way to the fire pit. He had placed it in the lee of a large boulder and a small crop of evergreens in anticipation of foul weather. He set the tea pot aside as he set about lighting a fire to boil water for tea and to cook breakfast. Those tasks done; he placed the tea pot on the flat rock he'd placed in the centre of the flames. The stone would get hot and heat the water.

Harry returned to the barn and rummaged through the food hamper. He retrieved a jar of beans and a packet of hard tack. The cook had surprised him by including a few goodies like the bottle of raspberry jam he was opening. He grunted in pleased anticipation.

Searching through his supplies he found a small saucepan he could use to heat the beans. Balancing the items, he walked over to the little bench and table Jake had made to serve as dining room. Leaving the hard tack and jam on the table he emptied the beans into the saucepan and retraced his steps outside.

The fire was crackling merrily and the wind forced the flames this way and that. Harry sat back on his heels and placed the pot of beans beside the teapot on the rock. He stood and looked about him. Saplings were bending in the wind but the sky was clear and Harry enjoyed the brisk morning air. The wind would calm down later, Harry knew.

I might just fashion a fishing pole and see if I can catch a trout or two fer me supper later, he thought. He glanced over at the root cellar and sighed. He wasn't particularly pleased about playing guard to the captain. He'd never liked the man. *There's something 'bout the man gives me the willies,* he thought, *can't put me finger on it but he's creepy, just plain creepy. And mean, ye can see it in his eyes. Still, tis easy work, all in all. I'll see to 'im after I fill me own belly.*

He looked toward the burned-out structure of the company house with its pile of charred wood beside it. *At least I won't 'ave far to go fer firewood,* he thought, *shame what 'e did though. Looks like it was a fine 'ouse afore Gallo torched it. Never would 'ave taken 'im fer a criminal and a murderer all the same.*

Harry's thoughts swung back to his intermittent work in the quarry and inevitably to the day Joe was injured so badly. He was deep in thought when the teapot began to whistle merrily on it's make-shift stove. Harry bent and moved it to the edge of the stone. He looked forward to a hot cup of tea to warm his bones and he wetted his lips in anticipation of the sweet jam. He stirred the pot of beans with a clean twig he'd prepared and waited for the food to come to a bubble before removing it as well as the teapot.

He'd made sure the firepit would post no danger to the surroundings and placing the food and water on a level bit of ground turned back to grab the bucket of water he'd placed nearby the night before. He put the fire out and walked away to eat his breakfast.

Entering the barn Harry noticed a stray cat lurking near the back wall. *Looks like I 'ave a bit of company* he smiled to himself as he set the breakfast items on the little table. Ignoring the cat, he went about retrieving what he needed from the hamper and was soon pouring hot tea into a metal mug. He lifted it to his mouth and drank deeply of the bitter brew.

Within minutes he was smacking his lips and patting his full stomach. *Simple fare but some good, I won't starve on this gig at least*, he thought back to a certain logging camp he once worked where the food was next to maggoty with rot and unfit to eat.

His eyes followed the cat as it inched toward him, hoping for a morsel of food. "Pssst" he called to the feline and was pleased when it came hesitantly toward him. "There you are," he said scaping a few beans unto the floor, "I saved ye a bit." He dunked the last piece of hard tack into his tea to soften the rock-hard bread and placed it on the floor as well. He laughed as the cat licked at it experimentally and sat back looking up into his face. "Ye don't look no worst fer wear. I 'ope ye stays. I could use a bit of company and every barn needs a cat to keep the mice away." He told the animal. "Go on now, eat it, that's all I gots to give ye."

He watched as the cat began to eat his offerings. "Better look after the prisoner," he told it as he stood up. The cat meowed its pleasure when he bent down to pet it's head and back. "Ye stay 'ere and I'll be back," he told the little creature. He stood a minute longer admiring the mix of colors on the tortoiseshell cat. "I'm gonna call ye Patches," he told it. "Ye stay put, Patches, I won't be long." He laughed at himself, "if anyone were to see me, they'd think I've gone off me rocker."

Harry poured the rest of the beans onto a tin plate and added a piece of the hard tack. He patted his pocket to assure himself he hadn't forgotten the pistol Langley had left with him. "Be right back," he told the cat again.

The wind had died down to a breeze he noted as he walked to the root cellar. There was no noise or anything to indicate the man imprisoned there. Harry laid the plate of food on the ground and moved to open the door. He pulled the pistol from his pocket and picked the plate up.

"Hey, ye, Gallo," he called, setting the plate down before lifting the hatch door, "I gots a bit of grub fer ye. Mind, I got the boss's pistol in hand so don't try nuddin'."

Gallo rose from the pile of hay that served as his bed and came to stand in the shaft of light pouring in from above. "I needs to use the outhouse," he demanded.

"Ye gots a bucket down there to do yer business in. Use that. I gots me orders not to take ye out of there lessen the boss is 'ere wit me," Harry told his prisoner, "Now do ye wants this plate of food or not?"

"For Christ's sakes I needs to take a shite," Gallo complained.

"Shit in the bucket and be careful not to knock it over," Harry suggested, "cuz ye ain't getting' out til the boss is 'ere to say ye can.

"Give me my grub then," Gallo ordered crossly, "and I'll be needing more water."

"I'd be mighty careful of me tone of voice if I was ye," Harry retorted, "ye don't want to aggravate yer keeper."

"Pass down that plate of food," Gallo demanded sulkily, "Even a dog t'would be treated better than this."

Harry leaned over the hole and carefully passed the plate of food as low as he dared.

"Ye should be grateful fer what ye gets after all ye done," Harry told him. "Langley's been right kind in me own opinion."

"Ye can shove yer opinion," Gallo growled as he snatched the plate of food, "What's this? Beans and hard tack again?"

"Why, tis the same food ye give the men what work the quarry day in and day out," Harry pointed out, "Per'aps ye think yer too good fer it, eh?"

Gallo threw the plate against the rock wall causing a huge din and clatter. "I ain't eatin' that slop," he shouted at Harry.

"Tis all the same to me," Harry retorted angrily, "ye can starve if ye wants, that ain't no concern of mine."

"I ain't 'ungry and I tole ye, go get me some water!" Gallo snarled.

"And I tole ye to watch yer frigging tone. Just fer that ye can wait til I'm good and ready. And if ye wants water ye best throw the pail up 'ere," Harry growled back.

Harry jumped when the metal pail sailed past his knees, barely avoiding hitting him. "So that's the way of it, eh? Well, ye can just sit there and stew in yer own juices. Ye might give a thought to the fact that yer every need depends on my good will toward ye. And mister, it ain't lookin' good." Harry slammed the hatch door closed and ignored the shouting comin' from the root cellar as he stomped away.

"God dang waste of food and a waste of me time," Harry spoke aloud. Nobody was around to hear the stream of curse words that rent the air as he walked back to the stream. He filled the pail with water and returned to the cellar. He stood a minute listening to Gallo's raucous rampage before softly placing the pail on the stoop and walking away.

That man ain't doin' 'isself no favors, he thought bitterly as he moved toward the barn. The cat had curled up on his bunk and he moved to sit beside it. "Where did ye come from?" he asked as he stroked the soft fur. "People could learn a thing or two from ye dumb beasts," he told it. "Ye knows enough not to bite the 'and that feeds ye, don't ye?" Harry sat petting the cat and letting his temper calm down.

"Fer two pins I'd tell Langley to find someone else to do this dirty job," he told Patches, "But see, it's like this, me damned ribs ain't 'ealed yet so I'm stuck 'tween a rock and a 'ard place."

The cat continued to purr as he stroked her. After several minutes Harry stood and walked over to his table where he gathered pot, plate, and utensils to take to the stream to clean them. It was hours later before he decided enough time had elapsed and Gallo might be a tad more civil. *I'll bring 'im 'is water, but I ain't givin' 'im another bite to eat 'til supper time,* he told himself.

As he suspected Gallo was suitably subdued when he opened the hatch to lower the pail of water.

Gallo came to stand in the light and reached up to take the pail of water, which slopped over the top, soaking his chest. Though he jumped backward at the sudden shock of cold water he merely uttered a curse and put the bucket down beside him.

"I ain't got but the two plates so if ye wants supper later ye better toss up that plate," Harry told Gallo and stood back from the opening.

The plate came sailing through the mouth of the cellar without incident.

"That's better," Harry said, "smart move on yer part. Make sure yer a deal more civil when I comes back wit yer supper. I ain't about to put up wit no shit from the likes of ye."

Gallo made no response and Harry dropped the hatch door back in place.

Chapter

69

Gallo had spent another miserable night curled up in the corner of his earthen prison. He was grateful for the straw he'd fashioned into a bed, but there was little comfort in his confinement. His moods swung back and forth between abject misery and boiling rage. He planned again and again how he would take revenge on Langley, Parsons, and several of his former employees. Worst of all were the nightmares that dogged his sleep, returning him to his bitter childhood and all the abuse he'd suffered. It had been long years since he'd remembered the incidents. Before the events following Joe's death, he had thought he'd banished the past forever. Now it came back to haunt him and he'd torn out many clumps of hair when he'd been in the throes of his night terrors.

The former mining captain paced his prison cell repeatedly. Though he had searched over and over he could find no weakness in the cellar that would allow his escape. He cursed the men who'd built it and cursed his ill luck in being caught out in his mad moment of aiming that sharp pebble at Peter's mare. Again, and again, he laid the blame for his follies at the feet of others. Jake came often to mind. The man was too alike in size and body type to the man who had once used Gallo as his own personal plaything. Shame filled his entire being as the memory came unbidden one more time. And with it came the impotent rage that, even after decades, Gallo could not expel. It was Jake's misfortune that he triggered that rage in the mining captain.

Gallo remembered again that day Jake had come to the captain's shack to confess to letting the cart get away from him. There was something in the man's stance that reminded Gallo again of that other man. *That was the left leg of the devil, that was,* Gallo thought, *as hateful and evil as Lucifer hisself.* His pacing continued as he sought to exorcise his memories. But the memories came like the caplin in spring – great waves of them, one after another, after another.

Gallo remembered his mother prostrate on the floor, weeping and begging the man to let them stay in the hovel they'd called home. There was but one room and it was as cold and drafty as a shanty in the winter.

She'd been unable to find work washing and cleaning fer the rich folk after the family she'd worked for denounced her as a thief. They had no money and no food when the man had come with his threats to put them out in the cold until they paid up the rent. His mother's only sin was her naive honesty and lack of schooling. Though she denied any wrong doing the folk she worked for would not believe her and cast her out. And there she was groveling before the man who could take away the only home Gallo had ever known.

She died not long after that and Gallo was well and truly alone in the world and at the mercies of that man. Gallo refused to name him, even in his own thoughts. It was as if by denying the man a name he could deny he ever existed. He was certain the man had somehow been reincarnated in Jake's body, so much was Jake like him, even down to the color of his eyes and hair. It was uncanny, and, deeply disturbing.

I'd been in my cups the day I 'ired 'im. Thought it was the devil 'imself come back. Thought I could teach 'im a lesson, Gallo remembered, *thought I could finally 'ave a bit of pay back for all the 'ell 'e put me through. But it t'weren't 'im, just a carbon copy of 'im.* Gallo sat on the straw and banged his head softly against the rock wall, as if in doing so he could dislodge the painful memories.

He had stayed on in the hovel after they came to take his mother's body away. McGrath had come that day and, in the days, afterward. Sometimes he brought food. Sometimes he tended to the wounds the man had inflicted. Then he'd stopped coming. That other man always came, sometimes with sweets and petting, but mostly with his unquenchable thirst to inflict pain and harm. Until that day, that day when . . . and then Gallo had run away. He made his bed in alleys and under bridges and stole what food he could get his hands on.

That preacher what found me, took me to that 'ouse with all them other b'ys. Thought everything would be okay, that I'd be fine, Gallop laughed a high and bitter laugh, *t'was just more of the same. They didn't beat me as often as that man had but ....* He stopped the thought before it could fully form. *But I learned me letters, 'elped me get work wit that bookkeeper and I learned lots of secrets. Secrets them uppity ups didn't want getting out . . . what difference did it make to them rich lords, t'was but a few pennies, a drop of water in the ocean. They 'ad so much, more than they'd ever need . .*

Gallo sat remembering his ejection from the bookkeeper's shop where he'd worked for years. Merchant's gossip guaranteed he'd not get another position. He made them uppity-ups pay. He'd lined his pockets but good at their expense. *Oh yes, I made 'em pay fer their sins.*

Much later he made his way West where eventually he found work with Dominion Limestone. They didn't know their agent at the time had a fondness for young boys. But Gallo knew and he used the knowledge to secure his own future.

That frigging 'alf-breed, tis all his doing. If 'e 'adn't come to work the quarry, makin' me remember things best left alone. Jesus, I needs a drink. Gallo hung his head. Rum was the only way he could sleep without nightmares tormenting him. And he'd been drinking pretty steadily since the day he'd hired Jake.

I wonder if I could talk that man, 'arry into a little nip. Just a nip is all I needs. Gallo fantasized about the bottles he'd stored in the kitchen of the company house, forgetting it was in shambles from the fire he'd set.

Gallo had one more ace up his sleeve. Nobody knew about the money he'd hidden in his satchel in the woods. *I will get outta this, just gotta bide me time,* he told himself. He regretted his words and curses on Harry that morning. *I gots to fix things between me and 'arry. I gots to. Might be my only 'ope.*

Harry wondered why Gallo was suddenly so friendly and cordial when he brought him his supper. He didn't give it a lot of thought but thanked his lucky stars the evening had not been a repeat of the morning's nastiness.

"Poor bugger fergot 'e burned the place down – not a jigger of rum to be 'ad," Harry thought as he walked away from the root cellar. Maybe this will work out yet. I've worked for worst. As long as 'e behaves 'imself that is.

Chapter

70

Jack was skipping flat stones out into the water. He was deep in thought and struggling with all the recent events; with good versus evil and other confusing thoughts. Phil snuck through the long grasses taking care not to step on any twigs in his aim to give his younger sibling a good scare.

"Gotcha!" Phil jumped, grabbing Jack by the shoulders. His brother threw him backward, fist coming up in the process. "Jumpin' dyin' Jackie-boy, ye're getting' some friggin' strong," he said as he just barely stopped himself from falling backward. "Hah! Gave ye a fright, admit it!"

Jack dropped his arm, "Jeepers Phil, whatcha do that fer?"

"Couldn't resist b'y, ye was so deep in thought ye didn't even hear me comin'," Phil grinned from ear to ear. "Knew I'd find ye here. Tis yer turn to shovel out the chicken coop. I did it last week and William the week afore."

"I knows it's my turn. I just wanted a bit of time on me own afore I did me chores," Jack protested, "wasn't gonna be long."

"Ye knows Da likes us to get the work done afore anythin' else," Phil remarked.

"He knows I'm down here. I asked him first, afore I came," Jack rebuffed his brother with a scowl. "Sometimes a body needs a bit of time to think."

"And what great philosophy are ye considerin'?" Phil teased.

"Philosophy? What are ye getting' on with?" Jack was nonplussed.

"Something Aunt Elsie taught me about, numbskull," Phil grinned. "It's the study of nature and why things are the way they are. Leastwise, that's what I think it is. Anyway, tis a great word, Phil- los-oh-fee. It's got my name in it so it must be good."

"Sounds like a load of rubbish to me," Jack retorted, frowning.

"Ask Aunt Elsie, I can't explain it like she can," Phil replied, "What's got ye all so bemused?" he asked.

Jack looked at his brother solemnly, in no mood to join in Phil's foolishness. "William is gone up to see Ginny most every day and every time ye sees Haldi ye gets all soft in the head. Pretty soon ye will be gone all the time, too. Are ye gonna marry 'er?" he asked.

"Fer frig sakes," Phil reddened, "It ain't nuddin' like William and Ginny and even if it t'were, Haldi lives too far away fer me to visit 'er like William visits Ginny. I don't even know if she likes me that way."

"What way?" Jack asked, confused by his brother's embarrassment.

"Geez, Jack, in the way, well, ye know, like Ma likes Da," Phil stammered, out of his depth.

"I seen ye chattin' with 'er after church," Jack accused his brother, "and I heard 'er silly giggling. Ye liked it!"

"What's wrong with that? She's sweet and funny, pretty too," Phil looked out to sea as he listed some of Haldi's attributes.

"She must think ye're funny too, judging by the way ye had 'er laughin'," Jack observed. "Ye was supposed to come troutin' wit me Sunday afternoon. I couldn't find ye anywhere. I spose ye were hangin' out with 'er after church. Ye don't got no time fer me and neither does William!"

"Is that what's got ye so deep in thought out here?" Phil asked. "Sure, ye knows ye're always gonna be my brother, my best buddy. Ye do know that, don't ye?"

Jack frowned again. "I don't get why ye're so keen on Haldi. Ye're always moonin' over 'er. Ye don't want to do anythin' fun no more," he complained.

"Jackie-boy, one of these days ye're gonna meet somebody who takes yer breath away. There ain't no way I can explain what this feels like. I think it's love," Phil confided, "being with Haldi just makes me feel all warm inside . . ."

"I ain't ever gonna act all squirrelly over anybody," Jack said vehemently, "I ain't ever gonna go off and ferget about ye or William or the girls, Jimmy either."

"Are ye mad at me, Jack?" Phil asked.

"Yes, I am! I don't understand. Ye don't talk to me any more like ye used to and ye and William are always talkin' like ye gots secrets I wouldn't understand," Jack grumbled.

"B'y I'm startin to be sorry fer comin' to look fer ye, Ye're some almighty cranky," Phil protested.

"Well go on back to the house. I don't need ye," Jack retorted.

"Nope, I ain't goin' anywhere til things are right between ye and me again," Phil planted his feet stubbornly in front of Jack. "C'mon b'y," Phil said poking Jack's shoulder with one finger.

Jack gave his brother a dirty look and Phil poked him again. "Stop it!" Jack demanded pushing Phil away.

"Why don't ye make me?" Phil rejoined, poking him once again.

Soon the brothers were on the sand wrestling and landing playful punches. Before long Phil had Jack in a headlock. "Say 'uncle'," he threatened, "say 'uncle' or I won't let ye go."

Jack surprised Phil with his strength and agility and the older boy was hard put to keep the youngster under control. "Say 'uncle' and I'll let ye go," he said again.

"I ain't givin' in. I ain't gonna say 'uncle', no sir," Jack said as he continued to struggle to free himself.

"Ooof!" Phil was surprised to find the tables turned when Jack's sudden movement flipped him on his back.

"I ain't ever gonna say 'uncle' again, ye hear me?" Jack stood panting and glaring at his older brother.

Phil lunged toward him but slipped in the sand, landing in an awkward position on his butt, legs splayed out. Jack began to point and laugh loudly, holding his belly as he did so. Slowly Phil got to his feet and began to brush the sand from his clothes.

"Ye just got lucky," he told Jack, "I will make ye say 'uncle' again. Ye knows I will."

Jack continued to laugh loudly, shaking his head at the same time. "Nope, ye ain't ever gonna make me say 'uncle' ever, ever again."

Jack's laughter subsided when he caught the gleam in Phil's eyes. He took off running, knowing Phil was about to test his prowess.

Chapter

71

Peter stood up and stretched, he was feeling better than he had since before the fall from his horse and the dizzy spells were coming less and less. Much as he hated to admit it, Hilda was right in her diagnosis. Rest was helping. He had put all thoughts of Gallo aside with great effort and practised banishing them each time a worry would creep unbidden to mind.

He heard the sounds of pots and pans rattling in the kitchen and knew Hilda was there preparing breakfast for her brood. He had come to admire the woman's skills at housekeeping and her devotion to her family. *Hank's a very lucky man,* he thought as he considered what if anything Hilda would allow him to do. *Perhaps I will take a stroll to the beach, if she will allow it,* Peter grinned at the thoughts of Hilda's tenacity and keen attention to every detail of his health and well-being.

"Good morn, Missus," Peter's said to Hilda's back as he entered the warm kitchen.

Hilda turned, a dishcloth in hand, "Good morn, to ye. "Ow did ye sleep? Are you feeling a mite better?" She asked.

"I am. The headache's not near so bad and I notice the dizziness is comin' less and less often," Peter enthused. "Thought I might take a walk to the beach, maybe dig fer a few clams later."

Hilda walked over and grabbed Peter by the chin. She examined his face closely, noting his eyes were clear and the pallor was no longer in evidence. Peter stood patiently enduring her examination.

"I spose a bit more fresh air would do ye good," she finally determined, "I could whip up a pot of clam chowder, if ye have any luck."

Peter grinned at her, "I would love some clam chowder!"

"Clam chowder?" Hank asked, coming into the room. "Ye knows how to give a man something to look forward to after a day of busting rocks! Morning, Peter."

Peter turned toward his cousin with laughter in his eyes. "It all depends if I find some. Hilda, ye best have a back up plan, in case I come back empty-handed," he warned. "Wouldn't want that man of yers to starve after a hard day's labor."

"So ye're going digging clams today?" Hank asked Peter, "are ye sure she's gonna let ye leave the house?"

"Sure, e's well enough," Hilda retorted, "or e'd be spending another day here, tied up, if need be."

"She been hard on ye, my friend?' Hank turned to Peter, "she's like that ye knows. Ye may know it even better than I after being trapped here with 'er the last couple of days."

Hilda swatted her husband with the cloth in her hand, "trapped, is it? Now I likes that. And after all I do fer ye." Her voice was cross but her tone did not match the twinkling of her eyes.

"Hank, b'y, I'd consider myself blessed to be married to a good woman like ye got here," Peter answered, "Ye should go down on yer knees to the good God in thanks fer all she does fer the likes of ye." Peter winked at Hilda as he spoke.

"I thank the Creator every day for 'er," Hank returned, "I knows where me bread is buttered."

"If the two of ye are finished with all yer nonsense take a seat, breakfast is nearly ready." Hilda ordered them.

The men sat at the long table. "So, ye finished loading that freighter yesterday. I didn't get a chance to ask ye last evening. Is work better then, since the association formed?" Peter asked.

"I ain't sure if it's the association or the fact Gallo ain't there to throw his weight around, but the men seem a lot happier," Hank replied. "Josiah was always a fair pit boss but now Langley's got 'im doing the job of the mining captain. I wonder if he will give 'im the position permanently."

"Time will tell, I suppose," Peter mused, "Langley's a better man than I first thought. I've had cause to change my opinion of the man after spending a bit of time with 'im and watching how he treats others."

"He ain't afraid to get 'is hands dirty. He ain't real friendly, but he ain't one to throw his weight around like he's better than the men what works fer 'im," Hank agreed.

"T'was good of him to let ye and the others off early to get them depositions written up," Peter responded, "When are ye going to do yers?"

"Today, in fact, if nuddin' changes. Josiah said we could go one at a time and we can leave right after the dinner break. I'm told Langley ain't even gonna dock our pay. That's mighty decent of 'im," Hank reported admiringly.

"That is decent of 'im. Course, he needs them documents prepared in time to send to St. John's," Peter replied, "he wants to see Gallo sent back to England, as do I. The depositions will help make a case against him when he finally stands up to be tried."

"Peter! Don't get thinking on all that!" Hilda pounced, "it gives me a 'eadache just considering all that wretch has done, never mind what thinkin' on it might do to yer poor noggin." She turned toward Hank, "and ye should know better to get 'im ponderin' on it! The two of ye give up that kind of talk!"

Hank turned a shade of red. Hilda had scolded him in their bedroom the night before about Peter's delicate condition and the need to keep him calm. Her ears were attuned to their conversations every time they sat together and she had noted the effects such talk had on her patient.

"Sorry, b'y, I wasn't thinkin'," Hank told Peter.

"That's the trouble, neither one of ye are taking all this seriously," Hilda grumbled, "Don't look at me like that, Peter. I see the pallor return every time ye gets discussing that man and the efforts to get 'im to the city. Now, I'm tellin' ye again. Leave off thinkin' or talkin' about that rogue! Everythin' will fall into place in the Lord's good time."

"Yes, ma'am," Peter said contritely, "It ain't easy to do, seeing as how he's still up there in that root cellar."

"I knows it ain't easy. But if ye wants to go help make arrangements to get 'im to the city ye gots to do as I say," Hilda commanded.

Peter did not answer but looked to Hank for his help and support.

"She's right," Hank said quietly, "ye've had too much on yer mind these past weeks. Ye needs to rest yer mind as well as yer body."

"Alright, then, let's talk of something else. Like where can I find a good spade to dig up clams? I'll need a bucket as well," Peter asked.

"I'll go out to the barn and get ye one afore I leaves fer work," Hank promised, "I gots to feed the animals anyway."

"No reason why I can't feed the animals, give me something to do," Peter suggested.

"Is that alright, Hilda?" Hank asked turning to his wife. He wasn't going to give her an opportunity to scold him again.

Hilda was stirring something in a pot on the stove but she came over to study Peter's face again. "I guess t'would be alright. But ye mind, Peter, if ye ain't back in this kitchen in good time I'll come lookin' fer ye myself."

Peter sighed, sometimes Hilda's restrictions were hard to bear. "The spade out in the barn?" he asked Hank instead.

"Yes, in the back corner. Ye'll find it there with the rest of the tools," Hank responded.

"I'm looking forward to digging clams, haven't done it in years," Peter commented. "Uncle John used to take me and my cousin, Jeremiah, clam digging years ago."

"Tis a good day fer it," Hank replied, "Sure hope ye get lots. Hilda makes a tasty clam chowder. Makes me mouth water just thinkin' about it."

"It t'would be a 'elp if ye could shell 'em afore ye brings 'em back 'ere," Hilda remarked, "and it t'would keep ye busy and out of trouble fer a bit."

"Listen to 'er," Hank chuckled, "Ye wouldn't know but ye're nuddin' but a wee lad." He turned toward Hilda, "Ye're some bossy, ye are!"

"Tis fer 'is own good," she retorted unrepentantly.

Peter chuckled too, "If I am fortunate to find any, I will make sure to shuck them afore I comes back."

A couple of hours later Peter was walking the beach searching for the tell-tale tiny holes in the sand, evidence that clams had buried themselves below. It was low tide, the perfect time for his hunt. Peter pounded the sand with his spade every time he noticed a depression in the sand. Peter gave a joyful sound as he spied just what he was searching for: a small squirt of water a few seconds after he'd tamped down on the surface with his shovel. Dropping the bucket, he pushed the spade into the sand and was pleased when he lifted a good-sized clam out. He spent an enjoyable morning digging clams and shucking shells. The bucket was nearly full when he turned to take a leisurely stroll back to his cousins' home.

Sea Gulls wheeled and landed on the shore. Peter stopped and looked back where he'd left the shells and watched in amusement as a gull lifted one after another searching for a meal.

"Sorry, b'y, ain't nothing in 'em," he sang out. The gull waddled around another minute or too before deciding it was a fruitless effort and flew off into the sky. Peter watched as it soared out over the water, carried gracefully on the wind. The gull flew up and down, circling, searching for food.

Peter breathed deeply, enjoying the scent of brine on the air and the quiet of the cove. He seldom took the time to really enjoy his surroundings, his mind always working overtime. He often thought of the men in mines and logging camps he'd helped in the past, or, conversely, his inability to help Luke and his family.

His plate had been full of late. He'd received letters begging his aid in other places across the island. Then there was this business with Gallo. Peter took Hilda's advice to heart and did his best to banish thoughts of the quarry, Gallo, and any court proceedings that may come and vowed to himself: *I will enjoy the day and this bit of peace. Heaven knows it comes seldom enough. Hilda was right. I need to do this more often.* He tilted his head back and let the sun warm his face.

He turned again to walk back to deliver his day's haul to Hilda. He swung the bucket a little as he went along, listening to the surf as the waves washed in and back out again. It was like music for his soul and he hungered for more of the same.

Chapter

72

Langley placed the depositions carefully on his desk in the captain's hut. He had to go to the cookhouse and arrange for another hamper to be made up to send up to Harry. *Thank God that freighter's loaded and gone*, he told himself, *Picton's got more brains than Gallo ever did. He sure knows better than to treat the men like slaves, the way that wretch did.* Langley scratched his head; *Still can't fathom how he ever managed to secure the position of mining captain.* Langley's face darkened and his scowl deepened as he recalled the rumours he'd heard about Gallo's sordid past. His disgust was still evident on his face when his pit boss tapped lightly on his door and peeked inside.

"Boss? Was told ye wanted to see me," Picton asked nervously, assuming the agent's obvious displeasure concerned his dealings with the freighter's captain.

"Yes, yes. Come on inside," Langley barked, his inner turmoil making him seem cross.

Josiah doffed his cap as he entered, "Were them papers not done up right?" he asked.

"Yes, ye did a fine job of it," Langley assured him. "I just needed to see ye because I have to go back to town again on other business. I think ye can run things while I'm away. It might take a few days but there won't be another shipment going out until the end of the month."

"Sure thing, boss," Josiah answered, relieved, "t'will be just the regular work. I can easily oversee it, been doin' it fer years."

"Good. I will need to count on ye for the next while until I have time to hire a new man to take over as captain. Right now, I need ye to find that man, Paddy. Tell 'im to come see me straight away," the agent ordered, "after that ye can carry on with whatever ye were doing."

Josiah ducked his head and left to do Langley's bidding. Soon it was Paddy knocking on the door.

"Come in!" Langley ordered brusquely.

"Josiah told me ye wanted me," Paddy said as he entered the shack.

"Yes, I was hopin' I could prevail upon ye once again," Langley began, "I need somebody to deliver a couple of hampers to Harry at the company house. Would ye be willing to do that after ye're finished today?"

"Don't mind a bit, fact is, tis not far from where I live," Paddy replied.

"I am glad I can count on ye," Langley answered, "and will ye kindly bring the empty hampers back here tomorrow? Ye can leave 'em at the cookhouse. Thank ye."

"No worries, boss. I'll take care of it. Is that all ye want?" Paddy asked.

"Well, if ye don't mind, if ye can give Harry a hand, Gallo's prison may need to be aired out. I just need ye to keep a weapon trained on 'im. Harry's only got two hands, and the man was injured and is still healing. Can't trust that Gallo would not try to take advantage of 'im," Langley explained.

"I can do that," Paddy said simply.

"Ye will be rewarded fer all yer troubles," Langley promised. "Ye have gone over and beyond yer duties to the company and I want ye to know it is appreciated."

"Where Gallo is concerned, believe me, it's my pleasure," Paddy said sincerely.

"Ye can go on back to yer work, that's all I wanted," the agent dismissed him.

Langley picked up the log book that itemized all the limestone shipments and placed it back in the drawer and locked it. He looked about the little shack, making sure he'd left nothing of importance laying around. He lifted the packet of depositions as he stood. Best see to them hampers, he told himself, time's awasting.

Langley stepped inside the cookhouse and strode purposefully to the kitchen.

"I need ye to make up another three or four hampers," he told the cook, "Make sure there's enough food fer two men for several days."

"Yes, sir! Do ye have any special instructions?" the man wiped his hands on his apron while he waited.

Langley looked around the tight quarters. He had noted on his initial visit the lack of variety and the inferior goods on display.

"Who does the ordering fer the operation?" he asked.

"Sir, I used to do it meself until Mr. Gallo came, then he insisted on taking it over," he explained.

"I want ye to take it on again," Langley ordered, "and make sure it's good food, not this substandard fare. The company pays the bill and I am authorized in their name. I will check on supplies from time to time to make sure the men are receiving what's due them."

"I'll be happy to take care of it," the cook grinned widely, sensing a more pleasing array of dishes in his future.

"Just remember I will be dining here from time to time and don't be buying an overabundance of beans or hard tack either," Langley grimaced, remembering the taste of the food.

"I will make sure there is more variety and better offerings," the cook promised.

"Ye needn't get too carried away," Langley warned, "plain fare is fine, but it should be of better quality than this," he waved his hand contemptuously toward the shelves of groceries.

"Yes, sir, I understand what ye're getting' at," the cook agreed.

"Go through yer stores and get rid of anything outdated," Langley went on, "Some of this food ain't worth giving to pigs, never mind hard-working men."

"It t'will be my great pleasure," the cook answered.

"Make sure the hampers are ready by the end of the work day," Langley continued, "there will be a man here to pick them up. Carry on!"

"Yes, sir! Thank ye, sir!" the cook's head bobbed like a marionette in his pleasure.

Langley strode out of the cookhouse and mounted his horse for the ride to town. It was still fairly early in the day and he was confident he would reach the telegraph office in time to send the telegram Brown had written for him. *With any luck I'll receive an answer today,* he thought as he rode out of the quarry.

The agent made the telegraph office his first stop when he got to town. Then he went directly to his office.

"Good mornin', Dawe," he greeted his office clerk, "do ye have anything of importance for me to deal with?"

"Good mornin' to ye, Sir," Dawe said, standing up, "no, sir, but I do have a letter for ye here from Dominion Limestone. Ye told me to let ye know straight away if anything come. It arrived in the post last evening, special delivery, Sir."

"Let's have it, then," Langley said anxiously, "it's of the utmost importance!"

Dawe placed the mail in Langley's outstretched hand. The agent's eyes greedily read the covering as he walked quickly to his office. It was a slim envelope and Langley was tearing it open as he walked to his desk.

He dropped heavily into his chair and impatiently withdrew the missive. Quickly he scanned the correspondence and smiled grimly. So, the naval ship is leaving within the month, he said to himself, and Morgan thinks it may be too late to get Gallo on it. Well, we'll see about that! If nothing else at least he can arrange to have 'im held in a gaol there in the city. Langley's hands gripped the letter tightly and he sighed his disappointment.

He stood and took the packet of depositions he'd been clutching when he entered and placed them in a drawer under lock and key. He left the correspondence he'd written along with Brown's letter on top of the desk.

He pulled the pile of blank paper that sat on the front corner of the desk toward him and began to write a letter to the naval authority in St. John's outlining Gallo's crimes and the need to have him bundled off to Britain. Langley took his time, carefully using every ounce of persuasion he possessed to enlist the man's assistance in delaying the sailing of the navy ship until he could get Gallo to the city. Satisfied, he placed the missive in an envelope and addressed it to the address Morgan had provided.

Langley shuffled through his correspondence and lifted Brown's letter to the church in St. John's and placed it on the pile he needed to mail. He dropped his letter to Morgan on top. He had used his time in the bunkhouse to craft letters to people of influence in the city and now he hastened to move on his intentions. His movements were jerky as he stood up. I will get the scoundrel to St. john's if it's the last thing I do, he vowed to himself.

He hurriedly replaced his hat on his head and pulled his jacket on. He strode purposefully to the door. "I have a couple of things to look after," he told Dawe, "I will return after dinner."

"Sir? If ye wish, I can take yer letters to the post," Dawe said eyeing the thick stack of letters Langley held tightly.

"No, this is something I need to look after personally," Langley refused the offer, "I will return some time after the noon hour." "Very good, Sir," Dawe replied softly. He got no response as he watched Langley hurry from the premises.

Chapter

73

The place was abuzz with chatter as Paddy dug into his food. Jake was one of the men sitting with him and Paddy listened to the conversation around him as he ate. It was gratifying to see Jake included in the chatter as the men discussed the many changes in the quarry and gossiped about the mining captain.

"Cook told me Langley's gonna make sure we gots decent food to eat," one of the men was saying.

"Anythin' will be better than this steady diet of beans and hard tack," another complained.

"Cook said the agent put 'im back in charge of buying the food. That's a good thing. We used to eat better back in the days afore Gallo got here," the first man remarked, "seems like everything will get better now he's gone."

"Pay's better, too," the second man observed, "bout time. Tis back-breaking work!"

"We gots that Parsons fella to thank fer that," the first man pointed out, "T'was a good thing, the association."

"Hard to think it all started with Joe gettin' killed," the first man said solemnly.

Jake shifted uncomfortably and Paddy was quick to change the subject. "Langley wants me to stop by the company property, give Harry a hand with some things up there. Said he might need help with the prisoner."

"I heard they're gonna send 'im off to Sin John's to the naval authority," the first man remarked. "Guess they can't keep 'im in that cellar forever."

"We needs somebody to keep bad blood in line around 'ere," another man piped up, we ain't got no gaols or nuddin' round 'ere."

"There's truth to that, guess we bin lucky there ain't much crime to speak of, least up to now," another joined in.

Paddy leaned over to Jake and gestured toward the door and the two men climbed from the bench and went outside.

"So, the agent wants ye back up there again this evening," Jake commented, "Ye've been having to spend a fair bit of time there."

"I think it's because I live so close to the company property," Paddy shrugged, "And he needed hampers brought up there again. T'was wondering if ye'd mind giving me a hand. I will give ye a lift home afterward."

"I'd rather not have any more confrontations with the cap'n," Jake said, hesitating.

"Ye won't have to see 'im a'tall. I just needs help with them hampers," Paddy replied.

"I s'pose I could do that. T'will it take long cuz I'd like to get home to Mary," Jake hedged.

"Shouldn't take much time a'tall. Tis just to drop them hampers off at the barn then I can take ye home," Paddy promised.

"Alright, s'pose I can do that much fer ye, seeing as ye're been so good at finding me work fer the winter," Jake grinned, alluding to the promise of woodworking and repairs to the burnt house that seemed to be a promising prospect.

"I hope that works out fer ye. How's the mare doing?" Paddy inquired. "I knows Mary was some pleased when she come out to yer barn to see 'er, Haldi, too."

"I've been walking 'er around the yard a bit more each day, seems to be getting' a lot better," Jake responded, "she's some sweet. She deserves a better master than the cap'n. I think he was hard on 'er. I seen evidence of 'er being abused, scars and such."

"With any luck her leg will heal and she will be able to stay with ye," Paddy commented, "can't think of a better place fer 'er."

"No creature deserves to be treated so harshly," Jake replied, "I'd like 'er to stay, if only fer the chance it will give 'er to mend and put a bit of weight on 'er bones. She's far too skinny. I dunno if he was feedin' 'er proper like."

Paddy clapped a hand on Jake's shoulder, "Well she's in good hands now. We best get back ta work. I'll see ye later."

Paddy dropped Jake off, as promised, and returned to the barn to meet Harry. "Guess we best get to it," he told him. "Has he given ye any trouble a'tall?"

"Yis, ye knows, 'ad a run-in with 'im right off the bat, but I took care of that right fast," Harry replied and proceeded to describe Gallo's fit the first morning he'd had to bring him breakfast. "ain't 'ad a lick of trouble from 'im ever since."

"Glad it's ye and not me," Paddy said ruefully. "I only spent a couple of days here with 'im. It ain't somethin' I'd want to be at steady."

"If me ribs weren't still giving me trouble, I'd 'ead back out to the loggin' camp," Harry told Paddy, "As it is I'm lucky to 'ave this gig. Ain't much I can do labor-wise."

"That's why Langley sent me up here to give ye a hand," Paddy replied, "he seems like a good sort, even if he's a might blunt and to the point. He don't beat around the bush do he?"

"I like it better that way, a man knows where he stands wit 'im," Harry remarked.

"Ye gots that right," Paddy agreed.

"Guess we should take 'im out of there, let 'im use the outhouse, 'ave a bit of a walk about," Harry suggested. "I don't 'ave no love fer the man but it ain't right to keep 'im down in that cellar fer so long."

Paddy said nothing. He did not share Harry's sympathies for the man after all he'd put Jake through but he didn't share his thoughts with his companion.

"If ye wants to hold the pistol on 'im, I'll put the ladder down so he can climb out," Paddy suggested, "don't know if the agent warned ye but he's mighty cunnin'."

"Yes, so 'e told me," Harry replied, "I will keep a close eye on 'im. His slop bucket will need to be emptied. Are ye willin' to go down there and get it?"

Paddy screwed his nose up at the thought, "Yeah, Langley said the cellar might need to be cleaned out. It's a two-man job fer sure. One of us has to keep the gun on 'im. Tis best ye do that. I might be tempted to use it on 'im."

"I could mebbe lock 'im in the outhouse while we do what needs doing," Harry suggested.

"Let's check it out, see if that might work," Paddy agreed. The pair walked first to the privy to investigate the possibility before heading to the root cellar. Harry lifted the wooden crossbar.

"Ye ready?" he asked Paddy.

"As ready as I'll ever be," Paddy replied. Harry entered the structure with his helper close behind him.

"Gallo? We gots company and ye best behave ye 'ear?" Harry called before lifting the trap door. "Paddy's gonna drop the ladder down so ye can climb out. I gots the pistol and I ain't afeared to use it."

Gallo made no response as Paddy eased the ladder down into the hole and stood back.

"Come on out," Harry called, "Ye're in fer a treat, Ye get a new prison fer a little bit."

Gallo blinked at the evening light as he climbed the ladder. He had to stand for a bit before his eyes adjusted to the sudden light.

"Alright, ye ready?" Harry asked his prisoner. "We'll take ye out to the outhouse and if ye behaves mebbe I'll let ye stretch yer legs a bit."

Gallo did not answer and Harry's motioned with the pistol for him to exit the building. Paddy and Harry both followed the captain to the outhouse and with the use of a nearby boulder locked him inside.

"Go on and do what ye gots to do in the cellar. I'll wait 'ere," Harry whispered in Paddy's ear. "This 'ere will work just fine," he said indicating the boulder. Paddy nodded and moved away.

The stench of human excrement assaulted Paddy's nose while he was descending the ladder. He soon found the offensive slop bucket and gingerly climbed back up the ladder making sure not to spill its contents on himself. *Next time I'll make 'im carry this out himself,* Paddy vowed silently. He walked carefully to the outhouse where he set the bucket down on the step. Harry nodded and jerked his head toward the barn where he planned to take Gallo for a walk. At Paddy's silent assent Harry called out, "Ye about finished in there? C'mon out and we'll take ye fer a little walk."

Paddy rolled the boulder away from the door and Gallo stood glaring at the men. "Take that pail and empty it first," Paddy ordered. Gallo scowled and lifted the slop bucket and turning dumped it out. "Bring it with ye," Paddy growled at his former boss and turned toward Harry. "Keep that weapon trained on 'im," he warned.

Gallo's fingers itched to drop the bucket as the trio walked to the barn. His eyes swept the land and took secret delight at the charred remains of the house. *That'll cost the company a pretty penny to fix up,* he thought vengefully. He was careful to map out his escape, should an opportunity present itself. Nobody said a word as they walked the short distance to the barn.

"Ye, stand right there and don't ye dare move," Harry ordered his prisoner once they were inside the doorway of the barn.

Gallo's eyes swept the stables and he started, "Where's my mare?" He asked insolently. "I knows she was 'ere. I saw that 'alf-breed leading 'er back 'ere."

Paddy swung angrily around to glare at the captain. "What do ye care 'bout the beast? I knows ye were nuddin' but hateful to 'er while ye did have 'er."

"She's my rightful property," Gallo's voice rose as he continued to search the structure for the mare.

"Settle down, mate," Harry barked, "yer mare's fine. Jake's takin' good care of 'er, ain't that right, Paddy?"

His reassurance only agitated the captain further.

"What's that 'alf-breed doing with me 'orse? Did 'e steal 'er?" "Naw, b'y, Langley 'ad 'im take 'er back to 'is place to look after 'er. She'd come up lame," Harry tried to explain. He watched the rage overtake his prisoner with consternation.

Gallo swung the slop bucket with all his might at Harry and missed, the bucket flying past Harry's head and landing with a clatter on the floor. Gallo did not see Paddy's fist but felt his knuckles connect with his chin and he staggered backwards.

Harry waved the pistol at him, "That's enough! Ye 'ear me!"

Gallo rubbed his chin and glared at his gaoler. His chest heaved and his anger threatened to overwhelm him again, despite the weapon in Harry's hand.

"Let's put 'im back in his hole. This was a mistake," Paddy rasped out. Paddy grabbed their prisoner by his upper arm. "Pick it up!" he ordered as he kicked the slop bucket at his feet. He waited until Gallo complied and grabbed the pail from his hand. "Now, go on, get goin'," he ordered. He gave Gallo a hard push.

Gallo staggered forward a half-step and then stood, stubbornly refusing to move. Paddy shoved him again. "Ye can either go easy or ye can go hard. I don't mind draggin' yer sorry carcass to that cellar and dropping ye into it," Paddy warned. It took a mere second before Gallo decided to cooperate, biding his time in the hopes that Harry would be alone the next time.

Gallo felt the pistol poke him in between his shoulder blades. "Ye best not give us no more trouble or I'll be 'anding this gun over to Paddy 'ere. I might 'esitate a second afore shootin ye, but 'e won't. Understand?"

The trio made the return trip to the root cellar quickly. Harry's pistol poking Gallo's back repeatedly to hurry him along. Gallo nearly fell into the cellar during his descent down the ladder. Paddy was quick to remove it. He dropped the slop pail down into the hole let the hatch door fall back into place.

The two men closed the door and dropped the cross-bar back in place.

Harry smiled apologetically at Paddy. "I see now why Langley don't want me takin' 'im out unless there's somebody 'ere wit me."

Paddy's eyes were still stormy with anger and he glared at his partner. "Ye can't trust that as far as ye can spit," he said.

"Why'd 'e git so mad 'bout Jake lookin' after 'is mare?" Harry wondered.

"He hates Jake with a passion. Don't know why," Paddy revealed, "it set 'im off knowing Jake has his horse."

"I never did get 'im some water or 'is supper," Harry commented, "ain't likely I'm goin' back in there tonight."

"Best leave 'im to cool off," Paddy replied, "he won't die overnight."

"I am sorry as 'ell bout all that," Harry apologized. "I didn't know e'd get so riled up."

"Why did ye want to bring 'im in the barn?" Paddy asked.

"Was thinkin' to kill two birds wit one stone," Harry replied ruefully, "thought we could get a bit of straw fer 'im to make 'is bed and mebbe grab 'is supper at the same time."

"We shoulda talked it out afore hand," Paddy responded. "If I comes back to help ye again we needs to have a better plan."

"Much as I need the work, I 'ope Langley can arrange to get 'im outta 'ere sooner rather than later," Harry responded.

"Time will tell," Paddy replied, "Well, b'y, tis been a long day. I'm gonna shove off now. If I were ye, I wouldn't try to bring 'im anything else tonight."

"Naw, I don't think I will," Harry answered, "Like Langley said, he could do wit a bit of fastin'."

Harry thought hard and long about Gallo's character as he set about getting his own supper and throughout the long evening with only the cat for company. *Nope, I ain't about to try to bring 'im nuddin',* he thought after giving it a lot of careful consideration, *the man's too quick to anger and that equals danger. He'll keep til mornin'.*

Chapter

74

Gallo paced furiously in his cell. The knowledge that the man he hated so bitterly had his mare ate at him and forced him to change the plans he had been formulating since the beginning of his imprisonment.

Langley 'ad no right to give 'im my mare. That friggin' 'alf-breed! Just wait til I gets loose they're all gonna pay, he swore to himself as he turned again and again in the tiny quarters. *I needs my friggin' 'orse!* He barely walked six paces before he was forced to turn around again. His anger had no outlet and grew quickly as his thoughts fueled his emotions.

Gallo thought back on the interchange in the barn and he cursed his lack of control. *If only I'd thrown that bucket at Paddy instead. That's the one that's buddies with that friggin' 'alf-breed. Better still if I'd thrown it at 'im whilest it was full.*

Gallo's loud cackle rent the air as he imagined Paddy covered in excrement and urine. *Let 'im just try to order me to empty it again, I'll be ready,* he promised himself. The prisoner took comfort in all the ways he could have taken revenge on Jake's friend. *Well, I ain't dead yet.* He rubbed his hands together in anticipation and hope that Paddy would appear at the root cellar again. *Next time I'll be ready for 'im.* The former mining captain took delight in his schemes. His entertainment was short-lived.

I won't get far without me 'orse. Damn the man. Thought she was in 'er stable, like always. Ain't no way I can git very far on foot. Gallo's thoughts returned to the day Paddy had guarded him. He'd heard the dog barking and knew if he were to run the men might just use dogs to track him down. *Jake's place ain't far from 'ere. I could make it that far. I could get me mare and get away from 'ere.*

Gallo had taken note of Harry's habit of wrapping an arm around his middle. It was done without thought and betrayed the fact he was injured. Gallo had also studied the yard around the barn and house. *There's lots of good lengths of lumber I could use to knock 'im out. I just needs to watch fer a chance.* Gallo schemed. *Wish I 'adn't thrown that bucket at 'im. It's gonna make it 'ard to fix things with 'im.*

Gallo continued to pace and plan. *Once I get me satchel I can go anywhere, maybe even leave this God-forsaken island. If I can git to the mainland, they'd never find me. That man I met, the one what sails on the merchant ship. I knows 'e could 'elp me get away.* His thoughts went round and round while he paced.

It was on the third day in town that Langley received the telegram he'd been hoping for. Morgan had been successful in having the naval ship's departure delayed. But another two weeks was not a lot of time. Langley dropped the telegram on his desk. It was time to visit the harbor and find out what ships were docked there and if any were sailing for the city. He could not wait any longer to make a decision. He strode out of his office to confer with his clerk.

"Dawe, what do ye know of the Fisherman's Mission?" Langley questioned him.

"Sir? The Fisherman's Mission?" Dawe was confused by the query. "Why the mission sails round the Northern coast of the island and up and round the Northern Peninsula to Labrador. Why do ye ask, sir? Are ye interested in making a donation?"

"No, Dawe, I have something I need to get to St. John's at the earliest opportunity. Have ye ever heard of one of the Mission ships coming near here?" Langley asked impatiently.

"Sir, yer best bet would be to see if one of the fishing vessels could meet up with the Mission ship, perhaps up the coast. I am unsure how far south the mission ships sail, but that would be my advice," Dawe replied. "Could be one of 'em might intercept her somewhere along the way."

"Thank ye, Dawe. I have to go out. Make sure ye check the telegraph office fer any telegrams later this morning. I am awaiting a very important message from the city," the agent tersely ordered.

Langley walked quickly to the livery stable and retrieved his steed. He mounted and rode quickly from the stables and through town until he came to the track leading to the deep-sea harbor at the far end of town. His sharp eyes searched the bay for any sign of a schooner, without success. He made for the small fishing shanties that lined the wharf and spied a lone fisherman sitting on a stump outside his hut. He rode his horse toward the fellow until he was abreast of the man's shack.

"Sir! Might I have a word with ye?" He asked the man.

"Good day to ye, sir," the man's dark, leathery skin creased as he grinned a toothless grin at Langley, "what do ye wants away down 'ere?"

"I need to know, have ye seen any sign of a schooner when ye were out on the bay?" Langley asked brusquely.

The man's gaze took in Langley's appearance and manner as he sized the agent up before answering. "I ain't been out today. I 'ad to make repairs to me dory, there," he said pointing to the small boat that was upside down on the beach, "but there be a small schooner fishing out round the point. I saw 'er yesterday. Could be she'd be makin' for Rocky 'arbor up the coast. Could be she's makin' to anchor 'ere. There ain't no tellin' where she's 'eadin or when she might come ashore."

"Could ye tell me how often the fishing schooners anchor here in this harbor?" Langley asked.

"There ain't no regularity 'bout it. Sometimes we gets as many as two or tree a week. Other times dere's weeks go by with nar a one docking 'ere," he replied.

"Do ye have any idea how long they remain in the harbor and where the sailors might go if they're here at anchor for any length of time?" Langley questioned him.

"Yer best bet is to ask at the tavern dere in town," the fisherman answered, "If they're waiting out a storm, sometimes they will come into town to slake their thirst, if ye knows what I means."

Langley smiled grimly, "I do take yer meanin' and I thank ye fer yer time." The agent reached into his pocket and retrieved a silver coin which he tossed to the man.

"Why thank ye, sir," the man said as he caught the coin in midair, "and 'ave a grand day, sir."

Langley turned his horse and walked it slowly along the beach, scanning for the schooner the fisherman had told him about. There was no sign of her and the agent kicked his steed to a canter and headed back to town. *Aw, well, it was a long shot at best. Worth checking into and it may yet pay off in the end. Might just as well check with Fargo at the tavern. I should have considered that before.* He thought as he rode along.

It was still early in the day and there was no sign of Fargo when Langley entered the establishment. He chose to have his dinner before returning to the office. The fresh air had given him an appetite and he ordered his meal. His thoughts tumbled as he considered the challenge of getting Gallo moved to the city. He lifted the cup and sipped his tea. *I must come back and have a word with Fargo this eve. The barkeep may well have advice I'd not yet considered.* He thought about how isolated his existence had been and vowed to change that. He knew few people in this town where he'd lived for over a year. Connections, he knew, would have made this problem of moving Gallo less of an issue. The agent wiped his mouth and tossed coins on the table to pay for his dinner and rose to return to his office.

"Sir, a boy came from the telegraph office with another message for ye," Dawe told him as soon as he'd entered. "I left it on yer desk."

Langley grunted and strode to his office. He dropped his hat on the desk and picked up the telegraph laying there. It was from Brown's friend in the city and the agent smiled in relief as he read it. At long last he had good news. The *Southern Cross*, a fishing schooner, should be making port right there in town and if Langley acted quickly, he could have Gallo on it and sailing to meet a mission ship returning to St. John's. Langley thought it likely it was the same schooner the fisherman had noticed yesterday.

"Dawe! Come in here! I have an important mission fer ye. Leave everything else at once!" Langley called to this clerk.

"Sir?" Dawe questioned after entering Langley's inner sanctum.

"This is of utmost importance, Dawe, I cannot stress that enough," Langley told him, "There's a fishing schooner, the *Southern Cross*, will be setting anchor here in the harbor. I need ye to get a message to the captain as soon as it sails into port. I don't care what it costs I need ye to keep it here until I return. Is that understood?"

Dawe nodded and the agent continued with his instructions. "Pay any price the skipper demands for his time. Pay one of the small boat fishermen to take a message to the skipper, if need be. Ye're not to come into the office on the morrow but stand on the shore all day if need be, until ye catch sight of that schooner. Do ye understand?"

"Yes, sir," Dawe replied, "Will ye write a message to be sent to the skipper?"

"Yes, I will do that right now, and then I need to rush off to the quarry again," Langley responded. "Leave me now, I have work to do."

Dawe quietly left the room and Langley sat leaning over his desk as he drafted a letter to be delivered to the ship's captain as well as a telegraph to send to Brown's contact at the medical mission in the city.

"Dawe!" he called again. "Here take this to the telegraph office. Tell them to send it posthaste. You needn't wait for a reply but come straight back." He instructed his clerk who hurried off to do his bidding.

Langley lingered over the letter to the schooner's captain. He had just finished signing it with a flourish when Dawe returned. The clerk stood patiently waiting for further instruction as the agent opened a drawer, drawing out a bank draft.

"Dawe, I am leaving ye this bank draft to pay fer any costs to get this letter to the schooner's captain. I will expect receipts for any monies ye need to spend," Langley's filled out the document and handed it to his clerk. "Do ye have any questions?"

Dawe took the bank draft and the letter and shook his head. "No sir, no questions. I'm not to come into the office on the morrow but stay on the shore until I see the *Southern Cross*. I'm to get this letter to the captain, hiring a small boat fisherman if need be. I take it yer letter explains all the details?" he asked.

"It does," Langley agreed. "I am entrusting this to yer care. Don't let me down."

"I will do as ye say to the smallest detail," Dawe said solemnly, "Ye can count on me, sir."

"Very good," Langley commented, "Now, there is urgent business I must address at the quarry. I am hoping to be back tomorrow evening or the day after that at the latest."

Chapter

75

Gallo clenched his teeth as he thought of all the plans he had made that would come to naught without his mare. His hands fisted at his sides as he paced. *God damned Langley! I will make 'im pay if it's the last thing I ever do.* He promised himself.

Gallo paced furiously as he listed all the wrong-doings that he'd suffered in the past week. *I gots to get 'arry on me side, somehow.* He cringed inwardly as he remembered throwing the empty slop bucket at his guard. He hated making apologies but he knew he could swallow his pride if need be. *I 'ates to grovel and beg, but grovel I will if it means gettin' outta 'ere and away where Langley and the company men will never find me.* Gallo continued to plot long into the night.

Harry sat on his bunk and stroked the cat by his side. He had been true to his word and had brought his prisoner neither supper nor water. He'd not had many dealings with the captain while he'd worked at the quarry, dealing instead with Josiah, the pit boss, whom he found much easier to contend with.

The cap'n, 'e always was a 'ard case, right prickly and moody. Wonder what makes a body so dang ornery and 'ard to get along with. Harry mused. *I sure 'ope he's calmed down afore I 'as to bring 'im 'is breakfast. I needs to 'ave a word wit Langley bout the ruckus tonight. He ain't gonna be pleased. I did exactly like 'e said. I didn't try to take 'im out of the root cellar by meself. Paddy was 'ere and can attest to the cap'n's mood and sudden rage.* Harry thought over the incident a little longer before shaking his head and laying down on the bunk. Within minutes he was sound asleep, the cat curled up beside him.

Gallo had rehearsed his apology and the words he planned to say to get Harry over to his side and was ready when he heard the latch opening on the hatch above him.

"Is that ye, 'arry?" he called out as soon as light entered the underground room. "I am mighty sorry fer tossing that bucket at ye. Mighty sorry, indeed. I ain't 'ad no cause to do that, specially after ye've been so good to me," he wheedled.

"So, ye're singing a different tune this morn, are ye," Harry retorted. "Guess a night with no supper and nuddin' to whet yer whistle 'elped ye realize ye get more bees with 'oney than wit vinegar, eh?"

"Ye was right to leave me stew," Gallo said fawningly, "I 'ad no right to do that."

"Hand up yer water pail and I'll get ye a drink of water," Harry growled, in no mood to be placated. "Ye didn't get any last evening because of all yer friggin' goings on."

Gallo lifted the tin pail high above his head, "Are ye gonna give me anythin' to eat, not that I deserves it," he cajoled.

"Ye will get yers after I eats me own breakfast, not before," Harry barked back, "ye know, ye got a lot of friggin' nerve, ye does."

"Said I was sorry, and I means it," Gallo repeated his apology.

"I'll get yer water and I'll bring it when I brings ye yer food," Harry replied, not accepting his prisoner's apology, "might be a while, but ye ain't going nowhere." Harry said nothing else as he let the hatch door drop.

Gallo was ready when Harry returned and handed him the full pail of water. "I seen ye holding yer middle. Are ye hurt?" He asked feigning innocence. "Must be 'ard to work at anything if ye're 'urt." He said conversationally. "I broke me ribs once, took a long time to 'eal."

"Ye don't worry about me. I'm just fine," Harry lied.

"Did ye bring me any food?" Gallo asked in a mild tone.

"I got yer food right 'ere. I got me pistol, too, just ye mind that." Harry advised.

"I ain't gonna give ye no trouble a'tall. T'was learning that Langley gave me mare to that 'alf-breed set me off. I didn't mean to 'it ye wit that slop bucket. I regrets that. I do," Gallo's honeyed tone attempted to lure Harry into conversation.

"Ye always was a crotchety son of a bitch," Harry told him.

"I knows I ain't easy to get along wit. Like to make it up to ye, if I could," Gallo coaxed.

"Ye ain't got nuddin' I'd want," Harry replied.

"What if I tole ye I gots money, a lot of money," Gallo lured, "if ye're 'urt ye won't be able to work. Couldn't ye relax and let yerself 'eal if ye had a parcel of money put by?"

"Ye ain't got nuddin'. Ye lost yer job and now ye're eatin' whatever I decides I wants to give ye. Ye're dependent on me. Don't ye ferget it!" Harry refuted. "From where I'm standin' ye're as poor as a church mouse. What 'ave ye got but empty promises. Look, 'ere's yer breakfast, just take it and shut yer mouth."

Gallo reached up to receive his plate of food. "Wait, just wait. I ain't lying. Afore I set fire to the 'ouse I loaded all me money and me few belongins in me saddle bags. I knew Langley would come after me. I ain't stupid. I 'ave the money 'idden in the woods. Ye 'elp me get outta 'ere I'll give ye 'alf."

"And why would I trust ye? Ye set the 'ouse out yonder aflame, could 'ave burned out 'alf the area. Ye think about that a'tall? No, course ye didn't. Ye're a selfish son of a bitch. And Joe, remember Joe? Tis yer fault 'e died. Joe was a friend of mine and I'd rather rot in 'ell than give ye the time of day!" Harry exploded angrily. He dropped the hatch door back in place. He heard the tin plate hit the wall again as he was closing the door on the root cellar.

"Hope ye starves, ye bastard," Harry said to the closed door, his sense of honor and duty highly offended. "What kinda man do ye take me fer? I may not 'ave much but I ain't the kind ye can bribe wit yer filthy coins."

Chapter

76

L angley hurried back toward the quarry his thoughts looping as he rode. He needed someone he could trust to accompany his prisoner on his voyage to the city. On a whim he decided to stop by the house and check on Harry. He hadn't seen him in a couple of days and concern over the man's injury had kept a sliver of doubt alive in the back of his mind.

The agent was mulling over the possibility of hiring Harry to make sure Gallo was handed over to the naval officers the minute the ship docked in St. John's. As he rounded the coastline, he could see the half-burned cottage in the distance. The quiet of the early evening and the breeze coming off the bay combined to make for an idyllic ride but one the agent could not enjoy as troubled thoughts continued to plague him.

Harry had just started a fire to heat his supper and that of his prisoner's as well when he spied Langley's black steed trotting up the lane. He poked the fire with a long stick to stir the coals and coax it into a roaring flame. He was going about the business of preparing the food when Langley rode up.

"Evenin' boss," Harry greeted. "Glad you came, got things I needs to tell ye about Gallo."

"Has he been causing ye some trouble?" Langley asked.

"Aw, yup, ye could say that," Harry replied and proceeded to describe Paddy's visit and the ensuing commotion in the barn.

"Ye needn't have bothered to let him get any exercise. If he was in a gaol in the city, he wouldn't get any," Langley commented. "Tis good there wasn't any harm done. I take it he's still safe and sound in the cellar?"

"Yis, sir! Still down there, cooling 'is 'eels and scheming 'is escape," Harry answered, "seems e's got money 'idden in the woods somewhere. The bastard tried to bribe me wit it. Said 'e would give me 'alf if I 'elped 'im escape."

Langley's face darkened at this news and he did not reply immediately but stood stroking his chin and looking off into the distance. Harry's refusal to be bribed convinced the agent of his trustworthiness and loyalty.

"I figured he'd done something like that. He'd removed the saddle from his horse the night we tracked him down in the woods. I wondered what would make him do such a thing. Now I know," Langley spoke softly as he considered the news.

"The cap'n's a cunning son of a bitch," Harry spat, "and as unpredictable as the weather."

"Well, he's shown his hand now," Langley grunted, "I stopped in to see how ye were faring. How are yer ribs? Getting' any better a'tall?"

"I'm alright, still 'aving to watch what I'm doing, but getting' better all the time," Harry answered.

"There's reason I'm askin'," Langley told him, "There's a good chance I can get Gallo on a fishing schooner headed up the coast. He will have to be transferred to another ship plying fer St. John's. I was wonderin' if ye're fit to go along with him. I need somebody to oversee his passage, make sure he's kept chained so he can't make good on his plans to get away."

"And once we git to St. John's, what then?" Harry asked.

"When ye get there, he will be handed over to the naval authority. They will arrange his passage back to England," Langley explained.

"I ain't ever bin to the city," Harry commented, "where would I stay? I gots no relations there."

"Ye would be paid well, if ye choose to go and the company will pay fer yer food and lodgings. Have ye ever sailed afore?" Langley asked in turn.

"I worked all kinds of gigs, even went up the coast on a sealing vessel one time," Harry divulged, "T'was only the one time though. Didn't fancy it a'tall, a'tall. Fellin' trees is what I likes better, even if it don't always pay well."

"Seems to me ye've done a lot of different jobs. This will be different. Do ye think ye're fit enough to make the journey?" Langley queried.

"Yeah, I could 'andle that," Harry responded. "How soon would I 'ave to leave?"

"It may be as soon as tomorrow, or the day after," Langley told him, "More likely the day after. I need to figure it out. I'm going to see if one of the men could build some kind of cage to put in the back of a wagon to secure the prisoner. That will take time. I'm hoping to get things in place today."

"Can't see why not, there ain't nuddin' to 'old me 'ere," Harry replied as he stirred the beans in the pot."

"Don't let on to Gallo, and if ye could, see if ye can't get more information out of him regarding where he hid his purse," Langley instructed, "not to worry if ye can't get him talking. I already have a fair idea where it is."

"I'll see to it, can't make ye any promises I will be able to git 'im talking though," Harry replied, "I think 'e knows how much I despise 'im. Do ye want any of these beans, boss? Tis near ready to eat."

"No, thank ye, beans are not something I have a fondness for," Langley declined, "Let me just take care of my horse and I will help ye bring him his supper before I leave."

"Thanks, boss, that'd be good. It ain't easy balancing 'is plate wit a pistol in my 'and," Harry remarked, "I can do it, but two 'ands is better."

Gallo heard the hatch door being lifted and stood when Harry called out to him. He came and stood in the shaft of light pouring down into the cellar.

"We got company," Harry told him cheerfully. "Mr. Langley is here to see 'ow ye're doing. I knows ye're gonna be on yer best behaviour, ain't that right?"

Gallo did not rise to the baiting but simply waited for Harry to lower the plate to him. He grabbed the plate roughly from Harry's hand. "Needs that piss pot emptied," he growled, "needs more water, too."

"Ye can stand back then whilst I lower the ladder. I'll come down and git 'em both. Bear in mind Mr. Langley's got that pistol aimed at yer sorry 'ead, so don't be trying nuddin'," Harry answered. He lowered the ladder and as Langley stood silently by climbed down into the hole. He grabbed the empty water pail in one hand and reached for the foul slop bucket. "I'll bring 'em back in a bit and take yer plate when I come back." Harry climbed halfway up the ladder and tossed the empty water pail before retrieving the second bucket.

"I'll stay here with Gallo while ye see to all that," Langley said gesturing with his head toward the stinking bucket. "No need for the two of us to be traipsing back and forth." Harry nodded and left to perform the vile chore. The captain skulked into a dark corner where he sat and balanced his plate on his knees. As much as it would give him great satisfaction to throw the food in Langley's face his belly forced him to ignore the agent and he ate hungrily.

Harry returned carefully carrying the full water pail. He dropped the empty slop bucket down into the cellar and climbed down with the water. "Give me yer plate if ye wants breakfast in the morning," He ordered Gallo. The mining captain stood in the half-light hesitating. "Well, give it ta me," Harry said again. Gallo pushed the plate into Harry's gut and turned away.

"Ye 'ave a good night, now," Harry taunted as he eased the hatch door in place. He wasn't sure but thought he'd heard Gallo's boot connecting with the slop bucket as they left.

Chapter
77

L angley decided to stop by Paddy's house before riding on to the quarry. He had other details to see to before he could call it a day. It was with some apprehension that Paddy looked up to see the agent riding into his yard. He was standing outside when his employer rode in. *What the devil is going on now,* he thought as the agent drew nearer.

"Hullo, boss, what brings ye here?" He asked, surprise obvious in his facial expression.

"It seems there is no end to the list of favors I require," Langley said with a weary look on his face, "but it involves yer friend, Jake, as well. If ye're not busy would ye be willing to accompany me to his home? I have no idea where he lives, and, like I said, it involves the two of ye."

Paddy's look of consternation had the agent make a hasty explanation: "I need someone to build a sort of cage to hold Gallo, and a wagon to carry them both into town."

"Sure, boss, let me hitch my horse back up and ye can follow me to Jake's place," Paddy consented, "won't take long."

It was Jake's turn to be surprised when unexpected company showed up. He was out in his barn when the dog's agitated barking alerted him somebody was coming.

"Smokey! Sit!" He commanded the dog and stood waiting as Paddy's wagon rolled into the yard followed by Langley's steed.

"Hey, Jake," Paddy greeted him, "The boss has some business he wants to discuss with us."

Langley dismounted and looked about the yard, "Nice place ye got here," he complimented Jake as he gazed around him. "Ye got a great spot."

"We like it," Jake replied, "Still got a lot of work yet to do."

"Ye've done a good job of it from what I can see. Sorry to interrupt yer evening," Langley apologized, "I'm just on my way back from town. It looks like I may be able to get Gallo aboard a ship and on his way to the city. That's why I'm here.

"I need a wagon to carry 'im to town and some sort of cage to make sure he cannot escape on the way. I thought of ye and Paddy seeing as ye have the skills I need and Paddy has a wagon," he explained.

"I can do that but I don't have a lot of time and I have to work tomorrow," Jake hedged.

"If ye can start on it right away, ye won't have to come to the quarry in the mornin'. I will pay ye fer yer work. Two men will make the job quicker, so I thought if ye and Paddy worked on it together perhaps it would be finished by tomorrow evening. Is that a possibility?" Langley queried.

Jake cast a quick glance at his friend, "ye need something built straight away?" he asked.

"I do. Ye did such a fine job of fixing up the barn for Harry. What do ye say?

"I will need time to gather up enough boards. I could maybe use some of the scorched boards from the house the cap'n tried to burn down. If that suits," Jake raked his fingers through his hair as he considered the challenge.

"I got a bit of lumber scraps over ta my place," Paddy offered, "betwixt and between we should be able to get enough to finish the job."

"How big do ye want it?" Jake asked.

"It don't have to be all that large, just big enough to keep the man confined until we get 'im into town," Langley replied. "and it will have to fit into Paddy's wagon."

Jake looked at Paddy before answering: "Don't see why not. Paddy, what do ye think?"

Paddy shrugged, "I'm willing to help ye wit it. I s'pose it don't have to be nuddin' fancy."

"No, just sturdy enough that Gallo won't be able to tip it over, or move it in any way. Like I said, it's to prevent him trying to escape." Langley answered.

"Then I think we have a deal," Jake said and stretched out his hand.

Langley grasped Jake's hand and then turned and extended his to Paddy. "I knew I could count on ye. I am much obliged."

"If ye wants to come now, we can go collect the wood ye'll need," Paddy suggested to Jake, "then we can get started on it first thing in the mornin'."

"I need to let Mary know," Jake replied, "I think that's a good idea."

"I'll leave the two of ye to it, then," Langley remarked, "I will come after I see to some things in the quarry tomorrow. I bid ye both a good evenin'."

Langley's mind was much relieved with all he had accomplished. He had one more item to tick off his list and he gave it some thought as he cantered into the quarry. Doc was in the surgery sipping tea when the knock came at his door.

"Mr. Langley, good evening, sir. Please, come in, come in," Doc invited.

"Good evening to ye," Langley greeted him. "I come begging a favor, if ye please."

"What's that, now?" Doc asked.

"I need some kind of binding to keep our prisoner fastened while he's transported aboard a ship," Langley explained, "I'm not certain what to tell ye. T'was hoping ye might have some ideas."

"I'm just having a cup of tea. Why don't ye sit and join me while we talk it over," Doc offered.

"Tea sounds wonderful, I'm just getting back from town," Langley told him.

The men sat and considered the issue while they sipped the hot brew. Several ideas were brought up and discarded as they tried to come up with a solution.

"The thing is, he'll be aboard a fishing vessel and I doubt very highly there will be any sort of cell where he could be held," Langley explained as he told Doc about the plan to send Gallo to the city. "Most fishing vessels have little room in the hold for anything but the fish they carry and for the supplies for the fishermen. He must be kept bound in some way. He's sly and I don't trust him. Like as not he'd even throw himself overboard to escape."

"Perhaps a simple band of leather round his wrists and ankles would be yer best bet," Doc advised. "Or chains, but where would ye get chains around here?"

Langley rubbed his chin, "I am sure there is a blacksmith in town. I'm certain of it. I may need to ask the man at the livery stables where I keep my horse. I just thought Ye may have something around here, seeing as ye seen to the company horses back in the day, I don't have a lot of time to have shackles made."

"Don't see why a few strips of rawhide wouldn't work just as well," Doc surmised. "I do have some of that."

"I'll take 'em. Better that than nothing. I've just been tryin' to make sure I have every detail worked out, shackles would be my preference, but leather thongs would not be easy for him to get out of, if they're tied tight enough," Langley remarked. "If ye could gather what ye have so I can see 'em. I am hopin' to have 'im on a ship and on his way by tomorrow night."

"Why don't ye come out to the barn with me after ye're finished yer tea. We'll have a look-see," Doc suggested.

"If ye don't mind, I haven't had my supper yet. If ye could gather together whatever ye find I'll look at it in the morning. Tis been a long day. I think I will have my supper and see myself to bed," Langley said.

"I take it ye'll be using the bunk again tonight," Doc assumed, "I'll have it all ready fer ye to look at first thing in the morning. Matter of fact, I'll see to it right now."

Langley laid his lanky frame on the bunk. His thoughts continue to cascade through his mind like a river rapids, turbulent, sometimes violent, and constantly rushing one upon another. *I have things set in motion with any bit of luck Gallo will soon be in the belly of a ship, or held fast in one way or another and well on his way to St. John's. Not much else to be done.* Langley turned on his side, dismissing the avalanche of thought that threatened to keep him awake. Soon he was in a deep sleep.

Chapter

78

A s much as Peter had enjoyed his interlude on the beach he was not given for such leisure and he looked forward to a bit of activity after all the quiet days. Hilda had pronounced him well on his way to mending and Peter began making plans to visit his uncle in the near future.

"I need to see Langley this morning," Peter announced. "There are things I must discuss with him. Do I have yer blessing?" He asked Hilda.

"Well now, I s'pose ye're well enough," Hilda retorted, "don't push yerself just cuz ye're feelin' good this mornin'. Ye best take care of yerself."

"Best take 'er warnin' to heart, Peter, or ye will pay dearly fer it," Hank teased, "Hilda ain't a woman ye wants to cross."

"T'would never enter my mind," Peter grinned at his cousin.

"Go on, I've had me fill of ye 'angin' round, underfoot all the time," Hilda said nonchalantly, "but do mind me, Peter, don't try to bite off more than ye can chew."

"I will take care not to overdo it," Peter promised, "I do appreciate all ye both have done. I'd like to be off to see uncle before I leave for the city. I promised him I'd come fer a visit. He's likely wondering what became of me."

"Ye're not planning on leaving today, are ye?" Hilda asked.

"Yes, that's what I was thinkin'. By the time I spend a bit of time with Uncle John it will be getting into the fall. I need to be underway long before the first snows fly," Peter explained. "I promise, Hilda, I will be well looked after at my uncle's place. Mildred, Uncle's cook and housekeeper, will be fussing I've no doubt at all. If it weren't fer the promise I'd made Uncle John I'd leave from here. Mildred's twice as strict as ye and that's sayin' something!"

Hilda grinned unapologetically. "Sounds like my kind of woman. She must be strong to keep the likes of ye under control."

"She is strong. She's been lookin' after me since I was a little lad," Peter told Hilda, "It will be like bein' here with ye. She won't want to let me out of her sight if Uncle's told her of my mishap. I'm hopin' he hasn't."

"I hope 'e 'as," Hilda smiled, "Ye single men are worst than children. I swear ye are. Don't know when to quit fer yer own good. I 'ope this past while has been a lesson to ye."

"I have learned a thing or two. Who knew a little spill like that could be so crippling?" Peter remarked.

"It was a bad spill. Ye lost a lot of blood," Hank reminded him, "I don't know if ye realize how bad ye really were."

"Well, I feel as strong as an ox today," Peter retorted. "But don't ye worry, Hilda, I won't be undoing all yer hard work nursing me back to health." He hastened to add.

"I'll be 'olding ye to that promise," Hilda replied.

"If ye're finished eating we should be off," Hank put in, "are ye comin' now or did ye plan to wait until later?"

"No, I'll follow ye. I imagine Langley's likely already there," Peter replied. "Hilda, thanks again fer everything. I will come back to get my things and then I'll be leaving to visit Uncle John."

"Glad ye need to come back afore ye leave. I'll be able to rest my mind that ye're really okay to ride into town," Hilda responded.

"I'm not sure how long I will be at the quarry, but I will come say good-bye to ye and the children before I leave." Peter reassured her.

"Alright, that's enough dawdling. Come on, if ye're comin'," Hank told Peter.

Peter found Langley in the captain's shack, just as he'd thought he would. It felt like an age since he'd seen him, the days had dragged by so slowly.

"Good mornin'," Langley greeted him, "Ye have the best timing. There's been a lot going on since last we spoke. I have much to tell ye."

Langley proceeded to fill Peter in on the many plans he had underway to get the captain transported to the city.

"Ye've been a busy man!" Peter exclaimed, "and he may be on that fishing schooner as soon as this very evening?"

"If all goes according to plan, yes," Langley affirmed, "there are a few small details I need to iron out. Ye wouldn't happen to know of a blacksmith if I should need one?"

"Actually, the man who looks after my uncle's stable has some experience with blacksmithing. Did yer horse throw a shoe?" Peter asked.

"No, I was thinkin' a blacksmith could fashion some kind of shackles fer the prisoner," Langley replied. "Yet, there may not be time enough fer that."

"As a matter of fact, I came to see ye about lookin' over Gallo's books. I'm hopin' I can do that at yer office in town. I promised my uncle a visit but my injury has kept me down here at Hank's place. I am planning to go into town later today. I know I offered to go over the books with ye," Peter paused waiting for the agent's answer.

"That would work fine fer me as well," Langley replied, "I have been away from the office since all this business with Gallo began. I can leave Picton in charge here until I get Gallo on a ship and away. I need to take care of business at the office as well."

"Shall we meet at yer office then?" Peter asked. "I can see about getting' some sort of shackles made, or if not, perhaps Uncle can make a suggestion to keep 'im bound until he reaches St. John's."

"I had Doc look around the barns up at the surgery. He gave me what he had," Langley stood up and rooted in a box. "What do ye think? Will this work?" He asked holding out the leather cuffs Doc had fashioned out of an old harness. "He also gave me rawhide strips to tie 'im up with, if need be."

"It could work," Peter mused, "but it wouldn't hurt to see if Benjamin has any ideas. He might be able to fashion proper shackles."

"I'm hopin' Jake and Paddy will have a cage ready later today. I will be headin' up there after I'm finished here," Langley answered. "I will make sure to bring the books along and perhaps we can meet after supper at my office?"

"Yes, I can meet ye there," Peter replied.

"Let's do that," Langley agreed. "If I am not yet there ye can wait at the tavern in town." Peter nodded his agreement and the two men parted ways.

Peter was riding into town thinking fondly of Hilda, Hank and their family as he rode. *I am a man well blessed*, he thought. *I do hope Uncle has not mentioned my fall to Mildred.* Peter shuddered. *I know she will be watching over me like a hawk if he has. She means well. I know she does but my God I need a bit of freedom after this past week!* Peter allowed his thoughts to consider all the ramifications of getting Gallo safely underway as he rode. It was getting late in the afternoon before he reached his uncle's home.

"Good evenin', sir. Tis good to see ye," Benjamin greeted him when he rode his mare into the stables.

"Hullo, Benjamin! Just the man I need to see," Peter greeted him, "I have somethin' I need to discuss with ye." Peter explained about Gallo and his need for a set of handcuffs or shackles to keep the prisoner bound. Benjamin turned to search his stable for old horse shoes he could heat and mold into shackles, Peter at his elbow.

"I'd need to heat up the forge. It will take time," the groomsman told him, "Let me see what I can come up with. Ye must be getting' hungry. Why don't ye go on and have yer supper. I'll be out here when yer finished."

"Thank ye, I knew I could count on ye," Peter patted the older man's shoulder before turning to go to the house.

"Can't promise nuddin' but I'll do me best," Benjamin retorted. "Go on. Mildred will be tickled pink to see ye."

"Well, look what the cat dragged in," Mildred said coyly when Peter appeared in the kitchen door, "thought ye'd forgotten ye said ye'd be back fer a visit."

"How could I ferget the best cook in all the world?" Peter grinned as he flattered her. "Is Uncle home yet?"

"Go on wit yer nonsense! No, yer uncle's not home yet, but we're expectin 'im any minute," Mildred replied, "He'll be some glad to see ye. We bin hearin' stories about a fire down near the quarry. Tis bin a worry."

"I am sorry ye were worried. I got caught up in work down there and couldn't get away," Peter excused himself.

"And I s'pose it has nuddin' to do with that crack you got when ye fell from yer horse?" Mildred retorted. "Did ye think I wouldn't hear about that?"

Peter groaned. "I'd hoped ye hadn't," he admitted. "I've been doing little aside from lounging around Hank's house like some lazy old barn cat."

Mildred placed the lid she'd been holding back on the pot and stepped over to have a closer look at Peter's face. "Are ye feelin alright?" she asked.

"Fine as kind," Peter responded, "Hank's wife, Hilda, wouldn't let me out of her sight. She made sure I didn't lift a finger to do anything at all." He complained. "I've had about enough of laying about the house."

"Good fer her," Mildred said without an ounce of sympathy, "hard knock like that ye're lucky to be alive. Glad ye had a good woman lookin' after ye."

"Believe me, I did. Hilda is a great nurse," Peter replied.

"Well, ye got good color and yer eyes are clear. How's yer head? Any headaches?" Mildred asked.

"Not fer a couple of days," Peter told her, "I feel great. I really do."

"Have a seat, tell me about all them goings on down around the quarry," Mildred invited. Peter sat where she'd indicated and told her all of the adventures he'd had since his last visit. He was in the midst of relating his news when his uncle came into the room.

"Uncle John! I didn't hear ye come in," Peter exclaimed, standing up to embrace him.

"Ye were too busy chatting. Glad to see ye're safe and sound. We thought we'd see ye long before this. We were worried," John responded, "especially after yer last visit."

"I am sorry, Uncle. Hilda and Hank convinced me to stay put at their house. They were afraid to let me out of their sight. I was having difficulties with dizziness and headaches that were rather troublesome," Peter explained. "They thought I might take another fall from my horse if I tried to ride back to town."

"Ye're here now, that's the main thing. I am glad ye listened to yer cousins, wouldn't want ye to take a chance fer the sake of a visit," John replied.

"I will be here for a fortnight at least, if ye don't mind having me," Peter answered.

"Listen to the lad," John laughed, speaking to Mildred. Turning to Peter he said, "ye must know ye will always be welcome here. Now, I want to hear all that has happened since we last spoke. Mildred, supper will be at the usual time?" He asked.

"Yes, ye go on to the parlour. It will be a while yet before it's ready. Would ye like me to bring ye tea?" Mildred asked in turn.

"Yes, tea would be lovely," John told her.

Peter began filling his uncle in on all the news about the fire and the efforts to have the captain transported to the city.

"The man seems to be no end of trouble," John commented, "he doesn't think afore he leaps, does he?"

"No, he is rather impulsive," Peter agreed, "and dangerous as well."

"No doubt in my mind a'tall. That man, Langley, was right to fire 'im. It's one thing to hit yer horse with a stone and quite another to drag ye off into the bush to bleed to death. That was not impulsive. He was tryin' to save his own skin," John opined, "and that's what makes 'im dangerous. Seems to me the man will always look out fer his own interest, no matter what it may cost others."

"Hopefully Langley will have him aboard the fishing schooner this evening, or by tomorrow. There's a few small details need to be worked out. He needs some kind of shackles to keep 'im bound during his voyage back to the city. I asked Benjamin to see if he could come up with somethin'," Peter replied. "He was settin' his forge alight when I came in."

"If there's a way he can do it, he will," John responded, "Benjamin can fashion almost anything from iron."

"I don't like to see a man bound, but Gallo is so cunning and cannot be trusted. I don't see another way around it. Fishing schooners are not known fer a lot of space. I know once he's aboard a ship bound fer England he will be properly contained in a brig of some sort," Peter confided.

"That will be the naval authority's concern," John replied, "I think it is wise to keep him shackled until he's delivered to the proper authorities."

"I have to meet Langley at his offices after supper. We shall see what we can accomplish between the two of us," Peter remarked.

"So ye have made a friend of this Langley, it seems. From what ye tell me he seems like a good man," John remarked.

"He is. I think the men of the quarry will be in good hands now," Peter replied.

Just then Mildred rang the dinner bell and the pair left off their discussion.

Chapter
79

"See, Jackie-boy, tis Sunday and I am here to keep me promise to ye," Phil bounded onto the section of beach that Jack thought of as his special place.

"What are ye doin' down here anyway. Told ye I'd come troutin' with ye."

"Don't see no fishin' poles," Jack said, somewhat petulantly, "And I had to walk home with Sarah cuz ye were too busy with Haldi – again!"

"Look, Jack, ye can stay mad if ye wants. I wasn't that long and I'm here now," Phil retorted.

Jack turned his back on his brother and cast his last stone out into the water. It skipped merrily several times before slipping beneath the waves. Phil stood silently watching his brother before he spoke again.

"Jack? Do ye want to go troutin' or not?" he asked. "I left the poles up on the bank, thought we'd walk up the beach to where the stream pours out into the bay."

"I do. I just been wonderin' why ye wants to spend so much time with that girl," Jack's tone was sorrowful when he answered. "Seems like everything is changin' and I don't like it."

"Jack, I promise ye, nothin' will ever change between us. Ye're my best buddy as well as me brother. That ain't ever goin' ta change," Phil vowed. "Haldi is different. I ain't got words to describe it. She's just special, ye know?"

"No, I don't know," Jack argued, "all I know is that ye're not here even when ye're here. Ye're always drifting off in space and half the time ye don't hear what I'm sayin' to ye."

"I will make sure to listen to every word ye say to me today. I give ye me word of honour," Phil answered.

"Do ye swear? No talkin' 'bout Haldi or love or any of that foolishness?" Jack asked.

Phil clapped him on the back and threw an arm around his shoulder, "I swear by all that is holy. I, Phil Kelly, will give my brother, Jack, my total and undivided attention from this day forward."

Jack looked up into his brother's eyes, "Ye know, ye shouldn't make promises ye can't keep," he teased.

"Alright then, I swear on me word of honor, ye will have my complete and undivided attention until something reminds me of Haldi's pretty eyes, or her soft curls, or the way she makes me laugh, or how tiny she is, or the whiteness of her teeth, or her soft voice, or the kindness in her touch . . . I could go on. Want me to?" Phil's eyes danced with merriment.

"Yuck! If that's what love does to a fella, I hope I never, ever, meet a soul that has me all fooled up like ye are!" Jack's voice was filled with passion and he imitated Phil's swooning, clutching his heart and making big eyes at his brother.

Phil grabbed Jack in a headlock and rubbed the top of his head, hard. "I will be sure to remind ye when yer time comes." Jack stumbled back a half step when Phil released him.

"It ain't ever gonna happen. That I promise ye," Jack said with feeling. "Come on, let's go get them poles. I want to catch a trout."

"What're ye waiting fer? Let's go!" Phil turned and climbed up the bank to retrieve their fishing poles.

They were standing in the cool water, trousers rolled up to their knees in quiet companionship until Jack excitedly cried out when he caught the first of their catch.

"Wow! He's beauty!" Phil exclaimed as Jack removed the hook and held it up for his brother to admire.

"Told ye I'd catch the first one," he bragged.

"Day's not over, I bet I catch more than ye do," Phil retorted.

"We'll see about that," Jack returned. He was quiet for several minutes after throwing his catch up onto the beach. Phil watched his line carefully, looking for his first fish and didn't notice Jack's gaze was no longer on his line but cast far out to sea.

"Phil? Do ye remember when Uncle Joe was here fishin' with us? I miss 'im so much," Jack's voice caught and he stopped talking.

Phil glanced over at his younger brother and sorrow filled his eyes. "Yeah, I remember. He wouldn't keep the small ones but put 'em back in the water ever so gently."

"I remember 'im sayin, 'there ye go, little brother, go and have a good life'," Jack's voice was tearful as he spoke.

"He had such a great love fer all living things," Phil murmured.

Jack swiped at the tears that had come unbidden to his eyes. "I was kinda havin' a chat with 'im afore ye came," he confessed. "I like to come down to the beach after church on Sundays. He meets me here sometimes."

"Uncle Joe loved the beach," Phil commented, "he loved the fields and forests, too."

"Wish he'd never died," Jack whispered.

"So do I," Phil agreed, "ye're a lot like 'im. Did ye know that?"

"Lots of folks tell me that I look like 'im but I ain't got 'is good heart," Jack replied.

"I think ye do. Ye're like 'im in yer mannerisms and in the way ye love the outdoors and all life," Phil told him.

"Everythin's bin changin' so fast since he died," Jack said softly, "Now William is goin' ta marry Ginny and move into 'is own house. Maybe one day ye will marry Haldi and move away, too."

"Maybe one day," Phil admitted, "that won't be fer a long, long time though."

"Are ye courtin' er?" Jack asked quietly.

"Not exactly," Phil replied, "I hope to court 'er one day soon, but we can't get married fer a long time. Sure, she ain't much older than ye. Her parents ain't about to let 'er get married fer a long time yet. So, stop yer worryin'. I'll be around for years, b'y."

"Da says William and Ginny will be livin' close by and we can visit 'im any time we wants," Jack said thoughtfully. "Will ye always be close by?"

"Jackie-boy, I just tole ye, it will be years afore we can marry, and that's if she'd have me. Maybe she don't think of me that way," Phil confided.

"Huh! I seen the way she looks at ye. She's got it bad for ye," Jack responded.

"Do ye think so? I dunno 'bout that," Phil replied.

"She'd be luck to have ye," Jack told his brother, "Ye're the best."

"I knows I'm the best fisherman," Phil chortled as he brought his catch up high above the surface of the water, "look at the size of 'im. He's bigger than yers!"

The brothers spent the rest of the afternoon competing for the biggest catch and spending an enjoyable day together. Jack's heart was considerably lighter when they climbed the bank to go home, and Phil was reminded of how Jack grieved still for their uncle. He made a pact with himself vowing to spend more time with this brother whom he was so fond of.

Chapter

80

angley stopped at Jake's to check on their process after leaving the quarry. He grunted with satisfaction when his horse carried him to the open doorway of the barn where the men were still at work. He was in time to watch them nail the last boards on the crate that would ensure his prisoner would be securely contained during the drive into town.

"That's it, sir, tis finished," Jake remarked, "Now all that's left is to heft it onto the wagon."

"Ye did a fine job. It looks sturdy enough," Langley observed. He added his muscle to the effort to hoist it up onto the back of Paddy's wagon. The trio stood back and looked at the enclosure with critical eyes.

"It should be pushed back a bit more so it sits in the centre. T'will be better balanced that way," Jake suggested. Paddy climbed into the back and between he and Jake pushed the heavy enclosure until they felt it would not tip off the back should the wagon hit any deep ruts in the roadway.

Jake pulled a handkerchief from his pocket and wiped the sweat from his brow. "That should serve yer purposes, sir, tis big enough fer a man to stand up in and sturdy enough to restrain the strongest man."

"Will ye takin' the cap'n up to town this eve?" Paddy asked.

"Yes, I want to make sure he's there when the schooner arrives," Langley answered.

"Will ye join us fer supper, sir?" Jake asked. "I took the liberty of askin' my wife to prepare a meal. It should be about ready by now."

Langley looked up at the sun to gage the time before answering. "I am much obliged. If it isn't too much trouble."

Jake grinned at his employer, "I know ye've been staying at the quarry and the food is not the best, thought ye would enjoy a home cooked meal."

"I am blessed to have a wonderful cook and brought a hamper from my home so I have not been sufferin' unduly," the agent replied. "Yet, hot food would be most welcome."

"Tis glad I am to hear it," Paddy put in, "was afeared ye would want to leave immediately, and there ain't a better cook than Mary in these parts."

"We have time, just enough to eat but then we must go. We have yet to pick up Harry and our prisoner," Langley responded.

Mary was standing at the stove when the three men came in. She turned as Jake was ushering Langley inside.

"Mary, I'd like ye to meet Mr. Langley, my employer," Jake spoke nervously as the men filed into the kitchen.

Mary bobbed a half-curtsey and self-consciously lifted a hand to brush back a wisp of hair. "Honored to meet ye, sir," she said softly. She turned when she heard the sound of a baby crying and her sister's soft crooning. "If ye will excuse me fer a moment," she said, rushing away to check on her infants.

Paddy sat comfortably on the bench behind the table while Jake seated his guest of honor at the head of the table. The men could hear whispered conversation from the bedroom and Langley looked around with interest.

"Did ye build all the furniture ye have here?" He asked, admiring the sideboard and the sturdy table and chairs.

"I did, yes," Jake answered, coloring slightly, "Tis a small house. I am hoping to add on a couple of rooms."

"Ye will need them if ye plan on having more children," Langley said wryly. The agent had continued his examination of the cozy room until Mary reappeared with Haldi in her wake carrying one of the twins in her arms.

"This here's my sister, Haldi," she told Langley, still somewhat overwhelmed by her guest's presence at her table. Haldi did not speak but smiled at the agent and settled into the rocking chair with the child enfolded in her arms. Mary bustled about setting dishes on the table.

"Everything's ready," she told the men, "I just needs to dish it up."

"Let me help ye," Jake said standing up. "It smells delicious. Paddy's been bragging ye up," he told Mary, "Mr. Langley is lookin' forward to samplin' yer cookin'."

"Oh, go on wit ye," Mary said, blushing. "I hope ye all like it. It's nuddin' fancy, just potatoes and meat."

"It smells divine and I thank ye," Langley told Mary, "I've been eating cold meals so something hot will be a nice change."

Mary carried the platter of roasted venison to the table while Jake followed with the huge bowl of potatoes. Soon the table was laid out with a feast normally eaten on a holiday.

"Haldi, she's fallen back to sleep, why don't ye lay her back in 'er bed and come join us," Mary told her sister. Haldi rose to obey her sister, her head lowered in shyness.

"I've been curious to see yer husband's work," Langley said glancing about the tiny but spotless room at the open shelving and superbly crafted sideboard. "I will have need of furniture and he does fine work."

"He is the best carpenter ye'll ever meet," Mary said proudly, overcoming her shyness to praise her spouse. "Oh, here she is," she said as Haldi joined them at table. "Sir, if ye will do us the honor of saying the grace," she said as she turned toward Langley.

Now it was the agent's turn to be nonplussed. "Madam, I think the honor belongs to yer husband," he discreetly turned the invitation aside.

Jake gave Mary a look of consternation before mumbling out a short prayer of thanks for the provisions before them. Soon conversation was limited as three hungry men dug into the food in front of them.

"Mary, ye outdid yerself," Paddy said, wiping his mouth with a napkin, "that was some good."

"It was delicious," Langley added his praise, "I thank ye fer the fine meal."

Mary blushed again at the praise, "Ye're both very welcome. I am so glad ye liked it," she said.

"Forgive us, Madam, but we must be off," Langley apologized, "I must be in town this evening to see to some matters." He turned to Jake, "Thank ye for yer work on that, er, cage. It is good it was done early enough that I could enjoy such fine food. Thank ye again."

Jake stood to accompany the men outside. "Take care driving the wagon with that contraption aboard," he said to Paddy. "I s'pose Harry will be keeping an eye on the cap'n during the trip?"

"Yes, Harry has agreed to accompany the prisoner to the city," Langley told him, "I'll be following behind on my horse. Gallo would be a fool to try anything."

Jake nodded as Paddy climbed up onto the wagon seat. Langley mounted his steed and waved farewell. "I'll be seeing ye," Paddy called as he flipped the reins. It was a short trip to company property and the root cellar. It gave Paddy the opportunity to see if the enclosure would be steady for the drive into town. It was.

Chapter

81

Harry heard the wagon as Paddy drove into the laneway. He had just finished washing the tin plates and pots and was carrying them back to store in the barn. He hurried to tidy up as the wagon drew closer, Langley closely following. Paddy drove the wagon across the field until he came abreast of the root cellar. Langley stopped at the barn and walked his horse inside where Harry was waiting.

"Good evening, sir. I was wonderin' if I should pack up this remaining food to take along?" Harry queried.

"Seeing as how I don't know exactly when ye'll be boarding the schooner it might be a good idea," Langley replied. "Might be ye have to wait til mornin', or even a day or two afterward. I don't know if the schooner has arrived in the harbour yet."

Harry bustled about filling the hamper as they discussed incidental details. "He ain't give me a lick of trouble since ye was here last," he reported. "Thought he'd try agin to talk me into takin' 'is bribe, but nope, bin right quiet. Makes me worry what 'e 'as up 'is sleeve. There, 'amper's packed and ready to go. Shall we go git 'im?"

"He may try again to make his escape. We'll have to take good care," Langley warned as they walked away from the barn.

Harry looked across the field where Paddy's wagon stood waiting. "Won't 'ave no chance of getting' outta that," he said, "that cage is well made by the looks of it."

"He will be secure once we get him inside it," Langley agreed. "Mind how he threw that pail at ye and be ready for anything," he warned.

"Between the three of us we should be able to manage it," Harry replied.

Langley had the pistol in his hand when they entered the root cellar. Paddy was standing just outside the door, waiting.

"Mister Gallo, ye 'ave company again. Mr. Langley's 'ere and 'e's got a surprise fer ye," Harry called out as he lifted the hatch. He dropped the ladder into place as he continued to talk to his prisoner. "Ye can climb on out of there. Ye're about to get a bit of fresh air," he coaxed the captain.

Gallo came to stand at the foot of the ladder, "What's 'e want wit me now?" he asked suspiciously. Harry had been far too cheerful for his liking and he was leery of what was to come.

"Ye were told to come up. Now!" Langley barked his order.

"Why don't ye come in and git me?" Gallo answered, in no mood to be compliant.

"The way I see it, ye can either climb up here or stay there. Harry won't be here in the morning nor will anyone else. Ye can come out or stay down there and rot," Langley snarled.

Gallo glared up at his former boss and then spat onto the earthen floor. "Just what do ye intend to do wit me?" he asked.

"I am not about to answer yer questions. I gave ye choices, pick one," the agent growled.

Gallo cursed and grabbed at the ladder and began to slowly climb out of his dungeon. He'd reached the top rung when his gaze fell on the wagon waiting outside the door. "What do ye plan to do wit me?" He asked again.

Langley glanced outside and realized Gallo had seen the wagon. "I'm movin' ye, that's all," he told him.

Gallo hesitated a moment before climbing out. "Where are ye takin' me?" he asked.

Langley waved the pistol in Gallo's face, "I told ye, I will not answer yer questions. Shut yer mouth. Outside, now!" He ordered.

Gallo stood still, considering. Harry was standing to his left side. He held a cudgel in one hand. The agent in front of him with his pistol and Paddy a few feet from the door. He debated his chances at an escape as he walked slowly through the door.

"Now, hold out yer hands," Langley instructed. It was then the former captain turned his head to see the cage in the back of the wagon and he panicked.

"Ye aren't puttin' me in that thing!" He cried out and kicked out at Langley, connecting with his shin. The agent winced and Gallo fell face down when Harry hit him from behind with the stout stick. Paddy was quick to jump on the fallen man keeping his knee firmly in the centre of his back while he pulled his arms behind him.

Langley pulled the leather thongs from his pocket. "Here, tie 'im up," he told Paddy as he passed him the strings. Soon, Paddy had Gallo's hands tied firmly behind his back and grabbing him by his upper arm, pulled him to his feet. Gallo was dazed by the smack Harry had given him and swayed slightly.

"Now, ye're going to climb up on that wagon and get in yer cage," Langley spoke softly, "and if ye give me any more trouble I'll put a bullet in ye. Do ye understand?"

Gallo gave a single and silent nod. He was aching from the blow to his head. *Ye'll pay fer that,* he thought as he scowled in Harry's direction. He took a step toward the wagon and took a secret glee as each of the men kept their distance. The door to the contraption stood open and Gallo entered and sat on the crude bench Jake had built into the make shift cell. Paddy jumped onto the wagon and hurried to drop the board in place after slamming the door. Gallo sat and sullenly glared at his captors. The men moved away from the wagon to talk out of earshot of their prisoner.

Langley breathed a sigh of relief and looked at Harry. "Thanks fer that. I knew the bastard would try somethin'." he told him, "Glad ye thought to arm yerself."

"Well, 'e made mention of my injury," Harry replied, "I bin afeared 'e might try somethin'."

"Are ye sure about traveling with him aboard ship?" Langley asked, doubt evident in his tone.

"What's 'e gonna do once we're aboard? 'E won't 'ave nowhere to go. Besides, there's sure to be plenty of fisherman aboard as well," Harry replied. "It will be okay, boss. I managed 'im 'ere on me own, right?"

"If he gets a chance to talk to any of the men aboard ship, he may talk one of 'em into takin' the bribe ye refused," Langley pointed out.

"Ye could 'ave a word with the skipper, or send 'im word the prisoner is to 'ave no chance to chat to any of the crew," Harry suggested.

"I already put that in letters to both the skipper of the schooner and the mission ship," Langley informed him.

"Then ye ain't got nuddin to worry about," Harry answered.

"Aye, but I will worry until I know he's been delivered to the naval authority in the city," Langley retorted.

Paddy had stood by listening through the exchange but now he spoke up, "Boss, we best git goin' if ye wants to be in town afore dark," he suggested.

"Yes, ye're right. Stop at the barn, Harry has a hamper that must be loaded onto the wagon. Let's go," Langley responded.

"Why don't ye climb aboard the wagon, yer leg must be smartin from that kick he gave ye," Paddy suggested.

"I'm fine. Wouldn't give the bastard the satisfaction of knowin' it hurts," Langley replied. "Ye two go on. I can catch up to ye in no time. Ye will need to take it slow until ye see how the wagon bears the load."

Paddy and Harry did as he suggested, stopping at the barn to retrieve the hamper before driving out of the field and onto the roadway.

They didn't see Langley rubbing his shin or his limp as he walked to the barn.

Chapter

82

Peter cupped his hands around his eyes as he pressed his face to the window of Langley's office. He had knocked several times but without an answer. The door was locked. Giving up he stood back and looked up and down the street. There was no sign of the agent. Shrugging he decided to make his way to the tavern to wait as they'd arranged.

He shoved open the roughly hewn door as he entered and stood peering about the dimly lit room. At a table sat a familiar figure. Peter waited as his eyes adjusted to the lighting and then strode across the room to greet the figure seated there.

"Pastor Brown, what are ye doing here?" Peter asked in surprise.

"Good evening, Mr. Parsons. I have been called back to the city. It seems the minister there has taken ill," the cleric explained. "I will be sailing aboard the *Southern Cross* to meet up with the mission ship sailing fer St. John's."

"This is most welcome news," Peter enthused, "Langley is arranging to have our prisoner transported on that very schooner. How very fortunate."

"I wondered if he had followed up. I'd given him a telegraph to send to the Royal National Mission, and a letter as well," Brown related, "Perhaps I can be of service."

"Langley has hired a man to accompany Gallo to St. John's," Peter informed the cleric, "would ye be willin' to take important letters to the naval authority regarding the prisoner? We need them kept safe and delivered as soon as the ship reaches the harbour in the city."

"Yes, of course," the minister agreed. "I take it the naval authority will be informed."

"Yes, letters will be sent as well as a telegraph once Gallo is aboard ship," Peter told the cleric.

"When will the prisoner be brought into town?" Brown asked.

"I believe Langley will arrive with him at some point this evening," Peter replied, "I was to meet with him at his office. He has not arrived as yet. We agreed I would wait here in that case."

"I hope the skipper of the schooner will accept an additional three passengers. Some skippers are more accommodating than others," the cleric commented.

"I guess it t'will depend on how much space is left. With a bit of luck this vessel will be one of the larger ships," Peter replied, "Ye have not been down to the harbour to enquire?"

"No, I only arrived a short time ago. Thought I'd best have supper afore I am aboard ship with the questionable cooking talent," Brown smiled.

Langley looked less than pleased when he entered the tavern a short time later. He didn't trust clerics for reasons he seldom shared with another living soul. Peter stood to greet him.

"Ye made it! Did ye have any trouble with yer prisoner?" He asked as he stretched out a hand.

"Not much to speak of," Langley replied while he tipped his hat to the minister. "Mr. Brown, I did not expect to see ye here."

"As I was just explaining to Mr. Parsons, I have been recalled to the city and must make haste," the churchman responded.

"Pastor Brown will be traveling with Harry and yer prisoner," Peter interjected.

Langley raised his eyebrows, "Is that so?" He asked the preacher.

"If there is room aboard the schooner, I plan to be on it," Brown answered. "I take it Mr. Gallo is here with ye?"

"He is. I was fortunate to employ the labour of a carpenter to build a cell, of sorts. He is outside, waiting with his guard and a driver." Langley agreed.

"It will be a long voyage for him, contained in such a way," the cleric remarked.

"I doubt there is a way to have the cage moved to the ship. He will be shackled and, if ye please, I would prefer he have no communication with anyone aboard ship," Langley said.

"I cannot, in good conscience, agree to yer wishes. As a man of God, I will confer with any soul in need of the Lord's healing," Brown replied.

Langley said nothing as he searched the man's face before finally saying, "Ye may have yer mission and I have mine. My duty is to see to it that Gallo is received by the naval authorities in the city to be imprisoned there until such time as his transport to England is arranged."

"I will not interfere in yer mission. I ask that you do me the honor to not interfere in mine," the pastor answered. Langley was tight-lipped as he gave his single nod of assent.

"Perhaps we should ride down to the harbour to check on the whereabouts of the vessel?" Peter asked Langley.

"Yes, I think it best to do that forthwith," Langley answered. The two men said farewell to the cleric and walked outside. Langley walked down the street a short way with Peter matching his stride until he came abreast of Paddy's wagon.

"I'd like a word with ye both," Langley said to guard and driver. "Come."

Harry and Paddy climbed down from the wagon seat and followed the agent as he led them away from Gallo. The group of men stopped several yards away and spoke in hushed tones.

"Mr. Parsons and I will ride out to the harbour to check on the progress of the ship. Will ye both stay with the wagon until we return? Do not let the prisoner have an opportunity to talk to anyone," Langley instructed.

"Not even Pastor Brown if he makes an appearance?" Peter asked.

"I fear the good cleric may be hoodwinked by the captain. I'd prefer he not be given the opportunity to try," Langley replied and then turned to Harry. "Perhaps it would be best if ye were to follow us away from here," Langley told Harry and Paddy, "there is a place better suits my need where ye can wait for us. Drive the wagon down the street," He pointed in the direction he wished them to go. "We will catch up to ye and then ye can follow us." He instructed the men.

Langley rode his horse along the harbour after leaving Gallo in the hands of Harry and Paddy, safely stored away on a secluded stretch of road, far from the tavern. He was delighted to spy the same fisherman he'd spoken with before.

"Good eve, sir," he greeted the man as he dropped down from his saddle. "Any news of the Southern Cross?"

"She lays at anchor just around the shoals dere," the man said pointing at the strip of land that jutted out into the bay. "I spoke with yer man, Shaw, and delivered yer letter to the skipper. He is awaiting yer, er, cargo."

"That is splendid, indeed," Langley enthused. "It is necessary that I speak with 'im. I wonder if ye would carry another message to the skipper?"

"There ain't no need. 'E said to tell ye 'e will bring a row boat to shore in the morning. The sea is too rough for me to take me craft out there tonight. Ye need to be 'ere at first light," the fisherman relayed his message.

Langley nodded, "Thank ye for yer help."

"Tis me pleasure, ye paid me well fer the service. Tis I who should be thanking ye," the fisherman flashed his toothless grin.

The men bid the fisherman a good night and returned to the wagon where Paddy and Harry waited. Langley discussed the developments with the three men and it was decided Paddy would follow him to his house where guard and guarded could spend the night in his bunkhouse.

"I will meet ye at the harbour in the morn," Peter told them. "I am hoping Benjamin will have the shackles made and I will bring them if he's finished."

"Until the morrow, then," Langley agreed and waved his good-bye.

Chapter

83

Jack woke and rubbed his eyes. He'd had many dreams, almost nightly since his uncle died and the dregs of last night's continued to stand out clearly in his mind's eye. *Aw, Uncle Joe, if only it were all real and not just a dream,* he thought as he pulled on trousers and socks and made his way to the door.

"Mornin' Jackie-boy," his mother greeted as Jack walked softly across the kitchen floor. "Did ye sleep well?"

Jack yawned and stretched, "Lots of dreams, agin, but least this time they was good dreams. No nightmares," he told Fannie. "I just gotta go outside. Is Da up?" He asked.

"Yes, he's out in the barn already. Did ye dream of yer uncle again?" Fannie asked.

"Yis, ma'am, I did. I'll tell ye about it when I comes back in," Jack replied.

Fanny nodded as Jack reached for the door knob. *At least he slept all night. Tis either that or I slept more soundly than usual. I didn't hear a peep all night long,* she thought, *poor Jack, he's taken Joe's death hard but bless 'is heart, he's handling it better than many 'is age.* Fanny stood to lift the heavy kettle off the stove. The water was hot and ready for making tea. Thoughts of Jack and the recent trouble with the fire tumbled through her mind. She sighed audibly. *He's getting to be a man grown so quickly. S'pose it had to happen with 'im joining the men to work the quarry.* Fanny smiled remembering the little lad he'd once been. *I knows he's havin trouble getting used to the idea of William marrying and now Phil's lost his heart to Haldi. Time is going by so fast. Seems like only a moment ago he was playing with Sarah right here in this kitchen.*

Mick interrupted Fanny's walk down memory lane when he came inside. "Mouser left me a gift again," he told Fanny, "Wish the girls could teach 'er to stop leavin' dead rodents on the doorjamb. It's an awful sound of crunching bone when I steps on one."

Fanny made a face at Mick as she pictured it. "Well, ye encouraged it. Ye wouldn't take my side. I would've told 'em 'no' when William brought that kitten home."

Mick grinned without repentance, "She is earning 'er keep. Ye gots to admit it. And living up to 'er name as well. She really is a real good mouser."

"As long as she's stays out in the barn, I can put up wit 'er I s'pose," she answered. "Mick, did ye hear Jack a'tall last night? I must've been some tired, didn't hear a sound all night."

"Jack? No, not last night. I did hear the baby a time or two but he went straight back to sleep. First time he slept through the night since he was born," Mick remarked. "Jack must've slept well too, didn't hear 'im either."

"He's not having nightmares so often," Fanny remarked, "Not like he was. I knows he's still missing his uncle. As fer little Jimmy, he's been sleeping through the night fer a week now and this is the first ye noticed!" She smiled at her spouse.

"Jack is fine, Fan. Ye needs to stop yer worryin' over 'im," Mick replied, "he's stronger than ye knows."

"He wears his heart on his sleeve, much like Joe did," Fanny remarked. "I know he will be fine. He's having trouble with his brothers getting' all mixed up with girls. I think he's finding it too much, too many changes so soon after his uncle's death."

"He has to learn, Fan, that's just life and one day it will be his turn to be all besotted," Mick said gently.

Their conversation was cut short when Jack re-entered the room. "There ye are, Da, I was out lookin' fer ye in the barn. William and Phil still in bed?"

"Yeah, but they'll be out shortly. I was awake with first light. Tis still early yet. Ye take after yer mudder, up with the birds most days, but ye slept a bit longer this mornin' too," Mick pointed out.

Jack looked from one parent to the other as he decided whether to tell them of the wonderful dreams he'd been having. Shyly his gaze stayed on Fannie's face as he spoke: "I was dreaming about

Uncle Joe; it was such a good dream I didn't want to wake up. He was here, in our yard, and he had his little lad with him. Little Joe was chasing baby chicks around the garden, trying to catch one and Uncle Joe was laughing so hard. I miss his laugh," Jack's voice trailed off as he looked off into the distance, remembering. "He told me I was much like Little Joe when I was small.

"Aunt Elsie was there too, chasing after Little Joe. She couldn't catch him and that made Uncle laugh even harder." Jack paused again. "He told me not to worry, that he was fine and that one day we'd meet again in heaven."

"And ye will, my son, ye will," Fanny was quick to answer, "what a lovely dream to have. Ye must tell Elsie all about it. It'd be a comfort to her, I think."

"We never told ye that the wee babe was to be named after his father," Mick said thoughtfully. "We thought it would be too painful a reminder fer yer aunt and uncle to talk about it."

"Uncle Joe told me," Jack said simply, "guess he wanted me to know his son had a name, his name. He doesn't want us to ferget, said it would be a comfort fer Aunt Elsie to talk about their baby and to call him by name."

"Yer uncle was always much wiser than I," Mick told Jack, "Sometimes we think not talkin' is best, but that ain't true. At least, it ain't always true."

"He wanted me to tell ye something," Jack told his father, "He wanted ye to know he thought ye were the best brother a man could have, bar none. That's what he said."

Mick's eyes were moist as he peered at his son. "Thank fer tellin' me, son. I hope ye and yer brothers stay close like me and Joe did. Family is what life's all about."

Fanny stood suddenly and turned her back to father and son as she busied herself at the stove. "Maybe ye should call yer brothers, Jack. They seem to be sleepin' a touch too soundly this morn."

"Sure, Ma," Jack said to her back and he wondered why her voice seemed a bit muffled. It wasn't like her to mumble her words.

Jack didn't tell anyone about the rest of his dreams. The ones where his uncle was reassuring him that his brothers would always, always love him, no matter what. He felt a bit ashamed that Joe had to remind him that he, too, had to be a good brother and not just to Phil and William but to his sisters and baby brother as well. He hadn't thought how his goin' off to work in the quarry had affected Sarah, nor how much she missed him. *Mind, now, ye ain't the only one's bin hurtin'*, Joe's voice repeated in his mind, *yer brothers and sisters are too.* Jack nodded as he took the message to heart. *I hope he comes to me in my dreams again. He explains about life and death and the Creator better than any preacher I ever heard.*

Jack crossed to the bedroom he shared with his older brothers. *Soon William will be moved away with Ginny. I best remember Uncle's advice to be a good brother,* he told himself as his hand grabbed William's shoulder and shook him.

"Time to git up," he spoke firmly. He reached into the top bunk to wake Phil as well. "C'mon git outta bed. Ma's got breakfast ready."

Jack smiled to himself as his brothers grunted and growled at him and then turned to leave the room.

Chapter

84

The morning dawned thick with fog as Harry rolled off the bunk and tentatively stretched his arms overhead. He winced as the familiar pain helped him remember he was not yet fully healed. He dropped his arms and peered into the bunk above him.

"Paddy, hey Paddy," he whispered urgently, "tis time we was up. The boss will be out 'ere any minute now."

Paddy winced, "Already? Seems like I jist closed me eyes," he complained. He dragged his legs out from under the thick quilt and allowed them to hang down from his bed as he willed himself awake. "Tis still dark, sure," he remarked, "no sign of light a'tall."

"Langley said we'd be leaving afore dawn," Harry reminded him.

"That friggin' cap'n kept me awake wit his snoring. Ye slept right through it," Paddy remarked.

"Couldn't 'ave bin that bad. I'm a light sleeper," Harry retorted.

"Ye lost yer hearin' then," Paddy responded, "t'was enough to wake the dead sure."

"I didn't 'ear a ting. I best go find an outhouse and check on the prisoner," Harry yawned. He walked past the wagon Paddy had driven into the stables and noticed the captain was still rolled tightly in the blanket he'd been given. He laid on the bench Jake had built into the cage. Langley would not allow his removal the night before. Harry scratched his head as he headed toward the door. He was opening it when it was pulled from his hands.

"Good, ye're up," Langley said as he stood in the half open doorway.

"Yes, I was jist goin' to go find an outhouse or some place to relieve meself," Harry answered, "Paddy's awake as well, still sittin' on 'is bunk."

"There's an outhouse around the back of the building. Tis easy to find. Any trouble from Gallo last night?" the agent asked.

"Paddy said 'e kept 'im awake wit 'is snorin' so I guess 'e was trouble of a sort, 'e was still wrapped up tight in 'is blanket when I went by," Harry replied, "Still safe and sound inside 'is cage."

Langley's steed heard his voice and whinnied a welcome. "I need to take care of my horse and get him saddled. We'll leave as soon as ye are ready," he told Harry, "Go on about yer business."

Langley's groom was already feeding the animal when his boss came into the stables. The agent ignored the wagon and its occupant as he moved past it to his horse's stall. "Make sure he has a feedbag ready for me to take. Get him saddled up. I need to leave very shortly," he instructed the groom. "I need ye to hitch yonder mare to that wagon when yer done." The groom nodded and moved to do as he was bid. Langley moved toward the back of the stable where the bunkhouse was located.

"Morning, Paddy," he greeted his driver. "I hope to be underway shortly. Harry tells me ye had no trouble with Gallo through the night."

"No, not a bit, unless ye consider 'is ruddy snorin'," Paddy replied sourly.

"Ye won't be hearin' 'im again, with any luck he will be off and on his way to St. John's before the day is done," Langley replied.

"Ye seen Harry then?" Paddy asked as he dropped down from his bunk.

"Yeah, I did. If ye need the outhouse it's out behind the stables. Harry's out there now," Langley told Paddy, "We'll leave when ye get back."

The thick fog made the trees look like phantoms stretching their finger-like branches skyward only to disappear into the morning mist. Langley led the wagon out through the tree-lined drive to the roadway. Gallo sat in his cage. He had caught fragments of the conversation around him and knew he was to be aboard a ship before the day was out. His thoughts were morose as he considered his fate and the unlikeliness of any possible escape. *God 'elp 'im if I gets loose. I'll make the devils pay, I will,* Gallo promised himself as he worked to loosen the rawhide strips that kept him bound. His wrists and hands were sore from the constant rubbing against the rough boards that made up his enclosure. He could see little of his surroundings but worked on in the faint hope of escape.

Paddy followed Langley's bobbing lantern and carefully guided the wagon. The sky had lightened but the fog made visibility difficult and the going was slow. Langley's steed increased its speed from a walk to a slow trot once they'd reached the main roadway. It was Peter's lantern that guided the travelers to the wharf where he stood waiting for them.

"Good morn'," Peter called out as they approached.

"Hullo, good morn' to ye," Langley answered. "Have ye seen any sign of the ship?"

"Nay, not a one, the fog's too thick. Sun's comin' up, with any bit of luck it t'will burn it off before long," Peter answered.

"Ye two stay here," the agent told Paddy and Harry. Langley dropped down from his saddle and walked toward Peter, leading his horse. "Did yer groom have any luck with making shackles?"

Peter rattled the contraption he held in his hand. "He did, and a fine job he made of 'em, too." He held the handcuffs out for Langley's inspection. "He made shackles to go 'round his ankles, too. They're in my saddlebag."

"I s'pose we'll have to wait to put shackles around his feet, at least until we get 'im aboard ship," Langley commented.

"T'would make it hard for 'im to climb the rigging," Peter agreed.

"If we were in St. John's he'd be walking a plank to board," Langley sighed, "we'll have to make do with what we got."

"If we were in the city the naval authority would already have 'im and we wouldn't have to deal with all this," Peter pointed out.

"Tis true," Langley agreed gazing out over the bay where the sun was lighting the sky but had yet to penetrate the mist.

"Come on over here," Langley called out to Paddy and Harry, "Gallo's fine where he is."

Soon the four men were talking and making plans on how to arrange getting their prisoner into the row boat once it arrived. They were in the midst of their discussions when Paddy spied a man walking out of the fog.

"Hullo, who's there?" he called.

"Good morn," Brown answered as he picked his way carefully toward the group of men. "Tis I, Pastor Brown."

Langley grimaced at Peter as the minister approached. It was Peter who was left to make introductions.

"So, ye're planning on makin' the same journey wit me and the cap'n?" Harry asked.

"I am," the cleric responded, "I will be with ye all the way to St. John's, God willing, and if the skipper agrees."

"Ye haven't made arrangements with 'im?" Langley enquired.

"No, I only arrived in town late yesterday afternoon, but I have made several such trips and I am hoping to have already made the skipper's acquaintance," Brown replied.

"I have paid fer the prisoner and his guard here," Langley said nodding toward Harry, "I expect they will be taken aboard first."

"I will wait, if I must. Still, I am hopeful to make the voyage today, if at all possible," Brown answered.

The men stood in awkward silence until Langley spoke up, "I must see to the prisoner. Gentlemen, I may require assistance," he said.

Brown sensing Langley's animosity replied, "I will just take a walk as we wait. It is likely to take some time."

Peter nodded at the minister before turning to follow the agent to the wagon. The four men continued their discussion once the cleric was out of earshot. Langley repeated his instructions to Harry regarding the need to keep Gallo away from the cleric, should he be able to join them aboard ship. They had been waiting a long time before the fog dispersed and Paddy spied the row boat making for shore.

"That could be yer boat there, hard to tell if it's a dory or a rowboat just yet," he remarked.

Langley lifted his hand to shade his eyes as he looked to where Paddy was pointing. Within minutes it became obvious it was the vessel they'd been waiting on.

"Alright, men, guess it's time," the agent commented. "Gallo," he barked, "We're going to take ye out of yer cage. There are four of us here now. Ye can't escape so put it out of yer mind. Do ye hear? My pistol will be aimed at yer head the whole time. Mind that."

It was Paddy who climbed onto the back of the wagon to release the man. He lifted the board that held the door fast and stood aside waiting for Gallo to emerge.

"Ye might just as well shoot me now, I ain't movin'. Ye ain't puttin' me aboard no ship," Gallo cried out.

"We'll see about that," Paddy answered and reaching in grabbed Gallo by his upper arm, pulling him off the bench. As before, Gallo kicked out aiming for Paddy's shins and missed. The two men tussled but Gallo, with arms still fastened behind his back was off balance and tumbled from the wagon.

Paddy stood still on the back of the wagon looking down at his adversary and panting from his efforts to manhandle the prisoner.

Harry leaned over the man sprawled on the ground, "Ye sure likes to make things 'ard on yerself, don't ye?"

Gallo rolled onto his side and laid still, waiting. When Harry came closer, he aimed his foot at his guard's groin but missed again as Harry turned aside and dodged his kick. Paddy jumped down from the wagon, enraged. He grabbed Gallo before he could make another move and dragged him roughly to his feet. He shook the man, "try that agin and I will knock the livin' day lights outta ye," he threatened.

"Give me them shackles," Langley said to Peter. Taking the handcuffs from Peter's hands the agent walked behind Gallo and fastened them around his wrists. "Will ye get the ankle chains as well?" He asked, looking at Peter. Peter began to walk away but stopped and returned. He handed his pistol to Harry. "Just in case ye may need it," he said before walking to his horse to retrieve them.

Gallo was glaring at the men, his eyes darting from face to face, hostility and antagonism evident on his face. "Ye best 'ope ye never sees me agin. If I ever gets back 'ere I'll kill the lot of ye," he threatened.

"Ye ain't ever settin' foot in these parts again," Langley told him, very softly. "Go ahead and make all yer plans fer vengeance, ye ain't ever going to live long enough to carry 'em out."

Peter returned, shackles rattling noisily as he handed them to Langley. "He made the chains long enough so he can walk, but he won't be able to kick nobody else," he said, "if he tries, he'll end up flat on his back."

"Hold 'im down," Langley told the men, "keep 'im still while I place these on his ankles."

Gallo fought hard as the men pushed him down, resisting every effort made to shackle his feet. In the end it proved fruitless and he lay panting on his stomach. Paddy's knee was between his should blades once again as Harry firmly held his thighs.

"Will 'e be able to make it to the rowboat?" Harry asked once Gallo was hauled to his feet once more.

"We'll carry 'im if we have to," Langley answered. He turned and grinned menacingly at his former mining captain. "And if we drops 'im in the water t'will be his own fault. What's it going to be, Gallo? Are ye going to walk like a man or be bundled aboard?"

Gallo's look of hatred met Langley's query. "I'll walk," he growled.

"Ye're smarter than ye look," Langley replied.

"There ye go, thanks," Harry said, returning Peter's pistol to him.

"Looks like we have more company," Peter remarked pointing to a small dory that was making for shore.

"That will be the fisherman I hired to take me out to the schooner," Langley replied. "I want to personally see to it that he's safely confined aboard ship. I didn't think there'd be room for all of us in the rowboat."

"Here comes the preacher," Paddy said, "You were wise to hire that fisherman."

Langley did not reply but watched as the two boats drew closer to shore. It took some doing but a short time later Gallo was sitting in the bow of the rowboat, Langley's pistol in Harry's hand as they made for the schooner in the distance.

Once aboard the ship, Langley sought out the skipper and gave him instructions regarding his prisoner. In a surprising turn, Langley had gracefully invited the cleric to join him in the dory to take him to the schooner to make his plea for passage. The agent was not pleased to learn the churchman would join Harry and Gallo on the schooner. That fact worried him and played on his mind.

At least he will guard the legal documents placed in his care, Langley thought as the fisherman rowed the dory back to shore, *and he was helpful in writing letters to make arrangements for the mission ship to collect that scoundrel. As ministers go, I've known worst.* Langley patted his pocket where the telegraph he'd written to inform the authorities of Gallo's departure and his estimated time of arrival in the city was waiting to be delivered. Grunting he turned his thoughts back to the company he worked for and the reams of paper and log books he had yet to pore over.

Chapter

85

Peter had stood next to Paddy on the shore and watched as the two small craft rowed out to the schooner.

"No point to us waiting 'round here," Peter said turning to Paddy. "What say ye to breakfast at the tavern in town? I'm to meet Langley at his office and I am famished. T'was an earlier start to the day than usual."

Paddy glanced at the man shame-faced, "I ain't brought no money. Can't pay fer food. Harry left me a bit of hard tack. I'll gnaw on that on me way home."

"I'd be grateful for a bit of company. T'would be a favor ye'd be doing me. I will pay," Peter coaxed.

Paddy hesitated and Peter rightly took it for pride. "The favor ye did fer Langley in getting' Gallo into town profited me as well. I'd like the chance to repay ye in this small way," he pointed out.

"Well now, I could eat, I s'pose and I daresay hard tack ain't all that appealing," Paddy reluctantly agreed. Peter nodded and the two men walked back to where their conveyance stood waiting.

"If ye follow me we'll go there directly," Peter replied as he climbed up into his saddle.

The tavern was empty of customers when the two men arrived. A young woman was wiping down tables and getting ready for the day. Paddy followed Peter to a table and sat in a chair across from him.

"Any chance of getting' breakfast?" Peter asked the woman.

"Tis early but cook will rustle up somethin' fer ye, I allow," she answered. "T'won't be nuddin' fancy but t'will fill yer bellies. Let me go ask."

Peter looked at Paddy and grinned. "Food is good here. I've yet to be disappointed."

In mere moments she returned, "Cook says she can give ye eggs and bread and a slice of ham if that suits ye," she told them.

"That sounds wonderful and could ye bring us a pot of tea?" Pete asked.

"I'll bring it out soon as the kettle boils," the woman bobbed and walked away.

"I ain't ever bin in here," Paddy remarked as he looked around the room. "Ain't got cause to come into town much." He looked back at Peter, "Do ye s'pose the cap'n will give Harry any trouble aboard ship?"

"He isn't one to make life easy on his captors," Peter replied. "But the skipper would not take kindly to 'im causing any trouble. Harry will have help there and from the fishermen, I daresay."

"I hope so. Harry's a good man. Don't know 'im real well. He sure is a funny duck," Paddy remarked.

"Why do ye say that?" Peter asked.

"He wants me to stop at the barn on me way home, seems he took in a stray cat he named Patches. He was right worried about 'er," Paddy related the conversation he'd had with Harry while they'd waited for the row boat to take Gallo away. "I promised 'im I'd take care of 'er."

Peter smiled. "He's a surprising character, that Harry," he remarked.

"He is that. He comes off like a rough and tumble sort, but he has a big soft spot. Least he does fer that cat," Paddy commented.

"Langley told me Gallo had tried to bribe him to help him escape the root cellar. Harry refused his bribe. That tells me he's a man of integrity and honesty," Peter replied.

"I can attest to that. He followed Langley's instructions to the letter and he don't hold no love fer the cap'n. He was workin' wit Joe the day he got hurt. Seems they was friends a long time. Harry wouldn't take kindly to Gallo tryin' to bribe 'im. He didn't mention nuddin' to me but I knows he holds the cap'n responsible fer Joe's death. He as much as told me that," Paddy replied.

"And rightly so, he did play a big part in causing the man's death," Peter agreed.

"Sure hope he makes the trip without too many shenanigans," Paddy responded, "he ain't finished healing from them busted ribs. T'wouldn't take much to overcome 'im."

"Langley wouldn't have had him as a guard fer the journey if he was concerned about that. Like I said, the skipper will make sure he can't cause no harm," Peter mused.

"I hope ye're right," Paddy replied. Just then the waiter arrived with a big pot of tea.

"I'll get yer table set, yer breakfast will be ready in a bit," she said as she set the pot on the table in front of them. The men were silent as she scurried back and forth bringing cups, flatware, and napkins.

"I'll ask Langley to make sure he gets word to ye once the ship arrives in St. John's. Now, tell me, how are ye finding things at the quarry since the association was formed," Peter invited as soon as they were alone again. Paddy began telling Peter about all the improvements being made and the men fell into a discussion about the quarry.

Chapter

86

J ake was cleaning out the chicken coop when Paddy's wagon rolled into the yard. His dog took to leaping and barking, as per usual when she wanted to alert her master of company. Jake laid the pitchfork against the wall and wandered outside to see what the fuss was about.

"Paddy, hullo, how was yer trip to town?" Jake greeted his friend. "What in the name of God have ye got there?"

Paddy climbed down from the wagon seat holding the cat tight against his chest. "Would ye mind tying Smokey on fer a bit?" He asked without answering.

Jake grabbed his dog by her collar as she leapt up on Paddy, obviously curious about the bundle in his arms. Jake had to pull the dog away, all the while the animal whined and tugged, trying to get to Paddy.

"There now, Smokey, sit! Quiet now!" Jake commanded the animal, all the while glancing back at the cat Paddy held tight against his chest.

"Thought mebbe ye could use a cat fer yer barn," Paddy remarked, "Harry asked me to take care of 'er but there's too many cats at our place as it is. I daresay they'd run 'er off."

Jake walked over to investigate the furry bundle. "She's right purdy, ain't she?" He asked as he reached out to stroke the cat's fur. "Come on, let's see how she likes the barn."

Paddy followed into the barn and held the feline until Jake closed the barn door. He knelt down before gently releasing her.

"Look at that, now," Jake exclaimed as Patches wound herself around his ankles. "She's some friendly, what?"

Paddy shook his head. "Somehow or other she took a shine to Harry and has been keepin' 'im company. He made me promise 'im I'd take care of finding 'er a home," Paddy explained.

"Seems like she's found one," Jake replied wonderingly as the cat continued to wind herself around his ankles, purring loudly. "I've been meanin' to get one fer the barn. Nuddin' like a cat to keep the mice and rodents away."

"She ain't shy, that's fer sure," Paddy remarked, "she didn't run away or nuddin' when I got to the barn and she was not one peck of trouble in the wagon neither. She wasn't even afeared of yer dog."

Jake leaned down to scratch her ears. "And what about yer trip? The cage worked out alright? I take it Gallo's on 'is way by now?"

"The cage was perfect. I think Langley was right. If we'd tried to move 'im without it he'd of likely tried to jump off the wagon and run away. Yeah, he's aboard a schooner sailing away by now I'd guess," Paddy replied.

Jake sighed a big sigh of relief. "Can't tell ye how glad I am to hear it."

"Ye're not alone in that," Paddy responded, "good riddance, I say."

"And he didn't give ye no trouble?" Jake asked.

"Wouldn't say that," Paddy answered and proceeded to describe the issues they'd had getting Gallo into the row boat and away. The two men continued their conversation as the cat explored her new domicile.

"Why don't ye come in the house. There's left over supper and ye can tell the women about the cat ye brought back. Haldi will love it. She had her own cat back home. What do ye say?" Jake asked.

"Now, ye knows, I ain't ever gonna refuse any food Mary's cooked," Paddy grinned.

Chapter

87

A crewman had dropped down into the rowboat as they pulled alongside the schooner and in short order had removed the shackles and rawhide strips that had bound Gallo's wrists only to replace them with manacles made for restraining troublesome sailors. At least his arms were no longer behind his back and he gained some use of his hands, though movement remained limited. It allowed for easier climbing of the rigging and Gallo was grateful for the mug of water he was given once aboard.

"Take 'im down below," the skipper ordered the crewman "there's room beside the head. Make sure ye attach his shackles to the side beam. He ain't gonna be makin' trouble aboard me ship." The skipper turned to Harry, "If ye wants to watch 'im down below ye can follow 'em or ye can stay above, tis up to ye."

"If it's all the same to ye, I'll just make sure he's well secured and then I'll make the journey above deck," Harry replied thinking about the stench of the ship's toilet and wanting to avoid it.

"Do as ye please, but stay out of the way. Tis a workin' schooner ye're on and the men have their work to do," the skipper replied.

"C'mon, let's go," the crewman said as he grabbed Gallo's upper arm to guide him.

Gallo hung his head as he was marched to the ladder leading below deck. His shackles clanged as he was prodded along. He was tired after a night with little sleep and his wrestling match on shore. Still, he made sure to pay attention to his surroundings as he shuffled along. He'd also paid close attention to the fishermen he'd encountered marking those he thought might be likely to be sympathetic to his plight.

"Well, now, e's held fast," Harry remarked as the sailor closed the iron ring after looping Gallo's ankle chain through it. Gallo was confined in a small space with just enough room for him to sit or lay down, as needed.

"Yis sir, 'e ain't going nowhere," the sailor agreed. Turning to Gallo he said, "Yer guard can bring ye water and food as he sees fit. Ye may as well get comfortable it will be days afore we meets up with the mission ship."

Gallo did not respond but glared at Harry as he sunk to the floor. "Are ye stayin' 'ere wit 'im or are ye comin' above deck?" the sailor asked Harry.

"I'm comin' above wit ye," Harry answered, "I've 'ad enough of 'is company." He reached into the small satchel he carried and pulled out a piece of hard tack. He placed it on the floor next to Gallo. "Ye can eat, or not, tis up to ye." He told his prisoner, then turned to follow the sailor.

Brown was leaning on the ships' rail when Harry appeared beside him. "Tis fair seas," he remarked, "a good beginning fer our voyage. Is the prisoner safely secured?"

"Yis, b'y, 'e is. I doubt there'll be any trouble from 'im aboard this ship. I 'ope the next skipper is as 'elpful," Harry replied. "Langley 'ad nuddin' to worry over as far as this first leg of the journey is concerned."

Harry gazed out at the vanishing horizon and prayed the calm seas and easy beginning were an omen of what was to come.

Chapter

88

L angley made straight for the telegraph office as soon as he'd reached town. After paying for the service, he retraced his steps to visit the tavern for breakfast before returning to his office. He had just finished giving Shaw his instructions for the day when Peter appeared.

"I take it Gallo is off and away to St. John's without any further trouble?" Peter enquired without preamble.

"He is. I have sent a telegraph to the authorities so they can look fer the ship's arrival. Tis a mercy to have him taken off my hands," Langley replied, "the skipper was most helpful, though it cost a few extra coins to ensure he is kept well-secured. Tis money well-spent in my estimation."

"Dominion Limestone will foot the bill?" Peter asked.

"Just to deliver him to St. John's, after that it's up to the naval authorities to finance his removal to London," Langley responded.

"Well, the company will recoup their monies in future. Gallo will no longer be able to steal from them," Peter commented.

"Yes, that is what I pointed out to Morgan in my letter when his thievery was first discovered," Langley replied. "When do ye plan to leave fer the city?"

"I will spend a fortnight at least visiting my uncle but must not wait overlong to depart. The trails across the island are rough at best and I do not wish to be caught in an early snow storm on the way," Peter answered. "I promised ye I would help go over the books for the quarry and I intend to do that while I am still here in town."

"It will be quite an undertaking. I noticed the books are irregular and not organized well. Still, with yer help we can resolve any discrepancies and cast light on where Gallo was pilfering monies," Langley remarked.

"His ill-gotten gains will not be unduly difficult to itemize, especially since records in own hand show his activities," Peter answered. "When would ye like to start on it?"

"I know the company is anxious for a full report but the day began unduly early because of the need to be on shore to meet the row boat at first light. If it is to your liking we could start on the morrow. There is much that needs doing here that I have been neglecting what with making arrangements for Gallo's incarceration and dealing with things in the quarry," Langley explained.

"There is one more piece of business waiting," Peter said apologetically, "With all the goings on I have yet to get the widow's agreement to the terms you specified."

Langley waved the statement away, "She will be compensated. I no longer feel the need for any legal document. I will see to it personally and place the monies in her hand myself when next I go to the quarry. I'd not forgotten."

"That is most generous of ye. What will become of the men in the quarry and the monies Gallo stole from their wages?" Peter asked.

"That, my dear sir, is something I have yet to figure out. Harry told me about the money Gallo hid in the woods. I will find it and once we have gone over the books will be able to add up the total. The men will receive what is rightfully theirs. Ye have my promise," Langley vowed.

"Have ye written to Morgan about that?" Peter enquired.

"No, as I said, I first have to go through the books. I also have to locate his stolen stash. I am hopeful there will be enough monies in it to cover the lost wages," Langley replied, "The man has left a lot of problems that I will need to deal with. I will write to Morgan once I know the situation more intimately."

"I shall leave ye to yer work," Peter replied, "I will return on the morrow to lend my efforts."

Langley nodded, "Thank ye, kindly, until the morrow then."

John was in his study when Peter returned. "Tis good ye're back a bit earlier than anticipated, he said after greeting him, "I had taken it on myself to telegraph a colleague in the city to ask him to make inquiries about Gallo. I felt it necessary after the rogue left ye fer dead. I wanted to know if he'd committed any crimes in the city." John nodded toward a missive on his desk. "I received his response just this morning."

Peter dropped into the chair in front of his uncle's' desk. "What did ye learn?" He asked curiously.

"Seems the man worked fer a bookkeeper in the city for nearly a decade. He was robbing his employer the whole time. When his misdeeds were discovered, he was fired," John related. "He left the city but not before attempting to murder his employer. He'd laid in wait fer 'im in a back alley. He had a knife. The bookkeeper was able to fend him off and the scoundrel managed to get away."

"So, he could face charges other than those levied by Dominion Limestone and myself," Peter commented.

"That's not all," John spoke gravely, "he was also blackmailing certain men of means. There is no proof, of course, there is only rumour that the men were involved in some rather distasteful behaviour and would not bring any charges against him. They are interested only in protecting their good names."

"Distasteful behaviour?" Peter questioned.

"Involving young boys," John cleared his throat before continuing, "depraved behaviour, ye might say."

Peter stared at his uncle, comprehension dawning. He did not speak.

"It is rumoured that Gallo himself was one that was badly used by such men. I know that does not excuse his crimes . . ." John's voice trailed off. "To make matters worse rumour has it that Gallo was able to blackmail these men because he was the one procuring youngsters for their entertainment."

"His fate is sealed, then." Peter said quietly.

"Yes, I daresay he will spend the rest of his life behind bars. Men of means have ways of exacting their revenge," John responded.

"What of the youngsters he procured? Did yer colleague have news of them?" Peter wanted to know.

"No. They were more likely orphans or children of very poor families," John said sadly.

"There is no justice for innocents in this world," Peter observed.

"It is a harsh life for too many," John agreed. "I have not asked, were ye able to have him put aboard the schooner?"

"Yes, Uncle, he is now beginning his journey to face his judges," Peter replied and described the morning's events leading up to Gallo's transport to the schooner. The men sat gravely discussing the former mining captain and his many crimes and making assumptions about his possible sentence and what, if anything, could be done for his victims.

Chapter
89

Harry woke to blue skies and choppy seas. The schooner was rolling with the waves, many of which splashed over the rails. He sat for a moment. Sleep had been fitful and his bones ached from laying on the hard surface of the deck. Harry shook off his slumber.

Last day aboard this vessel, I 'ope, Harry thought as he recalled the conversation, he'd had with the skipper the night before. Harry grabbed at the railing as the ship rolled again in the swells, nearly knocking him off his feet. *Now I remember why I 'ate sailing,* he thought as he lurched toward the bow. *I 'ope the Princess May is less apt to roll like this one does,* Harry thought as his stomach threatened to heave. Slowly he made his way to the ladder leading down to the hold. Harry gingerly climbed down hanging on tightly to every rung as he descended.

He stopped briefly beside Gallo who was sitting against the wall. "Ye don't seem any the worst fer wear," he told him. The captain did not answer but glared up into his guard's face. Harry double checked the shackles that were chained through the iron loop and, satisfied that his prisoner was still secure, moved toward the head.

Weren't no cause to chain me up down 'ere like a common criminal, Gallo thought as Harry moved away, *I ain't done nuddin' so wrong I deserves this.* The former captain thought back on his one and only chance to garner the help of one of the crewmen.

"What'd ye do to git ye chained up down 'ere like an animal?" a sailor had questioned him.

Gallo had jumped at the chance to exonerate himself and convince the fisherman to aid his escape.

"Look, man, I don't care what ye tells me," The crewman had answered, "I jist needs to use the head. If the captain 'ears tell of me chattin' wit ye a'tall he'll take a whip to me. No, b'y, I can't 'elp ye."

Gallo had sung out to every man that passed by him on their way to the toilet but it was only the one who had stopped, albeit briefly. *I will bide my time. Sooner or later, I will make me escape. P'rhaps once we get to St. John's harbour. Just as well to wait. I wouldn't want to be wanderin' 'round the woods if I did make it to shore.* Gallo wondered how far off the coast the ship was. *Too cold to swim, t'will be better to wait,* he continued his inner monologue and his plans as the ship was lifted again and again on the heavy swells.

"I'll be back with food fer ye and a cup of water," Harry told him on his return, "don't go anywhere."

Gallo spat at Harry's back as he walked away, his hatred for the man growing daily.

Pastor Brown was holding fast to the railing when Harry appeared beside him. "Ye was tellin' me ye've made this trip afore. Do ye tink we'll meet up wit the *Princess May* today?" Harry asked.

"The hospital ship usually makes berth at several ports long the north shores. Tis likely we will see 'er in St. Anthony," Brown replied, "the winds have been carrying us along at good speed, no reason why we won't make that outport today."

"Ye bin aboard the *Princess May* afore? Is it larger than this schooner? Harry queried. "I'm 'oping I won't be pitched forward and back like I 'ave aboard this one."

"No, I have not. I believe this is 'er maiden voyage. She was to sail up the Labrador coast dispensing medical care to outports on 'er way. She'll be makin' the return trip to St. John's by the time we board 'er," Brown responded. "Most of 'em are workin' fishing vessels but they also carry doctors and medical supplies. I 'ave found 'em to be satisfactory. The last one I was on 'ad an infirmary below deck to treat any sick or wounded fishermen. I imagine the *Princess May* will be much the same."

Harry looked out at the horizon. He could see nothing but sea all around. It was a lonely feeling. He could see no evidence of land anywhere.

"How is yer prisoner faring?" Brown asked, interrupting his thoughts.

"Gallo is as ill-tempered as ever. Not to worry, 'e won't come to no 'arm by my 'and," Harry replied, "Unless 'e forces me."

"I have no fear where ye're concerned. There are some t'would enjoy delivering retribution fer his crimes," the cleric remarked. "I've seen too many poor sods pay dearly fer crimes that were not theirs."

"The cap'n is no innocent," Harry insisted, "as much as 'e protests, 'e is as guilty as sin. I can promise ye that."

"Are any of us innocent?" Brown asked rhetorically.

Harry did not answer but shifted his weight from one leg to another. Such talk made him uncomfortable. "Ain't any of us saints but not many go 'round stealing, lighting fires, and tryin' to murder people," Harry said gruffly.

"Tis my mission to try to save wretches such as him," the churchman commented, "I'd like a chance to talk with him."

"Langley gave me strict instructions to keep Gallo away from ye," Harry told him, uneasy with the request.

"Ye have the keys to his shackles. What harm would it do fer me to talk with him?" Brown pressed.

"The cap'n is as sly and crafty as they come, t'would not be a good idea," Harry answered.

"I have dealt with prisoners before in my ministry. I promise ye, there is nothing he could say that I haven't heard before," Brown insisted.

"Sir, I knows yer a man of the cloth and I means no disrespect but I has to follow me orders," Harry responded, "let that be an end to it."

Brown said no more on the matter and Harry excused himself to see to Gallo's breakfast as well as his own.

Chapter

90

J enkins spat into the water as he stood for a minute watching the
Southern Cross approach. *Tree more aboard this little tub, tis about
to get even more crowded*, he thought as he watched the vessel. *As
long as dey don't git in me way it don't matter none to me.*

"Jenkins! Make the plank ready fer boardin'," the skipper called,
"be quick about it. I wants to get underway as soon as possible after
the passengers alight."

Jenkins moved to follow orders. The schooner's sails were full
as the winds swept her toward the harbour. The sailor knew it
would pull alongside his ship in mere minutes, such was her speed.
Crewmen were already in the rigging preparing to sail. Jenkins
hauled the heavy plank over to the side of the ship and waited. It
wasn't long before the *Southern Cross* was anchored beside them. He
called to another crewman for help. The sailors grunted as they
pushed the plank across to allow the men to board the hospital ship.
Jenkins was watching as the former mining captain shuffled along
the plank, his guard behind him with a pistol in his hand. It took
a minute before recognition made Jenkin's blood run cold. Gallo,
however, did not recognize him.

It took everything he had in him not to give the man a shove
into the water just as he neared the end of the plank. Jenkins
eyes narrowed as he gazed into the face that haunted his dreams,
turning them to nightmares. He was older, a lot older, but Jenkins
remembered all too well. *Tis no mistake, tis the devil 'imself,* Jenkins
told himself. *What did the bastard do now to land 'im in chains,* he
wondered as he watched Gallo's awkward hop from the plank onto

the deck, his guard right behind him. *Likely the same crimes that made 'im run away from the city.*

"I gots somethin' 'ere I needs ye to give yer skipper," Harry interrupted the sailor's thoughts, "if ye don't mind." Harry reached into his pocket for the letter Langley had given him for the skipper of the *Princess May.*

Jenkins reached out and took the missive. "If ye wait right 'ere, I'll go get the skipper," he told Harry. He didn't look back as he walked away.

Harry stood stock-still; his pistol pushed into Gallo's shoulder blades. The minister waited with them, one hand on the ship's railing.

"What do ye think?" Brown asked Harry, "Tis a slight bit bigger than the schooner that brought us here, eh?"

Harry glanced around, "Ain't a whole lot different, smells the same, just 'ope she ain't given to pitchin' me all about."

"Ye'll have yer sea legs soon, then it twon't bother ye so much," the cleric promised.

"I likes the feel of land beneath me feet. I ain't got much of a likin' fer sailing," Harry replied.

The men were listening as the skipper gave orders to his crew and the ship was made ready to raise her anchor. It was some time before the ship's captain stood in front of the three travelers.

"So, this 'ere's yer prisoner?" the skipper asked Harry needlessly as he glanced over Gallo's shackles and chains. "Read yer letter, he can go in the hold. I ain't got no brig on me ship but he can be fastened down below. Ye got the money fer yer passage?"

"I do, and will retrieve it as soon as we get the prisoner safely stowed away," Harry replied. "I gots me 'ands full as ye can see."

The skipper gave Harry a hard look before turning to shout at another crewman. "Hey, ye, Bishop, take these men below deck, see to it that this prisoner is well secured." He turned back to Harry, "Ye are responsible fer this man. Make sure he don't cause no misery fer me. Take 'im below and then come see me in me cabin."

Bishop proved to be the talkative sort and was eager to tell Harry all about his ship and the work they were engaged in. Harry was glad that he and Brown were to sleep in hammocks and not on the deck. The men threaded between narrow aisles and around gear as Bishop led them to the bow. Sacks of dried good were piled to the rafters near the bow leaving a small cubby opening where Bishop indicated Gallo would be contained.

"Aw shite, I fergot somethin', wait 'ere I'll be right back," he told Harry. Bishop returned holding an iron spike in one hand and a mallet in the other. "I'll 'ave to make it so 'e can't go traipsing all over the hold," he told Harry, "Captain's orders, see."

Harry gritted his teeth as the clang of the mallet hitting the spike resounded through the hold. Still, he was glad he would be free to come and go as the ship sailed to St. John's. Harry's ears continued to ring after Bishop was finished his task, but Gallo's chain was securely nailed to the floor and Harry breathed a sigh of relief. Neither man acknowledged Gallo as they walked away.

"C'mon, I'll show ye the infirmary," Bishop said proudly, "ain't many 'ospital ships and this one is outfitted fer just about anythin'."

Harry wondered if he'd find his way back to Gallo as they weaved in and out and past gear, and supplies of all kinds. "In 'ere," Bishop directed him and Harry stood in the small corridor leading into the infirmary.

"Tis a wonder," Harry remarked as his glance took in the small quarters. "And they fixes people up down 'ere?"

"Not always, depends what's wrong wit 'em. Sometimes they keeps folks 'ere that gots to be taken to a proper 'ospital," Bishop explained. "Tis good work they're doin' many a soul 'as perished fer want of a doctor."

Harry thoughts flew immediately to Joe and the lack of medical care in the area of the quarry on the West coast. He wondered momentarily if Joe's life might have been saved had there been such a ship nearby when Joe got hurt.

"I best get back to me duties," Bishop apologized, "if there's aught ye needs I'm yer man. Tisn't a big ship, ye won't have to go far to find me."

"Thanks fer yer 'elp and fer showin' me all this," Harry said waving his hand toward the infirmary, "tis a wondrous thing."

Harry followed the crewman through the labyrinth of corridors to the ladder and returned topside. He found the cleric still standing at the railing watching as sailors climbed further into the rigging preparing the sails to catch the merest puff of wind.

569

"Prisoner's looked after," Harry told him as he joined him at the railing, "shouldn't give us no trouble."

Brown nodded, "T'would be difficult fer the man to cause any trouble with both his hands and feet shackled like they are."

"He brought it on 'isself, kicking and hittin' out like 'e did," Harry replied unrepentantly.

"Be that as it may, it still ain't right fer a man to be treated like an animal," the churchman responded.

"Maybe if ye saw what 'e's capable of ye'd understand the need to keep 'is limbs manacled," Harry said gruffly. "I ain't 'ere to argue wit ye. If ye would please give me that bag I needs to go pay fer our passage."

Brown passed Harry his satchel without another word and Harry left him standing there.

Chapter

91

J enkins took another swig of the rum he'd concealed in his bag. It was frowned upon and sailors had been strictly forbidden to carry spirits aboard the hospital ship. The sailor grimaced as the fiery liquid flowed down his throat, warming his insides. The ship rocked gently and Jenkins replaced the plug in the bottle.

"Jesus, Mary, and Joseph," he muttered to himself as he lay back in his narrow bunk, "why the devil did the bastard show up in me life now, just when I thought he must be dead."

Jenkins listened to the snoring of his crewmates and his thoughts took him back to his first meeting with Gallo decades before. He'd been huddled under the bridge watching the small river that flowed beneath. He'd been overcome with terror remembering the fire that claimed the lives of his mother, younger brother, and baby sister. His father was a sailor and had been gone for months when the house went up in flames. With no family nearby and nowhere to live the boy found himself having to fend for himself.

Jenkins allowed himself to relive, momentarily, the weeks of hell that followed. He'd had to steal food to survive and often raced away as merchants chased after him through the narrow streets. But he was small and very quick and always managed to elude them. It was cold there, under that bridge, but the structure kept the rain off and offered a refuge of sorts.

Aw, Benny, if it weren't fer ye I'd of died of exposure or starvation, Jenkins thought as he remembered his young friend who'd helped him live on the merciless streets. It was Benny who taught him the survival skills every street urchin had to learn to survive. Thoughts of his friendship with the younger boy brought him a moment of comfort as he remembered the sweet with the bitter.

He'd been mesmerized watching the river trickle on its merry way when a sixth sense alerted him to the presence of the man. He'd been so kindly, offering the child food and drink and friendship.

Friendship! Jenkins sneered as the word was fraught with every nuance of irony. His 'friendship' with Gallo had helped him learn tough lessons: lessons of deceit, ruse, and abuse he'd ever had the misfortune to learn. Gallo had bided his time, coming night after night, building the boy's trust and confidence.

Benny never trusted 'im. Benny didn't trust nobody. If only I'd listened to Benny ... Jenkins's thoughts bubbled like hot water in a cauldron. *He was so kind ... in the beginning...*

Jenkins reached back under his bunk for the bottle. *And now he's here, aboard this very ship. Not so proud now, is he? No fine clothes and as helpless as the children he once had quaking in their boots . . .*

Jenkins took another swig of rum.

Revenge is mine saith the Lord, the words he'd once taken to heart bubbled up as if in warning.

Yeah? Where was God back then? Where? Jenkins argued, bitterly.

Come to me, all ye who are heavy burdened and I will give thee rest, came the message that had once been his comfort and his rock. A verse his mother had taught him. It was a verse that had not come to mind in many years. Jenkins swatted it away like a mosquito.

There had been months of pain, humiliation, confusion, and shame. *And then me Da came and found me.* Jenkins allowed himself to remember the short years they'd had together. *He come and took me to his ship. I was so proud to be a cabin boy and the skipper treated me right. I was right happy to serve 'im. He was right strict wit the crewmen, but he was fair.*

Inevitably he remembered the night his father was taken from him, swept overboard in a terrible storm, and he grieved anew.

Thought I'd gotten past all that. That I wouldn't have to think on dem days ever agin, Jenkins said to himself as he raised the bottle to his lips once again. He felt the rum doing its job and he replaced the plug and hid the bottle once again. Soon his snores competed with those of his fellow sailors. It was a troubled sleep.

Chapter

92

Sarah screamed as she narrowly avoided Jack's fingers on her back and raced away. Jack lurched to the left and gave chase after Rose. Fanny looked out the window and smiled as she watched her children play.

"Ye're it!" Jack called to Rose.

"Ye didn't catch me," Rose denied as she continued to run.

"Yis, I did!" Jack crowed, standing still to give his little sister a chance to come after him.

"He did catch ye, Rose. Now ye have to catch one of us," Sarah called.

"I don't wanna play no more," Rose pouted.

"Aw, c'mon, Rosie, come get me," Jack begged, "Look I'll stay right here."

Rose smiled widely and turned back to run after Jack. Her brother pretended to get away, keeping his strides short to match those of his sister. Rose's arm stretched out and her fingers barely grazed Jack's shirt.

"Now, ye're it," she shouted triumphantly.

This time Jack chose Sarah as his victim and raced after her pell-mell. It took no time before Sarah was it and the game continued on until Rose sank onto the ground panting and laughing.

"That's enough," Jack proclaimed, "game is over. What do ye want to play next?"

"I want to go to the beach," Sarah said decidedly, "Jack, would ye take us?"

"Better ask Ma first," Jack replied, "wait here, I'll go see."

Sarah walked over and sank down onto the grass beside her sister. Her eyes shone with happiness. It had been a long time since Jack had played with them and she'd missed him.

"Let's go," Jack called as he emerged from the house, "But, mind, Ma says we're not to be down there too long."

Sarah leapt to her feet. The beach was off-limits to her and Rose unless one of their older brothers, or another adult, took them. Jack had been given strict instructions not to let the girls wade in the water.

"Look, Jack, look! A ship!" Sarah chirped cheerfully.

Jack shaded his eyes with his hand as he looked to where Sarah was pointing.

"She's a big one. Must be a naval ship," Jack told his siters as they watched the vessel.

"Da says his daddy came here on a ship from Ireland," Sarah commented.

"What's Island?" Rose asked.

"Not island, eye-er-land," Jack corrected her.

"Where's eye-er-land?" Rose asked.

"It's a country far away across the sea," Jack replied.

The children stood watching the ship until it faded into the horizon and they could no longer make out the sails.

"I want to go to eye-er-land," Rose remarked.

"Tis too far away. To get there we'd have to go aboard a ship and stay on it fer a long, long time," Jack replied.

Rose considered this for a minute before commenting, "when I gets big I'm gonna go to eye-er-land."

"Why do you want to go to Ireland?" Sarah asked.

"I wants to see all the eyes," Rose answered matter-of-factly.

"No, silly, it ain't a land full of eyes," Jack chuckled, "Da says his father told 'im it's a land a lot like this one."

"Did his mommy come from eye-er-land too?" Rose asked.

"No, I don't think so, only his father," Jack told her.

"Where's did his mommy come from?" Rose asked curiously.

"I don't know, I ain't ever thought about it so I never asked him," Jack replied.

"Jack, Rose, come see," Sarah called. She was stooped down looking into a tidal pool in the crevice of the rocks.

"Ooooh, look," Rose squealed. She sat down on the flat rock beside Sarah, "what's that, Jack?" she asked.

"Tis a sea snail," Jack said, reaching to pick it up, "Look, Rose, the snail is at home. He carries his house on his back."

Rose looked inside the opening in the shell and touched it. The creature shrunk back away from her finger.

"I don't think he likes to be touched," Jack chuckled, "Perhaps we should put him nearer the water. The tide swept him in, but I think he likes it better in the sea. Least, that's what Uncle Joe told me." "Can I take him?" Rose asked, holding out her little hand.

"Just to the edge of the sand. Ma don't want ye getting' wet. Mind now, or ye'll get me in trouble," Jack told her, placing the shell in her hand.

"I won't," Rose answered and walked slowly to the water. She stooped down and gently placed the animal at the edge of the sand where the waves would carry it back out to sea. She walked back to her siblings, studying the sand for seashells or other treasures as she came.

"Rose, look what else we found," Sarah called out joyfully, "it's a star fish."

Jack reached out and lifted it from the water. "Look here, one of its arms must have broken off. Uncle Joe showed me one like it one time. He said they can grow new arms. See, that?" Jack finger touched the area where the new appendage was growing.

The children spent a long time watching the various sea life trapped in the small tidal pools and carrying several specimens back to the shoreline to be saved by the waves.

"Ooooh a sand dollar," Sarah cried excitedly. She showed the sea urchin to her little sister, "See the star on it? It looks like it fell from the skies."

The girls examined their find while Jack continued to comb the beach for other items of interest.

"Hey, Jack, girls," Phil called from the top of the bank, "Ma wants ye to come home now."

"We're comin'," Jack answered and turned to his sisters, "C'mon, ye heard Phil, we gots to go back home now."

"I don't wanna go home," Rose pleaded, "please, Jack, just a little longer."

"We can take our time walking up the beach, maybe we'll find something else," Jack comforted, "and I'll bring ye to the beach again another day."

"Ye promise?" Rose asked, tearfully.

"Yes, I said I would, didn't I?" Jack responded and leaning down wiped the tear from his sister's face with his finger. "C'mon, let's go." Jack folded his hand around his little sister's and lead them toward home.

"Thanks, Jack," Sarah spoke up, "fer takin' us to the beach. Maybe we can come again next Sunday?"

"We'll see," Jack replied, refusing to make a commitment.

Sarah smiled and grabbed Jack's other hand. "I missed ye," she told him.

Jack smiled back at her, remembering his uncle's message in the dream. "I've missed ye, too," he said.

Chapter

93

Stacks of paper nearly covered the desk as the two men bent over them studying carefully when Shaw knocked on the door. Langley lifted his head and called to his clerk to come in.

"Sir, this telegraph just came," Shaw said, holding out the message. He stepped closer and held it out to the agent.

"Thank ye, Shaw, ye may leave us now," Langley replied. He carefully read the message and then looked at Peter. "The transfer's been made. Gallo is now on the mission ship sailing fer St. John's. I'd asked the skipper to let me know."

"Wonderful news," Peter responded, "shouldn't take too much longer afore the *Princess May* makes berth in the city. Should we inform the naval authorities?"

"I already sent the one. I don't think it's necessary to send a second," Langley answered. "They will be watching out fer 'er."

"Remind me to tell ye about the conversation I had with my uncle. Seems Gallo's penchant fer stealing and violence was not new to 'im. Uncle told me he sent a letter to colleagues of his in the city to make inquiries," Peter told the agent, "And received a rather lengthy reply."

"I am not surprised in the least. Let's get on with this and ye can tell me about it over lunch," Langley suggested.

At lunch Peter filled Langley in on all he'd learned from his uncle. "So, there must still be some desire to prosecute 'im," he finished.

"I'd heard bits of gossip," Langley acknowledged, "but did not remember the miscreant's name. I am not given to listening to gossip, too often a man's name is ruined by talk that has no credence or basis in fact."

"That is my uncle's view as well. He has rescued many a man from an unjust sentence, brought about by idle talk" Peter replied, "but in this case there is no doubt. He has it on good authority."

"It will make the job of having 'im sent back to stand trial in England all the easier," Langley commented.

"Gallo will be dealt with but I cannot help but think of all the harm he's done, both here and in the city. Thank God there is no evidence of his abuse of children here. He has left a very bitter legacy in the city," Peter said, gravely.

"The men of means, as you call them, have no understanding of their wrongdoing and seek only to protect their own names," Langley spat out, "there ought to be laws against such aberrant behaviours."

"I agree, wholeheartedly. Tis something I have discussed with my uncle. The powerful would prefer to keep such unpleasantness hidden. My uncle has worked with many a destitute soul who has come afoul of the law. We've had long talks about the need for changes in the law to benefit the common man," Peter said, "and the need for protection of the innocents who are too often abused by the rich and powerful."

"I've heard talk about a home for boys in the city. My family is one that is championing the effort. Too many boys are left orphaned and homeless, and, as a result, become a nuisance to the citizenry, pillaging and robbing to feed themselves. It only gets worst as they grow up. Tis thought that an orphanage would greatly benefit society. I must say I agree with the sentiment." Langley confessed.

"I have been fighting the abuse of power for many a year. I've seen too many broken men and broken families," Peter remarked.

"I agree, too many fall by the wayside in this life. It is the responsibility of those of us who have had every advantage to help the poor," Langley replied.

"What then of this orphanage ye speak of? Is it to be a product of a church or is it a layman's initiative?" Peter asked.

"Tis something that been the topic of conversation for too many years. Tis said the Catholics are hoping to make it a reality," Langley revealed.

"Lord knows the church has monies enough to finance such an endeavor and it tis much needed," Peter replied. "Will the church run the institution? Who will take charge of it?" Peter asked.

"I do not know. It is still in the planning stage at this point," Langley answered.

"I am heartened to hear of it. Perhaps there is hope for humankind yet," Peter replied. "I pray it will prove to be a refuge."

"The churches all do their part to take care of the poor, but the need far exceeds the means," Langley pondered aloud, "if an orphanage is built, I hope it will be a benefit to all, and not just to the Catholics."

"Historically they do tend to take care of their own first, but then, so too do the protestants," Peter pointed out.

"And then there are individuals such as yourself who have made it their mission to make life better for the masses," Langley said pointedly.

"I have and I do not regret it," Peter replied, somewhat defensively, "I will not apologize."

"I do not expect you to apologize. Fact is I have come to respect your efforts," Langley confided. He chuckled, "I never expected I would one day be sitting here with ye over dinner."

'Life is a strange thing," Peter replied, "ye are not the man I first thought ye to be."

"I do hope ye mean that in a good way," Langley answered sardonically.

"I do, sir, I do," Peter answered, "ye have proved to be a far better man than I first imagined ye to be."

"Tis time to return to the office and back to the task at hand. I hope to have a report ready to send to Morgan by week's end. I appreciate your help with it. Tis a tedious business," Langley responded, ignoring Peter's compliments.

"It truly is my pleasure. It certainly has given me insight into yer business," Peter replied.

"It has opened my eyes as well to all the chicanery that has been going on fer far too long. I am grateful now that ye came to form that association. I'd have been none the wiser if not fer that," Langley remarked. "The more I uncover the more I see how widespread Gallo's thievery really was. I have ye to thank fer that."

"We are both all the wiser fer it," Peter replied, "no thanks are needed. Let us get back to it then."

Chapter

94

"Oh, Elsie, I'm so very happy," Fanny cried, "ye will be the finest teacher!"

"I don't know about that but I will try my best to live up to yer expectations," Elsie replied nervously. "I must admit it makes me very anxious. My heart beats something crazy every time I think of it."

"But ye're such a natural. Ye have a way with children and they listen to ye," Fanny refuted. "I can't wait to tell Mick! There is work to be done on the schoolhouse. I wouldn't want ye freezing when the winter comes."

"I am writing to Edward to remind him of his promise of help," Elsie told Fanny, "But we will need lots of men to work on it."

"That's right, I'd forgotten he'd told ye he'd build ye a new schoolhouse," Fanny replied, "and I know Mick and all his friends will come help with it."

"That's what I'm countin' on," Elsie smiled.

"A visit with Reverend McGrath would not be amiss," Fanny planned, "he may be able to help with school books and supplies."

"I have heard of a society that helps provide education for children here on the island. It's called the *Newfoundland School Society*. I hope the minister can assist me in reaching out to them," Elsie commented. "He would certainly know whom to write to. There is so much we'll need. I have to make a list. I also need a list of the children's names, ages, and progress thus far. Oh, Fanny, there's so much to do," she worried.

"I will help ye. Don't fret, all will be well," Fanny comforted.

"May I use the books ye have here? I must take an inventory of what's in the schoolhouse. What about slates for the children to write upon? Oh, my, Fanny, there is so much to think about," Elsie said, "I feel quite overwhelmed."

"Of course, ye can take whatever we may have that will assist ye. First things first," Fanny answered, "let's begin with counting the children then we'll have a better idea what is needed and the sum total."

"Yes, that is practical," Elsie agreed. "I'd hoped ye'd say that. I brought a bit of paper and my quill and ink."

"Ye see, ye're already makin' preparations," Fanny smiled at her sister-in-law.

Elsie rooted in the small bag takin' out of it the fine tools she's been gifted with many years before. "Let's begin with Sarah and Rose. Are the girls still wantin to go to school?" she asked.

"Sarah is very excited. She made a few friends she's been longin' to see," Fanny replied, "She's glad Miss Pearl won't be returning and is lookin' forward to school again. Rose follows her sister's example. They will be thrilled to know their beloved aunt will be teachin' them."

"They are both such good children and so smart," Elsie smiled, "It will be a joy to teach if all the children are as well-behaved as yers are."

"Ye helped with raising 'em, tis no wonder they are. They've had a bit of a jump on their classmates, havin' their teacher already helpin' 'em learn their letters," Fanny replied. "Now, let's see, there's Hank and Hilda's crowd. They have five that will be sure to come to school. Ginny, of course, finished the same year as William. I am unsure if their next oldest b'y will come or not. He may be sent off to work the quarry. I cannot remember his age. I know he's close in age to our Jack."

The women continued to make their list, going through the community house by house until the number of children was known.

"Heavens! Thirty-five! I never thought we had so many children in the community," Elsie exclaimed.

"And more to come. In no time little Jimmy will be school-aged and there are plenty more," Fanny responded. "The littlest ones will be easiest, but the oldest ones will need more attention. I'm afraid there is much they will need to catch up on."

"Miss Pearl did not have the temperament for teaching. Jack confided in me about her lack of patience and strict nature, and how Sarah was ill treated," Elsie responded. "Still, I was surprised when she left so abruptly with nary a warning."

"She was a bit of a snob, felt the city offered better opportunities fer 'er own advancement," Fanny sniffed, "she seemed to feel our children were too backward to learn. T'was like she felt it t'would be lowering 'erself to keep on teachin' here."

"There are too many teachers who should never take on the responsibilities. Tis true she did not seem to have much love for little ones," Elsie sympathized. "Sarah was always one who loved learning. It hurt my heart to see her losing that passion last year. I'm afraid that teacher may have done more harm than good."

"Poor little Sarah, she cried to stay home near the end, which was not like 'er," Fanny replied, "but I have talked yer ear off enough times over that travesty."

"If nothing else, by takin' on the role I can ensure that no more of our children will suffer at the hands of an ill-equipped teacher," Elsie remarked. "Let's not speak any more of Miss Pearl but pour our energies into makin' school a place of happiness and learnin'."

"I know ye will and I promise I will help ye in whatever manner I can," Fanny promised.

Chapter

95

angley sat in his parlour thinking over all he'd learned of Parsons in their time together. *He's good man, far better than I was given to believe, he thought as he stared into the flames of the fire place. We have more in common than I'd have thought possible. He doesn't know much about my family or my adoption. Oddly, I don't think it would make a difference to 'im.*

Langley allowed himself to remember the day he'd learned how he came to be Jonathan Langley's son, and his utter desolation. *It all makes sense now,* he thought *I could never've imagined why Mother acted so distant and cold toward me. T'was like she barely tolerated my existence. Lucky fer me Grandmother was there.*

Langley's thoughts turned to his paternal grandmother and grandfather and the saving grace they were in his life. He smiled as he remembered their great devotion and care of him. Like many times before he wondered briefly what would have become of him if they hadn't bestowed all their love and affection on him. And he thought of his father. *He was as proud of his only child as if I'd sprung from his own loins,* he thought fondly.

His thoughts turned melancholy as he remembered the woman he called mother. *She hated me, truly hated me. No matter how hard I tried to gain her affection I could never succeed. Her distrust and dislike for my birth parents ran deep. She would never forgive me fer being Indian.* He remembered sadly her funeral and how distraught his father had been after she'd died.

The word had come only the once and his father had blamed it on her suffering, trying to convince his son his mother had not been in her right mind. *Half-breed!* She had put every bit of venom she possessed into that one word. It had cut him deeply, leaving a wound that continued to fester long into adulthood. The scene as he'd stood beside her death bed to say good-bye was seared deeply into his memories.

Langley remembered Gallo spitting that same word at Jake with just as much hate and venom. *He doesn't look Mi'kmaq. His skin is whiter than mine. Tis a good thing Grandmother was Italian. It excused my black hair and dark complexion. If Jake is part Indian it makes sense that he would be careful to conceal it.*

Langley pondered the injustices visited upon the native people. *It stands to reason that many here are the offspring of mixed marriages. After all many a fisherman or the sons of merchants had little choice in a bride. Naturally they would tend to marry the women they met and fell in love with. Women of this wild and rugged land.*

He remembered again the whispered talk he'd walked in on when his mother was visiting with like-minded ladies. His mother had pursed her lips, agreeing that Indians should never mix with polite society. She'd never given away his secret, his father guaranteed that, as well as her own fear of the secret becoming known. As far as most people knew he was a Langley by blood.

Polite society Langley thought with a grimace. He remembered searching for his identity, to learn who he truly was. He'd visited the Mi'kMaq village only once. He never told his father. *They seemed happy enough, as kind and generous as many an Englishman were not. Such gentle people, too,* he thought as he remembered his visit. He never knew his mother's name. His father refused him that knowledge and all he knew of his sire was that he was once an employee of his father's company. One whom Jonathan Langley had taken a deep liking to. One who had confided in his father the birth of his bastard son. That was all the history he could learn. *Mother's maid was most pleased to let me know of it. She was cut from the same cloth as Mother, as cruel and as hard as she was,* Langley remembered. *My double sin, not only was I an Indian, but a bastard to boot!*

He remembered running to his grandmother for comfort and verification. *"Ye're our child, our very own boy,"* she'd told him, *"That woman should be ashamed to fill yer head with such hatefulness. Do not believe her. She is poisoned by too many years in service to yer Mother. And she is jealous of yer position in the household. Hate married to jealousy are a very bad thing, my son. Do not take them into yer heart."*

Langley smiled as he remembered the maid leaving the Langley household. His father had been generous to her and given her money enough to see her through her days. Langley was not sorry to see her go. Langley had to shake himself out of his reminiscences, *that, as Father would have said, is water under the bridge. I am more fortunate than most. Enough then of bitter old women and hateful servants. It is time to look to the future.* He thought again of Jake and vowed to help the young man.

Chapter
96

Gallo sat in his confined space staring down at his palms, remembering his trek across the island so many years ago.

'E deserved it, that bookkeeper. I ain't one bit sorry, not one little bit. Bled like a pig, the son of a bitch. 'E got what was comin' to 'im. I'd do it agin, yes sir I would. He thought back to the day he was fired and the knowledge that the bookkeeper had spread the word far and wide of his alleged pilfering of company funds. *They done that to me Mudder, I weren't about to let 'em do ta me the way they did 'er.* Gallo remembered his exit from the city. *Knew they'd come after me. I knows they would 'ave lynched me or worst but I fooled 'em. I got away.*

Gallo's memories took him forward in time and the years he'd spent at hard labour. *Couldn't get work at another bookkeeping shop, not even in another town. They'd look fer me there. I 'ad to 'ide somewhere they'd never think to look fer me.* Gallo grinned as he thought back. The mines were hungry for workers and he knew how to swing a pickaxe, even if it was hard work, work he'd never done before. *Them bunch at the quarry they gots no idea what 'ard work is. I knows. All them years in coal mines and iron ore mines, hard work, that. Still, it was safer to work underground where nobody knew me and nobody'd recognize me. It took years moving from place to place until I eventually ended up working at the quarry.* Gallo thought back on the man who was agent before Langley came on the scene.

I made 'im pay. Bastard didn't remember me but I remembered 'im. Dirty son of a bitch. I let 'im off easy. Gallo snickered out loud remembering the man's shock when he stood in front of his desk and lowered the boom. *Recognized the bastard when he visited the quarry, too bad his visit 'adn't come long afore it did, would 'ave saved me bustin' me arse fer so long. And that mining captain deserved to lose 'is job after the way 'e treated me. I ain't ever gonna put up wit it, not ever again. I ain't nobody's lackey!*

He scowled as he remembered the most recent events and his capture. He looked around him. *All I needs is one of 'em to 'elp me once we docks in St. John's. I got across the island once. I can do it agin. I just needs one sailor to 'elp me out of this. I knows most of 'em growed up much like I did.*

Gallo had been studying each sailor that passed his aisle on their way to the head. One or two had impressed him as being likely candidates to assist him in his schemes.

If I could stow aboard another ship, git back to the West coast, git my money I could git off this friggin' island, go some place new. Someplace where nobody knows me. Gallo schemed. *Afore I do I'm gonna git even wit that 'arry. Son of a bitch is so self-righteous. Thinks 'imself better than the likes of me. I'll show 'im. One good kick to them ribs of 'is will bring 'im down. Lucky fer 'im I don't have me knife. I'd slash 'is throat like I did that bookkeeper, watch 'im bleed like that bastard did.*

His memories moved forward and back, like a pendulum, none were happy. Gallo snickered again. *That little 'alf-breed was shaking in 'is boots. I 'ad 'im whipped, I did. All I 'ad to do was flash me knife and he was whimperin' like a baby. Served 'im right, rattin' me out like 'e did. Best thing I ever did, getting' out of that b'ys 'ome. Friggin' little 'alf-breed, should of used me knife on 'im.*

Gallo leaned back on the wall behind him. His face darkened as he thought back over all the injustices that had been meted out to him since he was born. His imagination took gruesome turns as he imagined how he would inflict pain on each and every person he perceived to be an enemy. There were many.

Chapter

97

Peter's heart was heavy as he laid in bed thinking over the discussion. His conversation with his Uncle John had been sobering, to say the least. *Once I arrive in the city, I will look into the plans to build an orphanage. Mayhap I can make a contribution of some kind.*

His thoughts turned to Luke and he wondered if his young friend had landed in a safe place. Inevitably those thoughts led him to remembering the collapse of his father's mine and the death of Luke's father. *Please, Papa, please, will ye help Luke's mother and his family? What will they do? Where will they go?* Peter remembered begging his father. *You can help them, Papa.* Sadness filled his heart as he remembered his father's refusal. *I didn't even get a chance to say good-bye.*

Peter remembered the gentleness of Luke's parents and how kind they both were. Luke's father was away more often than not, working the mine. They were so proud of their son. His walk down memory lane took him to remembering the first day he'd met his friend. Luke's mother was a cleaning woman and came thrice a week to clean the neighbor's home. That family had fallen on hard times and could no longer afford a live-in maid. Peter had overheard the gossip. He did not understand all the whispered speech but he knew enough to glean that much. He'd been out in the garden entertaining himself with observing the bugs and insects there when he'd been interrupted by the thin dark-haired boy.

Watcha doing? Peter remembered him asking. *Luke turned out to be as curious as I and a great deal more intelligent,* he thought, *had he had even the slightest bit of education he could have done well. My governess recognized it and encouraged it. I remember the many times she allowed Luke to sit in on my lessons. It made learning so much more fun and Luke was so grateful for the few books I gave him. We had so many. We had so much more than Luke's family.* Peter remembered his governess with fondness. *She was a wonderful woman.* His thoughts idled back over the few years he'd enjoyed Luke's friendship and his governess's efforts to help his friend. Peter was careful to keep Luke away from his father. Somehow, he knew intuitively he would not approve of him.

His thoughts turned to Luke's family home, if it could be called that, but humble as it was, it was filled with more love, understanding, and charity than Peter enjoyed in his own home. *I didn't get to visit there near as often as I would've liked. I wonder whatever became of them?*

Peter turned over and tried to banish the memories that always caused him so much sadness and discomfort. *I have the means now. When I get to the city, I will hire a man to make inquiries. It's possible I may be able to track them down.*

Peter thought about the inheritance left by his grandfather, an inheritance he could now access, since he'd reached the age stipulated in the will. He'd been planning what he would do with the monies for years, chief among those plans was to locate Luke and his family, if at all possible. *Still, there is fortune enough to make a contribution to the orphanage as well. Children should not be left out in the cold to do fer themselves; to be at the mercy of monsters like Gallo.*

Peter drifted off to sleep thinking of the ways he could make a difference in the city.

Chapter

98

Jenkins climbed down the ladder to the hold. He needed the head. He took a deep breath, hating to have to pass by the narrow corridor where Gallo was being held. His sleep had been troubled ever since the hateful man appeared on his ship. He'd used the toilet and had almost made it back past his abuser when the voice of his nightmares beckoned to him.

"Eh, ye there. Would like a word wit yea," Gallo called out.

Jenkins stopped. His thoughts ran amuck as his blood ran cold and the fear he'd known as a child threatened to unman him. *I ain't a lad no more,* he told himself as he fingered the dagger he kept in his hand every time he'd had to use the bathroom since the prisoner came aboard. He waited a moment, *there ain't no way I will show that piece of shite how much he still affects me!*

"Are ye still there?" Gallo called again, "Look, mate, we ain't got much time. I needs to talk wit ye."

Jenkin's lip curled as he stepped into the corridor. It was dimly lit and he could just barely make out the man who'd featured in many a night terror over the years.

"What do ye want?" the sailor asked.

"Look, if ye can see yer way clear to 'elpin' me git free once we dock in the city I can make it worth yer while," Gallo's voice held the familiar soft tones he'd once used to convince Jenkins to come with him so many years ago.

"And just why should I do that?" Jenkins asked, remaining in the shadows where Gallo could not read his face or his emotions.

"I gots money. A lot of money. I jist needs help to get away and I will pay ye well," Gallo's voice held a note of desperation.

"And where are ye keepin' all yer money? In yer boots?" Jenkins questioned, "it ain't like ye gots a purse wit ye."

"No, tis true, I ain't got it 'ere on me person, but I can git it," Gallo wheedled.

"And how many b'ys did ye 'ave to sell to git it?" Jenkins asked softly.

"What? I dunno what yer getting on wit. What b'ys?" Gallo growled, "I dunno what yer talkin' about."

"I s'pose ye don't remember the little lads ye lured from under bridges and back alleys. I s'pose ye don't remember sellin' 'em, sometimes to the highest bidder," Jenkins asked, his voice as silky as Gallo's had been back in the day.

"Ye gots me mixed up wit somebody else," Gallo denied.

Jenkins moved away and lifted a lantern down from where it was hanging near the head. Returning to Gallo he held the lantern high, allowing the light to shine down on the captive's face. Gallo was temporarily blinded by the sudden glare in his eyes. Jenkins stood still examining his former torturer.

"I was sittin' under a bridge, watching the river first time ye came," Jenkins reminded Gallo, "ye came every night, bringing me food and drink. Sometimes ye brought sweets. Ye did a good job of getting' me to trust ye."

Gallo was silent for several seconds. "I don't know ye and I dunno what yer talkin' about," he said.

"Ye knew all the men in high places. The men who would pay ye fer a new b'y. The more innocent the better. Did ye git more money fer bringing the youngest and most innocent? I weren't very old," Jenkins continued as if he hadn't heard Gallo.

"No, I ain't had nuddin' to do wit whatever 'appened to ye," Gallo began to panic, his voice rose and Jenkins watched as sweat broke out on the captain's forehead.

"Ye came that first time wit new clothes fer me to wear. Ye combed me hair and gave me a bright, shiny copper to put in me pocket. I never had no jacket wit a pocket afore. Ye tole me ye were takin' me to that candy store I liked. Ye said I could pick out whatever I liked, even some fer my friends. So, I went wit ye," Jenkins's voice was monotone, emotionless and terrifying.

"Ye told me ye'd look after me. Ye told me I could trust ye. Ye tole lie after lie after lie. Ye useless piece of gutter shite!" Jenkins' voice was ominously calm, steady, and bone chilling.

"And now, ye wants my help? Mine?" Jenkins questioned quietly. "Why would I ever do that?"

"Look 'ere, I gots no idea what yer goin' on wit. Ye got me mixed up wit someone else," Gallo growled, "I ain't 'ad nuddin' to do wit sellin' b'ys or girls either."

Jenkins allowed the lantern to sway as he leaned in closer, "Ye still gots the scar Benny give ye. He was one of the smart ones. He never believed ye and ye weren't expectin' someone so little to be armed, were ye?" Jenkins laughed a low laugh. "He got ye but good. Such a little pen knife but it did the job, didn't it?"

Gallo did not respond but unconsciously his fingers went to the small scar above his eye. His thoughts darkened as he remembered the night Jenkins referred to and the scrappy child who'd given him a fight like no other. Benny had gotten away. The blood had run into Gallo's eye and he was blinded just long enough. Gallo had never again attempted to capture him.

"Aw, I see ye remember," Jenkins said, "that was my friend, Benny. I always loved how he took ye down a peg or two." Slowly he lowered the lantern, placing it on the floor. His dagger glinted as he did so.

Without warning Jenkins's boot came up and connected with Gallo's jaw, knocking him backward. Jenkins could not remember the scuffle afterward. He did not know how he'd managed to bring the knife to bear. He'd limped away. Gallo had hit back with his manacled fists, the chain doing more damage than his fists. Gallo's blood soaked his shirt front and he'd staggered to the head to throw up. He'd paused briefly as he passed Gallo one last time. He stood standing over the body of the man he'd hated for most of his life. I killed 'im. I done killed 'im, Jenkins thought as he looked down at the inert body.

Jenkins hurried back to the ladder and climbed topside, his thoughts a whirl and his stomach sick with his deeds. He didn't feel the pain of the blows Gallo had managed to inflict as he fought desperately with his opponent.

Jenkins had one thought only in his mind as he made his way to the upper deck. He wanted his father and the comfort and security he'd found with him after his trials on the streets of the city. *I'm comin', Da, I'm comin',* he thought as he made his way up the ladder. There was a splash as his body was embraced by the sea.

Harry awoke groggily as the ship's bell tolled and men scurried to answer the call. "Man overboard! Man overboard!" The cry was taken up and repeated as the sailors leapt to the railings, searching for the missing man. Lanterns swung madly as the crewmen searched the waters around the ship. They found the bloodied dagger near the bow where Jenkins's shaky fingers had dropped it.

Chapter
99

T he eulogy the following morning was the saddest Harry had ever heard. One after another spoke about their fellow sailor and fisherman. They'd found the bloody dagger and all signs pointed to Jenkins as the person who had stabbed Gallo. The prisoner now lay below deck in the infirmary. He had yet to awaken.

"He give all 'is wages to the mission, fer the poor folk who needed doctoring," one sailor had told the gathering.

"He was always doin' somethin' like that," another put in, "he kept a few pennies in case he needed somethin' but mostly he give all 'is money away. Sometimes to street urchins when we was ashore." "If a man needed anythin' a'tall he'd be offerin' it," another sailor piped up, "sure he gave me money fer me family more than once, said 'e weren't likely to 'ave children and 'e wanted to make sure me brood was looked after. One time it was fer warm coats in winter another time it was fer coal fer to keep me 'ouse warm."

"He bought me new boots," the cabin boy sniffled, "he said I wouldn't be able to crawl up into the riggin' safely without 'em. Gave me part of 'is share of supper many a time. He said a b'y should never 'ave to go 'ungry."

The men stood quietly, somberly remembering the generosity of their crew mate. There wasn't a puff of breeze and the ship rocked gently on the ocean as if in tribute to the man.

"There ain't a man alive who was as good a sailor and as good a man as Jenkins. He will be sorely missed," the skipper spoke gruffly as his eyes passed over the faces of his crew. "Now, Pastor Brown, if ye will say a few words."

The minister stepped forward. He'd changed into his priestly robes for the occasion. His face was grave as he looked upon the mourners.

"The Lord has given. The Lord has taken away," he began. "Gordon Jenkins was by all accounts a good man. One who, perhaps, lost his way momentarily. We cannot know what caused such a good soul to resort to violence. Today we gather to ask the Lord's mercy upon his soul. We ask fer forgiveness for Your servant, Gordon Jenkins, O Lord, our God."

"I shall now read from the Book of Common Prayer, if any among ye have a copy," the pastor then recited:

"We therefore commit his Body to the Deep, to be turned into Corruption, looking for the resurrection of the Body (when the sea shall give up her dead), and the life of the world to come, through our Lord, Jesus Christ; who at his coming shall change our vile Body, that it may be like his glorious Body, according to the mighty working, whereby he is able to subdue all things to himself."

Pastor Brown looked up from the book in his hands and gazed once again at the mourners.

"Into yer hands, Oh Lord, we commit the soul of our brethren, Gordon Jenkins," the cleric finished.

The sailors shuffled uncomfortably, wanting only to get back to work and away from any further ritual. They were quick to move away as soon as the minister closed the book and gave his final blessings, indicating an end to the short service.

Chapter

100

arry remembered finding his prisoner bloodied and passed out in the small corridor. He'd yelled fer help and soon he and a crewman had undone the shackles around Gallo's legs and arms. His body was dead weight and the two men struggled to carry him into the infirmary. Harry's ribs ached anew from his exertions. He'd visited the sick bay several times since he'd found his captive.

Each time Gallo had been unresponsive and the doctor repeated what he'd initially told Harry. Gallo's wounds were deep and he had a raging fever. He'd lain for hours after Jenkins had left him for dead. He'd lost a great deal of blood, the doctor pointed out, and he had no idea if the man would live or die. The doctor feared he may have blood poisoning. On his last visit Gallo had began thrashing around in his sleep and Harry had been permitted to replace the shackles, just in case the prisoner awakened. His prisoner was now chained to the rough bunk he was laid upon.

Brown stood at the bedside, his eyes filled with compassion for the man chained like an animal, even in his weakened state. What would possess Jenkins to do such a thing? He wondered silently. By all accounts he was a man of mercy and great empathy. Gallo had to have done something terrible for the sailor to do this awful thing. Brown's thoughts continued in this vein, even as he regretted never having had an opportunity to minister to the sorry soul in front of him.

Gallo's eyes fluttered and he briefly tried to raise a hand to his face. *Where the 'ell am I?* He asked himself as he struggled to awaken. *It 'urts! Lard Jazus, it 'urts!* Slowly he opened his eyes. Brown stepped forward, leaning over the hurt man, he watched as Gallo's eyes, filled with pain and confusion, registered his presence.

"How are ye feelin'?" Brown asked, "Ye're in the infirmary. Doctor's been workin' on ye. We feared the worst."

Gallo's expression changed to one of distaste as his eyes locked on the cleric's collar.

"What the devil do ye want wit me?" Gallo croaked.

"I came to minister to ye, to bring ye what comfort I could," Brown answered.

"Git away from me," Gallo rasped, "I knows what ye lot are all about."

"Sir, ye've been hurt bad. I'll call the doctor to see to ye," Brown spoke soothingly, "ye're weak and don't know what ye're sayin'."

"Go to the devil, where ye belongs. I knows what's what," Gallo said tiredly, "I don't need no churchman botherin' me."

Brown hesitated for a moment before sadly turning away to summon the doctor. He later stood at the railing looking out to sea and remembering another man who held much the same attitude toward clerics as Gallo portrayed when he'd tried to minister to him. It was rumoured that man had been a victim in his youth of a cleric whom, in Brown's estimation, was unfit to wear the collar. His contempt of churchmen of every stripe was every bit as contemptuous as Gallo's. *I wonder ...*

Brown's thoughts disturbed him greatly. *Suffer the little children to come to me ...But whoso shall offend one of these little ones which believe in me, it were better for him that a millstone were hanged about his neck, and that he were drowned in the depth of the sea . . .*Brown thought of Jenkins body deep beneath the waves ... *t'was not ye that should die thus.*

His thoughts returned to Gallo. *How can I reach such hardened hearts and tortured souls? Oh, God, I am but a simple man, please, I beg of ye, come to my aid!*

Chapter

101

T he doctor lifted his patient's arm. The ominous red streak continued to snake up his arm despite his application of carbolic acid-soaked bandages. The medic shook his head. This is not good. If the sepsis is not arrested, and soon, he will not survive. He reapplied a new set of bandages as the patient tiredly looked on.

"It still 'urts," Gallo complained, "and these blasted chains keep me from sleepin' much. Can ye not remove 'em?"

"I am not at liberty to remove your bonds," the doctor told him, "Ye're being delivered to the naval authority for crimes ye committed. I can give ye somethin' fer the pain and to help ye sleep." "I ain't done no wrong to man nor beast," Gallo denied, "ye see before ye an innocent man."

"Guilt or innocence is not fer me to decide. The courts shall see to justice fer ye," the medic replied.

"It would 'elp me 'eal if ye could remove them shackles," Gallo pressed. "Ain't that yer job, to 'eal me?"

"I have done all that I can to heal ye," the doctor responded, "what is needed now is time and prayer."

"Prayer!" Gallo's voice dripped with contempt, "I ain't no prayin' man," he scoffed.

"Sir, I will not dispute with ye but I have seen more healing wrought by prayer than by medicine alone," the physician answered. He pressed a palm to Gallo's forehead. *The fever rages still*, he thought as he removed his hand, *perhaps it is the fever talking*. Aloud he said, "I shall return with somethin' fer the pain."

Gallo did not answer but turned his face away as the doctor left him. *A lot 'e knows. Some doctor that is. Tis likely 'e wishes me dead like they all do. Dem men what work the quarry, Langley, all of 'em.* And then his blood curdled as he remembered Jenkins's words. *I was doin' 'im a favor. Tis likely he'd of died of starvation 'ad I not found a way fer 'im to survive. It ain't my fault what 'appened to 'im. No, sir. I ain't done no wrong by them b'ys.* Gallo continued his denials, rationalizing, and self justification until he fell into a deep and haunted sleep.

Harry made his way to the infirmary with trepidation. Much as he disliked the captain, he had no desire for the man to die in this way. The doctor had filled him in on the patient's progress and Harry knew it was unlikely Gallo would survive the blood poisoning. Ironically, it was caused by the smallest nick of Jenkin's knife, not one of the far deeper wounds he'd sustained. Harry shook his head.

Never liked the man. He was bad news from the start. Still, I hates to see a body suffer, Harry thought. He wound his way through the aisles and corridors until he stood at the foot of Gallo's bunk. The man groaned from time to time as Harry watched. The bed was soaked in sweat and he thrashed about trying to move his limbs which were held fast. Harry was filled with pity for the man. He gazed at his prisoner a few minutes longer before walking away to find the doctor and get a report.

Chapter

102

"I'm gonna run ahead. I wants to visit Uncle Joe's grave. Phil, can Sarah walk wit ye?" Jack asked as the family prepared to leave for church.

Phil smiled at their little sister, "T'will be my pleasure," he said.

Jack ran ahead, he was wanting to pay a visit to the cemetery. Normally he felt more comfortable conversing with his uncle on the beach where they'd shared so many precious moments. He didn't know exactly why he felt moved to visit the grave. He just did. His legs carried him quickly through the field and up the road until he was kneeling at the graveside.

"Good morn, Uncle Joe. Tis a beautiful morning. Just the kind of day ye always loved. The sun is shining and the bay looks like a sheet of glass. I wanted to talk ta ye afore the church service, so much has bin happenin'. I s'pose ye knows Aunt Elsie is gonna be teachin' this year. Sarah and Rose are so excited.

"Uncle Joe, have ye seen the pig? Da says it's the biggest pig he ever seen. Aunt Elsie says there'll be meat enough for all of us and then some. And the garden's doing well, too. Mouser's done a good job runnin' them rabbits off.

"Da thinks he will soon make the trip to pick up that lumber fer building them dories. Soon our family will be goin' at fishin' in stead of busting rocks fer a livin'. I won't be able to go right away. Da says we has to wait a bit, see how it goes. I wish I could go right away; I hates the quarry.

"Guess ye knows about the association and how much better things are at the quarry these days, but I still hates it. Tis hard work.

Uncle Joe, did ye hear about the mining cap'n? He's bin up to a lot of no good. He burned down the company house and he tried to kill Mr. Parsons; the man who helped set up the association.

"Wish ye were here to help me understand why men do such awful things. Try as I might I just can't figure it out.

"William is gonna marry Ginny. I guess ye knows that, too. Phil is still sweet on Haldi. She's a nice girl, I think. Leastwise Phil thinks so. I bin doin' what ye tole me in my dream, tryin' me best to be a good brother and to cherish the time I got wit me brothers and sisters.

"Things ain't bin the same without ye here. I miss ye so much. I think about ye all the time. Aunt Elsie tole me about the dream she had, she misses ye something awful. She seems a bit better since ye came to 'er in that dream. I keep the wood box filled fer 'er and I takes care of the animals, course, Da helps me wit that, William and Phil, too."

Jack turned as he heard his brothers and Sarah talking as they approached the church.

"Uncle Joe? I gots to go to church now. I just wanted to talk to ye fer a bit afore the service. I wanted to thank ye fer all yer help. I knows ye're watching over all of us. Ma says as long as we remember ye will live on in all our hearts. It ain't the same a'tall but Ma says that's just life. Sometimes it will be full of joy and other times we will be tested. I wish God hadn't taken ye away. Couldn't God have given us some other kind of test?

"Anyway, Uncle Joe, ye knows what ye means to me and always will. I hope ye and little Joe are havin' fun up there in heaven. Aunt Elsie said he would be nearly my age now. We woulda had so much fun together! I gots to go but I will come again another time."

Chapter

103

Harry and Pastor Brown stood again at the railing. A crewman high in the rigging had called out the welcome announcement, 'Land ho'. The two men searched for the sight, without success. The wind had the sails billowed out and they were clipping along at a good pace.

"Won't be long now and we shall catch a glimpse of the city," Brown commented.

"Ye must 'ave better peepers than me. I ain't seen sight of 'er yet," Harry replied.

"Ye'll see it soon enough, I promise ye that," the cleric responded.

"I 'ope the naval authority is keepin' watch fer us," Harry said, "I will be blasted glad to be relieved of the prisoner."

"No improvement yet?" the minister asked.

"No, none whatsoever. He looks to be dead. Tis only when he moans that ye knows 'e is wit us still," Harry answered. "Doc thinks 'e ain't long fer this world."

"I know he's done some terrible things in his lifetime but tis sad to see 'im die without at least tryin' to make things right. Tis such a waste of a life. May God have mercy upon 'is soul," the churchman remarked.

"I ain't much of a prayin' man," Harry told the preacher, "But I 'ave said a prayer or two fer the repose of 'is soul."

"All prayer is heard. Gallo will need yer prayers and the prayers of all men of good will," Brown replied.

"Why do ye think some men do such evil and others do not?" Harry asked.

"Tis a mystery to me. Some would say we were given the gift of free will and we make our own decisions, our own choices. It ain't an easy question to answer," Brown responded. "Per'aps some men were shown good and evil and chose to follow the good path. Per'aps others knew only evil and naught else and followed that path. God only knows."

"That sailor, Jenkins, the men sing 'is praises and yet he stabbed Gallo several times and left 'im fer dead. Then he threw 'imself off the ship, what do ye make of all that?" Harry pressed.

"We cannot know fer sure that he did throw himself overboard. Could be he slipped off the railing," Brown disputed, "no one will ever know."

"Tis true enough. I never knew the man. Don't know Gallo well neither, come to that. I just can't wrap me 'ead around it all. Like ye said, tis a mystery and one this poor old brain just can't grasp," Harry remarked.

"That's where faith comes in. We cannot know the answers. God alone has that wisdom. We are mere mortals. I do wish Gallo would have allowed me to minister to 'im. I tried over and over but he kept rejecting me, and rejecting God," Brown spoke sorrowfully, "I fear fer 'is immortal soul. I truly do."

Harry did not respond and the men continued to stand gazing out to sea, searching for the land that lay beyond the horizon.

Chapter

104

"Well, that's that," Langley remarked as he closed the last log book. "There's proof enough of Gallo's thievery and I will be showing these to Morgan when he comes for his annual inspection."

"When will that be?" Peter asked as he leaned back in his chair.

"I expect he will turn up within the month. I am grateful to ye fer yer help. It would have taken me considerably longer without yer aid," Langley replied. "I need to get back to the quarry. I have yet to replace Gallo and I need to find the monies he hid."

"Would ye mind if I join ye? I have a bit of business to clear up myself," Peter asked.

"By all means. Can ye be ready at first light? I hope to leave in the morning," Langley responded.

"Yes. The sooner the better I have to prepare to leave fer the city within the week," Peter answered. "Care to join me fer dinner? I am feelin' a bit peckish."

Langley pulled the pocket watch from his vest and glanced at the time. "The morning has passed quickly. My apologies, I was not payin' much attention to the time. Yes, I could do with a bite to eat."

The two men gathered up papers and books and put them in order and then left for a much-needed meal.

Langley was waiting for Peter early the next morning. They'd agreed to meet outside his office. "What's takin' the man?" Langley grumbled to himself as he looked up and down the street. He heard him before he saw him. The hoofbeats resounded through the morning air as Peter guided his mare toward their meeting place.

"Sorry to keep ye waitin'," Peter apologized as he approached, "Mildred insisted on packin' a lunch fer me."

"I haven't been here long," Langley turned the apology aside. "Tis a beautiful morning fer a ride. Shall we?"

The sun was already high in the sky when Langley reached the quarry. Peter had ridden on to see Hilda and deliver the gifts he'd purchased as evidence of his appreciation. Josiah was in the captain's shack when Langley entered.

"Good day to ye, Sir," he greeted his boss.

"Good day. Do ye have aught to report? Is there anything I should know?" Langley questioned the pit boss.

"Only how grateful the men are fer the change in meals, and the quality as well," Josiah answered, "all has been well. We have enough limestone ready fer the next shipment. Tis as if the men are workin' harder than ever."

"Oh? And how do ye account fer that?" Langley asked.

"I'd say fair pay and fair play makes a difference," Josiah answered.

"Let that be a lesson to ye," Langley replied, "ye have hard workin' and decent men under ye. Keep treatin' 'em with the respect they deserve and ye won't go astray. I should tell ye, Morgan, one of the owners of this mine, will be visiting within the month. Let the men know to be on their best behaviour when he arrives. No cussing."

"Yis, sir, I will let 'em know. Is there aught else ye need from me?" Josiah queried.

"Just one thing, will ye take over the crusher and send that man Jake to talk with me," Langley instructed.

Josiah went directly to the machine and relieved Jake, sending him to the shack for a meeting with their boss. Jake tapped lightly on the door before opening it and stood in the open doorway.

"Ye wanted to see me boss?" he asked politely.

"Yes, yes. Come in and close the door. I have a bit of business to discuss with ye," Langley ordered.

Jake did as he was instructed and waited patiently as Langley looked over the papers sitting on his desk.

"I need one last favor of ye," Langley told him when he looked up. "Do ye remember the night ye tracked down Gallo fer me? Do ye remember the place in the woods where his mare was standing lame?"

"I've come to know them woods like the back of me hand. I track caribou there often, yes I remember," Jake told him.

"This must stay between ye and I," Langley began, "I have reason to believe Gallo hid something of value in those woods and I suspect it t'won't be far from where we found 'is mare. I need ye to help me find it. Can ye track it after so long?"

"On me own, no, but I have me dog. Smokey is wonderful fer tracking," Jake responded.

"I can meet ye at yer house in the morning. Don't bother comin' to the quarry. This is more important. Ye will get paid fer yer efforts. I will let yer pit boss know," Langley replied, "ye can go back to yer work. I will see ye in the morn."

"Yes, sir," Jake answered and turned to leave. "Sir, if ye please, have ye heard word of the cap'n since the ship left. Has he arrived in Sin John's?"

"No, I haven't heard as yet," Langley replied gazing carefully at Jake's face. "Somethin' tells me ye're anxious to know 'is whereabouts. I can promise ye, he won't ever bother ye again."

"He never bothered me, sir," Jake reddened as he made his denial.

"Would ye like me to let ye know what happens to 'im?" Langley asked quietly.

"Naw, I'm sorry, sir. T'was just being a busy-nose," Jake attempted to be nonchalant in his retort. "I best get back to work."

Jake hurried out the door as Langley watched. *Methinks thou doth protest too much,* he quoted Shakespeare silently to himself as he watched Jake leave. His suspicions of Jake's lineage played on his mind for several minutes before he turned back to the task at hand.

Chapter
105

J ake was awake earlier than usual. He'd been anxious ever since his brief meeting with Langley the day before. In the past several meetings with the man Paddy had been there, lending his silent support. He wondered once again if Gallo had told the agent about Jake's secret. Still, he must not want to fire me. Why would he ask again fer my assistance if he meant to do that?

Jake's insecurities kept him on tenterhooks as he waited nervously for Langley to appear. He had Smokey ready and groomed for the task. He'd also put the saddle on Gallo's mare, just in case. She could do with a bit more exercise, Jake thought. He'd been taking extra care of the mare's leg and felt it sufficiently healed for a proper ride. He didn't have long to wait.

"Aw good! I'd hoped ye would make use of the mare," Langley said as he walked his horse up to Jake who was waiting with the mare outside the barn. "I'd forgotten to tell ye to take 'er if she was healed well enough to ride."

"She seems fit enough," Jake answered, "she's had a good, long rest."

"And better care, no doubt," Langley retorted sardonically. "I need to address that, but it will keep fer now. If ye're ready we can be off."

Jake climbed up into the saddle. "Do ye want to lead, or shall I?"

"I have no memory of where we went that night. Ye better guide me, I'd get us lost, no doubt," Langley replied, "Ye knows this land better than I."

"Smokey, here girl! I guess we best stop first at the house. I need something of the cap'n's fer the dog to get 'is scent," Jake explained.

"As ye wish. Ye knows best," Langley responded.

The two men rode out with Jake in the lead. Smokey loped beside Jake as he rode. The sun had crested but was still low in the sky. Jake first led them back to the burned remains of the company house where he found an old, battered cap that the captain had once worn. He held the cap out for Smokey to sniff and when satisfied the dog had his scent climbed back into the saddle. They rode to the caribou trail and through the woods. He was quiet as they rode. He walked the mare slowly to ensure his dog could pick up the scent. It seemed a long time before Smokey's ears perked up and she barked one quick, sharp bark.

"Smokey, sit!" Jake commanded the shepherd, and dropped down to the ground. "We'll have to tie our horses here. We'll need to go on foot for a while," he told Langley. The agent nodded and climbed out of the saddle.

The dog whined as she waited impatiently for her master. Jake tethered the mare and turned back to the agent. "Ready?" he asked. At Langley's nod Jake bent down to the dog and held out the cap once more for her to sniff, "Okay girl, track!" he commanded.

Tree branches, still wet with dew, blocked Jake's path repeatedly as he followed his dog into the brush. He dodged around them as he trudged after the shepherd who was slowly making her way, nose to ground. When her ears perked and she gave a sharp yip Jake knew they were on the right track. It was hours before the dog hit paydirt. She whined and dug at the fallen leaf debris under a strangely shaped spruce tree. It wasn't long before the satchel Gallo had shallowly buried was in plain sight.

"Good girl! Good job!" Jake praised his canine. "Sir, is this what ye're searching fer?" he asked Langley as he pulled the bag out of the damp debris.

Langley stepped closed and took the sack from Jake's hand. He opened the bag and rooted inside. He withdrew his hand with the band of bank notes clutched in his fingers. "Bloody thief," he snarled lowly. He returned the money to the bag and grasping it tightly looked at Jake. "I'd be greatly in yer debt if ye would keep this find between us."

Jake nodded, "Sure, boss, whatever ye wants."

"Tis money the swine's been stealing from the company fer many a year," Langley said by way of explanation, "the man's greed knew no bounds."

"Is there anything more ye needs me to search fer?" Jake asked.

"No. This is all," Langley replied, "I thought it t'was long gone. I could never have found it without yer help. Thank ye."

"Tis no favor, sir, ye're paying me to do a job. I did it, with Smokey's help," Jake waved the thanks away.

"She's a fine animal, if she ever has pups, I'd like one," Langley observed. "Shall we head back? If ye will, I'd like a word with ye. We'll stop fer a bit at the company house, what's left of it."

"Yes, of course, whatever ye wants, boss," Jake replied. "I'll be sure to keep one of 'er young fer ye, if she has any."

Langley nodded and gestured for Jake to precede him. The return trip was much faster and soon they were riding into the field where the burned-out structure reminded both men of Gallo's treachery.

"There's things I need to speak of with ye," Langley began once the horses were tethered and the dog given water. "I am not a man known to beat around the bush so I will speak plainly, do not be offended." Jake did not answer but gave a short nod.

"I wanted to speak with ye man to man away from any busybodies and sharp ears," Langley began. "Ye seem to me to be a hard workin' and honest man. I could not help but notice Gallo referred to ye more than once as a 'half-breed'. Would ye tell me why he did?"

Jake's face paled and he sank down upon the wooden bench he'd fashioned for Harry. *This is it. Now he's got his money he got no use fer me. He's gonna fire me.* Jake's thoughts were like a burning torch in his mind, ignited and hot.

"Jake, I needs ye to answer my question," Langley said, gently.

Jake hung his head and his voice was whisper quiet, "Cuz I am. I am a half-breed. I am part Mic'maq," the admission filled Jake with shame anew.

"Gallo seemed to have an intense hatred fer ye," Langley responded, "much the same as others had fer me."

Jake lifted his head slowly, his face a picture of disbelief. "Sir?"

"'Tis only another 'half-breed' can understand all the injustices meted out by men such as Gallo," Langley commented softly, "do ye understand?"

"But, sir, ye're an important man. Why ye're the agent, the head boss of the quarry," Jake stammered, the thought that Langley might carry Indian blood was beyond his comprehension.

"I was adopted and raised by influential people. I never knew my Mic'maq relations. 'Tis not something that is common knowledge. I am trusting ye with it. I have been observing ye closely these many weeks and I feel ye are a good man," Langley disclosed quietly, "I hope I am right in my judgement of ye."

"I will never breathe a word of it to another living soul," Jake promised earnestly.

"What reason did Gallo have to treat ye with such contempt? I've watched ye and know ye to be a hard worker. It seems there was more to it than just his bigotry," Langley queried, wonderingly.

"I don't know why he hated me so. I only know he threatened me time and time again. He blamed me for Joe Kelly's death and threatened to fire me if I ever spoke of my part in his accident," Jake confessed. "He said I was to tell no one I was workin' that cart alone and if I did, he'd see to it I'd never get work again, not at the quarry, nor anywhere else."

A dark shadow fell over the agent's face as Jake confided in him. "That accident was months ago. He was holding that over yer head right up to the time he got himself fired?" Jake nodded but did not speak. Langley stood abruptly and paced the barn.

"There is little justice in this world for those of us they call 'savage'. My position allows me to ensure there is justice for those like yerself who work fer this company," Langley continued to pace as he talked. "Men like Gallo are unlearned, uncouth, and reprehensible. I cannot undo what harm he may have inflicted but I think a certain justice will be served if I give ye his mare and saddle – a small compensation fer what he put ye through. God knows I am familiar with the cruelty such hard-hearted people can inflict."

"I don't know what to say, sir," Jake whispered, ye're very generous."

"'Tis little enough, I've a feelin' ye put up with a lot from yer former captain. Also, know this, as long as I am the agent for

Dominion Limestone ye will never have to worry about yer job," Langley vowed.

"I am grateful fer that, sir. Tis been a heavy load to carry, worrying about providing fer me family if I was to lose my job, and especially if word got out about my Indian blood," Jake spoke so softly so that Langley had to listen carefully to hear him.

"Ye need worry no longer. Ye have my promise yer job is secure and yers as long as ye want it," Langley repeated his promise. "Now fer the matter of rebuilding the house and furnishing it. Have ye given it any more thought? I need yer answer. If ye'd prefer not to I will need to find another."

"Sir, once the quarry closes fer the winter I will have time to work on it. Right now, between the quarry and the farm I ain't got much time," Jake answered.

"Will it take long to finish? When I hire a new captain, he will be given the house to live in," Langley replied, "the sooner it is done the better."

"As I said, I can begin as soon as the quarry closes fer the season. I can have it closed in afore winter hits hard," Jake repeated. "Once she's closed in the weather will not matter."

"Tis fair enough. I cannot expect ye to be two places at once and there will be another freighter afore the month is out," Langley rubbed his chin as he considered. "Yes, that's fine. The new captain will have to make do with a bunk in the surgery until the house is fit to live in." He held out his hand, "We have a deal. Will ye shake on it?"

"Thank ye, Sir," Jake said as he shook the proffered hand.

Chapter
106

"Why do ye ask, Sarah?" Mick asked his daughter, surprised by the question about his parents.

"We was on the beach and saw a great ship sailing on the horizon. I 'membered ye tellin' us of yer Dad comin' from Ireland. Ye talk a lot about yer father but me and Rosie want to know about our grandmother. Ye said she wasn't from Ireland."

Mick was quiet for several minutes wondering how to answer the child's questions. "No, she was a woman of this island, native of the land," he answered quietly.

"I thought ye and Uncle Joe came here from over on the mainland," Sarah said.

"Yes, we did, but my mother's family moved back and forth. They hunted and fished here and had a house here as well as over on the mainland," Mick answered. "Me mother was born here."

"They had two houses? Were they rich?" Rose joined in the questioning.

"No, my sweet, they were not rich in the way of houses and things. They were rich in love, in understanding and wisdom," Mick's gaze was not upon his daughters but looking out at the bay through the tiny window.

"Yer mama lived here with ye and Ma when William and Phil were little, right?" Sarah asked.

Mick's eyes fell on his daughter, so much alike in her coloring and features as his mother. "That right, my ducky."

"She died here. I remember ye showin' us 'er her grave in the cemetery," Sarah remarked.

"Yes, she did. She lived with yer Ma and me after me Da died," Mick soberly responded. "Ye look a lot like her, Sarah."

"I do?" Sarah asked, pleased at the thought.

"Same color eyes, same hair. Ye have her smile, too," Mick told the child.

"And her gentle nature," Fanny piped in.

"Am I like her too?" Rose wanted to know.

Mick smiled. "Ye look like yer mama, ye have different coloring, but yer face is so much like yer mother's."

"Why does Sarah look like Grandmother and I do not?" Rose puzzled.

"Now, that's a question I cannot answer. Only God knows why he fashioned ye the way He did and I ain't about to question the Almighty," Mick laughed.

"Why did they have two houses?" Sarah asked.

"Because they followed the caribou and there was food here that they didn't have on the mainland, or it wasn't as plentiful over there," Mick tried to explain.

"Did ye go back and forth with yer parents?" Sarah asked.

"No, my ducky. Only me mother's family did that. When me parents married, they stayed over on the mainland. They didn't come back and forth," Mick replied. "I was born over there, so was me brothers and sisters."

"Yer sisters and yer brothers are still there?" Rose asked.

"Yes, t'was only yer Uncle Joe and me moved here. Ye have many cousins and relations over on da mainland," Mick answered.

"Why don't they ever visit? I want to see them," Sarah wanted to know.

"They are busy with makin' a livin' same as we are. There isn't time to visit," Mick responded, "t'would be nice if we could."

Fanny reached across the table and patted her husband's hand. "Maybe one day we can go back there and see them all."

"Ye never know what life will bring, maybe one day," Mick smiled as he answered his wife.

"Can we visit there, too?" Sarah asked, excited at the prospect of meeting her relations.

"We shall see what the future brings," Mick answered. He changed the subject, "Now, tell me are ye excited to be going back ta school?"

His tactics worked and soon the girls were chattering easily about the fast-approaching school year.

Chapter

107

Peter had not planned to return to the peninsula. He'd thought to leave his uncle's home and make his way back across the island to the city. For reasons he could not name he was drawn to return one more time. He'd spent thrice the time with the men of the quarry than he'd spent with any other group. Part of it, he knew, was because of his injury but that was not wholly the reason he'd decided to return for one last visit before making his way east.

He puzzled over it all as he rode toward Hank and Hilda's home after leaving Langley at the quarry. Something in him wanted to see the results of his work on behalf of the men of the quarry. He'd been thinking a lot about Luke and his family over the past several days. Partly because of the discussions with his uncle who continued to work on Peter to convince him to go and see his father. Peter smiled as he remembered his uncle's earnest pleas on his father's behalf. He'd half-convinced him to do just that. *Maybe tis time to let bygones be bygones,* he thought as he ruminated.

It was not just his uncle's urgings that had Peter reconsidering, his discussions with Langley had also played a major role. Looking through the books for the company had given Peter insights that he could apply to his father's business and explained, at least in part, why his father did not come to the aid of Luke's family. It didn't make things right, but at least he gained a better understanding. Peter continued to contemplate his father's behaviours as he rode.

Hilda was hanging clothes on the line when Peter rode into the yard. "Peter! Good day to ye! I didn't expect to see ye 'ere again so soon," she greeted, "Is everything alright?"

"All is well, there's naught to worry about," Peter reassured her. He patted his saddlebags, "I have something fer ye, and fer the little ones."

"Ye needn't be at that," Hilda scolded.

"I wanted to give ye somethin' to show my gratitude fer all ye done fer me," Peter responded, "ye took such good care of me and I wanted to show my appreciation."

"Go on wit ye, there weren't no need," Hilda replied. "Give me a moment to finish 'angin' up these clothes and I'll be in. Why don't ye put yer mare in the barn? I'll be there in a moment."

"I'll just tether her outside. I'm thinkin' I'd like to walk the beach fer a bit. It will be a while afore Hank gets home and I need to have a chat with 'im," Peter replied.

"Why don't ye let me make ye somethin' to eat afore ye goes off to the beach? Tis after dinner and ye must be 'ungry," Hilda issued her invitation.

"Mildred made me a lunch. I need a bit of solitude, but thank ye," Peter answered.

Hilda left the clothesline and walked over to where she could examine Peter's face more closely. "Well, ye're looking a whole lot better. Alright then, will ye be joining us fer supper?"

Peter grinned at the woman, "Ye knows I will. I'll hear the whistle blow at the quarry and will come back then."

"Alright then, enjoy yer walk," Hilda told him and turned back to finish hanging her laundry.

Peter crossed the fields and climbed down the bank until he was on the shore. It was a perfect day. Warm, but not too warm and Peter continued to examine the case for returning to his father's house. His visits had been few and far between over the past decade, mainly at Christmas and for special occasions.

Father's not a bad man, just a hard business man, he thought as he walked. 'Peter, ye can't be soft-hearted in this world or it t'will pull ye apart, destroy ye', he remembered his father lecture while he was still young. *He meant well; I know he did.*

Peter's thoughts continued in this vein as he walked the beach. He'd been closer to his mother and his father fought to toughen him up as he grew, seeing his empathetic nature as a burden and not a positive trait. He came to a place where the rock met the ocean in one long layer of flat shale upon another. He picked a spot and sat looking out over the bay and thinking.

Peter was deep in thought when the quarry bell rang out, echoing across the bay and signalling the end of another work day. He shook off his meandering thoughts and rose to return to his cousin's house.

"Peter! Tis good to see ye again," Hank's greeting was hardy as he shook his cousin's hand, "I didn't think we'd see ye afore next spring at the soonest."

"I finished up helping Langley with the books and wanted to see ye afore I leave. There's a bit of unfinished business I need to discuss with Mick Kelly. I promised 'im some advice and then things went all amuck what with Gallo's misdeeds," Peter explained, "T'was hoping ye would come with me to visit Mick after supper."

"I'd be happy to," Hank agreed, "I s'pose tis about the lobster fishin'?"

"Yes, Mick wanted my help to set up a sort of partnership and advice on how to fairly distribute any monies earned," Peter replied.

"Yeah, we've had many a discussion 'bout how to best do that," Hank remarked, "Well come on in the house. Hilda will have supper ready and we can go right afterward."

Peter walked over to his horse and dug into the saddlebags, removing several small packages. There was a long parcel, wrapped in burlap and tied behind the saddle. Peter unfastened it and took this as well before following Hank into the house.

"What's all this?" Hank asked curiously.

"Just a few little baubles fer the children and a gift fer Hilda fer helpin' me get better," Peter answered.

"Ye knows ye needn't have done all that," Hank objected.

"I recently came into an inheritance and wanted to share the wealth a little bit," Peter replied, "it gives me joy to do so."

Hank shrugged, his eyes remained on the long awkward package Peter was struggling to carry, his hands already full as he juggled it along with the smaller bags.

"Well, ye shouldn't have. Here, let me carry that fer ye." Hank took the long parcel from Peter just as he was about to drop it.

"Thanks, mate," Peter said.

Hilda was bustling around the kitchen while Ginny helped with getting supper on the table. She turned as the men came in, "Ain't that a nice surprise, Hank? Didn't expect we'd be seeing Peter again so soon, eh?"

"Tis good to see 'im, tis true. I was tellin' 'im he needn't come bearing gifts," Hank replied.

"No need at'all, at'all," Hilda agreed. "Put all that down in the parlour and come eat this while it's hot."

Peter enjoyed his visit with his cousins and had many a chuckle as the children kept up a steady stream of chatter throughout the meal, with many glances into the parlour where Peter had laid his packages upon the sofa.

"Okay, now, it's time fer gifts," Peter said when supper was over and was answered by shrieks of joy. He handed each of the children a little bag containing candy and little treats.

"Don't be eating that all at one time," Hilda scolded the youngest ones, "Ye can have one piece each and then give it to me to put away fer ye."

That was answered with a chorus of disappointed voices. "This way, ye can have something to look forward to every day, at least until it's all gone," Peter coaxed.

Soon, the candy put away, the youngsters raced outside to play. "And now, fer yers and Ginny's," Peter said retrieving the long parcel and laying it on the table.

"Ye open it, Ginny," Hilda instructed, "Really, Peter, there was no need!"

Peter ignored her as he watched Ginny untie the strings wound around the burlap-wrapped gift.

"Oh my!" Ginny exclaimed as she revealed three bolts of cloth, one of white lace, another of white cotton, and lastly one of a silky sky-blue fabric.

"I hope there will be enough," Peter commented, "I had the clerk at the dry goods store measure enough for a new dress fer each of ye. "I hope ye like it. I thought with Ginny getting' married ye'd need cloth fer new dresses fer 'er weddin'."

Ginny's eyes were filled with tears and she could not answer. Hilda reached out and stroked the soft blue fabric. "This is too much, Peter, really it is."

"Not at all," Peter argued, "If it t'were'n't fer the two of ye nursing me back to health I may not have made it. Ye saved me life, sure. Besides, like I was tellin' Hank, I come into an inheritance and wanted to share the wealth."

"Ye're too kind, ye really are," Hilda replied, "we didn't expect ye to do any more than ye already did. Like Hank and I both tole ye, ye did enough with helping set up that association."

"I wanted to do a bit more. Ye must let me have the joy of giving ye something fer all yer care of me," Peter replied. "Is there enough? Can ye make dresses out of it?"

"Yes, there's more than enough," Hilda answered, "t'was thoughtful of ye."

"I likely won't be here fer the weddin' this is by way of a weddin' gift. Please, just accept it and say no more," Peter responded.

"Was mighty good of ye, me son," Hank remarked, "Now, why don't we go see Mick and leave the women folk to sigh over their treasures?"

Ginny rose from the table and followed the men to the door, surprising Peter with a quick hug. "Thank ye so much," she said and rushed away without another word.

"Will ye be staying the night, Peter?' Hilda asked.

"Yes, if ye don't mind. I will leave in the morn to return to Uncle John's," he answered her.

"Of course, we don't mind," Hilda said gruffly, "Go on now and see to yer business." Peter smiled at his former nurse and the two men left.

Chapter

108

Harry was awoken early by a sailor shaking him by the shoulder and whispering urgently the need for him to come to the sick bay. He swung his legs out of the hammock and tried to sit up. The hammock tipped him until his toes touched the floor. He hung there for a few minutes as he shook off the last dregs of sleep. The *Princess May* had dropped anchor just outside the harbour the evening before. He listened to the commotion as sailors made ready to sail into port.

Harry was surprised to see the minister standing beside Gallo's hospital bed when he reached the sick bay. Gallo's eyes were wide open staring at the ceiling and yet his body lay stiff and unmoving.

"He's gone," the cleric told Harry. "I asked the doc to come get me when he thought death was imminent. I tried one last time to reach him. I could not." The cleric looked as though he hadn't had a wink of sleep and Harry said nothing as he looked at the man who had caused so much grief and sorrow.

"Would ye mind closing 'is eyes?" Harry asked the cleric, "Tis a mite unnerving to know 'im to be dead and yet there 'e lies wit 'is eyes wide open."

Brown leaned over the inert body and gently closed the eye lids. Harry glanced at the minister's face, it looked gaunt and weary. "Ye bin 'ere all night?" he asked.

"Couldn't sleep anyway, felt the need to keep the man company whether he wanted me or no," Brown answered, "no soul should be alone at such a time, no matter what deeds he committed in this life."

"T'was good of ye," Harry replied, "not sure if 'e deserved yer pity but t'was good of ye none the less."

"Tis only God can judge what he deserves. He's with his maker now and can cause no further harm," Brown intoned solemnly.

"Guess we needs ta let the naval authority know. What will 'appen to 'im now? I mean, what do we do wit 'is body?" Harry wondered.

"He will be buried in a pauper's grave, no doubt. Perhaps the naval authority will make the arrangements? I don't rightly know. He was to be handed over to the authorities, ye will have to ask them," Brown responded. "I'd like to give a funeral service, though none would attend. I need to learn about it from the admiral."

"Per'aps the skipper will know, 'as the doc declared 'im dead yet?" Harry asked.

"He left just afore ye got here to prepare the paper work. He didn't make a declaration but tis obvious, is it not?" Brown asked in turn.

Harry did not answer and the two men stood quietly as they waited for the doctor to return to make it official.

"Guess I'll go topside, see if the skipper 'as any idea what I should do 'bout 'is body," Harry told the cleric after the doctor had affirmed Gallo's passing.

"Bishop, hey!" Harry called out to the crewman, "will ye ask the skipper if I might 'ave a word wit 'im when 'e 'as a moment?"

"Sure thing, boss. I'll let 'im know ye needs to speak wit 'im. Is it true yer prisoner's dead?"

"Yeah, it tis," Harry answered, "died early in the morn this day."

"Aye, so ye won't be needin' to be lookin' after 'im no more," Bishop remarked.

"Only to see to it that 'is body is taken away," Harry answered.

"I'll go see the skipper straight away. Tis likely 'e already knows," Bishop replied, "Is there aught else ye needs me to tell im?"

"No, I just needs to make arrangements wit 'im," Harry answered.

Bishop bobbed his head and turned away to find the captain of the ship.

Harry turned back to watching the sailors scurrying about as the ship was made fast to its berth. *Bloody man was trouble in life and now 'e will be trouble in death as well,* he thought as he gazed at the shore, *will 'ave to send a telegram to Langley, let 'im know what's what.*

It was quite a while later before the skipper joined Harry at the railing.

"I sent the cabin boy to send a message to the naval authority. T'will likely be hours afore they comes aboard," the skipper told Harry. "Once the men are free of their duties we'll sew 'is body up in a shroud and bring it topside."

"Will they look after makin' arrangements fer 'is burial then?" Harry asked.

"Ye have the paperwork fer them? I got 'im to the city. Tis up to the powers that be to take it from here," the ship's master replied, "Ye will need to talk to 'em when they arrive. Tis out of me hands."

"I ain't never bin in a situation like this," Harry told him, "What will I do if they don't take 'is body?"

"They will take 'im. If the bugger had died a day or two ago, we would have buried 'im at sea. It ain't our job to look after it. They'll know what to do, never fear," the captain reassured him, "I never told 'em in the message that he was dead, only that we'd arrived wit a prisoner aboard. I didn't want 'em to drag their feet."

"That was wise of ye. I will 'ave the paper from yer doctor to give 'em, the death certificate, as well as the papers wit the charges aginst 'im. I doubt they'll need aught else," Harry replied.

"Nuddin' fer ye to do now but wait," the skipper responded, "I'll have 'is body brought topside within the hour."

"Thanks, fer all yer 'elp," Harry said as he stuck out his hand. The skipper shook his hand, grunted, and walked off to attend to the business of unloading his ship just as Pastor Brown was walking toward them. He held a thick packet in his hand.

"Parsons gave me these for safe keeping. He wanted me to deliver 'em to the naval authority. I don't know as they'll be needed now, tis depositions from witnesses of 'is crimes. But I will do as I promised 'im," the churchman explained. "Have the authorities been informed of the situation?"

"The skipper sent 'em a message," Harry replied without supplying further details, "captain says we'll likely be waitin' fer a long time afore they shows up."

"I will wait with ye. I know ye're not familiar with the city. If ye'd like I will guide ye to yer lodgings, once all is taken care of here," Brown offered.

"That would be a blessin'," Harry answered, "one I greatly appreciate, thank ye. I also need to send a telegram to Langley, let 'im know what's 'appened. Is there a telegraph office nearby?"

"Yes, we can do that on our way," the cleric affirmed.

"I am much obliged fer yer 'elp," Harry responded.

The men stood watching the sailors and waiting for the authorities to arrive. They didn't speak any further, both were lost in thought.

Chapter
109

"I will return in a day or two," Langley told Josiah near the end of the work day, "there is something I must take care of. When I return, I will hire a new mining captain. Ye may let the men know if there's any among them interested in the position, they may come see me when I return."

"Is there much more to it than ye already showed me?" the pit boss asked.

"There is. Ye'd need to order supplies fer the cookhouse, assign jobs, hire extra men when needed, ensure the machinery and tools are in good condition, there is a long list of responsibilities, some of it requiring careful bookkeeping," Langley answered, "are ye considering the position?"

"I was thinkin' on it," Josiah admitted, "the cap'n made it seem a lot more difficult and needed more book learnin' than I'd had."

"There is a need fer a certain level of understandin', of literacy," Langley answered carefully. "There is a deal more documentation than what I showed ye when the last freighter was loaded."

"I will give it some thought," Josiah replied, "could be I ain't qualified."

"Ye have a lot of the qualifications," Langley hedged, not wanting to discourage the man, "fair warning though, it would require a lot of reading and writing."

The pit boss held up both hands, "that leaves me out of it. I will let the men know."

"I want ye to understand yer value. If not fer all the years ye put up with Gallo this mine would not be doing as well as it tis. Do not underestimate yer worth. I've watched ye and ye are a good worker. The men respect ye and that tells me a lot. Ye're doing an excellent job as pit boss. It shall be rewarded," Langley encouraged him, "I cannot speak further of it but I want ye to know that."

Josiah blushed at the praise, "I should get back to work. I'll let the men know. Thanks, boss." The pit boss turned and left the building.

Langley sat for several minutes considering his conversation with his pit boss. *Ye shall be rewarded and I will be having a word with Morgan when he comes about a regular annual bonus for ye. Ye deserves that and more,* he thought.

The agent unlocked the desk drawer and withdrew the bank notes he'd laid there that morning. He was careful to keep the money near his person ever since Jake had led him to its hiding place. He tidied up the papers he'd been going through and replaced them in the desk before rising to leave. The quarry and the need to hire a new mining captain were much on his mind as he rode back to town.

The rain was coming down in buckets when he rode his horse into town the next morning. Langley's coat and hat kept the damp off but he was glad to reach his office. Shaw was sitting dutifully at his desk when the agent arrived.

"Morning, sir, glad to see ye're back. Is there aught ye need me to do fer ye?" the clerk asked.

"No, Shaw, ye have done a good job lookin' after the office in my absence. There are things I need to deal with and do not want to be disturbed. Carry on with yer work," Langley answered. He paused after hanging up his coat and hat and turned back to his clerk, "I want ye to know I am grateful fer yer loyalty and help through these past weeks. Thank ye."

Shaw looked up, surprised at this sudden and hitherto unacknowledged praise of his work and devotion, "Why thank ye, sir." The clerk was nonplussed and Langley smiled to himself as he closed the door.

He dropped Gallo's satchel on the floor beside his chair. It was dirty and stank from its shallow grave in the woods. Langley had given it only the hastiest of examinations the previous day. He had removed the few articles of clothing stored inside. He was much more interested in the paperwork, heavy purse, and bank notes inside. Now he removed these and set them on his desk.

He pushed the bag of coins aside and placed the band of bank notes in a drawer. He unfolded the papers and smoothed them out. *Well now, let's see what the scoundrel had here that proved important enough to hide,* he thought.

He read through the papers carefully and a look of intense distaste came over his face. It was an itemized list of names and the money Gallo had been extracting. Although the reasons for the blackmail was not documented, Langley felt certain he knew the reasons why.

When he'd finished reading through the papers, he put them aside. Only one page gave proof of Gallo's stockpiling of wealth. It was a bank document revealing Gallo's vast savings. *Ye were well on yer way to guaranteeing yer future,* the agent thought as he studied the document. The full amount shocked Langley and he carefully refolded it to keep until Morgan's visit. A good barrister would be needed to help close the account and disperse the funds.

Langley stood and walked to the window where he stayed for a long time, staring out at the pouring rain and contemplating the legal ramifications of Gallo's dirty money. *No doubt some of it is money he'd siphoned off from Dominion Limestone, and possibly from his former employers as well,* the agent thought. *This may prove to be a legal quagmire. If I see Parsons afore he leaves I will ask his advice.*

Langley returned to his desk and counted the bank notes and coin. It added up to a small fortune, one he knew would cover Gallo's thievery of wages. He placed the money in a drawer and locked it. He turned to company records to figure out the total for each worker. It was a monumental task and one he was busily conducting when Shaw knocked timidly on his door.

"What is it? I told ye I was not to be disturbed," Langley called through the closed door.

Shaw opened the door a crack, "I know. I'm sorry, sir but a telegram has just arrived marked urgent," he said.

"Come in," Langley spoke gruffly, "give it to me."

Shaw left the message on his desk and quickly returned to the outer office. Langley read through the short missive quickly and leapt to his feet. *No doubt Morgan will have been informed of this development. It will hasten his departure. He will want to discuss all of this in person, the agent thought. Dead! Well, that will save monies for the naval authority. They won't be needing to transport 'is body to England, a prisoner is one thing, a dead one another after all. T"will be a pauper's grave fer 'im, no doubt.*

Langley paced his office for a while before settling back in his chair. *All the more reason to add up Gallo's misappropriation of wages.* He sighed, another long evening in the office. He picked up the papers he'd been studying and continued with the task.

Chapter
110

Brown looked down upon the simple pine box that held Gallo's remains. Harry was the only mourner in the little chapel and Brown wondered if he could even call him that. Still, he was grateful that there was at least one soul for the simple funeral service. It had taken some doing to convince the naval authority to release Gallo's body to him for burial. He'd had to persuade them and succeeded only because no relatives stepped forward to claim him. *Tis a good thing McGrath had confided in me. He thought I didn't know it was Gallo he was speaking of.* The cleric smiled as he remembered the conversation. *Aw, McGrath, ye thought ye were being so discreet. Ye're a good soul, my friend, but ye have no talent fer discretion, though ye tried. It wasn't hard to put two and two together. If not fer ye telling me about his early life I'd not have had the ammunition to convince 'em the man had no living relations.*

The cleric pondered the wisdom in celebrating funeral rites for one who so obviously had no interest in things spiritual, or any belief in God, come to that. Still, it was partly because of the conversation he'd had with McGrath that had informed him Gallo had once been baptized. For the sake of his mother who had worked to raise her child in the faith, up to her own untimely death, he felt duty bound to continue. *Has there ever been a soul more in dire need of prayer than this poor fellow?* He asked himself. 'I did not come to call the righteous, but sinners to repentance' he quoted silently.

The minister gave the coffin a final pat and turned to walk to the altar. Harry stood awkwardly in his pew, the only occupant of the chapel. 'Where two or three are gathered in my name,' Brown quoted again. He looked out into the chapel and began his service. It was short but earnest as the cleric prayed over the remains.

Harry breathed a sigh of relief as Brown gave his final benedictions. He was glad it was over. He really hadn't wanted to come but when he ran into Brown at the little eating house he'd been prevailed upon and had little reason to refuse. He was alone in the city and had nothing much to occupy his time. In truth, he'd felt pity for the man Gallo had become. Harry was not a man given to judging others, no matter their crimes. He wasn't what folks would term a religious man, but he had his own belief system. *There, but fer the grace of God, go I,* he told himself. Brown paused beside Harry momentarily to ask him to stay and have a word with him. Harry nodded and Brown moved on.

The minister walked out of the chapel to see if the wagon that would convey Gallo's casket to its final resting place was there yet. He would not be buried in the church yard due to the serious nature of his crimes. Brown could not change church regulations; he did not have that authority. He was relieved to see the grave diggers were there with their wagon, ready to transport the body to potter's field.

Brown watched as the casket was loaded onto the wagon. There would be no graveside ceremony. He simply had no way of reaching the field where Gallo would be laid to rest. He sighed as he turned away. *I done me best, Lord, now I leave him in yer merciful hands.*

Harry was standing in the vestibule when Brown retraced his steps. "I will be out momentarily. Allow me to remove my vestments and then perhaps ye will join me fer a cup of tea in the rectory?" He asked. Harry gave his assent and the cleric walked quickly into the sacristy to remove his garments.

"I am grateful to ye fer comin'," Brown told Harry when he reappeared. "Tis always a sad business but this one t'was more difficult and desolate than most."

"Tis no trouble. It ain't like I gots much to do 'ere in this city. Don't know a soul other than yerself," Harry replied.

"There is somethin' I need to discuss with ye so I am glad ye agreed to come fer tea," the cleric told him.

Harry was apprehensive as he followed the minister to the rectory, a small and humble house not far from the chapel. *What does the man want wit me now?*

"Please, come in, welcome to our little home," the churchman invited his guest.

Harry looked around. Although it was a small house it seemed comfortable and furnished with plush couches and chairs. "Please, wait here, make yerself at home. I'll just see to the tea," Brown told him and left him sitting gingerly on the edge of the fine sofa in the little parlour

Harry fidgeted as he waited. He glanced around at the little porcelain ornaments and the paintings on the walls. He felt extremely uncomfortable and out of his depth.

"The housekeeper is making tea and will bring a tray shortly," Brown told Harry when he entered the room. "I will get right to the point. I know ye like straight talk. Our sexton will be leaving us within the fortnight and we need a man to take his place. The position offers a small wage and room and board. I know ye don't have any ties to hold ye to the West coast and thought ye might be interested. I know it isn't the kind of work ye're used to ..." Brown trailed off.

"Well now, I don't rightly know. What does a sexton do?" Harry asked.

"He keeps the church buildings in good repair, takes care of diggin' graves and looks after the church cemetery and rings the bell afore services, amongst other things," Brown explained. "I know ye hurt yerself and won't be up to digging graves fer a while, but we can work around that until ye're healed. Tis not hard work, except fer the grave digging. What do ye think?"

"I'd 'ave a roof over me 'ead, food to eat, and a bit of coin? Sounds like a plum position to me, almost too good to be true. Sure beats fallin' trees or splitting rocks fer a livin'," Harry commented. "Still, I ain't ever done work like that in me life."

"But ye're used to doing small repairs, are ye not?" the cleric asked.

"I've 'ad to turn me 'and to a lot of things, fixed up a cabin or two in me time," Harry agreed.

"I know ye to be an honest and hard-workin' man. I was impressed at how ye followed Langley's instructions, even if I didn't agree with them at times. It showed ye could be trusted, and ye were never mean or cruel to yer prisoner, neither. That speaks to yer character," Brown praised his companion. "We need a man we can depend on. I think ye're that man."

"I'd be a fool to say no to ye," Harry responded, "I ain't gettin' any younger and after seeing what 'appened to Joe, and comin' close to meetin' me end in the loggin' camp, well, it's made me wonder what I can go at that don't end with me either dead or 'urt real bad," Harry answered. "Will ye be expectin' me to join in the worship service every Sunday?"

Brown smiled at the plain-spoken man in front of him. "I will leave that up to ye. Of course, ye would be most welcome in the house of the Lord."

Harry nodded, "I ain't much fer all that God-talk and such, but mebbe ye will see me in yer church now and then."

Just then the housekeeper entered bearing a tray loaded with small sandwiches, cakes, tea pot and cups.

"Thank ye, Missus," Brown said as she set the tray on the small table near the sofa.

"So, are ye agreeable to taking the position?" the cleric asked Harry after the woman had left the room.

"I'm certainly willin' to give it a try," Harry answered.

The churchman smiled widely, "I'd hoped ye say that. Come, have something to eat. I'll show ye around after we're done."

Chapter

111

T he small chapel was filled with well wishers and Mary was
grateful. She had waited longer than she'd wanted to have her
little ones baptized. Her heart was warmed by the presence
of the Kelly family. As they waited for the service to begin, she
pondered the wondrous events and blessings received.

She thought back to the twin's illness and her fears for their
survival. It had given her a great deal of worry, especially since the
infants had yet to be christened. She gave thanks for the blessings
of good health as she gazed down at Lily. She glanced over at Jake
holding Liza and smiled at his calm demeanor. *What a difference time
had made to his attitudes toward church and worship. It helped a great deal
that Pastor McGrath was such a simple and gracious man.*

Paddy fidgeted in the pew. Mary smiled again. *He will make a
good godfather,* she thought as she watched him, *and I am so grateful
Haldi is here and will be their godmother.*

The gathering stood as the minister entered and stood upon
the altar. Mary listened intently to the prayers as the baptism ritual
commenced.

Mick and Fanny insisted upon hosting the celebration following
the services. Their home was not large, but it was a deal bigger than
Jake and Mary's humble abode, and much nearer to the chapel. Elsie
was rocking one of the twins while Haldi proudly held the other.

"Ye went to too much trouble," Mary told Fanny, "Yet, we do
appreciate all yer kindnesses."

"Nonsense! Mick and I were happy to have ye. Tis nice to have
something to celebrate, there's been too much heaviness these past

months. Besides, it's naught but a few sandwiches and cakes," Fanny retorted as she balanced her baby boy on her hip, "ye're not to worry, besides, I'll be callin' upon ye fer help with the weddin' feast."

"I'll be happy to help wit whatever ye needs," Mary replied.

Jimmy chortled and bounced up and down, his little finger pointing at the twin Elsie held in her arms. His mother smiled at him, "who's that, Jimmy?" Fanny walked over to stand where the child could easily see the other baby.

"This time next year the three of them will be toddling around and getting' into things," Elsie commented.

"I've no doubt a'tall about that," Fanny agreed, "Jimmy is already reaching fer things. He's a real busy-nose, gots ta know what's goin' on all around 'im."

"He's the spit of 'is father," Elsie smiled, "I cannot get over how much he is like Mick."

"Got 'is father's temperament, too," Fanny agreed.

"How old is he?" Haldi wanted to know.

"Just six months, day afore yesterday," Fanny replied, "and getting' heavier all the time." She shifted the baby to the opposite hip.

"He's adorable," Haldi remarked. "Ye have a lovely family."

"We 'ave been most blessed," Fanny responded, "Now, Jimmy, I'm gonna put ye down. Ye sit right here." She turned to call her daughters to her to enlist their help with child care as she bustled about seeing to the comfort of her guests.

The men were gathered in the yard as the women set about laying out a lunch inside.

"So, ye'll be going up the coast next weekend?" Jake asked Mick.

"Yes, we received word from Edward and we'll set out early to pick up the lumber," Mick answered, "First off we have to see about starting on building William's house so it t'will be ready fer 'im to bring 'is bride. Edward said in 'is letter that he will come back wit us to help with building it and the new school house fer Elsie. We gots a pile of work to do."

"We'll make short work of it," Phil replied, "ye knows every man about will show up and t'won't take long, afore ye know it both of 'em will be built."

"I'd be happy to lend a hand," Jake told Mick, turning to Paddy he said, "ye'll come too, won't ye?"

"Be happy to," Paddy agreed, "Fall is setting in and if ye wants 'em closed in afore weather turns bad the more help the better, right? Ye're goin' at William's first?"

"Elsie says she can manage in the old school house til we gets the new one erected," Mick replied, "so we'll start wit William's house first, yes."

"Thought ye'd be busy startin' work on the company house," Mick said, Are ye goin' ta have time, Jake?"

"Already got the old, burnt part tore off and the new rooms framed in. There's still a heap of work to do, but I will soon have it closed in and then I can work on the inside in me own good time," Jake replied.

"Ye ain't easy, are ye?" Mick queried, "ye're a busy man." "Jake ain't one to ever sit still," Paddy remarked, "if there's work to be done Jake's like a busy beaver, always at it."

"Joe was much the same," Mick remarked, "ye're cut from the same cloth. Tis easy to see why the two of ye hit it off."

"He was a good man, the best," Jake answered quietly.

There was a quiet pause as Joe's brother, nephews, and friends remembered him. Soon the men were trading stories about the man and the reminiscences continued until Sarah arrived to tell them to come eat.

Chapter

112

L angley pushed the papers aside and rubbed his face. He'd been tallying numbers long into the night for several days and he was weary. He'd created a list by seniority and had been busy calculating what each man was owed from the wages Gallo had pilfered. *Tis finally done! Damn the man, anyway! I know ye shouldn't think evil thoughts of the dead but damn 'im to hell anyway,* he thought.

He stood up and stretched, his hands going to his lower back. He walked over to the window and looked out onto the street. *The men are about to receive a nice surprise. I know there's not a one who could afford to lose such sums. I will make it right.* He stood and thought of the men of the quarry and their meager existences. It may seem a pittance to others but every penny will make a difference to 'em.

Langley walked to the door of his office and opening it, called out to his clerk, "Shaw, I need ye to go over these figures, make sure I've not made any errors," he said.

The clerk hastened to his boss's desk. "It ain't like ye to make a mistake, but I'll be happy to look 'em over," he said as he took the sheaf of papers from Langley's hand.

"I need to make certain the numbers are correct," Langley told him, "Take special care."

"I will, boss, I most certainly will," Shaw answered, then turned and left the room. *That's an uncommon man, right there. There's many would pocket that money without even feelin' a hint of wrongdoing in doing so. The world needs more honest men like that,* he thought as he walked to his own desk, God bless 'im.

Langley pulled his pocket watch from his vest and looked at the time. Past noon already! He walked to the coat rack and removed his overcoat and hat. He donned both as he made his way to the door.

"Shaw, I will be stepping out fer my dinner. Ye can leave that until after ye eat, if ye want. I need it done but it can wait til after yer repast," the agent told his clerk.

"Very good, sir. Thank ye, I am feelin' a mite peckish," Shaw admitted.

Langley nodded and left the offices, making his way to the tavern. He was glad to see Peter already seated when he entered.

"Sorry to keep ye waitin'," Langley apologized as he joined Parsons at table.

"I've only just arrived myself," Peter grinned, "thought it t'would be me arriving late once again."

"I wanted to finish my calculations of stolen wages so each man gets what's rightfully his. I lost track of the time," Langley explained.

"I have no such excuse, nor as noble a one," Peter responded.

"Are ye still planning to leave at week's end?" Langley inquired.

"I am," Peter replied, "I am weeks late in taking my leave, for obvious reasons."

"Well then, we must make the most of this time together," Langley answered, "I received a telegram from Harry. He's decided to take on the position of sexton in Brown's church in the city."

"The man is full of surprises," Peter smiled, "I wouldn't have taken him for a man willing to do such work."

"No, I wouldn't have either, but he will make a good sexton. He seems to have a rare talent for many things," Langley responded.

"That's the thing about the men of the quarry, many have talents the two of us would never have dreamed of. Have ye hired a new man to do the job of mining captain?" Peter probed.

"No, not as yet, I have been delayed in returning to the quarry. After Jake helped me find the stolen money, I was determined to sort out how much was owed to each man. There was something else in the satchel I need yer advice on, tis a legal matter" Langley answered.

"Ye know I never finished law school, but if I can advise ye I will," Peter replied, "What do ye require help with?"

"There was a paper from a bank where Gallo had been savin' his ill-gotten gains. I need to know how my company can access the monies stolen," Langley explained.

"Now, that is something best addressed with an experienced barrister," Peter responded, "tis an area of law I never studied."

"Should it be dealt with in St. John's?" Langley asked.

"Can you ensure the monies were those taken from Dominion Limestone?" Peter queried.

"That's the thing, the sum total is more than what was taken from the company. Some of it may have been monies stolen from previous employers of Gallo's," Langley answered.

"That is indeed a quagmire. My advice is to give it over to this man, Morgan. Let him have the headache of resolving it," Peter advised, "If some of the monies were taken from a previous employer they will have to be notified as well. I assume ye refer to the bookkeeper?"

"That is correct," Langley continued in a lowered voice, "there is a list of names, important names. I believe some of the monies were raised through extortion."

Peter's face turned grave as he answered, "T'will be a matter fer lawyers and courts to sort out. He really was a despicable character, wasn't he?"

"Yes, and that's puttin' it mildly," Langley agreed, "The reason I raise the issue is because ye once mentioned yer uncle is a barrister here in town."

"It couldn't hurt fer ye to see Uncle John. He may not be able to help but he could direct ye to the right avenues," Peter replied.

"That would be most helpful," Langley answered as he steepled his fingers and rested his chin upon them. "I am concerned with that list of names fallin' into the wrong hands. I have no proof, of course, but that's the rumour, that men of considerable wealth were engaging in illicit relations with young boys."

"It seems to be to be an open secret," Peter frowned, "how so many men of influence can turn a blind eye to such immoral behaviour is beyond me."

"Yes, ye mentioned the letter yer uncle received in answer to his queries concerning Gallo's character," Langley responded.

"Apparently there's to be a large orphanage built in the city. Perhaps Gallo's tainted profits could be put to good use in helping build it," Peter suggested.

"Unfortunately, I have no power or authority regarding that money," Langley replied, "but I can make the suggestion."

"Why don't ye come visit me at my uncle's home. I can introduce ye to him and we can have an informal discussion regarding it all," Peter offered.

"Yes, that seems a wise idea," Langley agreed, "would this evening be acceptable?"

"I don't see why not. I will let Mildred know we shall be having a guest for supper," Peter responded.

"I don't mean to intrude on yer supper hour," Langley hesitated.

"It t'will be a pleasure. Ye're in fer a treat. Mildred is an uncommon cook," Peter reassured him.

"After hearin' ye brag more than once of the woman's prowess in the kitchen I would be a fool to refuse," Langley grinned.

"Tis settled then, come after ye close yer office this evening. Speaking of eatin' I think it's time we ordered our dinner," Peter replied.

Chapter
113

Langley rode his horse over the familiar road to the peninsula. His mind was full from the conversation he'd had with Peter and John the evening before. He was satisfied that his best course of action was to lay out the difficulties to Morgan, when he arrived. His thoughts turned to the quarry and the unfinished business there. *I hope Charlie is one of the men placing his hat in the ring for the captain's job,* he thought as he rode, *Peter seems to feel he is well equipped to take on the position.*

The agent patted his thick saddle bags and looked forward to the men's reactions when he returned their stolen wages. *They will be well-pleased, I've no doubt,* he thought. He'd planned on having Josiah have the men meet him one by one to receive their money. He smiled in anticipation. *And I shall ensure they know Jake's role in recovering that satchel. He will have friends enough after I'm done.* Langley thought again about the young man who had been bullied relentlessly by the former captain. *He'll not have to worry ever again about his acceptance in the community,* he vowed. *Indian or no, many a family will be singing his praises from now on.*

Satisfied with his plans Langley kicked his steed into a gallop. The horse fairly flew over the miles between town and the peninsula and before long Langley was riding into the quarry once more.

"Good morn, sir," Josiah greeted him, "I have a list of names of the men who'd like to apply for the position of mining captain. Did ye want to start on it right away?"

"There is an important piece of business I must see to first," Langley replied. "I need to see each and every man that works here, one at a time if ye please. I'm afraid ye're about to have a busy day as ye will have to take over for each one."

Josiah paled, "Is somethin' wrong, boss?"

"There is much that has been wrong that I hope to put right this day," Langley answered mysteriously, "but naught fer ye to worry over. This will take most of the day to accomplish. I have a list here fer ye to go by. Once I've seen each one, I need to have a chat with ye." Langley reached into his pocket for the list he'd prepared. "Here ye go, start with Mick Kelly," he ordered his pit boss.

Langley had stored the packets of money in his desk when he'd first arrived, each one in alphabetical order. Now he retrieved the packet with Mick's name on it and laid it on top of the desk. He hadn't long to wait before the man was knocking on the door, a mystified look on his face.

"Ye wanted to see me?" Mick asked, standing in the doorway.

"I do, indeed," Langley answered, "please, come in." Mick entered and stood waiting. "I will be coming to the cookhouse later to give an explanation to all ye men. Right now, suffice it to say, yer wages have been short fer some time. I have the monies here. I just need ye to sign a paper sayin' ye received 'em then ye can get back to work." Langley pushed the envelope toward Mick, "here it is. Just sign there beside yer name."

"I don't understand. Me wages were short?"

Langley sighed, "Yes, Gallo mishandled yer pay and the pay of each and every man here. One other thing, Mick, I have a packet with Joe's name on it as well. I'd like to deliver it to his widow myself this evening. If ye would be so kind as to accompany me to her house."

Mick blinked, "Right after work?" he asked.

"Yes, if that suits," Langley affirmed.

Mick hefted the heavy packet in his hand while he walked back to Josiah. Langley had told him the total and he was in a state of pleasant shock as he made his way back. *I will be able to pay Edward fer the lumber after all. This will make building dories much easier. And William can start married life on a secure footing.* Mick's thoughts tumbled one over the other as he considered his fortune.

Langley met with man after man, promising each one he would address their questions at the special break in the cookhouse. The cookhouse was full when he arrived. Josiah had been informed to have the men quit an hour earlier than usual so he could deliver his explanations and answer their questions.

Langley walked to the front of the room and conversation slowly abated when he stood in front of the men.

"I know ye're all wondering why ye were each given a packet of money today. Some will have received more than others and there is reason for this. First let me explain where the funds came from and I ask ye to keep yer questions until I am finished speaking to ye.

"The former mining captain made many mistakes during his tenure with this company. One of those mistakes was the mishandling of yer wages. I went through the company records very carefully to calculate what was owed. The total was calculated by seniority and number of hours worked. Some have worked here fer many a year while others were hired more recently. You have my word of honor that the monies ye received was the correct amount.

"One other thing ye should know, it was thanks to yer fellow crew member, Jake O'Quinn, that these monies were recovered. Now, if ye have questions I will be glad to answer 'em."

The room erupted with queries until Langley held his hand up. "One at a time, if ye please. Charlie, if ye don't mind comin' up here. I understand ye know most of the men by name," Langley paused until Charlie joined him, "alright now, wait til yer name is called and I will do my best to answer all yer questions."

"What did Jake 'ave to do wit ye findin' wages the cap'n kept from us?" One of the men asked.

Langley was ready with a carefully prepared reply and when he finished speaking many a voice called out expressions of thanks to Jake.

It took the hour to answer the many questions and as the men filed out Langley turned to Charlie, "I haven't had a chance yet to study the list of applicants. I was wonderin' if you decided to apply for the job of mining captain?"

"I've been considerin' it," Charlie nodded.

"Yer name has come up a time or two as a man who would make a good captain," Langley told him, "I am going to be talking to whomever is throwing their cap in the ring, so to speak, tomorrow."

"Ye'll likely be seeing me, then," Charlie replied.

"Ye know the men well and they seem to respect ye," Langley noted, "might be good fit fer ye. Thank ye for coming up and helping me with this today."

"T'was no trouble," Charlie responded, "I've known these men most of me life. They're a good bunch."

"Yes, as I've learned over the past few weeks," Langley agreed.

"Ye should know, everything ye've done to make it better 'round here has been noticed, and it's appreciated," Charlie commented.

"T'was only reversing some of Gallo's bad management decisions. As far as I'm concerned, the man never was fit to be mining captain here," Langley retorted.

"Ye won't get an argument from me," Charlie conceded, "If that's all ye need, boss, I guess I'll get going, got lots to do at home this evening."

"Yes, that's all, I'll look forward to speaking with ye about that position," Langley answered.

Charlie nodded, "Good evening to ye, sir," he said and walked away.

Mick was standing outside waiting when Langley made his way from the cookhouse. "Mick, thank ye fer waiting," Langley greeted him, "I am ready to go now. Tis a nice evening fer a walk, I'll just lead my horse, if ye don't mind waiting one more moment while I fetch 'im."

Mick nodded and watched while Langley walked over to the steed, rubbing the animal's nose and speaking softly to it. *Tis a good thing I sent the lads on ahead of me to warn Elsie about the visit. She wouldn't thank me to be surprised by such an important visitor.* Mick watched as the man led the huge stallion toward him. *Fine lookin' beast he's got there.*

Langley engaged Mick in small talk as they walked, finding him easy to talk with and a fount of information about the quarry and local history.

"I'll look after yer horse fer ye, if ye'd like," Mick offered and pointed toward his sister-in-law's house, "that's Elsie's place right there. I told me b'ys to let 'er know ye were comin'."

"Thank ye," Langley said as he passed the horse's reins over, "he likely needs a bit of water, shouldn't be hungry, he's been grazing all day."

"I'll take care of it and tether 'im in the barn," Mick pointed again to indicate where the horse would be.

Langley nodded and walked off to meet with Joe Kelly's widow. *Parsons will hear, no doubt.* He smiled to himself, *He was mighty concerned with making certain she gets what's comin' to 'er.* He turned over in his mind his initial meetings with Peter Parsons and his early animosity toward the man. *He proved me wrong. Strange how it turned out – we're like best of friends these days.*

Langley reached the widow's house and gave a sharp rap on the door. He removed his hat when Elsie answered it.

"Good evenin' Missus, name's Langley, I'm the agent fer Dominion Limestone. I was told ye'd be expectin' me," he introduced himself.

"Yes, Jack told me ye were comin', please, come in," Elsie graciously welcomed him.

"My apologies fer not visiting much sooner. There's been quite a lot of trouble at the quarry recently," Langley excused himself.

"Yes, I am aware of the recent fire and the treachery of the mining captain," Elsie spoke stiffly, assuming the agent was there with what she termed 'blood money'.

Langley raised an eyebrow and Elsie's cheeks turned pink. "Ye must know, I do not want any money from yer company. It feels too much like blood money to me and I do not wish to accept it. I do not want payment fer my husband's death," she stammered, "it feels too much like profiting from his sufferin' and passin'."

"My dear lady, I am here to discuss that with ye, but I also come on another matter," Langley smoothly explained.

"Very well, please, be seated," Elsie replied, waving toward the little parlour.

Langley folded his tall form into the chair that was once Joe's and Elsie cringed as she lowered herself onto the little settee.

"Madam, the former mining captain cheated the men on their pay for the entire time he managed the mine," Langley began, mincing no words, "today each employee received what was owed him. I have here the monies that yer husband should have been paid."

"Joe was cheated out of his pay?" Elsie asked, stunned by the admission.

"Not just yer husband but every man employed at the quarry," Langley repeated. "I am speaking plainly so ye understand that this is not 'blood money' but money yer husband should have had fer long ago." He offered the packet with Joe's name on it to her. "If ye wish ye can ask yer relatives. They will tell ye every man at the quarry received what was owed them this very day."

Elsie took the packet and read Joe's name. "I don't understand."

"Gallo was stealing from the men as well as from the company," Langley explained, "now this is not common knowledge. I tell it to ye so ye understand this is money Joe earned. I trust ye to keep this bit of knowledge to yerself. The men do not know the depths of Gallo's treachery. I see no reason for it to become grist fer the rumour mill."

Elsie nodded, still bemused, "Tis a lot to take in," she said.

"I also need ye to know, there was much Gallo could have done that would have prevented yer husband's tragic accident. I need ye to understand it is not blood money but compensation fer the mismanagement that led to his death. Tis common fer widows to receive a small bursary in such a situation," Langley withdrew another envelope from his pocket. "This money is rightfully yers, and if ye're uncomfortable accepting it, then donate it to yer favorite cause, the church, maybe. This money has been earmarked fer ye. My company expects me to deliver it, which I am here to do."

Elsie shrank back as if stung, "But I do not want it," she repeated.

"Be that as it may, I cannot continue to have it in my possession," Langley spoke gently and softly, "do not keep it, if that is yer wish, do as I suggest and apply it to some needy cause, fer schoolbooks, perhaps." Langley had done his homework and knew about the need for school supplies and he congratulated himself for suggesting it when he noticed the widow seemed to reconsider.

"Think of it as a scholarship in yer husband's name, if ye wish. However, ye choose to use the money is yer concern," he said as he offered her the packet once again. This time Elsie did accept it.

"That is a fine idea. There are many children who would not have the chance at further education and my husband loved youngsters. Yes, a scholarship in his name would be a good use fer those funds," Elsie hesitantly agreed.

"A wise decision," Langley said warmly as he stood, "And may I say, I am sorry fer yer troubles, missus."

"Thank ye, kindly, and thank ye fer comin' to see me in person," Elsie's composure had returned and she rose to her feet.

"Madam, I could do no less," Langley replied, "I am late in comin' but ye will understand, I hope, that my plate has been rather full since I had to relieve Gallo of his position. I owe Peter Parsons my gratitude fer opening my eyes to the situation at the quarry. I regret I did not visit regularly, part of the blame fer yer husband's death lays on my shoulders."

Elsie smiled sadly, "there are many who feel the weight of responsibility fer Joe's death. What does it matter? He is gone and I have no appetite fer blame."

"Nevertheless, I am profoundly sorry. I need ye to know that," Langley responded.

"Thank ye," Elsie accepted the apology, "I do appreciate it."

"I must be off," Langley said as he turned toward the door. He paused with his hand on the doorknob, "Please, if there is aught that ye need, I am at yer service. I mean that sincerely."

Elsie thanked him again and the agent made his exit. Mick was watching for him as he walked toward the barn.

"Thank ye fer comin' to see Elsie," Mick told him as he approached.

"No need fer yer thanks. I should have come long ago," Langley replied, "as I told yer sister-in-law, part of the blame fer yer brother's death is mine."

"That's not how I see it. Gallo was mining captain and bears the brunt of it," Mick returned.

"I have been remiss in not visiting the quarry on a regular basis. Had I done so I might have been able to put things to right and yer brother may not have died," Langley responded. "I am sorry fer yer loss and fer the part my absence played in it."

"I thank ye fer the sentiment. What's done is done. Ye have made many changes to the way the quarry operates and that's enough," Mick replied.

"Ye have Peter Parsons to thank fer that. If not fer his assistance in formin' yer association my eyes might never have been opened," Langley insisted.

"I s'pose there's been plenty of blame to go around fer Joe's death," Mick commented. "Mistakes were made, but ye've done what ye could to correct 'em. Tis enough."

"Thank ye fer sayin' that," Langley replied, "I cannot absolve myself so easily. That is my burden to carry. I will not take up more of yer time. I will see ye at the quarry tomorrow."

Mick nodded and watched as the agent untied his steed and climbed into the saddle. He gave a wave as Langley turned the horse and rode away.

Chapter

114

Elsie hurried over to see Fanny and Mick shortly after Langley left. She wanted to ensure the packet of money was indeed money Joe had earned and not a story the agent had made up due to his own guilt.

"Glad to see ye, it's been quite a day," Mick greeted her, "come in, join us fer supper."

"Ye waited supper on me? Ye didn't have to do that," Elsie remarked.

"We haven't been waiting long," Fanny replied, "Come, sit."

"Aunt Elsie," Jack began excitedly, "the big boss called everyone into the cap'n's shack today. Every single man there, even me. He gave us all a packet of money!"

"That's why I'm late. He came to visit to give me Joe's earnings," Elsie said, relief evident in her tone, "he told me so but it seemed like a dream. Tis true then?"

"Yes, it is," Mick told her, "Tis a small fortune. He said Gallo had been mismanaging the wages and payin' us less than we was s'posed to get."

"It sure is welcome with the weddin' comin' up," Fanny commented, "and now Mick says he has enough to pay Edward fer the lumber he wanted."

"That is wonderful news! And William can start married life without a worry or a care," Elsie answered enthusiastically.

"It also means we can all give up workin' the quarry, if we're careful with the funds," Mick remarked, "we'll finish out the season and spend the winter getting' ready to go fishin' in the spring."

"Oh, Mick, that is terrific!" Elsie responded, "and it will mean a deal less worry for Fanny and for me as well."

"The association made a difference as far as safety is concerned," Mick replied, "but tis still dangerous work. Fishin' has its dangers as well, but not nigh as many as the quarry."

"Do ye really think ye can all quit the quarry?" Elsie asked

"It looks that way, Mick answered, "Now, Jack, don't get yer hopes up too high. I need time to chew it all over carefully."

"I won't, Da, but I sure hope that's right. If I have to work the quarry another year, I will, but I do hope I can go fishin' wit ye," Jack spoke so earnestly it brought a smile to his father's face.

"Time will tell. It seems an answer to all our prayers," Fanny reached out and patted Jack's shoulder, "Ye knows if ye father can help it none of ye will be going back there next year."

"What and miss developing my muscles shoveling limestone into carts?" Phil's face wore an exaggerated woebegone expression and the family all laughed.

"I'd quit there tomorrow if I could. I fer one won't miss it," William put in.

"T'won't be fer much longer," Mick replied, "afore ye know it the snow will fly and the rock will be too frozen to work."

"Thank God fer winter," William grumbled and was met with more laughter.

"Daddy, will ye teach me and Rose to fish too?" Sarah asked.

"Ye girls will be busy in school," Mick reminded her, "Besides, tis not work fer girls."

"I seen women working the flakes up along the shore," Fanny reminded him, "they help their men with salting the codfish and gettin' it ready fer market."

"Yes, tis true, but they ain't out pulling up heavy lobster traps," Mick retorted.

"There might come a day when ye see women doin' most everything a man can do," Fanny replied, "women are stronger than most men think they are."

"Now, Fan, do ye really want to be out on the water afore it's even full light, in the wind and the cold and no matter the weather?' Mick asked with a twinkle in his eyes.

"No, not at all, I'm just sayin' there may come a day when a woman can if she wants to," Fanny rebuffed him.

"I don't doubt it fer a minute," Mick replied, eyes still twinkling merrily, "sure young Haldi was doin' everythin' on 'er parents farm that these b'ys do here. I wouldn't be surprised if ye females take over the world one day."

Fanny stuck her tongue out at her husband, "likely do a better job of it, too!"

"She's an uncommon lass, Haldi," Phil remarked dreamily and William elbowed him in the ribs.

"We are blessed to be surrounded with uncommon females," Mick remarked, "and pretty as a picture, too." He winked at his wife.

"Enough of yer blather," Fanny declared, "eat yer soup."

"Maybe yer father would be willin' to take ye out fer a ride in the dory now and then," Elsie told Sarah, "If yer a good child and ye ask nicely."

"Would ye, Da?" Sarah eyed her father pleadingly.

"Perhaps when ye're a mite bigger," Mick agreed.

"Me too. Me too!" Rose piped up.

"When ye're a big girl, maybe," Mick agreed again.

"Why do ye want to go out in the dory, Sarah?" Jack asked.

"I ain't ever been out in a boat and I want to see what it's like," Sarah answered matter-of-factly.

"I wants to go to eye-er-land," Rose intoned seriously and was met with much laughter.

The banter and excitement continued throughout the meal. The excitement carried over as they went about their evening chores with lightened hearts and hope-filled souls.

Chapter
115

McGrath sipped his tea, his thoughts churning and meandering like river rapids, first to one thing and then another, most of it dark and disturbing. Langley had stopped by the previous evening for a hasty visit to inform him of Gallo's death. The captain had been very much on his mind ever since he'd helped write up the depositions which would sentence him to a life of imprisonment. He'd spent a restless night tossing and turning as the past haunted his sleep. He castigated himself again and again for not doing more during his tenure in his first church.

If only I hadn't been called away, per'aps I may have made a difference in the lad's life. That scoundrel of a landlord surely made life a misery fer George and his mother. I still believe t'was him that was terrorizing the boy. I have no proof, of course but who else would have left such scars? I knows his mother was as gentle a soul as I ever met and they had no other visitors save meself. McGrath's mind tripped back in time and his mind's eye pictured Gallo as the innocent child he once was. *Never did learn what became of the lad's father. Tis a sorry business, that. The allegations that 'is mother stole from 'er employer was just that, allegations and naught else. That poor woman! Wish I could've done more fer 'em than the few crusts of bread I was able to give 'em.*

McGrath took another sip of tea and thought again of all the injustices meted out to the defenseless, the poor and destitute. *Tis a cruel, cruel world. I will light a candle fer 'em both and remember 'em in the prayers fer the dead.* He laid the empty cup in its saucer and spoke sternly to himself as he made ready for the day ahead. He had his sermon to write and a parish to see to and could ill afford to spend his day in useless remembrances he told himself. He moved to his office and retrieved ink and paper but thoughts of Gallo's youth continued to plague him.

Aaargh! There's nuddin' fer it but to leave this fer later! He pushed the papers away and stood up again. *Prayer is what's needed. There will be no sermon til I leaves this is the hands of the Almighty!* The preacher left the room and calling out his intentions to his housekeeper left to visit the chapel.

It was hours later before McGrath felt serene enough to tackle the task of writing the sermon. Satisfied with what he'd written he replaced the lid on the ink pot and allowed himself to dream of the future.

William and Ginny had come to see him after the service the previous Sunday to ask him to read their banns concerning their intended marriage a month hence. McGrath smiled as he dwelt on the happy occasion, this was to be the first reading of the banns that would allow any of the community to voice their objections to the joining in matrimony of the two young people. *Tis naught but a formality. I knows there's naught a just cause fer refusing their nuptials.*

McGrath thought back over the years of ministering to the parish and the joy it was to watch youngsters grow up. He remembered the children Ginny and William once were and it gave him joy to contemplate their future life together.

He'd chatted with several members of the community after the services and was gratified to learn about the windfall each family had been given through Langley's efforts. *It t'was a fine thing he did here. T'was a day of celebrating good fortune. Does me heart good, it does. Thanks be to God!*

He thought about the families in the community, their struggles and trials and the way they helped one another and gave thanks. *God's in his heaven's and all's right with the world!*

The cleric allowed himself a few minutes more of joyful anticipation before getting up to see to his other duties.

Chapter

116

Hilda smiled to herself as she braided the sweet grass and incorporated the dried wild flowers into the wreath she was weaving. She pictured Ginny wearing it when she married William in just a few days. It t'will suit her blond hair and fair complexion. Hilda had been busily preparing for her daughter's wedding for several weeks and the house continued to be a hive of activity as the day approached.

T'was kind of Peter to buy the fabric fer 'er wedding finery. Fancy a man knowing just what to buy fer such an occasion! She began to hum as she put the finishing touches on the head piece. The wedding dress hung on the back of her bedroom door along with the dress she'd sewn for herself. *All is as ready as it'll ever be, Ginny will look so pretty.* Hilda's thoughts continued as she pictured the bride to be in all her glory.

I shall miss 'er, but glad am I that tis William she'll be marryin'. He will be a grand provider and take good care of our Ginny. Hilda smiled again as she thought of William and how awkward he was when he first came calling on Ginny. It wasn't long before her mind was journeying back in time to Ginny's childhood and her growing years. Hilda gave herself a shake, *enough of all that, now, sure they'll be just a stone's throw away and we shall see 'em often enough.*

The men had done a wonderful job of building a snug cottage for the young couple. There were just the two bedrooms but another would be added on when or if it was needed. Jake had surprised the young couple with a finely made table and benches. He'd said it was a tribute to Joe who would have made many a fine piece of furniture had he lived. The cabin was built halfway between the two households and both sets of parents were gratified with the nearby location. It sat on the edge of the Kelly property with enough land to provide vegetable gardens and room for a small barn, once the couple had chickens and animals to house.

William stood and gazed over the little homestead that would be his and Ginny's home. He'd come to drop off the blankets and linens his mother and aunt had been busily sewing the minute he'd announced their engagement. He knew Hilda had her own stack to add to the pile. *We shan't be needin' fer much. We are surely blessed.* William's nerves kicked up as he imagined the nuptials and the night to follow. He kicked a small stone in the path and tried to stop the dominoes in his head. *We will be happy here, I knows we will.*

Ginny was out in the fields with her younger brothers and sister picking marsh berries. The first frost always gave the berries a fuller flavor. The pail was nearly full and Ginny stood to stretch her back. She looked out over the marshland at the evergreen shrubs that grew everywhere and at the ocean in the distance. It was one of her favorite places for berry picking, producing the gooseberries that her father loved as well as the bright red berries they were currently harvesting. She was doing her best to keep busy, to keep anxious thoughts at bay. It was easy to keep busy as her wedding day drew nearer. It seemed there was no end of work to be done. Her mother had helped ensure they would have a good share of the jams they made to fill her own small pantry. Ginny was filled with satisfaction as she imagined the pies she would bake for William. Her cheeks burned as she remembered their stolen kisses and embraces.

She was growing used to the idea of being married, even while there was a strangeness in the newness of it and apprehension of leaving her parent's home. Ginny sat back on her heels and continued the task. Her thoughts ran riot while she worked and the breeze cooled the back of her neck as she worked.

Fanny sat with Elsie at her table chopping vegetables for the moose pies that would be on offer at the wedding feast. The moose was stewing in a large pot on the stove as they worked.

"She really is a pretty lass and the girls adore her. I couldn't have asked fer a better wife fer our William," Fanny remarked.

"T'was wise of them to pick that spot fer their house, close enough to visit but far enough away to give 'em a bit of privacy," Elsie commented.

"They are sensible, the two of 'em," Fanny replied, "I got no fear a'tall fer their future."

The women continued to chat as they worked, stockpiling a variety of food for the wedding feast.

Mick patted the headboard of the bed he and Phil had just finished sanding. *Tis not as fine a job as Joe would have made of it but it will serve the purpose.* His thoughts flew to his brother as he remembered all the times he'd helped him with one bit of woodworking or another.

"I'll go get the wagon and we can it load it up to take to William's place. Gee, it seems strange to think of him in 'is own house," Phil remarked as he stood admiring the finished product.

"He won't be far away at least," Mick replied, "Tis good we have land enough fer each of ye to have yer own place one day. I expect it won't be long afore ye come tellin' us ye're gonna marry Haldi. T'was a good thing ye got to meet 'er parents and get their permission to court 'er."

Phil colored as he answered, "Geez Da, she ain't near old enough to marry. We got at least a few years yet. Or are ye wantin' to get rid of me?" He laughed.

"Wait til ye get my age, then ye'll see how fast time goes by," Mick retorted, "Go and get the wagon then. We gots lots to do yet afore their weddin' day."

Mick watched as Phil walked away, *a few years will go by in the blink of an eye, ye'll see,* he silently said to his son's retreating back.

Chapter
117

T he wedding day dawned bright and beautiful and the first fall
of snow glittered in the sunlight. It would melt off again later in
the day, first snow never stayed for very long. Mick had moved
horse and buggy out into the yard and the mare stood pawing at the
snow to get to the sweet grass underneath. With the help of his sons,
he'd set up long boards on saw horses borrowed from neighbors to
serve as a table for the feast that evening. The horse shed would
work well as a temporary gathering place for people to eat and drink
and to get out of the wind, if need be.

Along the beach several large piles of driftwood, brush, and
debris waited to be lit for the bon fires that night. In households
all along the coast families were devouring breakfast and excitedly
looking forward to the party late in the day, after the wedding
ceremony. The day passed by quickly with many last-minute chores
to be done before the feasting began.

Charlie checked again on his instrument ensuring it was well in
tune. He'd be one of the musicians playing the jigs and reels. He'd
accepted the gig as mining captain and Jake was quickly finishing
up the fine company cottage where he'd eventually bring Constance
to live. Charlie brought the fiddle up, placing it under his chin and
passed the bow lightly over it. He played several notes before he was
satisfied it was in tune as he thought about his own wedding day and
the future that lay bright before him.

Jake raised his spoon to his mouth and swallowed the last bit
of porridge. He had yet to put the final finishes to the shelves he'd
made to add to the newlywed's kitchen. He finished his breakfast

and hurried outside to accomplish his task. It would be a surprise wedding gift that no one but his family knew about.

Mary looked forward to dancing once again with the love of her life. Jake had fashioned a playpen where the twins could sleep later. Mary thought back on her own wedding day and envisioned how this one would be. She sighed contentedly as she washed down the table and sideboard.

Paddy was preparing his work wagon to carry Jake, Mary, and Haldi to the wedding later and he whistled as he worked, laying thick piles of fresh hay in the back to cushion the hard boards.

Jack chased his sisters around the barn while they waited to get ready to leave for the chapel. The girls squealed as they ran from him and their shrieks pierced the air. Soon Phil was there calling for them to come get dressed.

Fanny bustled about the house, the table groaned under the weight of the many casseroles and plates of food neighbors had dropped off that morning. She'd laid out their Sunday finery in readiness to don and was just finished dressing the baby.

"Aw, Mick, ye look so fine," she told her husband when he emerged from their bedroom. "How's William doing?"

"He's as nervous as a long-tailed cat in a room full of rockin' chairs," he retorted, "never seen a bridegroom so antsy in me life."

"Takes after 'is father," Fanny grinned. "Elsie will be here any minute. She's going to fix the girls' hair fer me. Where are they?"

"Phil just went out to call 'em in," Mick answered, "they'll be here in a minute."

"Make sure to tell Jack to keep a close eye on them. I don't want them gettin' dirty afore we leaves fer church," Fanny told him. "My goodness, so much to do!"

Mick reached out to snag her around the waist as she went to pass him. "Ye done got all in readiness. There's naught to do but to get dressed and leave. Ye look so fine."

Fanny pushed at the hands that gripped her, "Mick, stop, I got to do my hair afore I dress," she objected.

Mick chuckled and hugged her closer, "Ye look right pretty already. Yer hair's fine."

"Let go of me," Fanny struggled to free herself just as Elsie opened the door.

"Am I interruptin' something?" Elsie asked coyly, "Maybe I should come back in a bit."

"Aw, Elsie, tell this brute of a man to release me," Fanny entreated.

Mick laughed and let her go. "Ye look wonderful," he told his sister-in-law.

"Tis a fine day fer a weddin'," Elsie ignored his compliment, "how can I help ye?" She asked Fanny.

"Phil just went to get the Jack and the girls. If ye would do their hair while I get ready, t'would be a blessin'," Fanny begged.

Within the hour the Kelly family were entering the little church. Fanny paused a moment to smooth William's lapels. "Ye look so handsome," she told her son, "Are ye ready?"

"As ready as I'll ever be. What's takin' Ginny and 'er family so long?" William asked.

Fanny smiled, "We ain't been here five minutes. Be patient. They'll be along soon. William, be happy, alright? Just be happy." Fanny's eyes misted over and she moved quickly away to join Elsie and her children in their pew.

William paced back and forth anxiously as Phil and their father winked at one another. McGrath stood waiting with them for the bride and her family and tried unsuccessfully to calm the groom's nerves.

"They're here," Jack called from where he stood in the open doorway.

"We best go sit," Mick told his sons.

McGrath took William's elbow, "It's time. Let's go." He led the young man to the front of the church. "Stand right here," he instructed him and moved away to the altar and turned to face the open doorway.

Hilda was first to appear with all her brood in line. The family walked easily to the front of the chapel and seated themselves across the aisle from the Kelly clan. Hilda waved to Fanny and Elsie as she took her place.

Jack came forward and removed the flute in his breast pocket. This was his gift to his brother and his bride and he'd been practising in secret for weeks. He had used his small windfall to purchase the instrument. He began to play a quiet, sedate tune as the bride entered on her father's arm.

William's eyes were moist and a great lump filled his throat as he gazed at his bride. Her hands shook and the leaves cascading from the little posy she carried trembled in turn. The green of the wreath that sat on her hair made her eyes seem all the more emerald as she stared at her groom. She turned to kiss her father's cheek before turning back to William. Both were a bundle of nerves and barely heard all the prayers the cleric intoned.

"What God has joined let no man put asunder," the pastor spoke solemnly as he wrapped the ribbon around their joined hands and tied it with a flourish "Ye may kiss yer bride."

The ceremony was over and Jack's flute piped the newly married couple out of the church.

Elsie's eyes filled with tears when William and Ginny led their families to the graveyard where they stood at Joe's burial place. She had not expected this, but neither had the rest of the Kelly family. It was something William had cooked up with Ginny in secret. Ginny had let her parents in on the secret but none else.

"I thank ye, Uncle Joe, fer all ye taught me and fer the good example ye always set," William spoke softly, "I hope me and Ginny are as good to one another as ye and Aunt Elsie always were. Ye will always have a place in our hearts and at our hearth."

"Tis sorry I am that I never knew ye really well, but ye fashioned the cradle I was laid in as an infant and I hope one day we shall lay our own babe in that wee cot. Thank ye fer teaching William and fer the blessin' ye were to all in our community," Ginny added. "I know ye will be dancin' and celebratin' with us as we begin our new life." She broke off a flower from the posy she held and laid it on Joe's grave.

No other words were spoken as the newlyweds and their families paid silent tribute to a man well-loved.

"Alright, then, Mrs. Kelly, shall we?" William smiled down into Ginny's eyes. He led his bride to the horse and buggy borrowed for the occasion.

"Thanks Ma and Da. We'll meet ye at the house." William turned the mare away to steal a bit of privacy before joining in the festivities at home.

"The little girls can climb on here with our brood," Hilda called, "wouldn't want 'em to ruin their weddin' finery."

"Thanks, Hilda, that would be much appreciated," Fanny answered, "Meet ye at home."

Mick helped Fanny and Elsie into the buggy and turned to Phil and Jack, "See ye at home, don't be gettin' up to no shenanigans."

Phil grinned as he looked at Jack, "Race ye!"

Mick shook his head as he climbed up onto the seat, "B'ys will be b'ys, I s'pose," he said as he grinned at Fanny.

"And now there will be one less gettin' up to mischief," she answered.

"Oh, he'll still get up to mischief, but now he has a wife to answer to," Mick retorted. He squeezed her hand and headed for home.

Chapter
118

Elsie was taken aback when Langley stood in front of her and held out his hand. "May I have this dance?"

She looked askance at Fanny seated beside her, completely taken aback and not knowing how to answer. The wedding feast was in full swing and around them people laughed, danced, and made merry.

"Go, dance," Fanny encouraged her. "Yes, it's okay fer ye to have a bit of fun."

Elsie glanced up at the tall man with his hand still outstretched and a quirky smile on his face. His eyes sparkled in the firelight as he waited for her response. Tentatively Elsie placed her hand in his. Vic was playing a soft ballad on his accordion while Charlie accompanied him on the fiddle.

Langley swept her into his arms, holding her at a respectful distance as they began to waltz on the hardened earth.

"Tis a lovely party," he smiled at her as he spoke, "I am glad I came. The food is wonderful, too."

"I am glad ye're enjoying yerself," Elsie answered demurely, "tis been a long while since we had a feast such as this."

"Long overdue, I'd say," Langley replied, "such hard-workin' people deserve a bit of pleasure."

"We have fine people fer neighbors and they're all so very kind," Elsie told him.

"As I have discovered these past months," Langley agreed. "T'was nice of Mick to invite me. I don't often get the opportunity to enjoy such music or such a feast."

"Ye must have been to many such parties in the city," Elsie pointed out.

"I am not usually given to joining in," Langley replied, "at least, not in the city. Perhaps the fine people here will invite me to future soirees."

"Ye're such a fine dancer I'd assumed ye were well-practised," Elsie retorted.

"In my youth I danced a time or two," Langley admitted, "I wouldn't say I was well-practised, however."

"I do love to dance. Joe and I danced a lot, even without a feast. He liked to dance me around the kitchen when he was in a good mood, which was often," Elsie eyes clouded over as she shared the memory.

"By all the accounts he was a very special soul," Langley answered.

"He was," Elsie's voice was low as she answered. "Very special."

"No doubt ye miss him greatly," Langley responded gently.

The music changed to a fast jig as the ballad came to an end and Elsie gently extracted her hand from his.

"I do. Thank ye fer the dance," Elsie said softly.

"The pleasure is mine," Langley bowed before moving away to join the knot of men gathered in the shed.

"Tis nice to see ye dance again," Fanny said when Elsie returned to her seat. Her sister-in-law nodded but said nothing as they sat watching the dancers. Mary had thrown her head back and was laughing at something Jake had said. Phil and Haldi danced near them and were smiling into one another's eyes. William and Ginny were holding court near the entrance to the shed.

Laughter and shrieking could be heard coming from the beach where the children played and bonfires lit up the night. Fanny had given Jack strict instruction to take every care that no harm befell his sisters and the youngsters were enjoying their freedom away from the adults.

"Phil, will ye come here," Fanny called when there was a pause in the music.

"Yes, Ma?" Phil queried when he reached her with Haldi in tow.

"Would ye mind going down to the beach and tellin' the girls tis time fer 'em to come home?" Fanny asked.

"Sure, Ma," Phil assured her and turning to Haldi said, "Want to come?" Haldi nodded and the pair strode off.

"I get the feelin' it won't be long afore ye're hosting Phil's weddin' feast," Elsie said smiling after them.

"She's a sweet girl but too young to marry any time soon. Give it a year or two and he'll be comin' to us fer our blessin'," Fanny agreed.

The women sat and watched their friends and neighbors enjoying the feast long into the night.

Chapter
119

P eter kicked his horse into a canter at the bottom of the hill. He'd ridden into a snow storm the day before and had to find lodging in the little village where he'd spent nights on other trips across the island. He was still at least a day's ride away from the city and his thoughts often wandered to the welcome he might find there. He knew his father continued to frown on the work he was doing to safeguard working men.

He only sees things in black and white, at least that's all I remember. I hope Uncle John is right and he has undergone a softening in his opinions. Still, Uncle is right, Father is not getting' any younger and I have no desire to continue this stalemate. We shall have to agree to disagree.

Peter's thoughts had continued in that vein for much of his trip. He tipped his head back studying the skies. *Hopefully these clear skies hold up until I reach the city. I really do not wish to be further delayed.* He'd sent a telegram to his parents and knew his mother would be worrying. The snowstorm had added another day and he would be later arriving than he had supposed when he'd sent the telegram.

The roadway was not much more than a rutted pathway in most places and he often had to slow his mare to a walk to ensure she did not come to harm during the journey. He was bone tired from the lengthy ride and looked forward to a long rest in his father's house. He hoped his brother would not be there. He had no wish to face both brother and father.

Michael is far too much like Father. Even if Father's attitudes have softened, Michael's likely have not. Uncle has not seen him in years and could not guess where he might stand. Peter thought back on his rocky relationship with his older brother. The long years between them did not help. Michael never wanted his little brother toddling along after him when they were young. They never understood one another and that did not improve as they grew. Peter sighed. *Luke was more like a brother than Michael ever was. He was a lot more fun, too. If he only knew what an influence he has been on my work. I think he'd be proud.*

Peter allowed himself to dwell on his friendship with Luke and his family and the lessons he'd learned from them as he covered the miles.

Peter rode his mare around the back of the estate to the stables and instructed the groomsman to take care of her and walked quickly back to the mansion that was his family home. He walked tiredly up the sweeping stairway to the grand front entrance and paused briefly on the doorstep before taking a deep breath and entering. Not a soul stirred and he walked softly to the parlour searching for his mother. He found her poring over a letter she was writing at the small French provincial desk in a corner of the room.

"Peter!" she exclaimed and rose quickly from her chair and ran to embrace him. Standing back, she peppered him with questions, "We thought ye would arrive long before this. I've been worried. How are ye? Ye must be so tired. Here, come, sit and tell me what ye've been doing. How was yer ride across the island? Have ye eaten? Are ye hungry?"

Peter laughed, "Mother, tis good to see ye. I will tell ye all about my adventures once Father joins us. How are ye? I've missed ye."

"Let me ring fer tea and then I will sit and visit with ye," his mother stood and rang the little bell she'd lifted from a side table.

"I thought it t'would be Christmas before we saw ye again! Tis been a long time," she admonished her son after sending the maid to the kitchen for a tea tray.

"I do apologize fer worryin' ye, Mother. I was delayed due to a small incident. My horse threw me and I sustained an injury. It took longer to heal that I first thought it might," Peter sought to explain without alarming his mother unduly.

"Peter! Ye should have wrote and told us." His mother scolded, "tis hard to believe that mare would rear. Why I used to ride her myself before your father made a gift of her to ye when ye were not much more than a boy. She was always such a gentle creature."

"She still is," Peter replied, "she was hurt by a flying rock and it scared her."

"A flying rock?" the woman looked puzzled.

"Well, t'was aimed by a man with a slingshot," Peter admitted.

"What kind of person would do such a thing? That is shocking behaviour," she proclaimed.

"All's well that ends well. I took a nasty spill and had to spend weeks with Hank and Hilda while I recovered," Peter explained, "I am fine now."

"Are ye sure? We should call a doctor to have a look at ye," his mother worried.

"That is really not necessary. I am fit and healthy, do not concern yerself any further," Peter comforted. He was relieved when the maid entered carrying a heavy tray and distracted his mother.

"If ye don't mind I will go to my room," Peter said to his mother after he'd had tea and a visit with her. "It was a long trip and I'd like to rest a bit afore dinner."

The lady rose with Peter and embraced him again. "It is good to have ye home. Yes, go rest. I will see ye at dinner."

It was hours later when Peter entered his father's office. He stood studying the man for several moments before he spoke. His father was standing with his back to Peter gazing out the window on the wide estate.

"Father? I'm here," Peter said softly.

His father turned and looked blankly at him for a moment before crossing the room. Peter was surprised when he folded him in his arms.

"We nearly lost ye," the older man said gruffly as he stood back, his hands on his son's upper arms as he gazed intently at his face.

"No, Father, was naught but a bump on the head. I was fine," Peter denied.

"Yer uncle wrote to me. T'was more than a little bump on the noggin," his father argued, "I didn't tell yer mother. I didn't want to worry 'er."

"Tis a good thing I'm as hard-headed as ye," Peter tried to make light of it, "takes more than a spill from a horse to keep a Parsons down, eh?"

His father grinned suddenly, "Yes, a very good thing, indeed! I hope ye're here fer a longer visit this time. I won't hear the end of it if ye race off as quickly as the last time."

"I do have a bit of business to look after up the coast," Peter began, "but it can wait a bit."

"I suppose ye'll be off to start another association or some such thing," the patriarch retorted.

"Yes, in fact, I will," Peter answered carefully.

"T'was in a discussion with another mine owner where an association was set up," his father commented, "he was tellin' me his profit margin has expanded, much to his surprise, and mine too, come to that."

"Happy labourers actually work faster and better," Peter replied. "T'is what I've been tryin' to tell ye and Michael fer some years now."

"I'll admit, I did not see the sense of it," the elder man responded, "yet, many a business man has been attesting to the improved morale and better bottom line. The proof is in the pudding, so to speak."

"I am glad ye are able to see the wisdom of it," Peter remarked.

The older man was silent for a moment as he studied his son's face. "I owe ye an apology," he said soberly.

"No, Father, no apologies are needed," Peter answered, "I was pig-headed and refused to see things from yer point of view. I am equally to blame."

"Ye were close to Luke and his family. I could have been more understanding of yer grief and confusion," his father apologized.

"Let's not dwell on it. Tis in the past, let it lay there," Peter told him.

"I have a surprise fer ye, one I think will bring ye joy," his father replied, "I hired a man to find Luke. It took some doing but he's been located, if ye'd like to visit him."

Peter's shocked expression was all the answer his father needed, "I'm not so hard-hearted as ye once judged me," he told his son while his eyes twinkled merrily.

"But where is he?" Peter asked. "I'd imagined his family was spread all over the country."

"No, he's not so far away as ye'd think," his father answered. "Why don't we go into dinner. We can discuss all this afterward."

Peter's eyes welled up as he digested the news and he pulled his father into a hard embrace.

Chapter

120

It was barely past dawn. Elsie scattered seed from her apron to the clucking chickens and stopped momentarily to gaze out over the bay where three dories bobbed on the water. Mick and the boys have had an early start. She smiled. *Aw, Joe, yer dreams fer the family have come true. How I wish ye were here to go fishin with 'em. Hard to believe a year has passed, so much has happened, Joe. I am enjoying teaching school and life is busy but I miss ye still, so much, so very much. I wish ye were here to share all my joys. I went from being childless to being a nurturer of many. Are ye watching Joe? Did ye see the pride in the little one's eyes with each new thing they discover, with each new thing they learn? Tis pure joy, Joe. It fills me with a satisfaction I've never known before.*

The chickens kept clucking noisily as they chased after the seed. Elsie lifted her eyes to the skies where heavy clouds were rolling in promising rain. She hugged herself as she walked back to her cottage to get ready for the day. *There is much to be grateful for even if my heart still aches for Joe and the life we had together.* She smiled as she thought of her most recent dream. *I love ye so much, my Joe, and I always, always will. How blessed am I to receive the messages ye send, messages of love and hope that sustain me through these days? It's not the same but tis a comfort to feel the connection we always had. God blessed us well, did He not?*

Elsie hung her apron on the hook and set about getting ready for the day ahead. The early moments spent in communion with her God and with Joe gave her strength to continue on with her solitary life.

Fanny sat watching Jimmy running around on his short chubby legs and gave thanks for the child who'd arrived late in life. *Just when*

I thought my child-bearing years were over God blessed me yet again. She smiled as her little son rose on his toes trying to reach the wooden horse Joe had carved for him. It was his favorite plaything. She set her knitting down and rose to retrieve the toy. She admired anew the details of the flying mane and tail and thought again how talented her brother-in-law had been. *Aw Joe, ye had a spirit that was bigger than life itself. Jimmy will know how blessed he was to have such an uncle; he will know ye, Joe, if only through the stories we tell 'im. That I promise ye. Ye will never, ever be forgotten as long as there is breath in my body. The world is less without ye in it but yer spirit lives on in all of us who knew and loved ye, especially Elsie.* Fanny's thoughts turned again as Elsie's name came to mind. *T'was a blessin' the day she started teachin'. She has so much love to give and she truly has a talent fer teachin', the children love her.* Fanny's thoughts percolated as she thought over the past year with all its heartaches and trials. *We shall prevail, with yer blessin's, Father of all. I thank ye fer yer care of us all.*

The little dory rocked violently as the swells began to gather. The wind had come up suddenly and Mick took note of the gathering clouds. They would soon have to turn the boat toward shore. *Just ye remember, no matter what storm clouds gather, God holds ye all in 'is hands.* Joe's voice came out of nowhere and Mick smiled to himself. *Ye're prayin' fer us all from beyond the pale. Yes, Joe, I will remember. 'All things will be worked fer good fer them that pray', isn't that what ye used to preach to me every time I would get discouraged? Aye, Joe, I remember. I ain't much of a prayin' man but I am tryin' me best to follow yer example. I miss ye, brother, more than words can say. Thank ye fer helpin'* get our *dream off the ground. Yes, Joe, I know, tis God I need to be thankin'. But I knows ye had a hand in it as well.* Mick smiled and took to the oars, turning the dory around he headed for land.

Jack sat in the dory with his father, giving thanks he'd never have to break his back piling rock in the quarry ever again. He pulled the salt and pepper cap down firmly on his head to ensure the wind would not take it. As he helped his father row back to shore, he thought back over the past year since his uncle died. *You see, now, Jackie-boy, don't ye? God really does work in mysterious ways. It t'was my death that put that chain of events in order. It led to Peter comin' to help form the association, which led to Langley discovering Gallo's thievery which led to the monies comin to help ye all set up fishin'. It led to yer Aunt*

Elsie teachin' school. It led to so many blessin's fer ye all. Do ye understand now? Do not doubt the power of God to bring all things to good. Keep the faith, Jackie-boy, always. Jack listened as his uncle's voice continued to guide him, just as it had when he was alive and well. *I will, Uncle Joe, I promise ye, I will.*

The wind had begun to whip the water into a frenzy and waves lashed the little craft. Mick looked over his shoulder and was relieved to see William and Phil were following him ashore, as were Jake and Paddy in their own little dory.

Paddy put all his strength into the oars as he and Jake made a run for land. It was uncanny how quickly the winds had picked up. The sea was a veritable tempest as they struck out for shore. Jake was rowing hard as well as they raced the storm to shore and safety.

God will give ye strength to meet whatever rough seas ye may encounter in this life. Jake shook his head, was he imagining things? *Is that ye, Joe?* He asked silently as he put every bit of his strength into reaching the little cove. *Who else would it be? Yes, tis I.* Jake grinned to himself, making Paddy wonder at his sudden mirth. *Tis glad I am to see ye out on the water wit me brother and 'is sons. Just wanted to remind ye, despite yer frequent doubt, God will never leave ye alone wit yer burdens. Remember that and remember he will always, always give ye the strength ye need, whether fer rowing yer boat to shore or raising that fine family of yers. Remember never let hate-filled and twisted people poison yer soul lest ye become twisted yerself! Ye're not alone, Jake, ye never were and never will be. Do ye hear me?* Jake nodded to himself as he listened to the voice that was not a voice. It was just as insistent as before when he'd absolved Jake of causing his death. Joe's voice continued to talk to him as he rowed, reassuring him and reminding him that self-forgiveness was as necessary to life as breath itself.

Elsie pulled her shawl more tightly around her shoulders as she left. Rose and Sarah were dancing with impatience as they walked with her to school. The wind whipped their skirts around their legs as they hurried. Elsie stopped, as she often did, just outside the cemetery next to the little chapel. Blue forget-me-nots covered Joe's grave. *I am here wit ye, lass, and I always will be. Be happy, lass, be happy. Live yer life. I'll be right here waitin' fer ye.*

Author's Notes

The Quarry is a work of fiction inspired by historical facts. Of course, there were no unions as such at that point in time. However Protective Associations began to be formed in the mid 1800s and lent a measure of security and work place safety to labourers.

In the early centuries, prior to 1815 Fishing Admirals and civil magistrates were responsible for dispensing justice, except in the more serious crimes, such as murder.

The *SS Southern Cross* was a fishing schooner that sank in the horrific storms of 1914, the same storms that caused the great sealing disaster.

In the late 1800s the Royal National Mission out of Britain sought to ease the suffering of fishermen and the people living in outport communities along the coasts of Newfoundland and Labrador. As part of the *Fisherman's Mission* hospital ships were dispatched to serve these small settlements. The *Princess May* was the second hospital ship to sail the North Atlantic to serve the Dominion of Newfoundland.

The eulogy for Jenkins is found in the Book of Common Prayer (1762 Edition).

The *Newfoundland School Society* was founded by Samuel Codner in 1823 and was first known as the *Society for Educating the Poor of Newfoundland*.

The Mi'kmaq people are an indigenous people who live in the Eastern provinces of Canada including Newfoundland & Labrador, Nova Scotia, New Brunswick and as far west as the Gaspe Peninsula of Quebec. They also inhabited lands now known as Boston, Massachusetts, New England, and Maine. There is archeological proof of their settlements as well as an oral history dating back over 10,000 years. The territory has been known as Mi'gma'gi (Mi'kma'ki) to the Mi'kmaq people.

For more information, please visit https://www.heritage.nf.ca

CPSIA information can be obtained
at www.ICGtesting.com
Printed in the USA
LVHW042014161021
700650LV00006B/320

9 780228 864677